HARRY POTTER

AND THE ORDER OF THE PHOENIX

Harry Potter

AND THE ORDER OF THE PHOENIX

BY

J. K. Rowling

ILLUSTRATIONS BY MARY GRANDPRÉ

SCHOLASTIC INC.

Arthur A. Levine Books hardcover edition
art directed by David Saylor,
published by Arthur A. Levine Books,
an imprint of Scholastic Inc.,
July 2003

ISBN 978-0-439-35807-1

Library of Congress Control Number: 2003102525

58 57   19 20/0

Printed in the U.S.A.   40

First Scholastic trade paperback printing, September 2004

To Neil, Jessica, and David,
who make my world magical

CONTENTS

HARRY POTTER

AND THE ORDER OF THE PHOENIX

DUDLEY DEMENTED

The hottest day of the summer so far was drawing to a close and a drowsy silence lay over the large, square houses of Privet Drive. Cars that were usually gleaming stood dusty in their drives and lawns that were once emerald green lay parched and yellowing; the use of hosepipes had been banned due to drought. Deprived of their usual car-washing and lawn-mowing pursuits, the inhabitants of Privet Drive had retreated into the shade of their cool houses, windows thrown wide in the hope of tempting in a nonexistent breeze. The only person left outdoors was a teenage boy who was lying flat on his back in a flower bed outside number four.

He was a skinny, black-haired, bespectacled boy who had the pinched, slightly unhealthy look of someone who has grown a lot in a short space of time. His jeans were torn and dirty, his T-shirt baggy and faded, and the soles of his trainers were peeling away from the uppers. Harry Potter's appearance did not endear him to the neighbors, who were the sort of people who thought scruffiness ought to be punishable by law, but as he had hidden himself behind a large hydrangea bush this evening he was quite invisible to passersby. In fact, the only way he would be spotted was if his Uncle Vernon or Aunt Petunia stuck their heads out of the living room window and looked straight down into the flower bed below.

On the whole, Harry thought he was to be congratulated on his idea of hiding here. He was not, perhaps, very comfortable lying on the hot, hard earth, but on the other hand, nobody was glaring at him, grinding their teeth so loudly that he could not hear the news, or shooting nasty questions at him, as had happened every time he had tried sitting down in the living room and watching television with his aunt and uncle.

Almost as though this thought had fluttered through the open window, Vernon Dursley, Harry's uncle, suddenly spoke. "Glad to see the boy's stopped trying to butt in. Where is he anyway?"

"I don't know," said Aunt Petunia unconcernedly. "Not in the house."

Uncle Vernon grunted.

"Watching the news . . ." he said scathingly. "I'd like to know what he's really up to. As if a normal boy cares what's on the news — Dudley hasn't got a clue what's going on, doubt he knows who the Prime Minister is! Anyway, it's not as if there'd be anything about *his lot* on *our* news —"

"Vernon, *shh!*" said Aunt Petunia. "The window's open!"

"Oh — yes — sorry, dear . . ."

The Dursleys fell silent. Harry listened to a jingle about Fruit 'N Bran breakfast cereal while he watched Mrs. Figg, a batty, cat-loving old lady from nearby Wisteria Walk, amble slowly past. She was frowning and muttering to herself. Harry was very pleased that he was concealed behind the bush; Mrs. Figg had recently taken to asking him around for tea whenever she met him in the street. She had rounded the corner and vanished from view before Uncle Vernon's voice floated out of the window again.

"Dudders out for tea?"

"At the Polkisses'," said Aunt Petunia fondly. "He's got so many little friends, he's so popular . . ."

Harry repressed a snort with difficulty. The Dursleys really were astonishingly stupid about their son, Dudley; they had swallowed all his dim-witted lies about having tea with a different member of his gang every night of the summer holidays. Harry knew perfectly well that Dudley had not been to tea anywhere; he and his gang spent every evening vandalizing the play park, smoking on street corners, and throwing stones at passing cars and children. Harry had seen them at it during his evening walks around Little Whinging; he had spent most of the holidays wandering the streets, scavenging newspapers from bins along the way.

The opening notes of the music that heralded the seven o'clock news reached Harry's ears and his stomach turned over. Perhaps tonight — after a month of waiting — would be the night —

"Record numbers of stranded holidaymakers fill airports as the Spanish baggage-handlers' strike reaches its second week —"

"Give 'em a lifelong siesta, I would," snarled Uncle Vernon over the end of the newsreader's sentence, but no matter: Outside in the flower bed, Harry's stomach seemed to unclench. If anything had happened, it would surely have been the first item on the news; death and destruction were more important than stranded holidaymakers. . . .

He let out a long, slow breath and stared up at the brilliant blue sky. Every day this summer had been the same: the tension, the expectation, the temporary relief, and then mounting tension again . . . and always, growing more insistent all the time, the question of *why* nothing had happened yet. . . .

He kept listening, just in case there was some small clue, not recognized for what it really was by the Muggles — an unexplained disappearance, perhaps, or some strange accident . . . but the baggage-handlers' strike was followed by news on the drought in the Southeast ("I hope he's listening next door!" bellowed Uncle Vernon, "with his sprinklers on at three in the morning!"); then a helicopter that had almost crashed in a field in Surrey, then a famous actress's divorce from her famous husband ("as if we're interested in their sordid affairs," sniffed Aunt Petunia, who had followed the case obsessively in every magazine she could lay her bony hands on).

Harry closed his eyes against the now blazing evening sky as the newsreader said, "And finally, Bungy the budgie has found a novel way of keeping cool this summer. Bungy, who lives at the Five Feathers in Barnsley, has learned to water-ski! Mary Dorkins went to find out more. . . ."

Harry opened his eyes again. If they had reached water-skiing budgerigars, there was nothing else worth hearing. He rolled cautiously onto his front and raised himself onto his knees and elbows, preparing to crawl out from under the window.

He had moved about two inches when several things happened in very quick succession.

A loud, echoing *crack* broke the sleepy silence like a gunshot; a cat streaked out from under a parked car and flew out of sight; a shriek, a bellowed oath, and the sound of breaking china came from the Dursleys' living room, and as though Harry had been waiting for this signal, he jumped to his feet, at the same time pulling from the waistband of his jeans a thin wooden wand as if he were unsheathing a sword. But before he could draw himself up to full height, the top of his head collided with the Dursleys' open window, and the resultant crash made Aunt Petunia scream even louder.

Harry felt as if his head had been split in two; eyes streaming, he swayed, trying to focus on the street and spot the source of the noise, but he had barely staggered upright again when two large purple hands reached through the open window and closed tightly around his throat.

"Put — it — away!" Uncle Vernon snarled into Harry's ear. *"Now! Before — anyone — sees!"*

"Get — off — me!" Harry gasped; for a few seconds they struggled, Harry pulling at his uncle's sausage-like fingers with his left hand, his right maintaining a firm grip on his raised wand. Then, as the pain in the top of Harry's head gave a particularly nasty throb, Uncle Vernon yelped and released Harry as though he had received an electric shock — some invisible force seemed to have surged through his nephew, making him impossible to hold.

Panting, Harry fell forward over the hydrangea bush, straightened up, and stared around. There was no sign of what had caused the loud cracking noise, but there were several faces peering through various nearby windows. Harry stuffed his wand hastily back into his jeans and tried to look innocent.

"Lovely evening!" shouted Uncle Vernon, waving at Mrs. Number Seven, who was glaring from behind her net curtains. "Did you hear that car backfire just now? Gave Petunia and me quite a turn!"

He continued to grin in a horrible, manic way until all the curious neighbors had disappeared from their various windows, then the grin became a grimace of rage as he beckoned Harry back toward him.

Harry moved a few steps closer, taking care to stop just short of the point at which Uncle Vernon's outstretched hands could resume their strangling.

"What the *devil* do you mean by it, boy?" asked Uncle Vernon in a croaky voice that trembled with fury.

"What do I mean by what?" said Harry coldly. He kept looking left and right up the street, still hoping to see the person who had made the cracking noise.

"Making a racket like a starting pistol right outside our —"

"I didn't make that noise," said Harry firmly.

Aunt Petunia's thin, horsey face now appeared beside Uncle Vernon's wide, purple one. She looked livid.

"Why were you lurking under our window?"

"Yes — yes, good point, Petunia! *What were you doing under our window, boy?*"

"Listening to the news," said Harry in a resigned voice.

His aunt and uncle exchanged looks of outrage.

"Listening to the news! *Again?*"

"Well, it changes every day, you see," said Harry.

"Don't you be clever with me, boy! I want to know what you're really up to — and don't give me any more of this *listening to the news* tosh! You know perfectly well that *your lot* . . ."

"Careful, Vernon!" breathed Aunt Petunia, and Uncle Vernon lowered his voice so that Harry could barely hear him, ". . . that *your lot* don't get on *our* news!"

"That's all you know," said Harry.

The Dursleys goggled at him for a few seconds, then Aunt Petunia said, "You're a nasty little liar. What are all those —" she too lowered her voice so that Harry had to lip-read the next word, "— *owls* — doing if they're not bringing you news?"

"Aha!" said Uncle Vernon in a triumphant whisper. "Get out of that one, boy! As if we didn't know you get all your news from those pestilential birds!"

Harry hesitated for a moment. It cost him something to tell the truth this time, even though his aunt and uncle could not possibly know how bad Harry felt at admitting it.

"The owls . . . aren't bringing me news," said Harry tonelessly.

"I don't believe it," said Aunt Petunia at once.

"No more do I," said Uncle Vernon forcefully.

"We know you're up to something funny," said Aunt Petunia.

"We're not stupid, you know," said Uncle Vernon.

"Well, *that's* news to me," said Harry, his temper rising, and before the Dursleys could call him back, he had wheeled about, crossed the front lawn, stepped over the low garden wall, and was striding off up the street.

He was in trouble now and he knew it. He would have to face his aunt and uncle later and pay the price for his rudeness, but he did not care very much just at the moment; he had much more pressing matters on his mind.

Harry was sure that the cracking noise had been made by someone Apparating or Disapparating. It was exactly the sound Dobby the house-elf made when he vanished into thin air. Was it possible that Dobby was here in Privet Drive? Could Dobby be following him right at this very moment? As this thought occurred he wheeled around and stared back down Privet Drive, but it appeared to be completely deserted again and Harry was sure that Dobby did not know how to become invisible. . . .

He walked on, hardly aware of the route he was taking, for he had pounded these streets so often lately that his feet carried him to his favorite haunts automatically. Every few steps he glanced back over his shoulder. Someone magical had been near him as he lay among Aunt Petunia's dying begonias, he was sure of it. Why hadn't they spoken to him, why hadn't they made contact, why were they hiding now?

And then, as his feeling of frustration peaked, his certainty leaked away.

Perhaps it hadn't been a magical sound after all. Perhaps he was so desperate for the tiniest sign of contact from the world to which he belonged that he was simply overreacting to perfectly ordinary noises. Could he be *sure* it hadn't been the sound of something breaking inside a neighbor's house?

Harry felt a dull, sinking sensation in his stomach and, before he knew it, the feeling of hopelessness that had plagued him all summer rolled over him once again. . . .

Tomorrow morning he would be awoken by the alarm at five

o'clock so that he could pay the owl that delivered the *Daily Prophet* —
but was there any point in continuing to take it? Harry merely glanced
at the front page before throwing it aside these days; when the idiots
who ran the paper finally realized that Voldemort was back it would
be headline news, and that was the only kind Harry cared about.

If he was lucky, there would also be owls carrying letters from his
best friends, Ron and Hermione, though any expectation he had had
that their letters would bring him news had long since been dashed.

*"We can't say much about you-know-what, obviously. . . ." "We've been
told not to say anything important in case our letters go astray. . . ."
"We're quite busy but I can't give you details here. . . ." "There's a fair
amount going on, we'll tell you everything when we see you. . . ."*

But when were they going to see him? Nobody seemed too bothered with a precise date. Hermione had scribbled, *"I expect we'll be
seeing you quite soon"* inside his birthday card, but how soon was soon?
As far as Harry could tell from the vague hints in their letters, Hermione and Ron were in the same place, presumably at Ron's parents'
house. He could hardly bear to think of the pair of them having fun
at the Burrow when he was stuck in Privet Drive. In fact, he was so
angry at them that he had thrown both their birthday presents of
Honeydukes chocolates away unopened, though he had regretted this
after eating the wilting salad Aunt Petunia had provided for dinner
that night.

And what were Ron and Hermione busy with? Why wasn't he,
Harry, busy? Hadn't he proved himself capable of handling much
more than they? Had they all forgotten what he had done? Hadn't it
been *he* who had entered that graveyard and watched Cedric being
murdered and been tied to that tombstone and nearly killed . . . ?

Don't think about that, Harry told himself sternly for the hundredth
time that summer. It was bad enough that he kept revisiting the graveyard in his nightmares, without dwelling on it in his waking moments
too.

He turned a corner into Magnolia Crescent; halfway along he passed the narrow alleyway down the side of a garage where he had first clapped eyes on his godfather. Sirius, at least, seemed to understand how Harry was feeling; admittedly his letters were just as empty of proper news as Ron and Hermione's, but at least they contained words of caution and consolation instead of tantalizing hints:

"I know this must be frustrating for you. . . ." "Keep your nose clean and everything will be okay. . . ." "Be careful and don't do anything rash. . . ."

Well, thought Harry, as he crossed Magnolia Crescent, turned into Magnolia Road, and headed toward the darkening play park, he had (by and large) done as Sirius advised; he had at least resisted the temptation to tie his trunk to his broomstick and set off for the Burrow by himself. In fact Harry thought his behavior had been very good considering how frustrated and angry he felt at being stuck in Privet Drive this long, reduced to hiding in flower beds in the hope of hearing something that might point to what Lord Voldemort was doing. Nevertheless, it was quite galling to be told not to be rash by a man who had served twelve years in the wizard prison, Azkaban, escaped, attempted to commit the murder he had been convicted for in the first place, then gone on the run with a stolen hippogriff. . . .

Harry vaulted over the locked park gate and set off across the parched grass. The park was as empty as the surrounding streets. When he reached the swings he sank onto the only one that Dudley and his friends had not yet managed to break, coiled one arm around the chain, and stared moodily at the ground. He would not be able to hide in the Dursleys' flower bed again. Tomorrow he would have to think of some fresh way of listening to the news. In the meantime, he had nothing to look forward to but another restless, disturbed night, because even when he escaped nightmares about Cedric he had unsettling dreams about long dark corridors, all finishing in dead ends and locked doors, which he supposed had something to do with the trapped feeling he had when he was awake. Often the old scar on his forehead prickled uncomfortably, but he did not fool himself that Ron or Hermione or Sirius would find that very interesting anymore. . . . In the past his scar hurting had warned that Voldemort was getting stronger again, but now that Voldemort was back they would probably remind him that its regular irritation was only to be expected. . . . Nothing to worry about . . . old news . . .

The injustice of it all welled up inside him so that he wanted to yell with fury. If it hadn't been for him, nobody would even have known Voldemort was back! And his reward was to be stuck in Little Whinging for four solid weeks, completely cut off from the magical world, reduced to squatting among dying begonias so that he could hear about water-skiing budgerigars! How could Dumbledore have forgotten him so easily? Why had Ron and Hermione got together without inviting him along too? How much longer was he supposed to endure Sirius telling him to sit tight and be a good boy; or resist the temptation to write to the stupid *Daily Prophet* and point out that Voldemort had returned? These furious thoughts whirled around in Harry's head, and his insides writhed with anger as a sultry, velvety night fell around him, the air full of the smell of warm, dry grass and the only sound that of the low grumble of traffic on the road beyond the park railings.

He did not know how long he had sat on the swing before the sound of voices interrupted his musings and he looked up. The streetlamps from the surrounding roads were casting a misty glow strong enough to silhouette a group of people making their way across the park. One of them was singing a loud, crude song. The others were laughing. A soft ticking noise came from several expensive racing bikes that they were wheeling along.

Harry knew who those people were. The figure in front was unmistakably his cousin, Dudley Dursley, wending his way home, accompanied by his faithful gang.

Dudley was as vast as ever, but a year's hard dieting and the discovery of a new talent had wrought quite a change in his physique. As Uncle Vernon delightedly told anyone who would listen, Dudley had recently become the Junior Heavyweight Inter-School Boxing Champion of the Southeast. "The noble sport," as Uncle Vernon called it, had made Dudley even more formidable than he had seemed to Harry in the primary school days when he had served as Dudley's first punching bag. Harry was not remotely afraid of his cousin anymore but he still didn't think that Dudley learning to punch harder and more accurately was cause for celebration. Neighborhood children all around were terrified of him — even more terrified than they were of "that Potter boy," who, they had been warned, was a hardened hooligan who attended St. Brutus's Secure Center for Incurably Criminal Boys.

Harry watched the dark figures crossing the grass and wondered whom they had been beating up tonight. *Look round,* Harry found himself thinking as he watched them. *Come on . . . look round . . . I'm sitting here all alone. . . . Come and have a go. . . .*

If Dudley's friends saw him sitting here, they would be sure to make a beeline for him, and what would Dudley do then? He wouldn't want to lose face in front of the gang, but he'd be terrified of provoking Harry. . . . It would be really fun to watch Dudley's dilemma; to taunt him, watch him, with him powerless to respond . . . and if any of the others tried hitting Harry, Harry was ready — he had his wand . . . let them try . . . He'd love to vent some of his frustration on the boys who had once made his life hell —

But they did not turn around, they did not see him, they were almost at the railings. Harry mastered the impulse to call after them. . . . Seeking a fight was not a smart move. . . . He must not use magic. . . . He would be risking expulsion again. . . .

Dudley's gang's voices died; they were out of sight, heading along Magnolia Road.

There you go, Sirius, Harry thought dully. *Nothing rash. Kept my nose clean. Exactly the opposite of what you'd have done . . .*

He got to his feet and stretched. Aunt Petunia and Uncle Vernon seemed to feel that whenever Dudley turned up was the right time to be home, and anytime after that was much too late. Uncle Vernon had threatened to lock Harry in the shed if he came home after Dudley again, so, stifling a yawn, still scowling, Harry set off toward the park gate.

Magnolia Road, like Privet Drive, was full of large, square houses with perfectly manicured lawns, all owned by large, square owners who drove very clean cars similar to Uncle Vernon's. Harry preferred Little Whinging by night, when the curtained windows made patches of jewel-bright colors in the darkness and he ran no danger of hearing disapproving mutters about his "delinquent" appearance when he passed the householders. He walked quickly, so that halfway along Magnolia Road Dudley's gang came into view again; they were saying their farewells at the entrance to Magnolia Crescent. Harry stepped into the shadow of a large lilac tree and waited.

". . . squealed like a pig, didn't he?" Malcolm was saying, to guffaws from the others.

"Nice right hook, Big D," said Piers.

"Same time tomorrow?" said Dudley.

"Round at my place, my parents are out," said Gordon.

"See you then," said Dudley.

"'Bye Dud!"

"See ya, Big D!"

Harry waited for the rest of the gang to move on before setting off again. When their voices had faded once more he headed around the corner into Magnolia Crescent and by walking very quickly he soon came within hailing distance of Dudley, who was strolling along at his ease, humming tunelessly.

"Hey, Big D!"

Dudley turned.

"Oh," he grunted. "It's you."

"How long have you been 'Big D' then?" said Harry.

"Shut it," snarled Dudley, turning away again.

"Cool name," said Harry, grinning and falling into step beside his cousin. "But you'll always be Ickle Diddykins to me."

"I said, SHUT IT!" said Dudley, whose ham-like hands had curled into fists.

"Don't the boys know that's what your mum calls you?"

"Shut your face."

"You don't tell *her* to shut her face. What about 'popkin' and 'Dinky Diddydums,' can I use them then?"

Dudley said nothing. The effort of keeping himself from hitting Harry seemed to be demanding all his self-control.

"So who've you been beating up tonight?" Harry asked, his grin fading. "Another ten-year-old? I know you did Mark Evans two nights ago —"

"He was asking for it," snarled Dudley.

"Oh yeah?"

"He cheeked me."

"Yeah? Did he say you look like a pig that's been taught to walk on its hind legs? 'Cause that's not cheek, Dud, that's true . . ."

A muscle was twitching in Dudley's jaw. It gave Harry enormous satisfaction to know how furious he was making Dudley; he felt as though he was siphoning off his own frustration into his cousin, the only outlet he had.

They turned right down the narrow alleyway where Harry had first seen Sirius and which formed a shortcut between Magnolia Crescent and Wisteria Walk. It was empty and much darker than the streets it linked because there were no streetlamps. Their footsteps were muffled between garage walls on one side and a high fence on the other.

"Think you're a big man carrying that thing, don't you?" Dudley said after a few seconds.

"What thing?"

"That — that thing you're hiding."

Harry grinned again.

"Not as stupid as you look, are you, Dud? But I s'pose if you were, you wouldn't be able to walk and talk at the same time. . . ."

Harry pulled out his wand. He saw Dudley look sideways at it.

"You're not allowed," Dudley said at once. "I know you're not. You'd get expelled from that freak school you go to."

"How d'you know they haven't changed the rules, Big D?"

"They haven't," said Dudley, though he didn't sound completely convinced. Harry laughed softly.

"You haven't got the guts to take me on without that thing, have you?" Dudley snarled.

"Whereas you just need four mates behind you before you can beat up a ten-year-old. You know that boxing title you keep banging on about? How old was your opponent? Seven? Eight?"

"He was sixteen for your information," snarled Dudley, "and he was out cold for twenty minutes after I'd finished with him and he was twice as heavy as you. You just wait till I tell Dad you had that thing out —"

"Running to Daddy now, are you? Is his ickle boxing champ frightened of nasty Harry's wand?"

"Not this brave at night, are you?" sneered Dudley.

"This *is* night, Diddykins. That's what we call it when it goes all dark like this."

"I mean when you're in bed!" Dudley snarled.

He had stopped walking. Harry stopped too, staring at his cousin. From the little he could see of Dudley's large face, he was wearing a strangely triumphant look.

"What d'you mean, I'm not brave in bed?" said Harry, completely nonplussed. "What — am I supposed to be frightened of pillows or something?"

"I heard you last night," said Dudley breathlessly. "Talking in your sleep. *Moaning.*"

"What d'you mean?" Harry said again, but there was a cold, plunging sensation in his stomach. He had revisited the graveyard last night in his dreams.

Dudley gave a harsh bark of laughter then adopted a high-pitched, whimpering voice. "'Don't kill Cedric! Don't kill Cedric!' Who's Cedric — your boyfriend?"

"I — you're lying —" said Harry automatically. But his mouth had gone dry. He knew Dudley wasn't lying — how else would he know about Cedric?

"'Dad! Help me, Dad! He's going to kill me, Dad! Boo-hoo!'"

"Shut up," said Harry quietly. "Shut up, Dudley, I'm warning you!"

"'Come and help me, Dad! Mum, come and help me! He's killed Cedric! Dad, help me! He's going to —' *Don't you point that thing at me!*"

Dudley backed into the alley wall. Harry was pointing the wand directly at Dudley's heart. Harry could feel fourteen years' hatred of Dudley pounding in his veins — what wouldn't he give to strike now, to jinx Dudley so thoroughly he'd have to crawl home like an insect, struck dumb, sprouting feelers —

"Don't ever talk about that again," Harry snarled. "D'you understand me?"

"Point that thing somewhere else!"

"I said, *do you understand me?*"

"*Point it somewhere else!*"

"DO YOU UNDERSTAND ME?"

"GET THAT THING AWAY FROM —"

Dudley gave an odd, shuddering gasp, as though he had been doused in icy water.

Something had happened to the night. The star-strewn indigo sky was suddenly pitch-black and lightless — the stars, the moon, the misty streetlamps at either end of the alley had vanished. The distant grumble of cars and the whisper of trees had gone. The balmy evening was suddenly piercingly, bitingly cold. They were surrounded by total, impenetrable, silent darkness, as though some giant hand had dropped a thick, icy mantle over the entire alleyway, blinding them.

For a split second Harry thought he had done magic without meaning to, despite the fact that he'd been resisting as hard as he could — then his reason caught up with his senses — he didn't have the power to turn off the stars. He turned his head this way and that, trying to see something, but the darkness pressed on his eyes like a weightless veil.

Dudley's terrified voice broke in Harry's ear.

"W-what are you d-doing? St-stop it!"

"I'm not doing anything! Shut up and don't move!"

"I c-can't see! I've g-gone blind! I —"

"I said shut up!"

Harry stood stock-still, turning his sightless eyes left and right. The cold was so intense that he was shivering all over; goose bumps had erupted up his arms, and the hairs on the back of his neck were standing up — he opened his eyes to their fullest extent, staring blankly around, unseeing . . .

It was impossible. . . . They couldn't be here. . . . Not in Little Whinging . . . He strained his ears. . . . He would hear them before he saw them. . . .

"I'll t-tell Dad!" Dudley whimpered. "W-where are you? What are you d-do — ?"

"Will you shut up?" Harry hissed, "I'm trying to lis —"

But he fell silent. He had heard just the thing he had been dreading.

There was something in the alleyway apart from themselves, something that was drawing long, hoarse, rattling breaths. Harry felt a horrible jolt of dread as he stood trembling in the freezing air.

"C-cut it out! Stop doing it! I'll h-hit you, I swear I will!"

"Dudley, shut —"

WHAM!

A fist made contact with the side of Harry's head, lifting Harry off his feet. Small white lights popped in front of Harry's eyes; for the second time in an hour he felt as though his head had been cleaved in two; next moment he had landed hard on the ground, and his wand had flown out of his hand.

"You moron, Dudley!" Harry yelled, his eyes watering with pain, as he scrambled to his hands and knees, now feeling around frantically in the blackness. He heard Dudley blundering away, hitting the alley fence, stumbling.

"DUDLEY, COME BACK! YOU'RE RUNNING RIGHT AT IT!"

There was a horrible squealing yell, and Dudley's footsteps stopped. At the same moment, Harry felt a creeping chill behind him that could mean only one thing. There was more than one.

"DUDLEY, KEEP YOUR MOUTH SHUT! WHATEVER YOU DO, KEEP YOUR MOUTH SHUT! Wand!" Harry muttered frantically, his hands flying over the ground like spiders. "Where's — wand — come on — *Lumos!*"

He said the spell automatically, desperate for light to help him in his search — and to his disbelieving relief, light flared inches from his right hand — the wand-tip had ignited. Harry snatched it up, scrambled to his feet, and turned around.

His stomach turned over.

A towering, hooded figure was gliding smoothly toward him, hovering over the ground, no feet or face visible beneath its robes, sucking on the night as it came.

Stumbling backward, Harry raised his wand.

"Expecto Patronum!"

A silvery wisp of vapor shot from the tip of the wand and the dementor slowed, but the spell hadn't worked properly; tripping over his feet, Harry retreated farther as the dementor bore down upon him, panic fogging his brain — *concentrate* —

A pair of gray, slimy, scabbed hands slid from inside the dementor's robes, reaching for him. A rushing noise filled Harry's ears.

"Expecto Patronum!"

His voice sounded dim and distant. . . . Another wisp of silver smoke, feebler than the last, drifted from the wand — he couldn't do it anymore, he couldn't work the spell —

There was laughter inside his own head, shrill, high-pitched laughter. . . . He could smell the dementor's putrid, death-cold breath, filling his own lungs, drowning him — *Think . . . something happy. . . .*

But there was no happiness in him. . . . The dementor's icy fingers were closing on his throat — the high-pitched laughter was growing louder and louder, and a voice spoke inside his head — *"Bow to death, Harry. . . . It might even be painless. . . . I would not know. . . . I have never died. . . ."*

He was never going to see Ron and Hermione again —

And their faces burst clearly into his mind as he fought for breath —

"EXPECTO PATRONUM!"

An enormous silver stag erupted from the tip of Harry's wand; its antlers caught the dementor in the place where the heart should have been; it was thrown backward, weightless as darkness, and as the stag charged, the dementor swooped away, batlike and defeated.

"THIS WAY!" Harry shouted at the stag. Wheeling around, he sprinted down the alleyway, holding the lit wand aloft. "DUDLEY? DUDLEY!"

He had run barely a dozen steps when he reached them: Dudley was curled on the ground, his arms clamped over his face; a second dementor was crouching low over him, gripping his wrists in its slimy hands, prizing them slowly, almost lovingly apart, lowering its hooded head toward Dudley's face as though about to kiss him. . . .

"GET IT!" Harry bellowed, and with a rushing, roaring sound, the silver stag he had conjured came galloping back past him. The dementor's eyeless face was barely an inch from Dudley's when the silver antlers caught it; the thing was thrown up into the air and, like its fellow, it soared away and was absorbed into the darkness. The stag cantered to the end of the alleyway and dissolved into silver mist.

Moon, stars, and streetlamps burst back into life. A warm breeze swept the alleyway. Trees rustled in neighboring gardens and the mundane rumble of cars in Magnolia Crescent filled the air again. Harry stood quite still, all his senses vibrating, taking in the abrupt return to normality. After a moment he became aware that his T-shirt was sticking to him; he was drenched in sweat.

He could not believe what had just happened. Dementors *here,* in Little Whinging . . .

Dudley lay curled up on the ground, whimpering and shaking. Harry bent down to see whether he was in a fit state to stand up, but then heard loud, running footsteps behind him; instinctively raising his wand again, he spun on his heel to face the newcomer.

Mrs. Figg, their batty old neighbor, came panting into sight. Her grizzled gray hair was escaping from its hairnet, a clanking string shopping bag was swinging from her wrist, and her feet were halfway out of her tartan carpet slippers. Harry made to stow his wand hurriedly out of sight, but —

"Don't put it away, idiot boy!" she shrieked. "What if there are more of them around? Oh, I'm going to *kill* Mundungus Fletcher!"

A PECK OF OWLS

What?" said Harry blankly.

"He left!" said Mrs. Figg, wringing her hands. "Left to see someone about a batch of cauldrons that fell off the back of a broom! I told him I'd flay him alive if he went, and now look! Dementors! It's just lucky I put Mr. Tibbles on the case! But we haven't got time to stand around! Hurry, now, we've got to get you back! Oh, the trouble this is going to cause! I will *kill* him!"

"But —"

The revelation that his batty old cat-obsessed neighbor knew what dementors were was almost as big a shock to Harry as meeting two of them down the alleyway. "You're — you're a *witch*?"

"I'm a Squib, as Mundungus knows full well, so how on earth was I supposed to help you fight off dementors? He left you completely without cover when I *warned* him —"

"This bloke Mundungus has been following me? Hang on — it was *him*! He Disapparated from the front of my house!"

"Yes, yes, *yes*, but luckily I'd stationed Mr. Tibbles under a car just in case, and Mr. Tibbles came and warned me, but by the time I got to your house you'd gone — and now — oh, *what's* Dumbledore going to say? You!" she shrieked at Dudley, still supine on the alley floor. "Get your fat bottom off the ground, quick!"

"You know Dumbledore?" said Harry, staring at her.

"Of course I know Dumbledore, who doesn't know Dumbledore? But come *on* — I'll be no help if they come back, I've never so much as Transfigured a teabag —"

She stooped down, seized one of Dudley's massive arms in her wizened hands, and tugged.

"Get *up*, you useless lump, get *up*!"

But Dudley either could not or would not move. He was still on the ground, trembling and ashen-faced, his mouth shut very tight.

"I'll do it." Harry took hold of Dudley's arm and heaved: With an enormous effort he managed to hoist Dudley to his feet. Dudley seemed to be on the point of fainting: His small eyes were rolling in their sockets and sweat was beading his face; the moment Harry let go of him he swayed dangerously.

"Hurry up!" said Mrs. Figg hysterically.

Harry pulled one of Dudley's massive arms around his own shoulders and dragged him toward the road, sagging slightly under his weight. Mrs. Figg tottered along in front of them, peering anxiously around the corner.

"Keep your wand out," she told Harry, as they entered Wisteria Walk. "Never mind the Statute of Secrecy now, there's going to be hell to pay anyway, we might as well be hanged for a dragon as an egg. Talk about the Reasonable Restriction of Underage Sorcery . . . This was *exactly* what Dumbledore was afraid of — what's that at the end of the street? Oh, it's just Mr. Prentice. . . . Don't put your wand away, boy, don't I keep telling you I'm no use?"

It was not easy to hold a wand steady and carry Dudley along at the same time. Harry gave his cousin an impatient dig in the ribs, but Dudley seemed to have lost all desire for independent movement. He was slumped on Harry's shoulder, his large feet dragging along the ground.

"Why didn't you tell me you're a Squib?" Harry asked Mrs. Figg, panting with the effort to keep walking. "All those times I came round your house — why didn't you say anything?"

"Dumbledore's orders. I was to keep an eye on you but not say anything, you were too young. I'm sorry I gave you such a miserable time, but the Dursleys would never have let you come if they'd thought you enjoyed it. It wasn't easy, you know. . . . But oh my word," she said tragically, wringing her hands once more, "when Dumbledore hears about this — how could Mundungus have left, he was supposed to be on duty until midnight — *where is he?* How am I going to tell Dumbledore what's happened, I can't Apparate —"

"I've got an owl, you can borrow her," Harry groaned, wondering whether his spine was going to snap under Dudley's weight.

"Harry, you don't understand! Dumbledore will need to act as quickly as possible, the Ministry have their own ways of detecting underage magic, they'll know already, you mark my words —"

"But I was getting rid of dementors, I had to use magic — they're going to be more worried what dementors were doing floating around Wisteria Walk, surely?"

"Oh my dear, I wish it were so but I'm afraid — MUNDUNGUS FLETCHER, I AM GOING TO KILL YOU!"

There was a loud *crack* and a strong smell of mingled drink and stale tobacco filled the air as a squat, unshaven man in a tattered overcoat materialized right in front of them. He had short bandy legs, long straggly ginger hair, and bloodshot baggy eyes that gave him the doleful look of a basset hound; he was also clutching a silvery bundle that Harry recognized at once as an Invisibility Cloak.

"'S' up, Figgy?" he said, staring from Mrs. Figg to Harry and Dudley. "What 'appened to staying undercover?"

"I'll give you undercover!" cried Mrs. Figg. "*Dementors,* you useless, skiving sneak thief!"

"Dementors?" repeated Mundungus, aghast. "Dementors here?"

"Yes, here, you worthless pile of bat droppings, here!" shrieked Mrs. Figg. "Dementors attacking the boy on your watch!"

"Blimey," said Mundungus weakly, looking from Mrs. Figg to Harry and back again. "Blimey, I . . ."

"And you off buying stolen cauldrons! Didn't I tell you not to go? *Didn't I?*"

"I — well, I —" Mundungus looked deeply uncomfortable. "It . . . it was a very good business opportunity, see . . ."

Mrs. Figg raised the arm from which her string bag dangled and whacked Mundungus around the face and neck with it; judging by the clanking noise it made it was full of cat food.

"Ouch — gerroff — gerroff, you mad old bat! Someone's gotta tell Dumbledore!"

"Yes — they — have!" yelled Mrs. Figg, still swinging the bag of cat food at every bit of Mundungus she could reach. "And — it — had — better — be — you — and — you — can — tell — him — why — you — weren't — there — to — help!"

"Keep your 'airnet on!" said Mundungus, his arms over his head, cowering. "I'm going, I'm going!"

And with another loud *crack,* he vanished.

"I hope Dumbledore *murders* him!" said Mrs. Figg furiously. "Now come *on,* Harry, what are you waiting for?"

Harry decided not to waste his remaining breath on pointing out that he could barely walk under Dudley's bulk. He gave the semiconscious Dudley a heave and staggered onward.

"I'll take you to the door," said Mrs. Figg, as they turned into Privet Drive. "Just in case there are more of them around. . . . Oh my word, what a catastrophe . . . and you had to fight them off yourself . . . and

Dumbledore said we were to keep you from doing magic at all costs. . . . Well, it's no good crying over spilled potion, I suppose . . . but the cat's among the pixies now . . ."

"So," Harry panted, "Dumbledore's . . . been having . . . me followed?"

"Of course he has," said Mrs. Figg impatiently. "Did you expect him to let you wander around on your own after what happened in June? Good Lord, boy, they told me you were intelligent. . . . Right . . . get inside and stay there," she said as they reached number four. "I expect someone will be in touch with you soon enough."

"What are you going to do?" asked Harry quickly.

"I'm going straight home," said Mrs. Figg, staring around the dark street and shuddering. "I'll need to wait for more instructions. Just stay in the house. Good night."

"Hang on, don't go yet! I want to know —"

But Mrs. Figg had already set off at a trot, carpet slippers flopping, string bag clanking.

"Wait!" Harry shouted after her; he had a million questions to ask anyone who was in contact with Dumbledore; but within seconds Mrs. Figg was swallowed by the darkness. Scowling, Harry readjusted Dudley on his shoulder and made his slow, painful way up number four's garden path.

The hall light was on. Harry stuck his wand back inside the waistband of his jeans, rang the bell, and watched Aunt Petunia's outline grow larger and larger, oddly distorted by the rippling glass in the front door.

"Diddy! About time too, I was getting quite — quite — *Diddy, what's the matter?*"

Harry looked sideways at Dudley and ducked out from under his arm just in time. Dudley swayed for a moment on the spot, his face pale green, then he opened his mouth at last and vomited all over the doormat.

"DIDDY! Diddy, what's the matter with you? Vernon? VERNON!"

Harry's uncle came galumphing out of the living room, walrus mustache blowing hither and thither as it always did when he was agitated. He hurried forward to help Aunt Petunia negotiate a weak-kneed Dudley over the threshold while avoiding stepping in the pool of sick.

"He's ill, Vernon!"

"What is it, son? What's happened? Did Mrs. Polkiss give you something foreign for tea?"

"Why are you all covered in dirt, darling? Have you been lying on the ground?"

"Hang on — you haven't been mugged, have you, son?"

Aunt Petunia screamed.

"Phone the police, Vernon! Phone the police! Diddy, darling, speak to Mummy! What did they do to you?"

In all the kerfuffle, nobody seemed to have noticed Harry, which suited him perfectly. He managed to slip inside just before Uncle Vernon slammed the door and while the Dursleys made their noisy progress down the hall toward the kitchen, Harry moved carefully and quietly toward the stairs.

"Who did it, son? Give us names. We'll get them, don't worry."

"Shh! He's trying to say something, Vernon! What is it, Diddy? Tell Mummy!"

Harry's foot was on the bottommost stair when Dudley found his voice.

"*Him.*"

Harry froze, foot on the stair, face screwed up, braced for the explosion.

"BOY! COME HERE!"

With a feeling of mingled dread and anger, Harry removed his foot slowly from the stair and turned to follow the Dursleys.

The scrupulously clean kitchen had an oddly unreal glitter after the darkness outside. Aunt Petunia was ushering Dudley into a chair; he was still very green and clammy looking. Uncle Vernon was standing in front of the draining board, glaring at Harry through tiny, narrowed eyes.

"What have you done to my son?" he said in a menacing growl.

"Nothing," said Harry, knowing perfectly well that Uncle Vernon wouldn't believe him.

"What did he do to you, Diddy?" Aunt Petunia said in a quavering voice, now sponging sick from the front of Dudley's leather jacket. "Was it — was it you-know-what, darling? Did he use — his *thing*?"

Slowly, tremulously, Dudley nodded.

"I didn't!" Harry said sharply, as Aunt Petunia let out a wail and Uncle Vernon raised his fists. "I didn't do anything to him, it wasn't me, it was —"

But at that precise moment a screech owl swooped in through the kitchen window. Narrowly missing the top of Uncle Vernon's head, it soared across the kitchen, dropped the large parchment envelope it was carrying in its beak at Harry's feet, and turned gracefully, the tips of its wings just brushing the top of the fridge, then zoomed outside again and off across the garden.

"OWLS!" bellowed Uncle Vernon, the well-worn vein in his temple pulsing angrily as he slammed the kitchen window shut. "OWLS AGAIN! I WILL NOT HAVE ANY MORE OWLS IN MY HOUSE!"

But Harry was already ripping open the envelope and pulling out the letter inside, his heart pounding somewhere in the region of his Adam's apple.

Dear Mr. Potter,

We have received intelligence that you performed the Patronus Charm at twenty-three minutes past nine this evening in a Muggle-inhabited area and in the presence of a Muggle.

The severity of this breach of the Decree for the Reasonable Restriction of Underage Sorcery has resulted in your expulsion from Hogwarts School of Witchcraft and Wizardry. Ministry representatives will be calling at your place of residence shortly to destroy your wand.

As you have already received an official warning for a previous offense under section 13 of the International Confederation of Wizards' Statute of Secrecy, we regret to inform you that your presence is required at a disciplinary hearing at the Ministry of Magic at 9 A.M. on August 12th.

Hoping you are well,

Yours sincerely,

Mafalda Hopkirk

IMPROPER USE OF MAGIC OFFICE
Ministry of Magic

Harry read the letter through twice. He was only vaguely aware of Uncle Vernon and Aunt Petunia talking in the vicinity. Inside his head, all was icy and numb. One fact had penetrated his consciousness like a paralyzing dart. He was expelled from Hogwarts. It was all over. He was never going back.

He looked up at the Dursleys. Uncle Vernon was purple-faced, shouting, his fists still raised; Aunt Petunia had her arms around Dudley, who was retching again.

Harry's temporarily stupefied brain seemed to reawaken. *Ministry representatives will be calling at your place of residence shortly to destroy your wand.* There was only one thing for it. He would have to run — now. Where he was going to go, Harry didn't know, but he was certain of one thing: At Hogwarts or outside it, he needed his wand. In an almost dreamlike state, he pulled his wand out and turned to leave the kitchen.

"Where d'you think you're going?" yelled Uncle Vernon. When Harry didn't reply, he pounded across the kitchen to block the doorway into the hall. "I haven't finished with you, boy!"

"Get out of the way," said Harry quietly.

"You're going to stay here and explain how my son —"

"If you don't get out of the way I'm going to jinx you," said Harry, raising the wand.

"You can't pull that one on me!" snarled Uncle Vernon. "I know you're not allowed to use it outside that madhouse you call a school!"

"The madhouse has chucked me out," said Harry. "So I can do whatever I like. You've got three seconds. One — two —"

A resounding *CRACK* filled the kitchen; Aunt Petunia screamed, Uncle Vernon yelled and ducked, but for the third time that night Harry was staring for the source of a disturbance he had not made. He spotted it at once: A dazed and ruffled-looking barn owl was sitting outside on the kitchen sill, having just collided with the closed window.

Ignoring Uncle Vernon's anguished yell of "OWLS!" Harry crossed the room at a run and wrenched the window open again. The owl stuck out its leg, to which a small roll of parchment was tied, shook its feathers, and took off the moment Harry had pulled off the letter. Hands shaking, Harry unfurled the second message, which was written very hastily and blotchily in black ink.

Harry —

Dumbledore's just arrived at the Ministry, and he's trying to sort it all out. DO NOT LEAVE YOUR AUNT AND UNCLE'S HOUSE. DO NOT DO ANY MORE MAGIC. DO NOT SURRENDER YOUR WAND.

Arthur Weasley

Dumbledore was trying to sort it all out. . . . What did that mean? How much power did Dumbledore have to override the Ministry of Magic? Was there a chance that he might be allowed back to Hogwarts, then? A small shoot of hope burgeoned in Harry's chest, almost immediately strangled by panic — how was he supposed to refuse to surrender his wand without doing magic? He'd have to duel with the Ministry representatives, and if he did that, he'd be lucky to escape Azkaban, let alone expulsion.

His mind was racing. . . . He could run for it and risk being captured by the Ministry, or stay put and wait for them to find him here. He was much more tempted by the former course, but he knew that Mr. Weasley had his best interests at heart . . . and, after all, Dumbledore had sorted out much worse than this before. . . .

"Right," Harry said, "I've changed my mind, I'm staying."

He flung himself down at the kitchen table and faced Dudley and Aunt Petunia. The Dursleys appeared taken aback at his abrupt change of mind. Aunt Petunia glanced despairingly at Uncle Vernon. The vein in Uncle Vernon's purple temple was throbbing worse than ever.

"Who are all these ruddy owls from?" he growled.

"The first one was from the Ministry of Magic, expelling me," said Harry calmly; he was straining his ears to catch noises outside in case the Ministry representatives were approaching, and it was easier and quieter to answer Uncle Vernon's questions than to have him start raging and bellowing. "The second one was from my friend Ron's dad, he works at the Ministry."

"*Ministry of Magic?*" bellowed Uncle Vernon. "People like you in *government*? Oh this explains everything, everything, no wonder the country's going to the dogs. . . ."

When Harry did not respond, Uncle Vernon glared at him, then spat, "And why have you been expelled?"

"Because I did magic."

"AHA!" roared Uncle Vernon, slamming his fist down on the top of the fridge, which sprang open; several of Dudley's low-fat snacks toppled out and burst on the floor. "So you admit it! *What did you do to Dudley?*"

"Nothing," said Harry, slightly less calmly. "That wasn't me —"

"*Was,*" muttered Dudley unexpectedly, and Uncle Vernon and Aunt Petunia instantly made flapping gestures at Harry to quiet him while they both bent low over Dudley.

"Go on, son," said Uncle Vernon, "what did he do?"

"Tell us, darling," whispered Aunt Petunia.

"Pointed his wand at me," Dudley mumbled.

"Yeah, I did, but I didn't use —" Harry began angrily, but . . .

"SHUT UP!" roared Uncle Vernon and Aunt Petunia in unison. "Go on, son," repeated Uncle Vernon, mustache blowing about furiously.

"All dark," Dudley said hoarsely, shuddering. "Everything dark. And then I h-heard . . . *things.* Inside m-my head . . ."

Uncle Vernon and Aunt Petunia exchanged looks of utter horror. If their least favorite thing in the world was magic, closely followed by neighbors who cheated more than they did on the hosepipe ban, people who heard voices were definitely in the bottom ten. They obviously thought Dudley was losing his mind.

"What sort of things did you hear, popkin?" breathed Aunt Petunia, very white-faced and with tears in her eyes.

But Dudley seemed incapable of saying. He shuddered again and shook his large blond head, and despite the sense of numb dread that had settled on Harry since the arrival of the first owl, he felt a certain curiosity. Dementors caused a person to relive the worst moments of their life. . . . What would spoiled, pampered, bullying Dudley have been forced to hear?

"How come you fell over, son?" said Uncle Vernon in an unnaturally quiet voice, the kind of voice he would adopt at the bedside of a very ill person.

"T-tripped," said Dudley shakily. "And then —"

He gestured at his massive chest. Harry understood: Dudley was remembering the clammy cold that filled the lungs as hope and happiness were sucked out of you.

"Horrible," croaked Dudley. "Cold. Really cold."

"Okay," said Uncle Vernon in a voice of forced calm, while Aunt Petunia laid an anxious hand on Dudley's forehead to feel his temperature. "What happened then, Dudders?"

"Felt . . . felt . . . felt . . . as if . . . as if . . ."

"As if you'd never be happy again," Harry supplied tonelessly.

"Yes," Dudley whispered, still trembling.

"So," said Uncle Vernon, voice restored to full and considerable volume as he straightened up. "So you put some crackpot spell on my son so he'd hear voices and believe he was — was doomed to misery, or something, did you?"

"How many times do I have to tell you?" said Harry, temper and voice rising together. "*It wasn't me!* It was a couple of dementors!"

"A couple of — what's this codswallop?"

"De — men — tors," said Harry slowly and clearly. "Two of them."

"And what the ruddy hell are dementors?"

"They guard the wizard prison, Azkaban," said Aunt Petunia.

Two seconds' ringing silence followed these words and then Aunt Petunia clapped her hand over her mouth as though she had let slip a disgusting swear word. Uncle Vernon was goggling at her. Harry's brain reeled. Mrs. Figg was one thing — but *Aunt Petunia*?

"How d'you know that?" he asked her, astonished.

Aunt Petunia looked quite appalled with herself. She glanced at Uncle Vernon in fearful apology, then lowered her hand slightly to reveal her horsey teeth.

"I heard — that awful boy — telling *her* about them — years ago," she said jerkily.

"If you mean my mum and dad, why don't you use their names?" said Harry loudly, but Aunt Petunia ignored him. She seemed horribly flustered.

Harry was stunned. Except for one outburst years ago, in the course of which Aunt Petunia had screamed that Harry's mother had been a freak, he had never heard her mention her sister. He was astounded that she had remembered this scrap of information about the magical world for so long, when she usually put all her energies into pretending it didn't exist.

Uncle Vernon opened his mouth, closed it again, opened it once more, shut it, then, apparently struggling to remember how to talk, opened it for a third time and croaked, "So — so — they — er — they — er — they actually exist, do they — er — dementy-whatsits?"

Aunt Petunia nodded.

Uncle Vernon looked from Aunt Petunia to Dudley to Harry as if hoping somebody was going to shout "April Fool!" When nobody did, he opened his mouth yet again, but was spared the struggle to find more words by the arrival of the third owl of the evening, which zoomed through the still-open window like a feathery cannonball and landed with a clatter on the kitchen table, causing all three of the Dursleys to jump with fright. Harry tore a second official-looking envelope from the owl's beak and ripped it open as the owl swooped back out into the night.

"Enough — effing — *owls* . . ." muttered Uncle Vernon distractedly, stomping over to the window and slamming it shut again.

Dear Mr. Potter,

Further to our letter of approximately twenty-two minutes ago, the Ministry of Magic has revised its decision to destroy your wand forthwith. You may retain your wand until your disciplinary hearing on 12th August, at which time an official decision will be taken.

Following discussions with the headmaster of Hogwarts School of Witchcraft and Wizardry, the Ministry has agreed that the question of your expulsion will also be decided at that time. You should therefore consider yourself suspended from school pending further inquiries.

With best wishes,

Yours sincerely,

Mafalda Hopkirk

IMPROPER USE OF MAGIC OFFICE
Ministry of Magic

Harry read this letter through three times in quick succession. The miserable knot in his chest loosened slightly at the thought that he was not definitely expelled, though his fears were by no means banished. Everything seemed to hang on this hearing on the twelfth of August.

"Well?" said Uncle Vernon, recalling Harry to his surroundings. "What now? Have they sentenced you to anything? Do your lot have the death penalty?" he added as a hopeful afterthought.

"I've got to go to a hearing," said Harry.

"And they'll sentence you there?"

"I suppose so."

"I won't give up hope, then," said Uncle Vernon nastily.

"Well, if that's all," said Harry, getting to his feet. He was desperate to be alone, to think, perhaps to send a letter to Ron, Hermione, or Sirius.

"NO, IT RUDDY WELL IS NOT ALL!" bellowed Uncle Vernon. "SIT BACK DOWN!"

"What *now?*" said Harry impatiently.

"DUDLEY!" roared Uncle Vernon. "I want to know exactly what happened to my son!"

"FINE!" yelled Harry, and in his temper, red and gold sparks shot out of the end of his wand, still clutched in his hand. All three Dursleys flinched, looking terrified.

"Dudley and I were in the alleyway between Magnolia Crescent and Wisteria Walk," said Harry, speaking fast, fighting to control his temper. "Dudley thought he'd be smart with me, I pulled out my wand but didn't use it. Then two dementors turned up —"

"But what ARE dementoids?" asked Uncle Vernon furiously. "What do they DO?"

"I told you — they suck all the happiness out of you," said Harry, "and if they get the chance, they kiss you —"

"Kiss you?" said Uncle Vernon, his eyes popping slightly. "*Kiss* you?"

"It's what they call it when they suck the soul out of your mouth." Aunt Petunia uttered a soft scream.

"His *soul?* They didn't take — he's still got his —"

She seized Dudley by the shoulders and shook him, as though testing to see whether she could hear his soul rattling around inside him.

"Of course they didn't get his soul, you'd know if they had," said Harry, exasperated.

"Fought 'em off, did you, son?" said Uncle Vernon loudly, with the appearance of a man struggling to bring the conversation back onto a plane he understood. "Gave 'em the old one-two, did you?"

"You can't give a dementor *the old one-two,*" said Harry through clenched teeth.

"Why's he all right, then?" blustered Uncle Vernon. "Why isn't he all empty, then?"

"Because I used the Patronus —"

WHOOSH. With a clattering, a whirring of wings, and a soft fall of dust, a fourth owl came shooting out of the kitchen fireplace.

"FOR GOD'S SAKE!" roared Uncle Vernon, pulling great clumps of hair out of his mustache, something he hadn't been driven to in a long time. "I WILL NOT HAVE OWLS HERE, I WILL NOT TOLERATE THIS, I TELL YOU!"

But Harry was already pulling a roll of parchment from the owl's leg. He was so convinced that this letter had to be from Dumbledore, explaining everything — the dementors, Mrs. Figg, what the Ministry was up to, how he, Dumbledore, intended to sort everything out — that for the first time in his life he was disappointed to see Sirius's handwriting. Ignoring Uncle Vernon's ongoing rant about owls and narrowing his eyes against a second cloud of dust as the most recent owl took off back up the chimney, Harry read Sirius's message.

> Arthur's just told us what's happened.
> Don't leave the house again, whatever you do.

Harry found this such an inadequate response to everything that had happened tonight that he turned the piece of parchment over, looking for the rest of the letter, but there was nothing there.

And now his temper was rising again. Wasn't *anybody* going to say "well done" for fighting off two dementors single-handedly? Both Mr. Weasley and Sirius were acting as though he'd misbehaved and they were saving their tellings-off until they could ascertain how much damage had been done.

"— a peck, I mean, pack of owls shooting in and out of my house and I won't have it, boy, I won't —"

"I can't stop the owls coming," Harry snapped, crushing Sirius's letter in his fist.

"I want the truth about what happened tonight!" barked Uncle Vernon. "If it was demenders who hurt Dudley, how come you've been expelled? You did you-know-what, you've admitted it!"

Harry took a deep, steadying breath. His head was beginning to ache again. He wanted more than anything to get out of the kitchen, away from the Dursleys.

"I did the Patronus Charm to get rid of the dementors," he said, forcing himself to remain calm. "It's the only thing that works against them."

"But what were dementoids *doing* in Little Whinging?" said Uncle Vernon in tones of outrage.

"Couldn't tell you," said Harry wearily. "No idea."

His head was pounding in the glare of the strip lighting now. His anger was ebbing away. He felt drained, exhausted. The Dursleys were all staring at him.

"It's you," said Uncle Vernon forcefully. "It's got something to do with you, boy, I know it. Why else would they turn up here? Why else would they be down that alleyway? You've got to be the only — the only —" Evidently he couldn't bring himself to say the word "wizard." "The only *you-know-what* for miles."

"I don't know why they were here. . . ."

But at these words of Uncle Vernon's, Harry's exhausted brain ground back into action. Why *had* the dementors come to Little Whinging? How *could* it be coincidence that they had arrived in the alleyway where Harry was? Had they been sent? Had the Ministry of Magic lost control of the dementors, had they deserted Azkaban and joined Voldemort, as Dumbledore had predicted they would?

"These demembers guard some weirdos' prison?" said Uncle Vernon, lumbering in the wake of Harry's train of thought.

"Yes," said Harry.

If only his head would stop hurting, if only he could just leave the kitchen and get to his dark bedroom and *think.* . . .

"Oho! They were coming to arrest you!" said Uncle Vernon, with the triumphant air of a man reaching an unassailable conclusion. "That's it, isn't it, boy? You're on the run from the law!"

"Of course I'm not," said Harry, shaking his head as though to scare off a fly, his mind racing now.

"Then why — ?"

"He must have sent them," said Harry quietly, more to himself than to Uncle Vernon.

"What's that? Who must have sent them?"

"Lord Voldemort," said Harry.

He registered dimly how strange it was that the Dursleys, who flinched, winced, and squawked if they heard words like "wizard," "magic," or "wand," could hear the name of the most evil wizard of all time without the slightest tremor.

"Lord — hang on," said Uncle Vernon, his face screwed up, a look of dawning comprehension in his piggy eyes. "I've heard that name . . . that was the one who . . ."

"Murdered my parents, yes," Harry said.

"But he's gone," said Uncle Vernon impatiently, without the slightest sign that the murder of Harry's parents might be a painful topic to anybody. "That giant bloke said so. He's gone."

"He's back," said Harry heavily.

It felt very strange to be standing here in Aunt Petunia's surgically clean kitchen, beside the top-of-the-range fridge and the wide-screen television, and talking calmly of Lord Voldemort to Uncle Vernon. The arrival of the dementors in Little Whinging seemed to have caused a breach in the great, invisible wall that divided the relentlessly non-magical world of Privet Drive and the world beyond. Harry's two lives had somehow become fused and everything had been turned upside down: The Dursleys were asking for details about the magical world and Mrs. Figg knew Albus Dumbledore; dementors were soaring around Little Whinging and he might never go back to Hogwarts. Harry's head throbbed more painfully.

"Back?" whispered Aunt Petunia.

She was looking at Harry as she had never looked at him before. And all of a sudden, for the very first time in his life, Harry fully appreciated that Aunt Petunia was his mother's sister. He could not have said why this hit him so very powerfully at this moment. All he knew was that he was not the only person in the room who had an inkling of what Lord Voldemort being back might mean. Aunt Petunia had never in her life looked at him like that before. Her large, pale eyes (so unlike her sister's) were not narrowed in dislike or anger: They were wide and fearful. The furious pretense that Aunt Petunia had maintained all Harry's life — that there was no magic and no world other than the world she inhabited with Uncle Vernon — seemed to have fallen away.

"Yes," Harry said, talking directly to Aunt Petunia now. "He came back a month ago. I saw him."

Her hands found Dudley's massive leather-clad shoulders and clutched them.

"Hang on," said Uncle Vernon, looking from his wife to Harry and back again, apparently dazed and confused by the unprecedented understanding that seemed to have sprung up between them. "Hang on. This Lord Voldything's back, you say."

"Yes."

"The one who murdered your parents."

"Yes."

"And now he's sending dismembers after you?"

"Looks like it," said Harry.

"I see," said Uncle Vernon, looking from his white-faced wife to Harry and hitching up his trousers. He seemed to be swelling, his great purple face stretching before Harry's eyes. "Well, that settles it," he said, his shirt front straining as he inflated himself, *"you can get out of this house, boy!"*

"What?" said Harry.

"You heard me — OUT!" Uncle Vernon bellowed, and even Aunt

Petunia and Dudley jumped. "OUT! OUT! I should've done it years ago! Owls treating the place like a rest home, puddings exploding, half the lounge destroyed, Dudley's tail, Marge bobbing around on the ceiling, and that flying Ford Anglia — OUT! OUT! You've had it! You're history! You're not staying here if some loony's after you, you're not endangering my wife and son, you're not bringing trouble down on us, if you're going the same way as your useless parents, I've had it! OUT!"

Harry stood rooted to the spot. The letters from the Ministry, Mr. Weasley, and Sirius were crushed in his left hand. *Don't leave the house again, whatever you do. DO NOT LEAVE YOUR AUNT AND UNCLE'S HOUSE.*

"You heard me!" said Uncle Vernon, bending forward now, so that his massive purple face came closer to Harry's, so that Harry actually felt flecks of spit hit his face. "Get going! You were all keen to leave half an hour ago! I'm right behind you! Get out and never darken our doorstep again! Why we ever kept you in the first place I don't know. Marge was right, it should have been the orphanage, we were too damn soft for our own good, thought we could squash it out of you, thought we could turn you normal, but you've been rotten from the beginning, and I've had enough — OWLS!"

The fifth owl zoomed down the chimney so fast it actually hit the floor before zooming into the air again with a loud screech. Harry raised his hand to seize the letter, which was in a scarlet envelope, but it soared straight over his head, flying directly at Aunt Petunia, who let out a scream and ducked, her arms over her face. The owl dropped the red envelope on her head, turned, and flew straight up the chimney again.

Harry darted forward to pick up the letter, but Aunt Petunia beat him to it.

"You can open it if you like," said Harry, "but I'll hear what it says anyway. That's a Howler."

"Let go of it, Petunia!" roared Uncle Vernon. "Don't touch it, it could be dangerous!"

"It's addressed to me," said Aunt Petunia in a shaking voice. "It's addressed to *me*, Vernon, look! *Mrs. Petunia Dursley, The Kitchen, Number Four, Privet Drive —*"

She caught her breath, horrified. The red envelope had begun to smoke.

"Open it!" Harry urged her. "Get it over with! It'll happen anyway —"

"No —"

Aunt Petunia's hand was trembling. She looked wildly around the kitchen as though looking for an escape route, but too late — the envelope burst into flames. Aunt Petunia screamed and dropped it.

An awful voice filled the kitchen, echoing in the confined space, issuing from the burning letter on the table.

"REMEMBER MY LAST, PETUNIA."

Aunt Petunia looked as though she might faint. She sank into the chair beside Dudley, her face in her hands. The remains of the envelope smoldered into ash in the silence.

"What is this?" Uncle Vernon said hoarsely. "What — I don't — Petunia?"

Aunt Petunia said nothing. Dudley was staring stupidly at his mother, his mouth hanging open. The silence spiraled horribly. Harry was watching his aunt, utterly bewildered, his head throbbing fit to burst.

"Petunia, dear?" said Uncle Vernon timidly. "P-Petunia?"

She raised her head. She was still trembling. She swallowed.

"The boy — the boy will have to stay, Vernon," she said weakly.

"W-what?"

"He stays," she said. She was not looking at Harry. She got to her feet again.

"He . . . but Petunia . . ."

"If we throw him out, the neighbors will talk," she said. She was regaining her usual brisk, snappish manner rapidly, though she was still very pale. "They'll ask awkward questions, they'll want to know where he's gone. We'll have to keep him."

Uncle Vernon was deflating like an old tire.

"But Petunia, dear —"

Aunt Petunia ignored him. She turned to Harry.

"You're to stay in your room," she said. "You're not to leave the house. Now get to bed."

Harry didn't move.

"Who was that Howler from?"

"Don't ask questions," Aunt Petunia snapped.

"Are you in touch with wizards?"

"I told you to get to bed!"

"What did it mean? Remember the last what?"

"Go to bed!"

"How come — ?"

"YOU HEARD YOUR AUNT, NOW GET TO BED!"

THE ADVANCE GUARD

I've just been attacked by dementors and I might be expelled from Hogwarts. I want to know what's going on and when I'm going to get out of here.

Harry copied these words onto three separate pieces of parchment the moment he reached the desk in his dark bedroom. He addressed the first to Sirius, the second to Ron, and the third to Hermione. His owl, Hedwig, was off hunting; her cage stood empty on the desk. Harry paced the bedroom waiting for her to come back, his head pounding, his brain too busy for sleep even though his eyes stung and itched with tiredness. His back ached from carrying Dudley home, and the two lumps on his head where the window and Dudley had hit him were throbbing painfully.

Up and down he paced, consumed with anger and frustration, grinding his teeth and clenching his fists, casting angry looks out at the empty, star-strewn sky every time he passed the window. Dementors sent to get him, Mrs. Figg and Mundungus Fletcher tailing him in secret, then suspension from Hogwarts and a hearing at the Ministry of Magic — and *still* no one was telling him what was going on.

And what, *what*, had that Howler been about? Whose voice had echoed so horribly, so menacingly, through the kitchen?

Why was he still trapped here without information? Why was everyone treating him like some naughty kid? *Don't do any more magic, stay in the house. . . .*

He kicked his school trunk as he passed it, but far from relieving his anger he felt worse, as he now had a sharp pain in his toe to deal with in addition to the pain in the rest of his body.

Just as he limped past the window, Hedwig soared through it with a soft rustle of wings like a small ghost.

"About time!" Harry snarled, as she landed lightly on top of her cage. "You can put that down, I've got work for you!"

Hedwig's large round amber eyes gazed reproachfully at him over the dead frog clamped in her beak.

"Come here," said Harry, picking up the three small rolls of parchment and a leather thong and tying the scrolls to her scaly leg. "Take these straight to Sirius, Ron, and Hermione and don't come back here without good long replies. Keep pecking them till they've written decent-length answers if you've got to. Understand?"

Hedwig gave a muffled hooting noise, beak still full of frog.

"Get going, then," said Harry.

She took off immediately. The moment she'd gone, Harry threw himself down onto his bed without undressing and stared at the dark ceiling. In addition to every other miserable feeling, he now felt guilty that he'd been irritable with Hedwig; she was the only friend he had at number four, Privet Drive. But he'd make it up to her when she came back with Sirius's, Ron's, and Hermione's answers.

They were bound to write back quickly; they couldn't possibly ignore a dementor attack. He'd probably wake up tomorrow to three fat letters full of sympathy and plans for his immediate removal to the Burrow. And with that comforting idea, sleep rolled over him, stifling all further thought.

* * *

But Hedwig didn't return next morning. Harry spent the day in his bedroom, leaving it only to go to the bathroom. Three times that day Aunt Petunia shoved food into his room through the cat flap Uncle Vernon had installed three summers ago. Every time Harry heard her approaching he tried to question her about the Howler, but he might as well have interrogated the doorknob for all the answers he got. Otherwise the Dursleys kept well clear of his bedroom. Harry couldn't see the point of forcing his company on them; another row would achieve nothing except perhaps making him so angry he'd perform more illegal magic.

So it went on for three whole days. Harry was filled alternately with restless energy that made him unable to settle to anything, during which he paced his bedroom again, furious at the whole lot of them for leaving him to stew in this mess, and with a lethargy so complete that he could lie on his bed for an hour at a time, staring dazedly into space, aching with dread at the thought of the Ministry hearing.

What if they ruled against him? What if he *was* expelled and his wand was snapped in half? What would he do, where would he go? He could not return to living full-time with the Dursleys, not now that he knew the other world, the one to which he really belonged. . . . Was it possible that he might be able to move into Sirius's house, as Sirius had suggested a year ago, before he had been forced to flee from the Ministry himself? Would he be allowed to live there alone, given that he was still underage? Or would the matter of where he went next be decided for him; had his breach of the International Statute of Secrecy been severe enough to land him in a cell in Azkaban? Whenever this thought occurred, Harry invariably slid off his bed and began pacing again.

On the fourth night after Hedwig's departure Harry was lying in one of his apathetic phases, staring at the ceiling, his exhausted mind quite blank, when his uncle entered his bedroom. Harry looked slowly around at him. Uncle Vernon was wearing his best suit and an expression of enormous smugness.

"We're going out," he said.

"Sorry?"

"We — that is to say, your aunt, Dudley, and I — are going out."

"Fine," said Harry dully, looking back at the ceiling.

"You are not to leave your bedroom while we are away."

"Okay."

"You are not to touch the television, the stereo, or any of our possessions."

"Right."

"You are not to steal food from the fridge."

"Okay."

"I am going to lock your door."

"You do that."

Uncle Vernon glared at Harry, clearly suspicious of this lack of argument, then stomped out of the room and closed the door behind him. Harry heard the key turn in the lock and Uncle Vernon's footsteps walking heavily down the stairs. A few minutes later he heard the slamming of car doors, the rumble of an engine, and the unmistakable sound of the car sweeping out of the drive.

Harry had no particular feeling about the Dursleys leaving. It made no difference to him whether they were in the house or not. He could not even summon the energy to get up and turn on his bedroom light. The room grew steadily darker around him as he lay listening to the night sounds through the window he kept open all the time, waiting for the blessed moment when Hedwig returned.

The empty house creaked around him. The pipes gurgled. Harry lay there in a kind of stupor, thinking of nothing, suspended in misery.

And then, quite distinctly, he heard a crash in the kitchen below.

He sat bolt upright, listening intently. The Dursleys couldn't be back, it was much too soon, and in any case he hadn't heard their car.

There was silence for a few seconds, and then he heard voices.

Burglars, he thought, sliding off the bed onto his feet — but a split second later it occurred to him that burglars would keep their voices down, and whoever was moving around in the kitchen was certainly not troubling to do so.

He snatched up his wand from his bedside table and stood facing his bedroom door, listening with all his might. Next moment he jumped as the lock gave a loud click and his door swung open.

Harry stood motionless, staring through the open door at the dark upstairs landing, straining his ears for further sounds, but none came. He hesitated for a moment and then moved swiftly and silently out of his room to the head of the stairs.

His heart shot upward into his throat. There were people standing in the shadowy hall below, silhouetted against the streetlight glowing through the glass door; eight or nine of them, all, as far as he could see, looking up at him.

"Lower your wand, boy, before you take someone's eye out," said a low, growling voice.

Harry's heart was thumping uncontrollably. He knew that voice, but he did not lower his wand.

"Professor Moody?" he said uncertainly.

"I don't know so much about 'Professor,'" growled the voice, "never got round to much teaching, did I? Get down here, we want to see you properly."

Harry lowered his wand slightly but did not relax his grip on it, nor did he move. He had very good reason to be suspicious. He had recently spent nine months in what he had thought was Mad-Eye Moody's company only to find out that it wasn't Moody at all, but an impostor; an impostor, moreover, who had tried to kill Harry before being unmasked. But before he could make a decision about what to do next, a second, slightly hoarse voice floated upstairs.

"It's all right, Harry. We've come to take you away."

Harry's heart leapt. He knew that voice too, though he hadn't heard it for more than a year.

"P-Professor Lupin?" he said disbelievingly. "Is that you?"

"Why are we all standing in the dark?" said a third voice, this one completely unfamiliar, a woman's. *"Lumos."*

A wand-tip flared, illuminating the hall with magical light. Harry blinked. The people below were crowded around the foot of the stairs, gazing intently up at him, some craning their heads for a better look.

Remus Lupin stood nearest to him. Though still quite young, Lupin looked tired and rather ill; he had more gray hair than when Harry had said good-bye to him, and his robes were more patched and shabbier than ever. Nevertheless, he was smiling broadly at Harry, who tried to smile back through his shock.

"Oooh, he looks just like I thought he would," said the witch who was holding her lit wand aloft. She looked the youngest there; she had a pale heart-shaped face, dark twinkling eyes, and short spiky hair that was a violent shade of violet. "Wotcher, Harry!"

"Yeah, I see what you mean, Remus," said a bald black wizard standing farthest back; he had a deep, slow voice and wore a single gold hoop in his ear. "He looks exactly like James."

"Except the eyes," said a wheezy-voiced, silver-haired wizard at the back. "Lily's eyes."

Mad-Eye Moody, who had long grizzled gray hair and a large chunk missing from his nose, was squinting suspiciously at Harry through his mismatched eyes. One of the eyes was small, dark, and beady, the other large, round, and electric blue — the magical eye that could see through walls, doors, and the back of Moody's own head.

"Are you quite sure it's him, Lupin?" he growled. "It'd be a nice lookout if we bring back some Death Eater impersonating him. We ought to ask him something only the real Potter would know. Unless anyone brought any Veritaserum?"

"Harry, what form does your Patronus take?" said Lupin.

"A stag," said Harry nervously.

"That's him, Mad-Eye," said Lupin.

Harry descended the stairs, very conscious of everybody still staring at him, stowing his wand into the back pocket of his jeans as he came.

"Don't put your wand there, boy!" roared Moody. "What if it ignited? Better wizards than you have lost buttocks, you know!"

"Who d'you know who's lost a buttock?" the violet-haired woman asked Mad-Eye interestedly.

"Never you mind, you just keep your wand out of your back pocket!" growled Mad-Eye. "Elementary wand safety, nobody bothers about it anymore. . . ." He stumped off toward the kitchen. "And I saw that," he added irritably, as the woman rolled her eyes at the ceiling.

Lupin held out his hand and shook Harry's.

"How are you?" he asked, looking at Harry closely.

"F-fine . . ."

Harry could hardly believe this was real. Four weeks with nothing, not the tiniest hint of a plan to remove him from Privet Drive, and suddenly a whole bunch of wizards was standing matter-of-factly in the house as though this were a long-standing arrangement. He glanced at the people surrounding Lupin; they were still gazing avidly at him. He felt very conscious of the fact that he had not combed his hair for four days.

"I'm — you're really lucky the Dursleys are out . . ." he mumbled.

"Lucky, ha!" said the violet-haired woman. "It was me that lured them out of the way. Sent a letter by Muggle post telling them they'd been short-listed for the All-England Best-Kept Suburban Lawn Competition. They're heading off to the prize-giving right now. . . . Or they think they are."

Harry had a fleeting vision of Uncle Vernon's face when he realized there was no All-England Best-Kept Suburban Lawn Competition.

"We are leaving, aren't we?" he asked. "Soon?"

"Almost at once," said Lupin, "we're just waiting for the all-clear."

"Where are we going? The Burrow?" Harry asked hopefully.

"Not the Burrow, no," said Lupin, motioning Harry toward the kitchen; the little knot of wizards followed, all still eyeing Harry curiously. "Too risky. We've set up headquarters somewhere undetectable. It's taken a while. . . ."

Mad-Eye Moody was now sitting at the kitchen table swigging from a hip flask, his magical eye spinning in all directions, taking in the Dursleys' many labor-saving appliances.

"This is Alastor Moody, Harry," Lupin continued, pointing toward Moody.

"Yeah, I know," said Harry uncomfortably; it felt odd to be introduced to somebody he'd thought he'd known for a year.

"And this is Nymphadora —"

"*Don't* call me Nymphadora, Remus," said the young witch with a shudder. "It's Tonks."

"— Nymphadora Tonks, who prefers to be known by her surname only," finished Lupin.

"So would you if your fool of a mother had called you 'Nymphadora,'" muttered Tonks.

"And this is Kingsley Shacklebolt" — he indicated the tall black wizard, who bowed — "Elphias Doge" — the wheezy-voiced wizard nodded — "Dedalus Diggle —"

"We've met before," squeaked the excitable Diggle, dropping his top hat.

"— Emmeline Vance" — a stately looking witch in an emerald-green shawl inclined her head — "Sturgis Podmore" — a square-jawed wizard with thick, straw-colored hair winked — "and Hestia Jones." A pink-cheeked, black-haired witch waved from next to the toaster.

Harry inclined his head awkwardly at each of them as they were introduced. He wished they would look at something other than him; it was as though he had suddenly been ushered onstage. He also wondered why so many of them were there.

"A surprising number of people volunteered to come and get you," said Lupin, as though he had read Harry's mind; the corners of his mouth twitched slightly.

"Yeah, well, the more the better," said Moody darkly. "We're your guard, Potter."

"We're just waiting for the signal to tell us it's safe to set off," said Lupin, glancing out of the kitchen window. "We've got about fifteen minutes."

"Very *clean,* aren't they, these Muggles?" said the witch called Tonks, who was looking around the kitchen with great interest. "My dad's Muggle-born and he's a right old slob. I suppose it varies, just like with wizards?"

"Er — yeah," said Harry. "Look" — he turned back to Lupin — "what's going on, I haven't heard anything from anyone, what's Vol — ?"

Several of the witches and wizards made odd hissing noises; Dedalus Diggle dropped his hat again, and Moody growled, *"Shut up!"*

"What?" said Harry.

"We're not discussing anything here, it's too risky," said Moody, turning his normal eye on Harry; his magical eye remained pointing up at the ceiling. *"Damn it,"* he added angrily, putting a hand up to the magical eye, "it keeps sticking — ever since that scum wore it —"

And with a nasty squelching sound much like a plunger being pulled from a sink, he popped out his eye.

"Mad-Eye, you do know that's disgusting, don't you?" said Tonks conversationally.

"Get me a glass of water, would you, Harry?" asked Moody.

Harry crossed to the dishwasher, took out a clean glass, and filled it with water at the sink, still watched eagerly by the band of wizards. Their relentless staring was starting to annoy him.

"Cheers," said Moody, when Harry handed him the glass. He dropped the magical eyeball into the water and prodded it up and down; the eye whizzed around, staring at them all in turn. "I want three-hundred-and-sixty degrees visibility on the return journey."

"How're we getting — wherever we're going?" Harry asked.

"Brooms," said Lupin. "Only way. You're too young to Apparate, they'll be watching the Floo Network, and it's more than our life's worth to set up an unauthorized Portkey."

"Remus says you're a good flier," said Kingsley Shacklebolt in his deep voice.

"He's excellent," said Lupin, who was checking his watch. "Anyway, you'd better go and get packed, Harry, we want to be ready to go when the signal comes."

"I'll come and help you," said Tonks brightly.

She followed Harry back into the hall and up the stairs, looking around with much curiosity and interest.

"Funny place," she said, "it's a bit *too* clean, d'you know what I mean? Bit unnatural. Oh, this is better," she added, as they entered Harry's bedroom and he turned on the light.

His room was certainly much messier than the rest of the house. Confined to it for four days in a very bad mood, Harry had not bothered tidying up after himself. Most of the books he owned were strewn over the floor where he'd tried to distract himself with each in turn and thrown it aside. Hedwig's cage needed cleaning out and was starting to smell, and his trunk lay open, revealing a jumbled mixture of Muggle clothes and wizard's robes that had spilled onto the floor around it.

Harry started picking up books and throwing them hastily into his trunk. Tonks paused at his open wardrobe to look critically at her reflection in the mirror on the inside of the door.

"You know, I don't think purple's really my color," she said pensively, tugging at a lock of spiky hair. "D'you think it makes me look a bit peaky?"

"Er —" said Harry, looking up at her over the top of *Quidditch Teams of Britain and Ireland.*

"Yeah, it does," said Tonks decisively. She screwed up her eyes in a strained expression as though she were struggling to remember something. A second later, her hair had turned bubble-gum pink.

"How did you do that?" said Harry, gaping at her as she opened her eyes again.

"I'm a Metamorphmagus," she said, looking back at her reflection and turning her head so that she could see her hair from all directions. "It means I can change my appearance at will," she added, spotting Harry's puzzled expression in the mirror behind her. "I was born one. I got top marks in Concealment and Disguise during Auror training without any study at all, it was great."

"You're an Auror?" said Harry, impressed. Being a Dark wizard catcher was the only career he'd ever considered after Hogwarts.

"Yeah," said Tonks, looking proud. "Kingsley is as well; he's a bit higher up than I am, though. I only qualified a year ago. Nearly failed on Stealth and Tracking, I'm dead clumsy, did you hear me break that plate when we arrived downstairs?"

"Can you learn how to be a Metamorphmagus?" Harry asked her, straightening up, completely forgetting about packing.

Tonks chuckled.

"Bet you wouldn't mind hiding that scar sometimes, eh?"

Her eyes found the lightning-shaped scar on Harry's forehead.

"No, I wouldn't mind," Harry mumbled, turning away. He did not like people staring at his scar.

"Well, you'll have to learn the hard way, I'm afraid," said Tonks. "Metamorphmagi are really rare, they're born, not made. Most wizards need to use a wand or potions to change their appearance. . . ."

But we've got to get going, Harry, we're supposed to be packing," she added guiltily, looking around at all the mess on the floor.

"Oh — yeah," said Harry, grabbing up a few more books.

"Don't be stupid, it'll be much quicker if I — *pack*!" cried Tonks, waving her wand in a long, sweeping movement over the floor.

Books, clothes, telescope, and scales all soared into the air and flew pell-mell into the trunk.

"It's not very neat," said Tonks, walking over to the trunk and looking down at the jumble inside. "My mum's got this knack of getting stuff to fit itself in neatly — she even gets the socks to fold themselves — but I've never mastered how she does it — it's a kind of flick —"

She flicked her wand hopefully; one of Harry's socks gave a feeble sort of wiggle and flopped back on top of the mess within.

"Ah, well," said Tonks, slamming the trunk's lid shut, "at least it's all in. That could do with a bit of cleaning, too — *Scourgify* —" She pointed her wand at Hedwig's cage; a few feathers and droppings vanished. "Well, that's a *bit* better — I've never quite got the hang of these sort of householdy spells. Right — got everything? Cauldron? Broom? Wow! A *Firebolt*?"

Her eyes widened as they fell on the broomstick in Harry's right hand. It was his pride and joy, a gift from Sirius, an international standard broomstick.

"And I'm still riding a Comet Two Sixty," said Tonks enviously. "Ah well . . . wand still in your jeans? Both buttocks still on? Okay, let's go. *Locomotor Trunk.*"

Harry's trunk rose a few inches into the air. Holding her wand like a conductor's baton, Tonks made it hover across the room and out of the door ahead of them, Hedwig's cage in her left hand. Harry followed her down the stairs carrying his broomstick.

Back in the kitchen, Moody had replaced his eye, which was spinning so fast after its cleaning it made Harry feel sick. Kingsley

Shacklebolt and Sturgis Podmore were examining the microwave and Hestia Jones was laughing at a potato peeler she had come across while rummaging in the drawers. Lupin was sealing a letter addressed to the Dursleys.

"Excellent," said Lupin, looking up as Tonks and Harry entered. "We've got about a minute, I think. We should probably get out into the garden so we're ready. Harry, I've left a letter telling your aunt and uncle not to worry —"

"They won't," said Harry.

"That you're safe —"

"That'll just depress them."

"— and you'll see them next summer."

"Do I have to?"

Lupin smiled but made no answer.

"Come here, boy," said Moody gruffly, beckoning Harry toward him with his wand. "I need to Disillusion you."

"You need to what?" said Harry nervously.

"Disillusionment Charm," said Moody, raising his wand. "Lupin says you've got an Invisibility Cloak, but it won't stay on while we're flying; this'll disguise you better. Here you go —"

He rapped Harry hard on the top of the head and Harry felt a curious sensation as though Moody had just smashed an egg there; cold trickles seemed to be running down his body from the point the wand had struck.

"Nice one, Mad-Eye," said Tonks appreciatively, staring at Harry's midriff.

Harry looked down at his body, or rather, what had been his body, for it didn't look anything like his anymore. It was not invisible; it had simply taken on the exact color and texture of the kitchen unit behind him. He seemed to have become a human chameleon.

"Come on," said Moody, unlocking the back door with his wand.

They all stepped outside onto Uncle Vernon's beautifully kept lawn.

"Clear night," grunted Moody, his magical eye scanning the heavens. "Could've done with a bit more cloud cover. Right, you," he barked at Harry, "we're going to be flying in close formation. Tonks'll be right in front of you, keep close on her tail. Lupin'll be covering you from below. I'm going to be behind you. The rest'll be circling us. We don't break ranks for anything, got me? If one of us is killed —"

"Is that likely?" Harry asked apprehensively, but Moody ignored him.

"— the others keep flying, don't stop, don't break ranks. If they take out all of us and you survive, Harry, the rear guard are standing by to take over; keep flying east and they'll join you."

"Stop being so cheerful, Mad-Eye, he'll think we're not taking this seriously," said Tonks, as she strapped Harry's trunk and Hedwig's cage into a harness hanging from her broom.

"I'm just telling the boy the plan," growled Moody. "Our job's to deliver him safely to headquarters and if we die in the attempt —"

"No one's going to die," said Kingsley Shacklebolt in his deep, calming voice.

"Mount your brooms, that's the first signal!" said Lupin sharply, pointing into the sky.

Far, far above them, a shower of bright red sparks had flared among the stars. Harry recognized them at once as wand sparks. He swung his right leg over his Firebolt, gripped its handle tightly, and felt it vibrating very slightly, as though it was as keen as he was to be up in the air once more.

"Second signal, let's go!" said Lupin loudly, as more sparks, green this time, exploded high above them.

Harry kicked off hard from the ground. The cool night air rushed through his hair as the neat square gardens of Privet Drive fell away, shrinking rapidly into a patchwork of dark greens and blacks, and every thought of the Ministry hearing was swept from his mind as though the rush of air had blown it out of his head. He felt as though his heart was going to explode with pleasure; he was flying again, flying away from Privet Drive as he'd been fantasizing about all summer, he was going home. . . . For a few glorious moments, all his problems seemed to recede into nothing, insignificant in the vast, starry sky.

"Hard left, hard left, there's a Muggle looking up!" shouted Moody from behind him. Tonks swerved and Harry followed her, watching his trunk swinging wildly beneath her broom. "We need more height. . . . Give it another quarter of a mile!"

Harry's eyes watered in the chill as they soared upward; he could see nothing below now but tiny pinpricks of light that were car headlights and streetlamps. Two of those tiny lights might belong to Uncle Vernon's car. . . . The Dursleys would be heading back to their empty house right now, full of rage about the nonexistent lawn competition . . . and Harry laughed aloud at the thought, though his voice was drowned by the flapping of the others' robes, the creaking of the harness holding his trunk and the cage, the *whoosh* of the wind in their ears as they sped through the air. He had not felt this alive in a month, or this happy. . . .

"Bearing south!" shouted Mad-Eye. "Town ahead!"

They soared right, so that they did not pass directly over the glittering spiderweb of lights below.

"Bear southeast and keep climbing, there's some low cloud ahead we can lose ourselves in!" called Moody.

"We're not going through clouds!" shouted Tonks angrily. "We'll get soaked, Mad-Eye!"

Harry was relieved to hear her say this; his hands were growing numb on the Firebolt's handle. He wished he had thought to put on a coat; he was starting to shiver.

They altered their course every now and then according to Mad-Eye's instructions. Harry's eyes were screwed up against the rush of icy wind that was starting to make his ears ache. He could remember being this cold on a broom only once before, during the Quidditch match against Hufflepuff in his third year, which had taken place in a storm. The guard around him was circling continuously like giant birds of prey. Harry lost track of time. He wondered how long they had been flying; it felt like an hour at least.

"Turning southwest!" yelled Moody. "We want to avoid the motorway!"

Harry was now so chilled that he thought longingly for a moment of the snug, dry interiors of the cars streaming along below, then, even more longingly, of traveling by Floo powder; it might be uncomfortable to spin around in fireplaces but it was at least warm in the flames. . . . Kingsley Shacklebolt swooped around him, bald pate and earring gleaming slightly in the moonlight. . . . Now Emmeline Vance was on his right, her wand out, her head turning left and right . . . then she too swooped over him, to be replaced by Sturgis Podmore. . . .

"We ought to double back for a bit, just to make sure we're not being followed!" Moody shouted.

"ARE YOU MAD, MAD-EYE?" Tonks screamed from the front. "We're all frozen to our brooms! If we keep going off course we're not going to get there until next week! We're nearly there now!"

"Time to start the descent!" came Lupin's voice. "Follow Tonks, Harry!"

Harry followed Tonks into a dive. They were heading for the largest collection of lights he had yet seen, a huge, sprawling, crisscrossing mass, glittering in lines and grids, interspersed with patches of deepest black. Lower and lower they flew, until Harry could see individual headlights and streetlamps, chimneys, and television aerials. He wanted to reach the ground very much, though he felt sure that someone would have to unfreeze him from his broom.

"Here we go!" called Tonks, and a few seconds later she had landed.

Harry touched down right behind her and dismounted on a patch of unkempt grass in the middle of a small square. Tonks was already unbuckling Harry's trunk. Shivering, Harry looked around. The grimy fronts of the surrounding houses were not welcoming; some of them had broken windows, glimmering dully in the light from the street-lamps, paint was peeling from many of the doors, and heaps of rubbish lay outside several sets of front steps.

"Where are we?" Harry asked, but Lupin said quietly, "In a minute."

Moody was rummaging in his cloak, his gnarled hands clumsy with cold.

"Got it," he muttered, raising what looked like a silver cigarette lighter into the air and clicking it.

The nearest streetlamp went out with a pop. He clicked the un-lighter again; the next lamp went out. He kept clicking until every lamp in the square was extinguished and the only light in the square came from curtained windows and the sickle moon overhead.

"Borrowed it from Dumbledore," growled Moody, pocketing the Put-Outer. "That'll take care of any Muggles looking out of the win-dow, see? Now, come on, quick."

He took Harry by the arm and led him from the patch of grass, across the road, and onto the pavement. Lupin and Tonks followed, carrying Harry's trunk between them, the rest of the guard, all with their wands out, flanking them.

The muffled pounding of a stereo was coming from an upper win-dow in the nearest house. A pungent smell of rotting rubbish came from the pile of bulging bin-bags just inside the broken gate.

"Here," Moody muttered, thrusting a piece of parchment toward Harry's Disillusioned hand and holding his lit wand close to it, so as to illuminate the writing. "Read quickly and memorize."

Harry looked down at the piece of paper. The narrow handwriting was vaguely familiar. It said:

The headquarters of the Order of the Phoenix may be found at number twelve, Grimmauld Place, London.

NUMBER TWELVE, GRIMMAULD PLACE

W hat's the Order of the — ?" Harry began.

"Not here, boy!" snarled Moody. "Wait till we're inside!"

He pulled the piece of parchment out of Harry's hand and set fire to it with his wand-tip. As the message curled into flames and floated to the ground, Harry looked around at the houses again. They were standing outside number eleven; he looked to the left and saw number ten; to the right, however, was number thirteen.

"But where's — ?"

"Think about what you've just memorized," said Lupin quietly.

Harry thought, and no sooner had he reached the part about number twelve, Grimmauld Place, than a battered door emerged out of nowhere between numbers eleven and thirteen, followed swiftly by dirty walls and grimy windows. It was as though an extra house had inflated, pushing those on either side out of its way. Harry gaped at it. The stereo in number eleven thudded on. Apparently the Muggles inside hadn't even felt anything.

"Come on, hurry," growled Moody, prodding Harry in the back.

Harry walked up the worn stone steps, staring at the newly materialized door. Its black paint was shabby and scratched. The silver door knocker was in the form of a twisted serpent. There was no keyhole or letterbox.

Lupin pulled out his wand and tapped the door once. Harry heard many loud, metallic clicks and what sounded like the clatter of a chain. The door creaked open.

"Get in quick, Harry," Lupin whispered. "But don't go far inside and don't touch anything."

Harry stepped over the threshold into the almost total darkness of the hall. He could smell damp, dust, and a sweetish, rotting smell; the place had the feeling of a derelict building. He looked over his shoulder and saw the others filing in behind him, Lupin and Tonks carrying his trunk and Hedwig's cage. Moody was standing on the top step and releasing the balls of light the Put-Outer had stolen from the street-lamps; they flew back to their bulbs and the square beyond glowed momentarily with orange light before Moody limped inside and closed the front door, so that the darkness in the hall became complete.

"Here —"

He rapped Harry hard over the head with his wand; Harry felt as though something hot was trickling down his back this time and knew that the Disillusionment Charm must have lifted.

"Now stay still, everyone, while I give us a bit of light in here," Moody whispered.

The others' hushed voices were giving Harry an odd feeling of foreboding; it was as though they had just entered the house of a dying person. He heard a soft hissing noise and then old-fashioned gas lamps sputtered into life all along the walls, casting a flickering insubstantial light over the peeling wallpaper and threadbare carpet of a long, gloomy hallway, where a cobwebby chandelier glimmered overhead and age-blackened portraits hung crooked on the walls. Harry heard something scuttling behind the baseboard. Both the chandelier and the candelabra on a rickety table nearby were shaped like serpents.

There were hurried footsteps and Ron's mother, Mrs. Weasley, emerged from a door at the far end of the hall. She was beaming in welcome as she hurried toward them, though Harry noticed that she was rather thinner and paler than she had been last time he had seen her.

"Oh, Harry, it's lovely to see you!" she whispered, pulling him into a rib-cracking hug before holding him at arm's length and examining him critically. "You're looking peaky; you need feeding up, but you'll have to wait a bit for dinner, I'm afraid. . . ."

She turned to the gang of wizards behind him and whispered urgently, "He's just arrived, the meeting's started. . . ."

The wizards behind Harry all made noises of interest and excitement and began filing past Harry toward the door through which Mrs. Weasley had just come; Harry made to follow Lupin, but Mrs. Weasley held him back.

"No, Harry, the meeting's only for members of the Order. Ron and Hermione are upstairs, you can wait with them until the meeting's over and then we'll have dinner. And keep your voice down in the hall," she added in an urgent whisper.

"Why?"

"I don't want to wake anything up."

"What d'you — ?"

"I'll explain later, I've got to hurry, I'm supposed to be at the meeting — I'll just show you where you're sleeping."

Pressing her finger to her lips, she led him on tiptoes past a pair of long, moth-eaten curtains, behind which Harry supposed there must be another door, and after skirting a large umbrella stand that looked as though it had been made from a severed troll's leg, they started up the dark staircase, passing a row of shrunken heads mounted on plaques on the wall. A closer look showed Harry that the heads belonged to house-elves. All of them had the same rather snoutlike nose.

Harry's bewilderment deepened with every step he took. What on earth were they doing in a house that looked as though it belonged to the Darkest of wizards?

"Mrs. Weasley, why — ?"

"Ron and Hermione will explain everything, dear, I've really got to dash," Mrs. Weasley whispered distractedly. "There" — they had reached the second landing — "you're the door on the right. I'll call you when it's over."

And she hurried off downstairs again.

Harry crossed the dingy landing, turned the bedroom doorknob, which was shaped like a serpent's head, and opened the door.

He caught a brief glimpse of a gloomy high-ceilinged, twin-bedded room, then there was a loud twittering noise, followed by an even louder shriek, and his vision was completely obscured by a large quantity of very bushy hair — Hermione had thrown herself onto him in a hug that nearly knocked him flat, while Ron's tiny owl, Pigwidgeon, zoomed excitedly round and round their heads.

"HARRY! Ron, he's here, Harry's here! We didn't hear you arrive! Oh, how *are* you? Are you all right? Have you been furious with us? I bet you have, I know our letters were useless — but we couldn't tell you anything, Dumbledore made us swear we wouldn't, oh, we've got so much to tell you, and you've got to tell us — the dementors! When we heard — and that Ministry hearing — it's just outrageous, I've looked it all up, they can't expel you, they just can't, there's provision in the Decree for the Restriction of Underage Sorcery for the use of magic in life-threatening situations —"

"Let him breathe, Hermione," said Ron, grinning, closing the door behind Harry. He seemed to have grown several more inches during their month apart, making him taller and more gangly looking than ever, though the long nose, bright red hair, and freckles were the same.

Hermione, still beaming, let go of Harry, but before she could say another word there was a soft whooshing sound and something white soared from the top of a dark wardrobe and landed gently on Harry's shoulder.

"Hedwig!"

The snowy owl clicked her beak and nibbled his ear affectionately as Harry stroked her feathers.

"She's been in a right state," said Ron. "Pecked us half to death when she brought your last letters, look at this —"

He showed Harry the index finger of his right hand, which sported a half-healed but clearly deep cut.

"Oh yeah," Harry said. "Sorry about that, but I wanted answers, you know. . . ."

"We wanted to give them to you, mate," said Ron. "Hermione was going spare, she kept saying you'd do something stupid if you were stuck all on your own without news, but Dumbledore made us —"

"— swear not to tell me," said Harry. "Yeah, Hermione's already said."

The warm glow that had flared inside him at the sight of his two best friends was extinguished as something icy flooded the pit of his stomach. All of a sudden — after yearning to see them for a solid month — he felt he would rather Ron and Hermione left him alone.

There was a strained silence in which Harry stroked Hedwig automatically, not looking at either of the others.

"He seemed to think it was best," said Hermione rather breathlessly. "Dumbledore, I mean."

"Right," said Harry. He noticed that her hands too bore the marks of Hedwig's beak and found that he was not at all sorry.

"I think he thought you were safest with the Muggles —" Ron began.

"Yeah?" said Harry, raising his eyebrows. "Have either of you been attacked by dementors this summer?"

"Well, no — but that's why he's had people from the Order of the Phoenix tailing you all the time —"

Harry felt a great jolt in his guts as though he had just missed a step going downstairs. So everyone had known he was being followed except him.

"Didn't work that well, though, did it?" said Harry, doing his utmost to keep his voice even. "Had to look after myself after all, didn't I?"

"He was so angry," said Hermione in an almost awestruck voice. "Dumbledore. We saw him. When he found out Mundungus had left before his shift had ended. He was scary."

"Well, I'm glad he left," Harry said coldly. "If he hadn't, I wouldn't have done magic and Dumbledore would probably have left me at Privet Drive all summer."

"Aren't you . . . aren't you worried about the Ministry of Magic hearing?" said Hermione quietly.

"No," Harry lied defiantly. He walked away from them, looking around, with Hedwig nestled contentedly on his shoulder, but this room was not likely to raise his spirits. It was dank and dark. A blank stretch of canvas in an ornate picture frame was all that relieved the bareness of the peeling walls and as Harry passed it he thought he heard someone lurking out of sight snigger.

"So why's Dumbledore been so keen to keep me in the dark?" Harry asked, still trying hard to keep his voice casual. "Did you — er — bother to ask him at all?"

He glanced up just in time to see them exchanging a look that told him he was behaving just as they had feared he would. It did nothing to improve his temper.

"We told Dumbledore we wanted to tell you what was going on," said Ron. "We did, mate. But he's really busy now, we've only seen him twice since we came here and he didn't have much time, he just made us swear not to tell you important stuff when we wrote, he said the owls might be intercepted —"

"He could still've kept me informed if he'd wanted to," Harry said shortly. "You're not telling me he doesn't know ways to send messages without owls."

Hermione glanced at Ron and then said, "I thought that too. But he didn't want you to know *anything*."

"Maybe he thinks I can't be trusted," said Harry, watching their expressions.

"Don't be thick," said Ron, looking highly disconcerted.

"Or that I can't take care of myself —"

"Of course he doesn't think that!" said Hermione anxiously.

"So how come I have to stay at the Dursleys' while you two get to join in everything that's going on here?" said Harry, the words tumbling over one another in a rush, his voice growing louder with every word. "How come you two are allowed to know everything that's going on — ?"

"We're not!" Ron interrupted. "Mum won't let us near the meetings, she says we're too young —"

But before he knew it, Harry was shouting.

"SO YOU HAVEN'T BEEN IN THE MEETINGS, BIG DEAL! YOU'VE STILL BEEN HERE, HAVEN'T YOU? YOU'VE STILL BEEN TOGETHER! ME, I'VE BEEN STUCK AT THE DURS-LEYS' FOR A MONTH! AND I'VE HANDLED MORE THAN YOU TWO'VE EVER MANAGED AND DUMBLEDORE KNOWS IT — WHO SAVED THE SORCERER'S STONE? WHO GOT RID OF RIDDLE? WHO SAVED BOTH YOUR SKINS FROM THE DEMENTORS?"

Every bitter and resentful thought that Harry had had in the past month was pouring out of him; his frustration at the lack of news, the hurt that they had all been together without him, his fury at being followed and not told about it: All the feelings he was half-ashamed of finally burst their boundaries. Hedwig took fright at the noise and soared off on top of the wardrobe again; Pigwidgeon twittered in alarm and zoomed even faster around their heads.

"WHO HAD TO GET PAST DRAGONS AND SPHINXES AND EVERY OTHER FOUL THING LAST YEAR? WHO SAW HIM COME BACK? WHO HAD TO ESCAPE FROM HIM? ME!"

Ron was standing there with his mouth half-open, clearly stunned and at a loss for anything to say, while Hermione looked on the verge of tears.

"BUT WHY SHOULD I KNOW WHAT'S GOING ON? WHY SHOULD ANYONE BOTHER TO TELL ME WHAT'S BEEN HAPPENING?"

"Harry, we wanted to tell you, we really did —" Hermione began.

"CAN'T'VE WANTED TO THAT MUCH, CAN YOU, OR YOU'D HAVE SENT ME AN OWL, BUT *DUMBLEDORE MADE YOU SWEAR* —"

"Well, he did —"

"FOUR WEEKS I'VE BEEN STUCK IN PRIVET DRIVE, NICKING PAPERS OUT OF BINS TO TRY AND FIND OUT WHAT'S BEEN GOING ON —"

"We wanted to —"

"I SUPPOSE YOU'VE BEEN HAVING A REAL LAUGH, HAVEN'T YOU, ALL HOLED UP HERE TOGETHER —"

"No, honest —"

"Harry, we're really sorry!" said Hermione desperately, her eyes now sparkling with tears. "You're absolutely right, Harry — I'd be furious if it was me!"

Harry glared at her, still breathing deeply, then turned away from them again, pacing up and down. Hedwig hooted glumly from the top of the wardrobe. There was a long pause, broken only by the mournful creak of the floorboards below Harry's feet.

"What *is* this place anyway?" he shot at Ron and Hermione.

"Headquarters of the Order of the Phoenix," said Ron at once.

"Is anyone going to bother telling me what the Order of the Phoenix — ?"

"It's a secret society," said Hermione quickly. "Dumbledore's in charge, he founded it. It's the people who fought against You-Know-Who last time."

"Who's in it?" said Harry, coming to a halt with his hands in his pockets.

"Quite a few people —"

"— we've met about twenty of them," said Ron, "but we think there are more. . . ."

Harry glared at them.

"Well?" he demanded, looking from one to the other.

"Er," said Ron. "Well what?"

"Voldemort!" said Harry furiously, and both Ron and Hermione winced. "What's happening? What's he up to? Where is he? What are we doing to stop him?"

"We've *told* you, the Order don't let us in on their meetings," said Hermione nervously. "So we don't know the details — but we've got a general idea —" she added hastily, seeing the look on Harry's face.

"Fred and George have invented Extendable Ears, see," said Ron. "They're really useful."

"Extendable — ?"

"Ears, yeah. Only we've had to stop using them lately because Mum found out and went berserk. Fred and George had to hide them all to stop Mum binning them. But we got a good bit of use out of them before Mum realized what was going on. We know some of the Order are following known Death Eaters, keeping tabs on them, you know —"

"— some of them are working on recruiting more people to the Order —" said Hermione.

"— and some of them are standing guard over something," said Ron. "They're always talking about guard duty."

"Couldn't have been me, could it?" said Harry sarcastically.

"Oh yeah," said Ron, with a look of dawning comprehension.

Harry snorted. He walked around the room again, looking anywhere but at Ron and Hermione. "So what have you two been doing, if you're not allowed in meetings?" he demanded. "You said you'd been busy."

"We have," said Hermione quickly. "We've been decontaminating this house, it's been empty for ages and stuff's been breeding in here. We've managed to clean out the kitchen, most of the bedrooms, and I think we're doing the drawing room tomo — AARGH!"

With two loud cracks, Fred and George, Ron's elder twin brothers, had materialized out of thin air in the middle of the room. Pigwidgeon twittered more wildly than ever and zoomed off to join Hedwig on top of the wardrobe.

"Stop *doing* that!" Hermione said weakly to the twins, who were as vividly red-haired as Ron, though stockier and slightly shorter.

"Hello, Harry," said George, beaming at him. "We thought we heard your dulcet tones."

"You don't want to bottle up your anger like that, Harry, let it all out," said Fred, also beaming. "There might be a couple of people fifty miles away who didn't hear you."

"You two passed your Apparation tests, then?" asked Harry grumpily.

"With distinction," said Fred, who was holding what looked like a piece of very long, flesh-colored string.

"It would have taken you about thirty seconds longer to walk down the stairs," said Ron.

"Time is Galleons, little brother," said Fred. "Anyway, Harry, you're interfering with reception. Extendable Ears," he added in response to

Harry's raised eyebrows, holding up the string, which Harry now saw was trailing out onto the landing. "We're trying to hear what's going on downstairs."

"You want to be careful," said Ron, staring at the ear. "If Mum sees one of them again . . ."

"It's worth the risk, that's a major meeting they're having," said Fred.

The door opened and a long mane of red hair appeared.

"Oh hello, Harry!" said Ron's younger sister, Ginny, brightly. "I thought I heard your voice."

Turning to Fred and George she said, "It's no go with the Extendable Ears, she's gone and put an Imperturbable Charm on the kitchen door."

"How d'you know?" said George, looking crestfallen.

"Tonks told me how to find out," said Ginny. "You just chuck stuff at the door and if it can't make contact the door's been Imperturbed. I've been flicking Dungbombs at it from the top of the stairs and they just soar away from it, so there's no way the Extendable Ears will be able to get under the gap."

Fred heaved a deep sigh. "Shame. I really fancied finding out what old Snape's been up to."

"Snape?" said Harry quickly. "Is he here?"

"Yeah," said George, carefully closing the door and sitting down on one of the beds; Fred and Ginny followed. "Giving a report. Top secret."

"Git," said Fred idly.

"He's on our side now," said Hermione reprovingly.

Ron snorted. "Doesn't stop him being a git. The way he looks at us when he sees us. . . ."

"Bill doesn't like him either," said Ginny, as though that settled the matter.

Harry was not sure his anger had abated yet; but his thirst for information was now overcoming his urge to keep shouting. He sank onto the bed opposite the others.

"Is Bill here?" he asked. "I thought he was working in Egypt."

"He applied for a desk job so he could come home and work for the Order," said Fred. "He says he misses the tombs, but," he smirked, "there are compensations. . . ."

"What d'you mean?"

"Remember old Fleur Delacour?" said George. "She's got a job at Gringotts to *eemprove 'er Eeenglish* —"

"— and Bill's been giving her a lot of private lessons," sniggered Fred.

"Charlie's in the Order too," said George, "but he's still in Romania, Dumbledore wants as many foreign wizards brought in as possible, so Charlie's trying to make contacts on his days off."

"Couldn't Percy do that?" Harry asked. The last he had heard, the third Weasley brother was working in the Department of International Magical Cooperation at the Ministry of Magic.

At these words all the Weasleys and Hermione exchanged darkly significant looks.

"Whatever you do, don't mention Percy in front of Mum and Dad," Ron told Harry in a tense voice.

"Why not?"

"Because every time Percy's name's mentioned, Dad breaks whatever he's holding and Mum starts crying," Fred said.

"It's been awful," said Ginny sadly.

"I think we're well shut of him," said George with an uncharacteristically ugly look on his face.

"What's happened?" Harry said.

"Percy and Dad had a row," said Fred. "I've never seen Dad row with anyone like that. It's normally Mum who shouts. . . ."

"It was the first week back after term ended," said Ron. "We were about to come and join the Order. Percy came home and told us he'd been promoted."

"You're kidding?" said Harry.

Though he knew perfectly well that Percy was highly ambitious, Harry's impression was that Percy had not made a great success of his first job at the Ministry of Magic. Percy had committed the fairly large oversight of failing to notice that his boss was being controlled by Lord Voldemort (not that the Ministry had believed that — they all thought that Mr. Crouch had gone mad).

"Yeah, we were all surprised," said George, "because Percy got into a load of trouble about Crouch, there was an inquiry and everything. They said Percy ought to have realized Crouch was off his rocker and informed a superior. But you know Percy, Crouch left him in charge, he wasn't going to complain. . . ."

"So how come they promoted him?"

"That's exactly what we wondered," said Ron, who seemed very keen to keep normal conversation going now that Harry had stopped yelling. "He came home really pleased with himself — even more pleased than usual if you can imagine that — and told Dad he'd been offered a position in Fudge's own office. A really good one for someone only a year out of Hogwarts — Junior Assistant to the Minister. He expected Dad to be all impressed, I think."

"Only Dad wasn't," said Fred grimly.

"Why not?" said Harry.

"Well, apparently Fudge has been storming round the Ministry checking that nobody's having any contact with Dumbledore," said George.

"Dumbledore's name's mud with the Ministry these days, see," said Fred. "They all think he's just making trouble saying You-Know-Who's back."

"Dad says Fudge has made it clear that anyone who's in league with Dumbledore can clear out their desks," said George.

"Trouble is, Fudge suspects Dad, he knows he's friendly with Dumbledore, and he's always thought Dad's a bit of a weirdo because of his Muggle obsession —"

"But what's this got to do with Percy?" asked Harry, confused.

"I'm coming to that. Dad reckons Fudge only wants Percy in his office because he wants to use him to spy on the family — and Dumbledore."

Harry let out a low whistle.

"Bet Percy loved that."

Ron laughed in a hollow sort of way.

"He went completely berserk. He said — well, he said loads of terrible stuff. He said he's been having to struggle against Dad's lousy reputation ever since he joined the Ministry and that Dad's got no ambition and that's why we've always been — you know — not had a lot of money, I mean —"

"What?" said Harry in disbelief, as Ginny made a noise like an angry cat.

"I know," said Ron in a low voice. "And it got worse. He said Dad was an idiot to run around with Dumbledore, that Dumbledore was heading for big trouble and Dad was going to go down with him, and that he — Percy — knew where his loyalty lay and it was with the Ministry. And if Mum and Dad were going to become traitors to the Ministry he was going to make sure everyone knew he didn't belong to our family anymore. And he packed his bags the same night and left. He's living here in London now."

Harry swore under his breath. He had always liked Percy least of Ron's brothers, but he had never imagined he would say such things to Mr. Weasley.

"Mum's been in a right state," said Ron. "You know — crying and stuff. She came up to London to try and talk to Percy but he slammed the door in her face. I dunno what he does if he meets Dad at work — ignores him, I s'pose."

"But Percy *must* know Voldemort's back," said Harry slowly. "He's not stupid, he must know your mum and dad wouldn't risk everything without proof —"

"Yeah, well, your name got dragged into the row," said Ron, shooting Harry a furtive look. "Percy said the only evidence was your word and . . . I dunno . . . he didn't think it was good enough."

"Percy takes the *Daily Prophet* seriously," said Hermione tartly, and the others all nodded.

"What are you talking about?" Harry asked, looking around at them all. They were all regarding him warily.

"Haven't — haven't you been getting the *Daily Prophet*?" Hermione asked nervously.

"Yeah, I have!" said Harry.

"Have you — er — been reading it thoroughly?" Hermione asked still more anxiously.

"Not cover to cover," said Harry defensively. "If they were going to report anything about Voldemort it would be headline news, wouldn't it!"

The others flinched at the sound of the name. Hermione hurried on, "Well, you'd need to read it cover to cover to pick it up, but they — um — they mention you a couple of times a week."

"But I'd have seen —"

"Not if you've only been reading the front page, you wouldn't," said Hermione, shaking her head. "I'm not talking about big articles. They just slip you in, like you're a standing joke."

"What d'you — ?"

"It's quite nasty, actually," said Hermione in a voice of forced calm. "They're just building on Rita's stuff."

"But she's not writing for them anymore, is she?"

"Oh no, she's kept her promise — not that she's got any choice," Hermione added with satisfaction. "But she laid the foundation for what they're trying to do now."

"Which is *what*?" said Harry impatiently.

"Okay, you know she wrote that you were collapsing all over the place and saying your scar was hurting and all that?"

"Yeah," said Harry, who was not likely to forget Rita Skeeter's stories about him in a hurry.

"Well, they're writing about you as though you're this deluded, attention-seeking person who thinks he's a great tragic hero or something," said Hermione, very fast, as though it would be less unpleasant for Harry to hear these facts quickly. "They keep slipping in snide comments about you. If some far-fetched story appears they say something like 'a tale worthy of Harry Potter' and if anyone has a funny accident or anything it's 'let's hope he hasn't got a scar on his forehead or we'll be asked to worship him next —'"

"I don't want anyone to worship —" Harry began hotly.

"I know you don't," said Hermione quickly, looking frightened. "I *know,* Harry. But you see what they're doing? They want to turn you into someone nobody will believe. Fudge is behind it, I'll bet anything. They want wizards on the street to think you're just some stupid boy who's a bit of a joke, who tells ridiculous tall stories because he loves being famous and wants to keep it going."

"I didn't ask — I didn't want — *Voldemort killed my parents!*" Harry spluttered. "I got famous because he murdered my family but couldn't kill me! Who wants to be famous for that? Don't they think I'd rather it'd never —"

"We *know,* Harry," said Ginny earnestly.

"And of course, they didn't report a word about the dementors attacking you," said Hermione. "Someone's told them to keep that quiet. That should've been a really big story, out-of-control dementors. They haven't even reported that you broke the International Statute of Secrecy — we thought they would, it would tie in so well with this image of you as some stupid show-off — we think they're biding their time until you're expelled, then they're really going to go to town — I mean, *if* you're expelled, obviously," she went on hastily, "you really shouldn't be, not if they abide by their own laws, there's no case against you."

They were back on the hearing and Harry did not want to think about it. He cast around for another change of subject, but was saved the necessity of finding one by the sound of footsteps coming up the stairs.

"Uh-oh."

Fred gave the Extendable Ear a hearty tug; there was another loud crack and he and George vanished. Seconds later, Mrs. Weasley appeared in the bedroom doorway.

"The meeting's over, you can come down and have dinner now, everyone's dying to see you, Harry. And who's left all those Dungbombs outside the kitchen door?"

"Crookshanks," said Ginny unblushingly. "He loves playing with them."

"Oh," said Mrs. Weasley, "I thought it might have been Kreacher, he keeps doing odd things like that. Now don't forget to keep your voices down in the hall. Ginny, your hands are filthy, what have you been doing? Go and wash them before dinner, please. . . ."

Ginny grimaced at the others and followed her mother out of the room, leaving Harry alone with Ron and Hermione again. Both of them were watching him apprehensively, as though they feared that he would start shouting again now that everyone else had gone. The sight of them looking so nervous made him feel slightly ashamed.

"Look . . ." he muttered, but Ron shook his head, and Hermione said quietly, "We knew you'd be angry, Harry, we really don't blame you, but you've got to understand, we *did* try and persuade Dumbledore —"

"Yeah, I know," said Harry grudgingly.

He cast around for a topic to change the subject from Dumbledore — the very thought of him made Harry's insides burn with anger again.

"Who's Kreacher?" he asked.

"The house-elf who lives here," said Ron. "Nutter. Never met one like him."

Hermione frowned at Ron.

"He's not a *nutter*, Ron —"

"His life's ambition is to have his head cut off and stuck up on a plaque just like his mother," said Ron irritably. "Is that normal, Hermione?"

"Well — well, if he is a bit strange, it's not his fault —"

Ron rolled his eyes at Harry.

"Hermione still hasn't given up on *spew* —"

"It's not 'spew'!" said Hermione heatedly. "It's the Society for the Promotion of Elfish Welfare, and it's not just me, Dumbledore says we should be kind to Kreacher too —"

"Yeah, yeah," said Ron. "C'mon, I'm starving."

He led the way out of the door and onto the landing, but before they could descend the stairs — "Hold it!" Ron breathed, flinging out an arm to stop Harry and Hermione walking any farther. "They're still in the hall, we might be able to hear something —"

The three of them looked cautiously over the banisters. The gloomy hallway below was packed with witches and wizards, including all of Harry's guard. They were whispering excitedly together. In the very center of the group Harry saw the dark, greasy-haired head and prominent nose of his least favorite teacher at Hogwarts, Professor Snape. Harry leaned farther over the banisters. He was very interested in what Snape was doing for the Order of the Phoenix. . . .

A thin piece of flesh-colored string descended in front of Harry's eyes. Looking up he saw Fred and George on the landing above, cautiously lowering the Extendable Ear toward the dark knot of people below. A moment later, however, they began to move toward the front door and out of sight.

"Dammit," Harry heard Fred whisper, as he hoisted the Extendable Ear back up again.

They heard the front door open and then close.

"Snape never eats here," Ron told Harry quietly. "Thank God. C'mon."

"And don't forget to keep your voice down in the hall, Harry," Hermione whispered.

As they passed the row of house-elf heads on the wall they saw Lupin, Mrs. Weasley, and Tonks at the front door, magically sealing its many locks and bolts behind those who had just left.

"We're eating down in the kitchen," Mrs. Weasley whispered, meeting them at the bottom of the stairs. "Harry, dear, if you'll just tiptoe across the hall, it's through this door here —"

CRASH.

"*Tonks!*" cried Mrs. Weasley exasperatedly, turning to look behind her.

"I'm sorry!" wailed Tonks, who was lying flat on the floor. "It's that stupid umbrella stand, that's the second time I've tripped over —"

But the rest of her words were drowned by a horrible, earsplitting, bloodcurdling screech.

The moth-eaten velvet curtains Harry had passed earlier had flown apart, but there was no door behind them. For a split second, Harry thought he was looking through a window, a window behind which an old woman in a black cap was screaming and screaming as though she was being tortured — then he realized it was simply a life-size portrait, but the most realistic, and the most unpleasant, he had ever seen in his life.

The old woman was drooling, her eyes were rolling, the yellowing skin of her face stretched taut as she screamed, and all along the hall behind them, the other portraits awoke and began to yell too, so that

Harry actually screwed up his eyes at the noise and clapped his hands over his ears.

Lupin and Mrs. Weasley darted forward and tried to tug the curtains shut over the old woman, but they would not close and she screeched louder than ever, brandishing clawed hands as though trying to tear at their faces.

"Filth! Scum! By-products of dirt and vileness! Half-breeds, mutants, freaks, begone from this place! How dare you befoul the house of my fathers —"

Tonks apologized over and over again, at the same time dragging the huge, heavy troll's leg back off the floor. Mrs. Weasley abandoned the attempt to close the curtains and hurried up and down the hall, Stunning all the other portraits with her wand. Then a man with long black hair came charging out of a door facing Harry.

"Shut up, you horrible old hag, shut UP!" he roared, seizing the curtain Mrs. Weasley had abandoned.

The old woman's face blanched.

"Yoooou!" she howled, her eyes popping at the sight of the man. *"Blood traitor, abomination, shame of my flesh!"*

"I said — shut — UP!" roared the man, and with a stupendous effort he and Lupin managed to force the curtains closed again.

The old woman's screeches died and an echoing silence fell.

Panting slightly and sweeping his long dark hair out of his eyes, Harry's godfather, Sirius, turned to face him.

"Hello, Harry," he said grimly, "I see you've met my mother."

THE ORDER OF
THE PHOENIX

Y our — ?"

"My dear old mum, yeah," said Sirius. "We've been trying to get her down for a month but we think she put a Permanent Sticking Charm on the back of the canvas. Let's get downstairs, quick, before they all wake up again."

"But what's a portrait of your mother doing here?" Harry asked, bewildered, as they went through the door from the hall and led the way down a flight of narrow stone steps, the others just behind them.

"Hasn't anyone told you? This was my parents' house," said Sirius. "But I'm the last Black left, so it's mine now. I offered it to Dumbledore for headquarters — about the only useful thing I've been able to do."

Harry, who had expected a better welcome, noted how hard and bitter Sirius's voice sounded. He followed his godfather to the bottom of the stairs and through a door leading into the basement kitchen.

It was scarcely less gloomy than the hall above, a cavernous room with rough stone walls. Most of the light was coming from a large fire at the far end of the room. A haze of pipe smoke hung in the air like battle fumes, through which loomed the menacing shapes of heavy iron pots and pans hanging from the dark ceiling. Many chairs had been crammed into the room for the meeting and a long wooden table stood in the middle of the room, littered with rolls of parchment, goblets, empty wine bottles, and a heap of what appeared to be rags. Mr. Weasley and his eldest son, Bill, were talking quietly with their heads together at the end of the table.

Mrs. Weasley cleared her throat. Her husband, a thin, balding, red-haired man, who wore horn-rimmed glasses, looked around and jumped to his feet.

"Harry!" Mr. Weasley said, hurrying forward to greet him and shaking his hand vigorously. "Good to see you!"

Over his shoulder Harry saw Bill, who still wore his long hair in a ponytail, hastily rolling up the lengths of parchment left on the table.

"Journey all right, Harry?" Bill called, trying to gather up twelve scrolls at once. "Mad-Eye didn't make you come via Greenland, then?"

"He tried," said Tonks, striding over to help Bill and immediately sending a candle toppling onto the last piece of parchment. "Oh no — *sorry* —"

"Here, dear," said Mrs. Weasley, sounding exasperated, and she repaired the parchment with a wave of her wand: In the flash of light caused by Mrs. Weasley's charm, Harry caught a glimpse of what looked like the plan of a building.

Mrs. Weasley had seen him looking. She snatched the plan off the table and stuffed it into Bill's heavily laden arms.

"This sort of thing ought to be cleared away promptly at the end of meetings," she snapped before sweeping off toward an ancient dresser from which she started unloading dinner plates.

Bill took out his wand, muttered *"Evanesco!"* and the scrolls vanished.

"Sit down, Harry," said Sirius. "You've met Mundungus, haven't you?"

The thing Harry had taken to be a pile of rags gave a prolonged, grunting snore and then jerked awake.

"Some'n say m' name?" Mundungus mumbled sleepily. "I 'gree with Sirius. . . ."

He raised a very grubby hand in the air as though voting, his droopy, bloodshot eyes unfocused. Ginny giggled.

"The meeting's over, Dung," said Sirius, as they all sat down around him at the table. "Harry's arrived."

"Eh?" said Mundungus, peering balefully at Harry through his matted ginger hair. "Blimey, so 'e 'as. Yeah . . . you all right, 'arry?"

"Yeah," said Harry.

Mundungus fumbled nervously in his pockets, still staring at Harry, and pulled out a grimy black pipe. He stuck it in his mouth, ignited the end of it with his wand, and took a deep pull on it. Great billowing clouds of greenish smoke obscured him in seconds.

"Owe you a 'pology," grunted a voice from the middle of the smelly cloud.

"For the last time, Mundungus," called Mrs. Weasley, "will you please *not* smoke that thing in the kitchen, especially not when we're about to eat!"

"Ah," said Mundungus. "Right. Sorry, Molly."

The cloud of smoke vanished as Mundungus stowed his pipe back in his pocket, but an acrid smell of burning socks lingered.

"And if you want dinner before midnight I'll need a hand," Mrs. Weasley said to the room at large. "No, you can stay where you are, Harry dear, you've had a long journey —"

"What can I do, Molly?" said Tonks enthusiastically, bounding forward.

Mrs. Weasley hesitated, looking apprehensive.

"Er — no, it's all right, Tonks, you have a rest too, you've done enough today —"

"No, no, I want to help!" said Tonks brightly, knocking over a chair as she hurried toward the dresser from which Ginny was collecting cutlery.

Soon a series of heavy knives were chopping meat and vegetables of their own accord, supervised by Mr. Weasley, while Mrs. Weasley stirred a cauldron dangling over the fire and the others took out plates, more goblets, and food from the pantry. Harry was left at the table with Sirius and Mundungus, who was still blinking mournfully at him.

"Seen old Figgy since?" he asked.

"No," said Harry, "I haven't seen anyone."

"See, I wouldn't 'ave left," said Mundungus, leaning forward, a pleading note in his voice, "but I 'ad a business opportunity —"

Harry felt something brush against his knees and started, but it was only Crookshanks, Hermione's bandy-legged ginger cat, who wound himself once around Harry's legs, purring, then jumped onto Sirius's lap and curled up. Sirius scratched him absentmindedly behind the ears as he turned, still grim-faced, to Harry.

"Had a good summer so far?"

"No, it's been lousy," said Harry.

For the first time, something like a grin flitted across Sirius's face.

"Don't know what you're complaining about, myself."

"*What?*" said Harry incredulously.

"Personally, I'd have welcomed a dementor attack. A deadly struggle for my soul would have broken the monotony nicely. You think you've had it bad, at least you've been able to get out and about, stretch your legs, get into a few fights. . . . I've been stuck inside for a month."

"How come?" asked Harry, frowning.

"Because the Ministry of Magic's still after me, and Voldemort will know all about me being an Animagus by now, Wormtail will have told him, so my big disguise is useless. There's not much I can do for the Order of the Phoenix . . . or so Dumbledore feels."

There was something about the slightly flattened tone of voice in which Sirius uttered Dumbledore's name that told Harry that Sirius was not very happy with the headmaster either. Harry felt a sudden upsurge of affection for his godfather.

"At least you've known what's been going on," he said bracingly.

"Oh yeah," said Sirius sarcastically. "Listening to Snape's reports, having to take all his snide hints that he's out there risking his life while I'm sat on my backside here having a nice comfortable time . . . asking me how the cleaning's going —"

"What cleaning?" asked Harry.

"Trying to make this place fit for human habitation," said Sirius, waving a hand around the dismal kitchen. "No one's lived here for ten years, not since my dear mother died, unless you count her old house-elf, and he's gone round the twist, hasn't cleaned anything in ages —"

"Sirius?" said Mundungus, who did not appear to have paid any attention to this conversation, but had been minutely examining an empty goblet. "This solid silver, mate?"

"Yes," said Sirius, surveying it with distaste. "Finest fifteenth-century goblin-wrought silver, embossed with the Black family crest."

"That'd come off, though," muttered Mundungus, polishing it with his cuff.

"Fred — George — NO, JUST CARRY THEM!" Mrs. Weasley shrieked.

Harry, Sirius, and Mundungus looked around and, a split second later, dived away from the table. Fred and George had bewitched a large cauldron of stew, an iron flagon of butterbeer, and a heavy wooden breadboard, complete with knife, to hurtle through the air toward them. The stew skidded the length of the table and came to a halt just before the end, leaving a long black burn on the wooden surface, the flagon of butterbeer fell with a crash, spilling its contents everywhere, and the bread knife slipped off the board and landed, point down and quivering ominously, exactly where Sirius's right hand had been seconds before.

"FOR HEAVEN'S SAKE!" screamed Mrs. Weasley. "THERE WAS NO NEED — I'VE HAD ENOUGH OF THIS — JUST BECAUSE YOU'RE ALLOWED TO USE MAGIC NOW YOU DON'T HAVE TO WHIP YOUR WANDS OUT FOR EVERY TINY LITTLE THING!"

"We were just trying to save a bit of time!" said Fred, hurrying forward and wrenching the bread knife out of the table. "Sorry Sirius, mate — didn't mean to —"

Harry and Sirius were both laughing. Mundungus, who had toppled backward off his chair, was swearing as he got to his feet. Crookshanks had given an angry hiss and shot off under the dresser, from whence his large yellow eyes glowed in the darkness.

"Boys," Mr. Weasley said, lifting the stew back into the middle of the table, "your mother's right, you're supposed to show a sense of responsibility now you've come of age —"

"— none of your brothers caused this sort of trouble!" Mrs. Weasley raged at the twins, slamming a fresh flagon of butterbeer onto the table and spilling almost as much again. "Bill didn't feel the need to Apparate every few feet! Charlie didn't Charm everything he met! Percy —"

She stopped dead, catching her breath with a frightened look at her husband, whose expression was suddenly wooden.

"Let's eat," said Bill quickly.

"It looks wonderful, Molly," said Lupin, ladling stew onto a plate for her and handing it across the table.

For a few minutes there was silence but for the chink of plates and cutlery and the scraping of chairs as everyone settled down to their food. Then Mrs. Weasley turned to Sirius and said, "I've been meaning to tell you, there's something trapped in that writing desk in the drawing room, it keeps rattling and shaking. Of course, it could just be a boggart, but I thought we ought to ask Alastor to have a look at it before we let it out."

"Whatever you like," said Sirius indifferently.

"The curtains in there are full of doxies too," Mrs. Weasley went on. "I thought we might try and tackle them tomorrow."

"I look forward to it," said Sirius. Harry heard the sarcasm in his voice, but he was not sure that anyone else did.

Opposite Harry, Tonks was entertaining Hermione and Ginny by transforming her nose between mouthfuls. Screwing up her eyes each time with the same pained expression she had worn back in Harry's bedroom, her nose swelled to a beaklike protuberance like Snape's, shrank to something resembling a button mushroom, and then sprouted a great deal of hair from each nostril. Apparently this was a regular mealtime entertainment, because after a while Hermione and Ginny started requesting their favorite noses.

"Do that one like a pig snout, Tonks . . ."

Tonks obliged, and Harry, looking up, had the fleeting impression that a female Dudley was grinning at him from across the table.

Mr. Weasley, Bill, and Lupin were having an intense discussion about goblins.

"They're not giving anything away yet," said Bill. "I still can't work out whether they believe he's back or not. 'Course, they might prefer not to take sides at all. Keep out of it."

"I'm sure they'd never go over to You-Know-Who," said Mr. Weasley, shaking his head. "They've suffered losses too. Remember that goblin family he murdered last time, somewhere near Nottingham?"

"I think it depends what they're offered," said Lupin. "And I'm not talking about gold; if they're offered freedoms we've been denying them for centuries they're going to be tempted. Have you still not had any luck with Ragnok, Bill?"

"He's feeling pretty anti-wizard at the moment," said Bill. "He hasn't stopped raging about the Bagman business, he reckons the Ministry did a cover-up, those goblins never got their gold from him, you know —"

A gale of laughter from the middle of the table drowned the rest of Bill's words. Fred, George, Ron, and Mundungus were rolling around in their seats.

". . . and then," choked Mundungus, tears running down his face, "and then, if you'll believe it, 'e says to me, 'e says, ''ere, Dung, where didja get all them toads from? 'Cos some son of a Bludger's gone and nicked all mine!' And I says, 'Nicked all your toads, Will, what next? So you'll be wanting some more, then?' And if you'll believe me, lads, the gormless gargoyle buys all 'is own toads back orf me for twice what 'e paid in the first place —"

"I don't think we need to hear any more of your business dealings, thank you very much, Mundungus," said Mrs. Weasley sharply, as Ron slumped forward onto the table, howling with laughter.

"Beg pardon, Molly," said Mundungus at once, wiping his eyes and winking at Harry. "But, you know, Will nicked 'em orf Warty Harris in the first place so I wasn't really doing nothing wrong —"

"I don't know where you learned about right and wrong, Mundungus, but you seem to have missed a few crucial lessons," said Mrs. Weasley coldly.

Fred and George buried their faces in their goblets of butterbeer; George was hiccuping. For some reason, Mrs. Weasley threw a very nasty look at Sirius before getting to her feet and going to fetch a large rhubarb crumble for pudding. Harry looked round at his godfather.

"Molly doesn't approve of Mundungus," said Sirius in an undertone.

"How come he's in the Order?" Harry said very quietly.

"He's useful," Sirius muttered. "Knows all the crooks — well, he would, seeing as he's one himself. But he's also very loyal to Dumble-

dore, who helped him out of a tight spot once. It pays to have someone like Dung around, he hears things we don't. But Molly thinks
inviting him to stay for dinner is going too far. She hasn't forgiven
him for slipping off duty when he was supposed to be tailing you."

Three helpings of rhubarb crumble and custard later and the waistband on Harry's jeans was feeling uncomfortably tight (which was
saying something, as the jeans had once been Dudley's). He lay down
his spoon in a lull in the general conversation. Mr. Weasley was leaning back in his chair, looking replete and relaxed, Tonks was yawning
widely, her nose now back to normal, and Ginny, who had lured
Crookshanks out from under the dresser, was sitting cross-legged on
the floor, rolling butterbeer corks for him to chase.

"Nearly time for bed, I think," said Mrs. Weasley on a yawn.

"Not just yet, Molly," said Sirius, pushing away his empty plate and
turning to look at Harry. "You know, I'm surprised at you. I thought
the first thing you'd do when you got here would be to start asking
questions about Voldemort."

The atmosphere in the room changed with the rapidity Harry as-
sociated with the arrival of dementors. Where seconds before it had
been sleepily relaxed, it was now alert, even tense. A frisson had gone
around the table at the mention of Voldemort's name. Lupin, who
had been about to take a sip of wine, lowered his goblet slowly, looking wary.

"I did!" said Harry indignantly. "I asked Ron and Hermione but
they said we're not allowed in the Order, so —"

"And they're quite right," said Mrs. Weasley. "You're too young."

She was sitting bolt upright in her chair, her fists clenched upon its
arms, every trace of drowsiness gone.

"Since when did someone have to be in the Order of the Phoenix
to ask questions?" asked Sirius. "Harry's been trapped in that Muggle
house for a month. He's got the right to know what's been happen —"

"Hang on!" interrupted George loudly.

"How come Harry gets his questions answered?" said Fred angrily.

"*We've* been trying to get stuff out of you for a month and you haven't told us a single stinking thing!" said George.

"*'You're too young, you're not in the Order,'*" said Fred, in a high-pitched voice that sounded uncannily like his mother's. "Harry's not even of age!"

"It's not my fault you haven't been told what the Order's doing," said Sirius calmly. "That's your parents' decision. Harry, on the other hand —"

"It's not down to you to decide what's good for Harry!" said Mrs. Weasley sharply. Her normally kindly face looked dangerous. "You haven't forgotten what Dumbledore said, I suppose?"

"Which bit?" Sirius asked politely, but with an air as though readying himself for a fight.

"The bit about not telling Harry more than he *needs to know,*" said Mrs. Weasley, placing a heavy emphasis on the last three words.

Ron, Hermione, Fred, and George's heads turned from Sirius to Mrs. Weasley as though following a tennis rally. Ginny was kneeling amid a pile of abandoned butterbeer corks, watching the conversation with her mouth slightly open. Lupin's eyes were fixed on Sirius.

"I don't intend to tell him more than he *needs to know,* Molly," said Sirius. "But as he was the one who saw Voldemort come back" (again, there was a collective shudder around the table at the name), "he has more right than most to —"

"He's not a member of the Order of the Phoenix!" said Mrs. Weasley. "He's only fifteen and —"

"— and he's dealt with as much as most in the Order," said Sirius, "and more than some —"

"No one's denying what he's done!" said Mrs. Weasley, her voice rising, her fists trembling on the arms of her chair. "But he's still —"

"He's not a child!" said Sirius impatiently.

"He's not an adult either!" said Mrs. Weasley, the color rising in her cheeks. "He's not *James,* Sirius!"

"I'm perfectly clear who he is, thanks, Molly," said Sirius coldly.

"I'm not sure you are!" said Mrs. Weasley. "Sometimes, the way you talk about him, it's as though you think you've got your best friend back!"

"What's wrong with that?" said Harry.

"What's wrong, Harry, is that you are *not* your father, however much you might look like him!" said Mrs. Weasley, her eyes still boring into Sirius. "You are still at school and adults responsible for you should not forget it!"

"Meaning I'm an irresponsible godfather?" demanded Sirius, his voice rising.

"Meaning you've been known to act rashly, Sirius, which is why Dumbledore keeps reminding you to stay at home and —"

"We'll leave my instructions from Dumbledore out of this, if you please!" said Sirius loudly.

"Arthur!" said Mrs. Weasley, rounding on her husband. "Arthur, back me up!"

Mr. Weasley did not speak at once. He took off his glasses and cleaned them slowly on his robes, not looking at his wife. Only when he had replaced them carefully on his nose did he say, "Dumbledore knows the position has changed, Molly. He accepts that Harry will have to be filled in to a certain extent now that he is staying at headquarters —"

"Yes, but there's a difference between that and inviting him to ask whatever he likes!"

"Personally," said Lupin quietly, looking away from Sirius at last, as Mrs. Weasley turned quickly to him, hopeful that finally she was about to get an ally, "I think it better that Harry gets the facts — not all the facts, Molly, but the general picture — from us, rather than a garbled version from . . . others."

His expression was mild, but Harry felt sure that Lupin, at least, knew that some Extendable Ears had survived Mrs. Weasley's purge.

"Well," said Mrs. Weasley, breathing deeply and looking around the table for support that did not come, "well . . . I can see I'm going to be overruled. I'll just say this: Dumbledore must have had his reasons for not wanting Harry to know too much, and speaking as someone who has got Harry's best interests at heart —"

"He's not your son," said Sirius quietly.

"He's as good as," said Mrs. Weasley fiercely. "Who else has he got?"

"He's got me!"

"Yes," said Mrs. Weasley, her lip curling. "The thing is, it's been rather difficult for you to look after him while you've been locked up in Azkaban, hasn't it?"

Sirius started to rise from his chair.

"Molly, you're not the only person at this table who cares about Harry," said Lupin sharply. "Sirius, sit *down*."

Mrs. Weasley's lower lip was trembling. Sirius sank slowly back into his chair, his face white.

"I think Harry ought to be allowed a say in this," Lupin continued. "He's old enough to decide for himself."

"I want to know what's been going on," Harry said at once.

He did not look at Mrs. Weasley. He had been touched by what she had said about his being as good as a son, but he was also impatient at her mollycoddling. . . . Sirius was right, he was *not* a child.

"Very well," said Mrs. Weasley, her voice cracking. "Ginny — Ron — Hermione — Fred — George — I want you out of this kitchen, now."

There was instant uproar.

"We're of age!" Fred and George bellowed together.

"If Harry's allowed, why can't I?" shouted Ron.

"Mum, I *want* to!" wailed Ginny.

"NO!" shouted Mrs. Weasley, standing up, her eyes overbright. "I absolutely forbid —"

"Molly, you can't stop Fred and George," said Mr. Weasley wearily. "They *are* of age —"

"They're still at school —"

"But they're legally adults now," said Mr. Weasley in the same tired voice.

Mrs. Weasley was now scarlet in the face.

"I — oh, all right then, Fred and George can stay, but Ron —"

"Harry'll tell me and Hermione everything you say anyway!" said Ron hotly. "Won't — won't you?" he added uncertainly, meeting Harry's eyes.

For a split second, Harry considered telling Ron that he wouldn't tell him a single word, that he could try a taste of being kept in the dark and see how he liked it. But the nasty impulse vanished as they looked at each other.

"'Course I will," Harry said. Ron and Hermione beamed.

"Fine!" shouted Mrs. Weasley. "Fine! Ginny — BED!"

Ginny did not go quietly. They could hear her raging and storming at her mother all the way up the stairs, and when she reached the hall Mrs. Black's earsplitting shrieks were added to the din. Lupin hurried off to the portrait to restore calm. It was only after he had returned, closing the kitchen door behind him and taking his seat at the table again, that Sirius spoke.

"Okay, Harry . . . what do you want to know?"

Harry took a deep breath and asked the question that had been obsessing him for a month.

"Where's Voldemort? What's he doing? I've been trying to watch the Muggle news," he said, ignoring the renewed shudders and winces at the name, "and there hasn't been anything that looks like him yet, no funny deaths or anything —"

"That's because there haven't been any suspicious deaths yet," said Sirius, "not as far as we know, anyway. . . . And we know quite a lot."

"More than he thinks we do anyway," said Lupin.

"How come he's stopped killing people?" Harry asked. He knew that Voldemort had murdered more than once in the last year alone.

"Because he doesn't want to draw attention to himself at the moment," said Sirius. "It would be dangerous for him. His comeback didn't come off quite the way he wanted it to, you see. He messed it up."

"Or rather, you messed it up for him," said Lupin with a satisfied smile.

"How?" Harry asked perplexedly.

"You weren't supposed to survive!" said Sirius. "Nobody apart from his Death Eaters was supposed to know he'd come back. But you survived to bear witness."

"And the very last person he wanted alerted to his return the moment he got back was Dumbledore," said Lupin. "And you made sure Dumbledore knew at once."

"How has that helped?" Harry asked.

"Are you kidding?" said Bill incredulously. "Dumbledore was the only one You-Know-Who was ever scared of!"

"Thanks to you, Dumbledore was able to recall the Order of the Phoenix about an hour after Voldemort returned," said Sirius.

"So what's the Order been doing?" said Harry, looking around at them all.

"Working as hard as we can to make sure Voldemort can't carry out his plans," said Sirius.

"How d'you know what his plans are?" Harry asked quickly.

"Dumbledore's got a shrewd idea," said Lupin, "and Dumbledore's shrewd ideas normally turn out to be accurate."

"So what does Dumbledore reckon he's planning?"

"Well, firstly, he wants to build up his army again," said Sirius. "In the old days he had huge numbers at his command; witches and wizards he'd bullied or bewitched into following him, his faithful Death Eaters, a great variety of Dark creatures. You heard him planning to recruit the giants; well, they'll be just one group he's after. He's certainly not going to try and take on the Ministry of Magic with only a dozen Death Eaters."

"So you're trying to stop him getting more followers?"

"We're doing our best," said Lupin.

"How?"

"Well, the main thing is to try and convince as many people as possible that You-Know-Who really has returned, to put them on their guard," said Bill. "It's proving tricky, though."

"Why?"

"Because of the Ministry's attitude," said Tonks. "You saw Cornelius Fudge after You-Know-Who came back, Harry. Well, he hasn't shifted his position at all. He's absolutely refusing to believe it's happened."

"But why?" said Harry desperately. "Why's he being so stupid? If Dumbledore —"

"Ah, well, you've put your finger on the problem," said Mr. Weasley with a wry smile. *"Dumbledore."*

"Fudge is frightened of him, you see," said Tonks sadly.

"Frightened of Dumbledore?" said Harry incredulously.

"Frightened of what he's up to," said Mr. Weasley. "You see, Fudge thinks Dumbledore's plotting to overthrow him. He thinks Dumbledore wants to be Minister of Magic."

"But Dumbledore doesn't want —"

"Of course he doesn't," said Mr. Weasley. "He's never wanted the Minister's job, even though a lot of people wanted him to take it when Millicent Bagnold retired. Fudge came to power instead, but he's never quite forgotten how much popular support Dumbledore had, even though Dumbledore never applied for the job."

"Deep down, Fudge knows Dumbledore's much cleverer than he is, a much more powerful wizard, and in the early days of his Ministry he was forever asking Dumbledore for help and advice," said Lupin. "But it seems that he's become fond of power now, and much more confident. He loves being Minister of Magic, and he's managed to convince himself that he's the clever one and Dumbledore's simply stirring up trouble for the sake of it."

"How can he think that?" said Harry angrily. "How can he think Dumbledore would just make it all up — that *I'd* make it all up?"

"Because accepting that Voldemort's back would mean trouble like the Ministry hasn't had to cope with for nearly fourteen years," said Sirius bitterly. "Fudge just can't bring himself to face it. It's so much more comfortable to convince himself Dumbledore's lying to destabilize him."

"You see the problem," said Lupin. "While the Ministry insists there is nothing to fear from Voldemort, it's hard to convince people he's back, especially as they really don't want to believe it in the first place. What's more, the Ministry's leaning heavily on the *Daily Prophet* not to report any of what they're calling Dumbledore's rumor-mongering, so most of the Wizarding community are completely unaware anything's happened, and that makes them easy targets for the Death Eaters if they're using the Imperius Curse."

"But you're telling people, aren't you?" said Harry, looking around at Mr. Weasley, Sirius, Bill, Mundungus, Lupin, and Tonks. "You're letting people know he's back?"

They all smiled humorlessly.

"Well, as everyone thinks I'm a mad mass murderer and the Ministry's put a ten-thousand-Galleon price on my head, I can hardly stroll up the street and start handing out leaflets, can I?" said Sirius restlessly.

"And I'm not a very popular dinner guest with most of the community," said Lupin. "It's an occupational hazard of being a werewolf."

"Tonks and Arthur would lose their jobs at the Ministry if they started shooting their mouths off," said Sirius, "and it's very important for us to have spies inside the Ministry, because you can bet Voldemort will have them."

"We've managed to convince a couple of people, though," said Mr. Weasley. "Tonks here, for one — she's too young to have been in the Order of the Phoenix last time, and having Aurors on our side is a huge advantage — Kingsley Shacklebolt's been a real asset too. He's in charge of the hunt for Sirius, so he's been feeding the Ministry information that Sirius is in Tibet."

"But if none of you's putting the news out that Voldemort's back —" Harry began.

"Who said none of us was putting the news out?" said Sirius. "Why d'you think Dumbledore's in such trouble?"

"What d'you mean?" Harry asked.

"They're trying to discredit him," said Lupin. "Didn't you see the *Daily Prophet* last week? They reported that he'd been voted out of the Chairmanship of the International Confederation of Wizards because he's getting old and losing his grip, but it's not true, he was voted out by Ministry wizards after he made a speech announcing Voldemort's return. They've demoted him from Chief Warlock on the Wizengamot — that's the Wizard High Court — and they're talking about taking away his Order of Merlin, First Class, too."

"But Dumbledore says he doesn't care what they do as long as they don't take him off the Chocolate Frog cards," said Bill, grinning.

"It's no laughing matter," said Mr. Weasley shortly. "If he carries on defying the Ministry like this, he could end up in Azkaban and the last thing we want is Dumbledore locked up. While You-Know-Who knows Dumbledore's out there and wise to what he's up to, he's going to go cautiously for a while. If Dumbledore's out of the way — well, You-Know-Who will have a clear field."

"But if Voldemort's trying to recruit more Death Eaters, it's bound to get out that he's come back, isn't it?" asked Harry desperately.

"Voldemort doesn't march up to people's houses and bang on their front doors, Harry," said Sirius. "He tricks, jinxes, and blackmails them. He's well-practiced at operating in secrecy. In any case, gathering followers is only one thing he's interested in, he's got other plans too, plans he can put into operation very quietly indeed, and he's concentrating on them at the moment."

"What's he after apart from followers?" Harry asked swiftly.

He thought he saw Sirius and Lupin exchange the most fleeting of looks before Sirius said, "Stuff he can only get by stealth."

When Harry continued to look puzzled, Sirius said, "Like a weapon. Something he didn't have last time."

"When he was powerful before?"

"Yes."

"Like what kind of weapon?" said Harry. "Something worse than the *Avada Kedavra* — ?"

"That's enough."

Mrs. Weasley spoke from the shadows beside the door. Harry had not noticed her return from taking Ginny upstairs. Her arms were crossed and she looked furious.

"I want you in bed, now. All of you," she added, looking around at Fred, George, Ron, and Hermione.

"You can't boss us —" Fred began.

"Watch me," snarled Mrs. Weasley. She was trembling slightly as she looked at Sirius. "You've given Harry plenty of information. Any more and you might just as well induct him into the Order straightaway."

"Why not?" said Harry quickly. "I'll join, I want to join, I want to fight —"

"No."

It was not Mrs. Weasley who spoke this time, but Lupin.

"The Order is comprised only of overage wizards," he said. "Wizards who have left school," he added, as Fred and George opened their mouths. "There are dangers involved of which you can have no idea, any of you . . . I think Molly's right, Sirius. We've said enough."

Sirius half-shrugged but did not argue. Mrs. Weasley beckoned imperiously to her sons and Hermione. One by one they stood up and Harry, recognizing defeat, followed suit.

THE NOBLE AND MOST
ANCIENT HOUSE OF BLACK

Mrs. Weasley followed them upstairs looking grim.

"I want you all to go straight to bed, no talking," she said as they reached the first landing. "We've got a busy day tomorrow. I expect Ginny's asleep," she added to Hermione, "so try not to wake her up."

"Asleep, yeah, right," said Fred in an undertone, after Hermione bade them good night and they were climbing to the next floor. "If Ginny's not lying awake waiting for Hermione to tell her everything they said downstairs, then I'm a flobberworm. . . ."

"All right, Ron, Harry," said Mrs. Weasley on the second landing, pointing them into their bedroom. "Off to bed with you."

"'Night," Harry and Ron said to the twins.

"Sleep tight," said Fred, winking.

Mrs. Weasley closed the door behind Harry with a sharp snap. The bedroom looked, if anything, even danker and gloomier than it had on first sight. The blank picture on the wall was now breathing very slowly and deeply, as though its invisible occupant was asleep. Harry put on his pajamas, took off his glasses, and climbed into his chilly bed while Ron threw Owl Treats up on top of the wardrobe to pacify Hedwig and Pigwidgeon, who were clattering around and rustling their wings restlessly.

"We can't let them out to hunt every night," Ron explained as he pulled on his maroon pajamas. "Dumbledore doesn't want too many owls swooping around the square, thinks it'll look suspicious. Oh yeah . . . I forgot. . . ."

He crossed to the door and bolted it.

"What're you doing that for?"

"Kreacher," said Ron as he turned off the light. "First night I was here he came wandering in at three in the morning. Trust me, you don't want to wake up and find him prowling around your room. Anyway . . ." He got into his bed, settled down under the covers, then turned to look at Harry in the darkness. Harry could see his outline by the moonlight filtering in through the grimy window. *"What d'you reckon?"*

Harry didn't need to ask what Ron meant.

"Well, they didn't tell us much we couldn't have guessed, did they?" he said, thinking of all that had been said downstairs. "I mean, all they've really said is that the Order's trying to stop people joining Vol —"

There was a sharp intake of breath from Ron.

"— *demort,*" said Harry firmly. "When are you going to start using his name? Sirius and Lupin do."

Ron ignored this last comment. "Yeah, you're right," he said. "We already knew nearly everything they told us, from using the Extendable Ears. The only new bit was —"

Crack.

"OUCH!"

"Keep your voice down, Ron, or Mum'll be back up here."

"You two just Apparated on my knees!"

"Yeah, well, it's harder in the dark —"

Harry saw the blurred outlines of Fred and George leaping down from Ron's bed. There was a groan of bedsprings and Harry's mattress descended a few inches as George sat down near his feet.

"So, got there yet?" said George eagerly.

"The weapon Sirius mentioned?" said Harry.

"Let slip, more like," said Fred with relish, now sitting next to Ron. "We didn't hear about *that* on the old Extendables, did we?"

"What d'you reckon it is?" said Harry.

"Could be anything," said Fred.

"But there can't be anything worse than the *Avada Kedavra* curse, can there?" said Ron. "What's worse than death?"

"Maybe it's something that can kill loads of people at once," suggested George.

"Maybe it's some particularly painful way of killing people," said Ron fearfully.

"He's got the Cruciatus Curse for causing pain," said Harry. "He doesn't need anything more efficient than that."

There was a pause and Harry knew that the others, like him, were wondering what horrors this weapon could perpetrate.

"So who d'you think's got it now?" asked George.

"I hope it's our side," said Ron, sounding slightly nervous.

"If it is, Dumbledore's probably keeping it," said Fred.

"Where?" said Ron quickly. "Hogwarts?"

"Bet it is!" said George. "That's where he hid the Sorcerer's Stone!"

"A weapon's going to be a lot bigger than the Stone, though!" said Ron.

"Not necessarily," said Fred.

"Yeah, size is no guarantee of power," said George. "Look at Ginny."

"What d'you mean?" said Harry.

"You've never been on the receiving end of one of her Bat-Bogey Hexes, have you?"

"Shhh!" said Fred, half-rising from the bed. "Listen!"

They fell silent. Footsteps were coming up the stairs again.

"Mum," said George, and without further ado there was a loud crack and Harry felt the weight vanish from the end of his bed. A few seconds later and they heard the floorboard creak outside their door; Mrs. Weasley was plainly listening to see whether they were talking or not.

Hedwig and Pigwidgeon hooted dolefully. The floorboard creaked again and they heard her heading upstairs to check on Fred and George.

"She doesn't trust us at all, you know," said Ron regretfully.

Harry was sure he would not be able to fall asleep; the evening had been so packed with things to think about that he fully expected to lie awake for hours mulling it all over. He wanted to continue talking to Ron, but Mrs. Weasley was now creaking back downstairs again, and once she had gone he distinctly heard others making their way upstairs. . . . In fact, many-legged creatures were cantering softly up and down outside the bedroom door, and Hagrid, the Care of Magical Creatures teacher, was saying, *"Beauties, aren' they, eh, Harry? We'll be studyin' weapons this term. . . ."* And Harry saw that the creatures had cannons for heads and were wheeling to face him. . . . He ducked. . . .

The next thing he knew, he was curled in a warm ball under his bedclothes, and George's loud voice was filling the room.

"Mum says get up, your breakfast is in the kitchen and then she needs you in the drawing room, there are loads more doxies than she thought and she's found a nest of dead puffskeins under the sofa."

Half an hour later, Harry and Ron, who had dressed and breakfasted quickly, entered the drawing room, a long, high-ceilinged room on the first floor with olive-green walls covered in dirty tapestries. The carpet exhaled little clouds of dust every time someone put their foot on it and the long, moss-green velvet curtains were buzzing as though swarming with invisible bees. It was around these that Mrs. Weasley,

Hermione, Ginny, Fred, and George were grouped, all looking rather peculiar, as they had tied cloths over their noses and mouths. Each of them was also holding a large bottle of black liquid with a nozzle at the end.

"Cover your faces and take a spray," Mrs. Weasley said to Harry and Ron the moment she saw them, pointing to two more bottles of black liquid standing on a spindle-legged table. "It's Doxycide. I've never seen an infestation this bad — *what* that house-elf's been doing for the last ten years —"

Hermione's face was half concealed by a tea towel but Harry distinctly saw her throw a reproachful look at Mrs. Weasley at these words.

"Kreacher's really old, he probably couldn't manage —"

"You'd be surprised what Kreacher can manage when he wants to, Hermione," said Sirius, who had just entered the room carrying a blood-stained bag of what appeared to be dead rats. "I've just been feeding Buckbeak," he added, in reply to Harry's inquiring look. "I keep him upstairs in my mother's bedroom. Anyway . . . this writing desk . . ."

He dropped the bag of rats onto an armchair, then bent over to examine the locked cabinet which, Harry now noticed for the first time, was shaking slightly.

"Well, Molly, I'm pretty sure this is a boggart," said Sirius, peering through the keyhole, "but perhaps we ought to let Mad-Eye have a shifty at it before we let it out — knowing my mother it could be something much worse."

"Right you are, Sirius," said Mrs. Weasley.

They were both speaking in carefully light, polite voices that told Harry quite plainly that neither had forgotten their disagreement of the night before.

A loud, clanging bell sounded from downstairs, followed at once by the cacophony of screams and wails that had been triggered the previous night by Tonks knocking over the umbrella stand.

"I keep telling them not to ring the doorbell!" said Sirius exasperatedly, hurrying back out of the room. They heard him thundering down the stairs as Mrs. Black's screeches echoed up through the house once more: *"Stains of dishonor, filthy half-breeds, blood traitors, children of filth . . ."*

"Close the door, please, Harry," said Mrs. Weasley.

Harry took as much time as he dared to close the drawing room door; he wanted to listen to what was going on downstairs. Sirius had obviously managed to shut the curtains over his mother's portrait because she had stopped screaming. He heard Sirius walking down the hall, then the clattering of the chain on the front door, and then a deep voice he recognized as Kingsley Shacklebolt's saying, "Hestia's just relieved me, so she's got Moody's cloak now, thought I'd leave a report for Dumbledore. . . ."

Feeling Mrs. Weasley's eyes on the back of his head, Harry regretfully closed the drawing room door and rejoined the doxy party.

Mrs. Weasley was bending over to check the page on doxies in *Gilderoy Lockhart's Guide to Household Pests,* which was lying open on the sofa.

"Right, you lot, you need to be careful, because doxies bite and their teeth are poisonous. I've got a bottle of antidote here, but I'd rather nobody needed it."

She straightened up, positioned herself squarely in front of the curtains, and beckoned them all forward.

"When I say the word, start spraying immediately," she said. "They'll come flying out at us, I expect, but it says on the sprays one good squirt will paralyze them. When they're immobilized, just throw them in this bucket."

She stepped carefully out of their line of fire and raised her own spray. "All right — *squirt!*"

Harry had been spraying only a few seconds when a fully grown doxy came soaring out of a fold in the material, shiny beetlelike wings whirring, tiny needle-sharp teeth bared, its fairylike body covered with thick black hair and its four tiny fists clenched with fury. Harry caught it full in the face with a blast of Doxycide; it froze in midair and fell, with a surprisingly loud *thunk,* onto the worn carpet below. Harry picked it up and threw it in the bucket.

"Fred, what are you doing?" said Mrs. Weasley sharply. "Spray that at once and throw it away!"

Harry looked around. Fred was holding a struggling doxy between his forefinger and thumb.

"Right-o," Fred said brightly, spraying the doxy quickly in the face so that it fainted, but the moment Mrs. Weasley's back was turned he pocketed it with a wink.

"We want to experiment with doxy venom for our Skiving Snack-boxes," George told Harry under his breath.

Deftly spraying two doxies at once as they soared straight for his nose, Harry moved closer to George and muttered out of the corner of his mouth, "What are Skiving Snackboxes?"

"Range of sweets to make you ill," George whispered, keeping a wary eye on Mrs. Weasley's back. "Not seriously ill, mind, just ill enough to get you out of a class when you feel like it. Fred and I have been developing them this summer. They're double-ended, color-coded chews. If you eat the orange half of the Puking Pastilles, you throw up. Moment you've been rushed out of the lesson for the hospital wing, you swallow the purple half —"

"'— which restores you to full fitness, enabling you to pursue the leisure activity of your own choice during an hour that would otherwise have been devoted to unprofitable boredom.' That's what we're putting in the adverts, anyway," whispered Fred, who had edged over out of Mrs. Weasley's line of vision and was now sweeping a few stray doxies from the floor and adding them to his pocket. "But they still need a bit of work. At the moment our testers are having a bit of trouble stopping puking long enough to swallow the purple end."

"Testers?"

"Us," said Fred. "We take it in turns. George did the Fainting Fancies — we both tried the Nosebleed Nougat —"

"Mum thought we'd been dueling," said George.

"Joke shop still on, then?" Harry muttered, pretending to be adjusting the nozzle on his spray.

"Well, we haven't had a chance to get premises yet," said Fred, dropping his voice even lower as Mrs. Weasley mopped her brow with her scarf before returning to the attack, "so we're running it as a mail-order service at the moment. We put advertisements in the *Daily Prophet* last week."

"All thanks to you, mate," said George. "But don't worry . . . Mum hasn't got a clue. She won't read the *Daily Prophet* anymore, 'cause of it telling lies about you and Dumbledore."

Harry grinned. He had forced the Weasley twins to take the thousand-Galleon prize money he had won in the Triwizard Tournament to help them realize their ambition to open a joke shop, but he was still glad to know that his part in furthering their plans was unknown to Mrs. Weasley, who did not think that running a joke shop was a suitable career for two of her sons.

The de-doxying of the curtains took most of the morning. It was past midday when Mrs. Weasley finally removed her protective scarf, sank into a sagging armchair, and sprang up again with a cry of disgust, having sat on the bag of dead rats. The curtains were no longer buzzing; they hung limp and damp from the intensive spraying; unconscious doxies lay crammed in the bucket at the foot of them beside a bowl of their black eggs, at which Crookshanks was now sniffing and Fred and George were shooting covetous looks.

"I think we'll tackle *those* after lunch."

Mrs. Weasley pointed at the dusty glass-fronted cabinets standing on either side of the mantelpiece. They were crammed with an odd assortment of objects: a selection of rusty daggers, claws, a coiled snakeskin, a number of tarnished silver boxes inscribed with languages Harry could not understand and, least pleasant of all, an ornate crystal bottle with a large opal set into the stopper, full of what Harry was quite sure was blood.

The clanging doorbell rang again. Everyone looked at Mrs. Weasley.

"Stay here," she said firmly, snatching up the bag of rats as Mrs. Black's screeches started up again from down below. "I'll bring up some sandwiches."

She left the room, closing the door carefully behind her. At once, everyone dashed over to the window to look down onto the doorstep. They could see the top of an unkempt gingery head and a stack of precariously balanced cauldrons.

"Mundungus!" said Hermione. "What's he brought all those cauldrons for?"

"Probably looking for a safe place to keep them," said Harry. "Isn't that what he was doing the night he was supposed to be tailing me? Picking up dodgy cauldrons?"

"Yeah, you're right!" said Fred, as the front door opened; Mundungus heaved his cauldrons through it and disappeared from view. "Blimey, Mum won't like that. . . ."

He and George crossed to the door and stood beside it, listening intently. Mrs. Black's screaming had stopped again.

"Mundungus is talking to Sirius and Kingsley," Fred muttered, frowning with concentration. "Can't hear properly . . . d'you reckon we can risk the Extendable Ears?"

"Might be worth it," said George. "I could sneak upstairs and get a pair —"

But at that precise moment there was an explosion of sound from downstairs that rendered Extendable Ears quite unnecessary. All of them could hear exactly what Mrs. Weasley was shouting at the top of her voice.

"WE ARE NOT RUNNING A HIDEOUT FOR STOLEN GOODS!"

"I love hearing Mum shouting at someone else," said Fred, with a satisfied smile on his face as he opened the door an inch or so to allow Mrs. Weasley's voice to permeate the room better. "It makes such a nice change."

"— COMPLETELY IRRESPONSIBLE, AS IF WE HAVEN'T GOT ENOUGH TO WORRY ABOUT WITHOUT YOU DRAGGING STOLEN CAULDRONS INTO THE HOUSE —"

"The idiots are letting her get into her stride," said George, shaking his head. "You've got to head her off early, otherwise she builds up a head of steam and goes on for hours. And she's been dying to have a go at Mundungus ever since he sneaked off when he was supposed to be following you, Harry — and there goes Sirius's mum again —"

Mrs. Weasley's voice was lost amid fresh shrieks and screams from the portraits in the hall. George made to shut the door to drown the noise, but before he could do so, a house-elf edged into the room.

Except for the filthy rag tied like a loincloth around its middle, it was completely naked. It looked very old. Its skin seemed to be several times too big for it and though it was bald like all house-elves, there was a quantity of white hair growing out of its large, batlike ears. Its eyes were a bloodshot and watery gray, and its fleshy nose was large and rather snoutlike.

The elf took absolutely no notice of Harry and the rest. Acting as though it could not see them, it shuffled hunchbacked, slowly and doggedly, toward the far end of the room, muttering under its breath all the while in a hoarse, deep voice like a bullfrog's, ". . . Smells like a drain and a criminal to boot, but she's no better, nasty old blood traitor with her brats messing up my Mistress's house, oh my poor Mistress, if she knew, if she knew the scum they've let in her house, what would she say to old Kreacher, oh the shame of it, Mudbloods and werewolves and traitors and thieves, poor old Kreacher, what can he do. . . ."

"Hello, Kreacher," said Fred very loudly, closing the door with a snap.

The house-elf froze in his tracks, stopped muttering, and then gave a very pronounced and very unconvincing start of surprise.

"Kreacher did not see Young Master," he said, turning around and bowing to Fred. Still facing the carpet, he added, perfectly audibly, "Nasty little brat of a blood traitor it is."

"Sorry?" said George. "Didn't catch that last bit."

"Kreacher said nothing," said the elf, with a second bow to George, adding in a clear undertone, "and there's its twin, unnatural little beasts they are."

Harry didn't know whether to laugh or not. The elf straightened up, eyeing them all very malevolently, and apparently convinced that they could not hear him as he continued to mutter.

". . . and there's the Mudblood, standing there bold as brass, oh if my Mistress knew, oh how she'd cry, and there's a new boy, Kreacher doesn't know his name, what is he doing here, Kreacher doesn't know . . ."

"This is Harry, Kreacher," said Hermione tentatively. "Harry Potter."

Kreacher's pale eyes widened and he muttered faster and more furiously than ever.

"The Mudblood is talking to Kreacher as though she is my friend, if Kreacher's Mistress saw him in such company, oh what would she say —"

"Don't call her a Mudblood!" said Ron and Ginny together, very angrily.

"It doesn't matter," Hermione whispered, "he's not in his right mind, he doesn't know what he's —"

"Don't kid yourself, Hermione, he knows *exactly* what he's saying," said Fred, eyeing Kreacher with great dislike.

Kreacher was still muttering, his eyes on Harry.

"Is it true? Is it Harry Potter? Kreacher can see the scar, it must be true, that's that boy who stopped the Dark Lord, Kreacher wonders how he did it —"

"Don't we all, Kreacher?" said Fred.

"What do you want anyway?" George asked.

Kreacher's huge eyes darted onto George.

"Kreacher is cleaning," he said evasively.

"A likely story," said a voice behind Harry.

Sirius had come back; he was glowering at the elf from the doorway. The noise in the hall had abated; perhaps Mrs. Weasley and Mundungus had moved their argument down into the kitchen. At the sight of Sirius, Kreacher flung himself into a ridiculously low bow that flattened his snoutlike nose on the floor.

"Stand up straight," said Sirius impatiently. "Now, what are you up to?"

"Kreacher is cleaning," the elf repeated. "Kreacher lives to serve the noble house of Black —"

"— and it's getting blacker every day, it's filthy," said Sirius.

"Master always liked his little joke," said Kreacher, bowing again, and continuing in an undertone, "Master was a nasty ungrateful swine who broke his mother's heart —"

"My mother didn't have a heart, Kreacher," Sirius snapped. "She kept herself alive out of pure spite."

Kreacher bowed again and said, "Whatever Master says," then muttered furiously, "Master is not fit to wipe slime from his mother's boots, oh my poor Mistress, what would she say if she saw Kreacher serving him, how she hated him, what a disappointment he was —"

"I asked you what you were up to," said Sirius coldly. "Every time you show up pretending to be cleaning, you sneak something off to your room so we can't throw it out."

"Kreacher would never move anything from its proper place in Master's house," said the elf, then muttered very fast, "Mistress would never forgive Kreacher if the tapestry was thrown out, seven centuries it's been in the family, Kreacher must save it, Kreacher will not let Master and the blood traitors and the brats destroy it —"

"I thought it might be that," said Sirius, casting a disdainful look at the opposite wall. "She'll have put another Permanent Sticking Charm on the back of it, I don't doubt, but if I can get rid of it I certainly will. Now go away, Kreacher."

It seemed that Kreacher did not dare disobey a direct order; nevertheless, the look he gave Sirius as he shuffled out past him was redolent of deepest loathing and he muttered all the way out of the room.

"— comes back from Azkaban ordering Kreacher around, oh my poor Mistress, what would she say if she saw the house now, scum living in it, her treasures thrown out, she swore he was no son of hers and he's back, they say he's a murderer too —"

"Keep muttering and I will be a murderer!" said Sirius irritably, and he slammed the door shut on the elf.

"Sirius, he's not right in the head," said Hermione pleadingly, "I don't think he realizes we can hear him."

"He's been alone too long," said Sirius, "taking mad orders from my mother's portrait and talking to himself, but he was always a foul little —"

"If you just set him free," said Hermione hopefully, "maybe —"

"We can't set him free, he knows too much about the Order," said Sirius curtly. "And anyway, the shock would kill him. You suggest to him that he leaves this house, see how he takes it."

Sirius walked across the room, where the tapestry Kreacher had been trying to protect hung the length of the wall. Harry and the others followed.

The tapestry looked immensely old; it was faded and looked as though doxies had gnawed it in places; nevertheless, the golden thread with which it was embroidered still glinted brightly enough to show them a sprawling family tree dating back (as far as Harry could tell) to the Middle Ages. Large words at the very top of the tapestry read:

THE NOBLE AND MOST ANCIENT HOUSE OF BLACK
"TOUJOURS PUR"

"You're not on here!" said Harry, after scanning the bottom of the tree.

"I used to be there," said Sirius, pointing at a small, round, charred hole in the tapestry, rather like a cigarette burn. "My sweet old mother blasted me off after I ran away from home — Kreacher's quite fond of muttering the story under his breath."

"You ran away from home?"

"When I was about sixteen," said Sirius. "I'd had enough."

"Where did you go?" asked Harry, staring at him.

"Your dad's place," said Sirius. "Your grandparents were really good about it; they sort of adopted me as a second son. Yeah, I camped out at your dad's during the school holidays, and then when I was seventeen I got a place of my own, my Uncle Alphard had left me a decent bit of gold — he's been wiped off here too, that's probably why — anyway, after that I looked after myself. I was always welcome at Mr. and Mrs. Potter's for Sunday lunch, though."

"But . . . why did you . . . ?"

"Leave?" Sirius smiled bitterly and ran a hand through his long, unkempt hair. "Because I hated the whole lot of them: my parents, with their pure-blood mania, convinced that to be a Black made you practically royal . . . my idiot brother, soft enough to believe them . . . that's him."

Sirius jabbed a finger at the very bottom of the tree, at the name

REGULUS BLACK. A date of death (some fifteen years previously) followed the date of birth.

"He was younger than me," said Sirius, "and a much better son, as I was constantly reminded."

"But he died," said Harry.

"Yeah," said Sirius. "Stupid idiot . . . he joined the Death Eaters."

"You're kidding!"

"Come on, Harry, haven't you seen enough of this house to tell what kind of wizards my family were?" said Sirius testily.

"Were — were your parents Death Eaters as well?"

"No, no, but believe me, they thought Voldemort had the right idea, they were all for the purification of the Wizarding race, getting rid of Muggle-borns and having purebloods in charge. They weren't alone either, there were quite a few people, before Voldemort showed his true colors, who thought he had the right idea about things. . . . They got cold feet when they saw what he was prepared to do to get power, though. But I bet my parents thought Regulus was a right little hero for joining up at first."

"Was he killed by an Auror?" Harry asked tentatively.

"Oh no," said Sirius. "No, he was murdered by Voldemort. Or on Voldemort's orders, more likely, I doubt Regulus was ever important enough to be killed by Voldemort in person. From what I found out after he died, he got in so far, then panicked about what he was being asked to do and tried to back out. Well, you don't just hand in your resignation to Voldemort. It's a lifetime of service or death."

"Lunch," said Mrs. Weasley's voice.

She was holding her wand high in front of her, balancing a huge tray loaded with sandwiches and cake on its tip. She was very red in the face and still looked angry. The others moved over to her, eager for some food, but Harry remained with Sirius, who had bent closer to the tapestry.

"I haven't looked at this for years. There's Phineas Nigellus . . . my great-great-grandfather, see? Least popular headmaster Hogwarts ever had . . . and Araminta Meliflua . . . cousin of my mother's . . . tried to force through a Ministry Bill to make Muggle-hunting legal . . . and dear Aunt Elladora . . . she started the family tradition of beheading house-elves when they got too old to carry tea trays . . . of course, anytime the family produced someone halfway decent they were disowned. I see Tonks isn't on here. Maybe that's why Kreacher won't take orders from her — he's supposed to do whatever anyone in the family asks him. . . ."

"You and Tonks are related?" Harry asked, surprised.

"Oh yeah, her mother, Andromeda, was my favorite cousin," said Sirius, examining the tapestry carefully. "No, Andromeda's not on here either, look —"

He pointed to another small round burn mark between two names, Bellatrix and Narcissa.

"Andromeda's sisters are still here because they made lovely, respectable pure-blood marriages, but Andromeda married a Muggle-born, Ted Tonks, so —"

Sirius mimed blasting the tapestry with a wand and laughed sourly. Harry, however, did not laugh; he was too busy staring at the names to the right of Andromeda's burn mark. A double line of gold embroidery linked Narcissa Black with Lucius Malfoy, and a single vertical gold line from their names led to the name Draco.

"You're related to the Malfoys!"

"The pure-blood families are all interrelated," said Sirius. "If you're only going to let your sons and daughters marry purebloods your choice is very limited, there are hardly any of us left. Molly and I are cousins by marriage and Arthur's something like my second cousin once removed. But there's no point looking for them on here — if ever a family was a bunch of blood traitors it's the Weasleys."

But Harry was now looking at the name to the left of Andromeda's burn: Bellatrix Black, which was connected by a double line to Rodolphus Lestrange.

"Lestrange . . ." Harry said aloud. The name had stirred something in his memory; he knew it from somewhere, but for a moment he couldn't think where, though it gave him an odd, creeping sensation in the pit of his stomach.

"They're in Azkaban," said Sirius shortly.

Harry looked at him curiously.

"Bellatrix and her husband Rodolphus came in with Barty Crouch, Junior," said Sirius in the same brusque voice. "Rodolphus's brother, Rabastan, was with them too."

And Harry remembered: He had seen Bellatrix Lestrange inside Dumbledore's Pensieve, the strange device in which thoughts and memories could be stored: a tall dark woman with heavy-lidded eyes, who had stood at her trial and proclaimed her continuing allegiance to Lord Voldemort, her pride that she had tried to find him after his downfall and her conviction that she would one day be rewarded for her loyalty.

"You never said she was your —"

"Does it matter if she's my cousin?" snapped Sirius. "As far as I'm concerned, they're not my family. *She's* certainly not my family. I haven't seen her since I was your age, unless you count a glimpse of her coming in to Azkaban. D'you think I'm proud of having relatives like her?"

"Sorry," said Harry quickly, "I didn't mean — I was just surprised, that's all —"

"It doesn't matter, don't apologize," Sirius mumbled at once. He turned away from the tapestry, his hands deep in his pockets. "I don't like being back here," he said, staring across the drawing room. "I never thought I'd be stuck in this house again."

Harry understood completely. He knew how he would feel if

forced, when he was grown up and thought he was free of the place forever, to return and live at number four, Privet Drive.

"It's ideal for headquarters, of course," Sirius said. "My father put every security measure known to Wizard-kind on it when he lived here. It's Unplottable, so Muggles could never come and call — as if they'd have wanted to — and now Dumbledore's added his protection, you'd be hard put to find a safer house anywhere. Dumbledore's Secret-Keeper for the Order, you know — nobody can find headquarters unless he tells them personally where it is — that note Moody showed you last night, that was from Dumbledore. . . ." Sirius gave a short, barklike laugh. "If my parents could see the use it was being put to now . . . well, my mother's portrait should give you some idea. . . ."

He scowled for a moment, then sighed.

"I wouldn't mind if I could just get out occasionally and do something useful. I've asked Dumbledore whether I can escort you to your hearing — as Snuffles, obviously — so I can give you a bit of moral support, what d'you think?"

Harry felt as though his stomach had sunk through the dusty carpet. He had not thought about the hearing once since dinner the previous evening; in the excitement of being back with the people he liked best, of hearing everything that was going on, it had completely flown his mind. At Sirius's words, however, the crushing sense of dread returned to him. He stared at Hermione and the Weasleys, all tucking into their sandwiches, and thought how he would feel if they went back to Hogwarts without him.

"Don't worry," Sirius said. Harry looked up and realized that Sirius had been watching him. "I'm sure they're going to clear you, there's definitely something in the International Statute of Secrecy about being allowed to use magic to save your own life."

"But if they do expel me," said Harry, quietly, "can I come back here and live with you?"

Sirius smiled sadly.

"We'll see."

"I'd feel a lot better about the hearing if I knew I didn't have to go back to the Dursleys," Harry pressed him.

"They must be bad if you prefer this place," said Sirius gloomily.

"Hurry up, you two, or there won't be any food left," Mrs. Weasley called.

Sirius heaved another great sigh, cast a dark look at the tapestry, and he and Harry went to join the others.

Harry tried his best not to think about the hearing while they emptied the glass cabinets that afternoon. Fortunately for him, it was a job that required a lot of concentration, as many of the objects in there seemed very reluctant to leave their dusty shelves. Sirius sustained a bad bite from a silver snuffbox; within seconds, his bitten hand had developed an unpleasant crusty covering like a tough brown glove.

"It's okay," he said, examining the hand with interest before tapping it lightly with his wand and restoring its skin to normal, "must be Wartcap powder in there."

He threw the box aside into the sack where they were depositing the debris from the cabinets; Harry saw George wrap his own hand carefully in a cloth moments later and sneak the box into his already doxy-filled pocket.

They found an unpleasant-looking silver instrument, something like a many-legged pair of tweezers, which scuttled up Harry's arm like a spider when he picked it up, and attempted to puncture his skin; Sirius seized it and smashed it with a heavy book entitled *Nature's Nobility: A Wizarding Genealogy*. There was a musical box that emitted a faintly sinister, tinkling tune when wound, and they all found themselves becoming curiously weak and sleepy until Ginny had the sense to slam the lid shut; also a heavy locket that none of them could open, a number of ancient seals and, in a dusty box, an Order of Merlin, First Class, that had been awarded to Sirius's grandfather for "Services to the Ministry."

"It means he gave them a load of gold," said Sirius contemptuously, throwing the medal into the rubbish sack.

Several times, Kreacher sidled into the room and attempted to smuggle things away under his loincloth, muttering horrible curses every time they caught him at it. When Sirius wrested a large golden ring bearing the Black crest from his grip Kreacher actually burst into furious tears and left the room sobbing under his breath and calling Sirius names Harry had never heard before.

"It was my father's," said Sirius, throwing the ring into the sack. "Kreacher wasn't *quite* as devoted to him as to my mother, but I still caught him snogging a pair of my father's old trousers last week."

Mrs. Weasley kept them all working very hard over the next few days. The drawing room took three days to decontaminate; finally the only undesirable things left in it were the tapestry of the Black family tree, which resisted all their attempts to remove it from the wall, and the rattling writing desk; Moody had not dropped by headquarters yet, so they could not be sure what was inside it.

They moved from the drawing room to a dining room on the ground floor where they found spiders large as saucers lurking in the dresser (Ron left the room hurriedly to make a cup of tea and did not return for an hour and a half). The china, which bore the Black crest and motto, was all thrown unceremoniously into a sack by Sirius, and the same fate met a set of old photographs in tarnished silver frames, all of whose occupants squealed shrilly as the glass covering them smashed.

Snape might refer to their work as "cleaning," but in Harry's opinion they were really waging war on the house, which was putting up a very good fight, aided and abetted by Kreacher. The house-elf kept appearing wherever they were congregated, his muttering becoming more and more offensive as he attempted to remove anything he could from the rubbish sacks. Sirius went as far as to threaten him with clothes, but Kreacher fixed him with a watery stare and said, "Master must do as Master wishes," before turning away and muttering very loudly, "but Master will not turn Kreacher away, no, because Kreacher knows what they are up to, oh yes, he is plotting against the Dark Lord, yes, with these Mudbloods and traitors and scum. . . ."

At which Sirius, ignoring Hermione's protests, seized Kreacher by the back of his loincloth and threw him bodily from the room.

The doorbell rang several times a day, which was the cue for Sirius's mother to start shrieking again, and for Harry and the others to attempt to eavesdrop on the visitor, though they gleaned very little from the brief glimpses and snatches of conversation they were able to sneak before Mrs. Weasley recalled them to their tasks. Snape flitted in and out of the house several times more, though to Harry's relief they never came face-to-face; he also caught sight of his Transfiguration teacher, Professor McGonagall, looking very odd in a Muggle dress and coat, though she also seemed too busy to linger.

Sometimes, however, the visitors stayed to help; Tonks joined them for a memorable afternoon in which they found a murderous old ghoul lurking in an upstairs toilet, and Lupin, who was staying in the house with Sirius but who left it for long periods to do mysterious work for the Order, helped them repair a grandfather clock that had developed the unpleasant habit of shooting heavy bolts at passersby. Mundungus redeemed himself slightly in Mrs. Weasley's eyes by rescuing Ron from an ancient set of purple robes that had tried to strangle him when he removed them from their wardrobe.

Despite the fact that he was still sleeping badly, still having dreams about corridors and locked doors that made his scar prickle, Harry was managing to have fun for the first time all summer. As long as he was busy he was happy; when the action abated, however, whenever he dropped his guard, or lay exhausted in bed watching blurred shadows move across the ceiling, the thought of the looming Ministry

hearing returned to him. Fear jabbed at his insides like needles as he wondered what was going to happen to him if he was expelled. The idea was so terrible that he did not dare voice it aloud, not even to Ron and Hermione, who, though he often saw them whispering together and casting anxious looks in his direction, followed his lead in not mentioning it. Sometimes he could not prevent his imagination showing him a faceless Ministry official who was snapping his wand in two and ordering him back to the Dursleys' . . . but he would not go. He was determined on that. He would come back here to Grimmauld Place and live with Sirius.

He felt as though a brick had dropped into his stomach when Mrs. Weasley turned to him during dinner on Wednesday evening and said quietly, "I've ironed your best clothes for tomorrow morning, Harry, and I want you to wash your hair tonight too. A good first impression can work wonders."

Ron, Hermione, Fred, George, and Ginny all stopped talking and looked over at him. Harry nodded and tried to keep eating his chops, but his mouth had become so dry he could not chew.

"How am I getting there?" he asked Mrs. Weasley, trying to sound unconcerned.

"Arthur's taking you to work with him," said Mrs. Weasley gently.

Mr. Weasley smiled encouragingly at Harry across the table.

"You can wait in my office until it's time for the hearing," he said.

Harry looked over at Sirius, but before he could ask the question, Mrs. Weasley had answered it.

"Professor Dumbledore doesn't think it's a good idea for Sirius to go with you, and I must say I —"

"— think he's *quite right*," said Sirius through clenched teeth.

Mrs. Weasley pursed her lips.

"When did Dumbledore tell you that?" Harry said, staring at Sirius.

"He came last night, when you were in bed," said Mr. Weasley.

Sirius stabbed moodily at a potato with his fork. Harry dropped his own eyes to his plate. The thought that Dumbledore had been in the house on the eve of his hearing and not asked to see him made him feel, if that were possible, even worse.

THE MINISTRY
OF MAGIC

Harry awoke at half-past five the next morning as abruptly and completely as if somebody had yelled in his ear. For a few moments he lay immobile as the prospect of the hearing filled every tiny particle of his brain, then, unable to bear it, he leapt out of bed and put on his glasses. Mrs. Weasley had laid out his freshly laundered jeans and T-shirt at the foot of his bed. Harry scrambled into them. The blank picture on the wall sniggered again.

Ron was lying sprawled on his back with his mouth wide open, fast asleep. He did not stir as Harry crossed the room, stepped out onto the landing, and closed the door softly behind him. Trying not to think of the next time he would see Ron, when they might no longer be fellow students at Hogwarts, Harry walked quietly down the stairs, past the heads of Kreacher's ancestors, and into the kitchen.

He had expected it to be empty, but it was not. When he reached the door he heard the soft rumble of voices on the other side and when he pushed it open he saw Mr. and Mrs. Weasley, Sirius, Lupin, and Tonks sitting there almost as though they were waiting for him.

All were fully dressed except Mrs. Weasley, who was wearing a quilted, purple dressing gown. She leapt to her feet the moment he entered.

"Breakfast," she said as she pulled out her wand and hurried over to the fire.

"M-m-morning, Harry," yawned Tonks. Her hair was blonde and curly this morning. "Sleep all right?"

"Yeah," said Harry.

"I've b-b-been up all night," she said, with another shuddering yawn. "Come and sit down. . . ."

She drew out a chair, knocking over the one beside it in the process.

"What do you want, Harry?" Mrs. Weasley called. "Porridge? Muffins? Kippers? Bacon and eggs? Toast?"

"Just — just toast, thanks," said Harry.

Lupin glanced at Harry, then said to Tonks, "What were you saying about Scrimgeour?"

"Oh . . . yeah . . . well, we need to be a bit more careful, he's been asking Kingsley and me funny questions. . . ."

Harry felt vaguely grateful that he was not required to join in the conversation. His insides were squirming. Mrs. Weasley placed a couple of pieces of toast and marmalade in front of him; he tried to eat, but it was like chewing carpet. Mrs. Weasley sat down on his other side and started fussing with his T-shirt, tucking in the label and smoothing out creases across the shoulders. He wished she wouldn't.

". . . and I'll have to tell Dumbledore I can't do night duty tomorrow, I'm just t-t-too tired," Tonks finished, yawning hugely again.

"I'll cover for you," said Mr. Weasley. "I'm okay, I've got a report to finish anyway. . . ."

Mr. Weasley was not wearing wizard's robes but a pair of pinstriped trousers and an old bomber jacket. He turned from Tonks to Harry.

"How are you feeling?"

Harry shrugged.

"It'll all be over soon," Mr. Weasley said bracingly. "In a few hours' time you'll be cleared."

Harry said nothing.

"The hearing's on my floor, in Amelia Bones's office. She's Head of the Department of Magical Law Enforcement and she's the one who'll be questioning you."

"Amelia Bones is okay, Harry," said Tonks earnestly. "She's fair, she'll hear you out."

Harry nodded, still unable to think of anything to say.

"Don't lose your temper," said Sirius abruptly. "Be polite and stick to the facts."

Harry nodded again.

"The law's on your side," said Lupin quietly. "Even underage wizards are allowed to use magic in life-threatening situations."

Something very cold trickled down the back of Harry's neck; for a moment he thought someone was putting a Disillusionment Charm on him again, then he realized that Mrs. Weasley was attacking his hair with a wet comb. She pressed hard on the top of his head.

"Doesn't it ever lie flat?" she said desperately.

Harry shook his head.

Mr. Weasley checked his watch and looked up at Harry.

"I think we'll go now," he said. "We're a bit early, but I think you'll be better off there than hanging around here."

"Okay," said Harry automatically, dropping his toast and getting to his feet.

"You'll be all right, Harry," said Tonks, patting him on the arm.

"Good luck," said Lupin. "I'm sure it will be fine."

"And if it's not," said Sirius grimly, "I'll see to Amelia Bones for you. . . ."

Harry smiled weakly. Mrs. Weasley hugged him.

"We've all got our fingers crossed," she said.

"Right," said Harry. "Well . . . see you later then."

He followed Mr. Weasley upstairs and along the hall. He could hear Sirius's mother grunting in her sleep behind her curtains. Mr. Weasley unbolted the door and they stepped out into the cold, gray dawn.

"You don't normally walk to work, do you?" Harry asked him, as they set off briskly around the square.

"No, I usually Apparate," said Mr. Weasley, "but obviously you can't, and I think it's best we arrive in a thoroughly non-magical fashion . . . makes a better impression, given what you're being disciplined for. . . ."

Mr. Weasley kept his hand inside his jacket as they walked. Harry knew it was clenched around his wand. The run-down streets were almost deserted, but when they arrived at the miserable little Underground station they found it already full of early morning commuters. As ever when he found himself in close proximity to Muggles going about their daily business, Mr. Weasley was hard put to contain his enthusiasm.

"Simply fabulous," he whispered, indicating the automatic ticket machines. "Wonderfully ingenious."

"They're out of order," said Harry, pointing at the sign.

"Yes, but even so . . ." said Mr. Weasley, beaming fondly at them.

They bought their tickets instead from a sleepy-looking guard (Harry handled the transaction, as Mr. Weasley was not very good with Muggle money) and five minutes later they were boarding an Underground train that rattled them off toward the center of London. Mr. Weasley kept anxiously checking and rechecking the Underground map above the windows.

"Four stops, Harry . . . three stops left now . . . two stops to go, Harry . . ."

They got off at a station in the very heart of London, swept from the train in a tide of besuited men and women carrying briefcases.

Up the escalator they went, through the ticket barrier (Mr. Weasley delighted with the way the stile swallowed his ticket), and emerged onto a broad street lined with imposing-looking buildings, already full of traffic.

"Where are we?" said Mr. Weasley blankly, and for one heart-stopping moment Harry thought they had gotten off at the wrong station despite Mr. Weasley's continual references to the map; but a second later he said, "Ah yes . . . this way, Harry," and led him down a side road.

"Sorry," he said, "but I never come by train and it all looks rather different from a Muggle perspective. As a matter of fact I've never even used the visitor's entrance before."

The farther they walked, the smaller and less imposing the buildings became, until finally they reached a street that contained several rather shabby-looking offices, a pub, and an overflowing dumpster. Harry had expected a rather more impressive location for the Ministry of Magic.

"Here we are," said Mr. Weasley brightly, pointing at an old red telephone box, which was missing several panes of glass and stood before a heavily graffittied wall. "After you, Harry."

He opened the telephone box door.

Harry stepped inside, wondering what on earth this was about. Mr. Weasley folded himself in beside Harry and closed the door. It was a tight fit; Harry was jammed against the telephone apparatus, which was hanging crookedly from the wall as though a vandal had tried to rip it off. Mr. Weasley reached past Harry for the receiver.

"Mr. Weasley, I think this might be out of order too," Harry said.

"No, no, I'm sure it's fine," said Mr. Weasley, holding the receiver above his head and peering at the dial. "Let's see . . . six . . ." he dialed the number, "two . . . four . . . and another four . . . and another two . . ."

As the dial whirred smoothly back into place, a cool female voice sounded inside the telephone box, not from the receiver in Mr. Weasley's hand, but as loudly and plainly as though an invisible woman were standing right beside them.

"Welcome to the Ministry of Magic. Please state your name and business."

"Er . . ." said Mr. Weasley, clearly uncertain whether he should talk into the receiver or not; he compromised by holding the mouthpiece to his ear, "Arthur Weasley, Misuse of Muggle Artifacts Office, here to escort Harry Potter, who has been asked to attend a disciplinary hearing. . . ."

"Thank you," said the cool female voice. "Visitor, please take the badge and attach it to the front of your robes."

There was a click and a rattle, and Harry saw something slide out of the metal chute where returned coins usually appeared. He picked it up: It was a square silver badge with *Harry Potter, Disciplinary Hearing* on it. He pinned it to the front of his T-shirt as the female voice spoke again.

"Visitor to the Ministry, you are required to submit to a search and present your wand for registration at the security desk, which is located at the far end of the Atrium."

The floor of the telephone box shuddered. They were sinking slowly into the ground. Harry watched apprehensively as the pavement rose up past the glass windows of the telephone box until darkness closed over their heads. Then he could see nothing at all; he could only hear a dull grinding noise as the telephone box made its way down through the earth. After about a minute, though it felt much longer to Harry, a chink of golden light illuminated his feet and, widening, rose up his body, until it hit him in the face and he had to blink to stop his eyes from watering.

"The Ministry of Magic wishes you a pleasant day," said the woman's voice.

The door of the telephone box sprang open and Mr. Weasley stepped out of it, followed by Harry, whose mouth had fallen open.

They were standing at one end of a very long and splendid hall with a highly polished, dark wood floor. The peacock-blue ceiling was inlaid with gleaming golden symbols that were continually moving and changing like some enormous heavenly notice board. The walls on each side were paneled in shiny dark wood and had many gilded fireplaces set into them. Every few seconds a witch or wizard would emerge from one of the left-hand fireplaces with a soft *whoosh;* on the right-hand side, short queues of wizards were forming before each fireplace, waiting to depart.

Halfway down the hall was a fountain. A group of golden statues, larger than life-size, stood in the middle of a circular pool. Tallest of them all was a noble-looking wizard with his wand pointing straight up in the air. Grouped around him were a beautiful witch, a centaur, a goblin, and a house-elf. The last three were all looking adoringly up at the witch and wizard. Glittering jets of water were flying from the ends of the two wands, the point of the centaur's arrow, the tip of the goblin's hat, and each of the house-elf's ears, so that the tinkling hiss of falling water was added to the pops and cracks of Apparators and the clatter of footsteps as hundreds of witches and wizards, most of whom were wearing glum, early-morning looks, strode toward a set of golden gates at the far end of the hall.

"This way," said Mr. Weasley.

They joined the throng, wending their way between the Ministry workers, some of whom were carrying tottering piles of parchment, others battered briefcases, still others reading the *Daily Prophet* as they walked. As they passed the fountain Harry saw silver Sickles and bronze Knuts glinting up at him from the bottom of the pool. A small, smudged sign beside it read:

All proceeds from the Fountain of Magical Brethren will be given to St. Mungo's Hospital for Magical Maladies and Injuries

If I'm not expelled from Hogwarts, I'll put in ten Galleons, Harry found himself thinking desperately.

"Over here, Harry," said Mr. Weasley, and they stepped out of the stream of Ministry employees heading for the golden gates, toward a desk on the left, over which hung a sign saying SECURITY. A badly shaven wizard in peacock-blue robes looked up as they approached and put down his *Daily Prophet.*

"I'm escorting a visitor," said Mr. Weasley, gesturing toward Harry.

"Step over here," said the wizard in a bored voice.

Harry walked closer to him and the wizard held up a long golden rod, thin and flexible as a car aerial, and passed it up and down Harry's front and back.

"Wand," grunted the security wizard at Harry, putting down the golden instrument and holding out his hand.

Harry produced his wand. The wizard dropped it onto a strange brass instrument, which looked something like a set of scales with only one dish. It began to vibrate. A narrow strip of parchment came speeding out of a slit in the base. The wizard tore this off and read the writing upon it.

"Eleven inches, phoenix-feather core, been in use four years. That correct?"

"Yes," said Harry nervously.

"I keep this," said the wizard, impaling the slip of parchment on a small brass spike. "You get this back," he added, thrusting the wand at Harry.

"Thank you."

"Hang on. . . ." said the wizard slowly.

His eyes had darted from the silver visitor's badge on Harry's chest to his forehead.

"Thank you, Eric," said Mr. Weasley firmly, and grasping Harry by the shoulder, he steered him away from the desk and back into the stream of wizards and witches walking through the golden gates.

Jostled slightly by the crowd, Harry followed Mr. Weasley through the gates into the smaller hall beyond, where at least twenty lifts stood behind wrought golden grilles. Harry and Mr. Weasley joined the crowd around one of them. A big, bearded wizard holding a large cardboard box stood nearby. The box was emitting rasping noises.

"All right, Arthur?" said the wizard, nodding at Mr. Weasley.

"What've you got there, Bob?" asked Mr. Weasley, looking at the box.

"We're not sure," said the wizard seriously. "We thought it was a bog-standard chicken until it started breathing fire. Looks like a serious breach of the Ban on Experimental Breeding to me."

With a great jangling and clattering a lift descended in front of them; the golden grille slid back and Harry and Mr. Weasley moved inside it with the rest of the crowd. Harry found himself jammed against the back wall of the lift. Several witches and wizards were looking at him curiously; he stared at his feet to avoid catching anyone's eye, flattening his fringe as he did so. The grilles slid shut with a crash and the lift ascended slowly, chains rattling all the while, while the same cool female voice Harry had heard in the telephone box rang out again.

"Level seven, Department of Magical Games and Sports, incorporating the British and Irish Quidditch League Headquarters, Official Gobstones Club, and Ludicrous Patents Office."

The lift doors opened; Harry glimpsed an untidy-looking corridor, with various posters of Quidditch teams tacked lopsidedly on the walls; one of the wizards in the lift, who was carrying an armful of broomsticks, extricated himself with difficulty and disappeared down the corridor. The doors closed, the lift juddered upward again, and the woman's voice said, "Level six, Department of Magical Transport, incorporating the Floo Network Authority, Broom Regulatory Control, Portkey Office, and Apparation Test Center."

Once again the lift doors opened and four or five witches and wizards got out; at the same time, several paper airplanes swooped into the lift. Harry stared up at them as they flapped idly around above his head; they were a pale violet color and he could see MINISTRY OF MAGIC stamped along the edges of their wings.

"Just Interdepartmental memos," Mr. Weasley muttered to him. "We used to use owls, but the mess was unbelievable . . . droppings all over the desks . . ."

As they clattered upward again, the memos flapped around the swaying lamp in the lift's ceiling.

"Level five, Department of International Magical Cooperation, incorporating the International Magical Trading Standards Body, the International Magical Office of Law, and the International Confederation of Wizards, British Seats."

When the doors opened, two of the memos zoomed out with a few more witches and wizards, but several more memos zoomed in, so that the light from the lamp in the ceiling flickered and flashed as they darted around it.

"Level four, Department for the Regulation and Control of Magical Creatures, incorporating Beast, Being, and Spirit Divisions, Goblin Liaison Office, and Pest Advisory Bureau."

"'S'cuse," said the wizard carrying the fire-breathing chicken and he left the lift pursued by a little flock of memos. The doors clanged shut yet again.

"Level three, Department of Magical Accidents and Catastrophes, including the Accidental Magic Reversal Squad, Obliviator Headquarters, and Muggle-Worthy Excuse Committee."

Everybody left the lift on this floor except Mr. Weasley, Harry, and a witch who was reading an extremely long piece of parchment that was trailing on the ground. The remaining memos continued to soar around the lamp as the lift juddered upward again, and then the doors opened and the voice said, "Level two, Department of Magical Law Enforcement, including the Improper Use of Magic Office, Auror Headquarters, and Wizengamot Administration Services."

"This is us, Harry," said Mr. Weasley, and they followed the witch out of the lift into a corridor lined with doors. "My office is on the other side of the floor."

"Mr. Weasley," said Harry, as they passed a window through which sunlight was streaming, "aren't we underground?"

"Yes, we are," said Mr. Weasley, "those are enchanted windows; Magical Maintenance decide what weather we're getting every day. We had two months of hurricanes last time they were angling for a pay raise. . . . Just round here, Harry."

They turned a corner, walked through a pair of heavy oak doors, and emerged in a cluttered, open area divided into cubicles, which were buzzing with talk and laughter. Memos were zooming in and out of cubicles like miniature rockets. A lopsided sign on the nearest cubicle read AUROR HEADQUARTERS.

Harry looked surreptitiously through the doorways as they passed. The Aurors had covered their cubicle walls with everything from pictures of wanted wizards and photographs of their families, to posters of their favorite Quidditch teams and articles from the *Daily Prophet*. A scarlet-robed man with a ponytail longer than Bill's was sitting with his boots up on his desk, dictating a report to his quill. A little farther along, a witch with a patch over her eye was talking over the top of her cubicle wall to Kingsley Shacklebolt.

"Morning, Weasley," said Kingsley carelessly, as they drew nearer. "I've been wanting a word with you, have you got a second?"

"Yes, if it really is a second," said Mr. Weasley, "I'm in rather a hurry."

They were talking to each other as though they hardly knew each other, and when Harry opened his mouth to say hello to Kingsley, Mr. Weasley stood on his foot. They followed Kingsley along the row and into the very last cubicle.

Harry received a slight shock; Sirius's face was blinking down at him from every direction. Newspaper cuttings and old photographs

— even the one of Sirius being best man at the Potters' wedding — papered the walls. The only Sirius-free space was a map of the world in which little red pins were glowing like jewels.

"Here," said Kingsley brusquely to Mr. Weasley, shoving a sheaf of parchment into his hand, "I need as much information as possible on flying Muggle vehicles sighted in the last twelve months. We've received information that Black might still be using his old motorcycle."

Kingsley tipped Harry an enormous wink and added, in a whisper, "Give him the magazine, he might find it interesting." Then he said in normal tones, "And don't take too long, Weasley, the delay on that firelegs report held our investigation up for a month."

"If you had read my report you would know that the term is 'fire-arms,'" said Mr. Weasley coolly. "And I'm afraid you'll have to wait for information on motorcycles, we're extremely busy at the moment." He dropped his voice and said, "If you can get away before seven, Molly's making meatballs."

He beckoned to Harry and led him out of Kingsley's cubicle, through a second set of oak doors, into another passage, turned left, marched along another corridor, turned right into a dimly lit and distinctly shabby corridor, and finally reached a dead end, where a door on the left stood ajar, revealing a broom cupboard, and a door on the right bore a tarnished brass plaque reading MISUSE OF MUGGLE ARTIFACTS.

Mr. Weasley's dingy office seemed to be slightly smaller than the broom cupboard. Two desks had been crammed inside it and there was barely room to move around them because of all the overflowing filing cabinets lining the walls, on top of which were tottering piles of files. The little wall space available bore witness to Mr. Weasley's obsessions; there were several posters of cars, including one of a dismantled engine, two illustrations of postboxes he seemed to have cut out of Muggle children's books, and a diagram showing how to wire a plug.

Sitting on top of Mr. Weasley's overflowing in-tray was an old toaster that was hiccuping in a disconsolate way and a pair of empty leather gloves that were twiddling their thumbs. A photograph of the Weasley family stood beside the in-tray. Harry noticed that Percy appeared to have walked out of it.

"We haven't got a window," said Mr. Weasley apologetically, taking off his bomber jacket and placing it on the back of his chair. "We've asked, but they don't seem to think we need one. Have a seat, Harry, doesn't look as if Perkins is in yet."

Harry squeezed himself into the chair behind Perkins's desk while Mr. Weasley rifled through the sheaf of parchment Kingsley Shacklebolt had given him.

"Ah," he said, grinning, as he extracted a copy of a magazine entitled *The Quibbler* from its midst, "yes . . ." He flicked through it. "Yes, he's right, I'm sure Sirius will find that very amusing — oh dear, what's this now?"

A memo had just zoomed in through the open door and fluttered to rest on top of the hiccuping toaster. Mr. Weasley unfolded it and read aloud, "'Third regurgitating public toilet reported in Bethnal Green, kindly investigate immediately.' This is getting ridiculous. . . ."

"A regurgitating toilet?"

"Anti-Muggle pranksters," said Mr. Weasley, frowning. "We had two last week, one in Wimbledon, one in Elephant and Castle. Muggles are pulling the flush and instead of everything disappearing — well, you can imagine. The poor things keep calling in those — those *pumbles,* I think they're called — you know, the ones who mend pipes and things —"

"Plumbers?"

"— exactly, yes, but of course they're flummoxed. I only hope we can catch whoever's doing it."

"Will it be Aurors who catch them?"

"Oh no, this is too trivial for Aurors, it'll be the ordinary Magical Law Enforcement Patrol — ah, Harry, this is Perkins."

A stooped, timid-looking old wizard with fluffy white hair had just entered the room, panting.

"Oh Arthur!" he said desperately, without looking at Harry. "Thank goodness, I didn't know what to do for the best, whether to wait here for you or not, I've just sent an owl to your home but you've obviously missed it — an urgent message came ten minutes ago —"

"I know about the regurgitating toilet," said Mr. Weasley.

"No, no, it's not the toilet, it's the Potter boy's hearing — they've changed the time and venue — it starts at eight o'clock now and it's down in old Courtroom Ten —"

"Down in old — but they told me — Merlin's beard —"

Mr. Weasley looked at his watch, let out a yelp, and leapt from his chair.

"Quick, Harry, we should have been there five minutes ago!"

Perkins flattened himself against the filing cabinets as Mr. Weasley left the office at a run, Harry on his heels.

"Why have they changed the time?" Harry said breathlessly as they hurtled past the Auror cubicles; people poked out their heads and stared as they streaked past. Harry felt as though he had left all his insides back at Perkins's desk.

"I've no idea, but thank goodness we got here so early, if you'd missed it it would have been catastrophic!"

Mr. Weasley skidded to a halt beside the lifts and jabbed impatiently at the down button.

"Come ON!"

The lift clattered into view and they hurried inside. Every time it stopped Mr. Weasley cursed furiously and pummelled the number nine button.

"Those courtrooms haven't been used in years," said Mr. Weasley angrily. "I can't think why they're doing it down there — unless — but no . . ."

A plump witch carrying a smoking goblet entered the lift at that moment, and Mr. Weasley did not elaborate.

"The Atrium," said the cool female voice and the golden grilles slid open, showing Harry a distant glimpse of the golden statues in the fountain. The plump witch got out and a sallow-skinned wizard with a very mournful face got in.

"Morning, Arthur," he said in a sepulchral voice as the lift began to descend. "Don't often see you down here. . . ."

"Urgent business, Bode," said Mr. Weasley, who was bouncing on the balls of his feet and throwing anxious looks over at Harry.

"Ah, yes," said Bode, surveying Harry unblinkingly. "Of course."

Harry barely had emotion to spare for Bode, but his unfaltering gaze did not make him feel any more comfortable.

"Department of Mysteries," said the cool female voice, and left it at that.

"Quick, Harry," said Mr. Weasley as the lift doors rattled open, and they sped up a corridor that was quite different from those above. The walls were bare; there were no windows and no doors apart from a plain black one set at the very end of the corridor. Harry expected them to go through it, but instead Mr. Weasley seized him by the arm and dragged him to the left, where there was an opening leading to a flight of steps.

"Down here, down here," panted Mr. Weasley, taking two steps at a time. "The lift doesn't even come down this far . . . *why* they're doing it there . . ."

They reached the bottom of the steps and ran along yet another corridor, which bore a great resemblance to that which led to Snape's dungeon at Hogwarts, with rough stone walls and torches in brackets. The doors they passed here were heavy wooden ones with iron bolts and keyholes.

"Courtroom . . . ten . . . I think . . . we're nearly . . . yes."

Mr. Weasley stumbled to a halt outside a grimy dark door with an immense iron lock and slumped against the wall, clutching at a stitch in his chest.

"Go on," he panted, pointing his thumb at the door. "Get in there."

"Aren't — aren't you coming with — ?"

"No, no, I'm not allowed. Good luck!"

Harry's heart was beating a violent tattoo against his Adam's apple. He swallowed hard, turned the heavy iron door handle, and stepped inside the courtroom.

THE HEARING

Harry gasped; he could not help himself. The large dungeon he had entered was horribly familiar. He had not only seen it before, he had *been* here before: This was the place he had visited inside Dumbledore's Pensieve, the place where he had watched the Lestranges sentenced to life imprisonment in Azkaban.

The walls were made of dark stone, dimly lit by torches. Empty benches rose on either side of him, but ahead, in the highest benches of all, were many shadowy figures. They had been talking in low voices, but as the heavy door swung closed behind Harry an ominous silence fell.

A cold male voice rang across the courtroom.

"You're late."

"Sorry," said Harry nervously. "I-I didn't know the time had changed."

"That is not the Wizengamot's fault," said the voice. "An owl was sent to you this morning. Take your seat."

Harry dropped his gaze to the chair in the center of the room, the arms of which were covered in chains. He had seen those chains spring to life and bind whoever sat between them. His footsteps echoed loudly as he walked across the stone floor. When he sat gingerly on the edge of the chair the chains clinked rather threateningly but did not bind him. Feeling rather sick he looked up at the people seated at the bench above.

There were about fifty of them, all, as far as he could see, wearing plum-colored robes with an elaborately worked silver W on the left-hand side of the chest and all staring down their noses at him, some with very austere expressions, others looks of frank curiosity.

In the very middle of the front row sat Cornelius Fudge, the Minister of Magic. Fudge was a portly man who often sported a lime-green bowler hat, though today he had dispensed with it; he had dispensed too with the indulgent smile he had once worn when he spoke to Harry. A broad, square-jawed witch with very short gray hair sat on Fudge's left; she wore a monocle and looked forbidding. On Fudge's right was another witch, but she was sitting so far back on the bench that her face was in shadow.

"Very well," said Fudge. "The accused being present — finally — let us begin. Are you ready?" he called down the row.

"Yes, sir," said an eager voice Harry knew. Ron's brother Percy was sitting at the very end of the front bench. Harry looked at Percy, expecting some sign of recognition from him, but none came. Percy's eyes, behind his horn-rimmed glasses, were fixed on his parchment, a quill poised in his hand.

"Disciplinary hearing of the twelfth of August," said Fudge in a ringing voice, and Percy began taking notes at once, "into offenses committed under the Decree for the Reasonable Restriction of Underage Sorcery and the International Statute of Secrecy by Harry James Potter, resident at number four, Privet Drive, Little Whinging, Surrey.

"Interrogators: Cornelius Oswald Fudge, Minister of Magic; Amelia Susan Bones, Head of the Department of Magical Law Enforcement; Dolores Jane Umbridge, Senior Undersecretary to the Minister. Court Scribe, Percy Ignatius Weasley —"

"— Witness for the defense, Albus Percival Wulfric Brian Dumbledore," said a quiet voice from behind Harry, who turned his head so fast he cricked his neck.

Dumbledore was striding serenely across the room wearing long midnight-blue robes and a perfectly calm expression. His long silver beard and hair gleamed in the torchlight as he drew level with Harry and looked up at Fudge through the half-moon spectacles that rested halfway down his very crooked nose.

The members of the Wizengamot were muttering. All eyes were now on Dumbledore. Some looked annoyed, others slightly frightened; two elderly witches in the back row, however, raised their hands and waved in welcome.

A powerful emotion had risen in Harry's chest at the sight of Dumbledore, a fortified, hopeful feeling rather like that which phoenix song gave him. He wanted to catch Dumbledore's eye, but Dumbledore was not looking his way; he was continuing to look up at the obviously flustered Fudge.

"Ah," said Fudge, who looked thoroughly disconcerted. "Dumbledore. Yes. You — er — got our — er — message that the time and — er — place of the hearing had been changed, then?"

"I must have missed it," said Dumbledore cheerfully. "However, due to a lucky mistake I arrived at the Ministry three hours early, so no harm done."

"Yes — well — I suppose we'll need another chair — I — Weasley, could you — ?"

"Not to worry, not to worry," said Dumbledore pleasantly; he took out his wand, gave it a little flick, and a squashy chintz armchair appeared out of nowhere next to Harry. Dumbledore sat down, put the tips of his long fingers together, and looked at Fudge over them with an expression of polite interest. The Wizengamot was still muttering and fidgeting restlessly; only when Fudge spoke again did they settle down.

"Yes," said Fudge again, shuffling his notes. "Well, then. So. The charges. Yes."

He extricated a piece of parchment from the pile before him, took a deep breath, and read, "The charges against the accused are as follows: That he did knowingly, deliberately, and in full awareness of the illegality of his actions, having received a previous written warning from the Ministry of Magic on a similar charge, produce a Patronus Charm in a Muggle-inhabited area, in the presence of a Muggle, on August the second at twenty-three minutes past nine, which constitutes an offense under paragraph C of the Decree for the Reasonable Restriction of Underage Sorcery, 1875, and also under section thirteen of the International Confederation of Wizards' Statute of Secrecy.

"You are Harry James Potter, of number four, Privet Drive, Little Whinging, Surrey?" Fudge said, glaring at Harry over the top of his parchment.

"Yes," Harry said.

"You received an official warning from the Ministry for using illegal magic three years ago, did you not?"

"Yes, but —"

"And yet you conjured a Patronus on the night of the second of August?" said Fudge.

"Yes," said Harry, "but —"

"Knowing that you are not permitted to use magic outside school while you are under the age of seventeen?"

"Yes, but —"

"Knowing that you were in an area full of Muggles?"

"Yes, but —"

"Fully aware that you were in close proximity to a Muggle at the time?"

"*Yes,*" said Harry angrily, "but I only used it because we were —"

The witch with the monocle on Fudge's left cut across him in a booming voice.

"You produced a fully fledged Patronus?"

"Yes," said Harry, "because —"

"A corporeal Patronus?"

"A — what?" said Harry.

"Your Patronus had a clearly defined form? I mean to say, it was more than vapor or smoke?"

"Yes," said Harry, feeling both impatient and slightly desperate, "it's a stag, it's always a stag."

"Always?" boomed Madam Bones. "You have produced a Patronus before now?"

"*Yes,*" said Harry, "I've been doing it for over a year —"

"And you are fifteen years old?"

"Yes, and —"

"You learned this at school?"

"Yes, Professor Lupin taught me in my third year, because of the —"

"Impressive," said Madam Bones, staring down at him, "a true Patronus at that age . . . very impressive indeed."

Some of the wizards and witches around her were muttering again; a few nodded, but others were frowning and shaking their heads.

"It's not a question of how impressive the magic was," said Fudge in a testy voice. "In fact, the more impressive the worse it is, I would have thought, given that the boy did it in plain view of a Muggle!"

Those who had been frowning now murmured in agreement, but it was the sight of Percy's sanctimonious little nod that goaded Harry into speech.

"I did it because of the dementors!" he said loudly, before anyone could interrupt him again.

He had expected more muttering, but the silence that fell seemed to be somehow denser than before.

"Dementors?" said Madam Bones after a moment, raising her thick eyebrows so that her monocle looked in danger of falling out. "What do you mean, boy?"

"I mean there were two dementors down that alleyway and they went for me and my cousin!"

"Ah," said Fudge again, smirking unpleasantly as he looked around at the Wizengamot, as though inviting them to share the joke. "Yes. Yes, I thought we'd be hearing something like this."

"Dementors in Little Whinging?" Madam Bones said in tones of great surprise. "I don't understand —"

"Don't you, Amelia?" said Fudge, still smirking. "Let me explain. He's been thinking it through and decided dementors would make a very nice little cover story, very nice indeed. Muggles can't see dementors, can they, boy? Highly convenient, highly convenient . . . so it's just your word and no witnesses. . . ."

"I'm not lying!" said Harry loudly, over another outbreak of muttering from the court. "There were two of them, coming from opposite ends of the alley, everything went dark and cold and my cousin felt them and ran for it —"

"Enough, enough!" said Fudge with a very supercilious look on his face. "I'm sorry to interrupt what I'm sure would have been a very well-rehearsed story —"

Dumbledore cleared his throat. The Wizengamot fell silent again.

"We do, in fact, have a witness to the presence of dementors in that alleyway," he said, "other than Dudley Dursley, I mean."

Fudge's plump face seemed to slacken, as though somebody had let air out of it. He stared down at Dumbledore for a moment or two, then, with the appearance of a man pulling himself back together, said, "We haven't got time to listen to more taradiddles, I'm afraid, Dumbledore. I want this dealt with quickly —"

"I may be wrong," said Dumbledore pleasantly, "but I am sure that under the Wizengamot Charter of Rights, the accused has the right to present witnesses for his or her case? Isn't that the policy of the Department of Magical Law Enforcement, Madam Bones?" he continued, addressing the witch in the monocle.

"True," said Madam Bones. "Perfectly true."

"Oh, very well, very well," snapped Fudge. "Where is this person?"

"I brought her with me," said Dumbledore. "She's just outside the door. Should I — ?"

"No — Weasley, you go," Fudge barked at Percy, who got up at once, hurried down the stone steps from the judge's balcony, and hastened past Dumbledore and Harry without glancing at them.

A moment later, Percy returned, followed by Mrs. Figg. She looked scared and more batty than ever. Harry wished she had thought to change out of her carpet slippers.

Dumbledore stood up and gave Mrs. Figg his chair, conjuring a second one for himself.

"Full name?" said Fudge loudly, when Mrs. Figg had perched herself nervously on the very edge of her seat.

"Arabella Doreen Figg," said Mrs. Figg in her quavery voice.

"And who exactly are you?" said Fudge, in a bored and lofty voice.

"I'm a resident of Little Whinging, close to where Harry Potter lives," said Mrs. Figg.

"We have no record of any witch or wizard living in Little Whinging other than Harry Potter," said Madam Bones at once. "That situation has always been closely monitored, given . . . given past events."

"I'm a Squib," said Mrs. Figg. "So you wouldn't have me registered, would you?"

"A Squib, eh?" said Fudge, eyeing her suspiciously. "We'll be checking that. You'll leave details of your parentage with my assistant, Weasley. Incidentally, can Squibs see dementors?" he added, looking left and right along the bench where he sat.

"Yes, we can!" said Mrs. Figg indignantly.

Fudge looked back down at her, his eyebrows raised. "Very well," he said coolly. "What is your story?"

"I had gone out to buy cat food from the corner shop at the end of Wisteria Walk, shortly after nine on the evening of the second of August," gabbled Mrs. Figg at once, as though she had learned what she was saying by heart, "when I heard a disturbance down the alleyway between Magnolia Crescent and Wisteria Walk. On approaching the mouth of the alleyway I saw dementors running —"

"Running?" said Madam Bones sharply. "Dementors don't run, they glide."

"That's what I meant to say," said Mrs. Figg quickly, patches of pink appearing in her withered cheeks. "Gliding along the alley toward what looked like two boys."

"What did they look like?" said Madam Bones, narrowing her eyes so that the monocle's edges disappeared into her flesh.

"Well, one was very large and the other one rather skinny —"

"No, no," said Madam Bones impatiently, "the dementors . . . describe them."

"Oh," said Mrs. Figg, the pink flush creeping up her neck now. "They were big. Big and wearing cloaks."

Harry felt a horrible sinking in the pit of his stomach. Whatever Mrs. Figg said to the contrary, it sounded to him as though the most she had ever seen was a picture of a dementor, and a picture could never convey the truth of what these beings were like: the eerie way they moved, hovering inches over the ground, or the rotting smell of them, or that terrible, rattling noise they made as they sucked on the surrounding air . . . A dumpy wizard with a large black mustache in the second row leaned close to his neighbor, a frizzy-haired witch, and whispered something in her ear. She smirked and nodded.

"Big and wearing cloaks," repeated Madam Bones coolly, while Fudge snorted derisively. "I see. Anything else?"

"Yes," said Mrs. Figg. "I felt them. Everything went cold, and this was a very warm summer's night, mark you. And I felt . . . as though all happiness had gone from the world . . . and I remembered . . . dreadful things. . . ."

Her voice shook and died.

Madam Bones' eyes widened slightly. Harry could see red marks under her eyebrow where the monocle had dug into it.

"What did the dementors do?" she asked, and Harry felt a rush of hope.

"They went for the boys," said Mrs. Figg, her voice stronger and more confident now, the pink flush ebbing away from her face. "One of them had fallen. The other was backing away, trying to repel the dementor. That was Harry. He tried twice and produced silver vapor. On the third attempt, he produced a Patronus, which charged down the first dementor and then, with his encouragement, chased away the second from his cousin. And that . . . that was what happened," Mrs. Figg finished, somewhat lamely.

Madam Bones looked down at Mrs. Figg in silence; Fudge was not looking at her at all, but fidgeting with his papers. Finally he raised his eyes and said, rather aggressively, "That's what you saw, is it?"

"That was what happened," Mrs. Figg repeated.

"Very well," said Fudge. "You may go."

Mrs. Figg cast a frightened look from Fudge to Dumbledore, then got up and shuffled off toward the door again. Harry heard it thud shut behind her.

"Not a very convincing witness," said Fudge loftily.

"Oh, I don't know," said Madam Bones in her booming voice. "She certainly described the effects of a dementor attack very accurately. And I can't imagine why she would say they were there if they weren't —"

"But dementors wandering into a Muggle suburb and just *happening* to come across a wizard?" snorted Fudge. "The odds on that must be very, very long, even Bagman wouldn't have bet —"

"Oh, I don't think any of us believe the dementors were there by coincidence," said Dumbledore lightly.

The witch sitting to the right of Fudge with her face in shadow moved slightly, but everyone else was quite still and silent.

"And what is that supposed to mean?" asked Fudge icily.

"It means that I think they were ordered there," said Dumbledore.

"I think we might have a record of it if someone had ordered a pair of dementors to go strolling through Little Whinging!" barked Fudge.

"Not if the dementors are taking orders from someone other than the Ministry of Magic these days," said Dumbledore calmly. "I have already given you my views on this matter, Cornelius."

"Yes, you have," said Fudge forcefully, "and I have no reason to believe that your views are anything other than bilge, Dumbledore. The dementors remain in place in Azkaban and are doing everything we ask them to."

"Then," said Dumbledore, quietly but clearly, "we must ask ourselves why somebody within the Ministry ordered a pair of dementors into that alleyway on the second of August."

In the complete silence that greeted these words, the witch to the right of Fudge leaned forward so that Harry saw her for the first time.

He thought she looked just like a large, pale toad. She was rather squat with a broad, flabby face, as little neck as Uncle Vernon, and a very wide, slack mouth. Her eyes were large, round, and slightly bulging. Even the little black velvet bow perched on top of her short curly hair put him in mind of a large fly she was about to catch on a long sticky tongue.

"The Chair recognizes Dolores Jane Umbridge, Senior Undersecretary to the Minister," said Fudge.

The witch spoke in a fluttery, girlish, high-pitched voice that took Harry aback; he had been expecting a croak.

"I'm sure I must have misunderstood you, Professor Dumbledore," she said with a simper that left her big, round eyes as cold as ever. "So silly of me. But it sounded for a teensy moment as though you were suggesting that the Ministry of Magic had ordered an attack on this boy!"

She gave a silvery laugh that made the hairs on the back of Harry's neck stand up. A few other members of the Wizengamot laughed with her. It could not have been plainer that not one of them was really amused.

"If it is true that the dementors are taking orders only from the Ministry of Magic, and it is also true that two dementors attacked Harry and his cousin a week ago, then it follows logically that somebody at the Ministry might have ordered the attacks," said Dumbledore politely. "Of course, these particular dementors may have been outside Ministry control —"

"There are no dementors outside Ministry control!" snapped Fudge, who had turned brick red.

Dumbledore inclined his head in a little bow.

"Then undoubtedly the Ministry will be making a full inquiry into why two dementors were so very far from Azkaban and why they attacked without authorization."

"It is not for you to decide what the Ministry of Magic does or does not do, Dumbledore!" snapped Fudge, now a shade of magenta of which Uncle Vernon would have been proud.

"Of course it isn't," said Dumbledore mildly. "I was merely expressing my confidence that this matter will not go uninvestigated."

He glanced at Madam Bones, who readjusted her monocle and stared back at him, frowning slightly.

"I would remind everybody that the behavior of these dementors, if indeed they are not figments of this boy's imagination, is not the subject of this hearing!" said Fudge. "We are here to examine Harry Potter's offenses under the Decree for the Reasonable Restriction of Underage Sorcery!"

"Of course we are," said Dumbledore, "but the presence of dementors in that alleyway is highly relevant. Clause seven of the Decree states that magic may be used before Muggles in exceptional circumstances, and as those exceptional circumstances include situations that threaten the life of the wizard or witch himself, or witches, wizards, or Muggles present at the time of the —"

"We are familiar with clause seven, thank you very much!" snarled Fudge.

"Of course you are," said Dumbledore courteously. "Then we are in agreement that Harry's use of the Patronus Charm in these circumstances falls precisely into the category of exceptional circumstances it describes?"

"If there were dementors, which I doubt —"

"You have heard from an eyewitness," Dumbledore interrupted. "If you still doubt her truthfulness, call her back, question her again. I am sure she would not object."

"I — that — not —" blustered Fudge, fiddling with the papers before him. "It's — I want this over with today, Dumbledore!"

"But naturally, you would not care how many times you heard from a witness, if the alternative was a serious miscarriage of justice," said Dumbledore.

"Serious miscarriage, my hat!" said Fudge at the top of his voice. "Have you ever bothered to tot up the number of cock-and-bull stories this boy has come out with, Dumbledore, while trying to cover up his flagrant misuse of magic out of school? I suppose you've forgotten the Hover Charm he used three years ago —"

"That wasn't me, it was a house-elf!" said Harry.

"YOU SEE?" roared Fudge, gesturing flamboyantly in Harry's direction. "A house-elf! In a Muggle house! I ask you —"

"The house-elf in question is currently in the employ of Hogwarts School," said Dumbledore. "I can summon him here in an instant to give evidence if you wish."

"I — not — I haven't got time to listen to house-elves! Anyway, that's not the only — he blew up his aunt, for God's sake!" Fudge shouted, banging his fist on the judge's bench and upsetting a bottle of ink.

"And you very kindly did not press charges on that occasion, accepting, I presume, that even the best wizards cannot always control their emotions," said Dumbledore calmly, as Fudge attempted to scrub the ink off his notes.

"And I haven't even started on what he gets up to at school —"

"— but as the Ministry has no authority to punish Hogwarts students for misdemeanors at school, Harry's behavior there is not relevant to this inquiry," said Dumbledore, politely as ever, but now with a suggestion of coolness behind his words.

"Oho!" said Fudge. "Not our business what he does at school, eh? You think so?"

"The Ministry does not have the power to expel Hogwarts students, Cornelius, as I reminded you on the night of the second of August," said Dumbledore. "Nor does it have the right to confiscate wands until charges have been successfully proven, again, as I reminded you on the night of the second of August. In your admirable haste to ensure that the law is upheld, you appear, inadvertently I am sure, to have overlooked a few laws yourself."

"Laws can be changed," said Fudge savagely.

"Of course they can," said Dumbledore, inclining his head. "And you certainly seem to be making many changes, Cornelius. Why, in the few short weeks since I was asked to leave the Wizengamot, it has already become the practice to hold a full criminal trial to deal with a simple matter of underage magic!"

A few of the wizards above them shifted uncomfortably in their seats. Fudge turned a slightly deeper shade of puce. The toadlike witch on his right, however, merely gazed at Dumbledore, her face quite expressionless.

"As far as I am aware, however," Dumbledore continued, "there is no law yet in place that says this court's job is to punish Harry for every bit of magic he has ever performed. He has been charged with a specific offense and he has presented his defense. All he and I can do now is to await your verdict."

Dumbledore put his fingertips together again and said no more. Fudge glared at him, evidently incensed. Harry glanced sideways at Dumbledore, seeking reassurance; he was not at all sure that Dumbledore was right in telling the Wizengamot, in effect, that it was about time they made a decision. Again, however, Dumbledore seemed oblivious to Harry's attempt to catch his eye. He continued to look up at the benches where the entire Wizengamot had fallen into urgent, whispered conversations.

Harry looked at his feet. His heart, which seemed to have swollen to an unnatural size, was thumping loudly under his ribs. He had expected the hearing to last longer than this. He was not at all sure that he had made a good impression. He had not really said very much. He ought to have explained more fully about the dementors, about how he had fallen over, about how both he and Dudley had nearly been kissed. . . .

Twice he looked up at Fudge and opened his mouth to speak, but his swollen heart was now constricting his air passages and both times he merely took a deep breath and looked back at his shoes.

Then the whispering stopped. Harry wanted to look up at the judges, but found that it was really much, much easier to keep examining his laces.

"Those in favor of clearing the accused of all charges?" said Madam Bones's booming voice.

Harry's head jerked upward. There were hands in the air, many of them . . . more than half! Breathing very fast, he tried to count, but before he could finish Madam Bones had said, "And those in favor of conviction?"

Fudge raised his hand; so did half a dozen others, including the witch on his right and the heavily mustached wizard and the frizzy-haired witch in the second row.

Fudge glanced around at them all, looking as though there was something large stuck in his throat, then lowered his own hand. He took two deep breaths and then said, in a voice distorted by suppressed rage, "Very well, very well . . . cleared of all charges."

"Excellent," said Dumbledore briskly, springing to his feet, pulling out his wand, and causing the two chintz armchairs to vanish. "Well, I must be getting along. Good day to you all."

And without looking once at Harry, he swept from the dungeon.

THE WOES OF
MRS. WEASLEY

Dumbledore's abrupt departure took Harry completely by surprise. He remained sitting where he was in the chained chair, struggling with his feelings of shock and relief. The Wizengamot were all getting to their feet, talking, and gathering up their papers and packing them away. Harry stood up. Nobody seemed to be paying him the slightest bit of attention except the toadlike witch on Fudge's right, who was now gazing down at him instead of at Dumbledore. Ignoring her, he tried to catch Fudge's eye, or Madam Bones's, wanting to ask whether he was free to go, but Fudge seemed quite determined not to notice Harry, and Madam Bones was busy with her briefcase, so he took a few tentative steps toward the exit and when nobody called him back, broke into a very fast walk.

He took the last few steps at a run, wrenched open the door, and almost collided with Mr. Weasley, who was standing right outside, looking pale and apprehensive.

"Dumbledore didn't say —"

"Cleared," Harry said, pulling the door closed behind him, "of all charges!"

Beaming, Mr. Weasley seized Harry by the shoulders.

"Harry, that's wonderful! Well, of course, they couldn't have found you guilty, not on the evidence, but even so, I can't pretend I wasn't —"

But Mr. Weasley broke off, because the courtroom door had just opened again. The Wizengamot were filing out.

"Merlin's beard," said Mr. Weasley wonderingly, pulling Harry aside to let them all pass, "you were tried by the full court?"

"I think so," said Harry quietly.

One or two of the passing wizards nodded to Harry as they passed and a few, including Madam Bones, said, "Morning, Arthur," to Mr. Weasley, but most averted their eyes. Cornelius Fudge and the toad-like witch were almost the last to leave the dungeon. Fudge acted as though Mr. Weasley and Harry were part of the wall, but again, the witch looked almost appraisingly at Harry as she passed. Last of all to pass was Percy. Like Fudge, he completely ignored his father and Harry; he marched past clutching a large roll of parchment and a handful of spare quills, his back rigid and his nose in the air. The lines around Mr. Weasley's mouth tightened slightly, but other than this he gave no sign that he had noticed his third son.

"I'm going to take you straight back so you can tell the others the good news," he said, beckoning Harry forward as Percy's heels disappeared up the stairs to the ninth level. "I'll drop you off on the way to that toilet in Bethnal Green. Come on. . . ."

"So what will you have to do about the toilet?" Harry asked, grinning. Everything suddenly seemed five times funnier than usual. It was starting to sink in: He was cleared, *he was going back to Hogwarts.*

"Oh, it's a simple enough anti-jinx," said Mr. Weasley as they mounted the stairs, "but it's not so much having to repair the damage, it's more the attitude behind the vandalism, Harry. Muggle-baiting might strike some wizards as funny, but it's an expression of something much deeper and nastier, and I for one —"

Mr. Weasley broke off in mid-sentence. They had just reached the ninth-level corridor, and Cornelius Fudge was standing a few feet away from them, talking quietly to a tall man with sleek blond hair and a pointed, pale face.

The second man turned at the sound of their footsteps. He too broke off in mid-conversation, his cold gray eyes narrowed and fixed upon Harry's face.

"Well, well, well . . . Patronus Potter," said Lucius Malfoy coolly.

Harry felt winded, as though he had just walked into something heavy. He had last seen those cool gray eyes through slits in a Death Eater's hood, and last heard that man's voice jeering in a dark graveyard while Lord Voldemort tortured him. He could not believe that Lucius Malfoy dared look him in the face; he could not believe that he was here, in the Ministry of Magic, or that Cornelius Fudge was talking to him, when Harry had told Fudge mere weeks ago that Malfoy was a Death Eater.

"The Minister was just telling me about your lucky escape, Potter," drawled Mr. Malfoy. "Quite astonishing, the way you continue to wriggle out of very tight holes. . . . *Snakelike,* in fact . . ."

Mr. Weasley gripped Harry's shoulder in warning.

"Yeah," said Harry, "yeah, I'm good at escaping. . . ."

Lucius Malfoy raised his eyes to Mr. Weasley's face.

"And Arthur Weasley too! What are you doing here, Arthur?"

"I work here," said Mr. Weasley shortly.

"Not *here,* surely?" said Mr. Malfoy, raising his eyebrows and glancing toward the door over Mr. Weasley's shoulder. "I thought you were up on the second floor. . . . Don't you do something that involves sneaking Muggle artifacts home and bewitching them?"

"No," said Mr. Weasley curtly, his fingers now biting into Harry's shoulder.

"What are *you* doing here anyway?" Harry asked Lucius Malfoy.

"I don't think private matters between myself and the Minister are any concern of yours, Potter," said Malfoy, smoothing the front of his robes; Harry distinctly heard the gentle clinking of what sounded like a full pocket of gold. "Really, just because you are Dumbledore's favorite boy, you must not expect the same indulgence from the rest of us. . . . Shall we go up to your office, then, Minister?"

"Certainly," said Fudge, turning his back on Harry and Mr. Weasley. "This way, Lucius."

They strode off together, talking in low voices. Mr. Weasley did not let go of Harry's shoulder until they had disappeared into the lift.

"Why wasn't he waiting outside Fudge's office if they've got business to do together?" Harry burst out furiously. "What was he doing down here?"

"Trying to sneak down to the courtroom, if you ask me," said Mr. Weasley, looking extremely agitated as he glanced over his shoulder as though making sure they could not be overheard. "Trying to find out whether you'd been expelled or not. I'll leave a note for Dumbledore when I drop you off, he ought to know Malfoy's been talking to Fudge again."

"What private business have they got together anyway?"

"Gold, I expect," said Mr. Weasley angrily. "Malfoy's been giving generously to all sorts of things for years. . . . Gets him in with the right people . . . then he can ask favors . . . delay laws he doesn't want passed . . . Oh, he's very well connected, Lucius Malfoy. . . ."

The lift arrived; it was empty except for a flock of memos that flapped around Mr. Weasley's head as he pressed the button for the Atrium and the doors clanged shut; he waved them away irritably.

"Mr. Weasley," said Harry slowly, "if Fudge is meeting Death Eaters like Malfoy, if he's seeing them alone, how do we know they haven't put the Imperius Curse on him?"

"Don't think it hadn't occurred to us, Harry," muttered Mr. Weasley. "But Dumbledore thinks Fudge is acting of his own accord at the moment — which, as Dumbledore says, is not a lot of comfort. . . . Best not talk about it anymore just now, Harry. . . ."

The doors slid open and they stepped out into the now almost-deserted Atrium. Eric the security man was hidden behind his *Daily Prophet* again. They had walked straight past the golden fountain before Harry remembered.

"Wait. . . ." he told Mr. Weasley, and pulling his money bag from his pocket, he turned back to the fountain.

He looked up into the handsome wizard's face, but up close, Harry thought he looked rather weak and foolish. The witch was wearing a vapid smile like a beauty contestant, and from what Harry knew of goblins and centaurs, they were most unlikely to be caught staring this soppily at humans of any description. Only the house-elf's attitude of creeping servility looked convincing. With a grin at the thought of what Hermione would say if she could see the statue of the elf, Harry turned his money bag upside down and emptied not just ten Galleons, but the whole contents into the pool at the statues' feet.

"I knew it!" yelled Ron, punching the air. "You always get away with stuff!"

"They were bound to clear you," said Hermione, who had looked positively faint with anxiety when Harry had entered the kitchen and was now holding a shaking hand over her eyes. "There was no case against you, none at all. . . ."

"Everyone seems quite relieved, though, considering they all knew I'd get off," said Harry, smiling.

Mrs. Weasley was wiping her face on her apron, and Fred, George, and Ginny were doing a kind of war dance to a chant that went *"He got off, he got off, he got off —"*

"That's enough, settle down!" shouted Mr. Weasley, though he too was smiling. "Listen, Sirius, Lucius Malfoy was at the Ministry —"

"What?" said Sirius sharply.

"He got off, he got off, he got off —"

"Be quiet, you three! Yes, we saw him talking to Fudge on level nine, then they went up to Fudge's office together. Dumbledore ought to know."

"Absolutely," said Sirius. "We'll tell him, don't worry."

"Well, I'd better get going, there's a vomiting toilet in Bethnal Green waiting for me. Molly, I'll be late, I'm covering for Tonks, but Kingsley might be dropping in for dinner —"

"He got off, he got off, he got off —"

"That's enough — Fred — George — Ginny!" said Mrs. Weasley, as Mr. Weasley left the kitchen. "Harry dear, come and sit down, have some lunch, you hardly ate breakfast. . . ."

Ron and Hermione sat themselves down opposite him looking happier than they had done since he had first arrived at number twelve, Grimmauld Place, and Harry's feeling of giddy relief, which had been somewhat dented by his encounter with Lucius Malfoy, swelled again. The gloomy house seemed warmer and more welcoming all of a sudden; even Kreacher looked less ugly as he poked his snoutlike nose into the kitchen to investigate the source of all the noise.

"'Course, once Dumbledore turned up on your side, there was no way they were going to convict you," said Ron happily, now dishing great mounds of mashed potatoes onto everyone's plates.

"Yeah, he swung it for me," said Harry. He felt that it would sound highly ungrateful, not to mention childish, to say, "I wish he'd talked to me, though. Or even *looked* at me."

And as he thought this, the scar on his forehead burned so badly that he clapped his hand to it.

"What's up?" said Hermione, looking alarmed.

"Scar," Harry mumbled. "But it's nothing. . . . It happens all the time now. . . ."

None of the others had noticed a thing; all of them were now helping themselves to food while gloating over Harry's narrow escape; Fred, George, and Ginny were still singing. Hermione looked rather anxious, but before she could say anything, Ron said happily, "I bet Dumbledore turns up this evening to celebrate with us, you know."

"I don't think he'll be able to, Ron," said Mrs. Weasley, setting a huge plate of roast chicken down in front of Harry. "He's really very busy at the moment."

"HE GOT OFF, HE GOT OFF, HE GOT OFF —"

"SHUT UP!" roared Mrs. Weasley.

Over the next few days Harry could not help noticing that there was one person within number twelve, Grimmauld Place, who did not seem wholly overjoyed that he would be returning to Hogwarts. Sirius had put up a very good show of happiness on first hearing the news, wringing Harry's hand and beaming just like the rest of them; soon, however, he was moodier and surlier than before, talking less to everybody, even Harry, and spending increasing amounts of time shut up in his mother's room with Buckbeak.

"Don't you go feeling guilty!" said Hermione sternly, after Harry had confided some of his feelings to her and Ron while they scrubbed out a moldy cupboard on the third floor a few days later. "You belong at Hogwarts and Sirius knows it. Personally, I think he's being selfish."

"That's a bit harsh, Hermione," said Ron, frowning as he attempted to prize off a bit of mold that had attached itself firmly to his finger, "you wouldn't want to be stuck inside this house without company."

"He'll have company!" said Hermione. "It's headquarters to the Order of the Phoenix, isn't it? He just got his hopes up that Harry would be coming to live here with him."

"I don't think that's true," said Harry, wringing out his cloth. "He wouldn't give me a straight answer when I asked him if I could."

"He just didn't want to get his own hopes up even more," said Hermione wisely. "And he probably felt a bit guilty himself, because I think a part of him was really hoping you'd be expelled. Then you'd both be outcasts together."

"Come off it!" said Harry and Ron together, but Hermione merely shrugged.

"Suit yourselves. But I sometimes think Ron's mum's right, and Sirius gets confused about whether you're you or your father, Harry."

"So you think he's touched in the head?" said Harry heatedly.

"No, I just think he's been very lonely for a long time," said Hermione simply.

At this point Mrs. Weasley entered the bedroom behind them.

"Still not finished?" she said, poking her head into the cupboard.

"I thought you might be here to tell us to have a break!" said Ron bitterly. "D'you know how much mold we've got rid of since we arrived here?"

"You were so keen to help the Order," said Mrs. Weasley, "you can do your bit by making headquarters fit to live in."

"I feel like a house-elf," grumbled Ron.

"Well, now that you understand what dreadful lives they lead, perhaps you'll be a bit more active in S.P.E.W.!" said Hermione hopefully, as Mrs. Weasley left them to it again. "You know, maybe it wouldn't be a bad idea to show people exactly how horrible it is to clean all the time — we could do a sponsored scrub of Gryffindor common room, all proceeds to S.P.E.W., it would raise awareness as well as funds —"

"I'll sponsor you to shut up about *spew*," Ron muttered irritably, but only so Harry could hear him.

Harry found himself daydreaming about Hogwarts more and more as the end of the holidays approached; he could not wait to see Hagrid again, to play Quidditch, even to stroll across the vegetable patches to the Herbology greenhouses. It would be a treat just to leave this dusty, musty house, where half of the cupboards were still bolted shut and Kreacher wheezed insults out of the shadows as you passed, though Harry was careful not to say any of this within earshot of Sirius.

The fact was that living at the headquarters of the anti-Voldemort movement was not nearly as interesting or exciting as Harry would have expected before he'd experienced it. Though members of the Order of the Phoenix came and went regularly, sometimes staying for meals, sometimes only for a few minutes' whispered conversation, Mrs. Weasley made sure that Harry and the others were kept well out of earshot (whether Extendable or normal) and nobody, not even Sirius, seemed to feel that Harry needed to know anything more than he had heard on the night of his arrival.

On the very last day of the holidays Harry was sweeping up Hedwig's owl droppings from the top of the wardrobe when Ron entered their bedroom carrying a couple of envelopes.

"Booklists have arrived," he said, throwing one of the envelopes up to Harry, who was standing on a chair. "About time, I thought they'd forgotten, they usually come much earlier than this. . . ."

Harry swept the last of the droppings into a rubbish bag and threw the bag over Ron's head into the wastepaper basket in the corner, which swallowed it and belched loudly. He then opened his letter: It contained two pieces of parchment, one the usual reminder that term started on the first of September, the other telling him which books he would need for the coming year.

"Only two new ones," he said, reading the list. "*The Standard Book of Spells, Grade 5,* by Miranda Goshawk and *Defensive Magical Theory,* by Wilbert Slinkhard."

Crack.

Fred and George Apparated right beside Harry. He was so used to them doing this by now that he didn't even fall off his chair.

"We were just wondering who assigned the Slinkhard book," said Fred conversationally.

"Because it means Dumbledore's found a new Defense Against the Dark Arts teacher," said George.

"And about time too," said Fred.

"What d'you mean?" Harry asked, jumping down beside them.

"Well, we overheard Mum and Dad talking on the Extendable Ears a few weeks back," Fred told Harry, "and from what they were saying, Dumbledore was having real trouble finding anyone to do the job this year."

"Not surprising, is it, when you look at what's happened to the last four?" said George.

"One sacked, one dead, one's memory removed, and one locked in a trunk for nine months," said Harry, counting them off on his fingers. "Yeah, I see what you mean."

"What's up with you, Ron?" asked Fred.

Ron did not answer. Harry looked around. Ron was standing very still with his mouth slightly open, gaping at his letter from Hogwarts.

"What's the matter?" said Fred impatiently, moving around Ron to look over his shoulder at the parchment.

Fred's mouth fell open too.

"Prefect?" he said, staring incredulously at the letter. *"Prefect?"*

George leapt forward, seized the envelope in Ron's other hand, and turned it upside down. Harry saw something scarlet and gold fall into George's palm.

"No way," said George in a hushed voice.

"There's been a mistake," said Fred, snatching the letter out of Ron's grasp and holding it up to the light as though checking for a watermark. "No one in their right mind would make Ron a prefect. . . ."

The twins' heads turned in unison and both of them stared at Harry.

"We thought you were a cert!" said Fred in a tone that suggested Harry had tricked them in some way.

"We thought Dumbledore was *bound* to pick you!" said George indignantly.

"Winning the Triwizard and everything!" said Fred.

"I suppose all the mad stuff must've counted against him," said George to Fred.

"Yeah," said Fred slowly. "Yeah, you've caused too much trouble, mate. Well, at least one of you's got their priorities right."

He strode over to Harry and clapped him on the back while giving Ron a scathing look.

"*Prefect* . . . ickle Ronnie the prefect . . ."

"Oh, Mum's going to be revolting," groaned George, thrusting the prefect badge back at Ron as though it might contaminate him.

Ron, who still had not said a word, took the badge, stared at it for a moment, and then held it out to Harry as though asking mutely for confirmation that it was genuine. Harry took it. A large P was superimposed on the Gryffindor lion. He had seen a badge just like this on Percy's chest on his very first day at Hogwarts.

The door banged open. Hermione came tearing into the room, her cheeks flushed and her hair flying. There was an envelope in her hand.

"Did you — did you get — ?"

She spotted the badge in Harry's hand and let out a shriek.

"I knew it!" she said excitedly, brandishing her letter. "Me too, Harry, me too!"

"No," said Harry quickly, pushing the badge back into Ron's hand. "It's Ron, not me."

"It — what?"

"Ron's prefect, not me," Harry said.

"*Ron?*" said Hermione, her jaw dropping. "But . . . are you sure? I mean —"

She turned red as Ron looked around at her with a defiant expression on his face.

"It's my name on the letter," he said.

"I . . ." said Hermione, looking thoroughly bewildered. "I . . . well . . . wow! Well done, Ron! That's really —"

"Unexpected," said George, nodding.

"No," said Hermione, blushing harder than ever, "no, it's not . . . Ron's done loads of . . . he's really . . ."

The door behind her opened a little wider and Mrs. Weasley backed into the room carrying a pile of freshly laundered robes.

"Ginny said the booklists had come at last," she said, glancing around at all the envelopes as she made her way over to the bed and started sorting the robes into two piles. "If you give them to me I'll take them over to Diagon Alley this afternoon and get your books while you're packing. Ron, I'll have to get you more pajamas, these are at least six inches too short, I can't believe how fast you're growing . . . what color would you like?"

"Get him red and gold to match his badge," said George, smirking.

"Match his what?" said Mrs. Weasley absently, rolling up a pair of maroon socks and placing them on Ron's pile.

"His *badge*," said Fred, with the air of getting the worst over quickly. "His lovely shiny new *prefect's badge*."

Fred's words took a moment to penetrate Mrs. Weasley's preoccupation about pajamas.

"His . . . but . . . Ron, you're not . . . ?"

Ron held up his badge.

Mrs. Weasley let out a shriek just like Hermione's.

"I don't believe it! I don't believe it! Oh, Ron, how wonderful! A prefect! That's everyone in the family!"

"What are Fred and I, next-door neighbors?" said George indignantly, as his mother pushed him aside and flung her arms around her youngest son.

"Wait until your father hears! Ron, I'm so proud of you, what wonderful news, you could end up Head Boy just like Bill and Percy, it's the first step! Oh, what a thing to happen in the middle of all this worry, I'm just thrilled, oh *Ronnie* —"

Fred and George were both making loud retching noises behind her back but Mrs. Weasley did not notice; arms tight around Ron's neck, she was kissing him all over his face, which had turned a brighter scarlet than his badge.

"Mum . . . don't . . . Mum, get a grip. . . ." he muttered, trying to push her away.

She let go of him and said breathlessly, "Well, what will it be? We gave Percy an owl, but you've already got one, of course."

"W-what do you mean?" said Ron, looking as though he did not dare believe his ears.

"You've got to have a reward for this!" said Mrs. Weasley fondly. "How about a nice new set of dress robes?"

"We've already bought him some," said Fred sourly, who looked as though he sincerely regretted this generosity.

"Or a new cauldron, Charlie's old one's rusting through, or a new rat, you always liked Scabbers —"

"Mum," said Ron hopefully, "can I have a new broom?"

Mrs. Weasley's face fell slightly; broomsticks were expensive.

"Not a really good one!" Ron hastened to add. "Just — just a new one for a change . . ."

Mrs. Weasley hesitated, then smiled.

"Of *course* you can. . . . Well, I'd better get going if I've got a broom to buy too. I'll see you all later. . . . Little Ronnie, a prefect! And don't forget to pack your trunks. . . . A prefect . . . Oh, I'm all of a dither!"

She gave Ron yet another kiss on the cheek, sniffed loudly, and bustled from the room.

Fred and George exchanged looks.

"You don't mind if we don't kiss you, do you, Ron?" said Fred in a falsely anxious voice.

"We could curtsy, if you like," said George.

"Oh, shut up," said Ron, scowling at them.

"Or what?" said Fred, an evil grin spreading across his face. "Going to put us in detention?"

"I'd love to see him try," sniggered George.

"He could if you don't watch out!" said Hermione angrily, at which Fred and George burst out laughing and Ron muttered, "Drop it, Hermione."

"We're going to have to watch our step, George," said Fred, pretending to tremble, "with these two on our case. . . ."

"Yeah, it looks like our law-breaking days are finally over," said George, shaking his head.

And with another loud *crack,* the twins Disapparated.

"Those two!" said Hermione furiously, staring up at the ceiling, through which they could now hear Fred and George roaring with laughter in the room upstairs. "Don't pay any attention to them, Ron, they're only jealous!"

"I don't think they are," said Ron doubtfully, also looking up at the ceiling. "They've always said only prats become prefects. . . . Still," he added on a happier note, "they've never had new brooms! I wish I could go with Mum and choose. . . . She'll never be able to afford a Nimbus, but there's the new Cleansweep out, that'd be great. . . . Yeah, I think I'll go and tell her I like the Cleansweep, just so she knows. . . ."

He dashed from the room, leaving Harry and Hermione alone.

For some reason, Harry found that he did not want to look at Hermione. He turned to his bed, picked up the pile of clean robes Mrs. Weasley had laid upon it, and crossed the room to his trunk.

"Harry?" said Hermione tentatively.

"Well done," said Harry, so heartily it did not sound like his voice at all, and still not looking at her. "Brilliant. Prefect. Great."

"Thanks," said Hermione. "Erm — Harry — could I borrow Hedwig so I can tell Mum and Dad? They'll be really pleased — I mean, prefect is something they can understand —"

"Yeah, no problem," said Harry, still in the horrible hearty voice that did not belong to him. "Take her!"

He leaned over his trunk, laid the robes on the bottom of it, and pretended to be rummaging for something while Hermione crossed to the wardrobe and called Hedwig down. A few moments passed; Harry heard the door close but remained bent double, listening; the only sounds he could hear were the blank picture on the wall sniggering again and the wastepaper basket in the corner coughing up the owl droppings.

He straightened up and looked behind him. Hermione and Hedwig had gone. Harry returned slowly to his bed and sank onto it, gazing unseeingly at the foot of the wardrobe.

He had forgotten completely about prefects being chosen in the fifth year. He had been too anxious about the possibility of being expelled to spare a thought for the fact that badges must be winging their way toward certain people. But if he *had* remembered . . . if he *had* thought about it . . . what would he have expected?

Not this, said a small and truthful voice inside his head.

Harry screwed up his face and buried it in his hands. He could not lie to himself; if he had known the prefect badge was on its way, he would have expected it to come to him, not Ron. Did this make him as arrogant as Draco Malfoy? Did he think himself superior to everyone else? Did he really believe he was *better* than Ron?

No, said the small voice defiantly.

Was that true? Harry wondered, anxiously probing his own feelings.

I'm better at Quidditch, said the voice. *But I'm not better at anything else.*

That was definitely true, Harry thought; he was no better than Ron in lessons. But what about outside lessons? What about those adventures he, Ron, and Hermione had had together since they had started at Hogwarts, often risking much worse than expulsion?

Well, Ron and Hermione were with me most of the time, said the voice in Harry's head.

Not all the time, though, Harry argued with himself. *They didn't fight*

Quirrell with me. They didn't take on Riddle and the basilisk. They didn't get rid of all those dementors the night Sirius escaped. They weren't in that graveyard with me, the night Voldemort returned. . . .

And the same feeling of ill usage that had overwhelmed him on the night he had arrived rose again. *I've definitely done more,* Harry thought indignantly. *I've done more than either of them!*

But maybe, said the small voice fairly, *maybe Dumbledore doesn't choose prefects because they've got themselves into a load of dangerous situations. . . . Maybe he chooses them for other reasons. . . . Ron must have something you don't. . . .*

Harry opened his eyes and stared through his fingers at the wardrobe's clawed feet, remembering what Fred had said.

"No one in their right mind would make Ron a prefect. . . ."

Harry gave a small snort of laughter. A second later he felt sickened with himself.

Ron had not asked Dumbledore to give him the prefect badge. This was not Ron's fault. Was he, Harry, Ron's best friend in the world, going to sulk because he didn't have a badge, laugh with the twins behind Ron's back, ruin this for Ron when, for the first time, he had beaten Harry at something?

At this point Harry heard Ron's footsteps on the stairs again. He stood up, straightened his glasses, and hitched a grin onto his face as Ron bounded back through the door.

"Just caught her!" he said happily. "She says she'll get the Cleansweep if she can."

"Cool," Harry said, and he was relieved to hear that his voice had stopped sounding hearty. "Listen — Ron — well done, mate."

The smile faded off Ron's face.

"I never thought it would be me!" he said, shaking his head, "I thought it would be you!"

"Nah, I've caused too much trouble," Harry said, echoing Fred.

"Yeah," said Ron, "yeah, I suppose. . . . Well, we'd better get our trunks packed, hadn't we?"

It was odd how widely their possessions seemed to have scattered themselves since they had arrived. It took them most of the afternoon to retrieve their books and belongings from all over the house and stow them back inside their school trunks. Harry noticed that Ron kept moving his prefect's badge around, first placing it on his bedside table, then putting it into his jeans pocket, then taking it out and laying it on his folded robes, as though to see the effect of the red on the black. Only when Fred and George dropped in and offered to attach it to his forehead with a Permanent Sticking Charm did he wrap it tenderly in his maroon socks and lock it in his trunk.

Mrs. Weasley returned from Diagon Alley around six o'clock, laden with books and carrying a long package wrapped in thick brown paper that Ron took from her with a moan of longing.

"Never mind unwrapping it now, people are arriving for dinner, I want you all downstairs," she said, but the moment she was out of sight Ron ripped off the paper in a frenzy and examined every inch of his new broom, an ecstatic expression on his face.

Down in the basement Mrs. Weasley had hung a scarlet banner over the heavily laden dinner table, which read CONGRATULATIONS RON AND HERMIONE — NEW PREFECTS. She looked in a better mood than Harry had seen her all holiday.

"I thought we'd have a little party, not a sit-down dinner," she told Harry, Ron, Hermione, Fred, George, and Ginny as they entered the room. "Your father and Bill are on their way, Ron, I've sent them both owls and they're *thrilled*," she added, beaming.

Fred rolled his eyes.

Sirius, Lupin, Tonks, and Kingsley Shacklebolt were already there and Mad-Eye Moody stumped in shortly after Harry had got himself a butterbeer.

"Oh, Alastor, I am glad you're here," said Mrs. Weasley brightly, as

Mad-Eye shrugged off his traveling cloak. "We've been wanting to ask you for ages — could you have a look in the writing desk in the drawing room and tell us what's inside it? We haven't wanted to open it just in case it's something really nasty."

"No problem, Molly . . ."

Moody's electric-blue eye swiveled upward and stared fixedly through the ceiling of the kitchen.

"Drawing room . . ." he growled, as the pupil contracted. "Desk in the corner? Yeah, I see it. . . . Yeah, it's a boggart. . . . Want me to go up and get rid of it, Molly?"

"No, no, I'll do it myself later," beamed Mrs. Weasley. "You have your drink. We're having a little bit of a celebration, actually. . . ." She gestured at the scarlet banner. "Fourth prefect in the family!" she said fondly, ruffling Ron's hair.

"Prefect, eh?" growled Moody, his normal eye on Ron and his magical eye swiveling around to gaze into the side of his head. Harry had the very uncomfortable feeling it was looking at him and moved away toward Sirius and Lupin.

"Well, congratulations," said Moody, still glaring at Ron with his normal eye, "authority figures always attract trouble, but I suppose Dumbledore thinks you can withstand most major jinxes or he wouldn't have appointed you. . . ."

Ron looked rather startled at this view of the matter but was saved the trouble of responding by the arrival of his father and eldest brother. Mrs. Weasley was in such a good mood she did not even complain that they had brought Mundungus with them too; he was wearing a long overcoat that seemed oddly lumpy in unlikely places and declined the offer to remove it and put it with Moody's traveling cloak.

"Well, I think a toast is in order," said Mr. Weasley, when everyone had a drink. He raised his goblet. "To Ron and Hermione, the new Gryffindor prefects!"

Ron and Hermione beamed as everyone drank to them and then applauded.

"I was never a prefect myself," said Tonks brightly from behind Harry as everybody moved toward the table to help themselves to food. Her hair was tomato-red and waist length today; she looked like Ginny's older sister. "My Head of House said I lacked certain necessary qualities."

"Like what?" said Ginny, who was choosing a baked potato.

"Like the ability to behave myself," said Tonks.

Ginny laughed; Hermione looked as though she did not know whether to smile or not and compromised by taking an extra large gulp of butterbeer and choking on it.

"What about you, Sirius?" Ginny asked, thumping Hermione on the back.

Sirius, who was right beside Harry, let out his usual barklike laugh.

"No one would have made me a prefect, I spent too much time in detention with James. Lupin was the good boy, he got the badge."

"I think Dumbledore might have hoped that I would be able to exercise some control over my best friends," said Lupin. "I need scarcely say that I failed dismally."

Harry's mood suddenly lifted. His father had not been a prefect either. All at once the party seemed much more enjoyable; he loaded up his plate, feeling unusually fond of everyone in the room.

Ron was rhapsodizing about his new broom to anybody who would listen.

". . . naught to seventy in ten seconds, not bad, is it? When you think the Comet Two Ninety's only naught to sixty and that's with a decent tailwind according to *Which Broomstick*?"

Hermione was talking very earnestly to Lupin about her view of elf rights.

"I mean, it's the same kind of nonsense as werewolf segregation, isn't it? It all stems from this horrible thing wizards have of thinking they're superior to other creatures. . . ."

Mrs. Weasley and Bill were having their usual argument about Bill's hair.

". . . getting really out of hand, and you're so good-looking, it would look much better shorter, wouldn't it, Harry?"

"Oh — I dunno —" said Harry, slightly alarmed at being asked his opinion; he slid away from them in the direction of Fred and George, who were huddled in a corner with Mundungus.

Mundungus stopped talking when he saw Harry, but Fred winked and beckoned Harry closer.

"It's okay," he told Mundungus, "we can trust Harry, he's our financial backer."

"Look what Dung's gotten us," said George, holding out his hand to Harry. It was full of what looked like shriveled black pods. A faint rattling noise was coming from them, even though they were completely stationary.

"Venomous Tentacula seeds," said George. "We need them for the Skiving Snackboxes but they're a Class C Non-Tradeable Substance so we've been having a bit of trouble getting hold of them."

"Ten Galleons the lot, then, Dung?" said Fred.

"Wiv all the trouble I went to to get 'em?" said Mundungus, his saggy, bloodshot eyes stretching even wider. "I'm sorry, lads, but I'm not taking a Knut under twenty."

"Dung likes his little joke," Fred said to Harry.

"Yeah, his best one so far has been six Sickles for a bag of knarl quills," said George.

"Be careful," Harry warned them quietly.

"What?" said Fred. "Mum's busy cooing over Prefect Ron, we're okay."

"But Moody could have his eye on you," Harry pointed out.

Mundungus looked nervously over his shoulder.

"Good point, that," he grunted. "All right, lads, ten it is, if you'll take 'em quick."

"Cheers, Harry!" said Fred delightedly, when Mundungus had emptied his pockets into the twins' outstretched hands and scuttled off toward the food. "We'd better get these upstairs. . . ."

Harry watched them go, feeling slightly uneasy. It had just occurred to him that Mr. and Mrs. Weasley would want to know how Fred and George were financing their joke shop business when, as was inevitable, they finally found out about it. Giving the twins his Triwizard winnings had seemed a simple thing to do at the time, but what if it led to another family row and a Percy-like estrangement? Would Mrs. Weasley still feel that Harry was as good as her son if she found out he had made it possible for Fred and George to start a career she thought quite unsuitable?

Standing where the twins had left him with nothing but a guilty weight in the pit of his stomach for company, Harry caught the sound of his own name. Kingsley Shacklebolt's deep voice was audible even over the surrounding chatter.

". . . why Dumbledore didn't make Potter a prefect?" said Kingsley.

"He'll have had his reasons," replied Lupin.

"But it would've shown confidence in him. It's what I'd've done," persisted Kingsley, "'specially with the *Daily Prophet* having a go at him every few days. . . ."

Harry did not look around; he did not want Lupin or Kingsley to know he had heard. He followed Mundungus back toward the table, though not remotely hungry. His pleasure in the party had evaporated as quickly as it had come; he wished he were upstairs in bed.

Mad-Eye Moody was sniffing at a chicken leg with what remained of his nose; evidently he could not detect any trace of poison, because he then tore a strip off it with his teeth.

". . . the handle's made of Spanish oak with anti-jinx varnish and in-built vibration control —" Ron was saying to Tonks.

Mrs. Weasley yawned widely.

"Well, I think I'll sort out that boggart before I turn in. . . . Arthur, I don't want this lot up too late, all right? 'Night, Harry, dear."

She left the kitchen. Harry set down his plate and wondered whether he could follow her without attracting attention.

"You all right, Potter?" grunted Moody.

"Yeah, fine," lied Harry.

Moody took a swig from his hip flask, his electric blue eye staring sideways at Harry.

"Come here, I've got something that might interest you," he said.

From an inner pocket of his robes Moody pulled a very tattered old Wizarding photograph.

"Original Order of the Phoenix," growled Moody. "Found it last night when I was looking for my spare Invisibility Cloak, seeing as Podmore hasn't had the manners to return my best one. . . . Thought people might like to see it."

Harry took the photograph. A small crowd of people, some waving at him, others lifting their glasses, looked back up at him.

"There's me," said Moody unnecessarily, pointing at himself. The Moody in the picture was unmistakable, though his hair was slightly less gray and his nose was intact. "And there's Dumbledore beside me, Dedalus Diggle on the other side . . . That's Marlene McKinnon, she was killed two weeks after this was taken, they got her whole family. That's Frank and Alice Longbottom —"

Harry's stomach, already uncomfortable, clenched as he looked at Alice Longbottom; he knew her round, friendly face very well, even though he had never met her, because she was the image of her son, Neville.

"Poor devils," growled Moody. "Better dead than what happened to them . . . and that's Emmeline Vance, you've met her, and that there's Lupin, obviously . . . Benjy Fenwick, he copped it too, we only ever found bits of him . . . shift aside there," he added, poking the picture, and the little photographic people edged sideways, so that those who were partially obscured could move to the front.

"That's Edgar Bones . . . brother of Amelia Bones, they got him and his family too, he was a great wizard . . . Sturgis Podmore, blimey, he looks young . . . Caradoc Dearborn, vanished six months after this, we never found his body . . . Hagrid, of course, looks exactly the same as ever . . . Elphias Doge, you've met him, I'd forgotten he used to wear that stupid hat . . . Gideon Prewett, it took five Death Eaters to kill him and his brother Fabian, they fought like heroes . . . budge along, budge along . . ."

The little people in the photograph jostled among themselves, and those hidden right at the back appeared at the forefront of the picture.

"That's Dumbledore's brother, Aberforth, only time I ever met him, strange bloke . . . That's Dorcas Meadowes, Voldemort killed her personally . . . Sirius, when he still had short hair . . . and . . . there you go, thought that would interest you!"

Harry's heart turned over. His mother and father were beaming up at him, sitting on either side of a small, watery-eyed man Harry recognized at once as Wormtail: He was the one who had betrayed their whereabouts to Voldemort and so helped bring about their deaths.

"Eh?" said Moody.

Harry looked up into Moody's heavily scarred and pitted face. Evidently Moody was under the impression he had just given Harry a bit of a treat.

"Yeah," said Harry, attempting to grin again. "Er . . . listen, I've just remembered, I haven't packed my . . ."

He was spared the trouble of inventing an object he had not packed; Sirius had just said, "What's that you've got there, Mad-Eye?" and Moody had turned toward him. Harry crossed the kitchen, slipped through the door and up the stairs before anyone could call him back.

He did not know why he had received such a shock; he had seen his parents' pictures before, after all, and he had met Wormtail . . . but to have them sprung on him like that, when he was least expecting it . . . No one would like that, he thought angrily. . . .

And then, to see them surrounded by all those other happy faces . . . Benjy Fenwick, who had been found in bits, and Gideon Prewett, who had died like a hero, and the Longbottoms, who had been tortured into madness . . . all waving happily out of the photograph forevermore, not knowing that they were doomed. . . . Well, Moody might find that interesting . . . he, Harry, found it disturbing. . . .

Harry tiptoed up the stairs in the hall past the stuffed elf heads, glad to be on his own again, but as he approached the first landing he heard noises. Someone was sobbing in the drawing room.

"Hello?" Harry said.

There was no answer but the sobbing continued. He climbed the remaining stairs two at a time, walked across the landing, and opened the drawing-room door.

Someone was cowering against the dark wall, her wand in her hand, her whole body shaking with sobs. Sprawled on the dusty old carpet in a patch of moonlight, clearly dead, was Ron.

All the air seemed to vanish from Harry's lungs; he felt as though he were falling through the floor; his brain turned icy cold — Ron dead, no, it couldn't be —

But wait a moment, it *couldn't* be — Ron was downstairs —

"Mrs. Weasley?" Harry croaked.

"R-r-riddikulus!" Mrs. Weasley sobbed, pointing her shaking wand at Ron's body.

Crack.

Ron's body turned into Bill's, spread-eagled on his back, his eyes wide open and empty. Mrs. Weasley sobbed harder than ever.

"R-riddikulus!" she sobbed again.

Crack.

Mr. Weasley's body replaced Bill's, his glasses askew, a trickle of blood running down his face.

"No!" Mrs. Weasley moaned. "No . . . *riddikulus! Riddikulus! RIDDIKULUS!"*

Crack. Dead twins. *Crack.* Dead Percy. *Crack.* Dead Harry . . .

"Mrs. Weasley, just get out of here!" shouted Harry, staring down at his own dead body on the floor. "Let someone else —"

"What's going on?"

Lupin had come running into the room, closely followed by Sirius, with Moody stumping along behind them. Lupin looked from Mrs. Weasley to the dead Harry on the floor and seemed to understand in an instant. Pulling out his own wand he said, very firmly and clearly, *"Riddikulus!"*

Harry's body vanished. A silvery orb hung in the air over the spot where it had lain. Lupin waved his wand once more and the orb vanished in a puff of smoke.

"Oh — oh — oh!" gulped Mrs. Weasley, and she broke into a storm of crying, her face in her hands.

"Molly," said Lupin bleakly, walking over to her, "Molly, don't . . ."

Next second she was sobbing her heart out on Lupin's shoulder.

"Molly, it was just a boggart," he said soothingly, patting her on the head. "Just a stupid boggart . . ."

"I see them d-d-dead all the time!" Mrs. Weasley moaned into his shoulder. "All the t-t-time! I d-d-dream about it . . ."

Sirius was staring at the patch of carpet where the boggart, pretending to be Harry's body, had lain. Moody was looking at Harry, who avoided his gaze. He had a funny feeling Moody's magical eye had followed him all the way out of the kitchen.

"D-d-don't tell Arthur," Mrs. Weasley was gulping now, mopping

her eyes frantically with her cuffs. "I d-d-don't want him to know. . . .
Being silly . . ."

Lupin handed her a handkerchief and she blew her nose.

"Harry, I'm so sorry, what must you think of me?" she said shakily.
"Not even able to get rid of a boggart . . ."

"Don't be stupid," said Harry, trying to smile.

"I'm just s-s-so worried," she said, tears spilling out of her eyes again.
"Half the f-f-family's in the Order, it'll b-b-be a miracle if we all come
through this. . . . and P-P-Percy's not talking to us. . . . What if something d-d-dreadful happens and we had never m-m-made up? And
what's going to happen if Arthur and I get killed, who's g-g-going to
look after Ron and Ginny?"

"Molly, that's enough," said Lupin firmly. "This isn't like last time.
The Order is better prepared, we've got a head start, we know what
Voldemort's up to —"

Mrs. Weasley gave a little squeak of fright at the sound of the name.

"Oh, Molly, come on, it's about time you got used to hearing it —
look, I can't promise no one's going to get hurt, nobody can promise
that, but we're much better off than we were last time, you weren't in
the Order then, you don't understand, last time we were outnumbered
twenty to one by the Death Eaters and they were picking us off one
by one. . . ."

Harry thought of the photograph again, of his parents' beaming
faces. He knew Moody was still watching him.

"Don't worry about Percy," said Sirius abruptly. "He'll come round.
It's a matter of time before Voldemort moves into the open; once he
does, the whole Ministry's going to be begging us to forgive them.
And I'm not sure I'll be accepting their apology," he added bitterly.

"And as for who's going to look after Ron and Ginny if you and
Arthur died," said Lupin, smiling slightly, "what do you think we'd
do, let them starve?"

Mrs. Weasley smiled tremulously.

"Being silly," she muttered again, mopping her eyes.

But Harry, closing his bedroom door behind him some ten minutes later, could not think Mrs. Weasley silly. He could still see his parents beaming up at him from the tattered old photograph, unaware that their lives, like so many of those around them, were drawing to a close. The image of the boggart posing as the corpse of each member of Mrs. Weasley's family in turn kept flashing before his eyes.

Without warning, the scar on his forehead seared with pain again and his stomach churned horribly.

"Cut it out," he said firmly, rubbing the scar as the pain receded again.

"First sign of madness, talking to your own head," said a sly voice from the empty picture on the wall.

Harry ignored it. He felt older than he had ever felt in his life, and it seemed extraordinary to him that barely an hour ago he had been worried about a joke shop and who had gotten a prefect's badge.

LUNA LOVEGOOD

Harry had a troubled night's sleep. His parents wove in and out of his dreams, never speaking; Mrs. Weasley sobbed over Kreacher's dead body watched by Ron and Hermione, who were wearing crowns, and yet again Harry found himself walking down a corridor ending in a locked door. He awoke abruptly with his scar prickling to find Ron already dressed and talking to him.

". . . better hurry up, Mum's going ballistic, she says we're going to miss the train. . . ."

There was a lot of commotion in the house. From what he heard as he dressed at top speed, Harry gathered that Fred and George had bewitched their trunks to fly downstairs to save the bother of carrying them, with the result that they had hurtled straight into Ginny and knocked her down two flights of stairs into the hall; Mrs. Black and Mrs. Weasley were both screaming at the top of their voices.

"— COULD HAVE DONE HER A SERIOUS INJURY, YOU IDIOTS —"

"— FILTHY HALF-BREEDS, BESMIRCHING THE HOUSE OF MY FATHERS —"

Hermione came hurrying into the room looking flustered just as Harry was putting on his trainers; Hedwig was swaying on her shoulder, and she was carrying a squirming Crookshanks in her arms.

"Mum and Dad just sent Hedwig back" — the owl fluttered obligingly over and perched on top of her cage — "are you ready yet?"

"Nearly — Ginny all right?" Harry asked, shoving on his glasses.

"Mrs. Weasley's patched her up," said Hermione. "But now Mad-Eye's complaining that we can't leave unless Sturgis Podmore's here, otherwise the guard will be one short."

"Guard?" said Harry. "We have to go to King's Cross with a guard?"

"*You* have to go to King's Cross with a guard," Hermione corrected him.

"Why?" said Harry irritably. "I thought Voldemort was supposed to be lying low, or are you telling me he's going to jump out from behind a dustbin to try and do me in?"

"I don't know, it's just what Mad-Eye says," said Hermione distractedly, looking at her watch. "But if we don't leave soon we're definitely going to miss the train. . . ."

"WILL YOU LOT GET DOWN HERE NOW, PLEASE!" Mrs. Weasley bellowed and Hermione jumped as though scalded and hurried out of the room. Harry seized Hedwig, stuffed her unceremoniously into her cage, and set off downstairs after Hermione, dragging his trunk.

Mrs. Black's portrait was howling with rage but nobody was bothering to close the curtains over her; all the noise in the hall was bound to rouse her again anyway.

"Harry, you're to come with me and Tonks," shouted Mrs. Weasley over the repeated screeches of *"MUDBLOODS! SCUM! CREATURES OF DIRT!"* "Leave your trunk and your owl, Alastor's going to deal with the luggage. . . . Oh, for heaven's sake, Sirius, Dumbledore said no!"

A bearlike black dog had appeared at Harry's side as Harry clambered over the various trunks cluttering the hall to get to Mrs. Weasley.

"Oh honestly . . ." said Mrs. Weasley despairingly, "well, on your own head be it!"

She wrenched open the front door and stepped out into the weak September sunlight. Harry and the dog followed her. The door slammed behind them and Mrs. Black's screeches were cut off instantly.

"Where's Tonks?" Harry said, looking around as they went down the stone steps of number twelve, which vanished the moment they reached the pavement.

"She's waiting for us just up here," said Mrs. Weasley stiffly, averting her eyes from the lolloping black dog beside Harry.

An old woman greeted them on the corner. She had tightly curled gray hair and wore a purple hat shaped like a porkpie.

"Wotcher, Harry," she said, winking. "Better hurry up, hadn't we, Molly?" she added, checking her watch.

"I know, I know," moaned Mrs. Weasley, lengthening her stride, "but Mad-Eye wanted to wait for Sturgis. . . . If only Arthur could have got us cars from the Ministry again . . . but Fudge wouldn't let him borrow so much as an empty ink bottle these days. . . . *How* Muggles can stand traveling without magic . . ."

But the great black dog gave a joyful bark and gamboled around them, snapping at pigeons, and chasing its own tail. Harry couldn't help laughing. Sirius had been trapped inside for a very long time. Mrs. Weasley pursed her lips in an almost Aunt Petunia-ish way.

It took them twenty minutes to reach King's Cross by foot and nothing more eventful happened during that time than Sirius scaring a couple of cats for Harry's entertainment. Once inside the station they lingered casually beside the barrier between platforms nine and ten until the coast was clear, then each of them leaned against it in turn and fell easily through onto platform nine and three quarters, where the Hogwarts Express stood belching sooty steam over a platform packed with departing students and their families. Harry inhaled the familiar smell and felt his spirits soar. . . . He was really going back. . . .

"I hope the others make it in time," said Mrs. Weasley anxiously, staring behind her at the wrought-iron arch spanning the platform, through which new arrivals would come.

"Nice dog, Harry!" called a tall boy with dreadlocks.

"Thanks, Lee," said Harry, grinning, as Sirius wagged his tail frantically.

"Oh good," said Mrs. Weasley, sounding relieved, "here's Alastor with the luggage, look . . ."

A porter's cap pulled low over his mismatched eyes, Moody came limping through the archway pushing a cart full of their trunks.

"All okay," he muttered to Mrs. Weasley and Tonks. "Don't think we were followed. . . ."

Seconds later, Mr. Weasley emerged onto the platform with Ron and Hermione. They had almost unloaded Moody's luggage cart when Fred, George, and Ginny turned up with Lupin.

"No trouble?" growled Moody.

"Nothing," said Lupin.

"I'll still be reporting Sturgis to Dumbledore," said Moody. "That's the second time he's not turned up in a week. Getting as unreliable as Mundungus."

"Well, look after yourselves," said Lupin, shaking hands all round. He reached Harry last and gave him a clap on the shoulder. "You too, Harry. Be careful."

"Yeah, keep your head down and your eyes peeled," said Moody, shaking Harry's hand too. "And don't forget, all of you — careful what you put in writing. If in doubt, don't put it in a letter at all."

"It's been great meeting all of you," said Tonks, hugging Hermione and Ginny. "We'll see you soon, I expect."

A warning whistle sounded; the students still on the platform started hurrying onto the train.

"Quick, quick," said Mrs. Weasley distractedly, hugging them at random and catching Harry twice. "Write. . . . Be good. . . . If you've forgotten anything we'll send it on. . . . Onto the train, now, hurry. . . ."

For one brief moment, the great black dog reared onto its hind legs and placed its front paws on Harry's shoulders, but Mrs. Weasley shoved Harry away toward the train door hissing, "For heaven's sake act more like a dog, Sirius!"

"See you!" Harry called out of the open window as the train began to move, while Ron, Hermione, and Ginny waved beside him. The figures of Tonks, Lupin, Moody, and Mr. and Mrs. Weasley shrank rapidly but the black dog was bounding alongside the window, wagging its tail; blurred people on the platform were laughing to see it chasing the train, and then they turned the corner, and Sirius was gone.

"He shouldn't have come with us," said Hermione in a worried voice.

"Oh lighten up," said Ron, "he hasn't seen daylight for months, poor bloke."

"Well," said Fred, clapping his hands together, "can't stand around chatting all day, we've got business to discuss with Lee. See you later," and he and George disappeared down the corridor to the right.

The train was gathering still more speed, so that the houses outside the window flashed past and they swayed where they stood.

"Shall we go and find a compartment, then?" Harry asked Ron and Hermione.

Ron and Hermione exchanged looks.

"Er," said Ron.

"We're — well — Ron and I are supposed to go into the prefect carriage," Hermione said awkwardly.

Ron wasn't looking at Harry; he seemed to have become intensely interested in the fingernails on his left hand.

"Oh," said Harry. "Right. Fine."

"I don't think we'll have to stay there all journey," said Hermione quickly. "Our letters said we just get instructions from the Head Boy and Girl and then patrol the corridors from time to time."

"Fine," said Harry again. "Well, I-I might see you later, then."

"Yeah, definitely," said Ron, casting a shifty, anxious look at Harry. "It's a pain having to go down there, I'd rather — but we have to — I mean, I'm not enjoying it, I'm not Percy," he finished defiantly.

"I know you're not," said Harry and he grinned. But as Hermione and Ron dragged their trunks, Crookshanks, and a caged Pigwidgeon off toward the engine end of the train, Harry felt an odd sense of loss. He had never traveled on the Hogwarts Express without Ron.

"Come on," Ginny told him, "if we get a move on we'll be able to save them places."

"Right," said Harry, picking up Hedwig's cage in one hand and the handle of his trunk in the other. They struggled off down the corridor, peering through the glass-paneled doors into the compartments they passed, which were already full. Harry could not help noticing that a lot of people stared back at him with great interest and that several of them nudged their neighbors and pointed him out. After he had met this behavior in five consecutive carriages he remembered that the *Daily Prophet* had been telling its readers all summer what a lying show-off he was. He wondered bleakly whether the people now staring and whispering believed the stories.

In the very last carriage they met Neville Longbottom, Harry's fellow fifth-year Gryffindor, his round face shining with the effort of pulling his trunk along and maintaining a one-handed grip on his struggling toad, Trevor.

"Hi, Harry," he panted. "Hi, Ginny. . . . Everywhere's full. . . . I can't find a seat. . . ."

"What are you talking about?" said Ginny, who had squeezed past Neville to peer into the compartment behind him. "There's room in this one, there's only Loony Lovegood in here —"

Neville mumbled something about not wanting to disturb anyone.

"Don't be silly," said Ginny, laughing, "she's all right."

She slid the door open and pulled her trunk inside it. Harry and Neville followed.

"Hi, Luna," said Ginny. "Is it okay if we take these seats?"

The girl beside the window looked up. She had straggly, waist-length, dirty-blond hair, very pale eyebrows, and protuberant eyes that gave her a permanently surprised look. Harry knew at once why Neville had chosen to pass this compartment by. The girl gave off an aura of distinct dottiness. Perhaps it was the fact that she had stuck her wand behind her left ear for safekeeping, or that she had chosen to wear a necklace of butterbeer caps, or that she was reading a magazine upside down. Her eyes ranged over Neville and came to rest on Harry. She nodded.

"Thanks," said Ginny, smiling at her.

Harry and Neville stowed the three trunks and Hedwig's cage in the luggage rack and sat down. The girl called Luna watched them over her upside-down magazine, which was called *The Quibbler*. She did not seem to need to blink as much as normal humans. She stared and stared at Harry, who had taken the seat opposite her and now wished he had not.

"Had a good summer, Luna?" Ginny asked.

"Yes," said Luna dreamily, without taking her eyes off Harry. "Yes, it was quite enjoyable, you know. *You're* Harry Potter," she added.

"I know I am," said Harry.

Neville chuckled. Luna turned her pale eyes upon him instead.

"And I don't know who you are."

"I'm nobody," said Neville hurriedly.

"No you're not," said Ginny sharply. "Neville Longbottom — Luna Lovegood. Luna's in my year, but in Ravenclaw."

"Wit beyond measure is man's greatest treasure," said Luna in a sing-song voice.

She raised her upside-down magazine high enough to hide her face and fell silent. Harry and Neville looked at each other with their eyebrows raised. Ginny suppressed a giggle.

The train rattled onward, speeding them out into open country. It was an odd, unsettled sort of day; one moment the carriage was full of sunlight and the next they were passing beneath ominously gray clouds.

"Guess what I got for my birthday?" said Neville.

"Another Remembrall?" said Harry, remembering the marblelike device Neville's grandmother had sent him in an effort to improve his abysmal memory.

"No," said Neville, "I could do with one, though, I lost the old one ages ago. . . . No, look at this. . . ."

He dug the hand that was not keeping a firm grip on Trevor into his schoolbag and after a little bit of rummaging pulled out what appeared to be a small gray cactus in a pot, except that it was covered with what looked like boils rather than spines.

"Mimbulus mimbletonia," he said proudly.

Harry stared at the thing. It was pulsating slightly, giving it the rather sinister look of some diseased internal organ.

"It's really, really rare," said Neville, beaming. "I don't know if there's one in the greenhouse at Hogwarts, even. I can't wait to show it to Professor Sprout. My great-uncle Algie got it for me in Assyria. I'm going to see if I can breed from it."

Harry knew that Neville's favorite subject was Herbology, but for the life of him he could not see what he would want with this stunted little plant.

"Does it — er — do anything?" he asked.

"Loads of stuff!" said Neville proudly. "It's got an amazing defensive mechanism — hold Trevor for me. . . ."

He dumped the toad into Harry's lap and took a quill from his schoolbag. Luna Lovegood's popping eyes appeared over the top of her upside-down magazine again, watching what Neville was doing. Neville held the *Mimbulus mimbletonia* up to his eyes, his tongue between his teeth, chose his spot, and gave the plant a sharp prod with the tip of his quill.

Liquid squirted from every boil on the plant, thick, stinking, dark-green jets of it; they hit the ceiling, the windows, and spattered Luna Lovegood's magazine. Ginny, who had flung her arms up in front of her face just in time, merely looked as though she was wearing a slimy green hat, but Harry, whose hands had been busy preventing the escape of Trevor, received a face full. It smelled like rancid manure.

Neville, whose face and torso were also drenched, shook his head to get the worst out of his eyes.

"S-sorry," he gasped. "I haven't tried that before. . . . Didn't realize it would be quite so . . . Don't worry, though, Stinksap's not poisonous," he added nervously, as Harry spat a mouthful onto the floor.

At that precise moment the door of their compartment slid open.

"Oh . . . hello, Harry," said a nervous voice. "Um . . . bad time?"

Harry wiped the lenses of his glasses with his Trevor-free hand. A very pretty girl with long, shiny black hair was standing in the doorway smiling at him: Cho Chang, the Seeker on the Ravenclaw Quidditch team.

"Oh . . . hi," said Harry blankly.

"Um . . ." said Cho. "Well . . . just thought I'd say hello . . . 'bye then."

She closed the door again, rather pink in the face, and departed. Harry slumped back in his seat and groaned. He would have liked Cho to discover him sitting with a group of very cool people laughing their heads off at a joke he had just told; he would not have chosen to be sitting with Neville and Loony Lovegood, clutching a toad and dripping in Stinksap.

"Never mind," said Ginny bracingly. "Look, we can get rid of all this easily." She pulled out her wand. *"Scourgify!"*

The Stinksap vanished.

"Sorry," said Neville again, in a small voice.

Ron and Hermione did not turn up for nearly an hour, by which time the food trolley had already gone by. Harry, Ginny, and Neville had finished their Pumpkin Pasties and were busy swapping Chocolate Frog cards when the compartment door slid open and they walked in, accompanied by Crookshanks and a shrilly hooting Pigwidgeon in his cage.

"I'm starving," said Ron, stowing Pigwidgeon next to Hedwig, grabbing a Chocolate Frog from Harry and throwing himself into the seat next to him. He ripped open the wrapper, bit off the Frog's head, and leaned back with his eyes closed as though he had had a very exhausting morning.

"Well, there are two fifth-year prefects from each House," said Hermione, looking thoroughly disgruntled as she took her seat. "Boy and girl from each."

"And guess who's a Slytherin prefect?" said Ron, still with his eyes closed.

"Malfoy," replied Harry at once, his worst fear confirmed.

"'Course," said Ron bitterly, stuffing the rest of the Frog into his mouth and taking another.

"And that complete *cow* Pansy Parkinson," said Hermione viciously. "How she got to be a prefect when she's thicker than a concussed troll . . ."

"Who's Hufflepuff?" Harry asked.

"Ernie Macmillan and Hannah Abbott," said Ron thickly.

"And Anthony Goldstein and Padma Patil for Ravenclaw," said Hermione.

"You went to the Yule Ball with Padma Patil," said a vague voice.

Everyone turned to look at Luna Lovegood, who was gazing unblinkingly at Ron over the top of *The Quibbler*. He swallowed his mouthful of Frog.

"Yeah, I know I did," he said, looking mildly surprised.

"She didn't enjoy it very much," Luna informed him. "She doesn't think you treated her very well, because you wouldn't dance with her. I don't think I'd have minded," she added thoughtfully, "I don't like dancing very much."

She retreated behind *The Quibbler* again. Ron stared at the cover with his mouth hanging open for a few seconds, then looked around at Ginny for some kind of explanation, but Ginny had stuffed her knuckles in her mouth to stop herself giggling. Ron shook his head, bemused, then checked his watch.

"We're supposed to patrol the corridors every so often," he told Harry and Neville, "and we can give out punishments if people are misbehaving. I can't wait to get Crabbe and Goyle for something. . . ."

"You're not supposed to abuse your position, Ron!" said Hermione sharply.

"Yeah, right, because Malfoy won't abuse it at all," said Ron sarcastically.

"So you're going to descend to his level?"

"No, I'm just going to make sure I get his mates before he gets mine."

"For heaven's sake, Ron —"

"I'll make Goyle do lines, it'll kill him, he hates writing," said Ron happily. He lowered his voice to Goyle's low grunt and, screwing up his face in a look of pained concentration, mimed writing in midair. *"I . . . must . . . not . . . look . . . like . . . a . . . baboon's . . . backside. . . ."*

Everyone laughed, but nobody laughed harder than Luna Love-good. She let out a scream of mirth that caused Hedwig to wake up and flap her wings indignantly and Crookshanks to leap up into the luggage rack, hissing. She laughed so hard that her magazine slipped out of her grasp, slid down her legs, and onto the floor.

"That was *funny*!"

Her prominent eyes swam with tears as she gasped for breath, staring at Ron. Utterly nonplussed, he looked around at the others, who were now laughing at the expression on Ron's face and at the ludicrously prolonged laughter of Luna Lovegood, who was rocking backward and forward, clutching her sides.

"Are you taking the mickey?" said Ron, frowning at her.

"Baboon's . . . backside!" she choked, holding her ribs.

Everyone else was watching Luna laughing, but Harry, glancing at the magazine on the floor, noticed something that made him dive for it. Upside down it had been hard to tell what the picture on the front was, but Harry now realized it was a fairly bad cartoon of Cornelius Fudge; Harry only recognized him because of the lime-green bowler hat. One of Fudge's hands was clenched around a bag of gold; the other hand was throttling a goblin. The cartoon was captioned: How Far Will Fudge Go to Gain Gringotts?

Beneath this were listed the titles of other articles inside the magazine.

CORRUPTION IN THE QUIDDITCH LEAGUE:
How the Tornados Are Taking Control

SECRETS OF THE ANCIENT RUNES REVEALED

SIRIUS BLACK: Villain or Victim?

"Can I have a look at this?" Harry asked Luna eagerly.

She nodded, still gazing at Ron, breathless with laughter.

Harry opened the magazine and scanned the index; until this moment he had completely forgotten the magazine Kingsley had handed Mr. Weasley to give to Sirius, but it must have been this edition of *The Quibbler*. He found the page and turned excitedly to the article.

This too was illustrated by a rather bad cartoon; in fact, Harry would not have known it was supposed to be Sirius if it hadn't been captioned. Sirius was standing on a pile of human bones with his wand out. The headline on the article read:

SIRIUS — Black As He's Painted?
Notorious Mass Murderer OR Innocent Singing Sensation?

Harry had to read this sentence several times before he was convinced that he had not misunderstood it. Since when had Sirius been a singing sensation?

> *For fourteen years Sirius Black has been believed guilty of the mass murder of twelve innocent Muggles and one wizard. Black's audacious escape from Azkaban two years ago has led to the widest manhunt ever conducted by the Ministry of Magic. None of us has ever questioned that he deserves to be recaptured and handed back to the dementors.*
>
> *BUT DOES HE?*
>
> *Startling new evidence has recently come to light that Sirius Black may not have committed the crimes for which he was sent to Azkaban. In fact, says Doris Purkiss, of 18 Acanthia Way, Little Norton, Black may not even have been present at the killings.*
>
> *"What people don't realize is that Sirius Black is a false name," says Mrs. Purkiss. "The man people*

*believe to be Sirius Black is actually Stubby Board-
man, lead singer of the popular singing group The
Hobgoblins, who retired from public life after being
struck in the ear by a turnip at a concert in Little Nor-
ton Church Hall nearly fifteen years ago. I recognized
him the moment I saw his picture in the paper. Now,
Stubby couldn't possibly have committed those
crimes, because on the day in question he happened
to be enjoying a romantic candlelit dinner with me. I
have written to the Minister of Magic and am expecting him to give Stubby, alias Sirius, a full pardon any
day now."*

Harry finished reading and stared at the page in disbelief. Perhaps
it was a joke, he thought, perhaps the magazine often printed spoof
items. He flicked back a few pages and found the piece on Fudge.

*Cornelius Fudge, the Minister of Magic, denied that
he had any plans to take over the running of the Wizarding bank, Gringotts, when he was elected Minister
of Magic five years ago. Fudge has always insisted
that he wants nothing more than to "cooperate
peacefully" with the guardians of our gold.*
    BUT DOES HE?
    *Sources close to the Minister have recently dis-
closed that Fudge's dearest ambition is to seize
control of the goblin gold supplies and that he will
not hesitate to use force if need be.*
    *"It wouldn't be the first time, either," said a
Ministry insider. "Cornelius 'Goblin-Crusher' Fudge,
that's what his friends call him, if you could hear him*

*when he thinks no one's listening, oh, he's always
talking about the goblins he's had done in; he's had
them drowned, he's had them dropped off buildings,
he's had them poisoned, he's had them cooked in
pies. . . ."*

Harry did not read any further. Fudge might have many faults but
Harry found it extremely hard to imagine him ordering goblins to be
cooked in pies. He flicked through the rest of the magazine. Pausing
every few pages he read an accusation that the Tutshill Tornados were
winning the Quidditch League by a combination of blackmail, illegal broom-tampering, and torture; an interview with a wizard who
claimed to have flown to the moon on a Cleansweep Six and brought
back a bag of moon frogs to prove it; and an article on ancient runes,
which at least explained why Luna had been reading *The Quibbler*
upside down. According to the magazine, if you turned the runes on
their heads they revealed a spell to make your enemy's ears turn into
kumquats. In fact, compared to the rest of the articles in *The Quibbler,* the suggestion that Sirius might really be the lead singer of The
Hobgoblins was quite sensible.

"Anything good in there?" asked Ron as Harry closed the magazine.

"Of course not," said Hermione scathingly, before Harry could answer, "*The Quibbler's* rubbish, everyone knows that."

"Excuse me," said Luna; her voice had suddenly lost its dreamy
quality. "My father's the editor."

"I — oh," said Hermione, looking embarrassed. "Well . . . it's got
some interesting . . . I mean, it's quite . . ."

"I'll have it back, thank you," said Luna coldly, and leaning forward
she snatched it out of Harry's hands. Rifling through it to page fifty-
seven, she turned it resolutely upside down again and disappeared
behind it, just as the compartment door opened for the third time.

Harry looked around; he had expected this, but that did not make the sight of Draco Malfoy smirking at him from between his cronies Crabbe and Goyle any more enjoyable.

"What?" he said aggressively, before Malfoy could open his mouth.

"Manners, Potter, or I'll have to give you a detention," drawled Malfoy, whose sleek blond hair and pointed chin were just like his father's. "You see, I, unlike you, have been made a prefect, which means that I, unlike you, have the power to hand out punishments."

"Yeah," said Harry, "but you, unlike me, are a git, so get out and leave us alone."

Ron, Hermione, Ginny, and Neville laughed. Malfoy's lip curled.

"Tell me, how does it feel being second-best to Weasley, Potter?" he asked.

"Shut up, Malfoy," said Hermione sharply.

"I seem to have touched a nerve," said Malfoy, smirking. "Well, just watch yourself, Potter, because I'll be *dogging* your footsteps in case you step out of line."

"Get out!" said Hermione, standing up.

Sniggering, Malfoy gave Harry a last malicious look and departed, Crabbe and Goyle lumbering in his wake. Hermione slammed the compartment door behind them and turned to look at Harry, who knew at once that she, like him, had registered what Malfoy had said and been just as unnerved by it.

"Chuck us another Frog," said Ron, who had clearly noticed nothing.

Harry could not talk freely in front of Neville and Luna. He exchanged another nervous look with Hermione and then stared out of the window.

He had thought Sirius coming with him to the station was a bit of a laugh, but suddenly it seemed reckless, if not downright dangerous. . . . Hermione had been right. . . . Sirius should not have come. What if Mr. Malfoy had noticed the black dog and told Draco, what if he had deduced that the Weasleys, Lupin, Tonks, and Moody knew where Sirius was hiding? Or had Malfoy's use of the word "dogging" been a coincidence?

The weather remained undecided as they traveled farther and farther north. Rain spattered the windows in a halfhearted way, then the sun put in a feeble appearance before clouds drifted over it once more. When darkness fell and lamps came on inside the carriages, Luna rolled up *The Quibbler,* put it carefully away in her bag, and took to staring at everyone in the compartment instead.

Harry was sitting with his forehead pressed against the train window, trying to get a first distant glimpse of Hogwarts, but it was a moonless night and the rain-streaked window was grimy.

"We'd better change," said Hermione at last. She and Ron pinned their prefect badges carefully to their chests. Harry saw Ron checking how it looked in the black window.

At last the train began to slow down and they heard the usual racket up and down it as everybody scrambled to get their luggage and pets assembled, ready for departure. Ron and Hermione were supposed to supervise all this; they disappeared from the carriage again, leaving Harry and the others to look after Crookshanks and Pigwidgeon.

"I'll carry that owl, if you like," said Luna to Harry, reaching out for Pigwidgeon as Neville stowed Trevor carefully in an inside pocket.

"Oh — er — thanks," said Harry, handing her the cage and hoisting Hedwig's more securely into his arms.

They shuffled out of the compartment feeling the first sting of the night air on their faces as they joined the crowd in the corridor. Slowly they moved toward the doors. Harry could smell the pine trees that lined the path down to the lake. He stepped down onto the platform and looked around, listening for the familiar call of "Firs' years over here . . . firs' years . . ."

But it did not come. Instead a quite different voice, a brisk female one, was calling, "First years line up over here, please! All first years to me!"

A lantern came swinging toward Harry and by its light he saw the prominent chin and severe haircut of Professor Grubbly-Plank, the witch who had taken over Hagrid's Care of Magical Creatures lessons for a while the previous year.

"Where's Hagrid?" he said out loud.

"I don't know," said Ginny, "but we'd better get out of the way, we're blocking the door."

"Oh yeah . . ."

Harry and Ginny became separated as they moved off along the platform and out through the station. Jostled by the crowd, Harry squinted through the darkness for a glimpse of Hagrid; he had to be here, Harry had been relying on it — seeing Hagrid again had been one of the things to which he had been looking forward most. But there was no sign of him at all.

He can't have left, Harry told himself as he shuffled slowly through a narrow doorway onto the road outside with the rest of the crowd. *He's just got a cold or something. . . .*

He looked around for Ron or Hermione, wanting to know what they thought about the reappearance of Professor Grubbly-Plank, but neither of them was anywhere near him, so he allowed himself to be shunted forward onto the dark rain-washed road outside Hogsmeade station.

Here stood the hundred or so horseless stagecoaches that always took the students above first year up to the castle. Harry glanced quickly at them, turned away to keep a lookout for Ron and Hermione, then did a double take.

The coaches were no longer horseless. There were creatures standing between the carriage shafts; if he had had to give them a name, he supposed he would have called them horses, though there was something reptilian about them, too. They were completely fleshless, their black coats clinging to their skeletons, of which every bone was visible. Their heads were dragonish, and their pupil-less eyes white and staring. Wings sprouted from each wither — vast, black leathery wings that looked as though they ought to belong to giant bats. Standing still and quiet in the gloom, the creatures looked eerie and sinister. Harry could not understand why the coaches were being pulled by these horrible horses when they were quite capable of moving along by themselves.

"Where's Pig?" said Ron's voice, right behind Harry.

"That Luna girl was carrying him," said Harry, turning quickly, eager to consult Ron about Hagrid. "Where d'you reckon —"

"— Hagrid is? I dunno," said Ron, sounding worried. "He'd better be okay. . . ."

A short distance away, Draco Malfoy, followed by a small gang of cronies including Crabbe, Goyle, and Pansy Parkinson, was pushing some timid-looking second years out of the way so that they could get a coach to themselves. Seconds later Hermione emerged panting from the crowd.

"Malfoy was being absolutely foul to a first year back there, I swear I'm going to report him, he's only had his badge three minutes and he's using it to bully people worse than ever. . . . Where's Crookshanks?"

"Ginny's got him," said Harry. "There she is. . . ."

Ginny had just emerged from the crowd, clutching a squirming Crookshanks.

"Thanks," said Hermione, relieving Ginny of the cat. "Come on, let's get a carriage together before they all fill up. . . ."

"I haven't got Pig yet!" Ron said, but Hermione was already heading off toward the nearest unoccupied coach. Harry remained behind with Ron.

"What *are* those things, d'you reckon?" he asked Ron, nodding at the horrible horses as the other students surged past them.

"What things?"

"Those horse —"

Luna appeared holding Pigwidgeon's cage in her arms; the tiny owl was twittering excitedly as usual.

"Here you are," she said. "He's a sweet little owl, isn't he?"

"Er . . . yeah . . . He's all right," said Ron gruffly. "Well, come on then, let's get in. . . . what were you saying, Harry?"

"I was saying, what are those horse things?" Harry said, as he, Ron, and Luna made for the carriage in which Hermione and Ginny were already sitting.

"What horse things?"

"The horse things pulling the carriages!" said Harry impatiently; they were, after all, about three feet from the nearest one; it was watching them with empty white eyes. Ron, however, gave Harry a perplexed look.

"What are you talking about?"

"I'm talking about — look!"

Harry grabbed Ron's arm and wheeled him about so that he was face-to-face with the winged horse. Ron stared straight at it for a second, then looked back at Harry.

"What am I supposed to be looking at?"

"At the — there, between the shafts! Harnessed to the coach! It's right there in front —"

But as Ron continued to look bemused, a strange thought occurred to Harry.

"Can't . . . can't you see them?"

"See what?"

"Can't you see what's pulling the carriages?"

Ron looked seriously alarmed now.

"Are you feeling all right, Harry?"

"I . . . yeah . . ."

Harry felt utterly bewildered. The horse was there in front of him, gleaming solidly in the dim light issuing from the station windows behind them, vapor rising from its nostrils in the chilly night air. Yet unless Ron was faking — and it was a very feeble joke if he was — Ron could not see it at all.

"Shall we get in, then?" said Ron uncertainly, looking at Harry as though worried about him.

"Yeah," said Harry. "Yeah, go on . . ."

"It's all right," said a dreamy voice from beside Harry as Ron vanished into the coach's dark interior. "You're not going mad or anything. I can see them too."

"Can you?" said Harry desperately, turning to Luna. He could see the bat-winged horses reflected in her wide, silvery eyes.

"Oh yes," said Luna, "I've been able to see them ever since my first day here. They've always pulled the carriages. Don't worry. You're just as sane as I am."

Smiling faintly, she climbed into the musty interior of the carriage after Ron. Not altogether reassured, Harry followed her.

THE SORTING HAT'S NEW SONG

arry did not want to tell the others that he and Luna were having the same hallucination, if that was what it was, so he said nothing about the horses as he sat down inside the carriage and slammed the door behind him. Nevertheless, he could not help watching the silhouettes of the horses moving beyond the window.

"Did everyone see that Grubbly-Plank woman?" asked Ginny. "What's she doing back here? Hagrid can't have left, can he?"

"I'll be quite glad if he has," said Luna. "He isn't a very good teacher, is he?"

"Yes, he is!" said Harry, Ron, and Ginny angrily.

Harry glared at Hermione; she cleared her throat and quickly said, "Erm . . . yes . . . he's very good."

"Well, we think he's a bit of a joke in Ravenclaw," said Luna, unfazed.

"You've got a rubbish sense of humor then," Ron snapped, as the wheels below them creaked into motion.

Luna did not seem perturbed by Ron's rudeness; on the contrary, she simply watched him for a while as though he were a mildly interesting television program.

Rattling and swaying, the carriages moved in convoy up the road. When they passed between the tall stone pillars topped with winged boars on either side of the gates to the school grounds, Harry leaned forward to try and see whether there were any lights on in Hagrid's cabin by the Forbidden Forest, but the grounds were in complete darkness. Hogwarts Castle, however, loomed ever closer: a towering mass of turrets, jet-black against the dark sky, here and there a window blazing fiery bright above them.

The carriages jingled to a halt near the stone steps leading up to the oak front doors and Harry got out of the carriage first. He turned again to look for lit windows down by the forest, but there was definitely no sign of life within Hagrid's cabin. Unwillingly, because he had half hoped they would have vanished, he turned his eyes instead upon the strange, skeletal creatures standing quietly in the chill night air, their blank white eyes gleaming.

Harry had once before had the experience of seeing something that Ron could not, but that had been a reflection in a mirror, something much more insubstantial than a hundred very solid-looking beasts strong enough to pull a fleet of carriages. If Luna was to be believed, the beasts had always been there but invisible; why, then, could Harry suddenly see them, and why could Ron not?

"Are you coming or what?" said Ron beside him.

"Oh . . . yeah," said Harry quickly, and they joined the crowd hurrying up the stone steps into the castle.

The entrance hall was ablaze with torches and echoing with footsteps as the students crossed the flagged stone floor for the double doors to the right, leading to the Great Hall and the start-of-term feast.

The four long House tables in the Great Hall were filling up under the starless black ceiling, which was just like the sky they could glimpse through the high windows. Candles floated in midair all along the tables, illuminating the silvery ghosts who were dotted about the Hall and the faces of the students talking eagerly to one another, exchanging summer news, shouting greetings at friends from other Houses, eyeing one another's new haircuts and robes. Again Harry noticed people putting their heads together to whisper as he passed; he gritted his teeth and tried to act as though he neither noticed nor cared.

Luna drifted away from them at the Ravenclaw table. The moment they reached Gryffindor's, Ginny was hailed by some fellow fourth years and left to sit with them; Harry, Ron, Hermione, and Neville found seats together about halfway down the table between Nearly Headless Nick, the Gryffindor House ghost, and Parvati Patil and Lavender Brown, the last two of whom gave Harry airy, overly friendly greetings that made him quite sure they had stopped talking about him a split second before. He had more important things to worry about, however: He was looking over the students' heads to the staff table that ran along the top wall of the Hall.

"He's not there."

Ron and Hermione scanned the staff table too, though there was no real need; Hagrid's size made him instantly obvious in any lineup.

"He can't have left," said Ron, sounding slightly anxious.

"Of course he hasn't," said Harry firmly.

"You don't think he's . . . *hurt,* or anything, do you?" said Hermione uneasily.

"No," said Harry at once.

"But where is he, then?"

There was a pause, then Harry said very quietly, so that Neville, Parvati, and Lavender could not hear, "Maybe he's not back yet. You know — from his mission — the thing he was doing over the summer for Dumbledore."

"Yeah . . . yeah, that'll be it," said Ron, sounding reassured, but Hermione bit her lip, looking up and down the staff table as though hoping for some conclusive explanation of Hagrid's absence.

"Who's *that*?" she said sharply, pointing toward the middle of the staff table.

Harry's eyes followed hers. They lit first upon Professor Dumbledore, sitting in his high-backed golden chair at the center of the long staff table, wearing deep-purple robes scattered with silvery stars and a matching hat. Dumbledore's head was inclined toward the woman sitting next to him, who was talking into his ear. She looked, Harry thought, like somebody's maiden aunt: squat, with short, curly, mouse-brown hair in which she had placed a horrible pink Alice band that matched the fluffy pink cardigan she wore over her robes. Then she turned her face slightly to take a sip from her goblet and he saw, with a shock of recognition, a pallid, toadlike face and a pair of prominent, pouchy eyes.

"It's that Umbridge woman!"

"Who?" said Hermione.

"She was at my hearing, she works for Fudge!"

"Nice cardigan," said Ron, smirking.

"She works for Fudge?" Hermione repeated, frowning. "What on earth's she doing here, then?"

"Dunno . . ."

Hermione scanned the staff table, her eyes narrowed.

"No," she muttered, "no, surely not . . ."

Harry did not understand what she was talking about but did not ask; his attention had just been caught by Professor Grubbly-Plank who had just appeared behind the staff table; she worked her way along to the very end and took the seat that ought to have been Hagrid's. That meant that the first years must have crossed the lake and reached the castle, and sure enough, a few seconds later, the doors from the entrance hall opened. A long line of scared-looking first years entered, led by Professor McGonagall, who was carrying a stool on which sat an ancient wizard's hat, heavily patched and darned with a wide rip near the frayed brim.

The buzz of talk in the Great Hall faded away. The first years lined up in front of the staff table facing the rest of the students, and Professor McGonagall placed the stool carefully in front of them, then stood back.

The first years' faces glowed palely in the candlelight. A small boy right in the middle of the row looked as though he was trembling. Harry recalled, fleetingly, how terrified he had felt when he had stood there, waiting for the unknown test that would determine to which House he belonged.

The whole school waited with bated breath. Then the rip near the hat's brim opened wide like a mouth and the Sorting Hat burst into song:

> In times of old when I was new
> And Hogwarts barely started
> The founders of our noble school
> Thought never to be parted:
> United by a common goal,
> They had the selfsame yearning,
> To make the world's best magic school
> And pass along their learning.
> "Together we will build and teach!"
> The four good friends decided
> And never did they dream that they
> Might someday be divided,
> For were there such friends anywhere
> As Slytherin and Gryffindor?
> Unless it was the second pair
> Of Hufflepuff and Ravenclaw?

So how could it have gone so wrong?
How could such friendships fail?
Why, I was there and so can tell
The whole sad, sorry tale.
Said Slytherin, "We'll teach just those
Whose ancestry is purest."
Said Ravenclaw, "We'll teach those whose
Intelligence is surest."
Said Gryffindor, "We'll teach all those
With brave deeds to their name."
Said Hufflepuff, "I'll teach the lot,
And treat them just the same."
These differences caused little strife
When first they came to light,
For each of the four founders had
A House in which they might
Take only those they wanted, so,
For instance, Slytherin
Took only pure-blood wizards
Of great cunning, just like him,
And only those of sharpest mind
Were taught by Ravenclaw
While the bravest and the boldest
Went to daring Gryffindor.
Good Hufflepuff, she took the rest,
And taught them all she knew,
Thus the Houses and their founders
Retained friendships firm and true.
So Hogwarts worked in harmony
For several happy years,
But then discord crept among us
Feeding on our faults and fears.

The Houses that, like pillars four,
Had once held up our school,
Now turned upon each other and,
Divided, sought to rule.
And for a while it seemed the school
Must meet an early end,
What with dueling and with fighting
And the clash of friend on friend
And at last there came a morning
When old Slytherin departed
And though the fighting then died out
He left us quite downhearted.
And never since the founders four
Were whittled down to three
Have the Houses been united
As they once were meant to be.
And now the Sorting Hat is here
And you all know the score:
I sort you into Houses
Because that is what I'm for,
But this year I'll go further,
Listen closely to my song:
Though condemned I am to split you
Still I worry that it's wrong,
Though I must fulfill my duty
And must quarter every year
Still I wonder whether Sorting
May not bring the end I fear.
Oh, know the perils, read the signs,
The warning history shows,
For our Hogwarts is in danger
From external, deadly foes

And we must unite inside her
Or we'll crumble from within.
I have told you, I have warned you. . . .
Let the Sorting now begin.

The hat became motionless once more; applause broke out, though it was punctured, for the first time in Harry's memory, with muttering and whispers. All across the Great Hall students were exchanging remarks with their neighbors and Harry, clapping along with everyone else, knew exactly what they were talking about.

"Branched out a bit this year, hasn't it?" said Ron, his eyebrows raised.

"Too right it has," said Harry.

The Sorting Hat usually confined itself to describing the different qualities looked for by each of the four Hogwarts Houses and its own role in sorting them; Harry could not remember it ever trying to give the school advice before.

"I wonder if it's ever given warnings before?" said Hermione, sounding slightly anxious.

"Yes, indeed," said Nearly Headless Nick knowledgeably, leaning across Neville toward her (Neville winced, it was very uncomfortable to have a ghost lean through you). "The hat feels itself honor-bound to give the school due warning whenever it feels —"

But Professor McGonagall, who was waiting to read out the list of first years' names, was giving the whispering students the sort of look that scorches. Nearly Headless Nick placed a see-through finger to his lips and sat primly upright again as the muttering came to an abrupt end. With a last frowning look that swept the four House tables, Professor McGonagall lowered her eyes to her long piece of parchment and called out,

"Abercrombie, Euan."

The terrified-looking boy Harry had noticed earlier stumbled

forward and put the hat on his head; it was only prevented from falling right down to his shoulders by his very prominent ears. The hat
considered for a moment, then the rip near the brim opened again
and shouted, *"GRYFFINDOR!"*

Harry clapped loudly with the rest of Gryffindor House as Euan
Abercrombie staggered to their table and sat down, looking as though
he would like very much to sink through the floor and never be looked
at again.

Slowly the long line of first years thinned; in the pauses between
the names and the Sorting Hat's decisions, Harry could hear Ron's
stomach rumbling loudly. Finally, "Zeller, Rose" was sorted into Hufflepuff, and Professor McGonagall picked up the hat and stool and
marched them away as Professor Dumbledore rose to his feet.

Harry was somehow soothed to see Dumbledore standing before
them all, whatever his recent bitter feelings toward his headmaster.
Between the absence of Hagrid and the presence of those dragonish
horses, he had felt that his return to Hogwarts, so long anticipated,
was full of unexpected surprises like jarring notes in a familiar song.
But this, at least, was how it was supposed to be: their headmaster rising to greet them all before the start-of-term feast.

"To our newcomers," said Dumbledore in a ringing voice, his arms
stretched wide and a beaming smile on his lips, "welcome! To our old
hands — welcome back! There is a time for speech making, but this
is not it. Tuck in!"

There was an appreciative laugh and an outbreak of applause as Dumbledore sat down neatly and threw his long beard over his shoulder so
as to keep it out of the way of his plate — for food had appeared out of
nowhere, so that the five long tables were groaning under joints and pies
and dishes of vegetables, bread, sauces, and flagons of pumpkin juice.

"Excellent," said Ron, with a kind of groan of longing, and he
seized the nearest plate of chops and began piling them onto his plate,
watched wistfully by Nearly Headless Nick.

"What were you saying before the Sorting?" Hermione asked the ghost. "About the hat giving warnings?"

"Oh yes," said Nick, who seemed glad of a reason to turn away from Ron, who was now eating roast potatoes with almost indecent enthusiasm. "Yes, I have heard the hat give several warnings before, always at times when it detects periods of great danger for the school. And always, of course, its advice is the same: Stand together, be strong from within."

"Ow kunnit nofe skusin danger ifzat?" said Ron.

His mouth was so full Harry thought it was quite an achievement for him to make any noise at all.

"I beg your pardon?" said Nearly Headless Nick politely, while Hermione looked revolted. Ron gave an enormous swallow and said, "How can it know if the school's in danger if it's a hat?"

"I have no idea," said Nearly Headless Nick. "Of course, it lives in Dumbledore's office, so I daresay it picks things up there."

"And it wants all the Houses to be friends?" said Harry, looking over at the Slytherin table, where Draco Malfoy was holding court. "Fat chance."

"Well, now, you shouldn't take that attitude," said Nick reprovingly. "Peaceful cooperation, that's the key. We ghosts, though we belong to separate Houses, maintain links of friendship. In spite of the competitiveness between Gryffindor and Slytherin, I would never dream of seeking an argument with the Bloody Baron."

"Only because you're terrified of him," said Ron.

Nearly Headless Nick looked highly affronted.

"Terrified? I hope I, Sir Nicholas de Mimsy-Porpington, have never been guilty of cowardice in my life! The noble blood that runs in my veins —"

"What blood?" asked Ron. "Surely you haven't still got — ?"

"It's a figure of speech!" said Nearly Headless Nick, now so annoyed his head was trembling ominously on his partially severed neck. "I assume I am still allowed to enjoy the use of whichever words I like, even if the pleasures of eating and drinking are denied me! But I am quite used to students poking fun at my death, I assure you!"

"Nick, he wasn't really laughing at you!" said Hermione, throwing a furious look at Ron.

Unfortunately, Ron's mouth was packed to exploding point again and all he could manage was "node iddum eentup sechew," which Nick did not seem to think constituted an adequate apology. Rising into the air, he straightened his feathered hat and swept away from them to the other end of the table, coming to rest between the Creevey brothers, Colin and Dennis.

"Well done, Ron," snapped Hermione.

"What?" said Ron indignantly, having managed, finally, to swallow his food. "I'm not allowed to ask a simple question?"

"Oh forget it," said Hermione irritably, and the pair of them spent the rest of the meal in huffy silence.

Harry was too used to their bickering to bother trying to reconcile them; he felt it was a better use of his time to eat his way steadily through his steak-and-kidney pie, then a large plateful of his favorite treacle tart.

When all the students had finished eating and the noise level in the hall was starting to creep upward again, Dumbledore got to his feet once more. Talking ceased immediately as all turned to face the headmaster. Harry was feeling pleasantly drowsy now. His four-poster bed was waiting somewhere above, wonderfully warm and soft. . . .

"Well, now that we are all digesting another magnificent feast, I beg a few moments of your attention for the usual start-of-term notices," said Dumbledore. "First years ought to know that the forest in the grounds is out of bounds to students — and a few of our older students ought to know by now too." (Harry, Ron, and Hermione exchanged smirks.)

"Mr. Filch, the caretaker, has asked me, for what he tells me is the four hundred and sixty-second time, to remind you all that magic is not permitted in corridors between classes, nor are a number of other things, all of which can be checked on the extensive list now fastened to Mr. Filch's office door.

"We have had two changes in staffing this year. We are very pleased to welcome back Professor Grubbly-Plank, who will be taking Care of Magical Creatures lessons; we are also delighted to introduce Professor Umbridge, our new Defense Against the Dark Arts teacher."

There was a round of polite but fairly unenthusiastic applause during which Harry, Ron, and Hermione exchanged slightly panicked looks; Dumbledore had not said for how long Grubbly-Plank would be teaching.

Dumbledore continued, "Tryouts for the House Quidditch teams will take place on the —"

He broke off, looking inquiringly at Professor Umbridge. As she was not much taller standing than sitting, there was a moment when nobody understood why Dumbledore had stopped talking, but then Professor Umbridge said, *"Hem, hem,"* and it became clear that she had got to her feet and was intending to make a speech.

Dumbledore only looked taken aback for a moment, then he sat back down smartly and looked alertly at Professor Umbridge as though he desired nothing better than to listen to her talk. Other members of staff were not as adept at hiding their surprise. Professor Sprout's eyebrows had disappeared into her flyaway hair, and Professor McGonagall's mouth was as thin as Harry had ever seen it. No new teacher had ever interrupted Dumbledore before. Many of the students were smirking; this woman obviously did not know how things were done at Hogwarts.

"Thank you, Headmaster," Professor Umbridge simpered, "for those kind words of welcome."

Her voice was high-pitched, breathy, and little-girlish and again, Harry felt a powerful rush of dislike that he could not explain to himself; all he knew was that he loathed everything about her, from her stupid voice to her fluffy pink cardigan. She gave another little throat-clearing cough (*"Hem, hem"*) and continued: "Well, it is lovely to be back at Hogwarts, I must say!" She smiled, revealing very pointed teeth. "And to see such happy little faces looking back at me!"

Harry glanced around. None of the faces he could see looked happy; on the contrary, they all looked rather taken aback at being addressed as though they were five years old.

"I am very much looking forward to getting to know you all, and I'm sure we'll be very good friends!"

Students exchanged looks at this; some of them were barely concealing grins.

"I'll be her friend as long as I don't have to borrow that cardigan," Parvati whispered to Lavender, and both of them lapsed into silent giggles.

Professor Umbridge cleared her throat again (*"Hem, hem"*), but when she continued, some of the breathiness had vanished from her voice. She sounded much more businesslike and now her words had a dull learned-by-heart sound to them.

"The Ministry of Magic has always considered the education of young witches and wizards to be of vital importance. The rare gifts with which you were born may come to nothing if not nurtured and honed by careful instruction. The ancient skills unique to the Wizarding community must be passed down through the generations lest we lose them forever. The treasure trove of magical knowledge amassed by our ancestors must be guarded, replenished, and polished by those who have been called to the noble profession of teaching."

Professor Umbridge paused here and made a little bow to her fellow staff members, none of whom bowed back. Professor McGonagall's dark eyebrows had contracted so that she looked positively hawklike, and Harry distinctly saw her exchange a significant glance with Professor Sprout as Umbridge gave another little *"Hem, hem"* and went on with her speech.

"Every headmaster and headmistress of Hogwarts has brought something new to the weighty task of governing this historic school, and that is as it should be, for without progress there will be stagnation and decay. There again, progress for progress's sake must be discouraged, for our tried and tested traditions often require no tinkering. A balance, then, between old and new, between permanence and change, between tradition and innovation . . ."

Harry found his attentiveness ebbing, as though his brain was slipping in and out of tune. The quiet that always filled the Hall when Dumbledore was speaking was breaking up as students put their heads together, whispering and giggling. Over at the Ravenclaw table, Cho Chang was chatting animatedly with her friends. A few seats along from Cho, Luna Lovegood had got out *The Quibbler* again. Meanwhile at the Hufflepuff table, Ernie Macmillan was one of the few still staring at Professor Umbridge, but he was glassy-eyed and Harry was sure he was only pretending to listen in an attempt to live up to the new prefect's badge gleaming on his chest.

Professor Umbridge did not seem to notice the restlessness of her audience. Harry had the impression that a full-scale riot could have broken out under her nose and she would have plowed on with her speech. The teachers, however, were still listening very attentively, and Hermione seemed to be drinking in every word Umbridge spoke, though judging by her expression, they were not at all to her taste.

". . . because some changes will be for the better, while others will come, in the fullness of time, to be recognized as errors of judgment. Meanwhile, some old habits will be retained, and rightly so, whereas others, outmoded and outworn, must be abandoned. Let us move forward, then, into a new era of openness, effectiveness, and accountability, intent on preserving what ought to be preserved, perfecting what needs to be perfected, and pruning wherever we find practices that ought to be prohibited."

She sat down. Dumbledore clapped. The staff followed his lead, though Harry noticed that several of them brought their hands together only once or twice before stopping. A few students joined in, but most had been taken unawares by the end of the speech, not having listened to more than a few words of it, and before they could start applauding properly, Dumbledore had stood up again.

"Thank you very much, Professor Umbridge, that was most illuminating," he said, bowing to her. "Now — as I was saying, Quidditch tryouts will be held . . ."

"Yes, it certainly was illuminating," said Hermione in a low voice.

"You're not telling me you enjoyed it?" Ron said quietly, turning a glazed face upon Hermione. "That was about the dullest speech I've ever heard, and I grew up with Percy."

"I said illuminating, not enjoyable," said Hermione. "It explained a lot."

"Did it?" said Harry in surprise. "Sounded like a load of waffle to me."

"There was some important stuff hidden in the waffle," said Hermione grimly.

"Was there?" said Ron blankly.

"How about 'progress for progress's sake must be discouraged'? How about 'pruning wherever we find practices that ought to be prohibited'?"

"Well, what does that mean?" said Ron impatiently.

"I'll tell you what it means," said Hermione ominously. "It means the Ministry's interfering at Hogwarts."

There was a great clattering and banging all around them; Dumbledore had obviously just dismissed the school, because everyone was standing up ready to leave the Hall. Hermione jumped up, looking flustered.

"Ron, we're supposed to show the first years where to go!"

"Oh yeah," said Ron, who had obviously forgotten. "Hey — hey you lot! Midgets!"

"Ron!"

"Well, they are, they're titchy. . . ."

"I know, but you can't call them midgets. . . . First years!" Hermione called commandingly along the table. "This way, please!"

A group of new students walked shyly up the gap between the Gryffindor and Hufflepuff tables, all of them trying hard not to lead the group. They did indeed seem very small; Harry was sure he had not appeared that young when he had arrived here. He grinned at them. A blond boy next to Euan Abercrombie looked petrified, nudged Euan, and whispered something in his ear. Euan Abercrombie looked equally frightened and stole a horrified look at Harry, who felt the grin slide off his face like Stinksap.

"See you later," he said to Ron and Hermione and he made his way out of the Great Hall alone, doing everything he could to ignore more whispering, staring, and pointing as he passed. He kept his eyes fixed ahead as he wove his way through the crowd in the entrance hall, then he hurried up the marble staircase, took a couple of concealed shortcuts, and had soon left most of the crowds behind.

He had been stupid not to expect this, he thought angrily, as he walked through much emptier upstairs corridors. Of course everyone was staring at him: He had emerged from the Triwizard maze two months ago clutching the dead body of a fellow student and claiming to have seen Lord Voldemort return to power. There had not been time last term to explain himself before everyone went home, even if he had felt up to giving the whole school a detailed account of the terrible events in that graveyard.

He had reached the end of the corridor to the Gryffindor common room and had come to a halt in front of the portrait of the Fat Lady before he realized that he did not know the new password.

"Er . . ." he said glumly, staring up at the Fat Lady, who smoothed the folds of her pink satin dress and looked sternly back at him.

"No password, no entrance," she said loftily.

"Harry, I know it!" someone panted from behind him, and he turned to see Neville jogging toward him. "Guess what it is? I'm actually going to be able to remember it for once —" He waved the stunted little cactus he had shown them on the train. *"Mimbulus mimbletonia!"*

"Correct," said the Fat Lady, and her portrait swung open toward them like a door, revealing a circular hole in the wall behind, through which Harry and Neville now climbed.

The Gryffindor common room looked as welcoming as ever, a cozy circular tower room full of dilapidated squashy armchairs and rickety old tables. A fire was crackling merrily in the grate and a few people were warming their hands before going up to their dormitories; on the other side of the room Fred and George Weasley were pinning something up on the notice board. Harry waved good night to them and headed straight for the door to the boys' dormitories; he was not in much of a mood for talking at the moment. Neville followed him.

Dean Thomas and Seamus Finnigan had reached the dormitory first and were in the process of covering the walls beside their beds with posters and photographs. They had been talking as Harry pushed open the door but stopped abruptly the moment they saw him. Harry wondered whether they had been talking about him, then whether he was being paranoid.

"Hi," he said, moving across to his own trunk and opening it.

"Hey, Harry," said Dean, who was putting on a pair of pajamas in the West Ham colors. "Good holiday?"

"Not bad," muttered Harry, as a true account of his holiday would have taken most of the night to relate and he could not face it. "You?"

"Yeah, it was okay," chuckled Dean. "Better than Seamus's anyway, he was just telling me."

"Why, what happened, Seamus?" Neville asked as he placed his *Mimbulus mimbletonia* tenderly on his bedside cabinet.

Seamus did not answer immediately; he was making rather a meal of ensuring that his poster of the Kenmare Kestrels Quidditch team was quite straight. Then he said, with his back still turned to Harry, "Me mam didn't want me to come back."

"What?" said Harry, pausing in the act of pulling off his robes.

"She didn't want me to come back to Hogwarts."

Seamus turned away from his poster and pulled his own pajamas out of his trunk, still not looking at Harry.

"But — why?" said Harry, astonished. He knew that Seamus's mother was a witch and could not understand, therefore, why she should have come over so Dursley-ish.

Seamus did not answer until he had finished buttoning his pajamas.

"Well," he said in a measured voice, "I suppose . . . because of you."

"What d'you mean?" said Harry quickly. His heart was beating rather fast. He felt vaguely as though something was closing in on him.

"Well," said Seamus again, still avoiding Harry's eyes, "she . . . er . . . well, it's not just you, it's Dumbledore too . . ."

"She believes the *Daily Prophet*?" said Harry. "She thinks I'm a liar and Dumbledore's an old fool?"

Seamus looked up at him. "Yeah, something like that."

Harry said nothing. He threw his wand down onto his bedside table, pulled off his robes, stuffed them angrily into his trunk, and pulled on his pajamas. He was sick of it; sick of being the person who was stared at and talked about all the time. If any of them knew, if any of them had the faintest idea what it felt like to be the one all these things had happened to . . . Mrs. Finnigan had no idea, the stupid woman, he thought savagely.

He got into bed and made to pull the hangings closed around him, but before he could do so, Seamus said, "Look . . . what *did* happen that night when . . . you know, when . . . with Cedric Diggory and all?"

Seamus sounded nervous and eager at the same time. Dean, who had been bending over his trunk, trying to retrieve a slipper, went oddly still and Harry knew he was listening hard.

"What are you asking me for?" Harry retorted. "Just read the *Daily Prophet* like your mother, why don't you? That'll tell you all you need to know."

"Don't you have a go at my mother," snapped Seamus.

"I'll have a go at anyone who calls me a liar," said Harry.

"Don't talk to me like that!"

"I'll talk to you how I want," said Harry, his temper rising so fast he snatched his wand back from his bedside table. "If you've got a problem sharing a dormitory with me, go and ask McGonagall if you can be moved, stop your mummy worrying —"

"Leave my mother out of this, Potter!"

"What's going on?"

Ron had appeared in the doorway. His wide eyes traveled from Harry, who was kneeling on his bed with his wand pointing at Seamus, to Seamus, who was standing there with his fists raised.

"He's having a go at my mother!" Seamus yelled.

"What?" said Ron. "Harry wouldn't do that — we met your mother, we liked her. . . ."

"That's before she started believing every word the stinking *Daily Prophet* writes about me!" said Harry at the top of his voice.

"Oh," said Ron, comprehension dawning across his freckled face. "Oh . . . right."

"You know what?" said Seamus heatedly, casting Harry a venomous look. "He's right, I don't want to share a dormitory with him anymore, he's a madman."

"That's out of order, Seamus," said Ron, whose ears were starting to glow red, always a danger sign.

"Out of order, am I?" shouted Seamus, who in contrast with Ron was turning paler. "You believe all the rubbish he's come out with about You-Know-Who, do you, you reckon he's telling the truth?"

"Yeah, I do!" said Ron angrily.

"Then you're mad too," said Seamus in disgust.

"Yeah? Well unfortunately for you, pal, I'm also a prefect!" said Ron, jabbing himself in the chest with a finger. "So unless you want detention, watch your mouth!"

Seamus looked for a few seconds as though detention would be a reasonable price to pay to say what was going through his mind; but with a noise of contempt he turned on his heel, vaulted into bed, and pulled the hangings shut with such violence that they were ripped from the bed and fell in a dusty pile to the floor. Ron glared at Seamus, then looked at Dean and Neville.

"Anyone else's parents got a problem with Harry?" he said aggressively.

"My parents are Muggles, mate," said Dean, shrugging. "They don't know nothing about no deaths at Hogwarts, because I'm not stupid enough to tell them."

"You don't know my mother, she'll weasel anything out of anyone!" Seamus snapped at him. "Anyway, your parents don't get the *Daily Prophet,* they don't know our headmaster's been sacked from the Wizengamot and the International Confederation of Wizards because he's losing his marbles —"

"My gran says that's rubbish," piped up Neville. "She says it's the *Daily Prophet* that's going downhill, not Dumbledore. She's canceled our subscription. We believe Harry," he said simply. He climbed into bed and pulled the covers up to his chin, looking owlishly over them at Seamus. "My gran's always said You-Know-Who would come back one day. She says if Dumbledore says he's back, he's back."

Harry felt a rush of gratitude toward Neville. Nobody else said anything. Seamus got out his wand, repaired the bed hangings, and vanished behind them. Dean got into bed, rolled over, and fell silent. Neville, who appeared to have nothing more to say either, was gazing fondly at his moonlit cactus.

Harry lay back on his pillows while Ron bustled around the next bed, putting his things away. He felt shaken by the argument with Seamus, whom he had always liked very much. How many more people were going to suggest that he was lying or unhinged?

Had Dumbledore suffered like this all summer, as first the Wizengamot, then the International Confederation of Wizards had thrown him from their ranks? Was it anger at Harry, perhaps, that had stopped Dumbledore getting in touch with him for months? The two of them were in this together, after all; Dumbledore had believed Harry, announced his version of events to the whole school and then to the wider Wizarding community. Anyone who thought Harry was a liar had to think that Dumbledore was too or else that Dumbledore had been hoodwinked. . . .

They'll know we're right in the end, thought Harry miserably, as Ron got into bed and extinguished the last candle in the dormitory. But he wondered how many attacks like Seamus's he would have to endure before that time came.

PROFESSOR UMBRIDGE

$\int$ eamus dressed at top speed next morning and left the dormitory before Harry had even put on his socks.

"Does he think he'll turn into a nutter if he stays in a room with me too long?" asked Harry loudly, as the hem of Seamus's robes whipped out of sight.

"Don't worry about it, Harry," Dean muttered, hoisting his school-bag onto his shoulder. "He's just . . ." But apparently he was unable to say exactly what Seamus was, and after a slightly awkward pause followed him out of the room.

Neville and Ron both gave Harry it's-his-problem-not-yours looks, but Harry was not much consoled. How much more of this was he going to have to take?

"What's the matter?" asked Hermione five minutes later, catching up with Harry and Ron halfway across the common room as they all headed toward breakfast. "You look absolutely — oh for heaven's sake."

She was staring at the common room notice board, where a large new sign had been put up.

GALLONS OF GALLEONS!
Pocket money failing to keep pace with your outgoings?
Like to earn a little extra gold?

➤━━━━━✦━━━━━◄

Contact Fred and George Weasley,
Gryffindor common room,
for simple, part-time, virtually painless jobs
(WE REGRET THAT ALL WORK IS UNDERTAKEN AT APPLICANT'S OWN RISK)

"They are the limit," said Hermione grimly, taking down the sign, which Fred and George had pinned up over a poster giving the date of the first Hogsmeade weekend in October. "We'll have to talk to them, Ron."

Ron looked positively alarmed.

"Why?"

"Because we're prefects!" said Hermione, as they climbed out through the portrait hole. "It's up to us to stop this kind of thing!"

Ron said nothing; Harry could tell from his glum expression that the prospect of stopping Fred and George doing exactly what they liked was not one that he found inviting.

"Anyway, what's up, Harry?" Hermione continued, as they walked down a flight of stairs lined with portraits of old witches and wizards, all of whom ignored them, being engrossed in their own conversation. "You look really angry about something."

"Seamus reckons Harry's lying about You-Know-Who," said Ron succinctly, when Harry did not respond.

Hermione, whom Harry had expected to react angrily on his behalf, sighed.

"Yes, Lavender thinks so too," she said gloomily.

"Been having a nice little chat with her about whether or not I'm a lying, attention-seeking prat, have you?" Harry said loudly.

"No," said Hermione calmly, "I told her to keep her big fat mouth shut about you, actually. And it would be quite nice if you stopped jumping down Ron's and my throats, Harry, because if you haven't noticed, we're on your side."

There was a short pause.

"Sorry," said Harry in a low voice.

"That's quite all right," said Hermione with dignity. Then she shook her head. "Don't you remember what Dumbledore said at the end-of-term feast last year?"

Harry and Ron both looked at her blankly, and Hermione sighed again.

"About You-Know-Who. He said, '*His gift for spreading discord and enmity is very great. We can fight it only by showing an equally strong bond of friendship and trust —*'"

"How do you remember stuff like that?" asked Ron, looking at her in admiration.

"I listen, Ron," said Hermione with a touch of asperity.

"So do I, but I still couldn't tell you exactly what —"

"The point," Hermione pressed on loudly, "is that this sort of thing is exactly what Dumbledore was talking about. You-Know-Who's only been back two months, and we've started fighting among ourselves. And the Sorting Hat's warning was the same — stand together, be united —"

"And Harry said it last night," retorted Ron, "if that means we're supposed to get matey with the Slytherins, fat chance."

"Well, I think it's a pity we're not trying for a bit of inter-House unity," said Hermione crossly.

They had reached the foot of the marble staircase. A line of fourth-year Ravenclaws was crossing the entrance hall; they caught sight of Harry and hurried to form a tighter group, as though frightened he might attack stragglers.

"Yeah, we really ought to be trying to make friends with people like that," said Harry sarcastically.

They followed the Ravenclaws into the Great Hall, looking instinctively at the staff table as they entered. Professor Grubbly-Plank was chatting to Professor Sinistra, the Astronomy teacher, and Hagrid was once again conspicuous only by his absence. The enchanted ceiling above them echoed Harry's mood; it was a miserable rain-cloud gray.

"Dumbledore didn't even mention how long that Grubbly-Plank woman's staying," he said, as they made their way across to the Gryffindor table.

"Maybe . . ." said Hermione thoughtfully.

"What?" said both Harry and Ron together.

"Well . . . maybe he didn't want to draw attention to Hagrid not being here."

"What d'you mean, draw attention to it?" said Ron, half laughing. "How could we not notice?"

Before Hermione could answer, a tall black girl with long, braided hair had marched up to Harry.

"Hi, Angelina."

"Hi," she said briskly, "good summer?" And without waiting for an answer, "Listen, I've been made Gryffindor Quidditch Captain."

"Nice one," said Harry, grinning at her; he suspected Angelina's pep talks might not be as long-winded as Oliver Wood's had been, which could only be an improvement.

"Yeah, well, we need a new Keeper now Oliver's left. Tryouts are on Friday at five o'clock and I want the whole team there, all right? Then we can see how the new person'll fit in."

"Okay," said Harry, and she smiled at him and departed.

"I'd forgotten Wood had left," said Hermione vaguely, sitting down beside Ron and pulling a plate of toast toward her. "I suppose that will make quite a difference to the team?"

"I s'pose," said Harry, taking the bench opposite. "He was a good Keeper. . . ."

"Still, it won't hurt to have some new blood, will it?" said Ron.

With a *whoosh* and a clatter, hundreds of owls came soaring in through the upper windows. They descended all over the Hall, bringing letters and packages to their owners and showering the breakfasters with droplets of water; it was clearly raining hard outside. Hedwig was nowhere to be seen, but Harry was hardly surprised; his only correspondent was Sirius, and he doubted Sirius would have anything new to tell him after only twenty-four hours apart. Hermione, however, had to move her orange juice aside quickly to make way for a large damp barn owl bearing a sodden *Daily Prophet* in its beak.

"What are you still getting that for?" said Harry irritably, thinking of Seamus, as Hermione placed a Knut in the leather pouch on the owl's leg and it took off again. "I'm not bothering . . . load of rubbish."

"It's best to know what the enemy are saying," said Hermione darkly, and she unfurled the newspaper and disappeared behind it, not emerging until Harry and Ron had finished eating.

"Nothing," she said simply, rolling up the newspaper and laying it down by her plate. "Nothing about you or Dumbledore or anything."

Professor McGonagall was now moving along the table handing out schedules.

"Look at today!" groaned Ron. "History of Magic, double Potions, Divination, and double Defense Against the Dark Arts . . . Binns, Snape, Trelawney, and that Umbridge woman all in one day! I wish Fred and George'd hurry up and get those Skiving Snackboxes sorted. . . ."

"Do mine ears deceive me?" said Fred, arriving with George and squeezing onto the bench beside Harry. "Hogwarts prefects surely don't wish to skive off lessons?"

"Look what we've got today," said Ron grumpily, shoving his schedule under Fred's nose. "That's the worst Monday I've ever seen."

"Fair point, little bro," said Fred, scanning the column. "You can have a bit of Nosebleed Nougat cheap if you like."

"Why's it cheap?" said Ron suspiciously.

"Because you'll keep bleeding till you shrivel up, we haven't got an antidote yet," said George, helping himself to a kipper.

"Cheers," said Ron moodily, pocketing his schedule, "but I think I'll take the lessons."

"And speaking of your Skiving Snackboxes," said Hermione, eyeing Fred and George beadily, "you can't advertise for testers on the Gryffindor notice board."

"Says who?" said George, looking astonished.

"Says me," said Hermione. "And Ron."

"Leave me out of it," said Ron hastily.

Hermione glared at him. Fred and George sniggered.

"You'll be singing a different tune soon enough, Hermione," said Fred, thickly buttering a crumpet. "You're starting your fifth year, you'll be begging us for a Snackbox before long."

"And why would starting fifth year mean I want a Skiving Snackbox?" asked Hermione.

"Fifth year's O.W.L. year," said George.

"So?"

"So you've got your exams coming up, haven't you? They'll be keeping your noses so hard to that grindstone they'll be rubbed raw," said Fred with satisfaction.

"Half our year had minor breakdowns coming up to O.W.L.s," said George happily. "Tears and tantrums . . . Patricia Stimpson kept coming over faint. . . ."

"Kenneth Towler came out in boils, d'you remember?" said Fred reminiscently.

"That's 'cause you put Bulbadox Powder in his pajamas," said George.

"Oh yeah," said Fred, grinning. "I'd forgotten. . . . Hard to keep track sometimes, isn't it?"

"Anyway, it's a nightmare of a year, the fifth," said George. "If you care about exam results anyway. Fred and I managed to keep our spirits up somehow."

"Yeah . . . you got, what was it, three O.W.L.s each?" said Ron.

"Yep," said Fred unconcernedly. "But we feel our futures lie outside the world of academic achievement."

"We seriously debated whether we were going to bother coming back for our seventh year," said George brightly, "now that we've got —"

He broke off at a warning look from Harry, who knew George had been about to mention the Triwizard winnings he had given them.

"— now that we've got our O.W.L.s," George said hastily. "I mean, do we really need N.E.W.T.s? But we didn't think Mum could take us leaving school early, not on top of Percy turning out to be the world's biggest prat."

"We're not going to waste our last year here, though," said Fred, looking affectionately around at the Great Hall. "We're going to use it to do a bit of market research, find out exactly what the average Hogwarts student requires from his joke shop, carefully evaluate the results of our research, and then produce the products to fit the demand."

"But where are you going to get the gold to start a joke shop?" asked Hermione skeptically. "You're going to need all the ingredients and materials — and premises too, I suppose. . . ."

Harry did not look at the twins. His face felt hot; he deliberately dropped his fork and dived down to retrieve it. He heard Fred say overhead, "Ask us no questions and we'll tell you no lies, Hermione. C'mon, George, if we get there early we might be able to sell a few Extendable Ears before Herbology."

Harry emerged from under the table to see Fred and George walking away, each carrying a stack of toast.

"What did that mean?" said Hermione, looking from Harry to Ron. "'Ask us no questions . . .' Does that mean they've already got some gold to start a joke shop?"

"You know, I've been wondering about that," said Ron, his brow furrowed. "They bought me a new set of dress robes this summer, and I couldn't understand where they got the Galleons. . . ."

Harry decided it was time to steer the conversation out of these dangerous waters.

"D'you reckon it's true this year's going to be really tough? Because of the exams?"

"Oh yeah," said Ron. "Bound to be, isn't it? O.W.L.s are really important, affect the jobs you can apply for and everything. We get career advice too, later this year, Bill told me. So you can choose what N.E.W.T.s you want to do next year."

"D'you know what you want to do after Hogwarts?" Harry asked the other two, as they left the Great Hall shortly afterward and set off toward their History of Magic classroom.

"Not really," said Ron slowly. "Except . . . well . . ."

He looked slightly sheepish.

"What?" Harry urged him.

"Well, it'd be cool to be an Auror," said Ron in an offhand voice.

"Yeah, it would," said Harry fervently.

"But they're, like, the elite," said Ron. "You've got to be really good. What about you, Hermione?"

"I don't know," said Hermione. "I think I'd really like to do something worthwhile."

"An Auror's worthwhile!" said Harry.

"Yes, it is, but it's not the only worthwhile thing," said Hermione thoughtfully. "I mean, if I could take S.P.E.W. further . . ."

Harry and Ron carefully avoided looking at each other.

History of Magic was by common consent the most boring subject ever devised by Wizard-kind. Professor Binns, their ghost teacher, had a wheezy, droning voice that was almost guaranteed to cause severe drowsiness within ten minutes, five in warm weather. He never varied the form of their lessons, but lectured them without pausing while they took notes, or rather, gazed sleepily into space. Harry and Ron had so far managed to scrape passes in this subject only by copying Hermione's notes before exams; she alone seemed able to resist the soporific power of Binns's voice.

Today they suffered three-quarters of an hour's droning on the subject of giant wars. Harry heard just enough within the first ten minutes to appreciate dimly that in another teacher's hands this subject might have been mildly interesting, but then his brain disengaged, and he spent the remaining thirty-five minutes playing hangman on a corner of his parchment with Ron, while Hermione shot them filthy looks out of the corner of her eye.

"How would it be," she asked them coldly as they left the classroom for break (Binns drifting away through the blackboard), "if I refused to lend you my notes this year?"

"We'd fail our O.W.L.s," said Ron. "If you want that on your conscience, Hermione . . ."

"Well, you'd deserve it," she snapped. "You don't even try to listen to him, do you?"

"We do try," said Ron. "We just haven't got your brains or your memory or your concentration — you're just cleverer than we are — is it nice to rub it in?"

"Oh, don't give me that rubbish," said Hermione, but she looked slightly mollified as she led the way out into the damp courtyard.

A fine misty drizzle was falling, so that the people standing in huddles around the yard looked blurred at the edges. Harry, Ron, and Hermione chose a secluded corner under a heavily dripping balcony, turning up the collars of their robes against the chilly September air and talking about what Snape was likely to set them in the first lesson of the year. They had got as far as agreeing that it was likely to be something extremely difficult, just to catch them off guard after a two-month holiday, when someone walked around the corner toward them.

"Hello, Harry!"

It was Cho Chang and what was more, she was on her own again. This was most unusual: Cho was almost always surrounded by a gang of giggling girls; Harry remembered the agony of trying to get her by herself to ask her to the Yule Ball.

"Hi," said Harry, feeling his face grow hot. *At least you're not covered in Stinksap this time,* he told himself. Cho seemed to be thinking along the same lines.

"You got that stuff off, then?"

"Yeah," said Harry, trying to grin as though the memory of their last meeting was funny as opposed to mortifying. "So did you . . . er . . . have a good summer?"

The moment he had said this he wished he hadn't: Cedric had been Cho's boyfriend and the memory of his death must have affected her holiday almost as badly as it had affected Harry's. . . . Something seemed to tauten in her face, but she said, "Oh, it was all right, you know. . . ."

"Is that a Tornados badge?" Ron demanded suddenly, pointing at the front of Cho's robes, to which a sky-blue badge emblazoned with a double gold T was pinned. "You don't support them, do you?"

"Yeah, I do," said Cho.

"Have you always supported them, or just since they started winning the league?" said Ron, in what Harry considered an unnecessarily accusatory tone of voice.

"I've supported them since I was six," said Cho coolly. "Anyway . . . see you, Harry."

She walked away. Hermione waited until Cho was halfway across the courtyard before rounding on Ron.

"You are so tactless!"

"What? I only asked her if —"

"Couldn't you tell she wanted to talk to Harry on her own?"

"So? She could've done, I wasn't stopping —"

"What on earth were you attacking her about her Quidditch team for?"

"Attacking? I wasn't attacking her, I was only —"

"Who *cares* if she supports the Tornados?"

"Oh, come on, half the people you see wearing those badges only bought them last season —"

"But what does it *matter*?"

"It means they're not real fans, they're just jumping on the bandwagon —"

"That's the bell," said Harry listlessly, because Ron and Hermione were bickering too loudly to hear it. They did not stop arguing all the way down to Snape's dungeon, which gave Harry plenty of time to reflect that between Neville and Ron he would be lucky ever to have two minutes' conversation with Cho that he could look back on without wanting to leave the country.

And yet, he thought, as they joined the queue lining up outside Snape's classroom door, she had chosen to come and talk to him, hadn't she? She had been Cedric's girlfriend; she could easily have hated Harry for coming out of the Triwizard maze alive when Cedric had died, yet she was talking to him in a perfectly friendly way, not as though she thought him mad, or a liar, or in some horrible way responsible for Cedric's death. . . . Yes, she had definitely chosen to come and talk to him, and that made the second time in two days . . . and at this thought, Harry's spirits rose. Even the ominous sound of Snape's dungeon door creaking open did not puncture the small, hopeful bubble that seemed to have swelled in his chest. He filed into the classroom behind Ron and Hermione and followed them to their usual table at the back, ignoring the huffy, irritable noises now issuing from both of them.

"Settle down," said Snape coldly, shutting the door behind him.

There was no real need for the call to order; the moment the class had heard the door close, quiet had fallen and all fidgeting stopped. Snape's mere presence was usually enough to ensure a class's silence.

"Before we begin today's lesson," said Snape, sweeping over to his desk and staring around at them all, "I think it appropriate to remind you that next June you will be sitting an important examination, during which you will prove how much you have learned about the composition and use of magical potions. Moronic though some of this class undoubtedly are, I expect you to scrape an 'Acceptable' in your O.W.L., or suffer my . . . displeasure."

His gaze lingered this time upon Neville, who gulped.

"After this year, of course, many of you will cease studying with me," Snape went on. "I take only the very best into my N.E.W.T. Potions class, which means that some of us will certainly be saying good-bye."

His eyes rested on Harry and his lip curled. Harry glared back, feeling a grim pleasure at the idea that he would be able to give up Potions after fifth year.

"But we have another year to go before that happy moment of farewell," said Snape softly, "so whether you are intending to attempt N.E.W.T. or not, I advise all of you to concentrate your efforts upon maintaining the high-pass level I have come to expect from my O.W.L. students.

"Today we will be mixing a potion that often comes up at Ordinary Wizarding Level: the Draught of Peace, a potion to calm anxiety and soothe agitation. Be warned: If you are too heavy-handed with the ingredients you will put the drinker into a heavy and sometimes irreversible sleep, so you will need to pay close attention to what you are doing." On Harry's left, Hermione sat up a little straighter, her expression one of the utmost attentiveness. "The ingredients and method" — Snape flicked his wand — "are on the blackboard" — (they appeared there) — "you will find everything you need" — he flicked his wand again — "in the store cupboard" — (the door of the said cupboard sprang open) — "you have an hour and a half. . . . Start."

Just as Harry, Ron, and Hermione had predicted, Snape could hardly have set them a more difficult, fiddly potion. The ingredients had to be added to the cauldron in precisely the right order and quantities; the mixture had to be stirred exactly the right number of times, firstly in clockwise, then in counterclockwise directions; the heat of the flames on which it was simmering had to be lowered to exactly the right level for a specific number of minutes before the final ingredient was added.

"A light silver vapor should now be rising from your potion," called Snape, with ten minutes left to go.

Harry, who was sweating profusely, looked desperately around the dungeon. His own cauldron was issuing copious amounts of dark gray steam; Ron's was spitting green sparks. Seamus was feverishly prodding the flames at the base of his cauldron with the tip of his wand, as they had gone out. The surface of Hermione's potion, however, was a shimmering mist of silver vapor, and as Snape swept by he looked down his hooked nose at it without comment, which meant that he could find nothing to criticize. At Harry's cauldron, however, Snape stopped, looking down at Harry with a horrible smirk on his face.

"Potter, what is this supposed to be?"

The Slytherins at the front of the class all looked up eagerly; they loved hearing Snape taunt Harry.

"The Draught of Peace," said Harry tensely.

"Tell me, Potter," said Snape softly, "can you read?"

Draco Malfoy laughed.

"Yes, I can," said Harry, his fingers clenched tightly around his wand.

"Read the third line of the instructions for me, Potter."

Harry squinted at the blackboard; it was not easy to make out the instructions through the haze of multicolored steam now filling the dungeon.

"'Add powdered moonstone, stir three times counterclockwise, allow to simmer for seven minutes, then add two drops of syrup of hellebore.'"

His heart sank. He had not added syrup of hellebore, but had proceeded straight to the fourth line of the instructions after allowing his potion to simmer for seven minutes.

"Did you do everything on the third line, Potter?"

"No," said Harry very quietly.

"I beg your pardon?"

"No," said Harry, more loudly. "I forgot the hellebore. . . ."

"I know you did, Potter, which means that this mess is utterly worthless. *Evanesco.*"

The contents of Harry's potion vanished; he was left standing foolishly beside an empty cauldron.

"Those of you who *have* managed to read the instructions, fill one flagon with a sample of your potion, label it clearly with your name, and bring it up to my desk for testing," said Snape. "Homework: twelve inches of parchment on the properties of moonstone and its uses in potion-making, to be handed in on Thursday."

While everyone around him filled their flagons, Harry cleared away his things, seething. His potion had been no worse than Ron's, which was now giving off a foul odor of bad eggs, or Neville's, which had achieved the consistency of just-mixed cement and which Neville was now having to gouge out of his cauldron, yet it was he, Harry, who would be receiving zero marks for the day's work. He stuffed his wand back into his bag and slumped down onto his seat, watching everyone else march up to Snape's desk with filled and corked flagons. When at long last the bell rang, Harry was first out of the dungeon and had already started his lunch by the time Ron and Hermione joined him in the Great Hall. The ceiling had turned an even murkier gray during the morning. Rain was lashing the high windows.

"That was really unfair," said Hermione consolingly, sitting down next to Harry and helping herself to shepherd's pie. "Your potion wasn't nearly as bad as Goyle's, when he put it in his flagon the whole thing shattered and set his robes on fire."

"Yeah, well," said Harry, glowering at his plate, "since when has Snape ever been fair to me?"

Neither of the others answered; all three of them knew that Snape and Harry's mutual enmity had been absolute from the moment Harry had set foot in Hogwarts.

"I did think he might be a bit better this year," said Hermione in a disappointed voice. "I mean . . . you know . . ." She looked carefully around; there were half a dozen empty seats on either side of them and nobody was passing the table. ". . . Now he's in the Order and everything."

"Poisonous toadstools don't change their spots," said Ron sagely. "Anyway, I've always thought Dumbledore was cracked trusting Snape, where's the evidence he ever really stopped working for You-Know-Who?"

"I think Dumbledore's probably got plenty of evidence, even if he doesn't share it with you, Ron," snapped Hermione.

"Oh, shut up, the pair of you," said Harry heavily, as Ron opened his mouth to argue back. Hermione and Ron both froze, looking angry and offended. "Can't you give it a rest?" he said. "You're always having a go at each other, it's driving me mad." And abandoning his shepherd's pie, he swung his schoolbag back over his shoulder and left them sitting there.

He walked up the marble staircase two steps at a time, past the many students hurrying toward lunch. The anger that had just flared so unexpectedly still blazed inside him, and the vision of Ron and

Hermione's shocked faces afforded him a sense of deep satisfaction. *Serve them right,* he thought. *Why can't they give it a rest? . . . Bickering all the time . . . It's enough to drive anyone up the wall. . . .*

He passed the large picture of Sir Cadogan the knight on a landing; Sir Cadogan drew his sword and brandished it fiercely at Harry, who ignored him.

"Come back, you scurvy dog, stand fast and fight!" yelled Sir Cadogan in a muffled voice from behind his visor, but Harry merely walked on, and when Sir Cadogan attempted to follow him by running into a neighboring picture, he was rebuffed by its inhabitant, a large and angry-looking wolfhound.

Harry spent the rest of the lunch hour sitting alone underneath the trapdoor at the top of North Tower, and consequently he was the first to ascend the silver ladder that led to Sybill Trelawney's classroom when the bell rang.

Divination was Harry's least favorite class after Potions, which was due mainly to Professor Trelawney's habit of predicting his premature death every few lessons. A thin woman, heavily draped in shawls and glittering with strings of beads, she always reminded Harry of some kind of insect, with her glasses hugely magnifying her eyes. She was busy putting copies of battered, leather-bound books on each of the spindly little tables with which her room was littered when Harry entered the room, but so dim was the light cast by the lamps covered by scarves and the low-burning, sickly-scented fire that she appeared not to notice him as he took a seat in the shadows. The rest of the class arrived over the next five minutes. Ron emerged from the trapdoor, looked around carefully, spotted Harry and made directly for him, or as directly as he could while having to wend his way between tables, chairs, and overstuffed poufs.

"Hermione and me have stopped arguing," he said, sitting down beside Harry.

"Good," grunted Harry.

"But Hermione says she thinks it would be nice if you stopped taking out your temper on us," said Ron.

"I'm not —"

"I'm just passing on the message," said Ron, talking over him. "But I reckon she's right. It's not our fault how Seamus and Snape treat you."

"I never said it —"

"Good day," said Professor Trelawney in her usual misty, dreamy voice, and Harry broke off, feeling both annoyed and slightly ashamed of himself again. "And welcome back to Divination. I have, of course, been following your fortunes most carefully over the holidays, and am delighted to see that you have all returned to Hogwarts safely — as, of course, I knew you would.

"You will find on the tables before you copies of *The Dream Oracle,* by Inigo Imago. Dream interpretation is a most important means of divining the future and one that may very probably be tested in your O.W.L. Not, of course, that I believe examination passes or failures are of the remotest importance when it comes to the sacred art of divination. If you have the Seeing Eye, certificates and grades matter very little. However, the headmaster likes you to sit the examination, so . . ."

Her voice trailed away delicately, leaving them all in no doubt that Professor Trelawney considered her subject above such sordid matters as examinations.

"Turn, please, to the introduction and read what Imago has to say on the matter of dream interpretation. Then divide into pairs. Use *The Dream Oracle* to interpret each other's most recent dreams. Carry on."

The one good thing to be said for this lesson was that it was not a double period. By the time they had all finished reading the introduction of the book, they had barely ten minutes left for dream interpretation. At the table next to Harry and Ron, Dean had paired up with Neville, who immediately embarked on a long-winded explanation of a nightmare involving a pair of giant scissors wearing his grandmother's best hat; Harry and Ron merely looked at each other glumly.

"I never remember my dreams," said Ron. "You say one."

"You must remember one of them," said Harry impatiently.

He was not going to share his dreams with anyone. He knew perfectly well what his regular nightmare about a graveyard meant, he did not need Ron or Professor Trelawney or the stupid *Dream Oracle* to tell him that. . . .

"Well, I had one that I was playing Quidditch the other night," said Ron, screwing up his face in an effort to remember. "What d'you reckon that means?"

"Probably that you're going to be eaten by a giant marshmallow or something," said Harry, turning the pages of *The Dream Oracle* without interest.

It was very dull work looking up bits of dreams in the *Oracle* and Harry was not cheered up when Professor Trelawney set them the task of keeping a dream diary for a month as homework. When the bell went, he and Ron led the way back down the ladder, Ron grumbling loudly.

"D'you realize how much homework we've got already? Binns set us a foot-and-a-half-long essay on giant wars, Snape wants a foot on the use of moonstones, and now we've got a month's dream diary from Trelawney! Fred and George weren't wrong about O.W.L. year, were they? That Umbridge woman had better not give us any. . . ."

When they entered the Defense Against the Dark Arts classroom they found Professor Umbridge already seated at the teacher's desk, wearing the fluffy pink cardigan of the night before and the black velvet bow on top of her head. Harry was again reminded forcibly of a large fly perched unwisely on top of an even larger toad.

The class was quiet as it entered the room; Professor Umbridge was, as yet, an unknown quantity and nobody knew yet how strict a disciplinarian she was likely to be.

"Well, good afternoon!" she said when finally the whole class had sat down.

A few people mumbled "Good afternoon," in reply.

"Tut, tut," said Professor Umbridge. "*That* won't do, now, will it? I should like you, please, to reply 'Good afternoon, Professor Umbridge.' One more time, please. Good afternoon, class!"

"Good afternoon, Professor Umbridge," they chanted back at her.

"There, now," said Professor Umbridge sweetly. "That wasn't too difficult, was it? Wands away and quills out, please."

Many of the class exchanged gloomy looks; the order "wands away" had never yet been followed by a lesson they had found interesting. Harry shoved his wand back inside his bag and pulled out quill, ink, and parchment. Professor Umbridge opened her handbag, extracted her own wand, which was an unusually short one, and tapped the blackboard sharply with it; words appeared on the board at once:

Defense Against the Dark Arts
A Return to Basic Principles

"Well now, your teaching in this subject has been rather disrupted and fragmented, hasn't it?" stated Professor Umbridge, turning to face the class with her hands clasped neatly in front of her. "The constant changing of teachers, many of whom do not seem to have followed any Ministry-approved curriculum, has unfortunately resulted in your being far below the standard we would expect to see in your O.W.L. year.

"You will be pleased to know, however, that these problems are now to be rectified. We will be following a carefully structured, theory-centered, Ministry-approved course of defensive magic this year. Copy down the following, please."

She rapped the blackboard again; the first message vanished and was replaced by:

Course aims:

1. *Understanding the principles underlying defensive magic.*
2. *Learning to recognize situations in which defensive magic can legally be used.*
3. *Placing the use of defensive magic in a context for practical use.*

For a couple of minutes the room was full of the sound of scratching quills on parchment. When everyone had copied down Professor Umbridge's three course aims she said, "Has everybody got a copy of *Defensive Magical Theory* by Wilbert Slinkhard?"

There was a dull murmur of assent throughout the class.

"I think we'll try that again," said Professor Umbridge. "When I ask you a question, I should like you to reply 'Yes, Professor Umbridge,' or 'No, Professor Umbridge.' So, has everyone got a copy of *Defensive Magical Theory* by Wilbert Slinkhard?"

"Yes, Professor Umbridge," rang through the room.

"Good," said Professor Umbridge. "I should like you to turn to page five and read chapter one, 'Basics for Beginners.' There will be no need to talk."

Professor Umbridge left the blackboard and settled herself in the chair behind the teacher's desk, observing them all with those pouchy toad's eyes. Harry turned to page five of his copy of *Defensive Magical Theory* and started to read.

It was desperately dull, quite as bad as listening to Professor Binns. He felt his concentration sliding away from him; he had soon read the same line half a dozen times without taking in more than the first few words. Several silent minutes passed. Next to him, Ron was absent-mindedly turning his quill over and over in his fingers, staring at the same spot on the page. Harry looked right and received a surprise to shake him out of his torpor. Hermione had not even opened her copy of *Defensive Magical Theory.* She was staring fixedly at Professor Umbridge with her hand in the air.

Harry could not remember Hermione ever neglecting to read when instructed to, or indeed resisting the temptation to open any book that came under her nose. He looked at her questioningly, but she merely shook her head slightly to indicate that she was not about to answer questions, and continued to stare at Professor Umbridge, who was looking just as resolutely in another direction.

After several more minutes had passed, however, Harry was not the only one watching Hermione. The chapter they had been instructed to read was so tedious that more and more people were choosing to watch Hermione's mute attempt to catch Professor Umbridge's eye than to struggle on with "Basics for Beginners."

When more than half the class were staring at Hermione rather than at their books, Professor Umbridge seemed to decide that she could ignore the situation no longer.

"Did you want to ask something about the chapter, dear?" she asked Hermione, as though she had only just noticed her.

"Not about the chapter, no," said Hermione.

"Well, we're reading just now," said Professor Umbridge, showing her small, pointed teeth. "If you have other queries we can deal with them at the end of class."

"I've got a query about your course aims," said Hermione.

Professor Umbridge raised her eyebrows.

"And your name is — ?"

"Hermione Granger," said Hermione.

"Well, Miss Granger, I think the course aims are perfectly clear if you read them through carefully," said Professor Umbridge in a voice of determined sweetness.

"Well, I don't," said Hermione bluntly. "There's nothing written up there about *using* defensive spells."

There was a short silence in which many members of the class turned their heads to frown at the three course aims still written on the blackboard.

"*Using* defensive spells?" Professor Umbridge repeated with a little laugh. "Why, I can't imagine any situation arising in my classroom that would require you to *use* a defensive spell, Miss Granger. You surely aren't expecting to be attacked during class?"

"We're not going to use magic?" Ron ejaculated loudly.

"Students raise their hands when they wish to speak in my class, Mr. — ?"

"Weasley," said Ron, thrusting his hand into the air.

Professor Umbridge, smiling still more widely, turned her back on him. Harry and Hermione immediately raised their hands too. Professor Umbridge's pouchy eyes lingered on Harry for a moment before she addressed Hermione.

"Yes, Miss Granger? You wanted to ask something else?"

"Yes," said Hermione. "Surely the whole point of Defense Against the Dark Arts is to practice defensive spells?"

"Are you a Ministry-trained educational expert, Miss Granger?" asked Professor Umbridge in her falsely sweet voice.

"No, but —"

"Well then, I'm afraid you are not qualified to decide what the 'whole point' of any class is. Wizards much older and cleverer than you have devised our new program of study. You will be learning about defensive spells in a secure, risk-free way —"

"What use is that?" said Harry loudly. "If we're going to be attacked it won't be in a —"

"*Hand,* Mr. Potter!" sang Professor Umbridge.

Harry thrust his fist in the air. Professor Umbridge promptly turned away from him again, but now several other people had their hands up too.

"And your name is?" Professor Umbridge said to Dean.

"Dean Thomas."

"Well, Mr. Thomas?"

"Well, it's like Harry said, isn't it?" said Dean. "If we're going to be attacked, it won't be risk-free —"

"I repeat," said Professor Umbridge, smiling in a very irritating fashion at Dean, "do you expect to be attacked during my classes?"

"No, but —"

Professor Umbridge talked over him.

"I do not wish to criticize the way things have been run in this school," she said, an unconvincing smile stretching her wide mouth, "but you have been exposed to some very irresponsible wizards in this class, very irresponsible indeed — not to mention," she gave a nasty little laugh, "extremely dangerous half-breeds."

"If you mean Professor Lupin," piped up Dean Thomas angrily, "he was the best we ever —"

"*Hand,* Mr. Thomas! As I was saying — you have been introduced to spells that have been complex, inappropriate to your age group, and potentially lethal. You have been frightened into believing that you are likely to meet Dark attacks every other day —"

"No we haven't," Hermione said, "we just —"

"*Your hand is not up, Miss Granger!*"

Hermione put up her hand; Professor Umbridge turned away from her.

"It is my understanding that my predecessor not only performed illegal curses in front of you, he actually performed them *on* you —"

"Well, he turned out to be a maniac, didn't he?" said Dean Thomas hotly. "Mind you, we still learned loads —"

"*Your hand is not up, Mr. Thomas!*" trilled Professor Umbridge. "Now, it is the view of the Ministry that a theoretical knowledge will be more than sufficient to get you through your examination, which, after all, is what school is all about. And your name is?" she added, staring at Parvati, whose hand had just shot up.

"Parvati Patil, and isn't there a practical bit in our Defense Against the Dark Arts O.W.L.? Aren't we supposed to show that we can actually do the countercurses and things?"

"As long as you have studied the theory hard enough, there is no reason why you should not be able to perform the spells under carefully controlled examination conditions," said Professor Umbridge dismissively.

"Without ever practicing them before?" said Parvati incredulously. "Are you telling us that the first time we'll get to do the spells will be during our exam?"

"I repeat, as long as you have studied the theory hard enough —"

"And what good's theory going to be in the real world?" said Harry loudly, his fist in the air again.

Professor Umbridge looked up.

"This is school, Mr. Potter, not the real world," she said softly.

"So we're not supposed to be prepared for what's waiting out there?"

"There is nothing waiting out there, Mr. Potter."

"Oh yeah?" said Harry. His temper, which seemed to have been bubbling just beneath the surface all day, was reaching boiling point.

"Who do you imagine wants to attack children like yourselves?" inquired Professor Umbridge in a horribly honeyed voice.

"Hmm, let's think . . ." said Harry in a mock thoughtful voice, "maybe *Lord Voldemort*?"

Ron gasped; Lavender Brown uttered a little scream; Neville slipped sideways off his stool. Professor Umbridge, however, did not flinch. She was staring at Harry with a grimly satisfied expression on her face.

"Ten points from Gryffindor, Mr. Potter."

The classroom was silent and still. Everyone was staring at either Umbridge or Harry.

"Now, let me make a few things quite plain."

Professor Umbridge stood up and leaned toward them, her stubby-fingered hands splayed on her desk.

"You have been told that a certain Dark wizard has returned from the dead —"

"He wasn't dead," said Harry angrily, "but yeah, he's returned!"

"Mr.-Potter-you-have-already-lost-your-House-ten-points-do-not-make-matters-worse-for-yourself," said Professor Umbridge in one breath without looking at him. "As I was saying, you have been informed that a certain Dark wizard is at large once again. *This is a lie.*"

"It is NOT a lie!" said Harry. "I saw him, I fought him!"

"Detention, Mr. Potter!" said Professor Umbridge triumphantly. "Tomorrow evening. Five o'clock. My office. I repeat, *this is a lie.* The Ministry of Magic guarantees that you are not in danger from any Dark wizard. If you are still worried, by all means come and see me outside class hours. If someone is alarming you with fibs about reborn Dark wizards, I would like to hear about it. I am here to help. I am your friend. And now, you will kindly continue your reading. Page five, 'Basics for Beginners.'"

Professor Umbridge sat down behind her desk again. Harry, however, stood up. Everyone was staring at him; Seamus looked half-scared, half-fascinated.

"Harry, no!" Hermione whispered in a warning voice, tugging at his sleeve, but Harry jerked his arm out of her reach.

"So, according to you, Cedric Diggory dropped dead of his own accord, did he?" Harry asked, his voice shaking.

There was a collective intake of breath from the class, for none of them, apart from Ron and Hermione, had ever heard Harry talk about what had happened on the night that Cedric had died. They stared avidly from Harry to Professor Umbridge, who had raised her eyes and was staring at him without a trace of a fake smile on her face.

"Cedric Diggory's death was a tragic accident," she said coldly.

"It was murder," said Harry. He could feel himself shaking. He had hardly talked to anyone about this, least of all thirty eagerly listening classmates. "Voldemort killed him, and you know it."

Professor Umbridge's face was quite blank. For a moment he thought she was going to scream at him. Then she said, in her softest, most sweetly girlish voice, "Come here, Mr. Potter, dear."

He kicked his chair aside, strode around Ron and Hermione and up to the teacher's desk. He could feel the rest of the class holding its breath. He felt so angry he did not care what happened next.

Professor Umbridge pulled a small roll of pink parchment out of her handbag, stretched it out on the desk, dipped her quill into a bottle of ink, and started scribbling, hunched over so that Harry could not see what she was writing. Nobody spoke. After a minute or so she rolled up the parchment and tapped it with her wand; it sealed itself seamlessly so that he could not open it.

"Take this to Professor McGonagall, dear," said Professor Umbridge, holding out the note to him.

He took it from her without saying a word and left the room, not even looking back at Ron and Hermione, and slamming the classroom door shut behind him. He walked very fast along the corridor, the note to McGonagall clutched tight in his hand, and turning a corner walked slap into Peeves the Poltergeist, a wide-faced little man floating on his back in midair, juggling several inkwells.

"Why, it's Potty Wee Potter!" cackled Peeves, allowing two of the inkwells to fall to the ground where they smashed and spattered the walls with ink; Harry jumped backward out of the way with a snarl.

"Get out of it, Peeves."

"Oooh, Crackpot's feeling cranky," said Peeves, pursuing Harry along the corridor, leering as he zoomed along above him. "What is it this time, my fine Potty friend? Hearing voices? Seeing visions? Speaking in" — Peeves blew a gigantic raspberry — "*tongues?*"

"I said, leave me ALONE!" Harry shouted, running down the

nearest flight of stairs, but Peeves merely slid down the banister on his back beside him.

> *"Oh, most think he's barking, the Potty wee lad,*
> *But some are more kindly and think he's just sad,*
> *But Peevesy knows better and says that he's mad —"*

"SHUT UP!"

A door to his left flew open and Professor McGonagall emerged from her office looking grim and slightly harassed.

"What on *earth* are you shouting about, Potter?" she snapped, as Peeves cackled gleefully and zoomed out of sight. "Why aren't you in class?"

"I've been sent to see you," said Harry stiffly.

"Sent? What do you mean, sent?"

He held out the note from Professor Umbridge. Professor McGonagall took it from him, frowning, slit it open with a tap of her wand, stretched it out, and began to read. Her eyes zoomed from side to side behind their square spectacles as she read what Umbridge had written, and with each line they became narrower.

"Come in here, Potter."

He followed her inside her study. The door closed automatically behind him.

"Well?" said Professor McGonagall, rounding on him. "Is this true?"

"Is what true?" Harry asked, rather more aggressively than he had intended. "Professor?" he added in an attempt to sound more polite.

"Is it true that you shouted at Professor Umbridge?"

"Yes," said Harry.

"You called her a liar?"

"Yes."

"You told her He-Who-Must-Not-Be-Named is back?"

"Yes."

Professor McGonagall sat down behind her desk, frowning at Harry. Then she said, "Have a biscuit, Potter."

"Have — what?"

"Have a biscuit," she repeated impatiently, indicating a tartan tin of cookies lying on top of one of the piles of papers on her desk. "And sit down."

There had been a previous occasion when Harry, expecting to be caned by Professor McGonagall, had instead been appointed by her to the Gryffindor Quidditch team. He sank into a chair opposite her and helped himself to a Ginger Newt, feeling just as confused and wrong-footed as he had done on that occasion.

Professor McGonagall set down Professor Umbridge's note and looked very seriously at Harry.

"Potter, you need to be careful."

Harry swallowed his mouthful of Ginger Newt and stared at her. Her tone of voice was not at all what he was used to; it was not brisk, crisp, and stern; it was low and anxious and somehow much more human than usual.

"Misbehavior in Dolores Umbridge's class could cost you much more than House points and a detention."

"What do you — ?"

"Potter, use your common sense," snapped Professor McGonagall, with an abrupt return to her usual manner. "You know where she comes from, you must know to whom she is reporting."

The bell rang for the end of the lesson. Overhead and all around came the elephantine sounds of hundreds of students on the move.

"It says here she's given you detention every evening this week, starting tomorrow," Professor McGonagall said, looking down at Umbridge's note again.

"Every evening this week!" Harry repeated, horrified. "But, Professor, couldn't you — ?"

"No, I couldn't," said Professor McGonagall flatly.

"But —"

"She is your teacher and has every right to give you detention. You will go to her room at five o'clock tomorrow for the first one. Just remember: Tread carefully around Dolores Umbridge."

"But I was telling the truth!" said Harry, outraged. "Voldemort's back, you know he is, Professor Dumbledore knows he is —"

"For heaven's sake, Potter!" said Professor McGonagall, straightening her glasses angrily (she had winced horribly when he had used Voldemort's name). "Do you really think this is about truth or lies? It's about keeping your head down and your temper under control!"

She stood up, nostrils wide and mouth very thin, and he stood too.

"Have another biscuit," she said irritably, thrusting the tin at him.

"No, thanks," said Harry coldly.

"Don't be ridiculous," she snapped.

He took one.

"Thanks," he said grudgingly.

"Didn't you listen to Dolores Umbridge's speech at the start-of-term feast, Potter?"

"Yeah," said Harry. "Yeah . . . she said . . . progress will be prohibited or . . . well, it meant that . . . that the Ministry of Magic is trying to interfere at Hogwarts."

Professor McGonagall eyed him for a moment, then sniffed, walked around her desk, and held open the door for him.

"Well, I'm glad you listen to Hermione Granger at any rate," she said, pointing him out of her office.

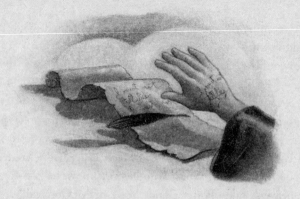

DETENTION WITH
DOLORES

Dinner in the Great Hall that night was not a pleasant experience for Harry. The news about his shouting match with Umbridge seemed to have traveled exceptionally fast even by Hogwarts standards. He heard whispers all around him as he sat eating between Ron and Hermione. The funny thing was that none of the whisperers seemed to mind him overhearing what they were saying about him — on the contrary, it was as though they were hoping he would get angry and start shouting again, so that they could hear his story firsthand.

"He says he saw Cedric Diggory murdered. . . ."

"He reckons he dueled with You-Know-Who. . . ."

"Come off it. . . ."

"Who does he think he's kidding?"

"Pur-*lease* . . ."

"What I don't get," said Harry in a shaking voice, laying down his knife and fork (his hands were trembling too much to hold them steady), "is why they all believed the story two months ago when Dumbledore told them. . . ."

"The thing is, Harry, I'm not sure they did," said Hermione grimly. "Oh, let's get out of here."

She slammed down her own knife and fork; Ron looked sadly at his half-finished apple pie but followed suit. People stared at them all the way out of the Hall.

"What d'you mean, you're not sure they believed Dumbledore?" Harry asked Hermione when they reached the first-floor landing.

"Look, you don't understand what it was like after it happened," said Hermione quietly. "You arrived back in the middle of the lawn clutching Cedric's dead body. . . . None of us saw what happened in the maze. . . . We just had Dumbledore's word for it that You-Know-Who had come back and killed Cedric and fought you."

"Which is the truth!" said Harry loudly.

"I know it is, Harry, so will you *please* stop biting my head off?" said Hermione wearily. "It's just that before the truth could sink in, everyone went home for the summer, where they spent two months reading about how you're a nutcase and Dumbledore's going senile!"

Rain pounded on the windowpanes as they strode along the empty corridors back to Gryffindor Tower. Harry felt as though his first day had lasted a week, but he still had a mountain of homework to do before bed. A dull pounding pain was developing over his right eye. He glanced out of a rain-washed window at the dark grounds as they turned into the Fat Lady's corridor. There was still no light in Hagrid's cabin.

"Mimbulus mimbletonia," said Hermione, before the Fat Lady could ask. The portrait swung open to reveal the hole behind and the three of them scrambled back through it.

The common room was almost empty; nearly everyone was still down at dinner. Crookshanks uncoiled himself from an armchair and trotted to meet them, purring loudly, and when Harry, Ron, and Hermione took their three favorite chairs at the fireside he leapt lightly into Hermione's lap and curled up there like a furry ginger cushion. Harry gazed into the flames, feeling drained and exhausted.

"*How* can Dumbledore have let this happen?" Hermione cried suddenly, making Harry and Ron jump; Crookshanks leapt off her, looking affronted. She pounded the arms of her chair in fury, so that bits of stuffing leaked out of the holes. "How can he let that terrible woman teach us? And in our O.W.L. year too!"

"Well, we've never had great Defense Against the Dark Arts teachers, have we?" said Harry. "You know what it's like, Hagrid told us, nobody wants the job, they say it's jinxed."

"Yes, but to employ someone who's actually refusing to let us do magic! *What's* Dumbledore playing at?"

"And she's trying to get people to spy for her," said Ron darkly. "Remember when she said she wanted us to come and tell her if we hear anyone saying You-Know-Who's back?"

"Of course she's here to spy on us all, that's obvious, why else would Fudge have wanted her to come?" snapped Hermione.

"Don't start arguing again," said Harry wearily, as Ron opened his mouth to retaliate. "Can't we just . . . Let's just do that homework, get it out of the way. . . ."

They collected their schoolbags from a corner and returned to the chairs by the fire. People were coming back from dinner now. Harry kept his face averted from the portrait hole, but could still sense the stares he was attracting.

"Shall we do Snape's stuff first?" said Ron, dipping his quill into his ink. "'*The properties . . . of moonstone . . . and its uses . . . in potion-making . . .*'" he muttered, writing the words across the top of his parchment as he spoke them. "There." He underlined the title, then looked up expectantly at Hermione.

"So what are the properties of moonstone and its uses in potion-making?"

But Hermione was not listening; she was squinting over into the far corner of the room, where Fred, George, and Lee Jordan were now sitting at the center of a knot of innocent-looking first years, all of whom were chewing something that seemed to have come out of a large pa-per bag that Fred was holding.

"No, I'm sorry, they've gone too far," she said, standing up and looking positively furious. "Come on, Ron."

"I — what?" said Ron, plainly playing for time. "No — come on, Hermione — we can't tell them off for giving out sweets. . . ."

"You know perfectly well that those are bits of Nosebleed Nougat or — or Puking Pastilles or —"

"Fainting Fancies?" Harry suggested quietly.

One by one, as though hit over the heads with invisible mallets, the first years were slumping unconscious in their seats; some slid right onto the floor, others merely hung over the arms of their chairs, their tongues lolling out. Most of the people watching were laughing; Her-mione, however, squared her shoulders and marched directly over to where Fred and George now stood with clipboards, closely observing the unconscious first years. Ron rose halfway out of his chair, hovered uncertainly for a moment or two, then muttered to Harry, "She's got it under control," before sinking as low in his chair as his lanky frame permitted.

"That's enough!" Hermione said forcefully to Fred and George, both of whom looked up in mild surprise.

"Yeah, you're right," said George, nodding, "this dosage looks strong enough, doesn't it?"

"I told you this morning, you can't test your rubbish on students!"

"We're paying them!" said Fred indignantly.

"I don't care, it could be dangerous!"

"Rubbish," said Fred.

"Calm down, Hermione, they're fine!" said Lee reassuringly as he walked from first year to first year, inserting purple sweets into their open mouths.

"Yeah, look, they're coming round now," said George.

A few of the first years were indeed stirring. Several looked so shocked to find themselves lying on the floor, or dangling off their chairs, that Harry was sure Fred and George had not warned them what the sweets were going to do.

"Feel all right?" said George kindly to a small dark-haired girl lying at his feet.

"I-I think so," she said shakily.

"Excellent," said Fred happily, but the next second Hermione had snatched both his clipboard and the paper bag of Fainting Fancies from his hands.

"It is NOT excellent!"

"'Course it is, they're alive, aren't they?" said Fred angrily.

"You can't do this, what if you made one of them really ill?"

"We're not going to make them ill, we've already tested them all on ourselves, this is just to see if everyone reacts the same —"

"If you don't stop doing it, I'm going to —"

"Put us in detention?" said Fred in an I'd-like-to-see-you-try-it voice.

"Make us write lines?" said George, smirking.

Onlookers all over the room were laughing. Hermione drew herself up to her full height; her eyes were narrowed and her bushy hair seemed to crackle with electricity.

"No," she said, her voice quivering with anger, "but I will write to your mother."

"You wouldn't," said George, horrified, taking a step back from her.

"Oh, yes, I would," said Hermione grimly. "I can't stop you eating the stupid things yourselves, but you're not giving them to first years."

Fred and George looked thunderstruck. It was clear that as far as they were concerned, Hermione's threat was way below the belt. With a last threatening look at them, she thrust Fred's clipboard and the bag of Fancies back into his arms and stalked back to her chair by the fire.

Ron was now so low in his seat that his nose was roughly level with his knees.

"Thank you for your support, Ron," Hermione said acidly.

"You handled it fine by yourself," Ron mumbled.

Hermione stared down at her blank piece of parchment for a few seconds, then said edgily, "Oh, it's no good, I can't concentrate now. I'm going to bed."

She wrenched her bag open; Harry thought she was about to put her books away, but instead she pulled out two misshapen woolly objects, placed them carefully on a table by the fireplace, covered them with a few screwed-up bits of parchment and a broken quill, and stood back to admire the effect.

"What in the name of Merlin are you doing?" said Ron, watching her as though fearful for her sanity.

"They're hats for house-elves," she said briskly, now stuffing her books back into her bag. "I did them over the summer. I'm a really slow knitter without magic, but now I'm back at school I should be able to make lots more."

"You're leaving out hats for the house-elves?" said Ron slowly. "And you're covering them up with rubbish first?"

"Yes," said Hermione defiantly, swinging her bag onto her back.

"That's not on," said Ron angrily. "You're trying to trick them into picking up the hats. You're setting them free when they might not want to be free."

"Of course they want to be free!" said Hermione at once, though her face was turning pink. "Don't you dare touch those hats, Ron!"

She left. Ron waited until she had disappeared through the door to the girls' dormitories, then cleared the rubbish off the woolly hats.

"They should at least see what they're picking up," he said firmly. "Anyway . . ." He rolled up the parchment on which he had written the title of Snape's essay. "There's no point trying to finish this now, I can't do it without Hermione, I haven't got a clue what you're supposed to do with moonstones, have you?"

Harry shook his head, noticing as he did so that the ache in his right temple was getting worse. He thought of the long essay on giant wars and the pain stabbed at him sharply. Knowing perfectly well that he would regret not finishing his homework tonight when the morning came, he piled his books back into his bag.

"I'm going to bed too."

He passed Seamus on the way to the door leading to the dormitories, but did not look at him. Harry had a fleeting impression that Seamus had opened his mouth to speak, but sped up, and reached the soothing peace of the stone spiral staircase without having to endure any more provocation.

The following day dawned just as leaden and rainy as the previous one. Hagrid was still absent from the staff table at breakfast.

"But on the plus side, no Snape today," said Ron bracingly.

Hermione yawned widely and poured herself some coffee. She looked mildly pleased about something, and when Ron asked her what she had to be so happy about, she simply said, "The hats have gone. Seems the house-elves do want freedom after all."

"I wouldn't bet on it," Ron told her cuttingly. "They might not count as clothes. They didn't look anything like hats to me, more like woolly bladders."

Hermione did not speak to him all morning.

Double Charms was succeeded by double Transfiguration. Professor Flitwick and Professor McGonagall both spent the first fifteen minutes of their lessons lecturing the class on the importance of O.W.L.s.

"What you must remember," said little Professor Flitwick squeakily, perched as ever on a pile of books so that he could see over the top of his desk, "is that these examinations may influence your futures for many years to come! If you have not already given serious thought to your careers, now is the time to do so. And in the meantime, I'm afraid, we shall be working harder than ever to ensure that you all do yourselves justice!"

They then spent more than an hour reviewing Summoning Charms, which according to Professor Flitwick were bound to come up in their O.W.L., and he rounded off the lesson by setting them their largest amount of Charms homework ever.

It was the same, if not worse, in Transfiguration.

"You cannot pass an O.W.L.," said Professor McGonagall grimly, "without serious application, practice, and study. I see no reason why everybody in this class should not achieve an O.W.L. in Transfiguration as long as they put in the work." Neville made a sad little disbelieving noise. "Yes, you too, Longbottom," said Professor McGonagall. "There's nothing wrong with your work except lack of confidence. So . . . today we are starting Vanishing Spells. These are easier than Conjuring Spells, which you would not usually attempt until N.E.W.T. level, but they are still among the most difficult magic you will be tested on in your O.W.L."

She was quite right; Harry found the Vanishing Spells horribly difficult. By the end of a double period, neither he nor Ron had managed to vanish the snails on which they were practicing, though Ron said hopefully that he thought his looked a bit paler. Hermione, on the other hand, successfully vanished her snail on the third attempt, earning her a ten-point bonus for Gryffindor from Professor McGonagall. She was the only person not given homework; everybody else was told to practice the spell overnight, ready for a fresh attempt on their snails the following afternoon.

Now panicking slightly about the amount of homework they had to do, Harry and Ron spent their lunch hour in the library looking up the uses of moonstones in potion-making. Still angry about Ron's slur on her woolly hats, Hermione did not join them. By the time they reached Care of Magical Creatures in the afternoon, Harry's head was aching again.

The day had become cool and breezy, and, as they walked down the sloping lawn toward Hagrid's cabin on the edge of the Forbidden Forest, they felt the occasional drop of rain on their faces. Professor Grubbly-Plank stood waiting for the class some ten yards from Hagrid's front door, a long trestle table in front of her laden with many twigs. As Harry and Ron reached her, a loud shout of laughter sounded behind them; turning, they saw Draco Malfoy striding toward them, surrounded by his usual gang of Slytherin cronies. He had clearly just said something highly amusing, because Crabbe, Goyle, Pansy Parkinson, and the rest continued to snigger heartily as they gathered around the trestle table. Judging by the fact that all of them kept looking over at Harry, he was able to guess the subject of the joke without too much difficulty.

"Everyone here?" barked Professor Grubbly-Plank, once all the Slytherins and Gryffindors had arrived. "Let's crack on then — who can tell me what these things are called?"

She indicated the heap of twigs in front of her. Hermione's hand shot into the air. Behind her back, Malfoy did a buck-toothed imitation of her jumping up and down in eagerness to answer a question. Pansy Parkinson gave a shriek of laughter that turned almost at once into a scream, as the twigs on the table leapt into the air and revealed themselves to be what looked like tiny pixieish creatures made of wood, each with knobbly brown arms and legs, two twiglike fingers at the end of each hand, and a funny, flat, barklike face in which a pair of beetle-brown eyes glittered.

"Ooooh!" said Parvati and Lavender, thoroughly irritating Harry: Anyone would have thought that Hagrid never showed them impressive creatures; admittedly the flobberworms had been a bit dull, but the salamanders and hippogriffs had been interesting enough, and the Blast-Ended Skrewts perhaps too much so.

"Kindly keep your voices down, girls!" said Professor Grubbly-Plank sharply, scattering a handful of what looked like brown rice among the stick-creatures, who immediately fell upon the food. "So — anyone know the names of these creatures? Miss Granger?"

"Bowtruckles," said Hermione. "They're tree-guardians, usually live in wand-trees."

"Five points for Gryffindor," said Professor Grubbly-Plank. "Yes, these are bowtruckles and, as Miss Granger rightly says, they generally live in trees whose wood is of wand quality. Anybody know what they eat?"

"Wood lice," said Hermione promptly, which explained why what Harry had taken for grains of brown rice were moving. "But fairy eggs if they can get them."

"Good girl, take another five points. So whenever you need leaves or wood from a tree in which a bowtruckle lodges, it is wise to have a gift of wood lice ready to distract or placate it. They may not look dangerous, but if angered they will gouge out human eyes with their fingers, which, as you can see, are very sharp and not at all desirable near the eyeballs. So if you'd like to gather closer, take a few wood lice and a bowtruckle — I have enough here for one between three — you can study them more closely. I want a sketch from each of you with all body parts labeled by the end of the lesson."

The class surged forward around the trestle table. Harry deliberately circled around the back so that he ended up right next to Professor Grubbly-Plank.

"Where's Hagrid?" he asked her, while everyone else was choosing bowtruckles.

"Never you mind," said Professor Grubbly-Plank repressively, which had been her attitude last time Hagrid had failed to turn up for a class too. Smirking all over his pointed face, Draco Malfoy leaned across Harry and seized the largest bowtruckle.

"Maybe," said Malfoy in an undertone, so that only Harry could hear him, "the stupid great oaf's got himself badly injured."

"Maybe you will if you don't shut up," said Harry out of the side of his mouth.

"Maybe he's been messing with stuff that's too *big* for him, if you get my drift."

Malfoy walked away, smirking over his shoulder at Harry, who suddenly felt sick. Did Malfoy know something? His father was a Death Eater, after all; what if he had information about Hagrid's fate that had not yet reached the Order's ears? He hurried back around the table to Ron and Hermione, who were squatting on the grass some distance away and attempting to persuade a bowtruckle to remain still long enough to draw it. Harry pulled out parchment and quill, crouched down beside the others, and related in a whisper what Malfoy had just said.

"Dumbledore would know if something had happened to Hagrid," said Hermione at once. "It's just playing into Malfoy's hands to look worried, it tells him we don't know exactly what's going on. We've got to ignore him, Harry. Here, hold the bowtruckle for a moment, just so I can draw its face. . . ."

"Yes," came Malfoy's clear drawl from the group nearest them, "Father was talking to the Minister just a couple of days ago, you know, and it sounds as though the Ministry's really determined to crack down on substandard teaching in this place. So even if that overgrown moron *does* show up again, he'll probably be sent packing straight away."

"OUCH!"

Harry had gripped the bowtruckle so hard that it had almost snapped; it had just taken a great retaliatory swipe at his hand with its sharp fingers, leaving two long deep cuts there. Harry dropped it; Crabbe and Goyle, who had already been guffawing at the idea of Hagrid being sacked, laughed still harder as the bowtruckle set off at full tilt toward the forest, a little, moving stickman soon swallowed up by the tree roots. When the bell echoed distantly over the grounds Harry rolled up his bloodstained bowtruckle picture and marched off to

Herbology with his hand wrapped in a handkerchief of Hermione's and Malfoy's derisive laughter still ringing in his ears.

"If he calls Hagrid a moron one more time . . ." snarled Harry.

"Harry, don't go picking a row with Malfoy, don't forget, he's a prefect now, he could make life difficult for you. . . ."

"Wow, I wonder what it'd be like to have a difficult life?" said Harry sarcastically. Ron laughed, but Hermione frowned. Together they traipsed across the vegetable patch. The sky still appeared unable to make up its mind whether it wanted to rain or not.

"I just wish Hagrid would hurry up and get back, that's all," said Harry in a low voice, as they reached the greenhouses. "And *don't* say that Grubbly-Plank woman's a better teacher!" he added threateningly.

"I wasn't going to," said Hermione calmly.

"Because she'll never be as good as Hagrid," said Harry firmly, fully aware that he had just experienced an exemplary Care of Magical Creatures lesson and was thoroughly annoyed about it.

The door of the nearest greenhouse opened and some fourth years spilled out of it, including Ginny.

"Hi," she said brightly as she passed. A few seconds later, Luna Lovegood emerged, trailing behind the rest of the class, a smudge of earth on her nose and her hair tied in a knot on the top of her head. When she saw Harry, her prominent eyes seemed to bulge excitedly and she made a beeline straight for him. Many of his classmates turned curiously to watch. Luna took a great breath and then said, without so much as a preliminary hello: "I believe He-Who-Must-Not-Be-Named is back, and I believe you fought him and escaped from him."

"Er — right," said Harry awkwardly. Luna was wearing what looked like a pair of orange radishes for earrings, a fact that Parvati and Lavender seemed to have noticed, as they were both giggling and pointing at her earlobes.

"You can laugh!" Luna said, her voice rising, apparently under the impression that Parvati and Lavender were laughing at what she had said rather than what she was wearing. "But people used to believe there were no such things as the Blibbering Humdinger or the Crumple-Horned Snorkack!"

"Well, they were right, weren't they?" said Hermione impatiently. "There *weren't* any such things as the Blibbering Humdinger or the Crumple-Horned Snorkack."

Luna gave her a withering look and flounced away, radishes swinging madly. Parvati and Lavender were not the only ones hooting with laughter now.

"D'you mind not offending the only people who believe me?" Harry asked Hermione as they made their way into class.

"Oh, for heaven's sake, Harry, you can do better than *her*," said Hermione. "Ginny's told me all about her, apparently she'll only believe in things as long as there's no proof at all. Well, I wouldn't expect anything else from someone whose father runs *The Quibbler*."

Harry thought of the sinister winged horses he had seen on the night he had arrived and how Luna had said she could see them too. His spirits sank slightly. Had she been lying? But before he could devote much more thought to the matter, Ernie Macmillan had stepped up to him.

"I want you to know, Potter," he said in a loud, carrying voice, "that it's not only weirdos who support you. I personally believe you one hundred percent. My family have always stood firm behind Dumbledore, and so do I."

"Er — thanks very much, Ernie," said Harry, taken aback but pleased. Ernie might be pompous on occasions like these, but Harry was in a mood to deeply appreciate a vote of confidence from somebody who was not wearing radishes in their ears. Ernie's words had certainly wiped the smile from Lavender Brown's face and, as he turned to talk to Ron and Hermione, Harry caught Seamus's expression, which looked both confused and defiant.

To nobody's surprise, Professor Sprout started their lesson by lecturing them about the importance of O.W.L.s. Harry wished all the teachers would stop doing this; he was starting to get an anxious, twisted feeling in his stomach every time he remembered how much homework he had to do, a feeling that worsened dramatically when Professor Sprout gave them yet another essay at the end of class. Tired and smelling strongly of dragon dung, Professor Sprout's preferred brand of fertilizer, the Gryffindors trooped back up to the castle, none of them talking very much; it had been another long day.

As Harry was starving, and he had his first detention with Umbridge at five o'clock, he headed straight for dinner without dropping off his bag in Gryffindor Tower so that he could bolt something down before facing whatever she had in store for him. He had barely reached the entrance of the Great Hall, however, when a loud and angry voice said, "Oy, Potter!"

"What now?" he muttered wearily, turning to face Angelina Johnson, who looked as though she was in a towering temper.

"I'll tell you what now," she said, marching straight up to him and poking him hard in the chest with her finger. "How come you've landed yourself in detention for five o'clock on Friday?"

"What?" said Harry. "Why . . . oh yeah, Keeper tryouts!"

"*Now* he remembers!" snarled Angelina. "Didn't I tell you I wanted to do a tryout with the *whole team,* and find someone who *fitted in with everyone*? Didn't I tell you I'd booked the Quidditch pitch specially? And now you've decided you're not going to be there!"

"I didn't decide not to be there!" said Harry, stung by the injustice of these words. "I got detention from that Umbridge woman, just because I told her the truth about You-Know-Who —"

"Well, you can just go straight to her and ask her to let you off on Friday," said Angelina fiercely, "and I don't care how you do it, tell her You-Know-Who's a figment of your imagination if you like, just *make sure you're there*!"

She stormed away.

"You know what?" Harry said to Ron and Hermione as they entered the Great Hall. "I think we'd better check with Puddlemere United whether Oliver Wood's been killed during a training session, because she seems to be channeling his spirit."

"What d'you reckon are the odds of Umbridge letting you off on Friday?" said Ron skeptically, as they sat down at the Gryffindor table.

"Less than zero," said Harry glumly, tipping lamb chops onto his plate and starting to eat. "Better try, though, hadn't I? I'll offer to do two more detentions or something, I dunno. . . ." He swallowed a mouthful of potato and added, "I hope she doesn't keep me too long this evening. You realize we've got to write three essays, practice Vanishing Spells for McGonagall, work out a countercharm for Flitwick, finish the bowtruckle drawing, and start that stupid dream diary for Trelawney?"

Ron moaned and for some reason glanced up at the ceiling.

"*And* it looks like it's going to rain."

"What's that got to do with our homework?" said Hermione, her eyebrows raised.

"Nothing," said Ron at once, his ears reddening.

At five to five Harry bade the other two good-bye and set off for Umbridge's office on the third floor. When he knocked on the door she said, "Come in," in a sugary voice. He entered cautiously, looking around.

He had known this office under three of its previous occupants. In the days when Gilderoy Lockhart had lived here it had been plastered in beaming portraits of its owner. When Lupin had occupied it, it was likely you would meet some fascinating Dark creature in a cage or tank if you came to call. In the impostor Moody's days it had been packed with various instruments and artifacts for the detection of wrongdoing and concealment.

Now, however, it looked totally unrecognizable. The surfaces had all been draped in lacy covers and cloths. There were several vases full of dried flowers, each residing on its own doily, and on one of the walls was a collection of ornamental plates, each decorated with a large Technicolored kitten wearing a different bow around its neck. These were so foul that Harry stared at them, transfixed, until Professor Umbridge spoke again.

"Good evening, Mr. Potter."

Harry started and looked around. He had not noticed her at first because she was wearing a luridly flowered set of robes that blended only too well with the tablecloth on the desk behind her.

"Evening," Harry said stiffly.

"Well, sit down," she said, pointing toward a small table draped in lace beside which she had drawn up a straight-backed chair. A piece of blank parchment lay on the table, apparently waiting for him.

"Er," said Harry, without moving. "Professor Umbridge? Er — before we start, I-I wanted to ask you a . . . a favor."

Her bulging eyes narrowed.

"Oh yes?"

"Well I'm . . . I'm on the Gryffindor Quidditch team. And I was supposed to be at the tryouts for the new Keeper at five o'clock on Friday and I was — was wondering whether I could skip detention that night and do it — do it another night . . . instead . . ."

He knew long before he reached the end of his sentence that it was no good.

"Oh no," said Umbridge, smiling so widely that she looked as though she had just swallowed a particularly juicy fly. "Oh no, no, no. This is your punishment for spreading evil, nasty, attention-seeking stories, Mr. Potter, and punishments certainly cannot be adjusted to suit the guilty one's convenience. No, you will come here at five o'clock tomorrow, and the next day, and on Friday too, and you will do your detentions as planned. I think it rather a good thing that you are missing something you really want to do. It ought to reinforce the lesson I am trying to teach you."

Harry felt the blood surge to his head and heard a thumping noise in his ears. So he told evil, nasty, attention-seeking stories, did he?

She was watching him with her head slightly to one side, still smiling widely, as though she knew exactly what he was thinking and was waiting to see whether he would start shouting again. With a massive effort Harry looked away from her, dropped his schoolbag beside the straight-backed chair, and sat down.

"There," said Umbridge sweetly, "we're getting better at controlling our temper already, aren't we? Now, you are going to be doing some lines for me, Mr. Potter. No, not with your quill," she added, as Harry bent down to open his bag. "You're going to be using a rather special one of mine. Here you are."

She handed him a long, thin black quill with an unusually sharp point.

"I want you to write *'I must not tell lies,'*" she told him softly.

"How many times?" Harry asked, with a creditable imitation of politeness.

"Oh, as long as it takes for the message to *sink in,*" said Umbridge sweetly. "Off you go."

She moved over to her desk, sat down, and bent over a stack of parchment that looked like essays for marking. Harry raised the sharp black quill and then realized what was missing.

"You haven't given me any ink," he said.

"Oh, you won't need ink," said Professor Umbridge with the merest suggestion of a laugh in her voice.

Harry placed the point of the quill on the paper and wrote: *I must not tell lies.*

He let out a gasp of pain. The words had appeared on the parchment in what appeared to be shining red ink. At the same time, the words had appeared on the back of Harry's right hand, cut into his skin as though traced there by a scalpel — yet even as he stared at the shining cut, the skin healed over again, leaving the place where it had been slightly redder than before but quite smooth.

Harry looked around at Umbridge. She was watching him, her wide, toadlike mouth stretched in a smile.

"Yes?"

"Nothing," said Harry quietly.

He looked back at the parchment, placed the quill upon it once more, wrote *I must not tell lies,* and felt the searing pain on the back of his hand for a second time; once again the words had been cut into his skin, once again they healed over seconds later.

And on it went. Again and again Harry wrote the words on the parchment in what he soon came to realize was not ink, but his own blood. And again and again the words were cut into the back of his hand, healed, and then reappeared the next time he set quill to parchment.

Darkness fell outside Umbridge's window. Harry did not ask when he would be allowed to stop. He did not even check his watch. He knew she was watching him for signs of weakness and he was not going to show any, not even if he had to sit here all night, cutting open his own hand with this quill. . . .

"Come here," she said, after what seemed hours.

He stood up. His hand was stinging painfully. When he looked down at it he saw that the cut had healed, but that the skin there was red raw.

"Hand," she said.

He extended it. She took it in her own. Harry repressed a shudder as she touched him with her thick, stubby fingers on which she wore a number of ugly old rings.

"Tut, tut, I don't seem to have made much of an impression yet," she said, smiling. "Well, we'll just have to try again tomorrow evening, won't we? You may go."

Harry left her office without a word. The school was quite deserted; it was surely past midnight. He walked slowly up the corridor then, when he had turned the corner and was sure that she would not hear him, broke into a run.

He had not had time to practice Vanishing Spells, had not written a single dream in his dream diary, and had not finished the drawing of the bowtruckle, nor had he written his essays. He skipped breakfast next morning to scribble down a couple of made-up dreams for Divination, their first lesson, and was surprised to find a disheveled Ron keeping him company.

"How come you didn't do it last night?" Harry asked, as Ron stared wildly around the common room for inspiration. Ron, who had been fast asleep when Harry got back to the dormitory, muttered something about "doing other stuff," bent low over his parchment, and scrawled a few words.

"That'll have to do," he said, slamming the diary shut, "I've said I dreamed I was buying a new pair of shoes, she can't make anything weird out of that, can she?"

They hurried off to North Tower together.

"How was detention with Umbridge, anyway? What did she make you do?"

Harry hesitated for a fraction of a second, then said, "Lines."

"That's not too bad, then, eh?" said Ron.

"Nope," said Harry.

"Hey — I forgot — did she let you off for Friday?"

"No," said Harry.

Ron groaned sympathetically.

It was another bad day for Harry; he was one of the worst in Transfiguration, not having practiced Vanishing Spells at all. He had to give up his lunch hour to complete the picture of the bowtruckle, and meanwhile, Professors McGonagall, Grubbly-Plank, and Sinistra gave them yet more homework, which he had no prospect of finishing that evening because of his second detention with Umbridge. To cap it all, Angelina Johnson tracked him down at dinner again and, on learning that he would not be able to attend Friday's Keeper tryouts, told him she was not at all impressed by his attitude and that she expected players who wished to remain on the team to put training before their other commitments.

"I'm in detention!" Harry yelled after her as she stalked away. "D'you think I'd rather be stuck in a room with that old toad or playing Quidditch?"

"At least it's only lines," said Hermione consolingly, as Harry sank back onto his bench and looked down at his steak-and-kidney pie, which he no longer fancied very much. "It's not as if it's a dreadful punishment, really. . . ."

Harry opened his mouth, closed it again, and nodded. He was not really sure why he was not telling Ron and Hermione exactly what was happening in Umbridge's room: He only knew that he did not want to see their looks of horror; that would make the whole thing seem worse and therefore more difficult to face. He also felt dimly that this was between himself and Umbridge, a private battle of wills, and he was not going to give her the satisfaction of hearing that he had complained about it.

"I can't believe how much homework we've got," said Ron miserably.

"Well, why didn't you do any last night?" Hermione asked him. "Where were you anyway?"

"I was . . . I fancied a walk," said Ron shiftily.

Harry had the distinct impression that he was not alone in concealing things at the moment.

The second detention was just as bad as the previous one. The skin on the back of Harry's hand became irritated more quickly now, red and inflamed; Harry thought it unlikely to keep healing as effectively for long. Soon the cut would remain etched in his hand and Umbridge would, perhaps, be satisfied. He let no moan of pain escape him, however, and from the moment of entering the room to the moment of his dismissal, again past midnight, he said nothing but "Good evening" and "Good night."

His homework situation, however, was now desperate, and when he returned to the Gryffindor common room he did not, though exhausted, go to bed, but opened his books and began Snape's moonstone essay. It was half-past two by the time he had finished it. He knew he had done a poor job, but there was no help for it; unless he had something to give in he would be in detention with Snape next. He then dashed off answers to the questions Professor McGonagall had set them, cobbled together something on the proper handling of bowtruckles for Professor Grubbly-Plank, and staggered up to bed, where he fell fully clothed on top of the bed covers and fell asleep immediately.

Thursday passed in a haze of tiredness. Ron seemed very sleepy too, though Harry could not see why he should be. Harry's third detention passed in the same way as the previous two, except that after two hours the words *I must not tell lies* did not fade from the back of Harry's hand, but remained scratched there, oozing droplets of blood. The pause in the pointed quill's scratching made Professor Umbridge look up.

"Ah," she said softly, moving around her desk to examine his hand herself. "Good. That ought to serve as a reminder to you, oughtn't it? You may leave for tonight."

"Do I still have to come back tomorrow?" said Harry, picking up his schoolbag with his left hand rather than his smarting right.

"Oh yes," said Professor Umbridge, smiling widely as before. "Yes, I think we can etch the message a little deeper with another evening's work."

He had never before considered the possibility that there might be another teacher in the world he hated more than Snape, but as he walked back toward Gryffindor Tower he had to admit he had found a contender. *She's evil,* he thought, as he climbed a staircase to the seventh floor, *she's an evil, twisted, mad, old —*

"Ron?"

He had reached the top of the stairs, turned right, and almost walked into Ron, who was lurking behind a statue of Lachlan the Lanky, clutching his broomstick. He gave a great leap of surprise when he saw Harry and attempted to hide his new Cleansweep Eleven behind his back.

"What are you doing?"

"Er — nothing. What are *you* doing?"

Harry frowned at him.

"Come on, you can tell me! What are you hiding here for?"

"I'm — I'm hiding from Fred and George, if you must know," said Ron. "They just went past with a bunch of first years, I bet they're testing stuff on them again, I mean, they can't do it in the common room now, can they, not with Hermione there."

He was talking in a very fast, feverish way.

"But what have you got your broom for, you haven't been flying, have you?" Harry asked.

"I — well — well, okay, I'll tell you, but don't laugh, all right?" Ron said defensively, turning redder with every second. "I-I thought I'd try out for Gryffindor Keeper now I've got a decent broom. There. Go on. Laugh."

"I'm not laughing," said Harry. Ron blinked. "It's a brilliant idea! It'd be really cool if you got on the team! I've never seen you play Keeper, are you good?"

"I'm not bad," said Ron, who looked immensely relieved at Harry's reaction. "Charlie, Fred, and George always made me Keep for them when they were training during the holidays."

"So you've been practicing tonight?"

"Every evening since Tuesday . . . just on my own, though, I've been trying to bewitch Quaffles to fly at me, but it hasn't been easy and I don't know how much use it'll be." Ron looked nervous and anxious. "Fred and George are going to laugh themselves stupid when I turn up for the tryouts. They haven't stopped taking the mickey out of me since I got made a prefect."

"I wish I was going to be there," said Harry bitterly, as they set off together toward the common room.

"Yeah, so do — Harry, what's that on the back of your hand?"

Harry, who had just scratched his nose with his free right hand, tried to hide it, but had as much success as Ron with his Cleansweep.

"It's just a cut — it's nothing — it's —"

But Ron had grabbed Harry's forearm and pulled the back of Harry's hand up level with his eyes. There was a pause, during which he stared at the words carved into the skin, then he released Harry, looking sick.

"I thought you said she was giving you lines?"

Harry hesitated, but after all, Ron had been honest with him, so he told Ron the truth about the hours he had been spending in Umbridge's office.

"The old hag!" Ron said in a revolted whisper as they came to a halt in front of the Fat Lady, who was dozing peacefully with her head against her frame. "She's sick! Go to McGonagall, say something!"

"No," said Harry at once. "I'm not giving her the satisfaction of knowing she's got to me."

"*Got to you?* You can't let her get away with this!"

"I don't know how much power McGonagall's got over her," said Harry.

"Dumbledore, then, tell Dumbledore!"

"No," said Harry flatly.

"Why not?"

"He's got enough on his mind," said Harry, but that was not the true reason. He was not going to go to Dumbledore for help when Dumbledore had not spoken to him once since last June.

"Well, I reckon you should —" Ron began, but he was interrupted by the Fat Lady, who had been watching them sleepily and now burst out, "Are you going to give me the password or will I have to stay awake all night waiting for you to finish your conversation?"

Friday dawned sullen and sodden as the rest of the week. Though Harry glanced toward the staff table automatically when he entered the Great Hall, it was without real hope of seeing Hagrid and he turned his mind immediately to his more pressing problems, such as the mountainous pile of homework he had to do and the prospect of yet another detention with Umbridge.

Two things sustained Harry that day. One was the thought that it was almost the weekend; the other was that, dreadful though his final detention with Umbridge was sure to be, he had a distant view of the Quidditch pitch from her window and might, with luck, be able to see something of Ron's tryout. These were rather feeble rays of light, it was true, but Harry was grateful for anything that might lighten his present darkness; he had never had a worse first week of term at Hogwarts.

At five o'clock that evening he knocked on Professor Umbridge's office door for what he sincerely hoped would be the final time, was told to enter and did so. The blank parchment lay ready for him on the lace-covered table, the pointed black quill beside it.

"You know what to do, Mr. Potter," said Umbridge, smiling sweetly over at him.

Harry picked up the quill and glanced through the window. If he just shifted his chair an inch or so to the right . . . On the pretext of shifting himself closer to the table he managed it. He now had a distant view of the Gryffindor Quidditch team soaring up and down the pitch, while half a dozen black figures stood at the foot of the three high goalposts, apparently awaiting their turn to Keep. It was impossible to tell which one was Ron at this distance.

I must not tell lies, Harry wrote. The cut in the back of his right hand opened and began to bleed afresh.

I must not tell lies. The cut dug deeper, stinging and smarting.

I must not tell lies. Blood trickled down his wrist.

He chanced another glance out of the window. Whoever was defending the goalposts now was doing a very poor job indeed. Katie Bell scored twice in the few seconds Harry dared watch. Hoping very much that the Keeper wasn't Ron, he dropped his eyes back to the parchment dotted with blood.

I must not tell lies.

I must not tell lies.

He looked up whenever he thought he could risk it, when he could hear the scratching of Umbridge's quill or the opening of a desk drawer. The third person to try out was pretty good, the fourth was terrible, the fifth dodged a Bludger exceptionally well but then fumbled an easy save. The sky was darkening so that Harry doubted he would be able to watch the sixth and seventh people at all.

I must not tell lies.

I must not tell lies.

The parchment was now shining with drops of blood from the back of his hand, which was searing with pain. When he next looked up, night had fallen and the Quidditch pitch was no longer visible.

"Let's see if you've gotten the message yet, shall we?" said Umbridge's soft voice half an hour later.

She moved toward him, stretching out her short be-ringed fingers for his arm. And then, as she took hold of him to examine the words now cut into his skin, pain seared, not across the back of his hand, but across the scar on his forehead. At the same time, he had a most peculiar sensation somewhere around his midriff.

He wrenched his arm out of her grip and leapt to his feet, staring at her. She looked back at him, a smile stretching her wide, slack mouth.

"Yes, it hurts, doesn't it?" she said softly.

He did not answer. His heart was thumping very hard and fast. Was she talking about his hand or did she know what he had just felt in his forehead?

"Well, I think I've made my point, Mr. Potter. You may go."

He caught up his schoolbag and left the room as quickly as he could.

Stay calm, he told himself as he sprinted up the stairs. *Stay calm, it doesn't necessarily mean what you think it means. . . .*

"*Mimbulus mimbletonia!*" he gasped at the Fat Lady, who swung forward once more.

A roar of sound greeted him. Ron came running toward him, beaming all over his face and slopping butterbeer down his front from the goblet he was clutching.

"Harry, I did it, I'm in, I'm Keeper!"

"What? Oh — brilliant!" said Harry, trying to smile naturally, while his heart continued to race and his hand throbbed and bled.

"Have a butterbeer." Ron pressed a bottle onto him. "I can't believe it — where's Hermione gone?"

"She's there," said Fred, who was also swigging butterbeer, and pointed to an armchair by the fire. Hermione was dozing in it, her drink tipping precariously in her hand.

"Well, she said she was pleased when I told her," said Ron, looking slightly put out.

"Let her sleep," said George hastily. It was a few moments before Harry noticed that several of the first years gathered around them bore unmistakable signs of recent nosebleeds.

"Come here, Ron, and see if Oliver's old robes fit you," called Katie Bell. "We can take off his name and put yours on instead. . . ."

As Ron moved away, Angelina came striding up to Harry.

"Sorry I was a bit short with you earlier, Potter," she said abruptly. "It's stressful, this managing lark, you know, I'm starting to think I was a bit hard on Wood sometimes." She was watching Ron over the rim of her goblet with a slight frown on her face.

"Look, I know he's your best mate, but he's not fabulous," she said bluntly. "I think with a bit of training he'll be all right, though. He comes from a family of good Quidditch players. I'm banking on him turning out to have a bit more talent than he showed today, to be honest. Vicky Frobisher and Geoffrey Hooper both flew better this evening, but Hooper's a real whiner, he's always moaning about something or other, and Vicky's involved in all sorts of societies, she admitted herself that if training clashed with her Charm Club she'd put Charms first. Anyway, we're having a practice session at two o'clock tomorrow, so just make sure you're there this time. And do me a favor and help Ron as much as you can, okay?"

He nodded and Angelina strolled back to Alicia Spinnet. Harry moved over to sit next to Hermione, who awoke with a jerk as he put down his bag.

"Oh, Harry, it's you. . . . Good about Ron, isn't it?" she said blearily. "I'm just so — so — so tired," she yawned. "I was up until one o'clock making more hats. They're disappearing like mad!"

And sure enough, now that he looked, Harry saw that there were woolly hats concealed all around the room where unwary elves might accidentally pick them up.

"Great," said Harry distractedly; if he did not tell somebody soon, he would burst. "Listen, Hermione, I was just up in Umbridge's office and she touched my arm . . ."

Hermione listened closely. When Harry had finished she said slowly, "You're worried that You-Know-Who's controlling her like he controlled Quirrell?"

"Well," said Harry, dropping his voice, "it's a possibility, isn't it?"

"I suppose so," said Hermione, though she sounded unconvinced. "But I don't think he can be *possessing* her the way he possessed Quirrell, I mean, he's properly alive again now, isn't he, he's got his own body, he wouldn't need to share someone else's. He could have her under the Imperius Curse, I suppose. . . ."

Harry watched Fred, George, and Lee Jordan juggling empty butterbeer bottles for a moment. Then Hermione said, "But last year your scar hurt when nobody was touching you, and didn't Dumbledore say it had to do with what You-Know-Who was feeling at the time? I mean, maybe this hasn't got anything to do with Umbridge at all, maybe it's just coincidence it happened while you were with her?"

"She's evil," said Harry flatly. "Twisted."

"She's horrible, yes, but . . . Harry, I think you ought to tell Dumbledore your scar hurt."

It was the second time in two days he had been advised to go to Dumbledore and his answer to Hermione was just the same as his answer to Ron.

"I'm not bothering him with this. Like you just said, it's not a big deal. It's been hurting on and off all summer — it was just a bit worse tonight, that's all —"

"Harry, I'm sure Dumbledore would *want* to be bothered by this —"

"Yeah," said Harry, before he could stop himself, "that's the only bit of me Dumbledore cares about, isn't it, my scar?"

"Don't say that, it's not true!"

"I think I'll write and tell Sirius about it, see what he thinks —"

"Harry, you can't put something like that in a letter!" said Hermione, looking alarmed. "Don't you remember, Moody told us to be careful what we put in writing! We just can't guarantee owls aren't being intercepted anymore!"

"All right, all right, I won't tell him, then!" said Harry irritably. He got to his feet. "I'm going to bed. Tell Ron for me, will you?"

"Oh no," said Hermione, looking relieved, "if you're going that means I can go without being rude too, I'm absolutely exhausted and I want to make some more hats tomorrow. Listen, you can help me if you like, it's quite fun, I'm getting better, I can do patterns and bobbles and all sorts of things now."

Harry looked into her face, which was shining with glee, and tried to look as though he was vaguely tempted by this offer.

"Er . . . no, I don't think I will, thanks," he said. "Er — not tomorrow. I've got loads of homework to do. . . ."

And he traipsed off to the boys' stairs, leaving her looking slightly disappointed behind him.

PERCY AND PADFOOT

Harry was the first to awake in his dormitory next morning. He lay for a moment watching dust swirl in the chink of sunlight falling through the gap in his four-poster's hangings and savored the thought that it was Saturday. The first week of term seemed to have dragged on forever, like one gigantic History of Magic lesson.

Judging by the sleepy silence and the freshly minted look of that beam of sunlight, it was just after daybreak. He pulled open the curtains around his bed, got up, and started to dress. The only sound apart from the distant twittering of birds was the slow, deep breathing of his fellow Gryffindors. He opened his schoolbag carefully, pulled out parchment and quill, and headed out of the dormitory for the common room.

Making straight for his favorite squashy old armchair beside the now extinct fire, Harry settled himself down comfortably and unrolled his parchment while looking around the room. The detritus of crumpled-up bits of parchment, old Gobstones, empty ingredient jars, and candy wrappers that usually covered the common room at the end of each day was gone, as were all Hermione's elf hats. Wondering vaguely how many elves had now been set free whether they wanted to be or not, Harry uncorked his ink bottle, dipped his quill into it, and then held it suspended an inch above the smooth yellowish surface of his parchment, thinking hard. . . . But after a minute or so he found himself staring into the empty grate, at a complete loss for what to say.

He could now appreciate how hard it had been for Ron and Hermione to write him letters over the summer. How was he supposed to tell Sirius everything that had happened over the past week and pose all the questions he was burning to ask without giving potential letter-thieves a lot of information he did not want them to have?

He sat quite motionless for a while, gazing into the fireplace, then, finally coming to a decision, he dipped his quill into the ink bottle once more and set it resolutely upon the parchment.

> *Dear Snuffles,*
>
> *Hope you're okay, the first week back here's been terrible, I'm really glad it's the weekend.*
>
> *We've got a new Defense Against the Dark Arts teacher, Professor Umbridge. She's nearly as nice as your mum. I'm writing because that thing I wrote to you about last summer happened again last night when I was doing a detention with Umbridge.*
>
> *We're all missing our biggest friend, we hope he'll be back soon. Please write back quickly.*
>
> *Best,*
>
> *Harry*

Harry reread this letter several times, trying to see it from the point of view of an outsider. He could not see how they would know what he was talking about — or who he was talking to — just from reading this letter. He did hope Sirius would pick up the hint about Hagrid and tell them when he might be back: Harry did not want to ask directly in case it drew too much attention to what Hagrid might be up to while he was not at Hogwarts.

Considering it was a very short letter it had taken a long time to write; sunlight had crept halfway across the room while he had been working on it, and he could now hear distant sounds of movement from the dormitories above. Sealing the parchment carefully he climbed through the portrait hole and headed off for the Owlery.

"I would *not* go that way if I were you," said Nearly Headless Nick, drifting disconcertingly through a wall just ahead of him as he walked down the passage. "Peeves is planning an amusing joke on the next person to pass the bust of Paracelsus halfway down the corridor."

"Does it involve Paracelsus falling on top of the person's head?" asked Harry.

"Funnily enough, it *does*," said Nearly Headless Nick in a bored voice. "Subtlety has never been Peeves's strong point. I'm off to try and find the Bloody Baron. . . . He might be able to put a stop to it. . . . See you, Harry. . . ."

"Yeah, 'bye," said Harry and instead of turning right, he turned left, taking a longer but safer route up to the Owlery. His spirits rose as he walked past window after window showing brilliantly blue sky; he had training later, he would be back on the Quidditch pitch at last —

Something brushed his ankles. He looked down and saw the caretaker's skeletal gray cat, Mrs. Norris, slinking past him. She turned lamplike yellow eyes upon him for a moment before disappearing behind a statue of Wilfred the Wistful.

"I'm not doing anything wrong," Harry called after her. She had the unmistakable air of a cat that was off to report to her boss, yet Harry could not see why; he was perfectly entitled to walk up to the Owlery on a Saturday morning.

The sun was high in the sky now and when Harry entered the

Owlery the glassless windows dazzled his eyes; thick silvery beams of sunlight crisscrossed the circular room in which hundreds of owls nestled on rafters, a little restless in the early morning light, some clearly just returned from hunting. The straw-covered floor crunched a little as he stepped across tiny animal bones, craning his neck for a sight of Hedwig.

"There you are," he said, spotting her somewhere near the very top of the vaulted ceiling. "Get down here, I've got a letter for you."

With a low hoot she stretched her great white wings and soared down onto his shoulder.

"Right, I know this says 'Snuffles' on the outside," he told her, giving her the letter to clasp in her beak and, without knowing exactly why, whispering, "but it's for Sirius, okay?"

She blinked her amber eyes once and he took that to mean that she understood.

"Safe flight, then," said Harry and he carried her to one of the windows; with a moment's pressure on his arm Hedwig took off into the blindingly bright sky. He watched her until she became a tiny black speck and vanished, then switched his gaze to Hagrid's hut, clearly visible from this window, and just as clearly uninhabited, the chimney smokeless, the curtains drawn.

The treetops of the Forbidden Forest swayed in a light breeze. Harry watched them, savoring the fresh air on his face, thinking about Quidditch later . . . and then he saw it. A great, reptilian winged horse, just like the ones pulling the Hogwarts carriages, with leathery black wings spread wide like a pterodactyl's, rose up out of the trees like a grotesque, giant bird. It soared in a great circle and then plunged once more into the trees. The whole thing had happened so quickly Harry could hardly believe what he had seen, except that his heart was hammering madly.

The Owlery door opened behind him. He leapt in shock, and turning quickly, saw Cho Chang holding a letter and a parcel in her hands.

"Hi," said Harry automatically.

"Oh . . . hi," she said breathlessly. "I didn't think anyone would be up here this early. . . . I only remembered five minutes ago, it's my mum's birthday."

She held up the parcel.

"Right," said Harry. His brain seemed to have jammed. He wanted to say something funny and interesting, but the memory of that terrible winged horse was fresh in his mind.

"Nice day," he said, gesturing to the windows. His insides seemed to shrivel with embarrassment. The weather. He was talking about the *weather.* . . .

"Yeah," said Cho, looking around for a suitable owl. "Good Quidditch conditions. I haven't been out all week, have you?"

"No," said Harry.

Cho had selected one of the school barn owls. She coaxed it down onto her arm where it held out an obliging leg so that she could attach the parcel.

"Hey, has Gryffindor got a new Keeper yet?" she asked.

"Yeah," said Harry. "It's my friend Ron Weasley, d'you know him?"

"The Tornado-hater?" said Cho rather coolly. "Is he any good?"

"Yeah," said Harry, "I think so. I didn't see his tryout, though, I was in detention."

Cho looked up, the parcel only half-attached to the owl's legs.

"That Umbridge woman's foul," she said in a low voice. "Putting you in detention just because you told the truth about how — how — how he died. Everyone heard about it, it was all over the school. You were really brave standing up to her like that."

Harry's insides reinflated so rapidly he felt as though he might actually float a few inches off the dropping-strewn floor. Who cared about a stupid flying horse, Cho thought he had been really brave. . . . For a moment he considered accidentally-on-purpose showing her his cut hand as he helped her tie her parcel onto her owl. . . . But the very instant that this thrilling thought occurred, the Owlery door opened again.

Filch, the caretaker, came wheezing into the room. There were purple patches on his sunken, veined cheeks, his jowls were aquiver and his thin gray hair disheveled; he had obviously run here. Mrs. Norris came trotting at his heels, gazing up at the owls overhead and mewing hungrily. There was a restless shifting of wings from above, and a large brown owl snapped his beak in a menacing fashion.

"Aha!" said Filch, taking a flat-footed step toward Harry, his pouchy cheeks trembling with anger. "I've had a tip-off that you are intending to place a massive order for Dungbombs!"

Harry folded his arms and stared at the caretaker.

"Who told you I was ordering Dungbombs?"

Cho was looking from Harry to Filch, also frowning; the barn owl on her arm, tired of standing on one leg, gave an admonitory hoot but she ignored it.

"I have my sources," said Filch in a self-satisfied hiss. "Now hand over whatever it is you're sending."

Feeling immensely thankful that he had not dawdled in posting off the letter, Harry said, "I can't, it's gone."

"*Gone?*" said Filch, his face contorting with rage.

"Gone," said Harry calmly.

Filch opened his mouth furiously, mouthed for a few seconds, then raked Harry's robes with his eyes. "How do I know you haven't got it in your pocket?"

"Because —"

"I saw him send it," said Cho angrily.

Filch rounded on her.

"You saw him — ?"

"That's right, I saw him," she said fiercely.

There was a moment's pause in which Filch glared at Cho and Cho

glared right back, then the caretaker turned and shuffled back toward
the door. He stopped with his hand on the handle and looked back
at Harry.

"If I get so much as a whiff of a Dungbomb . . ."

He stumped off down the stairs. Mrs. Norris cast a last longing
look at the owls and followed him.

Harry and Cho looked at each other.

"Thanks," Harry said.

"No problem," said Cho, finally fixing the parcel to the barn owl's
other leg, her face slightly pink. "You *weren't* ordering Dungbombs,
were you?"

"No," said Harry.

"I wonder why he thought you were, then?" she said, as she carried
the owl to the window.

Harry shrugged; he was quite as mystified by that as she was,
though, oddly, it was not bothering him very much at the moment.

They left the Owlery together. At the entrance of a corridor that
led toward the west wing of the castle, Cho said, "I'm going this way.
Well, I'll . . . I'll see you around, Harry."

"Yeah . . . see you."

She smiled at him and departed. He walked on, feeling quietly
elated. He had managed to have an entire conversation with her and
not embarrassed himself once. . . . *You were really brave standing up to
her like that.* . . . She had called him brave. . . . She did not hate him
for being alive. . . .

Of course, she had preferred Cedric, he knew that. . . . Though if
he'd only asked her to the ball before Cedric had, things might have
turned out differently. . . . She had seemed sincerely sorry that she had
to refuse when Harry had asked her. . . .

"Morning," Harry said brightly to Ron and Hermione, joining
them at the Gryffindor table in the Great Hall.

"What are you looking so pleased about?" said Ron, eyeing Harry in surprise.

"Erm . . . Quidditch later," said Harry happily, pulling a large platter of bacon and eggs toward him.

"Oh . . . yeah . . ." said Ron. He put down the bit of toast he was eating and took a large swig of pumpkin juice. Then he said, "Listen . . . you don't fancy going out a bit earlier with me, do you? Just to — er — give me some practice before training? So I can, you know, get my eye in a bit . . ."

"Yeah, okay," said Harry.

"Look, I don't think you should," said Hermione seriously, "you're both really behind on homework as it —"

But she broke off; the morning post was arriving and, as usual, the *Daily Prophet* was soaring toward her in the beak of a screech owl, which landed perilously close to the sugar bowl and held out a leg; Hermione pushed a Knut into its leather pouch, took the newspaper, and scanned the front page critically as the owl took off again.

"Anything interesting?" said Ron; Harry smiled — he knew Ron was keen to get her off the subject of homework.

"No," she sighed, "just some guff about the bass player in the Weird Sisters getting married. . . ."

She opened the paper and disappeared behind it. Harry devoted himself to another helping of eggs and bacon; Ron was staring up at the high windows, looking slightly preoccupied.

"Wait a moment," said Hermione suddenly. "Oh no . . . Sirius!"

"What's happened?" said Harry, and he snatched at the paper so violently that it ripped down the middle so that he and Hermione were holding half each.

"*The Ministry of Magic has received a tip-off from a reliable source that Sirius Black, notorious mass murderer . . . blah blah blah . . . is currently hiding in London!*" Hermione read from her half in an anguished whisper.

"Lucius Malfoy, I'll bet anything," said Harry in a low, furious voice. "He *did* recognize Sirius on the platform. . . ."

"What?" said Ron, looking alarmed. "You didn't say —"

"Shh!" said the other two.

". . . *Ministry warns Wizarding community that Black is very dangerous . . . killed thirteen people . . . broke out of Azkaban . . .*' the usual rubbish," Hermione concluded, laying down her half of the paper and looking fearfully at Harry and Ron. "Well, he just won't be able to leave the house again, that's all," she whispered. "Dumbledore did warn him not to."

Harry looked down glumly at the bit of the *Prophet* he had torn off. Most of the page was devoted to an advertisement for Madame Malkin's Robes for All Occasions, which was apparently having a sale.

"Hey!" he said, flattening it down so Hermione and Ron could both see it. "Look at this!"

"I've got all the robes I want," said Ron.

"No," said Harry, "look . . . this little piece here . . ."

Ron and Hermione bent closer to read it; the item was barely an inch long and placed right at the bottom of a column. It was headlined:

TRESPASS AT MINISTRY

Sturgis Podmore, 38, of number two, Laburnum Gardens, Clapham, has appeared in front of the Wizengamot charged with trespass and attempted robbery at the Ministry of Magic on 31st August. Podmore was arrested by Ministry of Magic watchwizard Eric Munch, who found him attempting to force his way through a top-security door at one o'clock in the morning. Podmore, who refused to speak in his own defense, was convicted on both charges and sentenced to six months in Azkaban.

"Sturgis Podmore?" said Ron slowly, "but he's that bloke who looks like his head's been thatched, isn't he? He's one of the Ord —"

"Ron, *shh!*" said Hermione, casting a terrified look around them.

"Six months in Azkaban!" whispered Harry, shocked. "Just for trying to get through a door!"

"Don't be silly, it wasn't just for trying to get through a door — what on earth was he doing at the Ministry of Magic at one o'clock in the morning?" breathed Hermione.

"D'you reckon he was doing something for the Order?" Ron muttered.

"Wait a moment. . . ." said Harry slowly. "Sturgis was supposed to come and see us off, remember?"

The other two looked at him.

"Yeah, he was supposed to be part of our guard going to King's Cross, remember? And Moody was all annoyed because he didn't turn up, so that doesn't seem like he was supposed to be on a job for them, does it?"

"Well, maybe they didn't expect him to get caught," said Hermione.

"It could be a frame-up!" Ron exclaimed excitedly. "No — listen!" he went on, dropping his voice dramatically at the threatening look on Hermione's face. "The Ministry suspects he's one of Dumbledore's lot so — I dunno — they *lured* him to the Ministry, and he wasn't trying to get through a door at all! Maybe they've just made something up to get him!"

There was a pause while Harry and Hermione considered this. Harry thought it seemed far-fetched; Hermione, on the other hand, looked rather impressed and said, "Do you know, I wouldn't be at all surprised if that were true."

She folded up her half of the newspaper thoughtfully. When Harry laid down his knife and fork she seemed to come out of a reverie.

"Right, well, I think we should tackle that essay for Sprout on Self-Fertilizing Shrubs first, and if we're lucky we'll be able to start McGonagall's Inanimatus Conjurus before lunch. . . ."

Harry felt a small twinge of guilt at the thought of the pile of homework awaiting him upstairs, but the sky was a clear, exhilarating blue, and he had not been on his Firebolt all week. . . .

"I mean, we can do it tonight," said Ron, as he and Harry walked down the sloping lawns toward the Quidditch pitch, their broomsticks over their shoulders, Hermione's dire warnings that they would fail all their O.W.L.s still ringing in their ears. "And we've got tomorrow. She gets too worked up about work, that's her trouble. . . ." There was a pause and he added, in a slightly more anxious tone, "D'you think she meant it when she said we weren't copying from her?"

"Yeah, I do," said Harry. "Still, this is important too, we've got to practice if we want to stay on the Quidditch team. . . ."

"Yeah, that's right," said Ron in a heartened tone. "And we *have* got plenty of time to do it all. . . ."

Harry glanced over to his right as they approached the Quidditch pitch, to where the trees of the Forbidden Forest were swaying darkly. Nothing flew out of them; the sky was empty but for a few distant owls fluttering around the Owlery Tower. He had enough to worry about; the flying horse wasn't doing him any harm: He pushed it out of his mind.

They collected balls from the cupboard in the changing room and set to work, Ron guarding the three tall goalposts, Harry playing Chaser and trying to get the Quaffle past Ron. Harry thought Ron was pretty good; he blocked three-quarters of the goals Harry attempted to put past him and played better the longer they practiced. After a couple of hours they returned to the school, where they ate lunch, during which Hermione made it quite clear that she thought they were irresponsible, then returned to the Quidditch pitch for the real training session. All their teammates but Angelina were already in the changing room when they entered.

"All right, Ron?" said George, winking at him.

"Yeah," said Ron, who had become quieter and quieter all the way down to the pitch.

"Ready to show us all up, Ickle Prefect?" said Fred, emerging tousle-haired from the neck of his Quidditch robes, a slightly malicious grin on his face.

"Shut up," said Ron, stony-faced, pulling on his own team robes for the first time. They fitted him well considering they had been Oliver Wood's, who was rather broader in the shoulder.

"Okay everyone," said Angelina, entering from the Captain's office, already changed. "Let's get to it; Alicia and Fred, if you can just bring the ball crate out for us. Oh, and there are a couple of people out there watching but I want you to just ignore them, all right?"

Something in her would-be casual voice made Harry think he might know who the uninvited spectators were, and sure enough, when they left the changing room for the bright sunlight of the pitch it was to a storm of catcalls and jeers from the Slytherin Quidditch team and assorted hangers-on, who were grouped halfway up the empty stands and whose voices echoed loudly around the stadium.

"What's that Weasley's riding?" Malfoy called in his sneering drawl. "Why would anyone put a Flying Charm on a moldy old log like that?"

Crabbe, Goyle, and Pansy Parkinson guffawed and shrieked with laughter. Ron mounted his broom and kicked off from the ground and Harry followed him, watching his ears turn red from behind.

"Ignore them," he said, accelerating to catch up with Ron. "We'll see who's laughing after we play them. . . ."

"Exactly the attitude I want, Harry," said Angelina approvingly, soaring around them with the Quaffle under her arm and slowing to hover on the spot in front of her airborne team. "Okay everyone, we're going to start with some passes just to warm up, the whole team please —"

"Hey, Johnson, what's with that hairstyle anyway?" shrieked Pansy Parkinson from below. "Why would anyone want to look like they've got worms coming out of their head?"

Angelina swept her long braided hair out of her face and said calmly, "Spread out, then, and let's see what we can do. . . ."

Harry reversed away from the others to the far side of the pitch. Ron fell back toward the opposite goal. Angelina raised the Quaffle with one hand and threw it hard to Fred, who passed to George, who passed to Harry, who passed to Ron, who dropped it.

The Slytherins, led by Malfoy, roared and screamed with laughter. Ron, who had pelted toward the ground to catch the Quaffle before it landed, pulled out of the dive untidily, so that he slipped sideways on his broom, and returned to playing height, blushing. Harry saw Fred and George exchange looks, but uncharacteristically neither of them said anything, for which he was grateful.

"Pass it on, Ron," called Angelina, as though nothing had happened.

Ron threw the Quaffle to Alicia, who passed back to Harry, who passed to George. . . .

"Hey, Potter, how's your scar feeling?" called Malfoy. "Sure you don't need a lie-down? It must be, what, a whole week since you were in the hospital wing, that's a record for you, isn't it?"

Fred passed to Angelina; she reverse passed to Harry, who had not been expecting it, but caught it in the very tips of his fingers and passed it quickly to Ron, who lunged for it and missed by inches.

"Come on now, Ron," said Angelina crossly, as Ron dived for the ground again, chasing the Quaffle. "Pay attention."

It would have been hard to say whether Ron's face or the Quaffle was a deeper scarlet when he returned again to playing height. Malfoy and the rest of the Slytherin team were howling with laughter.

On his third attempt, Ron caught the Quaffle; perhaps out of relief he passed it on so enthusiastically that it soared straight through Katie's outstretched hands and hit her hard in the face.

"Sorry!" Ron groaned, zooming forward to see whether he had done any damage.

"Get back in position, she's fine!" barked Angelina. "But as you're passing to a teammate, do *try* not to knock her off her broom, won't you? We've got Bludgers for that!"

Katie's nose was bleeding. Down below the Slytherins were stamping their feet and jeering. Fred and George converged on Katie.

"Here, take this," Fred told her, handing her something small and purple from out of his pocket. "It'll clear it up in no time."

"All right," called Angelina, "Fred, George, go and get your bats and a Bludger; Ron, get up to the goalposts, Harry, release the Snitch when I say so. We're going to aim for Ron's goal, obviously."

Harry zoomed off after the twins to fetch the Snitch.

"Ron's making a right pig's ear of things, isn't he?" muttered George, as the three of them landed at the crate containing the balls and opened it to extract one of the Bludgers and the Snitch.

"He's just nervous," said Harry. "He was fine when I was practicing with him this morning."

"Yeah, well, I hope he hasn't peaked too soon," said Fred gloomily.

They returned to the air. When Angelina blew her whistle, Harry released the Snitch and Fred and George let fly the Bludger; from that moment on, Harry was barely aware of what the others were doing. It was his job to recapture the tiny fluttering golden ball that was worth a hundred and fifty points to the Seeker's team and doing so required enormous speed and skill. He accelerated, rolling and swerving in and out of the Chasers, the warm autumn air whipping his face and the distant yells of the Slytherins so much meaningless roaring in his ears. . . . But too soon, the whistle brought him to a halt again.

"Stop — *stop* — STOP!" screamed Angelina. "Ron — you're not covering your middle post!"

Harry looked around at Ron, who was hovering in front of the left-hand hoop, leaving the other two completely unprotected.

"Oh . . . sorry . . ."

"You keep shifting around while you're watching the Chasers!" said Angelina. "Either stay in center position until you have to move to defend a hoop, or else circle the hoops, but don't drift vaguely off to one side, that's how you let in the last three goals!"

"Sorry . . ." Ron repeated, his red face shining like a beacon against the bright blue sky.

"And Katie, can't you do something about that nosebleed?"

"It's just getting worse!" said Katie thickly, attempting to stem the flow with her sleeve.

Harry glanced around at Fred, who was looking anxious and checking his pockets. He saw Fred pull out something purple, examine it for a second, and then look around at Katie, evidently horrorstruck.

"Well, let's try again," said Angelina. She was ignoring the Slytherins, who had now set up a chant of *"Gryffindor are losers, Gryffindor are losers,"* but there was a certain rigidity about her seat on the broom nevertheless.

This time they had been flying for barely three minutes when Angelina's whistle sounded. Harry, who had just sighted the Snitch circling the opposite goalpost, pulled up feeling distinctly aggrieved.

"What now?" he said impatiently to Alicia, who was nearest.

"Katie," she said shortly.

Harry turned and saw Angelina, Fred, and George all flying as fast as they could toward Katie. Harry and Alicia sped toward her too. It was plain that Angelina had stopped training just in time; Katie was now chalk-white and covered in blood.

"She needs the hospital wing," said Angelina.

"We'll take her," said Fred. "She — er — might have swallowed a Blood Blisterpod by mistake —"

"Well, there's no point continuing with no Beaters and a Chaser gone," said Angelina glumly, as Fred and George zoomed off toward the castle supporting Katie between them. "Come on, let's go and get changed."

The Slytherins continued to chant as they trailed back into the changing rooms.

"How was practice?" asked Hermione rather coolly half an hour later, as Harry and Ron climbed through the portrait hole into the Gryffindor common room.

"It was —" Harry began.

"Completely lousy," said Ron in a hollow voice, sinking into a chair beside Hermione. She looked up at Ron and her frostiness seemed to melt.

"Well, it was only your first one," she said consolingly, "it's bound to take time to —"

"Who said it was me who made it lousy?" snapped Ron.

"No one," said Hermione, looking taken aback, "I thought —"

"You thought I was bound to be rubbish?"

"No, of course I didn't! Look, you said it was lousy so I just —"

"I'm going to get started on some homework," said Ron angrily and stomped off to the staircase to the boys' dormitories and vanished from sight. Hermione turned to Harry.

"*Was* he lousy?"

"No," said Harry loyally.

Hermione raised her eyebrows.

"Well, I suppose he could've played better," Harry muttered, "but it was only the first training session, like you said. . . ."

Neither Harry nor Ron seemed to make much headway with their homework that night. Harry knew Ron was too preoccupied with how badly he had performed at Quidditch practice and he himself was having difficulty in getting the chant of *"Gryffindor are losers"* out of his head.

They spent the whole of Sunday in the common room, buried in their books while the room around them filled up, then emptied: It was another clear, fine day and most of their fellow Gryffindors spent the day out in the grounds, enjoying what might well be some of the last sunshine that year. By the evening Harry felt as though somebody had been beating his brain against the inside of his skull.

"You know, we probably should try and get more homework done during the week," Harry muttered to Ron, as they finally laid aside Professor McGonagall's long essay on the Inanimatus Conjurus spell and turned miserably to Professor Sinistra's equally long and difficult essay about Jupiter's moons.

"Yeah," said Ron, rubbing slightly bloodshot eyes and throwing his fifth spoiled bit of parchment into the fire beside them. "Listen . . . shall we just ask Hermione if we can have a look at what she's done?"

Harry glanced over at her; she was sitting with Crookshanks on her lap and chatting merrily to Ginny as a pair of knitting needles flashed in midair in front of her, now knitting a pair of shapeless elf socks.

"No," he said heavily, "you know she won't let us."

And so they worked on while the sky outside the windows became steadily darker; slowly, the crowd in the common room began to thin again. At half-past eleven, Hermione wandered over to them, yawning.

"Nearly done?"

"No," said Ron shortly.

"Jupiter's biggest moon is Ganymede, not Callisto," she said, pointing over Ron's shoulder at a line in his Astronomy essay, "and it's Io that's got the volcanos."

"Thanks," snarled Ron, scratching out the offending sentences.

"Sorry, I only —"

"Yeah, well, if you've just come over here to criticize —"

"Ron —"

"I haven't got time to listen to a sermon, all right, Hermione, I'm up to my neck in it here —"

"No — look!"

Hermione was pointing to the nearest window. Harry and Ron both looked over. A handsome screech owl was standing on the windowsill, gazing into the room at Ron.

"Isn't that Hermes?" said Hermione, sounding amazed.

"Blimey, it is!" said Ron quietly, throwing down his quill and getting to his feet. "What's Percy writing to me for?"

He crossed to the window and opened it; Hermes flew inside, landed upon Ron's essay, and held out a leg to which a letter was attached. Ron took it off and the owl departed at once, leaving inky footprints across Ron's drawing of the moon Io.

"That's definitely Percy's handwriting," said Ron, sinking back into his chair and staring at the words on the outside of the scroll: *To Ronald Weasley, Gryffindor House, Hogwarts.* He looked up at the other two. "What d'you reckon?"

"Open it!" said Hermione eagerly. Harry nodded.

Ron unrolled the scroll and began to read. The farther down the parchment his eyes traveled, the more pronounced became his scowl. When he had finished reading, he looked disgusted. He thrust the letter at Harry and Hermione, who leaned toward each other to read it together:

Dear Ron,

    I have only just heard (from no less a person than the Minister of Magic himself, who has it from your new teacher, Professor Umbridge) that you have become a Hogwarts prefect.

    I was most pleasantly surprised when I heard this news and must firstly offer my congratulations. I must admit that I have always been afraid that you would take what we might call the "Fred and George" route, rather than following in my footsteps, so you can imagine my feelings on hearing you have stopped flouting authority and have decided to shoulder some real responsibility.

But I want to give you more than congratulations, Ron, I want to give you some advice, which is why I am sending this at night rather than by the usual morning post. Hopefully you will be able to read this away from prying eyes and avoid awkward questions.

From something the Minister let slip when telling me you are now a prefect, I gather that you are still seeing a lot of Harry Potter. I must tell you, Ron, that nothing could put you in danger of losing your badge more than continued fraternization with that boy. Yes, I am sure you are surprised to hear this — no doubt you will say that Potter has always been Dumbledore's favorite — but I feel bound to tell you that Dumbledore may not be in charge at Hogwarts much longer and the people who count have a very different — and probably more accurate — view of Potter's behavior. I shall say no more here, but if you look at the Daily Prophet tomorrow you will get a good idea of the way the wind is blowing — and see if you can spot yours truly!

Seriously, Ron, you do not want to be tarred with the same brush as Potter, it could be very damaging to your future prospects, and I am talking here about life after school too. As you must be aware, given that our father escorted him to court, Potter had a disciplinary hearing this summer in front of the whole Wizengamot and he did not come out of it looking too good. He got off on a mere technicality if you ask me and many of the people I've spoken to remain convinced of his guilt.

It may be that you are afraid to sever ties with Potter — I know that he can be unbalanced and, for all I know, violent — but if you have any worries about this, or have spotted anything else in Potter's behavior that is troubling you, I urge you to speak to Dolores Umbridge, a really delightful woman, who I know will be only too happy to advise you.

This leads me to my other bit of advice. As I have hinted

above, Dumbledore's regime at Hogwarts may soon be over. Your loyalty, Ron, should be not to him, but to the school and the Ministry. I am very sorry to hear that so far Professor Umbridge is encountering very little cooperation from staff as she strives to make those necessary changes within Hogwarts that the Ministry so ardently desires (although she should find this easier from next week — again, see the Prophet *tomorrow!). I shall say only this — a student who shows himself willing to help Professor Umbridge now may be very well placed for Head Boyship in a couple of years!*

I am sorry that I was unable to see more of you over the summer. It pains me to criticize our parents, but I am afraid I can no longer live under their roof while they remain mixed up with the dangerous crowd around Dumbledore (if you are writing to Mother at any point, you might tell her that a certain Sturgis Podmore, who is a great friend of Dumbledore's, has recently been sent to Azkaban for trespass at the Ministry. Perhaps that will open their eyes to the kind of petty criminals with whom they are currently rubbing shoulders). I count myself very lucky to have escaped the stigma of association with such people — the Minister really could not be more gracious to me — and I do hope, Ron, that you will not allow family ties to blind you to the misguided nature of our parents' beliefs and actions either. I sincerely hope that, in time, they will realize how mistaken they were and I shall, of course, be ready to accept a full apology when that day comes.

Please think over what I have said most carefully, particularly the bit about Harry Potter, and congratulations again on becoming prefect.

Your brother,

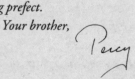

Harry looked up at Ron.

"Well," he said, trying to sound as though he found the whole thing a joke, "if you want to — er — what is it?" (He checked Percy's letter.) "Oh yeah — 'sever ties' with me, I swear I won't get violent."

"Give it back," said Ron, holding out his hand. "He is —" Ron said jerkily, tearing Percy's letter in half, "the world's" — he tore it into quarters — "biggest" — he tore it into eighths — "*git.*" He threw the pieces into the fire.

"Come on, we've got to get this finished some time before dawn," he said briskly to Harry, pulling Professor Sinistra's essay back toward him.

Hermione was looking at Ron with an odd expression on her face.

"Oh, give them here," she said abruptly.

"What?" said Ron.

"Give them to me, I'll look through them and correct them," she said.

"Are you serious? Ah, Hermione, you're a lifesaver," said Ron, "what can I — ?"

"What you can say is, 'We promise we'll never leave our homework this late again,'" she said, holding out both hands for their essays, but she looked slightly amused all the same.

"Thanks a million, Hermione," said Harry weakly, passing over his essay and sinking back into his armchair, rubbing his eyes.

It was now past midnight and the common room was deserted but for the three of them and Crookshanks. The only sound was that of Hermione's quill scratching out sentences here and there on their essays and the ruffle of pages as she checked various facts in the reference books strewn across the table. Harry was exhausted. He also felt an odd, sick, empty feeling in his stomach that had nothing to do with tiredness and everything to do with the letter now curling blackly in the heart of the fire.

He knew that half the people inside Hogwarts thought him

strange, even mad; he knew that the *Daily Prophet* had been making snide allusions to him for months, but there was something about seeing it written down like that in Percy's writing, about knowing that Percy was advising Ron to drop him and even to tell tales on him to Umbridge, that made his situation real to him as nothing else had. He had known Percy for four years, had stayed in his house during the summers, shared a tent with him during the Quidditch World Cup, had even been awarded full marks by him in the second task of the Triwizard Tournament last year, yet now, Percy thought him unbalanced and possibly violent.

And with a surge of sympathy for his godfather, Harry thought that Sirius was probably the only person he knew who could really understand how he felt at the moment, because Sirius was in the same situation; nearly everyone in the Wizarding world thought Sirius a dangerous murderer and a great Voldemort supporter and he had had to live with that knowledge for fourteen years. . . .

Harry blinked. He had just seen something in the fire that could not have been there. It had flashed into sight and vanished immediately. No . . . it could not have been. . . . He had imagined it because he had been thinking about Sirius. . . .

"Okay, write that down," Hermione said to Ron, pushing his essay and a sheet covered in her own writing back to Ron, "and then copy out this conclusion that I've written for you."

"Hermione, you are honestly the most wonderful person I've ever met," said Ron weakly, "and if I'm ever rude to you again —"

"— I'll know you're back to normal," said Hermione. "Harry, yours is okay except for this bit at the end, I think you must have misheard Professor Sinistra, Europa's covered in *ice,* not mice — Harry?"

Harry had slid off his chair onto his knees and was now crouching on the singed and threadbare hearthrug, gazing into the flames.

"Er — Harry?" said Ron uncertainly. "Why are you down there?"

"Because I've just seen Sirius's head in the fire," said Harry.

He spoke quite calmly; after all, he had seen Sirius's head in this very fire the previous year and talked to it too. Nevertheless, he could not be sure that he had really seen it this time. . . . It had vanished so quickly. . . .

"Sirius's head?" Hermione repeated. "You mean like when he wanted to talk to you during the Triwizard Tournament? But he wouldn't do that now, it would be too — *Sirius!*"

She gasped, gazing at the fire; Ron dropped his quill. There in the middle of the dancing flames sat Sirius's head, long dark hair falling around his grinning face.

"I was starting to think you'd go to bed before everyone else had disappeared," he said. "I've been checking every hour."

"You've been popping into the fire every hour?" Harry said, half laughing.

"Just for a few seconds to check if the coast was clear yet."

"But what if you'd been seen?" said Hermione anxiously.

"Well, I think a girl — first year by the look of her — might've got a glimpse of me earlier, but don't worry," Sirius said hastily, as Hermione clapped a hand to her mouth. "I was gone the moment she looked back at me and I'll bet she just thought I was an oddly shaped log or something."

"But Sirius, this is taking an awful risk —" Hermione began.

"You sound like Molly," said Sirius. "This was the only way I could come up with of answering Harry's letter without resorting to a code — and codes are breakable."

At the mention of Harry's letter, Hermione and Ron had both turned to stare at him.

"You didn't say you'd written to Sirius!" said Hermione accusingly.

"I forgot," said Harry, which was perfectly true; his meeting with Cho in the Owlery had driven everything before it out of his mind. "Don't look at me like that, Hermione, there was no way anyone would have got secret information out of it, was there, Sirius?"

"No, it was very good," said Sirius, smiling. "Anyway, we'd better be quick, just in case we're disturbed — your scar."

"What about — ?" Ron began, but Hermione said quickly, "We'll tell you afterward, go on, Sirius."

"Well, I know it can't be fun when it hurts, but we don't think it's anything to really worry about. It kept aching all last year, didn't it?"

"Yeah, and Dumbledore said it happened whenever Voldemort was feeling a powerful emotion," said Harry, ignoring, as usual, Ron and Hermione's winces. "So maybe he was just, I dunno, really angry or something the night I had that detention."

"Well, now he's back it's bound to hurt more often," said Sirius.

"So you don't think it had anything to do with Umbridge touching me when I was in detention with her?" Harry asked.

"I doubt it," said Sirius. "I know her by reputation and I'm sure she's no Death Eater —"

"She's foul enough to be one," said Harry darkly and Ron and Hermione nodded vigorously in agreement.

"Yes, but the world isn't split into good people and Death Eaters," said Sirius with a wry smile. "I know she's a nasty piece of work, though — you should hear Remus talk about her."

"Does Lupin know her?" asked Harry quickly, remembering Umbridge's comments about dangerous half-breeds during her first lesson.

"No," said Sirius, "but she drafted a bit of anti-werewolf legislation two years ago that makes it almost impossible for him to get a job."

Harry remembered how much shabbier Lupin looked these days and his dislike of Umbridge deepened even further.

"What's she got against werewolves?" said Hermione angrily.

"Scared of them, I expect," said Sirius, smiling at her indignation. "Apparently she loathes part-humans; she campaigned to have mer-people rounded up and tagged last year too. Imagine wasting your time and energy persecuting merpeople when there are little toerags like Kreacher on the loose —"

Ron laughed but Hermione looked upset.

"Sirius!" she said reproachfully. "Honestly, if you made a bit of an effort with Kreacher I'm sure he'd respond, after all, you are the only member of his family he's got left, and Professor Dumbledore said —"

"So what are Umbridge's lessons like?" Sirius interrupted. "Is she training you all to kill half-breeds?"

"No," said Harry, ignoring Hermione's affronted look at being cut off in her defense of Kreacher. "She's not letting us use magic at all!"

"All we do is read the stupid textbook," said Ron.

"Ah, well, that figures," said Sirius. "Our information from inside the Ministry is that Fudge doesn't want you trained in combat."

"Trained in combat?" repeated Harry incredulously. "What does he think we're doing here, forming some sort of wizard army?"

"That's exactly what he thinks you're doing," said Sirius, "or rather, that's exactly what he's afraid Dumbledore's doing — forming his own private army, with which he will be able to take on the Ministry of Magic."

There was a pause at this, then Ron said, "That's the stupidest thing I've ever heard, including all the stuff that Luna Lovegood comes out with."

"So we're being prevented from learning Defense Against the Dark Arts because Fudge is scared we'll use spells against the Ministry?" said Hermione, looking furious.

"Yep," said Sirius. "Fudge thinks Dumbledore will stop at nothing to seize power. He's getting more paranoid about Dumbledore by the day. It's a matter of time before he has Dumbledore arrested on some trumped-up charge."

This reminded Harry of Percy's letter.

"D'you know if there's going to be anything about Dumbledore in the *Daily Prophet* tomorrow? Only Ron's brother Percy reckons there will be —"

"I don't know," said Sirius, "I haven't seen anyone from the Order all weekend, they're all busy. It's just been Kreacher and me here. . . ."

There was a definite note of bitterness in Sirius's voice.

"So you haven't had any news about Hagrid, either?"

"Ah . . ." said Sirius, "well, he was supposed to be back by now, no one's sure what's happened to him." Then, seeing their stricken faces, he added quickly, "But Dumbledore's not worried, so don't you three get yourselves in a state; I'm sure Hagrid's fine."

"But if he was supposed to be back by now . . ." said Hermione in a small, worried voice.

"Madame Maxime was with him, we've been in touch with her and she says they got separated on the journey home — but there's nothing to suggest he's hurt or — well, nothing to suggest he's not perfectly okay."

Unconvinced, Harry, Ron, and Hermione exchanged worried looks.

"Listen, don't go asking too many questions about Hagrid," said Sirius hastily, "it'll just draw even more attention to the fact that he's not back, and I know Dumbledore doesn't want that. Hagrid's tough, he'll be okay." And when they did not appear cheered by this, Sirius added, "When's your next Hogsmeade weekend anyway? I was thinking, we got away with the dog disguise at the station, didn't we? I thought I could —"

"NO!" said Harry and Hermione together, very loudly.

"Sirius, didn't you see the *Daily Prophet*?" said Hermione anxiously.

"Oh that," said Sirius, grinning, "they're always guessing where I am, they haven't really got a clue —"

"Yeah, but we think this time they have," said Harry. "Something Malfoy said on the train made us think he knew it was you, and his father was on the platform, Sirius — you know, Lucius Malfoy — so don't come up here, whatever you do, if Malfoy recognizes you again —"

"All right, all right, I've got the point," said Sirius. He looked most displeased. "Just an idea, thought you might like to get together —"

"I would, I just don't want you chucked back in Azkaban!" said Harry.

There was a pause in which Sirius looked out of the fire at Harry, a crease between his sunken eyes.

"You're less like your father than I thought," he said finally, a definite coolness in his voice. "The risk would've been what made it fun for James."

"Look —"

"Well, I'd better get going, I can hear Kreacher coming down the stairs," said Sirius, but Harry was sure he was lying. "I'll write to tell you a time I can make it back into the fire, then, shall I? If you can stand to risk it?"

There was a tiny *pop,* and the place where Sirius's head had been was flickering flame once more.

THE HOGWARTS
HIGH INQUISITOR

They had expected to have to comb Hermione's *Daily Prophet* carefully next morning to find the article Percy had mentioned in his letter. However, the departing delivery owl had barely cleared the top of the milk jug when Hermione let out a huge gasp and flattened the newspaper to reveal a large photograph of Dolores Umbridge, smiling widely and blinking slowly at them from beneath the headline:

MINISTRY SEEKS EDUCATIONAL REFORM
DOLORES UMBRIDGE APPOINTED FIRST-EVER "HIGH INQUISITOR"

"'High Inquisitor'?" said Harry darkly, his half-eaten bit of toast slipping from his fingers. "What does *that* mean?"

Hermione read aloud:

"*In a surprise move last night the Ministry of Magic passed new legislation giving itself an unprecedented level of control at Hogwarts School of Witchcraft and Wizardry.*

"'*The Minister has been growing uneasy about goings-on at Hogwarts for some time,' said Junior Assistant to the Minister, Percy Weasley. 'He is now responding to concerns voiced by anxious parents, who feel the school may be moving in a direction they do not approve.'*

"This is not the first time in recent weeks Fudge has used new laws to effect improvements at the Wizarding school. As recently as August 30th Educational Decree Twenty-two was passed, to ensure that, in the event of the current headmaster being unable to provide a candidate for a teaching post, the Ministry should select an appropriate person.

"'That's how Dolores Umbridge came to be appointed to the teaching staff at Hogwarts,' said Weasley last night. 'Dumbledore couldn't find anyone, so the Minister put in Umbridge and of course, she's been an immediate success —'"

"She's been a WHAT?" said Harry loudly.

"Wait, there's more," said Hermione grimly.

"'— an immediate success, totally revolutionizing the teaching of Defense Against the Dark Arts and providing the Minister with on-the-ground feedback about what's really happening at Hogwarts.'

"It is this last function that the Ministry has now formalized with the passing of Educational Decree Twenty-three, which creates the new position of 'Hogwarts High Inquisitor.'

"'This is an exciting new phase in the Minister's plan to get to grips with what some are calling the "falling standards" at Hogwarts,' said Weasley. 'The Inquisitor will have powers to inspect her fellow educators and make sure that they are coming up to scratch. Professor Umbridge has been offered this position in addition to her own teaching post, and we are delighted to say that she has accepted.'

"The Ministry's new moves have received enthusiastic support from parents of students at Hogwarts.

"'I feel much easier in my mind now that I know that Dumbledore is being subjected to fair and objective evaluation,' said Mr. Lucius Malfoy, 41, speaking from his Wiltshire mansion last night. 'Many of us with our children's best interests at heart have been concerned about some of*

Dumbledore's eccentric decisions in the last few years and will be glad to know that the Ministry is keeping an eye on the situation.'

"Among those 'eccentric decisions' are undoubtedly the controversial staff appointments previously described in this newspaper, which have included the hiring of werewolf Remus Lupin, half-giant Rubeus Hagrid, and delusional ex-Auror 'Mad-Eye' Moody.

"Rumors abound, of course, that Albus Dumbledore, once Supreme Mugwump of the International Confederation of Wizards and Chief Warlock of the Wizengamot, is no longer up to the task of managing the prestigious school of Hogwarts.

"'I think the appointment of the Inquisitor is a first step toward ensuring that Hogwarts has a headmaster in whom we can all repose confidence,' said a Ministry insider last night.

"Wizengamot elders Griselda Marchbanks and Tiberius Ogden have resigned in protest at the introduction of the post of Inquisitor to Hogwarts.

"'Hogwarts is a school, not an outpost of Cornelius Fudge's office,' said Madam Marchbanks. 'This is a further disgusting attempt to discredit Albus Dumbledore.' (For a full account of Madam Marchbanks' alleged links to subversive goblin groups, turn to page 17.)"

Hermione finished reading and looked across the table at the other two.

"So now we know how we ended up with Umbridge! Fudge passed this 'Educational Decree' and forced her on us! And now he's given her the power to inspect other teachers!" Hermione was breathing fast and her eyes were very bright. "I can't believe this. It's *outrageous*. . . ."

"I know it is," said Harry. He looked down at his right hand, clenched upon the tabletop, and saw the faint white outline of the words Umbridge had forced him to cut into his skin.

But a grin was unfurling on Ron's face.

"What?" said Harry and Hermione together, staring at him.

"Oh, I can't wait to see McGonagall inspected," said Ron happily. "Umbridge won't know what's hit her."

"Well, come on," said Hermione, jumping up, "we'd better get going, if she's inspecting Binns's class we don't want to be late. . . ."

But Professor Umbridge was not inspecting their History of Magic lesson, which was just as dull as the previous Monday, nor was she in Snape's dungeon when they arrived for double Potions, where Harry's moonstone essay was handed back to him with a large, spiky black D scrawled in an upper corner.

"I have awarded you the grades you would have received if you presented this work in your O.W.L.," said Snape with a smirk, as he swept among them, passing back their homework. "This should give you a realistic idea of what to expect in your examination."

Snape reached the front of the class and turned to face them.

"The general standard of this homework was abysmal. Most of you would have failed had this been your examination. I expect to see a great deal more effort for this week's essay on the various varieties of venom antidotes, or I shall have to start handing out detentions to those dunces who get D's."

He smirked as Malfoy sniggered and said in a carrying whisper, "Some people got *D's*? Ha!"

Harry realized that Hermione was looking sideways to see what grade he had received; he slid his moonstone essay back into his bag as quickly as possible, feeling that he would rather keep that information private.

Determined not to give Snape an excuse to fail him this lesson, Harry read and reread every line of the instructions on the blackboard at least three times before acting on them. His Strengthening Solution was not precisely the clear turquoise shade of Hermione's but it was at least blue rather than pink, like Neville's, and he delivered a flask of it to Snape's desk at the end of the lesson with a feeling of mingled defiance and relief.

"Well, that wasn't as bad as last week, was it?" said Hermione, as they climbed the steps out of the dungeon and made their way across the entrance hall toward lunch. "And the homework didn't go too badly either, did it?"

When neither Ron nor Harry answered, she pressed on, "I mean, all right, I didn't expect the top grade, not if he's marking to O.W.L. standard, but a pass is quite encouraging at this stage, wouldn't you say?"

Harry made a noncommittal noise in his throat.

"Of course, a lot can happen between now and the exam, we've got plenty of time to improve, but the grades we're getting now are a sort of baseline, aren't they? Something we can build on . . ."

They sat down together at the Gryffindor table.

"Obviously, I'd have been *thrilled* if I'd gotten an O —"

"Hermione," said Ron sharply, "if you want to know what grades we got, ask."

"I don't — I didn't mean — well, if you want to tell me —"

"I got a P," said Ron, ladling soup into his bowl. "Happy?"

"Well, that's nothing to be ashamed of," said Fred, who had just arrived at the table with George and Lee Jordan and was sitting down on Harry's right. "Nothing wrong with a good healthy P."

"But," said Hermione, "doesn't P stand for . . ."

"'Poor,' yeah," said Lee Jordan. "Still, better than D, isn't it? 'Dreadful'?"

Harry felt his face grow warm and faked a small coughing fit over his roll. When he emerged from this he was sorry to find that Hermione was still in full flow about O.W.L. grades.

"So top grade's O for 'Outstanding,'" she was saying, "and then there's A —"

"No, E," George corrected her, "E for 'Exceeds Expectations.' And I've always thought Fred and I should've got E in everything, because we exceeded expectations just by turning up for the exams."

They all laughed except Hermione, who plowed on, "So after E, it's A for 'Acceptable,' and that's the last pass grade, isn't it?"

"Yep," said Fred, dunking an entire roll in his soup, transferring it to his mouth, and swallowing it whole.

"Then you get P for 'Poor'" — Ron raised both his arms in mock celebration — "and D for 'Dreadful.'"

"And then T," George reminded him.

"T?" asked Hermione, looking appalled. "Even lower than a D? What on earth does that stand for?"

"'Troll,'" said George promptly.

Harry laughed again, though he was not sure whether or not George was joking. He imagined trying to conceal from Hermione that he had received T's in all his O.W.L.s and immediately resolved to work harder from now on.

"You lot had an inspected lesson yet?" Fred asked them.

"No," said Hermione at once, "have you?"

"Just now, before lunch," said George. "Charms."

"What was it like?" Harry and Hermione asked together.

Fred shrugged.

"Not that bad. Umbridge just lurked in the corner making notes on a clipboard. You know what Flitwick's like, he treated her like a guest, didn't seem to bother him at all. She didn't say much. Asked Alicia a couple of questions about what the classes are normally like, Alicia told her they were really good, that was it."

"I can't see old Flitwick getting marked down," said George, "he usually gets everyone through their exams all right."

"Who've you got this afternoon?" Fred asked Harry.

"Trelawney —"

"A T if ever I saw one —"

"— and Umbridge herself."

"Well, be a good boy and keep your temper with Umbridge today," said George. "Angelina'll do her nut if you miss any more Quidditch practices."

But Harry did not have to wait for Defense Against the Dark Arts to meet Professor Umbridge. He was pulling out his dream diary in a seat at the very back of the shadowy Divination room when Ron elbowed him in the ribs and, looking round, he saw Professor Umbridge emerging through the trapdoor in the floor. The class, which had been talking cheerily, fell silent at once. The abrupt fall in the noise level made Professor Trelawney, who had been wafting about handing out *Dream Oracles,* look round.

"Good afternoon, Professor Trelawney," said Professor Umbridge with her wide smile. "You received my note, I trust? Giving the time and date of your inspection?"

Professor Trelawney nodded curtly and, looking very disgruntled, turned her back on Professor Umbridge and continued to give out books. Still smiling, Professor Umbridge grasped the back of the nearest armchair and pulled it to the front of the class so that it was a few inches behind Professor Trelawney's seat. She then sat down, took her clipboard from her flowery bag, and looked up expectantly, waiting for the class to begin.

Professor Trelawney pulled her shawls tight about her with slightly trembling hands and surveyed the class through her hugely magnifying lenses. "We shall be continuing our study of prophetic dreams today," she said in a brave attempt at her usual mystic tones, though her voice shook slightly. "Divide into pairs, please, and interpret each other's latest nighttime visions with the aid of the *Oracle.*"

She made as though to sweep back to her seat, saw Professor Umbridge sitting right beside it, and immediately veered left toward Parvati and Lavender, who were already deep in discussion about Parvati's most recent dream.

Harry opened his copy of *The Dream Oracle,* watching Umbridge covertly. She was making notes on her clipboard now. After a few minutes she got to her feet and began to pace the room in Trelawney's wake, listening to her conversations with students and posing questions here and there. Harry bent his head hurriedly over his book.

"Think of a dream, quick," he told Ron, "in case the old toad comes our way."

"I did it last time," Ron protested, "it's your turn, you tell me one."

"Oh, I dunno . . ." said Harry desperately, who could not remember dreaming anything at all over the last few days. "Let's say I dreamed I was . . . drowning Snape in my cauldron. Yeah, that'll do. . . ."

Ron chortled as he opened his *Dream Oracle*.

"Okay, we've got to add your age to the date you had the dream, the number of letters in the subject . . . would that be 'drowning' or 'cauldron' or 'Snape'?"

"It doesn't matter, pick any of them," said Harry, chancing a glance behind him. Professor Umbridge was now standing at Professor Trelawney's shoulder making notes while the Divination teacher questioned Neville about his dream diary.

"What night did you dream this again?" Ron said, immersed in calculations.

"I dunno, last night, whenever you like," Harry told him, trying to listen to what Umbridge was saying to Professor Trelawney. They were only a table away from him and Ron now. Professor Umbridge was making another note on her clipboard and Professor Trelawney was looking extremely put out.

"Now," said Umbridge, looking up at Trelawney, "you've been in this post how long, exactly?"

Professor Trelawney scowled at her, arms crossed and shoulders hunched as though wishing to protect herself as much as possible from the indignity of the inspection. After a slight pause in which she seemed to decide that the question was not so offensive that she could reasonably ignore it, she said in a deeply resentful tone, "Nearly sixteen years."

"Quite a period," said Professor Umbridge, making a note on her clipboard. "So it was Professor Dumbledore who appointed you?"

"That's right," said Professor Trelawney shortly.

Professor Umbridge made another note.

"And you are a great-great-granddaughter of the celebrated Seer Cassandra Trelawney?"

"Yes," said Professor Trelawney, holding her head a little higher.

Another note on the clipboard.

"But I think — correct me if I am mistaken — that you are the first in your family since Cassandra to be possessed of second sight?"

"These things often skip — er — three generations," said Professor Trelawney.

Professor Umbridge's toadlike smile widened.

"Of course," she said sweetly, making yet another note. "Well, if you could just predict something for me, then?"

She looked up inquiringly, still smiling. Professor Trelawney had stiffened as though unable to believe her ears.

"I don't understand you," said Professor Trelawney, clutching convulsively at the shawl around her scrawny neck.

"I'd like you to make a prediction for me," said Professor Umbridge very clearly.

Harry and Ron were not the only people watching and listening sneakily from behind their books now; most of the class were staring transfixed at Professor Trelawney as she drew herself up to her full height, her beads and bangles clinking.

"The Inner Eye does not See upon command!" she said in scandalized tones.

"I see," said Professor Umbridge softly, making yet another note on her clipboard.

"I — but — but . . . *wait!*" said Professor Trelawney suddenly, in an attempt at her usual ethereal voice, though the mystical effect was ruined somewhat by the way it was shaking with anger. "I . . . I think I *do* see something . . . something that concerns *you*. . . . Why, I sense something . . . something dark . . . some grave peril . . ."

Professor Trelawney pointed a shaking finger at Professor Umbridge who continued to smile blandly at her, eyebrows raised.

"I am afraid . . . I am afraid that you are in grave danger!" Professor Trelawney finished dramatically.

There was a pause. Professor Umbridge's eyebrows were still raised.

"Right," she said softly, scribbling on her clipboard once more. "Well, if that's really the best you can do . . ."

She turned away, leaving Professor Trelawney standing rooted to the spot, her chest heaving. Harry caught Ron's eye and knew that Ron was thinking exactly the same as he was: They both knew that Professor Trelawney was an old fraud, but on the other hand, they loathed Umbridge so much that they felt very much on Trelawney's side — until she swooped down on them a few seconds later, that was.

"Well?" she said, snapping her long fingers under Harry's nose, uncharacteristically brisk. "Let me see the start you've made on your dream diary, please."

And by the time she had interpreted Harry's dreams at the top of her voice (all of which, even the ones that involved eating porridge, apparently foretold a gruesome and early death), he was feeling much less sympathetic toward her. All the while, Professor Umbridge stood a few feet away, making notes on that clipboard, and when the bell rang she descended the silver ladder first so that she was waiting for them all when they reached their Defense Against the Dark Arts lesson ten minutes later.

She was humming and smiling to herself when they entered the room. Harry and Ron told Hermione, who had been in Arithmancy, exactly what had happened in Divination while they all took out their copies of *Defensive Magical Theory,* but before Hermione could ask any questions Professor Umbridge had called them all to order and silence fell.

"Wands away," she instructed them all smilingly, and those people who had been hopeful enough to take them out sadly returned them to their bags. "As we finished chapter one last lesson, I would like you all to turn to page nineteen today and commence chapter two, 'Common Defensive Theories and Their Derivation.' There will be no need to talk."

Still smiling her wide, self-satisfied smile, she sat down at her desk. The class gave an audible sigh as it turned, as one, to page nineteen. Harry wondered dully whether there were enough chapters in the book to keep them reading through all this year's lessons and was on the point of checking the contents when he noticed that Hermione had her hand in the air again.

Professor Umbridge had noticed too, and what was more, she seemed to have worked out a strategy for just such an eventuality. Instead of trying to pretend she had not noticed Hermione, she got to her feet and walked around the front row of desks until they were face-to-face, then she bent down and whispered, so that the rest of the class could not hear, "What is it this time, Miss Granger?"

"I've already read chapter two," said Hermione.

"Well then, proceed to chapter three."

"I've read that too. I've read the whole book."

Professor Umbridge blinked but recovered her poise almost instantly.

"Well, then, you should be able to tell me what Slinkhard says about counterjinxes in chapter fifteen."

"He says that counterjinxes are improperly named," said Hermione promptly. "He says 'counterjinx' is just a name people give their jinxes when they want to make them sound more acceptable."

Professor Umbridge raised her eyebrows, and Harry knew she was impressed against her will.

"But I disagree," Hermione continued.

Professor Umbridge's eyebrows rose a little higher and her gaze became distinctly colder.

"You disagree?"

"Yes, I do," said Hermione, who, unlike Umbridge, was not whispering, but speaking in a clear, carrying voice that had by now attracted the rest of the class's attention. "Mr. Slinkhard doesn't like jinxes, does he? But I think they can be very useful when they're used defensively."

"Oh, you do, do you?" said Professor Umbridge, forgetting to whisper and straightening up. "Well, I'm afraid it is Mr. Slinkhard's opinion, and not yours, that matters within this classroom, Miss Granger."

"But —" Hermione began.

"That is enough," said Professor Umbridge. She walked back to the front of the class and stood before them, all the jauntiness she had shown at the beginning of the lesson gone. "Miss Granger, I am going to take five points from Gryffindor House."

There was an outbreak of muttering at this.

"What for?" said Harry angrily.

"Don't you get involved!" Hermione whispered urgently to him.

"For disrupting my class with pointless interruptions," said Professor Umbridge smoothly. "I am here to teach you using a Ministry-approved method that does not include inviting students to give their opinions on matters about which they understand very little. Your previous teachers in this subject may have allowed you more license, but as none of them — with the possible exception of Professor Quirrell, who did at least appear to have restricted himself to age-appropriate subjects — would have passed a Ministry inspection —"

"Yeah, Quirrell was a great teacher," said Harry loudly, "there was just that minor drawback of him having Lord Voldemort sticking out of the back of his head."

This pronouncement was followed by one of the loudest silences Harry had ever heard. Then —

"I think another week's detentions would do you some good, Mr. Potter," said Umbridge sleekly.

* * *

The cut on the back of Harry's hand had barely healed and by the following morning, it was bleeding again. He did not complain during the evening's detention; he was determined not to give Umbridge the satisfaction; over and over again he wrote *I must not tell lies* and not a sound escaped his lips, though the cut deepened with every letter.

The very worst part of this second week's worth of detentions was, just as George had predicted, Angelina's reaction. She cornered him just as he arrived at the Gryffindor table for breakfast on Tuesday and shouted so loudly that Professor McGonagall came sweeping down upon the pair of them from the staff table.

"Miss Johnson, how *dare* you make such a racket in the Great Hall! Five points from Gryffindor!"

"But Professor — he's gone and landed himself in detention *again* —"

"What's this, Potter?" said Professor McGonagall sharply, rounding on Harry. "Detention? From whom?"

"From Professor Umbridge," muttered Harry, not meeting Professor McGonagall's beady, square-framed eyes.

"Are you telling me," she said, lowering her voice so that the group of curious Ravenclaws behind them could not hear, "that after the warning I gave you last Monday you lost your temper in Professor Umbridge's class again?"

"Yes," Harry muttered, speaking to the floor.

"Potter, you must get a grip on yourself! You are heading for serious trouble! Another five points from Gryffindor!"

"But — what? Professor, no!" Harry said, furious at this injustice. "I'm already being punished by *her,* why do you have to take points as well?"

"Because detentions do not appear to have any effect on you whatsoever!" said Professor McGonagall tartly. "No, not another word of complaint, Potter! And as for you, Miss Johnson, you will confine your shouting matches to the Quidditch pitch in future or risk losing the team Captaincy!"

She strode back toward the staff table. Angelina gave Harry a look of deepest disgust and stalked away, upon which Harry flung himself onto the bench beside Ron, fuming.

"She's taken points off Gryffindor because I'm having my hand sliced open every night! How is that fair, *how*?"

"I know, mate," said Ron sympathetically, tipping bacon onto Harry's plate, "she's bang out of order."

Hermione, however, merely rustled the pages of her *Daily Prophet* and said nothing.

"You think McGonagall was right, do you?" said Harry angrily to the picture of Cornelius Fudge obscuring Hermione's face.

"I wish she hadn't taken points from you, but I think she's right to warn you not to lose your temper with Umbridge," said Hermione's voice, while Fudge gesticulated forcefully from the front page, clearly giving some kind of speech.

Harry did not speak to Hermione all through Charms, but when they entered Transfiguration he forgot his anger; Professor Umbridge and her clipboard were sitting in a corner and the sight of her drove the memory of breakfast right out of his head.

"Excellent," whispered Ron, as they sat down in their usual seats. "Let's see Umbridge get what she deserves."

Professor McGonagall marched into the room without giving the slightest indication that she knew Professor Umbridge was there.

"That will do," she said and silence fell immediately. "Mr. Finnigan, kindly come here and hand back the homework — Miss Brown, please take this box of mice — don't be silly, girl, they won't hurt you — and hand one to each student —"

"Hem, hem," said Professor Umbridge, employing the same silly little cough she had used to interrupt Dumbledore on the first night of term. Professor McGonagall ignored her. Seamus handed back Harry's essay; Harry took it without looking at him and saw, to his relief, that he had managed an A.

"Right then, everyone, listen closely — Dean Thomas, if you do that to the mouse again I shall put you in detention — most of you have now successfully vanished your snails and even those who were left with a certain amount of shell have the gist of the spell. Today we shall be —"

"Hem, hem," said Professor Umbridge.

"Yes?" said Professor McGonagall, turning round, her eyebrows so close together they seemed to form one long, severe line.

"I was just wondering, Professor, whether you received my note telling you of the date and time of your inspec —"

"Obviously I received it, or I would have asked you what you are doing in my classroom," said Professor McGonagall, turning her back firmly on Professor Umbridge. Many of the students exchanged looks of glee. "As I was saying, today we shall be practicing the altogether more difficult vanishment of mice. Now, the Vanishing Spell —"

"Hem, hem."

"I wonder," said Professor McGonagall in cold fury, turning on Professor Umbridge, "how you expect to gain an idea of my usual teaching methods if you continue to interrupt me? You see, I do not generally permit people to talk when I am talking."

Professor Umbridge looked as though she had just been slapped in the face. She did not speak, but straightened the parchment on her clipboard and began scribbling furiously. Looking supremely unconcerned, Professor McGonagall addressed the class once more.

"As I was saying, the Vanishing Spell becomes more difficult with the complexity of the animal to be vanished. The snail, as an invertebrate, does not present much of a challenge; the mouse, as a mammal, offers a much greater one. This is not, therefore, magic you can accomplish with your mind on your dinner. So — you know the incantation, let me see what you can do. . . ."

"How she can lecture me about not losing my temper with Umbridge!" Harry said to Ron under his voice, but he was grinning; his anger with Professor McGonagall had quite evaporated.

Professor Umbridge did not follow Professor McGonagall around the class as she had followed Professor Trelawney; perhaps she thought that Professor McGonagall would not permit it. She did, however, take many more notes while she sat in her corner, and when Professor McGonagall finally told them all to pack away, rose with a grim expression on her face.

"Well, it's a start," said Ron, holding up a long, wriggling mouse tail and dropping it back into the box Lavender was passing around.

As they filed out of the classroom, Harry saw Professor Umbridge approach the teacher's desk; he nudged Ron, who nudged Hermione in turn, and the three of them deliberately fell back to eavesdrop.

"How long have you been teaching at Hogwarts?" Professor Umbridge asked.

"Thirty-nine years this December," said Professor McGonagall brusquely, snapping her bag shut.

Professor Umbridge made a note.

"Very well," she said, "you will receive the results of your inspection in ten days' time."

"I can hardly wait," said Professor McGonagall in a coldly indifferent voice, and she strode off toward the door. "Hurry up, you three," she added, sweeping Harry, Ron, and Hermione before her. Harry could not help giving her a faint smile and could have sworn he received one in return.

He had thought that the next time he would see Umbridge would be in his detention that evening, but he was wrong. When they walked down the lawns toward the forest for Care of Magical Creatures, they found her and her clipboard waiting for them beside Professor Grubbly-Plank.

"You do not usually take this class, is that correct?" Harry heard her ask as they arrived at the trestle table where the group of captive bowtruckles were scrabbling around for wood lice like so many living twigs.

"Quite correct," said Professor Grubbly-Plank, hands behind her back and bouncing on the balls of her feet. "I am a substitute teacher standing in for Professor Hagrid."

Harry exchanged uneasy looks with Ron and Hermione. Malfoy was whispering with Crabbe and Goyle; he would surely love this opportunity to tell tales on Hagrid to a member of the Ministry.

"Hmm," said Professor Umbridge, dropping her voice, though Harry could still hear her quite clearly, "I wonder — the headmaster seems strangely reluctant to give me any information on the matter — can *you* tell me what is causing Professor Hagrid's very extended leave of absence?"

Harry saw Malfoy look up eagerly.

"'Fraid I can't," said Professor Grubbly-Plank breezily. "Don't know anything more about it than you do. Got an owl from Dumbledore, would I like a couple of weeks teaching work, accepted — that's as much as I know. Well . . . shall I get started then?"

"Yes, please do," said Professor Umbridge, scribbling upon her clipboard.

Umbridge took a different tack in this class and wandered among the students, questioning them on magical creatures. Most people were able to answer well and Harry's spirits lifted somewhat; at least the class was not letting Hagrid down.

"Overall," said Professor Umbridge, returning to Professor Grubbly-Plank's side after a lengthy interrogation of Dean Thomas, "how do you, as a temporary member of staff — an objective outsider, I suppose you might say — how do you find Hogwarts? Do you feel you receive enough support from the school management?"

"Oh, yes, Dumbledore's excellent," said Professor Grubbly-Plank heartily. "No, I'm very happy with the way things are run, very happy indeed."

Looking politely incredulous, Umbridge made a tiny note on her clipboard and went on, "And what are you planning to cover with this class this year — assuming, of course, that Professor Hagrid does not return?"

"Oh, I'll take them through the creatures that most often come up in O.W.L.," said Professor Grubbly-Plank. "Not much left to do — they've studied unicorns and nifflers, I thought we'd cover porlocks and kneazles, make sure they can recognize crups and knarls, you know. . . ."

"Well, *you* seem to know what you're doing, at any rate," said Professor Umbridge, making a very obvious tick on her clipboard. Harry did not like the emphasis she put on *"you"* and liked it even less when she put her next question to Goyle: "Now, I hear there have been injuries in this class?"

Goyle gave a stupid grin. Malfoy hastened to answer the question. "That was me," he said. "I was slashed by a hippogriff."

"A hippogriff?" said Professor Umbridge, now scribbling frantically.

"Only because he was too stupid to listen to what Hagrid told him to do," said Harry angrily.

Both Ron and Hermione groaned. Professor Umbridge turned her head slowly in Harry's direction.

"Another night's detention, I think," she said softly. "Well, thank you very much, Professor Grubbly-Plank, I think that's all I need here. You will be receiving the results of your inspection within ten days."

"Jolly good," said Professor Grubbly-Plank, and Professor Umbridge set off back across the lawn to the castle.

* * *

It was nearly midnight when Harry left Umbridge's office that night, his hand now bleeding so severely that it was staining the scarf he had wrapped around it. He expected the common room to be empty when he returned, but Ron and Hermione had sat up waiting for him. He was pleased to see them, especially as Hermione was disposed to be sympathetic rather than critical.

"Here," she said anxiously, pushing a small bowl of yellow liquid toward him, "soak your hand in that, it's a solution of strained and pickled murtlap tentacles, it should help."

Harry placed his bleeding, aching hand into the bowl and experienced a wonderful feeling of relief. Crookshanks curled around his legs, purring loudly, and then leapt into his lap and settled down.

"Thanks," he said gratefully, scratching behind Crookshanks's ears with his left hand.

"I still reckon you should complain about this," said Ron in a low voice.

"No," said Harry flatly.

"McGonagall would go nuts if she knew —"

"Yeah, she probably would," said Harry. "And how long d'you reckon it'd take Umbridge to pass another Decree saying anyone who complains about the High Inquisitor gets sacked immediately?"

Ron opened his mouth to retort but nothing came out and after a moment he closed it again in a defeated sort of way.

"She's an awful woman," said Hermione in a small voice. "*Awful.* You know, I was just saying to Ron when you came in . . . we've got to do something about her."

"I suggested poison," said Ron grimly.

"No . . . I mean, something about what a dreadful teacher she is, and how we're not going to learn any defense from her at all," said Hermione.

"Well, what can we do about that?" said Ron, yawning. "'S too late, isn't it? She got the job, she's here to stay, Fudge'll make sure of that."

"Well," said Hermione tentatively. "You know, I was thinking to-day. . . ." She shot a slightly nervous look at Harry and then plunged on, "I was thinking that — maybe the time's come when we should just — just do it ourselves."

"Do what ourselves?" said Harry suspiciously, still floating his hand in the essence of murtlap tentacles.

"Well — learn Defense Against the Dark Arts ourselves," said Hermione.

"Come off it," groaned Ron. "You want us to do extra work? D'you realize Harry and I are behind on homework again and it's only the second week?"

"But this is much more important than homework!" said Hermione.

Harry and Ron goggled at her.

"I didn't think there was anything in the universe more important than homework," said Ron.

"Don't be silly, of course there is!" said Hermione, and Harry saw, with an ominous feeling, that her face was suddenly alight with the kind of fervor that S.P.E.W. usually inspired in her. "It's about pre-paring ourselves, like Harry said in Umbridge's first lesson, for what's waiting out there. It's about making sure we really can defend our-selves. If we don't learn anything for a whole year —"

"We can't do much by ourselves," said Ron in a defeated voice. "I mean, all right, we can go and look jinxes up in the library and try and practice them, I suppose —"

"No, I agree, we've gone past the stage where we can just learn things out of books," said Hermione. "We need a teacher, a proper one, who can show us how to use the spells and correct us if we're going wrong."

"If you're talking about Lupin . . ." Harry began.

"No, no, I'm not talking about Lupin," said Hermione. "He's too busy with the Order and anyway, the most we could see him is during Hogsmeade weekends and that's not nearly often enough."

"Who, then?" said Harry, frowning at her.

Hermione heaved a very deep sigh.

"Isn't it obvious?" she said. "I'm talking about *you*, Harry."

There was a moment's silence. A light night breeze rattled the windowpanes behind Ron and the fire guttered.

"About me what?" said Harry.

"I'm talking about *you* teaching us Defense Against the Dark Arts."

Harry stared at her. Then he turned to Ron, ready to exchange the exasperated looks they sometimes shared when Hermione elaborated on far-fetched schemes like S.P.E.W. To Harry's consternation, however, Ron did not look exasperated. He was frowning slightly, apparently thinking. Then he said, "That's an idea."

"What's an idea?" said Harry.

"You," said Ron. "Teaching us to do it."

"But . . ."

Harry was grinning now, sure the pair of them were pulling his leg.

"But I'm not a teacher, I can't —"

"Harry, you're the best in the year at Defense Against the Dark Arts," said Hermione.

"Me?" said Harry, now grinning more broadly than ever. "No I'm not, you've beaten me in every test —"

"Actually, I haven't," said Hermione coolly. "You beat me in our third year — the only year we both sat the test and had a teacher who actually knew the subject. But I'm not talking about test results, Harry. Look what you've *done*!"

"How d'you mean?"

"You know what, I'm not sure I want someone this stupid teaching me," Ron said to Hermione, smirking slightly. He turned to Harry. "Let's think," he said, pulling a face like Goyle concentrating. "Uh . . . first year — you saved the Stone from You-Know-Who."

"But that was luck," said Harry, "that wasn't skill —"

"Second year," Ron interrupted, "you killed the basilisk and destroyed Riddle."

"Yeah, but if Fawkes hadn't turned up I —"

"Third year," said Ron, louder still, "you fought off about a hundred dementors at once —"

"You know that was a fluke, if the Time-Turner hadn't —"

"Last year," Ron said, almost shouting now, "you fought off You-Know-Who again —"

"Listen to me!" said Harry, almost angrily, because Ron and Hermione were both smirking now. "Just listen to me, all right? It sounds great when you say it like that, but all that stuff was luck — I didn't know what I was doing half the time, I didn't plan any of it, I just did whatever I could think of, and I nearly always had help —"

Ron and Hermione were still smirking and Harry felt his temper rise; he wasn't even sure why he was feeling so angry.

"Don't sit there grinning like you know better than I do, I was there, wasn't I?" he said heatedly. "I know what went on, all right? And I didn't get through any of that because I was brilliant at Defense Against the Dark Arts, I got through it all because — because help came at the right time, or because I guessed right — but I just blundered through it all, I didn't have a clue what I was doing — STOP LAUGHING!"

The bowl of murtlap essence fell to the floor and smashed. He became aware that he was on his feet, though he couldn't remember standing up. Crookshanks streaked away under a sofa; Ron and Hermione's smiles had vanished.

"*You don't know what it's like!* You — neither of you — you've never had to face him, have you? You think it's just memorizing a bunch of spells and throwing them at him, like you're in class or something? The whole time you know there's nothing between you and dying except your own — your own brain or guts or whatever — like you can think straight when you know you're about a second from being murdered, or tortured, or watching your friends die — they've never taught us that in their classes, what it's like to deal with things like that — and you two sit there acting like I'm a clever little boy to be standing here, alive, like Diggory was stupid, like he messed up — you just don't get it, that could just as easily have been me, it would have been if Voldemort hadn't needed me —"

"We weren't saying anything like that, mate," said Ron, looking aghast. "We weren't having a go at Diggory, we didn't — you've got the wrong end of the —"

He looked helplessly at Hermione, whose face was stricken.

"Harry," she said timidly, "don't you see? This . . . this is exactly why we need you. . . . We need to know what it's r-really like . . . facing him . . . facing V-Voldemort."

It was the first time she had ever said Voldemort's name, and it was this, more than anything else, that calmed Harry. Still breathing hard, he sank back into his chair, becoming aware as he did so that his hand was throbbing horribly again. He wished he had not smashed the bowl of murtlap essence.

"Well . . . think about it," said Hermione quietly. "Please?"

Harry could not think of anything to say. He was feeling ashamed of his outburst already. He nodded, hardly aware of what he was agreeing to.

Hermione stood up.

"Well, I'm off to bed," she said in a voice that was clearly as natural as she could make it. "Erm . . . 'night."

Ron had gotten to his feet too.

"Coming?" he said awkwardly to Harry.

"Yeah," said Harry. "In . . . in a minute. I'll just clear this up."

He indicated the smashed bowl on the floor. Ron nodded and left.

"Reparo," Harry muttered, pointing his wand at the broken pieces

of china. They flew back together, good as new, but there was no returning the murtlap essence to the bowl.

He was suddenly so tired that he was tempted to sink back into his armchair and sleep there, but instead he got to his feet and followed Ron upstairs. His restless night was punctuated once more by dreams of long corridors and locked doors, and he awoke next day with his scar prickling again.

IN THE HOG'S HEAD

Hermione made no mention of Harry giving Defense Against the Dark Arts lessons for two whole weeks after her original suggestion. Harry's detentions with Umbridge were finally over (he doubted whether the words now etched on the back of his hand would ever fade entirely); Ron had had four more Quidditch practices and not been shouted at during the last two; and all three of them had managed to vanish their mice in Transfiguration (Hermione had actually progressed to vanishing kittens), before the subject was broached again, on a wild, blustery evening at the end of September, when the three of them were sitting in the library, looking up potion ingredients for Snape.

"I was wondering," Hermione said suddenly, "whether you'd thought any more about Defense Against the Dark Arts, Harry."

"'Course I have," said Harry grumpily. "Can't forget it, can we, with that hag teaching us —"

"I meant the idea Ron and I had" — Ron cast her an alarmed, threatening kind of look; she frowned at him — "oh, all right, the idea *I* had, then — about you teaching us."

Harry did not answer at once. He pretended to be perusing a page of *Asiatic Anti-Venoms,* because he did not want to say what was in his mind.

The fact was that he had given the matter a great deal of thought over the past fortnight. Sometimes it seemed an insane idea, just as it had on the night Hermione had proposed it, but at others, he had found himself thinking about the spells that had served him best in his various encounters with Dark creatures and Death Eaters — found himself, in fact, subconsciously planning lessons. . . .

"Well," he said slowly, when he could not pretend to find Asiatic anti-venoms interesting much longer, "yeah, I — I've thought about it a bit."

"And?" said Hermione eagerly.

"I dunno," said Harry, playing for time. He looked up at Ron.

"I thought it was a good idea from the start," said Ron, who seemed keener to join in this conversation now that he was sure that Harry was not going to start shouting again.

Harry shifted uncomfortably in his chair.

"You did listen to what I said about a load of it being luck, didn't you?"

"Yes, Harry," said Hermione gently, "but all the same, there's no point pretending that you're not good at Defense Against the Dark Arts, because you are. You were the only person last year who could throw off the Imperius Curse completely, you can produce a Patronus, you can do all sorts of stuff that full-grown wizards can't, Viktor always said —"

Ron looked around at her so fast he appeared to crick his neck; rubbing it, he said, "Yeah? What did Vicky say?"

"Ho ho," said Hermione in a bored voice. "He said Harry knew how to do stuff even he didn't, and he was in the final year at Durmstrang."

Ron was looking at Hermione suspiciously.

"You're not still in contact with him, are you?"

"So what if I am?" said Hermione coolly, though her face was a little pink. "I can have a pen pal if I —"

"He didn't only want to be your pen pal," said Ron accusingly.

Hermione shook her head exasperatedly and, ignoring Ron, who was continuing to watch her, said to Harry, "Well, what do you think? Will you teach us?"

"Just you and Ron, yeah?"

"Well," said Hermione, now looking a mite anxious again. "Well . . . now, don't fly off the handle again, Harry, please. . . . But I really think you ought to teach anyone who wants to learn. I mean, we're talking about defending ourselves against V-Voldemort — oh, don't be pathetic, Ron — it doesn't seem fair if we don't offer the chance to other people."

Harry considered this for a moment, then said, "Yeah, but I doubt anyone except you two would want to be taught by me. I'm a nutter, remember?"

"Well, I think you might be surprised how many people would be interested in hearing what you've got to say," said Hermione seriously. "Look," she leaned toward him; Ron, who was still watching her with a frown on his face, leaned forward to listen too, "you know the first weekend in October's a Hogsmeade weekend? How would it be if we tell anyone who's interested to meet us in the village and we can talk it over?"

"Why do we have to do it outside school?" said Ron.

"Because," said Hermione, returning to the diagram of the Chinese Chomping Cabbage she was copying, "I don't think Umbridge would be very happy if she found out what we were up to."

Harry had been looking forward to the weekend trip into Hogsmeade, but there was one thing worrying him. Sirius had maintained a stony silence since he had appeared in the fire at the beginning of

September; Harry knew they had made him angry by saying that they did not want him to come — but he still worried from time to time that Sirius might throw caution to the winds and turn up anyway. What were they going to do if the great black dog came bounding up the street toward them in Hogsmeade, perhaps under the nose of Draco Malfoy?

"Well, you can't blame him for wanting to get out and about," said Ron, when Harry discussed his fears with him and Hermione. "I mean, he's been on the run for over two years, hasn't he, and I know that can't have been a laugh, but at least he was free, wasn't he? And now he's just shut up all the time with that lunatic elf."

Hermione scowled at Ron, but otherwise ignored the slight on Kreacher.

"The trouble is," she said to Harry, "until V-Voldemort — oh for heaven's *sake*, Ron — comes out into the open, Sirius is going to have to stay hidden, isn't he? I mean, the stupid Ministry isn't going to realize Sirius is innocent until they accept that Dumbledore's been telling the truth about him all along. And once the fools start catching real Death Eaters again it'll be obvious Sirius isn't one . . . I mean, he hasn't got the Mark, for one thing."

"I don't reckon he'd be stupid enough to turn up," said Ron bracingly. "Dumbledore'd go mad if he did and Sirius listens to Dumbledore even if he doesn't like what he hears."

When Harry continued to look worried, Hermione said, "Listen, Ron and I have been sounding out people who we thought might want to learn some proper Defense Against the Dark Arts, and there are a couple who seem interested. We've told them to meet us in Hogsmeade."

"Right," said Harry vaguely, his mind still on Sirius.

"Don't worry, Harry," Hermione said quietly. "You've got enough on your plate without Sirius too."

She was quite right, of course; he was barely keeping up with his homework, though he was doing much better now that he was no longer spending every evening in detention with Umbridge. Ron was even further behind with his work than Harry, because while they both had Quidditch practices twice a week, Ron also had prefect duties. However, Hermione, who was taking more subjects than either of them, had not only finished all her homework but was also finding time to knit more elf clothes. Harry had to admit that she was getting better; it was now almost always possible to distinguish between the hats and the socks.

The morning of the Hogsmeade visit dawned bright but windy. After breakfast they queued up in front of Filch, who matched their names to the long list of students who had permission from their parents or guardian to visit the village. With a slight pang, Harry remembered that if it hadn't been for Sirius, he would not have been going at all.

When Harry reached Filch, the caretaker gave a great sniff as though trying to detect a whiff of something from Harry. Then he gave a curt nod that set his jowls aquiver again and Harry walked on, out onto the stone steps and the cold, sunlit day.

"Er — why was Filch sniffing you?" asked Ron, as he, Harry, and Hermione set off at a brisk pace down the wide drive to the gates.

"I suppose he was checking for the smell of Dungbombs," said Harry with a small laugh. "I forgot to tell you . . ."

And he recounted the story of sending his letter to Sirius and Filch bursting in seconds later, demanding to see the letter. To his slight surprise, Hermione found this story highly interesting, much more, indeed, than he did himself.

"He said he was tipped off you were ordering Dungbombs? But who had tipped him off?"

"I dunno," said Harry, shrugging. "Maybe Malfoy, he'd think it was a laugh."

They walked between the tall stone pillars topped with winged

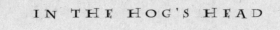

boars and turned left onto the road into the village, the wind whipping their hair into their eyes.

"Malfoy?" said Hermione, very skeptically. "Well . . . yes . . . maybe . . ."

And she remained deep in thought all the way into the outskirts of Hogsmeade.

"Where are we going anyway?" Harry asked. "The Three Broomsticks?"

"Oh — no," said Hermione, coming out of her reverie, "no, it's always packed and really noisy. I've told the others to meet us in the Hog's Head, that other pub, you know the one, it's not on the main road. I think it's a bit . . . you know . . . *dodgy* . . . but students don't normally go in there, so I don't think we'll be overheard."

They walked down the main street past Zonko's Joke Shop, where they were unsurprised to see Fred, George, and Lee Jordan, past the post office, from which owls issued at regular intervals, and turned up a side street at the top of which stood a small inn. A battered wooden sign hung from a rusty bracket over the door, with a picture upon it of a wild boar's severed head leaking blood onto the white cloth around it. The sign creaked in the wind as they approached. All three of them hesitated outside the door.

"Well, come on," said Hermione slightly nervously. Harry led the way inside.

It was not at all like the Three Broomsticks, whose large bar gave an impression of gleaming warmth and cleanliness. The Hog's Head bar comprised one small, dingy, and very dirty room that smelled strongly of something that might have been goats. The bay windows were so encrusted with grime that very little daylight could permeate the room, which was lit instead with the stubs of candles sitting on rough wooden tables. The floor seemed at first glance to be earthy, though as Harry stepped onto it he realized that there was stone beneath what seemed to be the accumulated filth of centuries.

Harry remembered Hagrid mentioning this pub in his first year: *"Yeh get a lot o' funny folk in the Hog's Head,"* he had said, explaining how he had won a dragon's egg from a hooded stranger there. At the time Harry had wondered why Hagrid had not found it odd that the stranger kept his face hidden throughout their encounter; now he saw that keeping your face hidden was something of a fashion in the Hog's Head. There was a man at the bar whose whole head was wrapped in dirty gray bandages, though he was still managing to gulp endless glasses of some smoking, fiery substance through a slit over his mouth. Two figures shrouded in hoods sat at a table in one of the windows; Harry might have thought them dementors if they had not been talking in strong Yorkshire accents; in a shadowy corner beside the fireplace sat a witch with a thick, black veil that fell to her toes. They could just see the tip of her nose because it caused the veil to protrude slightly.

"I don't know about this, Hermione," Harry muttered, as they crossed to the bar. He was looking particularly at the heavily veiled witch. "Has it occurred to you Umbridge might be under that?"

Hermione cast an appraising eye at the veiled figure.

"Umbridge is shorter than that woman," she said quietly. "And anyway, even if Umbridge *does* come in here there's nothing she can do to stop us, Harry, because I've double- and triple-checked the school rules. We're not out-of-bounds; I specifically asked Professor Flitwick whether students were allowed to come in the Hog's Head, and he said yes, but he advised me strongly to bring our own glasses. And I've looked up everything I can think of about study groups and homework groups and they're definitely allowed. I just don't think it's a good idea if we *parade* what we're doing."

"No," said Harry dryly, "especially as it's not exactly a homework group you're planning, is it?"

The barman sidled toward them out of a back room. He was a grumpy-looking old man with a great deal of long gray hair and beard. He was tall and thin and looked vaguely familiar to Harry.

"What?" he grunted.

"Three butterbeers, please," said Hermione.

The man reached beneath the counter and pulled up three very dusty, very dirty bottles, which he slammed on the bar.

"Six Sickles," he said.

"I'll get them," said Harry quickly, passing over the silver. The barman's eyes traveled over Harry, resting for a fraction of a second on his scar. Then he turned away and deposited Harry's money in an ancient wooden till whose drawer slid open automatically to receive it. Harry, Ron, and Hermione retreated to the farthest table from the bar and sat down, looking around, while the man in the dirty gray bandages rapped the counter with his knuckles and received another smoking drink from the barman.

"You know what?" Ron murmured, looking over at the bar with enthusiasm. "We could order anything we liked in here, I bet that bloke would sell us anything, he wouldn't care. I've always wanted to try firewhisky —"

"You — are — a — *prefect*," snarled Hermione.

"Oh," said Ron, the smile fading from his face. "Yeah . . ."

"So who did you say is supposed to be meeting us?" Harry asked, wrenching open the rusty top of his butterbeer and taking a swig.

"Just a couple of people," Hermione repeated, checking her watch and then looking anxiously toward the door. "I told them to be here about now and I'm sure they all know where it is — oh look, this might be them now —"

The door of the pub had opened. A thick band of dusty sunlight split the room in two for a moment and then vanished, blocked by the incoming rush of a crowd of people.

First came Neville with Dean and Lavender, who were closely followed by Parvati and Padma Patil with (Harry's stomach did a back flip) Cho and one of her usually giggling girlfriends, then (on her own and looking so dreamy that she might have walked in by accident)

Luna Lovegood; then Katie Bell, Alicia Spinnet, and Angelina John-son, Colin and Dennis Creevey, Ernie Macmillan, Justin Finch-Fletchley, Hannah Abbott, and a Hufflepuff girl with a long plait down her back whose name Harry did not know; three Ravenclaw boys he was pretty sure were called Anthony Goldstein, Michael Cor-ner, and Terry Boot; Ginny, followed by a tall skinny blond boy with an upturned nose whom Harry recognized vaguely as being a member of the Hufflepuff Quidditch team, and bringing up the rear, Fred and George Weasley with their friend Lee Jordan, all three of whom were carrying large paper bags crammed with Zonko's merchandise.

"A couple of people?" said Harry hoarsely to Hermione. "A *couple of people?*"

"Yes, well, the idea seemed quite popular," said Hermione happily. "Ron, do you want to pull up some more chairs?"

The barman had frozen in the act of wiping out a glass with a rag so filthy it looked as though it had never been washed. Possibly he had never seen his pub so full.

"Hi," said Fred, reaching the bar first and counting his companions quickly. "Could we have . . . twenty-five butterbeers, please?"

The barman glared at him for a moment, then, throwing down his rag irritably as though he had been interrupted in something very im-portant, he started passing up dusty butterbeers from under the bar.

"Cheers," said Fred, handing them out. "Cough up, everyone, I haven't got enough gold for all of these. . . ."

Harry watched numbly as the large chattering group took their beers from Fred and rummaged in their robes to find coins. He could not imagine what all these people had turned up for until the horrible thought occurred to him that they might be expecting some kind of speech, at which he rounded on Hermione.

"What have you been telling people?" he said in a low voice. "What are they expecting?"

"I've told you, they just want to hear what you've got to say," said Hermione soothingly; but Harry continued to look at her so furiously that she added quickly, "You don't have to do anything yet, I'll speak to them first."

"Hi, Harry," said Neville, beaming and taking a seat opposite Harry.

Harry tried to smile back, but did not speak; his mouth was exceptionally dry. Cho had just smiled at him and sat down on Ron's right. Her friend, who had curly reddish-blonde hair, did not smile, but gave Harry a thoroughly mistrustful look that told Harry plainly that, given her way, she would not be here at all.

In twos and threes the new arrivals settled around Harry, Ron, and Hermione, some looking rather excited, others curious, Luna Lovegood gazing dreamily into space. When everybody had pulled up a chair, the chatter died out. Every eye was upon Harry.

"Er," said Hermione, her voice slightly higher than usual out of nerves. "Well — er — hi."

The group focused its attention on her instead, though eyes continued to dart back regularly to Harry.

"Well . . . erm . . . well, you know why you're here. Erm . . . well, Harry here had the idea — I mean" — Harry had thrown her a sharp look — "I had the idea — that it might be good if people who wanted to study Defense Against the Dark Arts — and I mean, really study it, you know, not the rubbish that Umbridge is doing with us" — (Hermione's voice became suddenly much stronger and more confident) — "because nobody could call that Defense Against the Dark Arts" — "Hear, hear," said Anthony Goldstein, and Hermione looked heartened — "well, I thought it would be good if we, well, took matters into our own hands."

She paused, looked sideways at Harry, and went on, "And by that I mean learning how to defend ourselves properly, not just theory but the real spells —"

"You want to pass your Defense Against the Dark Arts O.W.L. too though, I bet?" said Michael Corner.

"Of course I do," said Hermione at once. "But I want more than that, I want to be properly trained in Defense because . . . because . . ." She took a great breath and finished, "Because Lord Voldemort's back."

The reaction was immediate and predictable. Cho's friend shrieked and slopped butterbeer down herself, Terry Boot gave a kind of involuntary twitch, Padma Patil shuddered, and Neville gave an odd yelp that he managed to turn into a cough. All of them, however, looked fixedly, even eagerly, at Harry.

"Well . . . that's the plan anyway," said Hermione. "If you want to join us, we need to decide how we're going to —"

"Where's the proof You-Know-Who's back?" said the blond Hufflepuff player in a rather aggressive voice.

"Well, Dumbledore believes it —" Hermione began.

"You mean, Dumbledore believes *him*," said the blond boy, nodding at Harry.

"Who are *you*?" said Ron rather rudely.

"Zacharias Smith," said the boy, "and I think we've got the right to know exactly what makes *him* say You-Know-Who's back."

"Look," said Hermione, intervening swiftly, "that's really not what this meeting was supposed to be about —"

"It's okay, Hermione," said Harry.

It had just dawned upon him why there were so many people there. He felt that Hermione should have seen this coming. Some of these people — maybe even most of them — had turned up in the hope of hearing Harry's story firsthand.

"What makes me say You-Know-Who's back?" he asked, looking Zacharias straight in the face. "I saw him. But Dumbledore told the whole school what happened last year, and if you didn't believe him, you don't believe me, and I'm not wasting an afternoon trying to convince anyone."

The whole group seemed to have held its breath while Harry spoke. Harry had the impression that even the barman was listening in. He was wiping the same glass with the filthy rag; it was becoming steadily dirtier.

Zacharias said dismissively, "All Dumbledore told us last year was that Cedric Diggory got killed by You-Know-Who and that you brought Diggory's body back to Hogwarts. He didn't give us details, he didn't tell us exactly how Diggory got murdered, I think we'd all like to know —"

"If you've come to hear exactly what it looks like when Voldemort murders someone I can't help you," Harry said. His temper, always so close to the surface these days, was rising again. He did not take his eyes from Zacharias Smith's aggressive face, determined not to look at Cho. "I don't want to talk about Cedric Diggory, all right? So if that's what you're here for, you might as well clear out."

He cast an angry look in Hermione's direction. This was, he felt, all her fault; she had decided to display him like some sort of freak and of course they had all turned up to see just how wild his story was. . . . But none of them left their seats, not even Zacharias Smith, though he continued to gaze intently at Harry.

"So," said Hermione, her voice very high-pitched again. "So . . . like I was saying . . . if you want to learn some defense, then we need to work out how we're going to do it, how often we're going to meet, and where we're going to —"

"Is it true," interrupted the girl with the long plait down her back, looking at Harry, "that you can produce a Patronus?"

There was a murmur of interest around the group at this.

"Yeah," said Harry slightly defensively.

"A corporeal Patronus?"

The phrase stirred something in Harry's memory.

"Er — you don't know Madam Bones, do you?" he asked.

The girl smiled.

"She's my auntie," she said. "I'm Susan Bones. She told me about your hearing. So — is it really true? You make a stag Patronus?"

"Yes," said Harry.

"Blimey, Harry!" said Lee, looking deeply impressed. "I never knew that!"

"Mum told Ron not to spread it around," said Fred, grinning at Harry. "She said you got enough attention as it was."

"She's not wrong," mumbled Harry and a couple of people laughed. The veiled witch sitting alone shifted very slightly in her seat.

"And did you kill a basilisk with that sword in Dumbledore's office?" demanded Terry Boot. "That's what one of the portraits on the wall told me when I was in there last year. . . ."

"Er — yeah, I did, yeah," said Harry.

Justin Finch-Fletchley whistled, the Creevey brothers exchanged awestruck looks, and Lavender Brown said "wow" softly. Harry was feeling slightly hot around the collar now; he was determinedly looking anywhere but at Cho.

"And in our first year," said Neville to the group at large, "he saved that Sorcerous Stone —"

"Sorcerer's," hissed Hermione.

"Yes, that, from You-Know-Who," finished Neville.

Hannah Abbott's eyes were as round as Galleons.

"And that's not to mention," said Cho (Harry's eyes snapped onto her, she was looking at him, smiling; his stomach did another somersault), "all the tasks he had to get through in the Triwizard Tournament last year — getting past dragons and merpeople and acromantulas and things. . . ."

There was a murmur of impressed agreement around the table.

Harry's insides were squirming. He was trying to arrange his face so that he did not look too pleased with himself. The fact that Cho had just praised him made it much, much harder for him to say the thing he had sworn to himself he would tell them.

"Look," he said and everyone fell silent at once, "I . . . I don't want to sound like I'm trying to be modest or anything, but . . . I had a lot of help with all that stuff. . . ."

"Not with the dragon, you didn't," said Michael Corner at once. "That was a seriously cool bit of flying. . . ."

"Yeah, well —" said Harry, feeling it would be churlish to disagree.

"And nobody helped you get rid of those dementors this summer," said Susan Bones.

"No," said Harry, "no, okay, I know I did bits of it without help, but the point I'm trying to make is —"

"Are you trying to weasel out of showing us any of this stuff?" said Zacharias Smith.

"Here's an idea," said Ron loudly, before Harry could speak, "why don't you shut your mouth?"

Perhaps the word "weasel" had affected Ron particularly strongly; in any case, he was now looking at Zacharias as though he would like nothing better than to thump him. Zacharias flushed.

"Well, we've all turned up to learn from him, and now he's telling us he can't really do any of it," he said.

"That's not what he said," snarled Fred Weasley.

"Would you like us to clean out your ears for you?" inquired George, pulling a long and lethal-looking metal instrument from inside one of the Zonko's bags.

"Or any part of your body, really, we're not fussy where we stick this," said Fred.

"Yes, well," said Hermione hastily, "moving on . . . the point is, are we agreed we want to take lessons from Harry?"

There was a murmur of general agreement. Zacharias folded his arms and said nothing, though perhaps this was because he was too busy keeping an eye on the instrument in George's hand.

"Right," said Hermione, looking relieved that something had at last been settled. "Well, then, the next question is how often we do it. I really don't think there's any point in meeting less than once a week —"

"Hang on," said Angelina, "we need to make sure this doesn't clash with our Quidditch practice."

"No," said Cho, "nor with ours."

"Nor ours," added Zacharias Smith.

"I'm sure we can find a night that suits everyone," said Hermione, slightly impatiently, "but you know, this is rather important, we're talking about learning to defend ourselves against V-Voldemort's Death Eaters —"

"Well said!" barked Ernie Macmillan, whom Harry had been expecting to speak long before this. "Personally I think this is really important, possibly more important than anything else we'll do this year, even with our O.W.L.s coming up!"

He looked around impressively, as though waiting for people to cry, "Surely not!" When nobody spoke, he went on, "I, personally, am at a loss to see why the Ministry has foisted such a useless teacher upon us at this critical period. Obviously they are in denial about the return of You-Know-Who, but to give us a teacher who is trying to actively prevent us from using defensive spells —"

"We think the reason Umbridge doesn't want us trained in Defense Against the Dark Arts," said Hermione, "is that she's got some . . . some mad idea that Dumbledore could use the students in the school as a kind of private army. She thinks he'd mobilize us against the Ministry."

Nearly everybody looked stunned at this news; everybody except

Luna Lovegood, who piped up, "Well, that makes sense. After all, Cornelius Fudge has got his own private army."

"What?" said Harry, completely thrown by this unexpected piece of information.

"Yes, he's got an army of heliopaths," said Luna solemnly.

"No, he hasn't," snapped Hermione.

"Yes, he has," said Luna.

"What are heliopaths?" asked Neville, looking blank.

"They're spirits of fire," said Luna, her protuberant eyes widening so that she looked madder than ever. "Great tall flaming creatures that gallop across the ground burning everything in front of —"

"They don't exist, Neville," said Hermione tartly.

"Oh yes they do!" said Luna angrily.

"I'm sorry, but where's the *proof* of that?" snapped Hermione.

"There are plenty of eyewitness accounts, just because you're so narrow-minded you need to have everything shoved under your nose before you —"

"Hem, hem," said Ginny in such a good imitation of Professor Umbridge that several people looked around in alarm and then laughed. "Weren't we trying to decide how often we're going to meet and get Defense lessons?"

"Yes," said Hermione at once, "yes, we were, you're right. . . ."

"Well, once a week sounds cool," said Lee Jordan.

"As long as —" began Angelina.

"Yes, yes, we know about the Quidditch," said Hermione in a tense voice. "Well, the other thing to decide is where we're going to meet. . . ."

This was rather more difficult; the whole group fell silent.

"Library?" suggested Katie Bell after a few moments.

"I can't see Madam Pince being too chuffed with us doing jinxes in the library," said Harry.

"Maybe an unused classroom?" said Dean.

"Yeah," said Ron, "McGonagall might let us have hers, she did when Harry was practicing for the Triwizard. . . ."

But Harry was pretty certain that McGonagall would not be so accommodating this time. For all that Hermione had said about study and homework groups being allowed, he had the distinct feeling this one might be considered a lot more rebellious.

"Right, well, we'll try to find somewhere," said Hermione. "We'll send a message round to everybody when we've got a time and a place for the first meeting."

She rummaged in her bag and produced parchment and a quill, then hesitated, rather as though she was steeling herself to say something.

"I-I think everybody should write their name down, just so we know who was here. But I also think," she took a deep breath, "that we all ought to agree not to shout about what we're doing. So if you sign, you're agreeing not to tell Umbridge — or anybody else — what we're up to."

Fred reached out for the parchment and cheerfully put down his signature, but Harry noticed at once that several people looked less than happy at the prospect of putting their names on the list.

"Er . . ." said Zacharias slowly, not taking the parchment that George was trying to pass him. "Well . . . I'm sure Ernie will tell me when the meeting is."

But Ernie was looking rather hesitant about signing too. Hermione raised her eyebrows at him.

"I — well, we are *prefects*," Ernie burst out. "And if this list was found . . . well, I mean to say . . . you said yourself, if Umbridge finds out . . ."

"You just said this group was the most important thing you'd do this year," Harry reminded him.

"I — yes," said Ernie, "yes, I do believe that, it's just . . ."

"Ernie, do you really think I'd leave that list lying around?" said Hermione testily.

"No. No, of course not," said Ernie, looking slightly less anxious. "I — yes, of course I'll sign."

Nobody raised objections after Ernie, though Harry saw Cho's friend give her a rather reproachful look before adding her name. When the last person — Zacharias — had signed, Hermione took the parchment back and slipped it carefully into her bag. There was an odd feeling in the group now. It was as though they had just signed some kind of contract.

"Well, time's ticking on," said Fred briskly, getting to his feet. "George, Lee, and I have got items of a sensitive nature to purchase, we'll be seeing you all later."

In twos and threes the rest of the group took their leave too. Cho made rather a business of fastening the catch on her bag before leaving, her long dark curtain of hair swinging forward to hide her face, but her friend stood beside her, arms folded, clicking her tongue, so that Cho had little choice but to leave with her. As her friend ushered her through the door, Cho looked back and waved at Harry.

"Well, I think that went quite well," said Hermione happily, as she, Harry, and Ron walked out of the Hog's Head into the bright sunlight a few moments later, Harry and Ron still clutching their bottles of butterbeer.

"That Zacharias bloke's a wart," said Ron, who was glowering after the figure of Smith just discernible in the distance.

"I don't like him much either," admitted Hermione, "but he overheard me talking to Ernie and Hannah at the Hufflepuff table and he seemed really interested in coming, so what could I say? But the more people the better really — I mean, Michael Corner and his friends wouldn't have come if he hadn't been going out with Ginny —"

Ron, who had been draining the last few drops from his butterbeer bottle, gagged and sprayed butterbeer down his front.

"He's WHAT?" said Ron, outraged, his ears now resembling curls of raw beef. "She's going out with — my sister's going — what d'you mean, Michael Corner?"

"Well, that's why he and his friends came, I think — well, they're obviously interested in learning Defense, but if Ginny hadn't told Michael what was going on —"

"When did this — when did she — ?"

"They met at the Yule Ball and they got together at the end of last year," said Hermione composedly. They had turned into the High Street and she paused outside Scrivenshaft's Quill Shop, where there was a handsome display of pheasant-feather quills in the window. "Hmm . . . I could do with a new quill."

She turned into the shop. Harry and Ron followed her.

"Which one was Michael Corner?" Ron demanded furiously.

"The dark one," said Hermione.

"I didn't like him," said Ron at once.

"Big surprise," said Hermione under her breath.

"But," said Ron, following Hermione along a row of quills in copper pots, "I thought Ginny fancied Harry!"

Hermione looked at him rather pityingly and shook her head.

"Ginny *used* to fancy Harry, but she gave up on him months ago. Not that she doesn't *like* you, of course," she added kindly to Harry while she examined a long black-and-gold quill.

Harry, whose head was still full of Cho's parting wave, did not find this subject quite as interesting as Ron, who was positively quivering with indignation, but it did bring something home to him that until now he had not really registered.

"So that's why she talks now?" he asked Hermione. "She never used to talk in front of me."

"Exactly," said Hermione. "Yes, I think I'll have this one. . . ."

She went up to the counter and handed over fifteen Sickles and two Knuts, Ron still breathing down her neck.

"Ron," she said severely as she turned and trod on his feet, "this is exactly why Ginny hasn't told you she's seeing Michael, she knew you'd take it badly. So don't harp on about it, for heaven's sake."

"What d'you mean, who's taking anything badly? I'm not going to *harp on* about anything . . ."

Ron continued to chunter under his breath all the way down the street. Hermione rolled her eyes at Harry and then said in an undertone, while Ron was muttering imprecations about Michael Corner, "And talking about Michael and Ginny . . . what about Cho and you?"

"What d'you mean?" said Harry quickly.

It was as though boiling water was rising rapidly inside him; a burning sensation that was causing his face to smart in the cold — had he been that obvious?

"Well," said Hermione, smiling slightly, "she just couldn't keep her *eyes* off you, could she?"

Harry had never before appreciated just how beautiful the village of Hogsmeade was.

EDUCATIONAL DECREE NUMBER TWENTY-FOUR

Harry felt happier for the rest of the weekend than he had done all term. He and Ron spent much of Sunday catching up with all their homework again, and although this could hardly be called fun, the last burst of autumn sunshine persisted, so rather than sitting hunched over tables in the common room, they took their work outside and lounged in the shade of a large beech tree on the edge of the lake. Hermione, who of course was up to date with all her work, brought more wool outside with her and bewitched her knitting needles so that they flashed and clicked in midair beside her, producing more hats and scarves.

The knowledge that they were doing something to resist Umbridge and the Ministry, and that he was a key part of the rebellion, gave Harry a feeling of immense satisfaction. He kept reliving Saturday's meeting in his mind: all those people, coming to him to learn Defense Against the Dark Arts . . . and the looks on their faces as they had heard some of the things he had done . . . and Cho praising his performance in the Triwizard Tournament. . . . The knowledge that all those people did not think him a lying weirdo, but someone to be admired, buoyed him up so much that he was still cheerful on Monday morning, despite the imminent prospect of all his least favorite classes.

He and Ron headed downstairs from their dormitory together, discussing Angelina's idea that they were to work on a new move called the Sloth Grip Roll during that night's Quidditch practice, and not until they were halfway across the sunlit common room did they notice the addition to the room that had already attracted the attention of a small group of people.

A large sign had been affixed to the Gryffindor notice board, so large that it covered everything else on there — the lists of secondhand spellbooks for sale, the regular reminders of school rules from Argus Filch, the Quidditch team training schedule, the offers to barter certain Chocolate Frog cards for others, the Weasleys' new advertisement for testers, the dates of the Hogsmeade weekends, and the lost-and-found notices. The new sign was printed in large black letters and there was a highly official-looking seal at the bottom beside a neat and curly signature.

—————— BY ORDER OF ——————

The High Inquisitor of Hogwarts

All Student Organizations, Societies, Teams, Groups, and Clubs are henceforth disbanded.

An Organization, Society, Team, Group, or Club is hereby defined as a regular meeting of three or more students.

Permission to re-form may be sought from the High Inquisitor (Professor Umbridge).

No Student Organization, Society, Team, Group, or Club may exist without the knowledge and approval of the High Inquisitor.

Any student found to have formed, or to belong to, an Organization, Society, Team, Group, or Club that has not been approved by the High Inquisitor will be expelled.

The above is in accordance with
Educational Decree Number Twenty-four.

Signed:

Dolores Jane Umbridge

HIGH INQUISITOR

Harry and Ron read the notice over the heads of some anxious-looking second years.

"Does this mean they're going to shut down the Gobstones Club?" one of them asked his friend.

"I reckon you'll be okay with Gobstones," Ron said darkly, making the second year jump. "I don't think we're going to be as lucky, though, do you?" he asked Harry as the second years hurried away.

Harry was reading the notice through again. The happiness that had filled him since Saturday was gone. His insides were pulsing with rage.

"This isn't a coincidence," he said, his hands forming fists. "She knows."

"She can't," said Ron at once.

"There were people listening in that pub. And let's face it, we don't know how many of the people who turned up we can trust. . . . Any of them could have run off and told Umbridge. . . ."

And he had thought they believed him, thought they even admired him . . .

"Zacharias Smith!" said Ron at once, punching a fist into his hand. "Or — I thought that Michael Corner had a really shifty look too —"

"I wonder if Hermione's seen this yet?" Harry said, looking around at the door to the girls' dormitories.

"Let's go and tell her," said Ron. He bounded forward, pulled open the door, and set off up the spiral staircase.

He was on the sixth stair when it happened. There was a loud, wailing, klaxonlike sound and the steps melted together to make a long, smooth stone slide. There was a brief moment when Ron tried to keep running, arms working madly like windmills, then he toppled over backward and shot down the newly created slide, coming to rest on his back at Harry's feet.

"Er — I don't think we're allowed in the girls' dormitories," said Harry, pulling Ron to his feet and trying not to laugh.

Two fourth-year girls came zooming gleefully down the stone slide.

"Oooh, who tried to get upstairs?" they giggled happily, leaping to their feet and ogling Harry and Ron.

"Me," said Ron, who was still rather disheveled. "I didn't realize that would happen. It's not fair!" he added to Harry, as the girls headed off for the portrait hole, still giggling madly. "Hermione's allowed in our dormitory, how come we're not allowed — ?"

"Well, it's an old-fashioned rule," said Hermione, who had just slid neatly onto a rug in front of them and was now getting to her feet, "but it says in *Hogwarts: A History* that the founders thought boys were less trustworthy than girls. Anyway, why were you trying to get in there?"

"To see you — look at this!" said Ron, dragging her over to the notice board.

Hermione's eyes slid rapidly down the notice. Her expression became stony.

"Someone must have blabbed to her!" Ron said angrily.

"They can't have done," said Hermione in a low voice.

"You're so naive," said Ron, "you think just because you're all honorable and trustworthy —"

"No, they can't have done because I put a jinx on that piece of parchment we all signed," said Hermione grimly. "Believe me, if anyone's run off and told Umbridge, we'll know exactly who they are and they will really regret it."

"What'll happen to them?" said Ron eagerly.

"Well, put it this way," said Hermione, "it'll make Eloise Midgen's acne look like a couple of cute freckles. Come on, let's get down to breakfast and see what the others think. . . . I wonder whether this has been put up in all the Houses?"

It was immediately apparent on entering the Great Hall that Umbridge's sign had not only appeared in Gryffindor Tower. There was a peculiar intensity about the chatter and an extra measure of movement in the Hall as people scurried up and down their tables conferring on what they had read. Harry, Ron, and Hermione had barely taken their seats when Neville, Dean, Fred, George, and Ginny descended upon them.

"Did you see it?"

"D'you reckon she knows?"

"What are we going to do?"

They were all looking at Harry. He glanced around to make sure there were no teachers near them.

"We're going to do it anyway, of course," he said quietly.

"Knew you'd say that," said George, beaming and thumping Harry on the arm.

"The prefects as well?" said Fred, looking quizzically at Ron and Hermione.

"Of course," said Hermione coolly.

"Here comes Ernie and Hannah Abbott," said Ron, looking over his shoulder. "*And* those Ravenclaw blokes and Smith . . . and no one looks very spotty."

Hermione looked alarmed.

"Never mind spots, the idiots can't come over here now, it'll look really suspicious — sit down!" she mouthed to Ernie and Hannah, gesturing frantically to them to rejoin the Hufflepuff table. "Later! We'll — talk — to — you — *later*!"

"I'll tell Michael," said Ginny impatiently, swinging herself off her bench. "The fool, honestly . . ."

She hurried off toward the Ravenclaw table; Harry watched her go. Cho was sitting not far away, talking to the curly-haired friend she had brought along to the Hog's Head. Would Umbridge's notice scare her off meeting them again?

But the full repercussions of the sign were not felt until they were leaving the Great Hall for History of Magic.

"Harry! *Ron!*"

It was Angelina and she was hurrying toward them looking perfectly desperate.

"It's okay," said Harry quietly, when she was near enough to hear him. "We're still going to —"

"You realize she's including Quidditch in this?" Angelina said over him. "We have to go and ask permission to re-form the Gryffindor team!"

"What?" said Harry.

"No way," said Ron, appalled.

"You read the sign, it mentions teams too! So listen, Harry . . . I am saying this for the last time. . . . Please, *please* don't lose your temper with Umbridge again or she might not let us play anymore!"

"Okay, okay," said Harry, for Angelina looked as though she was on the verge of tears. "Don't worry, I'll behave myself. . . ."

"Bet Umbridge is in History of Magic," said Ron grimly, as they set off for Binns's lesson. "She hasn't inspected Binns yet. . . . Bet you anything she's there. . . ."

But he was wrong; the only teacher present when they entered was Professor Binns, floating an inch or so above his chair as usual and preparing to continue his monotonous drone on giant wars. Harry did not even attempt to follow what he was saying today; he doodled idly on his parchment ignoring Hermione's frequent glares and nudges, until a particularly painful poke in the ribs made him look up angrily.

"*What?*"

She pointed at the window. Harry looked around. Hedwig was perched on the narrow window ledge, gazing through the thick glass at him, a letter tied to her leg. Harry could not understand it; they had just had breakfast, why on earth hadn't she delivered the letter then, as usual? Many of his classmates were pointing out Hedwig to each other too.

"Oh, I've always loved that owl, she's so beautiful," Harry heard Lavender sigh to Parvati.

He glanced around at Professor Binns who continued to read his notes, serenely unaware that the class's attention was even less focused upon him than usual. Harry slipped quietly off his chair, crouched down, and hurried along the row to the window, where he slid the catch and opened it very slowly.

He had expected Hedwig to hold out her leg so that he could remove the letter and then fly off to the Owlery, but the moment the window was open wide enough she hopped inside, hooting dolefully. He closed the window with an anxious glance at Professor Binns, crouched low again, and sped back to his seat with Hedwig on his shoulder. He regained his seat, transferred Hedwig to his lap, and made to remove the letter tied to her leg.

It was only then that he realized that Hedwig's feathers were oddly ruffled; some were bent the wrong way, and she was holding one of her wings at an odd angle.

"She's hurt!" Harry whispered, bending his head low over her. Hermione and Ron leaned in closer; Hermione even put down her quill. "Look — there's something wrong with her wing —"

Hedwig was quivering; when Harry made to touch the wing she

gave a little jump, all her feathers on end as though she was inflating herself, and gazed at him reproachfully.

"Professor Binns," said Harry loudly, and everyone in the class turned to look at him. "I'm not feeling well."

Professor Binns raised his eyes from his notes, looking amazed, as always, to find the room in front of him full of people.

"Not feeling well?" he repeated hazily.

"Not at all well," said Harry firmly, getting to his feet while concealing Hedwig behind his back. "So I think I'll need to go to the hospital wing."

"Yes," said Professor Binns, clearly very much wrong-footed. "Yes . . . yes, hospital wing . . . well, off you go, then, Perkins . . ."

Once outside the room Harry returned Hedwig to his shoulder and hurried off up the corridor, pausing to think only when he was out of sight of Binns's door. His first choice of somebody to cure Hedwig would have been Hagrid, of course, but as he had no idea where Hagrid was, his only remaining option was to find Professor Grubbly-Plank and hope she would help.

He peered out of a window at the blustery, overcast grounds. There was no sign of her anywhere near Hagrid's cabin; if she was not teaching, she was probably in the staffroom. He set off downstairs, Hedwig hooting feebly as she swayed on his shoulder.

Two stone gargoyles flanked the staffroom door. As Harry approached, one of them croaked, "You should be in class, sunny Jim."

"This is urgent," said Harry curtly.

"Ooooh, *urgent*, is it?" said the other gargoyle in a high-pitched voice. "Well, that's put *us* in our place, hasn't it?"

Harry knocked; he heard footsteps and then the door opened and he found himself face-to-face with Professor McGonagall.

"You haven't been given another detention!" she said at once, her square spectacles flashing alarmingly.

"No, Professor!" said Harry hastily.

"Well then, why are you out of class?"

"It's *urgent,* apparently," said the second gargoyle snidely.

"I'm looking for Professor Grubbly-Plank," Harry explained. "It's my owl, she's injured."

"Injured owl, did you say?"

Professor Grubbly-Plank appeared at Professor McGonagall's shoulder, smoking a pipe and holding a copy of the *Daily Prophet.*

"Yes," said Harry, lifting Hedwig carefully off his shoulder, "she turned up after the other post owls and her wing's all funny, look —"

Professor Grubbly-Plank stuck her pipe firmly between her teeth and took Hedwig from Harry while Professor McGonagall watched.

"Hmm," said Professor Grubbly-Plank, her pipe waggling slightly as she talked. "Looks like something's attacked her. Can't think what would have done it, though. . . . Thestrals will sometimes go for birds, of course, but Hagrid's got the Hogwarts thestrals well trained not to touch owls . . ."

Harry neither knew nor cared what thestrals were, he just wanted to know that Hedwig was going to be all right. Professor McGonagall, however, looked sharply at Harry and said, "Do you know how far this owl's traveled, Potter?"

"Er," said Harry. "From London, I think."

He met her eyes briefly and knew that she understood "London" to mean "number twelve, Grimmauld Place" by the way her eyebrows had joined in the middle.

Professor Grubbly-Plank pulled a monocle out of the inside of her robes and screwed it into her eye to examine Hedwig's wing closely. "I should be able to sort this out if you leave her with me, Potter," she said. "She shouldn't be flying long distances for a few days, in any case."

"Er — right — thanks," said Harry, just as the bell rang for break.

"No problem," said Professor Grubbly-Plank gruffly, turning back into the staffroom.

"Just a moment, Wilhelmina!" said Professor McGonagall. "Potter's letter!"

"Oh yeah!" said Harry, who had momentarily forgotten the scroll tied to Hedwig's leg. Professor Grubbly-Plank handed it over and then disappeared into the staffroom carrying Hedwig, who was staring at Harry as though unable to believe he would give her away like this. Feeling slightly guilty, he turned to go, but Professor McGonagall called him back.

"Potter!"

"Yes, Professor?"

She glanced up and down the corridor; there were students coming from both directions.

"Bear in mind," she said quickly and quietly, her eyes on the scroll in his hand, "that channels of communication in and out of Hogwarts may be being watched, won't you?"

"I —" said Harry, but the flood of students rolling along the corridor was almost upon him. Professor McGonagall gave him a curt nod and retreated into the staffroom, leaving Harry to be swept out into the courtyard with the crowd. Here he spotted Ron and Hermione already standing in a sheltered corner, their cloak collars turned up against the wind. Harry slit open the scroll as he hurried toward them and found five words in Sirius's handwriting:

Today, same time, same place.

"Is Hedwig okay?" asked Hermione anxiously, the moment he was within earshot.

"Where did you take her?" asked Ron.

"To Grubbly-Plank," said Harry. "And I met McGonagall. . . . Listen. . . ."

And he told them what Professor McGonagall had said. To his

surprise, neither of the others looked shocked; on the contrary, they exchanged significant looks.

"What?" said Harry, looking from Ron to Hermione and back again.

"Well, I was just saying to Ron . . . what if someone had tried to intercept Hedwig? I mean, she's never been hurt on a flight before, has she?"

"Who's the letter from anyway?" asked Ron, taking the note from Harry.

"Snuffles," said Harry quietly.

"'Same time, same place'? Does he mean the fire in the common room?"

"Obviously," said Hermione, also reading the note. She looked uneasy. "I just hope nobody else has read this. . . ."

"But it was still sealed and everything," said Harry, trying to convince himself as much as her. "And nobody would understand what it meant if they didn't know where we'd spoken to him before, would they?"

"I don't know," said Hermione anxiously, hitching her bag back over her shoulder as the bell rang again. "It wouldn't be exactly difficult to reseal the scroll by magic. . . . And if anyone's watching the Floo Network . . . but I don't really see how we can warn him not to come without *that* being intercepted too!"

They trudged down the stone steps to the dungeons for Potions, all three of them lost in thought, but as they reached the bottom of the stairs they were recalled to themselves by the voice of Draco Malfoy, who was standing just outside Snape's classroom door, waving around an official-looking piece of parchment and talking much louder than was necessary so that they could hear every word.

"Yeah, Umbridge gave the Slytherin Quidditch team permission to continue playing straightaway, I went to ask her first thing this morning. Well, it was pretty much automatic, I mean, she knows my father really well, he's always popping in and out of the Ministry. . . . It'll be interesting to see whether Gryffindor are allowed to keep playing, won't it?"

"Don't rise," Hermione whispered imploringly to Harry and Ron, who were both watching Malfoy, faces set and fists clenched. "It's what he wants. . . ."

"I mean," said Malfoy, raising his voice a little more, his gray eyes glittering malevolently in Harry and Ron's direction, "if it's a question of influence with the Ministry, I don't think they've got much chance. . . . From what my father says, they've been looking for an excuse to sack Arthur Weasley for years. . . . And as for Potter . . . My father says it's a matter of time before the Ministry has him carted off to St. Mungo's. . . . apparently they've got a special ward for people whose brains have been addled by magic. . . ."

Malfoy made a grotesque face, his mouth sagging open and his eyes rolling. Crabbe and Goyle gave their usual grunts of laughter, Pansy Parkinson shrieked with glee.

Something collided hard with Harry's shoulder, knocking him sideways. A split second later he realized that Neville had just charged past him, heading straight for Malfoy.

"Neville, *no!*"

Harry leapt forward and seized the back of Neville's robes; Neville struggled frantically, his fists flailing, trying desperately to get at Malfoy who looked, for a moment, extremely shocked.

"Help me!" Harry flung at Ron, managing to get an arm around Neville's neck and dragging him backward, away from the Slytherins. Crabbe and Goyle were now flexing their arms, closing in front of Malfoy, ready for the fight. Ron hurried forward and seized Neville's arms; together, he and Harry succeeded in dragging Neville back into the Gryffindor line. Neville's face was scarlet; the pressure Harry was exerting on his throat rendered him quite incomprehensible, but odd words spluttered from his mouth.

"Not . . . funny . . . don't . . . Mungo's . . . show . . . him . . ."

The dungeon door opened. Snape appeared there. His black eyes swept up the Gryffindor line to the point where Harry and Ron were wrestling with Neville.

"Fighting, Potter, Weasley, Longbottom?" Snape said in his cold, sneering voice. "Ten points from Gryffindor. Release Longbottom, Potter, or it will be detention. Inside, all of you."

Harry let go of Neville, who stood panting and glaring at him.

"I had to stop you," Harry gasped, picking up his bag. "Crabbe and Goyle would've torn you apart."

Neville said nothing, he merely snatched up his own bag and stalked off into the dungeon.

"What in the name of Merlin," said Ron slowly, as they followed Neville, "was *that* about?"

Harry did not answer. He knew exactly why the subject of people who were in St. Mungo's because of magical damage to their brains was highly distressing to Neville, but he had sworn to Dumbledore that he would not tell anyone Neville's secret. Even Neville did not know that Harry knew.

Harry, Ron, and Hermione took their usual seats at the back of the class and pulled out parchment, quills, and their copies of *One Thousand Magical Herbs and Fungi*. The class around them was whispering about what Neville had just done, but when Snape closed the dungeon door with an echoing bang everybody fell silent immediately.

"You will notice," said Snape in his low, sneering voice, "that we have a guest with us today."

He gestured toward the dim corner of the dungeon, and Harry saw Professor Umbridge sitting there, clipboard on her knee. He glanced sideways at Ron and Hermione, his eyebrows raised. Snape and Umbridge, the two teachers he hated most . . . it was hard to decide which he wanted to triumph over the other.

"We are continuing with our Strengthening Solutions today, you will find your mixtures as you left them last lesson, if correctly made they should have matured well over the weekend — instructions" — he waved his wand again — "on the board. Carry on."

Professor Umbridge spent the first half hour of the lesson making notes in her corner. Harry was very interested in hearing her question Snape, so interested, that he was becoming careless with his potion again.

"Salamander blood, Harry!" Hermione moaned, grabbing his wrist to prevent him adding the wrong ingredient for the third time. "Not pomegranate juice!"

"Right," said Harry vaguely, putting down the bottle and continuing to watch the corner. Umbridge had just gotten to her feet. "Ha," he said softly, as she strode between two lines of desks toward Snape, who was bending over Dean Thomas's cauldron.

"Well, the class seems fairly advanced for their level," she said briskly to Snape's back. "Though I would question whether it is advisable to teach them a potion like the Strengthening Solution. I think the Ministry would prefer it if that was removed from the syllabus."

Snape straightened up slowly and turned to look at her.

"Now . . . how long have you been teaching at Hogwarts?" she asked, her quill poised over her clipboard.

"Fourteen years," Snape replied. His expression was unfathomable. His eyes on Snape, Harry added a few drops to his potion; it hissed menacingly and turned from turquoise to orange.

"You applied first for the Defense Against the Dark Arts post, I believe?" Professor Umbridge asked Snape.

"Yes," said Snape quietly.

"But you were unsuccessful?"

Snape's lip curled.

"Obviously."

Professor Umbridge scribbled on her clipboard.

"And you have applied regularly for the Defense Against the Dark Arts post since you first joined the school, I believe?"

"Yes," said Snape quietly, barely moving his lips. He looked very angry.

"Do you have any idea why Dumbledore has consistently refused to appoint you?" asked Umbridge.

"I suggest you ask him," said Snape jerkily.

"Oh I shall," said Professor Umbridge with a sweet smile.

"I suppose this is relevant?" Snape asked, his black eyes narrowed.

"Oh yes," said Professor Umbridge. "Yes, the Ministry wants a thorough understanding of teachers' — er — backgrounds. . . ."

She turned away, walked over to Pansy Parkinson and began questioning her about the lessons. Snape looked around at Harry and their eyes met for a second. Harry hastily dropped his gaze to his potion, which was now congealing foully and giving off a strong smell of burned rubber.

"No marks again, then, Potter," said Snape maliciously, emptying Harry's cauldron with a wave of his wand. "You will write me an essay on the correct composition of this potion, indicating how and why you went wrong, to be handed in next lesson, do you understand?"

"Yes," said Harry furiously. Snape had already given them homework, and he had Quidditch practice this evening; this would mean another couple of sleepless nights. It did not seem possible that he had awoken that morning feeling very happy. All he felt now was a fervent desire for this day to end as soon as possible.

"Maybe I'll skive off Divination," he said glumly as they stood again in the courtyard after lunch, the wind whipping at the hems of robes and brims of hats. "I'll pretend to be ill and do Snape's essay instead, then I won't have to stay up half the night. . . ."

"You can't skive off Divination," said Hermione severely.

"Hark who's talking, you walked out of Divination, you hate Trelawney!" said Ron indignantly.

"I don't *hate* her," said Hermione loftily. "I just think she's an absolutely appalling teacher and a real old fraud. . . . But Harry's already missed History of Magic and I don't think he ought to miss anything else today!"

There was too much truth in this to ignore, so half an hour later Harry took his seat in the hot, over-perfumed atmosphere of the Divination classroom feeling angry at everybody. Professor Trelawney was handing out copies of *The Dream Oracle* yet again; he would surely be much better employed doing Snape's punishment essay than sitting here trying to find meaning in a lot of made-up dreams.

It seemed, however, that he was not the only person in Divination who was in a temper. Professor Trelawney slammed a copy of the *Oracle* down on the table between Harry and Ron and swept away, her lips pursed; she threw the next copy of the *Oracle* at Seamus and Dean, narrowly avoiding Seamus's head, and thrust the final one into Neville's chest with such force that he slipped off his pouf.

"Well, carry on!" said Professor Trelawney loudly, her voice high pitched and somewhat hysterical. "You know what to do! Or am I such a substandard teacher that you have never learned how to open a book?"

The class stared perplexedly at her and then at each other. Harry, however, thought he knew what was the matter. As Professor Trelawney flounced back to the high-backed teacher's chair, her magnified eyes full of angry tears, he leaned his head closer to Ron's and muttered, "I think she's got the results of her inspection back."

"Professor?" said Parvati Patil in a hushed voice (she and Lavender had always rather admired Professor Trelawney). "Professor, is there anything — er — wrong?"

"Wrong!" cried Professor Trelawney in a voice throbbing with emotion. "Certainly not! I have been insulted, certainly. . . . Insinuations have been made against me. . . . Unfounded accusations levelled . . . but no, there is nothing wrong, certainly not. . . ."

She took a great shuddering breath and looked away from Parvati, angry tears spilling from under her glasses.

"I say nothing," she choked, "of sixteen years' devoted service. . . . It has passed, apparently, unnoticed. . . . But I shall not be insulted, no, I shall not!"

"But Professor, who's insulting you?" asked Parvati timidly.

"The establishment!" said Professor Trelawney in a deep, dramatic, wavering voice. "Yes, those with eyes too clouded by the Mundane to See as I See, to Know as I Know . . . Of course, we Seers have always been feared, always persecuted. . . . It is — alas — our fate. . . ."

She gulped, dabbed at her wet cheeks with the end of her shawl, and then pulled a small, embroidered handkerchief from her sleeve, into which she blew her nose very hard with a sound like Peeves blowing a raspberry. Ron sniggered. Lavender shot him a disgusted look.

"Professor," said Parvati, "do you mean . . . is it something Professor Umbridge . . . ?"

"Do not speak to me about that woman!" cried Professor Trelawney, leaping to her feet, her beads rattling and her spectacles flashing. "Kindly continue with your work!"

And she spent the rest of the lesson striding among them, tears still leaking from behind her glasses, muttering what sounded like threats under her breath.

" . . . may well choose to leave . . . the indignity of it . . . on probation . . . we shall see . . . how she dares . . ."

"You and Umbridge have got something in common," Harry told Hermione quietly when they met again in Defense Against the Dark Arts. "She obviously reckons Trelawney's an old fraud too. . . . Looks like she's put her on probation."

Umbridge entered the room as he spoke, wearing her black velvet bow and an expression of great smugness.

"Good afternoon, class."

"Good afternoon, Professor Umbridge," they chanted drearily.

"Wands away, please . . ."

But there was no answering flurry of movement this time; nobody had bothered to take out their wands.

"Please turn to page thirty-four of *Defensive Magical Theory* and read the third chapter, entitled 'The Case for Non-Offensive Responses to Magical Attack.' There will be —"

"— no need to talk," Harry, Ron, and Hermione said together under their breaths.

"No Quidditch practice," said Angelina in hollow tones when Harry, Ron, and Hermione entered the common room that night after dinner.

"But I kept my temper!" said Harry, horrified. "I didn't say anything to her, Angelina, I swear, I —"

"I know, I know," said Angelina miserably. "She just said she needed a bit of time to consider."

"Consider what?" said Ron angrily. "She's given the Slytherins permission, why not us?"

But Harry could imagine how much Umbridge was enjoying holding the threat of no Gryffindor Quidditch team over their heads and could easily understand why she would not want to relinquish that weapon over them too soon.

"Well," said Hermione, "look on the bright side — at least now you'll have time to do Snape's essay!"

"That's a bright side, is it?" snapped Harry, while Ron stared incredulously at Hermione. "No Quidditch practice and extra Potions?"

Harry slumped down into a chair, dragged his Potions essay reluctantly from his bag, and set to work.

It was very hard to concentrate; even though he knew that Sirius was not due in the fire until much later he could not help glancing

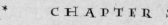 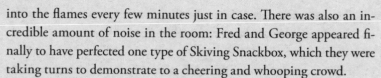

into the flames every few minutes just in case. There was also an incredible amount of noise in the room: Fred and George appeared finally to have perfected one type of Skiving Snackbox, which they were taking turns to demonstrate to a cheering and whooping crowd.

First, Fred would take a bite out of the orange end of a chew, at which he would vomit spectacularly into a bucket they had placed in front of them. Then he would force down the purple end of the chew, at which the vomiting would immediately cease. Lee Jordan, who was assisting the demonstration, was lazily vanishing the vomit at regular intervals with the same Vanishing Spell Snape kept using on Harry's potions.

What with the regular sounds of retching, cheering, and Fred and George taking advance orders from the crowd, Harry was finding it exceptionally difficult to focus on the correct method for Strengthening Solutions. Hermione was not helping matters; the cheers and sound of vomit hitting the bottom of Fred and George's bucket were punctuated by loud and disapproving sniffs that Harry found, if anything, more distracting.

"Just go and stop them, then!" he said irritably, after crossing out the wrong weight of powdered griffin claw for the fourth time.

"I can't, they're not *technically* doing anything wrong," said Hermione through gritted teeth. "They're quite within their rights to eat the foul things themselves, and I can't find a rule that says the other idiots aren't entitled to buy them, not unless they're proven to be dangerous in some way, and it doesn't look as though they are. . . ."

She, Harry, and Ron watched George projectile-vomit into the bucket, gulp down the rest of the chew, and straighten up, beaming with his arms wide to protracted applause.

"You know, I don't get why Fred and George only got three O.W.L.s each," said Harry, watching as Fred, George, and Lee collected gold from the eager crowd. "They really know their stuff. . . ."

"Oh, they only know flashy stuff that's no real use to anyone," said Hermione disparagingly.

"No real use?" said Ron in a strained voice. "Hermione, they've got about twenty-six Galleons already. . . ."

It was a long while before the crowd around the Weasleys dispersed, and then Fred, Lee, and George sat up counting their takings even longer, so that it was well past midnight when Harry, Ron, and Hermione finally had the common room to themselves again. At long last, Fred closed the doorway to the boys' dormitories behind him, rattling his box of Galleons ostentatiously so that Hermione scowled. Harry, who was making very little progress with his Potions essay, decided to give it up for the night. As he put his books away, Ron, who was dozing lightly in an armchair, gave a muffled grunt, awoke, looked blearily into the fire and said, "Sirius!"

Harry whipped around; Sirius's untidy dark head was sitting in the fire again.

"Hi," he said, grinning.

"Hi," chorused Harry, Ron, and Hermione, all three kneeling down upon the hearthrug. Crookshanks purred loudly and approached the fire, trying, despite the heat, to put his face close to Sirius's.

"How're things?" said Sirius.

"Not that good," said Harry, as Hermione pulled Crookshanks back to stop him singeing his whiskers. "The Ministry's forced through another decree, which means we're not allowed to have Quidditch teams —"

"— or secret Defense Against the Dark Arts groups?" said Sirius.

There was a short pause.

"How did you know about that?" Harry demanded.

"You want to choose your meeting places more carefully," said Sirius, grinning still more broadly. "The Hog's Head, I ask you . . ."

"Well, it was better than the Three Broomsticks!" said Hermione defensively. "That's always packed with people —"

"— which means you'd have been harder to overhear," said Sirius. "You've got a lot to learn, Hermione."

"Who overheard us?" Harry demanded.

"Mundungus, of course," said Sirius, and when they all looked puzzled he laughed. "He was the witch under the veil."

"That was Mundungus?" Harry said, stunned. "What was he doing in the Hog's Head?"

"What do you think he was doing?" said Sirius impatiently. "Keeping an eye on you, of course."

"I'm still being followed?" asked Harry angrily.

"Yeah, you are," said Sirius, "and just as well, isn't it, if the first thing you're going to do on your weekend off is organize an illegal defense group."

But he looked neither angry nor worried; on the contrary, he was looking at Harry with distinct pride.

"Why was Dung hiding from us?" asked Ron, sounding disappointed. "We'd've liked to've seen him."

"He was banned from the Hog's Head twenty years ago," said Sirius, "and that barman's got a long memory. We lost Moody's spare Invisibility Cloak when Sturgis was arrested, so Dung's been dressing as a witch a lot lately. . . . Anyway . . . First of all, Ron — I've sworn to pass on a message from your mother."

"Oh yeah?" said Ron, sounding apprehensive.

"She says on no account whatsoever are you to take part in an illegal secret Defense Against the Dark Arts group. She says you'll be expelled for sure and your future will be ruined. She says there will be plenty of time to learn how to defend yourself later and that you are too young to be worrying about that right now. She also" — Sirius's eyes turned to the other two — "advises Harry and Hermione not to proceed with the group, though she accepts that she has no authority over either of them and simply begs them to remember that she has their best interests at heart. She would have written all this to you, but if the owl had been intercepted you'd all have been in real trouble, and she can't say it for herself because she's on duty tonight."

"On duty doing what?" said Ron quickly.

"Never you mind, just stuff for the Order," said Sirius. "So it's fallen to me to be the messenger and make sure you tell her I passed it all on, because I don't think she trusts me to."

There was another pause in which Crookshanks, mewing, attempted to paw Sirius's head, and Ron fiddled with a hole in the hearthrug.

"So you want me to say I'm not going to take part in the defense group?" he muttered finally.

"Me? Certainly not!" said Sirius, looking surprised. "I think it's an excellent idea!"

"You do?" said Harry, his heart lifting.

"Of course I do!" said Sirius. "D'you think your father and I would've lain down and taken orders from an old hag like Umbridge?"

"But — last term all you did was tell me to be careful and not take risks —"

"Last year all the evidence was that someone inside Hogwarts was trying to kill you, Harry!" said Sirius impatiently. "This year we know that there's someone outside Hogwarts who'd like to kill us all, so I think learning to defend yourselves properly is a very good idea!"

"And if we do get expelled?" Hermione asked, a quizzical look on her face.

"Hermione, this whole thing was your idea!" said Harry, staring at her.

"I know it was. . . . I just wondered what Sirius thought," she said, shrugging.

"Well, better expelled and able to defend yourselves than sitting safely in school without a clue," said Sirius.

"Hear, hear," said Harry and Ron enthusiastically.

"So," said Sirius, "how are you organizing this group? Where are you meeting?"

"Well, that's a bit of a problem now," said Harry. "Dunno where we're going to be able to go. . . ."

"How about the Shrieking Shack?" suggested Sirius.

"Hey, that's an idea!" said Ron excitedly, but Hermione made a skeptical noise and all three of them looked at her, Sirius's head turning in the flames.

"Well, Sirius, it's just that there were only four of you meeting in the Shrieking Shack when you were at school," said Hermione, "and all of you could transform into animals and I suppose you could all have squeezed under a single Invisibility Cloak if you'd wanted to. But there are twenty-eight of us and none of us is an Animagus, so we wouldn't need so much an Invisibility Cloak as an Invisibility Marquee —"

"Fair point," said Sirius, looking slightly crestfallen. "Well, I'm sure you'll come up with somewhere. . . . There used to be a pretty roomy secret passageway behind that big mirror on the fourth floor, you might have enough space to practice jinxes in there —"

"Fred and George told me it's blocked," said Harry, shaking his head. "Caved in or something."

"Oh . . ." said Sirius, frowning. "Well, I'll have a think and get back to —"

He broke off. His face was suddenly tense, alarmed. He turned sideways, apparently looking into the solid brick wall of the fireplace.

"Sirius?" said Harry anxiously.

But he had vanished. Harry gaped at the flames for a moment, then turned to look at Ron and Hermione.

"Why did he — ?"

Hermione gave a horrified gasp and leapt to her feet, still staring at the fire.

A hand had appeared amongst the flames, groping as though to catch hold of something; a stubby, short-fingered hand covered in ugly old-fashioned rings. . . .

The three of them ran for it; at the door of the boys' dormitory Harry looked back. Umbridge's hand was still making snatching movements amongst the flames, as though she knew exactly where Sirius's hair had been moments before and was determined to seize it.

DUMBLEDORE'S ARMY

U mbridge has been reading your mail, Harry. There's no other explanation."

"You think Umbridge attacked Hedwig?" he said, outraged.

"I'm almost certain of it," said Hermione grimly. "Watch your frog, it's escaping."

Harry pointed his wand at the bullfrog that had been hopping hopefully toward the other side of the table — "*Accio!*" — and it zoomed gloomily back into his hand.

Charms was always one of the best lessons in which to enjoy a private chat: There was generally so much movement and activity that the danger of being overheard was very slight. Today, with the room full of croaking bullfrogs and cawing ravens, and with a heavy downpour of rain clattering and pounding against the classroom windows, Harry, Ron, and Hermione's whispered discussion about how Umbridge had nearly caught Sirius went quite unnoticed.

"I've been suspecting this ever since Filch accused you of ordering Dungbombs, because it seemed such a stupid lie," Hermione whispered. "I mean, once your letter had been read, it would have been quite clear you *weren't* ordering them, so you wouldn't have been in trouble at all — it's a bit of a feeble joke, isn't it? But then I thought, what if somebody just wanted an excuse to read your mail? Well then, it would be a perfect way for Umbridge to manage it — tip off Filch, let him do the dirty work and confiscate the letter, then either find a way of stealing it from him or else demand to see it — I don't think Filch would object, when's he ever stuck up for a student's rights? Harry, you're squashing your frog."

Harry looked down; he was indeed squeezing his bullfrog so tightly its eyes were popping; he replaced it hastily upon the desk.

"It was a very, very close call last night," said Hermione. "I just wonder if Umbridge knows how close it was. *Silencio!*"

The bullfrog on which she was practicing her Silencing Charm was struck dumb mid-croak and glared at her reproachfully.

"If she'd caught Snuffles . . ."

Harry finished the sentence for her.

"He'd probably be back in Azkaban this morning." He waved his wand without really concentrating; his bullfrog swelled like a green balloon and emitted a high-pitched whistle.

"*Silencio!*" said Hermione hastily, pointing her wand at Harry's frog, which deflated silently before them. "Well, he mustn't do it again, that's all. I just don't know how we're going to let him know. We can't send him an owl."

"I don't reckon he'll risk it again," said Ron. "He's not stupid, he knows she nearly got him. *Silencio!*"

The large and ugly raven in front of him let out a derisive caw.

"*Silencio! SILENCIO!*"

The raven cawed more loudly.

"It's the way you're moving your wand," said Hermione, watching Ron critically. "You don't want to wave it, it's more a sharp *jab*."

"Ravens are harder than frogs," said Ron testily.

"Fine, let's swap," said Hermione, seizing Ron's raven and replacing it with her own fat bullfrog. *"Silencio!"* The raven continued to open and close its sharp beak, but no sound came out.

"Very good, Miss Granger!" said Professor Flitwick's squeaky little voice and Harry, Ron, and Hermione all jumped. "Now, let me see you try, Mr. Weasley!"

"Wha — ? Oh — oh, right," said Ron, very flustered. "Er — *Silencio!*" He jabbed at the bullfrog so hard that he poked it in the eye; the frog gave a deafening croak and leapt off the desk.

It came as no surprise to any of them that Harry and Ron were given additional practice of the Silencing Charm for homework.

They were allowed to remain inside over break due to the downpour outside. They found seats in a noisy and overcrowded classroom on the first floor in which Peeves was floating dreamily up near the chandelier, occasionally blowing an ink pellet at the top of somebody's head. They had barely sat down when Angelina came struggling toward them through the groups of gossiping students.

"I've got permission!" she said. "To re-form the Quidditch team!"

"Excellent!" said Ron and Harry together.

"Yeah," said Angelina, beaming. "I went to McGonagall and I *think* she might have appealed to Dumbledore — anyway, Umbridge had to give in. Ha! So I want you down at the pitch at seven o'clock tonight, all right, because we've got to make up time, you realize we're only three weeks away from our first match?"

She squeezed away from them, narrowly dodged an ink pellet from Peeves, which hit a nearby first year instead, and vanished from sight.

Ron's smile slipped slightly as he looked out of the window, which was now opaque with hammering rain.

"Hope this clears up . . . What's up with you, Hermione?"

She too was gazing at the window, but not as though she really saw it. Her eyes were unfocused and there was a frown on her face.

"Just thinking . . ." she said, still frowning at the rain-washed window.

"About Siri . . . Snuffles?" said Harry.

"No . . . not exactly . . ." said Hermione slowly. "More . . . wondering . . . I suppose we're doing the right thing . . . I think . . . aren't we?"

Harry and Ron looked at each other.

"Well, that clears that up," said Ron. "It would've been really annoying if you hadn't explained yourself properly."

Hermione looked at him as though she had only just realized he was there.

"I was just wondering," she said, her voice stronger now, "whether we're doing the right thing, starting this Defense Against the Dark Arts group."

"What!" said Harry and Ron together.

"Hermione, it was your idea in the first place!" said Ron indignantly.

"I know," said Hermione, twisting her fingers together. "But after talking to Snuffles . . ."

"But he's all for it!" said Harry.

"Yes," said Hermione, staring at the window again. "Yes, that's what made me think maybe it wasn't a good idea after all. . . ."

Peeves floated over them on his stomach, peashooter at the ready; automatically all three of them lifted their bags to cover their heads until he had passed.

"Let's get this straight," said Harry angrily, as they put their bags back on the floor, "Sirius agrees with us, so you don't think we should do it anymore?"

Hermione looked tense and rather miserable. Now staring at her own hands she said, "Do you honestly trust his judgment?"

"Yes, I do!" said Harry at once. "He's always given us great advice!"

An ink pellet whizzed past them, striking Katie Bell squarely in the ear. Hermione watched Katie leap to her feet and start throwing things at Peeves; it was a few moments before Hermione spoke again and it sounded as though she was choosing her words very carefully.

"You don't think he has become . . . sort of . . . reckless . . . since he's been cooped up in Grimmauld Place? You don't think he's . . . kind of . . . living through us?"

"What d'you mean, 'living through us'?" Harry retorted.

"I mean . . . well, I think he'd love to be forming secret defense societies right under the nose of someone from the Ministry. . . . I think he's really frustrated at how little he can do where he is . . . so I think he's keen to kind of . . . egg us on."

Ron looked utterly perplexed.

"Sirius is right," he said, "you *do* sound just like my mother."

Hermione bit her lip and did not answer. The bell rang just as Peeves swooped down upon Katie and emptied an entire ink bottle over her head.

The weather did not improve as the day wore on, so that at seven o'clock that evening, when Harry and Ron went down to the Quidditch pitch for practice, they were soaked through within minutes, their feet slipping and sliding on the sodden grass. The sky was a deep, thundery gray and it was a relief to gain the warmth and light of the changing rooms, even if they knew the respite was only temporary. They found Fred and George debating whether to use one of their own Skiving Snackboxes to get out of flying.

"— but I bet she'd know what we'd done," Fred said out of the corner of his mouth. "If only I hadn't offered to sell her some Puking Pastilles yesterday —"

"We could try the Fever Fudge," George muttered, "no one's seen that yet —"

"Does it work?" inquired Ron hopefully, as the hammering of rain on the roof intensified and wind howled around the building.

"Well, yeah," said Fred, "your temperature'll go right up —"

"— but you get these massive pus-filled boils too," said George, "and we haven't worked out how to get rid of them yet."

"I can't see any boils," said Ron, staring at the twins.

"No, well, you wouldn't," said Fred darkly, "they're not in a place we generally display to the public —"

"— but they make sitting on a broom a right pain in the —"

"All right, everyone, listen up," said Angelina loudly, emerging from the Captain's office. "I know it's not ideal weather, but there's a good chance we'll be playing Slytherin in conditions like this so it's a good idea to work out how we're going to cope with them. Harry, didn't you do something to your glasses to stop the rain fogging them up when we played Hufflepuff in that storm?"

"Hermione did it," said Harry. He pulled out his wand, tapped his glasses and said, *"Impervius!"*

"I think we all ought to try that," said Angelina. "If we could just keep the rain off our faces it would really help visibility — all together, come on — *Impervius!* Okay. Let's go."

They all stowed their wands back in the inside pockets of their robes, shouldered their brooms, and followed Angelina out of the changing rooms.

They squelched through the deepening mud to the middle of the pitch; visibility was still very poor even with the Impervius Charm; light was fading fast and curtains of rain were sweeping the grounds.

"All right, on my whistle," shouted Angelina.

Harry kicked off from the ground, spraying mud in all directions, and shot upward, the wind pulling him slightly off course. He had no idea how he was going to see the Snitch in this weather; he was having enough difficulty seeing the one Bludger with which they were practicing; a minute into the practice it almost unseated him and he had to use the Sloth Grip Roll to avoid it. Unfortunately Angelina did not see this; in fact, she did not appear to be able to see anything; none of them had a clue what the others were doing. The wind was picking up; even at a distance Harry could hear the swishing, pounding sounds of the rain pummeling the surface of the lake.

Angelina kept them at it for nearly an hour before conceding defeat. She led her sodden and disgruntled team back into the changing rooms, insisting that the practice had not been a waste of time, though without any real conviction in her voice. Fred and George were looking particularly annoyed; both were bandy-legged and winced with every movement. Harry could hear them complaining in low voices as he toweled his hair dry.

"I think a few of mine have ruptured," said Fred in a hollow voice.

"Mine haven't," said George, wincing. "They're throbbing like mad . . . feel bigger if anything . . ."

"OUCH!" said Harry.

He pressed the towel to his face, his eyes screwed tight with pain. The scar on his forehead had seared again, more painfully than in months.

"What's up?" said several voices.

Harry emerged from behind his towel; the changing room was blurred because he was not wearing his glasses; but he could still tell that everyone's face was turned toward him.

"Nothing," he muttered, "I — poked myself in the eye, that's all. . . ."

But he gave Ron a significant look and the two of them hung back as the rest of the team filed back outside, muffled in their cloaks, their hats pulled low over their ears.

"What happened?" said Ron, the moment that Alicia had disappeared through the door. "Was it your scar?"

Harry nodded.

"But . . ." Looking scared, Ron strode across to the window and stared out into the rain, "He — he can't be near us now, can he?"

"No," Harry muttered, sinking onto a bench and rubbing his

forehead. "He's probably miles away. It hurt because . . . he's . . . angry."

Harry had not meant to say that at all, and heard the words as though a stranger had spoken them — yet he knew at once that they were true. He did not know how he knew it, but he did; Voldemort, wherever he was, whatever he was doing, was in a towering temper.

"Did you see him?" said Ron, looking horrified. "Did you . . . get a vision, or something?"

Harry sat quite still, staring at his feet, allowing his mind and his memory to relax in the aftermath of the pain. . . .

A confused tangle of shapes, a howling rush of voices . . .

"He wants something done, and it's not happening fast enough," he said.

Again, he felt surprised to hear the words coming out of his mouth, and yet quite certain that they were true.

"But . . . how do you know?" said Ron.

Harry shook his head and covered his eyes with his hands, pressing down upon them with his palms. Little stars erupted in them. He felt Ron sit down on the bench beside him and knew Ron was staring at him.

"Is this what it was about last time?" said Ron in a hushed voice. "When your scar hurt in Umbridge's office? You-Know-Who was angry?"

Harry shook his head.

"What is it, then?"

Harry was thinking himself back. He had been looking into Umbridge's face. . . . His scar had hurt . . . and he had had that odd feeling in his stomach . . . a strange, leaping feeling . . . a *happy* feeling. . . . But, of course, he had not recognized it for what it was, as he had been feeling so miserable himself. . . .

"Last time, it was because he was pleased," he said. "Really pleased.

He thought . . . something good was going to happen. And the night before we came back to Hogwarts . . ." He thought back to the moment when his scar had hurt so badly in his and Ron's bedroom in Grimmauld Place. "He was furious. . . ."

He looked around at Ron, who was gaping at him.

"You could take over from Trelawney, mate," he said in an awed voice.

"I'm not making prophecies," said Harry.

"No, you know what you're doing?" Ron said, sounding both scared and impressed. "Harry, *you're reading You-Know-Who's mind.* . . ."

"No," said Harry, shaking his head. "It's more like . . . his mood, I suppose. I'm just getting flashes of what mood he's in. . . . Dumbledore said something like this was happening last year. . . . He said that when Voldemort was near me, or when he was feeling hatred, I could tell. Well, now I'm feeling it when he's pleased too. . . ."

There was a pause. The wind and rain lashed at the building.

"You've got to tell someone," said Ron.

"I told Sirius last time."

"Well, tell him about this time!"

"Can't, can I?" said Harry grimly. "Umbridge is watching the owls and the fires, remember?"

"Well then, Dumbledore —"

"I've just told you, he already knows," said Harry shortly, getting to his feet, taking his cloak off his peg, and swinging it around himself. "There's no point telling him again."

Ron did up the fastening of his own cloak, watching Harry thoughtfully.

"Dumbledore'd want to know," he said.

Harry shrugged.

"C'mon . . . we've still got Silencing Charms to practice . . ."

They hurried back through the dark grounds, sliding and stumbling up the muddy lawns, not talking. Harry was thinking hard.

What was it that Voldemort wanted done that was not happening quickly enough?

"He's got other plans . . . plans he can put into operation very quietly indeed . . . stuff he can only get by stealth . . . like a weapon. Something he didn't have last time."

He had not thought about those words in weeks; he had been too absorbed in what was going on at Hogwarts, too busy dwelling on the ongoing battles with Umbridge, the injustice of all the Ministry interference. . . . But now they came back to him and made him wonder. . . . Voldemort's anger would make sense if he was no nearer laying hands on the weapon, whatever it was. . . . Had the Order thwarted him, stopped him from seizing it? Where was it kept? Who had it now?

"Mimbulus mimbletonia," said Ron's voice and Harry came back to his senses just in time to clamber through the portrait hole into the common room.

It appeared that Hermione had gone to bed early, leaving Crookshanks curled in a nearby chair and an assortment of knobbly, knitted elf hats lying on a table by the fire. Harry was rather grateful that she was not around because he did not much want to discuss his scar hurting and have her urge him to go to Dumbledore too. Ron kept throwing him anxious glances, but Harry pulled out his Potions book and set to work to finish his essay, though he was only pretending to concentrate and, by the time that Ron said he was going to bed too, had written hardly anything.

Midnight came and went while Harry was reading and rereading a passage about the uses of scurvy-grass, lovage, and sneezewort and not taking in a word of it. . . .

These plantes are moste efficacious in the inflaming of the braine, and are therefore much used in Confusing and Befuddlement Draughts, where the wizard is desirous of producing hot-headedness and recklessness. . . .

. . . Hermione said Sirius was becoming reckless cooped up in Grimmauld Place. . . .

. . . moste efficacious in the inflaming of the braine, and are therefore much used . . .

. . . the *Daily Prophet* would think his brain was inflamed if they found out that he knew what Voldemort was feeling . . .

. . . therefore much used in Confusing and Befuddlement Draughts . . .

. . . confusing was the word, all right; *why* did he know what Voldemort was feeling? What was this weird connection between them, which Dumbledore had never been able to explain satisfactorily?

. . . where the wizard is desirous . . .

. . . how he would like to sleep . . .

. . . of producing hot-headedness . . .

. . . It was warm and comfortable in his armchair before the fire, with the rain still beating heavily on the windowpanes and Crookshanks purring and the crackling of the flames. . . .

The book slipped from Harry's slack grip and landed with a dull thud on the hearthrug. His head fell sideways. . . .

He was walking once more along a windowless corridor, his footsteps echoing in the silence. As the door at the end of the passage loomed larger his heart beat fast with excitement. . . . If he could only open it . . . enter beyond . . .

He stretched out his hand. . . . His fingertips were inches from it. . . .

"Harry Potter, sir!"

He awoke with a start. The candles had all been extinguished in the common room, but there was something moving close by.

"Whozair?" said Harry, sitting upright in his chair. The fire was almost extinguished, the room very dark.

"Dobby has your owl, sir!" said a squeaky voice.

"Dobby?" said Harry thickly, peering through the gloom toward the source of the voice.

Dobby the house-elf was standing beside the table on which Hermione had left her half a dozen knitted hats. His large, pointed ears were now sticking out from beneath what looked like all the hats that Hermione had ever knitted; he was wearing one on top of the other, so that his head seemed elongated by two or three feet, and on the very topmost bobble sat Hedwig, hooting serenely and obviously cured.

"Dobby volunteered to return Harry Potter's owl!" said the elf squeakily, with a look of positive adoration on his face. "Professor Grubbly-Plank says she is all well now, sir!"

He sank into a deep bow so that his pencil-like nose brushed the threadbare surface of the hearthrug and Hedwig gave an indignant hoot and fluttered onto the arm of Harry's chair.

"Thanks, Dobby!" said Harry, stroking Hedwig's head and blinking hard, trying to rid himself of the image of the door in his dream. . . . It had been very vivid. . . . Looking back at Dobby, he noticed that the elf was also wearing several scarves and innumerable socks, so that his feet looked far too big for his body.

"Er . . . have you been taking *all* the clothes Hermione's been leaving out?"

"Oh no, sir," said Dobby happily, "Dobby has been taking some for Winky too, sir."

"Yeah, how is Winky?" asked Harry.

Dobby's ears drooped slightly.

"Winky is still drinking lots, sir," he said sadly, his enormous round green eyes, large as tennis balls, downcast. "She still does not care for clothes, Harry Potter. Nor do the other house-elves. None of them will clean Gryffindor Tower anymore, not with the hats and socks hidden everywhere, they finds them insulting, sir. Dobby does it all himself, sir, but Dobby does not mind, sir, for he always hopes to meet Harry Potter and tonight, sir, he has got his wish!" Dobby sank into a deep bow again. "But Harry Potter does not seem happy," Dobby went on, straightening up again and looking timidly at Harry. "Dobby heard him muttering in his sleep. Was Harry Potter having bad dreams?"

"Not really bad," said Harry, yawning and rubbing his eyes. "I've had worse."

The elf surveyed Harry out of his vast, orblike eyes. Then he said very seriously, his ears drooping, "Dobby wishes he could help Harry Potter, for Harry Potter set Dobby free and Dobby is much, much happier now. . . ."

Harry smiled.

"You can't help me, Dobby, but thanks for the offer. . . ."

He bent and picked up his Potions book. He'd have to try and finish the essay tomorrow. He closed the book and as he did so the firelight illuminated the thin white scars on the back of his hand — the result of his detention with Umbridge.

"Wait a moment — there *is* something you can do for me, Dobby," said Harry slowly.

The elf looked around, beaming.

"Name it, Harry Potter, sir!"

"I need to find a place where twenty-eight people can practice Defense Against the Dark Arts without being discovered by any of the teachers. Especially," Harry clenched his hand on the book, so that the scars shone pearly white, "Professor Umbridge."

He expected the elf's smile to vanish, his ears to droop; he expected him to say that this was impossible, or else that he would try, but his hopes were not high. . . . What he had not expected was for Dobby to give a little skip, his ears waggling happily, and clap his hands together.

"Dobby knows the perfect place, sir!" he said happily. "Dobby heard tell of it from the other house-elves when he came to Hogwarts, sir. It is known by us as the Come and Go Room, sir, or else as the Room of Requirement!"

"Why?" said Harry curiously.

"Because it is a room that a person can only enter," said Dobby seriously, "when they have real need of it. Sometimes it is there, and sometimes it is not, but when it appears, it is always equipped for the seeker's needs. Dobby has used it, sir," said the elf, dropping his voice and looking guilty, "when Winky has been very drunk. He has hidden her in the Room of Requirement and he has found antidotes to butterbeer there, and a nice elf-sized bed to settle her on while she sleeps it off, sir. . . . And Dobby knows Mr. Filch has found extra cleaning materials there when he has run short, sir, and —"

"— and if you really needed a bathroom," said Harry, suddenly remembering something Dumbledore had said at the Yule Ball the previous Christmas, "would it fill itself with chamber pots?"

"Dobby expects so, sir," said Dobby, nodding earnestly. "It is a most amazing room, sir."

"How many people know about it?" said Harry, sitting up straighter in his chair.

"Very few, sir. Mostly people stumbles across it when they needs it, sir, but often they never finds it again, for they do not know that it is always there waiting to be called into service, sir."

"It sounds brilliant," said Harry, his heart racing. "It sounds perfect, Dobby. When can you show me where it is?"

"Anytime, Harry Potter, sir," said Dobby, looking delighted at Harry's enthusiasm. "We could go now, if you like!"

For a moment Harry was tempted to go now; he was halfway out of his seat, intending to hurry upstairs for his Invisibility Cloak when, not for the first time, a voice very much like Hermione's whispered in his ear: *reckless*. It was, after all, very late, and he was exhausted.

"Not tonight, Dobby," said Harry reluctantly, sinking back into his chair. "This is really important. . . . I don't want to blow it, it'll need proper planning. . . . Listen, can you just tell me exactly where this Room of Requirement is and how to get in there?"

Their robes billowed and swirled around them as they splashed across the flooded vegetable patch to double Herbology, where they could hardly hear what Professor Sprout was saying over the hammering of raindrops hard as hailstones on the greenhouse roof. The afternoon's Care of Magical Creatures lesson was to be relocated from the storm-swept grounds to a free classroom on the ground floor and, to their intense relief, Angelina sought out her team at lunch to tell them that Quidditch practice was canceled.

"Good," said Harry quietly, when she told him, "because we've found somewhere to have our first Defense meeting. Tonight, eight o'clock, seventh floor opposite that tapestry of Barnabas the Barmy being clubbed by those trolls. Can you tell Katie and Alicia?"

She looked slightly taken aback but promised to tell the others; Harry returned hungrily to his sausages and mash. When he looked up to take a drink of pumpkin juice, he found Hermione watching him.

"What?" he said thickly.

"Well . . . it's just that Dobby's plans aren't always that safe. Don't you remember when he lost you all the bones in your arm?"

"This room isn't just some mad idea of Dobby's; Dumbledore knows about it too, he mentioned it to me at the Yule Ball."

Hermione's expression cleared.

"Dumbledore told you about it?"

"Just in passing," said Harry, shrugging.

"Oh well, that's all right then," said Hermione briskly and she raised no more objections.

Together with Ron they had spent most of the day seeking out those people who had signed their names to the list in the Hog's Head and telling them where to meet that evening. Somewhat to Harry's disappointment, it was Ginny who managed to find Cho Chang and her friend first; however, by the end of dinner he was confident that the news had been passed to every one of the twenty-five people who had turned up in the Hog's Head.

At half-past seven Harry, Ron, and Hermione left the Gryffindor common room, Harry clutching a certain piece of aged parchment in his hand. Fifth years were allowed to be out in the corridors until nine o'clock, but all three of them kept looking around nervously as they made their way up to the seventh floor.

"Hold it," said Harry warningly, unfolding the piece of parchment at the top of the last staircase, tapping it with his wand, and muttering, "I solemnly swear that I am up to no good."

A map of Hogwarts appeared upon the blank surface of the parchment. Tiny black moving dots, labeled with names, showed where various people were.

"Filch is on the second floor," said Harry, holding the map close to his eyes and scanning it closely, "and Mrs. Norris is on the fourth."

"And Umbridge?" said Hermione anxiously.

"In her office," said Harry, pointing. "Okay, let's go."

They hurried along the corridor to the place Dobby had described to Harry, a stretch of blank wall opposite an enormous tapestry depicting Barnabas the Barmy's foolish attempt to train trolls for the ballet.

"Okay," said Harry quietly, while a moth-eaten troll paused in his relentless clubbing of the would-be ballet teacher to watch. "Dobby said to walk past this bit of wall three times, concentrating hard on what we need."

They did so, turning sharply at the window just beyond the blank stretch of wall, then at the man-size vase on its other side. Ron had screwed up his eyes in concentration, Hermione was whispering something under her breath, Harry's fists were clenched as he stared ahead of him.

We need somewhere to learn to fight. . . . he thought. *Just give us a place to practice . . . somewhere they can't find us . . .*

"Harry," said Hermione sharply, as they wheeled around after their third walk past.

A highly polished door had appeared in the wall. Ron was staring at it, looking slightly wary. Harry reached out, seized the brass handle, pulled open the door, and led the way into a spacious room lit with flickering torches like those that illuminated the dungeons eight floors below.

The walls were lined with wooden bookcases, and instead of chairs there were large silk cushions on the floor. A set of shelves at the far end of the room carried a range of instruments such as Sneakoscopes, Secrecy Sensors, and a large, cracked Foe-Glass that Harry was sure had hung, the previous year, in the fake Moody's office.

"These will be good when we're practicing Stunning," said Ron enthusiastically, prodding one of the cushions with his foot.

"And just look at these books!" said Hermione excitedly, running a finger along the spines of the large leather-bound tomes. "*A Compendium of Common Curses and Their Counter-Actions . . . The Dark Arts Outsmarted . . . Self-Defensive Spellwork . . .* wow . . ." She looked around at Harry, her face glowing, and he saw that the presence of hundreds of books had finally convinced Hermione that what they were doing was right. "Harry, this is wonderful, there's everything we need here!"

And without further ado she slid *Jinxes for the Jinxed* from its shelf, sank onto the nearest cushion, and began to read.

There was a gentle knock on the door. Harry looked around; Ginny, Neville, Lavender, Parvati, and Dean had arrived.

"Whoa," said Dean, staring around, impressed. "What is this place?"

Harry began to explain, but before he had finished more people had arrived, and he had to start all over again. By the time eight o'clock arrived, every cushion was occupied. Harry moved across to the door and turned the key protruding from the lock; it clicked in a satisfyingly loud way and everybody fell silent, looking at him. Hermione carefully marked her page of *Jinxes for the Jinxed* and set the book aside.

"Well," said Harry, slightly nervously. "This is the place we've found for practices, and you've — er — obviously found it okay —"

"It's fantastic!" said Cho, and several people murmured their agreement.

"It's bizarre," said Fred, frowning around at it. "We once hid from Filch in here, remember, George? But it was just a broom cupboard then. . . ."

"Hey, Harry, what's this stuff?" asked Dean from the rear of the room, indicating the Sneakoscopes and the Foe-Glass.

"Dark Detectors," said Harry, stepping between the cushions to reach them. "Basically they all show when Dark wizards or enemies are around, but you don't want to rely on them too much, they can be fooled. . . ."

He gazed for a moment into the cracked Foe-Glass; shadowy figures were moving around inside it, though none was recognizable. He turned his back on it.

"Well, I've been thinking about the sort of stuff we ought to do first and — er —" He noticed a raised hand. "What, Hermione?"

"I think we ought to elect a leader," said Hermione.

"Harry's leader," said Cho at once, looking at Hermione as though she were mad, and Harry's stomach did yet another back flip.

"Yes, but I think we ought to vote on it properly," said Hermione, unperturbed. "It makes it formal and it gives him authority. So — everyone who thinks Harry ought to be our leader?"

Everybody put up their hands, even Zacharias Smith, though he did it very halfheartedly.

"Er — right, thanks," said Harry, who could feel his face burning. "And — *what,* Hermione?"

"I also think we ought to have a name," she said brightly, her hand still in the air. "It would promote a feeling of team spirit and unity, don't you think?"

"Can we be the Anti-Umbridge League?" said Angelina hopefully.

"Or the Ministry of Magic Are Morons Group?" suggested Fred.

"I was thinking," said Hermione, frowning at Fred, "more of a name that didn't tell everyone what we were up to, so we can refer to it safely outside meetings."

"The Defense Association?" said Cho. "The D.A. for short, so nobody knows what we're talking about?"

"Yeah, the D.A.'s good," said Ginny. "Only let's make it stand for Dumbledore's Army because that's the Ministry's worst fear, isn't it?"

There was a good deal of appreciative murmuring and laughter at this.

"All in favor of the D.A.?" said Hermione bossily, kneeling up on her cushion to count. "That's a majority — motion passed!"

She pinned the piece of paper with all of their names on it on the wall and wrote DUMBLEDORE'S ARMY across the top in large letters.

"Right," said Harry, when she had sat down again, "shall we get practicing then? I was thinking, the first thing we should do is *Expelliarmus,* you know, the Disarming Charm. I know it's pretty basic but I've found it really useful —"

"Oh *please,*" said Zacharias Smith, rolling his eyes and folding his arms. "I don't think *Expelliarmus* is exactly going to help us against You-Know-Who, do you?"

"I've used it against him," said Harry quietly. "It saved my life last June."

Smith opened his mouth stupidly. The rest of the room was very quiet.

"But if you think it's beneath you, you can leave," Harry said.

Smith did not move. Nor did anybody else.

"Okay," said Harry, his mouth slightly drier than usual with all those eyes upon him, "I reckon we should all divide into pairs and practice."

It felt very odd to be issuing instructions, but not nearly as odd as seeing them followed. Everybody got to their feet at once and divided up. Predictably, Neville was left partnerless.

"You can practice with me," Harry told him. "Right — on the count of three, then — one, two, three —"

The room was suddenly full of shouts of *"Expelliarmus!"*: Wands flew in all directions, missed spells hit books on shelves and sent them flying into the air. Harry was too quick for Neville, whose wand went spinning out of his hand, hit the ceiling in a shower of sparks, and landed with a clatter on top of a bookshelf, from which Harry retrieved it with a Summoning Charm. Glancing around he thought he had been right to suggest that they practice the basics first; there was a lot of shoddy spellwork going on; many people were not succeeding in disarming their opponents at all, but merely causing them to jump backward a few paces or wince as the feeble spell whooshed over them.

"Expelliarmus!" said Neville, and Harry, caught unawares, felt his wand fly out of his hand.

"I DID IT!" said Neville gleefully. "I've never done it before — I DID IT!"

"Good one!" said Harry encouragingly, deciding not to point out that in a real duel situation Neville's opponent was unlikely to be staring in the opposite direction with his wand held loosely at his side. "Listen, Neville, can you take it in turns to practice with Ron and Hermione for a couple of minutes so I can walk around and see how the rest are doing?"

Harry moved off into the middle of the room. Something very odd was happening to Zacharias Smith; every time he opened his mouth to disarm Anthony Goldstein, his own wand would fly out of his hand, yet Anthony did not seem to be making a sound. Harry did not have to look far for the solution of the mystery, however; Fred and George were several feet from Smith and taking it in turns to point their wands at his back.

"Sorry, Harry," said George hastily, when Harry caught his eye. "Couldn't resist . . ."

Harry walked around the other pairs, trying to correct those who were doing the spell wrong. Ginny was teamed with Michael Corner; she was doing very well, whereas Michael was either very bad or unwilling to jinx her. Ernie Macmillan was flourishing his wand unnecessarily, giving his partner time to get in under his guard; the Creevey brothers were enthusiastic but erratic and mainly responsible for all the books leaping off the shelves around them. Luna Lovegood was similarly patchy, occasionally sending Justin Finch-Fletchley's wand spinning out of his hand, at other times merely causing his hair to stand on end.

"Okay, stop!" Harry shouted. *"Stop! STOP!"*

I need a whistle, he thought, and immediately spotted one lying on top of the nearest row of books. He caught it up and blew hard. Everyone lowered their wands.

"That wasn't bad," said Harry, "but there's definite room for improvement." Zacharias Smith glared at him. "Let's try again. . . ."

He moved off around the room again, stopping here and there to make suggestions. Slowly the general performance improved. He avoided going near Cho and her friend for a while, but after walking twice around every other pair in the room felt he could not ignore them any longer.

"Oh no," said Cho rather wildly as he approached. *"Expelliarmious!* I mean, *Expellimellius!* I — oh, sorry, Marietta!"

Her curly-haired friend's sleeve had caught fire; Marietta extinguished it with her own wand and glared at Harry as though it was his fault.

"You made me nervous, I was doing all right before then!" Cho told Harry ruefully.

"That was quite good," Harry lied, but when she raised her eyebrows he said, "Well, no, it was lousy, but I know you can do it properly, I was watching from over there. . . ."

She laughed. Her friend Marietta looked at them rather sourly and turned away.

"Don't mind her," Cho muttered. "She doesn't really want to be here but I made her come with me. Her parents have forbidden her to do anything that might upset Umbridge, you see — her mum works for the Ministry."

"What about your parents?" asked Harry.

"Well, they've forbidden me to get on the wrong side of Umbridge too," said Cho, drawing herself up proudly. "But if they think I'm not going to fight You-Know-Who after what happened to Cedric —"

She broke off, looking rather confused, and an awkward silence fell between them; Terry Boot's wand went whizzing past Harry's ear and hit Alicia Spinnet hard on the nose.

"Well, my father is *very* supportive of any anti-Ministry action!" said Luna Lovegood proudly from just behind Harry; evidently she had been eavesdropping on his conversation while Justin Finch-Fletchley attempted to disentangle himself from the robes that had flown up over his head. "He's always saying he'd believe anything of Fudge, I mean, the number of goblins Fudge has had assassinated! And of course he uses the Department of Mysteries to develop terrible poisons, which he feeds secretly to anybody who disagrees with him. And then there's his Umgubular Slashkilter —"

"Don't ask," Harry muttered to Cho as she opened her mouth, looking puzzled. She giggled.

"Hey, Harry," Hermione called from the other end of the room, "have you checked the time?"

He looked down at his watch and received a shock — it was already ten past nine, which meant they needed to get back to their common rooms immediately or risk being caught and punished by

Filch for being out-of-bounds. He blew his whistle; everybody stopped shouting, *"Expelliarmus!"* and the last couple of wands clattered to the floor.

"Well, that was pretty good," said Harry, "but we've overrun, we'd better leave it here. Same time, same place next week?"

"Sooner!" said Dean Thomas eagerly and many people nodded in agreement.

Angelina, however, said quickly, "The Quidditch season's about to start, we need team practices too!"

"Let's say next Wednesday night, then," said Harry, "and we can decide on additional meetings then. . . . Come on, we'd better get going. . . ."

He pulled out the Marauder's Map again and checked it carefully for signs of teachers on the seventh floor. He let them all leave in threes and fours, watching their tiny dots anxiously to see that they returned safely to their dormitories: the Hufflepuffs to the basement corridor that also led to the kitchens, the Ravenclaws to a tower on the west side of the castle, and the Gryffindors along the corridor to the seventh floor and the Fat Lady's portrait.

"That was really, really good, Harry," said Hermione, when finally it was just her, Harry, and Ron left.

"Yeah, it was!" said Ron enthusiastically, as they slipped out of the door and watched it melt back into stone behind them. "Did you see me disarm Hermione, Harry?"

"Only once," said Hermione, stung. "I got you loads more than you got me —"

"I did not only get you once, I got you at least three times —"

"Well, if you're counting the one where you tripped over your own feet and knocked the wand out of my hand —"

They argued all the way back to the common room, but Harry was not listening to them. He had one eye on the Marauder's Map, but he was also thinking of how Cho had said he made her nervous. . . .

THE LION AND
THE SERPENT

Harry felt as though he were carrying some kind of talisman inside his chest over the following two weeks, a glowing secret that supported him through Umbridge's classes and even made it possible for him to smile blandly as he looked into her horrible bulging eyes. He and the D.A. were resisting her under her very nose, doing the very thing that she and the Ministry most feared, and whenever he was supposed to be reading Wilbert Slinkhard's book during her lessons he dwelled instead on satisfying memories of their most recent meetings, remembering how Neville had successfully disarmed Hermione, how Colin Creevey had mastered the Impediment Jinx after three meetings' hard effort, how Parvati Patil had produced such a good Reductor Curse that she had reduced the table carrying all the Sneakoscopes to dust.

He was finding it almost impossible to fix a regular night of the week for D.A. meetings, as they had to accommodate three separate Quidditch teams' practices, which were often rearranged depending on the weather conditions; but Harry was not sorry about this, he had a feeling that it was probably better to keep the timing of their meetings unpredictable. If anyone was watching them, it would be hard to make out a pattern.

Hermione soon devised a very clever method of communicating the time and date of the next meeting to all the members in case they needed to change it at short notice, because it would look so suspicious if people from different Houses were seen crossing the Great Hall to talk to each other too often. She gave each of the members of the D.A. a fake Galleon (Ron became very excited when he saw the basket at first, convinced that she was actually giving out gold).

"You see the numerals around the edge of the coins?" Hermione said, holding one up for examination at the end of their fourth meeting. The coin gleamed fat and yellow in the light from the torches. "On real Galleons that's just a serial number referring to the goblin who cast the coin. On these fake coins, though, the numbers will change to reflect the time and date of the next meeting. The coins will grow hot when the date changes, so if you're carrying them in a pocket you'll be able to feel them. We take one each, and when Harry sets the date of the next meeting he'll change the numbers on *his* coin, and because I've put a Protean Charm on them, they'll all change to mimic his."

A blank silence greeted Hermione's words. She looked around at all the faces upturned to her, rather disconcerted.

"Well — I thought it was a good idea," she said uncertainly, "I mean, even if Umbridge asked us to turn out our pockets, there's nothing fishy about carrying a Galleon, is there? But . . . well, if you don't want to use them . . ."

"You can do a Protean Charm?" said Terry Boot.

"Yes," said Hermione.

"But that's . . . that's N.E.W.T. standard, that is," he said weakly.

"Oh," said Hermione, trying to look modest. "Oh . . . well . . . yes, I suppose it is. . . ."

"How come you're not in Ravenclaw?" he demanded, staring at Hermione with something close to wonder. "With brains like yours?"

"Well, the Sorting Hat did seriously consider putting me in Ravenclaw during my Sorting," said Hermione brightly, "but it decided on Gryffindor in the end. So does that mean we're using the Galleons?"

There was a murmur of assent and everybody moved forward to collect one from the basket. Harry looked sideways at Hermione.

"You know what these remind me of?"

"No, what's that?"

"The Death Eaters' scars. Voldemort touches one of them, and all their scars burn, and they know they've got to join him."

"Well . . . yes," said Hermione quietly. "That *is* where I got the idea . . . but you'll notice I decided to engrave the date on bits of metal rather than on our members' skin. . . ."

"Yeah . . . I prefer your way," said Harry, grinning, as he slipped his Galleon into his pocket. "I suppose the only danger with these is that we might accidentally spend them."

"Fat chance," said Ron, who was examining his own fake Galleon with a slightly mournful air. "I haven't got any real Galleons to confuse it with."

As the first Quidditch match of the season, Gryffindor versus Slytherin, drew nearer, their D.A. meetings were put on hold because Angelina insisted on almost daily practices. The fact that the Quidditch Cup had not been held for so long added considerably to the interest and excitement surrounding the forthcoming game. The Ravenclaws and Hufflepuffs were taking a lively interest in the outcome, for they, of course, would be playing both teams over the coming year; and the Heads of House of the competing teams, though they attempted to disguise it under a decent pretense of sportsmanship, were determined to see their side's victory. Harry realized how much Professor McGonagall cared about beating Slytherin when she abstained from giving them homework in the week leading up to the match.

"I think you've got enough to be getting on with at the moment," she said loftily. Nobody could quite believe their ears until she looked directly at Harry and Ron and said grimly, "I've become accustomed to seeing the Quidditch Cup in my study, boys, and I really don't want to have to hand it over to Professor Snape, so use the extra time to practice, won't you?"

Snape was no less obviously partisan: He had booked the Quidditch pitch for Slytherin practice so often that the Gryffindors had difficulty getting on it to play. He was also turning a deaf ear to the many reports of Slytherin attempts to hex Gryffindor players in the corridors. When Alicia Spinnet turned up in the hospital wing with her eyebrows growing so thick and fast that they obscured her vision and obstructed her mouth, Snape insisted that she must have attempted a Hair-Thickening Charm on herself and refused to listen to the fourteen eyewitnesses who insisted that they had seen the Slytherin Keeper, Miles Bletchley, hit her from behind with a jinx while she worked in the library.

Harry felt optimistic about Gryffindor's chances; they had, after all, never lost to Malfoy's team. Admittedly Ron was still not performing to Wood's standard, but he was working extremely hard to improve. His greatest weakness was a tendency to lose confidence when he made a blunder; if he let in one goal he became flustered and was therefore likely to miss more. On the other hand, Harry had seen Ron make some truly spectacular saves when he was on form: During one memorable practice, he had hung one-handed from his broom and kicked the Quaffle so hard away from the goal hoop that it soared the length of the pitch and through the center hoop at the other end. The rest of the team felt this save compared favorably with one made recently by Barry Ryan, the Irish International Keeper, against Poland's top Chaser, Ladislaw Zamojski. Even Fred had said that Ron might yet make him and George proud, and that they were seriously considering admitting that he was related to them, something he assured Ron they had been trying to deny for four years.

The only thing really worrying Harry was how much Ron was allowing the tactics of the Slytherin team to upset him before they even got onto the pitch. Harry, of course, had endured their snide comments for more than four years, so whispers of, "Hey, Potty, I heard Warrington's sworn to knock you off your broom on Saturday," far from chilling his blood, made him laugh. "Warrington's aim's so pathetic I'd be more worried if he was aiming for the person next to me," he retorted, which made Ron and Hermione laugh and wiped the smirk off Pansy Parkinson's face.

But Ron had never endured a relentless campaign of insults, jeers, and intimidation. When Slytherins, some of them seventh years and considerably larger than he was, muttered as they passed in the corridors, "Got your bed booked in the hospital wing, Weasley?" he did not laugh, but turned a delicate shade of green. When Draco Malfoy imitated Ron dropping the Quaffle (which he did whenever they were within sight of each other), Ron's ears glowed red and his hands shook so badly that he was likely to drop whatever he was holding at the time too.

October extinguished itself in a rush of howling winds and driving rain and November arrived, cold as frozen iron, with hard frosts every morning and icy drafts that bit at exposed hands and faces. The skies and the ceiling of the Great Hall turned a pale, pearly gray, the mountains around Hogwarts became snowcapped, and the temperature in the castle dropped so far that many students wore their thick protective dragon skin gloves in the corridors between lessons.

The morning of the match dawned bright and cold. When Harry awoke he looked around at Ron's bed and saw him sitting bolt upright, his arms around his knees, staring fixedly into space.

"You all right?" said Harry.

Ron nodded but did not speak. Harry was reminded forcibly of the time that Ron had accidentally put a slug-vomiting charm on himself. He looked just as pale and sweaty as he had done then, not to mention as reluctant to open his mouth.

"You just need some breakfast," Harry said bracingly. "C'mon."

The Great Hall was filling up fast when they arrived, the talk louder and the mood more exuberant than usual. As they passed the Slytherin table there was an upsurge of noise; Harry looked around and saw that nearly everyone there was wearing, in addition to the usual green-and-silver scarves and hats, silver badges in the shape of what seemed to be crowns. For some reason many of them waved at Ron, laughing uproariously. Harry tried to see what was written on the badges as he walked by, but he was too concerned to get Ron past their table quickly to linger long enough to read them.

They received a rousing welcome at the Gryffindor table, where everyone was wearing red and gold, but far from raising Ron's spirits the cheers seemed to sap the last of his morale; he collapsed onto the nearest bench looking as though he were facing his final meal.

"I must've been mental to do this," he said in a croaky whisper. *"Mental."*

"Don't be thick," said Harry firmly, passing him a choice of cereals. "You're going to be fine. It's normal to be nervous."

"I'm rubbish," croaked Ron. "I'm lousy. I can't play to save my life. What was I thinking?"

"Get a grip," said Harry sternly. "Look at that save you made with your foot the other day, even Fred and George said it was brilliant —"

Ron turned a tortured face to Harry.

"That was an accident," he whispered miserably. "I didn't mean to do it — I slipped off my broom when none of you were looking and I was trying to get back on and I kicked the Quaffle by accident."

"Well," said Harry, recovering quickly from this unpleasant surprise, "a few more accidents like that and the game's in the bag, isn't it?"

Hermione and Ginny sat down opposite them wearing red-and-gold scarves, gloves, and rosettes.

"How're you feeling?" Ginny asked Ron, who was now staring into the dregs of milk at the bottom of his empty cereal bowl as though seriously considering attempting to drown himself in them.

"He's just nervous," said Harry.

"Well, that's a good sign, I never feel you perform as well in exams if you're not a bit nervous," said Hermione heartily.

"Hello," said a vague and dreamy voice from behind them. Harry looked up: Luna Lovegood had drifted over from the Ravenclaw table. Many people were staring at her and a few openly laughing and pointing; she had managed to procure a hat shaped like a life-size lion's head, which was perched precariously on her head.

"I'm supporting Gryffindor," said Luna, pointing unnecessarily at her hat. "Look what it does. . . ."

She reached up and tapped the hat with her wand. It opened its mouth wide and gave an extremely realistic roar that made everyone in the vicinity jump.

"It's good, isn't it?" said Luna happily. "I wanted to have it chewing up a serpent to represent Slytherin, you know, but there wasn't time. Anyway . . . good luck, Ronald!"

She drifted away. They had not quite recovered from the shock of Luna's hat before Angelina came hurrying toward them, accompanied by Katie and Alicia, whose eyebrows had mercifully been returned to normal by Madam Pomfrey.

"When you're ready," she said, "we're going to go straight down to the pitch, check out conditions and change."

"We'll be there in a bit," Harry assured her. "Ron's just got to have some breakfast."

It became clear after ten minutes, however, that Ron was not capable of eating anything more and Harry thought it best to get him down to the changing rooms. As they rose from the table, Hermione got up too, and taking Harry's arm, she drew him to one side.

"Don't let Ron see what's on those Slytherins' badges," she whispered urgently.

Harry looked questioningly at her, but she shook her head warningly; Ron had just ambled over to them, looking lost and desperate.

"Good luck, Ron," said Hermione, standing on tiptoe and kissing him on the cheek. "And you, Harry —"

Ron seemed to come to himself slightly as they walked back across the Great Hall. He touched the spot on his face where Hermione had kissed him, looking puzzled, as though he was not quite sure what had just happened. He seemed too distracted to notice much around him, but Harry cast a curious glance at the crown-shaped badges as they passed the Slytherin table, and this time he made out the words etched onto them:

With an unpleasant feeling that this could mean nothing good, he hurried Ron across the entrance hall, down the stone steps, and out into the icy air.

The frosty grass crunched under their feet as they hurried down the sloping lawns toward the stadium. There was no wind at all and the sky was a uniform pearly white, which meant that visibility would be good without the drawback of direct sunlight in the eyes. Harry pointed out these encouraging factors to Ron as they walked, but he was not sure that Ron was listening.

Angelina had changed already and was talking to the rest of the team when they entered. Harry and Ron pulled on their robes (Ron attempted to do his up back-to-front for several minutes before Alicia took pity on him and went to help) and then sat down to listen to the pre-match talk while the babble of voices outside grew steadily louder as the crowd came pouring out of the castle toward the pitch.

"Okay, I've only just found out the final lineup for Slytherin," said Angelina, consulting a piece of parchment. "Last year's Beaters, Derrick and Bole, have left now, but it looks as though Montague's replaced them with the usual gorillas, rather than anyone who can fly particularly well. They're two blokes called Crabbe and Goyle, I don't know much about them —"

"We do," said Harry and Ron together.

"Well, they don't look bright enough to tell one end of a broom from another," said Angelina, pocketing her parchment, "but then I was always surprised Derrick and Bole managed to find their way onto the pitch without signposts."

"Crabbe and Goyle are in the same mold," Harry assured her.

They could hear hundreds of footsteps mounting the banked benches of the spectators' stands now. Some people were singing, though Harry could not make out the words. He was starting to feel nervous, but he knew his butterflies were as nothing to Ron's, who was clutching his stomach and staring straight ahead again, his jaw set and his complexion pale gray.

"It's time," said Angelina in a hushed voice, looking at her watch. "C'mon everyone . . . good luck."

The team rose, shouldered their brooms, and marched in single file out of the changing room and into the dazzling sky. A roar of sound greeted them in which Harry could still hear singing, though it was muffled by the cheers and whistles.

The Slytherin team were standing waiting for them. They too were wearing those silver crown-shaped badges. The new captain, Montague, was built along the same lines as Dudley, with massive forearms like hairy hams. Behind him lurked Crabbe and Goyle, almost as large, blinking stupidly, swinging their new Beaters' bats. Malfoy stood to one side, the sunlight gleaming on his white-blond head. He caught Harry's eye and smirked, tapping the crown-shaped badge on his chest.

"Captains shake hands," ordered the umpire, Madam Hooch, as Angelina and Montague reached each other. Harry could tell that Montague was trying to crush Angelina's fingers, though she did not wince. "Mount your brooms. . . ."

Madam Hooch placed her whistle in her mouth and blew.

The balls were released and the fourteen players shot upward; out of the corner of his eye Harry saw Ron streak off toward the goal hoops. He zoomed higher, dodging a Bludger, and set off on a wide lap of the pitch, gazing around for a glint of gold; on the other side of the stadium, Draco Malfoy was doing exactly the same.

"And it's Johnson, Johnson with the Quaffle, what a player that girl is, I've been saying it for years but she still won't go out with me —"

"JORDAN!" yelled Professor McGonagall.

"Just a fun fact, Professor, adds a bit of interest — and she's ducked Warrington, she's passed Montague, she's — ouch — been hit from behind by a Bludger from Crabbe. . . . Montague catches the Quaffle, Montague heading back up the pitch and — nice Bludger there from George Weasley, that's a Bludger to the head for Montague, he drops the Quaffle, caught by Katie Bell, Katie Bell of Gryffindor reverse passes to Alicia Spinnet and Spinnet's away —"

Lee Jordan's commentary rang through the stadium and Harry listened as hard as he could through the wind whistling in his ears and the din of the crowd, all yelling and booing and singing —

"— dodges Warrington, avoids a Bludger — close call, Alicia — and the crowd are loving this, just listen to them, what's that they're singing?"

And as Lee paused to listen the song rose loud and clear from the sea of green and silver in the Slytherin section of the stands:

Weasley cannot save a thing,
He cannot block a single ring,
That's why Slytherins all sing:
Weasley is our King.

Weasley was born in a bin,
He always lets the Quaffle in,
Weasley will make sure we win,
Weasley is our King.

"— and Alicia passes back to Angelina!" Lee shouted, and as Harry swerved, his insides boiling at what he had just heard, he knew Lee was trying to drown out the sound of the singing. "Come on now, Angelina — looks like she's got just the Keeper to beat! — SHE SHOOTS — SHE — aaaah . . ."

Bletchley, the Slytherin Keeper, had saved the goal; he threw the Quaffle to Warrington who sped off with it, zigzagging in between Alicia and Katie; the singing from below grew louder and louder as he drew nearer and nearer Ron —

Weasley is our King,
Weasley is our King,
He always lets the Quaffle in,
Weasley is our King.

Harry could not help himself: Abandoning his search for the Snitch, he turned his Firebolt toward Ron, a lone figure at the far end of the pitch, hovering before the three goal hoops while the massive Warrington pelted toward him . . .

"— and it's Warrington with the Quaffle, Warrington heading for goal, he's out of Bludger range with just the Keeper ahead —"

A great swell of song rose from the Slytherin stands below:

Weasley cannot save a thing,
He cannot block a single ring . . .

"— so it's the first test for new Gryffindor Keeper, Weasley, brother of Beaters, Fred and George, and a promising new talent on the team — come on, Ron!"

But the scream of delight came from the Slytherin end: Ron had dived wildly, his arms wide, and the Quaffle had soared between them, straight through Ron's central hoop.

"Slytherin score!" came Lee's voice amid the cheering and booing from the crowds below. "So that's ten-nil to Slytherin — bad luck, Ron . . ."

The Slytherins sang even louder:

> *WEASLEY WAS BORN IN A BIN,*
> *HE ALWAYS LETS THE QUAFFLE IN . . .*

"— and Gryffindor back in possession and it's Katie Bell tanking up the pitch —" cried Lee valiantly, though the singing was now so deafening that he could hardly make himself heard above it.

> *WEASLEY WILL MAKE SURE WE WIN,*
> *WEASLEY IS OUR KING . . .*

"Harry, WHAT ARE YOU DOING?" screamed Angelina, soaring past him to keep up with Katie. "GET GOING!"

Harry realized that he had been stationary in midair for more than a minute, watching the progress of the match without sparing a thought for the whereabouts of the Snitch; horrified, he went into a dive and started circling the pitch again, staring around, trying to ignore the chorus now thundering through the stadium:

WEASLEY IS OUR KING,
WEASLEY IS OUR KING...

There was no sign of the Snitch anywhere he looked; Malfoy was still circling the stadium just like Harry. They passed midway around the pitch going in opposite directions and Harry heard Malfoy singing loudly,

WEASLEY WAS BORN IN A BIN...

"— and it's Warrington again," bellowed Lee, "who passes to Pucey, Pucey's off past Spinnet, come on now Angelina, you can take him — turns out you can't — but nice Bludger from Fred Weasley, I mean, George Weasley, oh who cares, one of them anyway, and Warrington drops the Quaffle and Katie Bell — er — drops it too — so that's Montague with the Quaffle, Slytherin Captain Montague takes the Quaffle, and he's off up the pitch, come on now Gryffindor, block him!"

Harry zoomed around the end of the stadium behind the Slytherin goal hoops, willing himself not to look at what was going on at Ron's end; as he sped past the Slytherin Keeper, he heard Bletchley singing along with the crowd below,

WEASLEY CANNOT SAVE A THING...

"— and Pucey's dodged Alicia again, and he's heading straight for goal, stop it, Ron!"

Harry did not have to look to see what had happened: There was a terrible groan from the Gryffindor end, coupled with fresh screams and applause from the Slytherins. Looking down, Harry saw the pug-faced Pansy Parkinson right at the front of the stands, her back to the pitch as she conducted the Slytherin supporters who were roaring:

THAT'S WHY SLYTHERINS ALL SING:
WEASLEY IS OUR KING.

But twenty–nil was nothing, there was still time for Gryffindor to catch up or catch the Snitch, a few goals and they would be in the lead as usual, Harry assured himself, bobbing and weaving through the other players in pursuit of something shiny that turned out to be Montague's watch strap. . . .

But Ron let in two more goals. There was an edge of panic in Harry's desire to find the Snitch now. If he could just get it soon and finish the game quickly . . .

"— and Katie Bell of Gryffindor dodges Pucey, ducks Montague, nice swerve, Katie, and she throws to Johnson, Angelina Johnson takes the Quaffle, she's past Warrington, she's heading for goal, come on now Angelina — GRYFFINDOR SCORE! It's forty–ten, forty–ten to Slytherin and Pucey has the Quaffle. . . ."

Harry could hear Luna's ludicrous lion hat roaring amidst the Gryffindor cheers and felt heartened; only thirty points in it, that was nothing, they could pull back easily. Harry ducked a Bludger that Crabbe had sent rocketing in his direction and resumed his frantic scouring of the pitch for the Snitch, keeping one eye on Malfoy in case he showed signs of having spotted it, but Malfoy, like him, was continuing to soar around the stadium, searching fruitlessly . . .

"— Pucey throws to Warrington, Warrington to Montague, Montague back to Pucey — Johnson intervenes, Johnson takes the Quaffle, Johnson to Bell, this looks good — I mean bad — Bell's hit by a Bludger from Goyle of Slytherin and it's Pucey in possession again . . ."

WEASLEY WAS BORN IN A BIN,
HE ALWAYS LETS THE QUAFFLE IN,
WEASLEY WILL MAKE SURE WE WIN —

But Harry had seen it at last: The tiny fluttering Golden Snitch was hovering feet from the ground at the Slytherin end of the pitch.

He dived. . . .

In a matter of seconds, Malfoy was streaking out of the sky on Harry's left, a green-and-silver blur lying flat on his broom. . . .

The Snitch skirted the foot of one of the goal hoops and scooted off toward the other side of the stands; its change of direction suited Malfoy, who was nearer. Harry pulled his Firebolt around, he and Malfoy were now neck and neck . . .

Feet from the ground, Harry lifted his right hand from his broom, stretching toward the Snitch . . . to his right, Malfoy's arm extended too, reaching, groping . . .

It was over in two breathless, desperate, windswept seconds — Harry's fingers closed around the tiny, struggling ball — Malfoy's fingernails scrabbled the back of Harry's hand hopelessly — Harry pulled his broom upward, holding the struggling ball in his hand and the Gryffindor spectators screamed their approval. . . .

They were saved, it did not matter that Ron had let in those goals, nobody would remember as long as Gryffindor had won —

WHAM!

A Bludger hit Harry squarely in the small of the back and he flew forward off his broom; luckily he was only five or six feet above the ground, having dived so low to catch the Snitch, but he was winded all the same as he landed flat on his back on the frozen pitch. He heard Madam Hooch's shrill whistle, an uproar in the stands compounded of catcalls, angry yells and jeering, a thud, then Angelina's frantic voice.

"Are you all right?"

"'Course I am," said Harry grimly, taking her hand and allowing her to pull him to his feet. Madam Hooch was zooming toward one of the Slytherin players above him, though he could not see who it was at this angle.

"It was that thug, Crabbe," said Angelina angrily. "He whacked the Bludger at you the moment he saw you'd got the Snitch — but we won, Harry, we won!"

Harry heard a snort from behind him and turned around, still holding the Snitch tightly in his hand: Draco Malfoy had landed close by; white-faced with fury, he was still managing to sneer.

"Saved Weasley's neck, haven't you?" he said to Harry. "I've never seen a worse Keeper . . . but then he was *born in a bin*. . . . Did you like my lyrics, Potter?"

Harry did not answer; he turned away to meet the rest of the team who were now landing one by one, yelling and punching the air in triumph, all except Ron, who had dismounted from his broom over by the goalposts and was making his way slowly back to the changing rooms alone.

"We wanted to write another couple of verses!" Malfoy called, as Katie and Alicia hugged Harry. "But we couldn't find rhymes for fat and ugly — we wanted to sing about his mother, see —"

"Talk about sour grapes," said Angelina, casting Malfoy a disgusted look.

"— we couldn't fit in *useless loser* either — for his father, you know —"

Fred and George had realized what Malfoy was talking about. Halfway through shaking Harry's hand they stiffened, looking around at Malfoy.

"Leave it," said Angelina at once, taking Fred by the arm. "Leave it, Fred, let him yell, he's just sore he lost, the jumped-up little —"

"— but you like the Weasleys, don't you, Potter?" said Malfoy, sneering. "Spend holidays there and everything, don't you? Can't see how you stand the stink, but I suppose when you've been dragged up by Muggles even the Weasleys' hovel smells okay —"

Harry grabbed hold of George; meanwhile it was taking the combined efforts of Angelina, Alicia, and Katie to stop Fred leaping on

Malfoy, who was laughing openly. Harry looked around for Madam Hooch, but she was still berating Crabbe for his illegal Bludger attack.

"Or perhaps," said Malfoy, leering as he backed away, "you can remember what *your* mother's house stank like, Potter, and Weasley's pigsty reminds you of it —"

Harry was not aware of releasing George, all he knew was that a second later both of them were sprinting at Malfoy. He had completely forgotten the fact that all the teachers were watching: All he wanted to do was cause Malfoy as much pain as possible. With no time to draw out his wand, he merely drew back the fist clutching the Snitch and sank it as hard as he could into Malfoy's stomach —

"Harry! HARRY! GEORGE! *NO!*"

He could hear girls' voices screaming, Malfoy yelling, George swearing, a whistle blowing, and the bellowing of the crowd around him, but he did not care, not until somebody in the vicinity yelled *"IMPEDIMENTA!"* and only when he was knocked over backward by the force of the spell did he abandon the attempt to punch every inch of Malfoy he could reach. . . .

"What do you think you're doing?" screamed Madam Hooch, as Harry leapt to his feet again; it was she who had hit him with the Impediment Jinx. She was holding her whistle in one hand and a wand in the other, her broom lay abandoned several feet away. Malfoy was curled up on the ground, whimpering and moaning, his nose bloody; George was sporting a swollen lip; Fred was still being forcibly restrained by the three Chasers, and Crabbe was cackling in the background. "I've never seen behavior like it — back up to the castle, both of you, and straight to your Head of House's office! Go! *Now!*"

Harry and George marched off the pitch, both panting, neither saying a word to each other. The howling and jeering of the crowd grew fainter and fainter until they reached the entrance hall, where they could hear nothing except the sound of their own footsteps. Harry became aware that something was still struggling in his right hand, the knuckles of which he had bruised against Malfoy's jaw; looking down he saw the Snitch's silver wings protruding from between his fingers, struggling for release.

They had barely reached the door of Professor McGonagall's office when she came marching along the corridor behind them. She was wearing a Gryffindor scarf, but tore it from her throat with shaking hands as she strode toward them, looking livid.

"In!" she said furiously, pointing to the door. Harry and George entered. She strode around behind her desk and faced them, quivering with rage as she threw the Gryffindor scarf aside onto the floor.

"*Well?*" she said. "I have never seen such a disgraceful exhibition. Two onto one! Explain yourselves!"

"Malfoy provoked us," said Harry stiffly.

"Provoked you?" shouted Professor McGonagall, slamming a fist onto her desk so that her tartan biscuit tin slid sideways off it and burst open, littering the floor with Ginger Newts. "He'd just lost, hadn't he, of course he wanted to provoke you! But what on earth he can have said that justified what you two —"

"He insulted my parents," snarled George. "And Harry's mother."

"But instead of leaving it to Madam Hooch to sort out, you two decided to give an exhibition of Muggle dueling, did you?" bellowed Professor McGonagall. "Have you any idea what you've — ?"

"*Hem, hem.*"

George and Harry both spun around. Dolores Umbridge was standing in the doorway wrapped in a green tweed cloak that greatly enhanced her resemblance to a giant toad, and smiling in the horribly sickly, ominous way that Harry had come to associate with imminent misery.

"May I help, Professor McGonagall?" asked Professor Umbridge in her most poisonously sweet voice.

Blood rushed into Professor McGonagall's face.

"Help?" she repeated in a constricted voice. "What do you mean, 'help'?"

Professor Umbridge moved forward into the office, still smiling her sickly smile.

"Why, I thought you might be grateful for a little extra authority."

Harry would not have been surprised to see sparks fly from Professor McGonagall's nostrils.

"You thought wrong," she said, turning her back on Umbridge. "Now, you two had better listen closely. I do not care what provocation Malfoy offered you, I do not care if he insulted every family member you possess, your behavior was disgusting and I am giving each of you a week's worth of detention! Do not look at me like that, Potter, you deserve it! And if either of you ever —"

"*Hem, hem.*"

Professor McGonagall closed her eyes as though praying for patience as she turned her face toward Professor Umbridge again.

"*Yes?*"

"I think they deserve rather more than detentions," said Umbridge, smiling still more broadly.

Professor McGonagall's eyes flew open. "But unfortunately," she said, with an attempt at a reciprocal smile that made her look as though she had lockjaw, "it is what I think that counts, as they are in my House, Dolores."

"Well, *actually,* Minerva," simpered Umbridge, "I think you'll find that what I think *does* count. Now, where is it? Cornelius just sent it. . . . I mean," she gave a little false laugh as she rummaged in her handbag, "the *Minister* just sent it. . . . Ah yes . . ."

She had pulled out a piece of parchment that she now unfurled, clearing her throat fussily before starting to read what it said.

"*Hem, hem* . . . 'Educational Decree Number Twenty-five . . .'"

"Not another one!" exclaimed Professor McGonagall violently.

"Well, yes," said Umbridge, still smiling. "As a matter of fact, Minerva, it was you who made me see that we *needed* a further amendment. . . . You remember how you overrode me, when I was unwilling to allow the Gryffindor Quidditch team to re-form? How you took the case to Dumbledore, who insisted that the team be allowed to play? Well, now, I couldn't have that. I contacted the Minister at once, and he quite agreed with me that the High Inquisitor has to have the power to strip pupils of privileges, or she — that is to say, I — would have less authority than common teachers! And you see now, don't you, Minerva, how right I was in attempting to stop the Gryffindor team re-forming? *Dreadful* tempers . . . Anyway, I was reading out our amendment . . . *hem, hem* . . . 'The High Inquisitor will henceforth have supreme authority over all punishments, sanctions, and removal of privileges pertaining to the students of Hogwarts, and the power to alter such punishments, sanctions, and removals of privileges as may have been ordered by other staff members. Signed, Cornelius Fudge, Minister of Magic, Order of Merlin First Class, etc., etc. . . .'"

She rolled up the parchment and put it back into her handbag, still smiling.

"So . . . I really think I will have to ban these two from playing Quidditch ever again," she said, looking from Harry to George and back again.

Harry felt the Snitch fluttering madly in his hand.

"Ban us?" he said, and his voice sounded strangely distant. "From playing . . . ever again?"

"Yes, Mr. Potter, I think a lifelong ban ought to do the trick," said Umbridge, her smile widening still further as she watched him struggle to comprehend what she had said. "You *and* Mr. Weasley here. And I think, to be safe, this young man's twin ought to be stopped too — if his teammates had not restrained him, I feel sure he would have attacked young Mr. Malfoy as well. I will want their broomsticks confiscated, of course; I shall keep them safely in my office, to make sure there is no infringement of my ban. But I am not unreasonable, Professor McGonagall," she continued, turning back to Professor McGonagall who was now standing as still as though carved from ice, staring at her. "The rest of the team can continue playing, I saw no signs of violence from any of *them*. Well . . . good afternoon to you."

And with a look of the utmost satisfaction Umbridge left the room, leaving a horrified silence in her wake.

"Banned," said Angelina in a hollow voice, late that evening in the common room. "*Banned*. No Seeker and no Beaters . . . What on earth are we going to do?"

It did not feel as though they had won the match at all. Everywhere Harry looked there were disconsolate and angry faces; the team themselves were slumped around the fire, all apart from Ron, who had not been seen since the end of the match.

"It's just so unfair," said Alicia numbly. "I mean, what about Crabbe and that Bludger he hit after the whistle had been blown? Has she banned *him*?"

"No," said Ginny miserably; she and Hermione were sitting on either side of Harry. "He just got lines, I heard Montague laughing about it at dinner."

"And banning Fred when he didn't even do anything!" said Alicia furiously, pummeling her knee with her fist.

"It's not my fault I didn't," said Fred, with a very ugly look on his face. "I would've pounded the little scumbag to a pulp if you three hadn't been holding me back."

Harry stared miserably at the dark window. Snow was falling. The Snitch he had caught earlier was now zooming around and around the common room; people were watching its progress as though hypnotized and Crookshanks was leaping from chair to chair, trying to catch it.

"I'm going to bed," said Angelina, getting slowly to her feet.

"Maybe this will all turn out to have been a bad dream. . . . Maybe I'll wake up tomorrow and find we haven't played yet. . . ."

She was soon followed by Alicia and Katie. Fred and George sloped off to bed some time later, glowering at everyone they passed, and Ginny went not long after that. Only Harry and Hermione were left beside the fire.

"Have you seen Ron?" Hermione asked in a low voice.

Harry shook his head.

"I think he's avoiding us," said Hermione. "Where do you think he — ?"

But at that precise moment, there was a creaking sound behind them as the Fat Lady swung forward and Ron came clambering through the portrait hole. He was very pale indeed and there was snow in his hair. When he saw Harry and Hermione he stopped dead in his tracks.

"Where have you been?" said Hermione anxiously, springing up.

"Walking," Ron mumbled. He was still wearing his Quidditch things.

"You look frozen," said Hermione. "Come and sit down!"

Ron walked to the fireside and sank into the chair farthest from Harry's, not looking at him. The stolen Snitch zoomed over their heads.

"I'm sorry," Ron mumbled, looking at his feet.

"What for?" said Harry.

"For thinking I can play Quidditch," said Ron. "I'm going to resign first thing tomorrow."

"If you resign," said Harry testily, "there'll only be three players left on the team." And when Ron looked puzzled, he said, "I've been given a lifetime ban. So've Fred and George."

"What?" Ron yelped.

Hermione told him the full story; Harry could not bear to tell it again. When she had finished, Ron looked more anguished than ever.

"This is all my fault —"

"You didn't *make* me punch Malfoy," said Harry angrily.

"— if I wasn't so lousy at Quidditch —"

"— it's got nothing to do with that —"

"— it was that song that wound me up —"

"— it would've wound anyone up —"

Hermione got up and walked to the window, away from the argument, watching the snow swirling down against the pane.

"Look, drop it, will you!" Harry burst out. "It's bad enough without you blaming yourself for everything!"

Ron said nothing but sat gazing miserably at the damp hem of his robes. After a while he said in a dull voice, "This is the worst I've ever felt in my life."

"Join the club," said Harry bitterly.

"Well," said Hermione, her voice trembling slightly. "I can think of one thing that might cheer you both up."

"Oh yeah?" said Harry skeptically.

"Yeah," said Hermione, turning away from the pitch-black, snow-flecked window, a broad smile spreading across her face. "Hagrid's back."

HAGRID'S TALE

Harry sprinted up to the boys' dormitory to fetch the Invisibility Cloak and the Marauder's Map from his trunk; he was so quick that he and Ron were ready to leave at least five minutes before Hermione hurried back down from the girls' dormitories, wearing scarf, gloves, and one of her own knobbly elf hats.

"Well, it's cold out there!" she said defensively, as Ron clicked his tongue impatiently.

They crept through the portrait hole and covered themselves hastily in the Cloak — Ron had grown so much he now needed to crouch to prevent his feet showing — then, moving slowly and cautiously, they proceeded down the many staircases, pausing at intervals to check the map for signs of Filch or Mrs. Norris. They were lucky; they saw nobody but Nearly Headless Nick, who was gliding along absentmindedly humming something that sounded horribly like "Weasley Is Our King." They crept across the entrance hall and then out into the silent, snowy grounds. With a great leap of his heart, Harry saw little golden squares of light ahead and smoke coiling up from Hagrid's chimney. He set off at a quick march, the other two jostling and bumping along behind him, and they crunched excitedly through the thickening snow until at last they reached the wooden front door; when Harry raised his fist and knocked three times, a dog started barking frantically inside.

"Hagrid, it's us!" Harry called through the keyhole.

"Shoulda known!" said a gruff voice.

They beamed at one another under the Cloak; they could tell that Hagrid's voice was pleased. "Bin home three seconds . . . Out the way, Fang . . . *Out the way,* yeh dozy dog . . ."

The bolt was drawn back, the door creaked open, and Hagrid's head appeared in the gap.

Hermione screamed.

"Merlin's beard, keep it down!" said Hagrid hastily, staring wildly over their heads. "Under that Cloak, are yeh? Well, get in, get in!"

"I'm sorry!" Hermione gasped, as the three of them squeezed past Hagrid into the house and pulled the Cloak off themselves so he could see them. "I just — oh, *Hagrid*!"

"It's nuthin', it's nuthin'!" said Hagrid hastily, shutting the door behind them and hurrying to close all the curtains, but Hermione continued to gaze up at him in horror.

Hagrid's hair was matted with congealed blood, and his left eye had been reduced to a puffy slit amid a mass of purple-and-black bruises. There were many cuts on his face and hands, some of them still bleeding, and he was moving gingerly, which made Harry suspect broken ribs. It was obvious that he had only just got home; a thick black traveling cloak lay over the back of a chair and a haversack large enough to carry several small children leaned against the wall inside the door. Hagrid himself, twice the size of a normal man and three times as broad, was now limping over to the fire and placing a copper kettle over it.

"What happened to you?" Harry demanded, while Fang danced around them all, trying to lick their faces.

"Told yeh, *nuthin'*," said Hagrid firmly. "Want a cuppa?"

"Come off it," said Ron, "you're in a right state!"

"I'm tellin' yeh, I'm fine," said Hagrid, straightening up and turning to beam at them all, but wincing. "Blimey, it's good ter see you three again — had good summers, did yeh?"

"Hagrid, you've been attacked!" said Ron.

"Fer the las' time, it's nuthin'!" said Hagrid firmly.

"Would you say it was nothing if one of us turned up with a pound of mince instead of a face?" Ron demanded.

"You ought to go and see Madam Pomfrey, Hagrid," said Hermione anxiously. "Some of those cuts look nasty."

"I'm dealin' with it, all righ'?" said Hagrid repressively.

He walked across to the enormous wooden table that stood in the middle of his cabin and twitched aside a tea towel that had been lying on it. Underneath was a raw, bloody, green-tinged steak slightly larger than the average car tire.

"You're not going to eat that, are you, Hagrid?" said Ron, leaning in for a closer look. "It looks poisonous."

"It's s'posed ter look like that, it's dragon meat," Hagrid said. "An' I didn' get it ter eat."

He picked up the steak and slapped it over the left side of his face. Greenish blood trickled down into his beard as he gave a soft moan of satisfaction.

"Tha's better. It helps with the stingin', yeh know."

"So are you going to tell us what's happened to you?" Harry asked.

"Can', Harry. Top secret. More'n me job's worth ter tell yeh that."

"Did the giants beat you up, Hagrid?" asked Hermione quietly.

Hagrid's fingers slipped on the dragon steak, and it slid squelchily onto his chest.

"Giants?" said Hagrid, catching the steak before it reached his belt and slapping it back over his face. "Who said anythin' abou' giants?

Who yeh bin talkin' to? Who's told yeh what I've — who's said I've bin — eh?"

"We guessed," said Hermione apologetically.

"Oh, yeh did, did yeh?" said Hagrid, fixing her sternly with the eye that was not hidden by the steak.

"It was kind of . . . obvious," said Ron. Harry nodded.

Hagrid glared at them, then snorted, threw the steak onto the table again and strode back to the kettle, which was now whistling.

"Never known kids like you three fer knowin' more'n yeh oughta," he muttered, splashing boiling water into three of his bucket-shaped mugs. "An' I'm not complimentin' yeh, neither. Nosy, some'd call it. Interferin'."

But his beard twitched.

"So you have been to look for giants?" said Harry, grinning as he sat down at the table.

Hagrid set tea in front of each of them, sat down, picked up his steak again, and slapped it back over his face.

"Yeah, all righ'," he grunted, "I have."

"And you found them?" said Hermione in a hushed voice.

"Well, they're not that difficult ter find, ter be honest," said Hagrid. "Pretty big, see."

"Where are they?" said Ron.

"Mountains," said Hagrid unhelpfully.

"So why don't Muggles — ?"

"They do," said Hagrid darkly. "O'ny their deaths are always put down ter mountaineerin' accidents, aren' they?"

He adjusted the steak a little so that it covered the worst of the bruising.

"Come on, Hagrid, tell us what you've been up to!" said Ron. "Tell us about being attacked by the giants and Harry can tell you about being attacked by the dementors —"

Hagrid choked in his mug and dropped his steak at the same time; a large quantity of spit, tea, and dragon blood was sprayed over the table as Hagrid coughed and spluttered and the steak slid, with a soft *splat,* onto the floor.

"Whadda yeh mean, attacked by dementors?" growled Hagrid.

"Didn't you know?" Hermione asked him, wide-eyed.

"I don' know anything that's been happenin' since I left. I was on a secret mission, wasn' I, didn' wan' owls followin' me all over the place — ruddy dementors! Yeh're not serious?"

"Yeah, I am, they turned up in Little Whinging and attacked my cousin and me, and then the Ministry of Magic expelled me —"

"WHAT?"

"— and I had to go to a hearing and everything, but tell us about the giants first."

"You were *expelled*?"

"Tell us about your summer and I'll tell you about mine."

Hagrid glared at him through his one open eye. Harry looked right back, an expression of innocent determination on his face.

"Oh, all righ'," Hagrid said in a resigned voice.

He bent down and tugged the dragon steak out of Fang's mouth.

"Oh, Hagrid, don't, it's not hygien —" Hermione began, but Hagrid had already slapped the meat back over his swollen eye. He took another fortifying gulp of tea and then said, "Well, we set off righ' after term ended —"

"Madame Maxime went with you, then?" Hermione interjected.

"Yeah, tha's right," said Hagrid, and a softened expression appeared on the few inches of face that were not obscured by beard or green steak. "Yeah, it was jus' the pair of us. An' I'll tell yeh this, she's not afraid of roughin' it, Olympe. Yeh know, she's a fine, well-dressed woman, an' knowin' where we was goin' I wondered 'ow she'd feel abou' clamberin' over boulders an' sleepin' in caves an' tha', bu' she never complained once."

"You knew where you were going?" Harry asked. "You knew where the giants were?"

"Well, Dumbledore knew, an' he told us," said Hagrid.

"Are they hidden?" asked Ron. "Is it a secret, where they are?"

"Not really," said Hagrid, shaking his shaggy head. "It's jus' that mos' wizards aren' bothered where they are, s' long as it's a good long way away. But where they are's very difficult ter get ter, fer humans anyway, so we needed Dumbledore's instructions. Took us abou' a month ter get there —"

"A *month*?" said Ron, as though he had never heard of a journey lasting such a ridiculously long time. "But — why couldn't you just grab a Portkey or something?"

There was an odd expression in Hagrid's unobscured eye as he squinted at Ron; it was almost pitying.

"We're bein' watched, Ron," he said gruffly.

"What d'you mean?"

"Yeh don' understand," said Hagrid. "The Ministry's keepin' an eye on Dumbledore an' anyone they reckon's in league with him, an' —"

"We know about that," said Harry quickly, keen to hear the rest of Hagrid's story. "We know about the Ministry watching Dumbledore —"

"So you couldn't use magic to get there?" asked Ron, looking thunderstruck. "You had to act like Muggles *all the way*?"

"Well, not exactly all the way," said Hagrid cagily. "We jus' had ter be careful, 'cause Olympe an' me, we stick out a bit —"

Ron made a stifled noise somewhere between a snort and a sniff and hastily took a gulp of tea.

"— so we're not hard ter follow. We was pretendin' we was goin' on holiday together, so we got inter France an' we made like we was headin' fer where Olympe's school is, 'cause we knew we was bein' tailed by someone from the Ministry. We had to go slow, 'cause I'm not really s'posed ter use magic an' we knew the Ministry'd be lookin' fer a reason ter run us in. But we managed ter give the berk tailin' us the slip round abou' Dee-John —"

"Ooooh, Dijon?" said Hermione excitedly. "I've been there on holiday, did you see — ?"

She fell silent at the look on Ron's face.

"We chanced a bit o' magic after that, and it wasn' a bad journey. Ran inter a couple o' mad trolls on the Polish border, an' I had a sligh' disagreement with a vampire in a pub in Minsk, but apart from tha', couldn't'a bin smoother.

"An' then we reached the place, an' we started trekkin' up through the mountains, lookin' fer signs of 'em . . .

"We had ter lay off the magic once we got near 'em. Partly 'cause they don' like wizards an' we didn' want ter put their backs up too soon, and partly 'cause Dumbledore had warned us You-Know-Who was bound ter be after the giants an' all. Said it was odds on he'd sent a messenger off ter them already. Told us ter be very careful of drawin' attention ter ourselves as we got nearer in case there was Death Eaters around."

Hagrid paused for a long draught of tea.

"Go on!" said Harry urgently.

"Found 'em," said Hagrid baldly. "Went over a ridge one nigh' an' there they was, spread ou' underneath us. Little fires burnin' below an' huge shadows . . . It was like watchin' bits o' the mountain movin'."

"How big are they?" asked Ron in a hushed voice.

"'Bout twenty feet," said Hagrid casually. "Some o' the bigger ones mighta bin twenty-five."

"And how many were there?" asked Harry.

"I reckon abou' seventy or eighty," said Hagrid.

"Is that all?" said Hermione.

"Yep," said Hagrid sadly, "eighty left, an' there was loads once, musta bin a hundred diff'rent tribes from all over the world. But they've bin dyin' out fer ages. Wizards killed a few, o' course, but mostly they killed each other, an' now they're dyin' out faster than ever. They're not made ter live bunched up together like tha'. Dumbledore says it's our fault, it was the wizards who forced 'em to go an' made 'em live a good long way from us an' they had no choice but ter stick together fer their own protection."

"So," said Harry, "you saw them and then what?"

"Well, we waited till morning, didn' want ter go sneakin' up on 'em in the dark, fer our own safety," said Hagrid. "'Bout three in the mornin' they fell asleep jus' where they was sittin'. We didn' dare sleep. Fer one thing, we wanted ter make sure none of 'em woke up an' came up where we were, an' fer another, the snorin' was unbelievable. Caused an avalanche near mornin'.

"Anyway, once it was light we wen' down ter see 'em."

"Just like that?" said Ron, looking awestruck. "You just walked right into a giant camp?"

"Well, Dumbledore'd told us how ter do it," said Hagrid. "Give the Gurg gifts, show some respect, yeh know."

"Give the *what* gifts?" asked Harry.

"Oh, the Gurg — means the chief."

"How could you tell which one was the Gurg?" asked Ron.

Hagrid grunted in amusement.

"No problem," he said. "He was the biggest, the ugliest, an' the laziest. Sittin' there waitin' ter be brought food by the others. Dead goats an' such like. Name o' Karkus. I'd put him at twenty-two, twenty-three feet, an' the weight of a couple o' bull elephants. Skin like rhino hide an' all."

"And you just walked up to him?" said Hermione breathlessly.

"Well . . . *down* ter him, where he was lyin' in the valley. They was in this dip between four pretty high mountains, see, beside a mountain lake, an' Karkus was lyin' by the lake roarin' at the others ter feed him an' his wife. Olympe an' I went down the mountainside —"

"But didn't they try and kill you when they saw you?" asked Ron incredulously.

"It was def'nitely on some of their minds," said Hagrid, shrugging, "but we did what Dumbledore told us ter do, which was ter hold our gift up high an' keep our eyes on the Gurg an' ignore the others. So tha's what we did. An' the rest of 'em went quiet an' watched us pass an' we got right up ter Karkus's feet an' we bowed an' put our present down in front o' him."

"What do you give a giant?" asked Ron eagerly. "Food?"

"Nah, he can get food all righ' fer himself," said Hagrid. "We took him magic. Giants like magic, jus' don't like us usin' it against 'em. Anyway, that firs' day we gave him a branch o' Gubraithian fire."

Hermione said "wow" softly, but Harry and Ron both frowned in puzzlement.

"A branch of — ?"

"Everlasting fire," said Hermione irritably, "you ought to know that by now, Professor Flitwick's mentioned it at least twice in class!"

"Well anyway," said Hagrid quickly, intervening before Ron could answer back, "Dumbledore'd bewitched this branch to burn ever-more, which isn' somethin' any wizard could do, an' so I lies it down in the snow by Karkus's feet and says, 'A gift to the Gurg of the giants from Albus Dumbledore, who sends his respectful greetings.'"

"And what did Karkus say?" asked Harry eagerly.

"Nothin'," said Hagrid. "Didn' speak English."

"You're kidding!"

"Didn' matter," said Hagrid imperturbably, "Dumbledore had warned us tha' migh' happen. Karkus knew enough to yell fer a cou-ple o' giants who knew our lingo an' they translated fer us."

"And did he like the present?" asked Ron.

"Oh yeah, it went down a storm once they understood what it was," said Hagrid, turning his dragon steak over to press the cooler side to his swollen eye. "Very pleased. So then I said, 'Albus Dumbledore asks the Gurg to speak with his messenger when he returns tomorrow with another gift.'"

"Why couldn't you speak to them that day?" asked Hermione.

"Dumbledore wanted us ter take it very slow," said Hagrid. "Let 'em see we kept our promises. *We'll come back tomorrow with another present,* an' then we do come back with another present — gives a good impression, see? An' gives them time ter test out the firs' present an' find out it's a good one, an' get 'em eager fer more. In any case, giants like Karkus — overload 'em with information an' they'll kill yeh jus' to simplify things. So we bowed outta the way an' went off an' found ourselves a nice little cave ter spend that night in, an' the followin' mornin' we went back an' this time we found Karkus sittin' up waitin' fer us lookin' all eager."

"And you talked to him?"

"Oh yeah. Firs' we presented him with a nice battle helmet — goblin-made an' indestructible, yeh know — an' then we sat down an' we talked."

"What did he say?"

"Not much," said Hagrid. "Listened mostly. But there were good signs. He'd heard o' Dumbledore, heard he'd argued against the killin' of the last giants in Britain. Karkus seemed ter be quite int'rested in what Dumbledore had ter say. An' a few o' the others, 'specially the ones who had some English, they gathered round an' listened too. We were hopeful when we left that day. Promised ter come back next day with another present.

"But that night it all wen' wrong."

"What d'you mean?" said Ron quickly.

"Well, like I say, they're not meant ter live together, giants," said Hagrid sadly. "Not in big groups like that. They can' help themselves, they half kill each other every few weeks. The men fight each other an' the women fight each other, the remnants of the old tribes fight each other, an' that's even without squabbles over food an' the best fires an' sleepin' spots. Yeh'd think, seein' as how their whole race is abou' finished, they'd lay off each other, but . . ."

Hagrid sighed deeply.

"That night a fight broke out, we saw it from the mouth of our cave, lookin' down on the valley. Went on fer hours, yeh wouldn' believe the noise. An' when the sun came up the snow was scarlet an' his head was lyin' at the bottom o' the lake."

"Whose head?" gasped Hermione.

"Karkus's," said Hagrid heavily. "There was a new Gurg, Golgomath." He sighed deeply. "Well, we hadn' bargained on a new Gurg two days after we'd made friendly contact with the firs' one, an' we had a funny feelin' Golgomath wouldn' be so keen ter listen to us, but we had ter try."

"You went to speak to him?" asked Ron incredulously. "After you'd watched him rip off another giant's head?"

"'Course we did," said Hagrid, "we hadn' gone all that way ter give up after two days! We wen' down with the next present we'd meant ter give ter Karkus.

"I knew it was no go before I'd opened me mouth. He was sitting there wearin' Karkus's helmet, leerin' at us as we got nearer. He's massive, one o' the biggest ones there. Black hair an' matchin' teeth an' a necklace o' bones. Human-lookin' bones, some of 'em. Well, I gave it a go — held out a great roll o' dragon skin — an' said 'A gift fer the Gurg of the giants —' Nex' thing I knew, I was hangin' upside down in the air by me feet, two of his mates had grabbed me."

Hermione clapped her hands to her mouth.

"How did you get out of *that*?" asked Harry.

"Wouldn'ta done if Olympe hadn' bin there," said Hagrid. "She pulled out her wand an' did some o' the fastes' spellwork I've ever seen.

Ruddy marvelous. Hit the two holdin' me right in the eyes with Conjunctivitus Curses an' they dropped me straightaway — bu' we were in trouble then, 'cause we'd used magic against 'em, an' that's what giants hate abou' wizards. We had ter leg it an' we knew there was no way we was going ter be able ter march inter camp again."

"Blimey, Hagrid," said Ron quietly.

"So how come it's taken you so long to get home if you were only there for three days?" asked Hermione.

"We didn' leave after three days!" said Hagrid, looking outraged. "Dumbledore was relyin' on us!"

"But you've just said there was no way you could go back!"

"Not by daylight, we couldn', no. We just had ter rethink a bit. Spent a couple o' days lyin' low up in the cave an' watchin'. An' wha' we saw wasn' good."

"Did he rip off more heads?" asked Hermione, sounding squeamish.

"No," said Hagrid. "I wish he had."

"What d'you mean?"

"I mean we soon found out he didn' object ter all wizards — just us."

"Death Eaters?" said Harry quickly.

"Yep," said Hagrid darkly. "Couple of 'em were visitin' him ev'ry day, bringin' gifts ter the Gurg, an' he wasn' dangling them upside down."

"How d'you know they were Death Eaters?" said Ron.

"Because I recognized one of 'em," Hagrid growled. "Macnair, remember him? Bloke they sent ter kill Buckbeak? Maniac, he is. Likes killin' as much as Golgomath, no wonder they were gettin' on so well."

"So Macnair's persuaded the giants to join You-Know-Who?" said Hermione desperately.

"Hold yer hippogriffs, I haven' finished me story yet!" said Hagrid indignantly, who, considering he had not wanted to tell them anything in the first place, now seemed to be rather enjoying himself. "Me an' Olympe talked it over an' we agreed, jus' 'cause the Gurg looked like favorin' You-Know-Who didn' mean all of 'em would. We had ter try an' persuade some o' the others, the ones who hadn' wanted Golgomath as Gurg."

"How could you tell which ones they were?" asked Ron.

"Well, they were the ones bein' beaten to a pulp, weren' they?" said Hagrid patiently. "The ones with any sense were keepin' outta Golgomath's way, hidin' out in caves roun' the gully jus' like we were. So we decided we'd go pokin' round the caves by night an' see if we couldn' persuade a few o' them."

"You went poking around dark caves looking for giants?" said Ron with awed respect in his voice.

"Well, it wasn' the giants who worried us most," said Hagrid. "We were more concerned abou' the Death Eaters. Dumbledore had told us before we wen' not ter tangle with 'em if we could avoid it, an' the trouble was they knew we was around — 'spect Golgomath told him abou' us. At night when the giants were sleepin' an' we wanted ter be creepin' inter the caves, Macnair an' the other one were sneakin' round the mountains lookin' fer us. I was hard put to stop Olympe jumpin' out at them," said Hagrid, the corners of his mouth lifting his wild beard. "She was rarin' ter attack 'em. . . . She's somethin' when she's roused, Olympe. . . . Fiery, yeh know . . . 'spect it's the French in her . . ."

Hagrid gazed misty-eyed into the fire. Harry allowed him thirty seconds' reminiscence before clearing his throat loudly.

"So what happened? Did you ever get near any of the other giants?"

"What? Oh . . . oh yeah, we did. Yeah, on the third night after Karkus was killed, we crept outta the cave we'd bin hidin' in and headed back down inter the gully, keepin' our eyes skinned fer the Death Eaters. Got inside a few o' the caves, no go — then, in abou' the sixth one, we found three giants hidin'."

"Cave must've been cramped," said Ron.

"Wasn' room ter swing a kneazle," said Hagrid.

"Didn't they attack you when they saw you?" asked Hermione.

"Probably woulda done if they'd bin in any condition," said Hagrid, "but they was badly hurt, all three o' them. Golgomath's lot had beaten 'em unconscious; they'd woken up an' crawled inter the nearest shelter they could find. Anyway, one o' them had a bit of English an' 'e translated fer the others, an' what we had ter say didn' seem ter go down too badly. So we kep' goin' back, visitin' the wounded. . . . I reckon we had abou' six or seven o' them convinced at one poin'."

"Six or seven?" said Ron eagerly. "Well that's not bad — are they going to come over here and start fighting You-Know-Who with us?"

But Hermione said, "What do you mean 'at one point,' Hagrid?"

Hagrid looked at her sadly.

"Golgomath's lot raided the caves. The ones tha' survived didn' wan' no more ter to do with us after that."

"So . . . so there aren't any giants coming?" said Ron, looking disappointed.

"Nope," said Hagrid, heaving a deep sigh as he turned over his steak again and applied the cooler side to his face, "but we did wha' we wanted ter do, we gave 'em Dumbledore's message an' some o' them heard it an' I 'spect some o' them'll remember it. Jus' maybe, them that don' want ter stay around Golgomath'll move outta the mountains, an' there's gotta be a chance they'll remember Dumbledore's friendly to 'em. . . . Could be they'll come . . ."

Snow was filling up the window now. Harry became aware that the knees of his robes were soaked through; Fang was drooling with his head in Harry's lap.

"Hagrid?" said Hermione quietly after a while.

"Mmm?"

"Did you . . . was there any sign of . . . did you hear anything about your . . . your . . . mother while you were there?"

Hagrid's unobscured eye rested upon her, and Hermione looked rather scared.

"I'm sorry . . . I . . . forget it —"

"Dead," Hagrid grunted. "Died years ago. They told me."

"Oh . . . I'm . . . I'm really sorry," said Hermione in a very small voice.

Hagrid shrugged his massive shoulders. "No need," he said shortly. "Can' remember her much. Wasn' a great mother."

They were silent again. Hermione glanced nervously at Harry and Ron, plainly wanting them to speak.

"But you still haven't explained how you got in this state, Hagrid," Ron said, gesturing toward Hagrid's bloodstained face.

"Or why you're back so late," said Harry. "Sirius says Madame Maxime got back ages ago —"

"Who attacked you?" said Ron.

"I haven' bin attacked!" said Hagrid emphatically. "I —"

But the rest of his words were drowned in a sudden outbreak of rapping on the door. Hermione gasped; her mug slipped through her fingers and smashed on the floor; Fang yelped. All four of them stared at the window beside the doorway. The shadow of somebody small and squat rippled across the thin curtain.

"It's her!" Ron whispered.

"Get under here!" Harry said quickly; seizing the Invisibility Cloak he whirled it over himself and Hermione while Ron tore around the table and dived beneath the Cloak as well. Huddled together they backed away into a corner. Fang was barking madly at the door. Hagrid looked thoroughly confused.

"Hagrid, hide our mugs!"

Hagrid seized Harry's and Ron's mugs and shoved them under the cushion in Fang's basket. Fang was now leaping up at the door; Hagrid pushed him out of the way with his foot and pulled it open.

Professor Umbridge was standing in the doorway wearing her

green tweed cloak and a matching hat with earflaps. Lips pursed, she leaned back so as to see Hagrid's face; she barely reached his navel.

"*So,*" she said slowly and loudly, as though speaking to somebody deaf. "You're Hagrid, are you?"

Without waiting for an answer she strolled into the room, her bulging eyes rolling in every direction.

"Get away," she snapped, waving her handbag at Fang, who had bounded up to her and was attempting to lick her face.

"Er — I don' want ter be rude," said Hagrid, staring at her, "but who the ruddy hell are you?"

"My name is Dolores Umbridge."

Her eyes were sweeping the cabin. Twice they stared directly into the corner where Harry stood, sandwiched between Ron and Hermione.

"Dolores Umbridge?" Hagrid said, sounding thoroughly confused. "I thought you were one o' them Ministry — don' you work with Fudge?"

"I was Senior Undersecretary to the Minister, yes," said Umbridge, now pacing around the cabin, taking in every tiny detail within, from the haversack against the wall to the abandoned traveling cloak. "I am now the Defense Against the Dark Arts teacher —"

"Tha's brave of yeh," said Hagrid, "there's not many'd take tha' job anymore —"

"— and Hogwarts High Inquisitor," said Umbridge, giving no sign that she had heard him.

"Wha's that?" said Hagrid, frowning.

"Precisely what I was going to ask," said Umbridge, pointing at the broken shards of china on the floor that had been Hermione's mug.

"Oh," said Hagrid, with a most unhelpful glance toward the corner where Harry, Ron, and Hermione stood hidden, "oh, tha' was . . . was Fang. He broke a mug. So I had ter use this one instead."

Hagrid pointed to the mug from which he had been drinking, one hand still clamped over the dragon steak pressed to his eye. Umbridge stood facing him now, taking in every detail of his appearance instead of the cabin's.

"I heard voices," she said quietly.

"I was talkin' ter Fang," said Hagrid stoutly.

"And was he talking back to you?"

"Well . . . in a manner o' speakin'," said Hagrid, looking uncomfortable. "I sometimes say Fang's near enough human —"

"There are three sets of footprints in the snow leading from the castle doors to your cabin," said Umbridge sleekly.

Hermione gasped; Harry clapped a hand over her mouth. Luckily, Fang was sniffing loudly around the hem of Professor Umbridge's robes, and she did not appear to have heard.

"Well, I on'y jus' got back," said Hagrid, waving an enormous hand at the haversack. "Maybe someone came ter call earlier an' I missed 'em."

"There are no footsteps leading away from your cabin door."

"Well I . . . I don' know why that'd be. . . ." said Hagrid, tugging nervously at his beard and again glancing toward the corner where Harry, Ron, and Hermione stood, as though asking for help. "Erm . . ."

Umbridge wheeled around and strode the length of the cabin, looking around carefully. She bent and peered under the bed. She opened Hagrid's cupboards. She passed within two inches of where Harry, Ron, and Hermione stood pressed against the wall; Harry actually pulled in his stomach as she walked by. After looking carefully inside the enormous cauldron Hagrid used for cooking she wheeled around again and said, "What has happened to you? How did you sustain those injuries?"

Hagrid hastily removed the dragon steak from his face, which in Harry's opinion was a mistake, because the black-and-purple bruising

all around his eye was now clearly visible, not to mention the large
amount of fresh and congealed blood on his face. "Oh, I . . . had a bit
of an accident," he said lamely.

"What sort of accident?"

"I-I tripped."

"You tripped," she repeated coolly.

"Yeah, tha's right. Over . . . over a friend's broomstick. I don' fly,
meself. Well, look at the size o' me, I don' reckon there's a broomstick
that'd hold me. Friend o' mine breeds Abraxan horses, I dunno if
you've ever seen 'em, big beasts, winged, yeh know, I've had a bit of a
ride on one o' them an' it was —"

"Where have you been?" asked Umbridge, cutting coolly through
Hagrid's babbling.

"Where've I . . . ?"

"Been, yes," she said. "Term started more than two months ago.
Another teacher has had to cover your classes. None of your colleagues
has been able to give me any information as to your whereabouts. You
left no address. Where have you been?"

There was a pause in which Hagrid stared at her with his newly un-
covered eye. Harry could almost hear his brain working furiously.

"I — I've been away for me health," he said.

"For your health," said Umbridge. Her eyes traveled over Hagrid's
discolored and swollen face; dragon blood dripped gently onto his
waistcoat in the silence. "I see."

"Yeah," said Hagrid, "bit o' — o' fresh air, yeh know —"

"Yes, as gamekeeper fresh air must be so difficult to come by," said
Umbridge sweetly. The small patch of Hagrid's face that was not black
or purple flushed.

"Well — change o' scene, yeh know —"

"Mountain scenery?" said Umbridge swiftly.

She knows, Harry thought desperately.

"Mountains?" Hagrid repeated, clearly thinking fast. "Nope, South of France fer me. Bit o' sun an' . . . an' sea."

"Really?" said Umbridge. "You don't have much of a tan."

"Yeah . . . well . . . sensitive skin," said Hagrid, attempting an ingratiating smile. Harry noticed that two of his teeth had been knocked out. Umbridge looked at him coldly; his smile faltered. Then she hoisted her handbag a little higher into the crook of her arm and said, "I shall, of course, be informing the Minister of your late return."

"Righ'," said Hagrid, nodding.

"You ought to know too that as High Inquisitor it is my unfortunate but necessary duty to inspect my fellow teachers. So I daresay we shall meet again soon enough."

She turned sharply and marched back to the door.

"You're inspectin' us?" Hagrid echoed blankly, looking after her.

"Oh yes," said Umbridge softly, looking back at him with her hand on the door handle. "The Ministry is determined to weed out unsatisfactory teachers, Hagrid. Good night."

She left, closing the door behind her with a snap. Harry made to pull off the Invisibility Cloak but Hermione seized his wrist.

"Not yet," she breathed in his ear. "She might not be gone yet."

Hagrid seemed to be thinking the same way; he stumped across the room and pulled back the curtain an inch or so.

"She's goin' back ter the castle," he said in a low voice. "Blimey . . . inspectin' people, is she?"

"Yeah," said Harry, pulling the Cloak off. "Trelawney's on probation already. . . ."

"Um . . . what sort of thing are you planning to do with us in class, Hagrid?" asked Hermione.

"Oh, don' you worry abou' that, I've got a great load o' lessons planned," said Hagrid enthusiastically, scooping up his dragon steak from the table and slapping it over his eye again. "I've bin keepin' a couple o' creatures saved fer yer O.W.L. year, you wait, they're some-thin' really special."

"Erm . . . special in what way?" asked Hermione tentatively.

"I'm not sayin'," said Hagrid happily. "I don' want ter spoil the surprise."

"Look, Hagrid," said Hermione urgently, dropping all pretense, "Professor Umbridge won't be at all happy if you bring anything to class that's too dangerous —"

"Dangerous?" said Hagrid, looking genially bemused. "Don' be silly, I wouldn' give yeh anythin' dangerous! I mean, all righ', they can look after themselves —"

"Hagrid, you've got to pass Umbridge's inspection, and to do that it would really be better if she saw you teaching us how to look after porlocks, how to tell the difference between knarls and hedgehogs, stuff like that!" said Hermione earnestly.

"But tha's not very interestin', Hermione," said Hagrid. "The stuff I've got's much more impressive, I've bin bringin' 'em on fer years, I reckon I've got the on'y domestic herd in Britain —"

"Hagrid . . . please . . ." said Hermione, a note of real desperation in her voice. "Umbridge is looking for any excuse to get rid of teach-ers she thinks are too close to Dumbledore. Please, Hagrid, teach us something dull that's bound to come up in our O.W.L. . . . ."

But Hagrid merely yawned widely and cast a one-eyed look of longing toward the vast bed in the corner.

"Lis'en, it's bin a long day an' it's late," he said, patting Hermione gently on the shoulder, so that her knees gave way and hit the floor with a thud. "Oh — sorry —" He pulled her back up by the neck of her robes. "Look, don' you go worryin' abou' me, I promise yeh I've got really good stuff planned fer yer lessons now I'm back. . . . Now you lot had better get back up to the castle, an' don' forget ter wipe yer footprints out behind yeh!"

"I dunno if you got through to him," said Ron a short while later when, having checked that the coast was clear, they walked back up to the castle through the thickening snow, leaving no trace behind them due to the Obliteration Charm Hermione was performing as they went.

"Then I'll go back again tomorrow," said Hermione determinedly. "I'll plan his lessons for him if I have to. I don't care if she throws out Trelawney but she's not taking Hagrid!"

THE EYE OF THE SNAKE

Hermione plowed her way back to Hagrid's cabin through two feet of snow on Sunday morning. Harry and Ron wanted to go with her, but their mountain of homework had reached an alarming height again, so they grudgingly remained in the common room, trying to ignore the gleeful shouts drifting up from the grounds outside, where students were enjoying themselves skating on the frozen lake, tobogganing, and worst of all, bewitching snowballs to zoom up to Gryffindor Tower and rap hard on the windows.

"Oy!" bellowed Ron, finally losing patience and sticking his head out of the window, "I am a prefect and if one more snowball hits this window — OUCH!"

He withdrew his head sharply, his face covered in snow.

"It's Fred and George," he said bitterly, slamming the window behind him. "Gits . . ."

Hermione returned from Hagrid's just before lunch, shivering slightly, her robes damp to the knees.

"So?" said Ron, looking up when she entered. "Got all his lessons planned for him?"

"Well, I tried," she said dully, sinking into a chair beside Harry. She pulled out her wand and gave it a complicated little wave so that hot air streamed out of the tip; she then pointed this at her robes, which began to steam as they dried out. "He wasn't even there when I arrived, I was knocking for at least half an hour. And then he came stumping out of the forest —"

Harry groaned. The Forbidden Forest was teeming with the kind of creatures most likely to get Hagrid the sack. "What's he keeping in there? Did he say?" asked Harry.

"No," said Hermione miserably. "He says he wants them to be a surprise. I tried to explain about Umbridge, but he just doesn't get it. He kept saying nobody in their right mind would rather study knarls than chimaeras — oh I don't think he's *got* a chimaera," she added at the appalled look on Harry and Ron's faces, "but that's not for lack of trying from what he said about how hard it is to get eggs. . . . I don't know how many times I told him he'd be better off following Grubbly-Plank's plan, I honestly don't think he listened to half of what I said. He's in a bit of a funny mood, you know. He still won't say how he got all those injuries. . . ."

Hagrid's reappearance at the staff table at breakfast next day was not greeted by enthusiasm from all students. Some, like Fred, George, and Lee, roared with delight and sprinted up the aisle between the Gryffindor and Hufflepuff tables to wring Hagrid's enormous hand; others, like Parvati and Lavender, exchanged gloomy looks and shook their heads. Harry knew that many of them preferred Professor Grubbly-Plank's lessons, and the worst of it was that a very small, un-biased part of him knew that they had good reason: Grubbly-Plank's idea of an interesting class was not one where there was a risk that somebody might have their head ripped off.

It was with a certain amount of apprehension that Harry, Ron, and Hermione headed down to Hagrid's on Tuesday, heavily muffled against the cold. Harry was worried, not only about what Hagrid might have decided to teach them, but also about how the rest of the class, particularly Malfoy and his cronies, would behave if Umbridge was watching them.

However, the High Inquisitor was nowhere to be seen as they struggled through the snow toward Hagrid, who stood waiting for them on the edge of the forest. He did not present a reassuring sight; the bruises that had been purple on Saturday night were now tinged with green and yellow and some of his cuts still seemed to be bleeding. Harry could not understand this: Had Hagrid perhaps been attacked by some creature whose venom prevented the wounds it inflicted from healing? As though to complete the ominous picture, Hagrid was carrying what looked like half a dead cow over his shoulder.

"We're workin' in here today!" Hagrid called happily to the approaching students, jerking his head back at the dark trees behind him. "Bit more sheltered! Anyway, they prefer the dark. . . ."

"What prefers the dark?" Harry heard Malfoy say sharply to Crabbe and Goyle, a trace of panic in his voice. "What did he say prefers the dark — did you hear?"

Harry remembered the only occasion on which Malfoy had entered the forest before now; he had not been very brave then either. He smiled to himself; after the Quidditch match anything that caused Malfoy discomfort was all right with him.

"Ready?" said Hagrid happily, looking around at the class. "Right, well, I've bin savin' a trip inter the forest fer yer fifth year. Thought we'd go an' see these creatures in their natural habitat. Now, what we're studyin' today is pretty rare, I reckon I'm probably the on'y person in Britain who's managed ter train 'em —"

"And you're sure they're trained, are you?" said Malfoy, the panic in his voice even more pronounced now. "Only it wouldn't be the first time you'd brought wild stuff to class, would it?"

The Slytherins murmured agreement and a few Gryffindors looked as though they thought Malfoy had a fair point too.

"'Course they're trained," said Hagrid, scowling and hoisting the dead cow a little higher on his shoulder.

"So what happened to your face, then?" demanded Malfoy.

"Mind yer own business!" said Hagrid, angrily. "Now if yeh've finished askin' stupid questions, follow me!"

He turned and strode straight into the forest. Nobody seemed much disposed to follow. Harry glanced at Ron and Hermione, who sighed but nodded, and the three of them set off after Hagrid, leading the rest of the class.

They walked for about ten minutes until they reached a place where the trees stood so closely together that it was as dark as twilight and there was no snow on the ground at all. Hagrid deposited his half a cow with a grunt on the ground, stepped back, and turned to face his class again, most of whom were creeping toward him from tree to tree, peering around nervously as though expecting to be set upon at any moment.

"Gather roun', gather roun'," said Hagrid encouragingly. "Now, they'll be attracted by the smell o' the meat but I'm goin' ter give 'em a call anyway, 'cause they'll like ter know it's me. . . ."

He turned, shook his shaggy head to get the hair out of his face, and gave an odd, shrieking cry that echoed through the dark trees like the call of some monstrous bird. Nobody laughed; most of them looked too scared to make a sound.

Hagrid gave the shrieking cry again. A minute passed in which the class continued to peer nervously over their shoulders and around trees for a first glimpse of whatever it was that was coming. And then, as Hagrid shook his hair back for a third time and expanded his enormous chest, Harry nudged Ron and pointed into the black space between two gnarled yew trees.

A pair of blank, white, shining eyes were growing larger through the gloom and a moment later the dragonish face, neck, and then skeletal body of a great, black, winged horse emerged from the darkness. It looked around at the class for a few seconds, swishing its long black tail, then bowed its head and began to tear flesh from the dead cow with its pointed fangs.

A great wave of relief broke over Harry. Here at last was proof that he had not imagined these creatures, that they were real: Hagrid knew about them too. He looked eagerly at Ron, but Ron was still staring around into the trees and after a few seconds he whispered, "Why doesn't Hagrid call again?"

Most of the rest of the class were wearing expressions as confused and nervously expectant as Ron's and were still gazing everywhere but at the horse standing feet from them. There were only two other people who seemed to be able to see them: a stringy Slytherin boy standing just behind Goyle was watching the horse eating with an expression of great distaste on his face, and Neville, whose eyes were following the swishing progress of the long black tail.

"Oh, an' here comes another one!" said Hagrid proudly, as a second black horse appeared out of the dark trees, folded its leathery wings closer to its body, and dipped its head to gorge on the meat. "Now . . . put yer hands up, who can see 'em?"

Immensely pleased to feel that he was at last going to understand the mystery of these horses, Harry raised his hand. Hagrid nodded at him.

"Yeah . . . yeah, I knew you'd be able ter, Harry," he said seriously. "An' you too, Neville, eh? An' —"

"Excuse me," said Malfoy in a sneering voice, "but what exactly are we supposed to be seeing?"

For answer, Hagrid pointed at the cow carcass on the ground. The whole class stared at it for a few seconds, then several people gasped and Parvati squealed. Harry understood why: Bits of flesh stripping themselves away from the bones and vanishing into thin air had to look very odd indeed.

"What's doing it?" Parvati demanded in a terrified voice, retreating behind the nearest tree. "What's eating it?"

"Thestrals," said Hagrid proudly and Hermione gave a soft "oh!" of comprehension at Harry's shoulder. "Hogwarts has got a whole herd of 'em in here. Now, who knows — ?"

"But they're really, really unlucky!" interrupted Parvati, looking alarmed. "They're supposed to bring all sorts of horrible misfortune on people who see them. Professor Trelawney told me once —"

"No, no, no," said Hagrid, chuckling, "tha's jus' superstition, that is, they aren' unlucky, they're dead clever an' useful! 'Course, this lot don' get a lot o' work, it's mainly jus' pullin' the school carriages unless Dumbledore's takin' a long journey an' don' want ter Apparate — an' here's another couple, look —"

Two more horses came quietly out of the trees, one of them passing very close to Parvati, who shivered and pressed herself closer to the tree, saying, "I think I felt something, I think it's near me!"

"Don' worry, it won' hurt yeh," said Hagrid patiently. "Righ', now, who can tell me why some o' you can see them an' some can't?"

Hermione raised her hand.

"Go on then," said Hagrid, beaming at her.

"The only people who can see thestrals," she said, "are people who have seen death."

"Tha's exactly right," said Hagrid solemnly, "ten points ter Gryffindor. Now, thestrals —"

"Hem, hem."

Professor Umbridge had arrived. She was standing a few feet away from Harry, wearing her green hat and cloak again, her clipboard at the ready. Hagrid, who had never heard Umbridge's fake cough before, was gazing in some concern at the closest thestral, evidently under the impression that it had made the sound.

"Hem, hem."

"Oh hello!" Hagrid said, smiling, having located the source of the noise.

"You received the note I sent to your cabin this morning?" said

Umbridge, in the same loud, slow voice she had used with him earlier, as though she was addressing somebody both foreign and very slow. "Telling you that I would be inspecting your lesson?"

"Oh yeah," said Hagrid brightly. "Glad yeh found the place all righ'! Well, as you can see — or, I dunno — can you? We're doin' thestrals today —"

"I'm sorry?" said Umbridge loudly, cupping her hand around her ear and frowning. "What did you say?"

Hagrid looked a little confused.

"Er — *thestrals*!" he said loudly. "Big — er — winged horses, yeh know!"

He flapped his gigantic arms hopefully. Professor Umbridge raised her eyebrows at him and muttered as she made a note on her clipboard, "*'has . . . to . . . resort . . . to . . . crude . . . sign . . . language . . .'*"

"Well . . . anyway . . ." said Hagrid, turning back to the class and looking slightly flustered. "Erm . . . what was I sayin'?"

"*'Appears . . . to . . . have . . . poor . . . short . . . term . . . memory . . .'*" muttered Umbridge, loudly enough for everyone to hear her. Draco Malfoy looked as though Christmas had come a month early; Hermione, on the other hand, had turned scarlet with suppressed rage.

"Oh yeah," said Hagrid, throwing an uneasy glance at Umbridge's clipboard, but plowing on valiantly. "Yeah, I was gonna tell yeh how come we got a herd. Yeah, so, we started off with a male an' five females. This one," he patted the first horse to have appeared, "name o' Tenebrus, he's my special favorite, firs' one born here in the forest —"

"Are you aware," Umbridge said loudly, interrupting him, "that the Ministry of Magic has classified thestrals as 'dangerous'?"

Harry's heart sank like a stone, but Hagrid merely chuckled.

"Thestrals aren' dangerous! All righ', they might take a bite outta you if yeh really annoy them —"

"*'Shows . . . signs . . . of . . . pleasure . . . at . . . idea . . . of . . . violence . . .'*" muttered Umbridge, scribbling on her clipboard again.

"No — come on!" said Hagrid, looking a little anxious now. "I mean, a dog'll bite if yeh bait it, won' it — but thestrals have jus' got a bad reputation because o' the death thing — people used ter think they were bad omens, didn' they? Jus' didn' understand, did they?"

Umbridge did not answer; she finished writing her last note, then looked up at Hagrid and said, again very loudly and slowly, "Please continue teaching as usual. I am going to walk" — she mimed walking — Malfoy and Pansy Parkinson were having silent fits of laughter — "among the students" — she pointed around at individual members of the class — "and ask them questions." She pointed at her mouth to indicate talking.

Hagrid stared at her, clearly at a complete loss to understand why she was acting as though he did not understand normal English. Hermione had tears of fury in her eyes now.

"You hag, you evil hag!" she whispered, as Umbridge walked toward Pansy Parkinson. "I know what you're doing, you awful, twisted, vicious —"

"Erm . . . anyway," said Hagrid, clearly struggling to regain the flow of his lesson, "so — thestrals. Yeah. Well, there's loads o' good stuff abou' them. . . ."

"Do you find," said Professor Umbridge in a ringing voice to Pansy Parkinson, "that you are able to understand Professor Hagrid when he talks?"

Just like Hermione, Pansy had tears in her eyes, but these were tears of laughter; indeed, her answer was almost incoherent because she was trying to suppress her giggles. "No . . . because . . . well . . . it sounds . . . like grunting a lot of the time. . . ."

Umbridge scribbled on her clipboard. The few unbruised bits of Hagrid's face flushed, but he tried to act as though he had not heard Pansy's answer.

"Er . . . yeah . . . good stuff abou' thestrals. Well, once they're

tamed, like this lot, yeh'll never be lost again. 'Mazin' senses o' direction, jus' tell 'em where yeh want ter go —"

"Assuming they can understand you, of course," said Malfoy
loudly, and Pansy Parkinson collapsed in a fit of renewed giggles.
Professor Umbridge smiled indulgently at them and then turned to
Neville.

"You can see the thestrals, Longbottom, can you?" she said.

Neville nodded.

"Whom did you see die?" she asked, her tone indifferent.

"My . . . my grandad," said Neville.

"And what do you think of them?" she said, waving her stubby
hand at the horses, who by now had stripped a great deal of the carcass down to bone.

"Erm," said Neville nervously, with a glance at Hagrid. "Well,
they're . . . er . . . okay. . . ."

"'Students . . . are . . . too . . . intimidated . . . to . . . admit . . . they
. . . are . . . frightened. . . .'" muttered Umbridge, making another
note on her clipboard.

"No!" said Neville, looking upset, "no, I'm not scared of them — !"

"It's quite all right," said Umbridge, patting Neville on the shoulder with what she evidently intended to be an understanding smile,
though it looked more like a leer to Harry. "Well, Hagrid," she turned
to look up at him again, speaking once more in that loud, slow
voice, "I think I've got enough to be getting along with. . . . You
will receive" — she mimed taking something from the air in front
of her — "the results of your inspection" — she pointed at the clipboard — "in ten days' time." She held up ten stubby little fingers,
then, her smile wider and more toadlike than ever before beneath her
green hat, she bustled from their midst, leaving Malfoy and Pansy
Parkinson in fits of laughter, Hermione actually shaking with fury,
and Neville looking confused and upset.

"That foul, lying, twisting old gargoyle!" stormed Hermione half an hour later, as they made their way back up to the castle through the channels they had made earlier in the snow. "You see what she's up to? It's her thing about half-breeds all over again — she's trying to make out Hagrid's some kind of dim-witted troll, just because he had a giantess for a mother — and oh, it's not fair, that really wasn't a bad lesson at all — I mean, all right, if it had been Blast-Ended Skrewts again, but thestrals are fine — in fact, for Hagrid, they're really good!"

"Umbridge said they're dangerous," said Ron.

"Well, it's like Hagrid said, they can look after themselves," said Hermione impatiently, "and I suppose a teacher like Grubbly-Plank wouldn't usually show them to us before N.E.W.T. level, but, well, they *are* very interesting, aren't they? The way some people can see them and some can't! I wish I could."

"Do you?" Harry asked her quietly.

She looked horrorstruck.

"Oh Harry — I'm sorry — no, of course I don't — that was a really stupid thing to say —"

"It's okay," he said quickly, "don't worry. . . ."

"I'm surprised so many people *could* see them," said Ron. "Three in a class —"

"Yeah, Weasley, we were just wondering," said a malicious voice nearby. Unheard by any of them in the muffling snow, Malfoy, Crabbe, and Goyle were walking along right behind them. "D'you reckon if you saw someone snuff it you'd be able to see the Quaffle better?"

He, Crabbe, and Goyle roared with laughter as they pushed past on their way to the castle and then broke into a chorus of "Weasley Is Our King." Ron's ears turned scarlet.

"Ignore them, just ignore them," intoned Hermione, pulling out her wand and performing the charm to produce hot air again, so that she could melt them an easier path through the untouched snow between them and the greenhouses.

December arrived, bringing with it more snow and a positive avalanche of homework for the fifth years. Ron and Hermione's prefect duties also became more and more onerous as Christmas approached. They were called upon to supervise the decoration of the castle ("You try putting up tinsel when Peeves has got the other end and is trying to strangle you with it," said Ron), to watch over first and second years spending their break times inside because of the bitter cold ("And they're cheeky little snotrags, you know, we definitely weren't that rude when we were in first year," said Ron), and to patrol the corridors in shifts with Argus Filch, who suspected that the holiday spirit might show itself in an outbreak of wizard duels ("He's got dung for brains, that one," said Ron furiously). They were so busy that Hermione had stopped knitting elf hats and was fretting that she was down to her last three.

"All those poor elves I haven't set free yet, having to stay over during Christmas because there aren't enough hats!"

Harry, who had not had the heart to tell her that Dobby was taking everything she made, bent lower over his History of Magic essay. In any case, he did not want to think about Christmas. For the first time in his school career, he very much wanted to spend the holidays away from Hogwarts. Between his Quidditch ban and worry about whether or not Hagrid was going to be put on probation, he felt highly resentful toward the place at the moment. The only thing he really looked forward to were the D.A. meetings, and they would have to stop over the holidays, as nearly everybody in the D.A. would be spending the time with their families. Hermione was going skiing with her parents, something that greatly amused Ron, who had never before heard of Muggles strapping narrow strips of wood to their feet to slide down mountains. Ron, meanwhile, was going home to the Burrow. Harry endured several days of jealousy before Ron said, in response to Harry asking how Ron was going to get home for Christmas, "But you're coming too! Didn't I say? Mum wrote and told me to invite you weeks ago!"

Hermione rolled her eyes, but Harry's spirits soared: The thought of Christmas at the Burrow was truly wonderful, only slightly marred by Harry's guilty feeling that he would not be able to spend the holiday with Sirius. He wondered whether he could possibly persuade Mrs. Weasley to invite his godfather for the festivities too, but apart from the fact that he doubted whether Dumbledore would permit Sirius to leave Grimmauld Place, he could not help but feel that Mrs. Weasley might not want him; they were so often at loggerheads. Sirius had not contacted Harry at all since his last appearance in the fire, and although Harry knew that with Umbridge on the constant watch it would be unwise to attempt to contact him, he did not like to think of Sirius alone in his mother's old house, perhaps pulling a lonely cracker with Kreacher.

Harry arrived early in the Room of Requirement for the last D.A. meeting before the holidays and was very glad he had, because when the lamps burst into light he saw that Dobby had taken it upon himself to decorate the place for Christmas. He could tell the elf had done it, because nobody else would have strung a hundred golden baubles from the ceiling, each showing a picture of Harry's face and bearing the legend HAVE A VERY HARRY CHRISTMAS!

Harry had only just managed to get the last of them down before the door creaked open and Luna Lovegood entered, looking dreamy as always.

"Hello," she said vaguely, looking around at what remained of the decorations. "These are nice, did you put them up?"

"No," said Harry, "it was Dobby the house-elf."

"Mistletoe," said Luna dreamily, pointing at a large clump of white berries placed almost over Harry's head. He jumped out from under it. "Good thinking," said Luna very seriously. "It's often infested with nargles."

Harry was saved the necessity of asking what nargles were by the arrival of Angelina, Katie, and Alicia. All three of them were breathless and looked very cold.

"Well," said Angelina dully, pulling off her cloak and throwing it into a corner, "we've replaced you."

"Replaced me?" said Harry blankly.

"You and Fred and George," she said impatiently. "We've got another Seeker!"

"Who?" said Harry quickly.

"Ginny Weasley," said Katie.

Harry gaped at her.

"Yeah, I know," said Angelina, pulling out her wand and flexing her arm. "But she's pretty good, actually. Nothing on you, of course," she said, throwing him a very dirty look, "but as we can't have you . . ."

Harry bit back the retort he was longing to utter: Did she imagine for a second that he did not regret his expulsion from the team a hundred times more than she did?

"And what about the Beaters?" he asked, trying to keep his voice even.

"Andrew Kirke," said Alicia without enthusiasm, "and Jack Sloper. Neither of them are brilliant, but compared with the rest of the idiots who turned up . . ."

The arrival of Ron, Hermione, and Neville brought this depressing discussion to an end and within five minutes, the room was full enough to prevent him seeing Angelina's burning, reproachful looks.

"Okay," he said, calling them all to order. "I thought this evening we should just go over the things we've done so far, because it's the last meeting before the holidays and there's no point starting anything new right before a three-week break —"

"We're not doing anything new?" said Zacharias Smith, in a disgruntled whisper loud enough to carry through the room. "If I'd known that, I wouldn't have come. . . ."

"We're all really sorry Harry didn't tell you, then," said Fred loudly.

Several people sniggered. Harry saw Cho laughing and felt the familiar swooping sensation in his stomach, as though he had missed a step going downstairs.

"We can practice in pairs," said Harry. "We'll start with the Impediment Jinx, just for ten minutes, then we can get out the cushions and try Stunning again."

They all divided up obediently; Harry partnered Neville as usual. The room was soon full of intermittent cries of *"Impedimenta!"* People froze for a minute or so, during which their partners would stare aimlessly around the room watching other pairs at work, then would unfreeze and take their turn at the jinx.

Neville had improved beyond all recognition. After a while, when Harry had unfrozen three times in a row, he had Neville join Ron and Hermione again so that he could walk around the room and watch the others. When he passed Cho she beamed at him; he resisted the temptation to walk past her several more times.

After ten minutes on the Impediment Jinx, they laid out cushions all over the floor and started practicing Stunning again. Space was really too confined to allow them all to work this spell at once; half the group observed the others for a while, then swapped over. Harry felt himself positively swelling with pride as he watched them all. True, Neville did Stun Padma Patil rather than Dean, at whom he had been aiming, but it was a much closer miss than usual, and everybody else had made enormous progress.

At the end of an hour, Harry called a halt.

"You're getting really good," he said, beaming around at them. "When we get back from the holidays we can start doing some of the big stuff — maybe even Patronuses."

There was a murmur of excitement. The room began to clear in the usual twos and threes; most people wished Harry a Happy Christmas as they went. Feeling cheerful, he collected up the cushions with Ron and Hermione and stacked them neatly away. Ron and Hermione left before he did; he hung back a little, because Cho was still there and he was hoping to receive a Merry Christmas from her.

"No, you go on," he heard her say to her friend Marietta, and his heart gave a jolt that seemed to take it into the region of his Adam's apple.

He pretended to be straightening the cushion pile. He was quite sure they were alone now and waited for her to speak. Instead, he heard a hearty sniff.

He turned and saw Cho standing in the middle of the room, tears pouring down her face.

"Wha — ?"

He didn't know what to do. She was simply standing there, crying silently.

"What's up?" he said feebly.

She shook her head and wiped her eyes on her sleeve. "I'm — sorry," she said thickly. "I suppose . . . it's just . . . learning all this stuff. . . . It just makes me . . . wonder whether . . . if *he'd* known it all . . . he'd still be alive. . . ."

Harry's heart sank right back past its usual spot and settled somewhere around his navel. He ought to have known. She wanted to talk about Cedric.

"He did know this stuff," Harry said heavily. "He was really good at it, or he could never have got to the middle of that maze. But if Voldemort really wants to kill you, you don't stand a chance."

She hiccuped at the sound of Voldemort's name, but stared at Harry without flinching.

"*You* survived when you were just a baby," she said quietly.

"Yeah, well," said Harry wearily, moving toward the door, "I dunno why, nor does anyone else, so it's nothing to be proud of."

"Oh don't go!" said Cho, sounding tearful again. "I'm really sorry to get all upset like this. . . . I didn't mean to. . . ."

She hiccuped again. She was very pretty even when her eyes were red and puffy. Harry felt thoroughly miserable. He'd have been so pleased just with a Merry Christmas. . . .

"I know it must be horrible for you," she said, mopping her eyes on her sleeve again. "Me mentioning Cedric, when you saw him die. . . . I suppose you just want to forget about it. . . ."

Harry did not say anything to this; it was quite true, but he felt heartless saying it.

"You're a r-really good teacher, you know," said Cho, with a watery smile. "I've never been able to Stun anything before."

"Thanks," said Harry awkwardly.

They looked at each other for a long moment. Harry felt a burning desire to run from the room and, at the same time, a complete inability to move his feet.

"Mistletoe," said Cho quietly, pointing at the ceiling over his head.

"Yeah," said Harry. His mouth was very dry. "It's probably full of nargles, though."

"What are nargles?"

"No idea," said Harry. She had moved closer. His brain seemed to have been Stunned. "You'd have to ask Loony. Luna, I mean."

Cho made a funny noise halfway between a sob and a laugh. She was even nearer him now. He could have counted the freckles on her nose.

"I really like you, Harry."

He could not think. A tingling sensation was spreading throughout him, paralyzing his arms, legs, and brain.

She was much too close. He could see every tear clinging to her eyelashes. . . .

He returned to the common room half an hour later to find Hermione and Ron in the best seats by the fire; nearly everybody else had gone to bed. Hermione was writing a very long letter; she had already filled half a roll of parchment, which was dangling from the edge of the table. Ron was lying on the hearthrug, trying to finish his Transfiguration homework.

"What kept you?" he asked, as Harry sank into the armchair next to Hermione's.

Harry did not answer. He was in a state of shock. Half of him wanted to tell Ron and Hermione what had just happened, but the other half wanted to take the secret with him to the grave.

"Are you all right, Harry?" Hermione asked, peering at him over the tip of her quill.

Harry gave a halfhearted shrug. In truth, he didn't know whether he was all right or not.

"What's up?" said Ron, hoisting himself up on his elbow to get a clearer view of Harry. "What's happened?"

Harry didn't quite know how to set about telling them, and still wasn't sure whether he wanted to. Just as he had decided not to say anything, Hermione took matters out of his hands.

"Is it Cho?" she asked in a businesslike way. "Did she corner you after the meeting?"

Numbly surprised, Harry nodded. Ron sniggered, breaking off when Hermione caught his eye.

"So — er — what did she want?" he asked in a mock casual voice.

"She —" Harry began, rather hoarsely; he cleared his throat and tried again. "She — er —"

"Did you kiss?" asked Hermione briskly.

Ron sat up so fast that he sent his ink bottle flying all over the rug. Disregarding this completely he stared avidly at Harry.

"Well?" he demanded.

Harry looked from Ron's expression of mingled curiosity and hilarity to Hermione's slight frown, and nodded.

"HA!"

Ron made a triumphant gesture with his fist and went into a raucous peal of laughter that made several timid-looking second years over beside the window jump. A reluctant grin spread over Harry's face as he watched Ron rolling around on the hearthrug. Hermione gave Ron a look of deep disgust and returned to her letter.

"Well?" Ron said finally, looking up at Harry. "How was it?"

Harry considered for a moment.

"Wet," he said truthfully.

Ron made a noise that might have indicated jubilation or disgust, it was hard to tell.

"Because she was crying," Harry continued heavily.

"Oh," said Ron, his smile fading slightly. "Are you that bad at kissing?"

"Dunno," said Harry, who hadn't considered this, and immediately felt rather worried. "Maybe I am."

"Of course you're not," said Hermione absently, still scribbling away at her letter.

"How do you know?" said Ron in a sharp voice.

"Because Cho spends half her time crying these days," said Hermione vaguely. "She does it at mealtimes, in the loos, all over the place."

"You'd think a bit of kissing would cheer her up," said Ron, grinning.

"Ron," said Hermione in a dignified voice, dipping the point of her quill into her ink pot, "you are the most insensitive wart I have ever had the misfortune to meet."

"What's that supposed to mean?" said Ron indignantly. "What sort of person cries while someone's kissing them?"

"Yeah," said Harry, slightly desperately, "who does?"

Hermione looked at the pair of them with an almost pitying expression on her face.

"Don't you understand how Cho's feeling at the moment?" she asked.

"No," said Harry and Ron together.

Hermione sighed and laid down her quill.

"Well, obviously, she's feeling very sad, because of Cedric dying. Then I expect she's feeling confused because she liked Cedric and now she likes Harry, and she can't work out who she likes best. Then she'll be feeling guilty, thinking it's an insult to Cedric's memory to be kissing Harry at all, and she'll be worrying about what everyone else might say about her if she starts going out with Harry. And she probably can't work out what her feelings toward Harry are anyway, because he was the one who was with Cedric when Cedric died, so that's all very mixed up and painful. Oh, and she's afraid she's going to be thrown off the Ravenclaw Quidditch team because she's been flying so badly."

A slightly stunned silence greeted the end of this speech, then Ron said, "One person can't feel all that at once, they'd explode."

"Just because you've got the emotional range of a teaspoon doesn't mean we all have," said Hermione nastily, picking up her quill again.

"She was the one who started it," said Harry. "I wouldn't've — she just sort of came at me — and next thing she's crying all over me — I didn't know what to do —"

"Don't blame you, mate," said Ron, looking alarmed at the very thought.

"You just had to be nice to her," said Hermione, looking up anxiously. "You were, weren't you?"

"Well," said Harry, an unpleasant heat creeping up his face, "I sort of — patted her on the back a bit."

Hermione looked as though she was restraining herself from rolling her eyes with extreme difficulty.

"Well, I suppose it could have been worse," she said. "Are you going to see her again?"

"I'll have to, won't I?" said Harry. "We've got D.A. meetings, haven't we?"

"You know what I mean," said Hermione impatiently.

Harry said nothing. Hermione's words opened up a whole new vista of frightening possibilities. He tried to imagine going somewhere with Cho — Hogsmeade, perhaps — and being alone with her for hours at a time. Of course, she would have been expecting him to ask her out after what had just happened. . . . The thought made his stomach clench painfully.

"Oh well," said Hermione distantly, buried in her letter once more, "you'll have plenty of opportunities to ask her. . . ."

"What if he doesn't want to ask her?" said Ron, who had been watching Harry with an unusually shrewd expression on his face.

"Don't be silly," said Hermione vaguely, "Harry's liked her for ages, haven't you, Harry?"

He did not answer. Yes, he had liked Cho for ages, but whenever he had imagined a scene involving the two of them it had always featured a Cho who was enjoying herself, as opposed to a Cho who was sobbing uncontrollably into his shoulder.

"Who're you writing the novel to anyway?" Ron asked Hermione, trying to read the bit of parchment now trailing on the floor. Hermione hitched it up out of sight.

"Viktor."

"*Krum?*"

"How many other Viktors do we know?"

Ron said nothing, but looked disgruntled. They sat in silence for another twenty minutes, Ron finishing his Transfiguration essay with many snorts of impatience and crossings-out, Hermione writing steadily to the very end of the parchment, rolling it up carefully and sealing it, and Harry staring into the fire, wishing more than anything that Sirius's head would appear there and give him some advice about girls. But the fire merely crackled lower and lower, until the red-hot embers crumbled into ash and, looking around, Harry saw that they were, yet again, the last in the common room.

"Well, 'night," said Hermione, yawning widely, and she set off up the girls' staircase.

"What does she see in Krum?" Ron demanded as he and Harry climbed the boys' stairs.

"Well," said Harry, considering the matter, "I s'pose he's older, isn't he . . . and he's an international Quidditch player. . . ."

"Yeah, but apart from that," said Ron, sounding aggravated. "I mean he's a grouchy git, isn't he?"

"Bit grouchy, yeah," said Harry, whose thoughts were still on Cho.

They pulled off their robes and put on pajamas in silence; Dean, Seamus, and Neville were already asleep. Harry put his glasses on his bedside table and got into bed but did not pull the hangings closed around his four-poster; instead he stared at the patch of starry sky visible through the window next to Neville's bed. If he had known, this time last night, that in twenty-four hours' time he would have kissed Cho Chang . . .

"'Night," grunted Ron, from somewhere to his right.

"'Night," said Harry.

Maybe next time . . . if there was a next time . . . she'd be a bit happier. He ought to have asked her out; she had probably been expecting it and was now really angry with him . . . or was she lying in bed, still crying about Cedric? He did not know what to think. Hermione's explanation had made it all seem more complicated rather than easier to understand.

That's what they should teach us here, he thought, turning over onto his side, *how girls' brains work . . . it'd be more useful than Divination anyway. . . .*

Neville snuffled in his sleep. An owl hooted somewhere out in the night.

Harry dreamed he was back in the D.A. room. Cho was accusing him of luring her there under false pretenses; she said that he had promised her a hundred and fifty Chocolate Frog cards if she showed up. Harry protested. . . . Cho shouted, *"Cedric gave me loads of Chocolate Frog cards, look!"* And she pulled out fistfuls of cards from inside her robes and threw them into the air, and then turned into Hermione, who said, *"You did promise her, you know, Harry. . . . I think you'd better give her something else instead. . . . How about your Firebolt?"* And Harry was protesting that he could not give Cho his Firebolt because Umbridge had it, and anyway the whole thing was ridiculous, he'd only come to the D.A. room to put up some Christmas baubles shaped like Dobby's head. . . .

The dream changed. . . .

His body felt smooth, powerful, and flexible. He was gliding between shining metal bars, across dark, cold stone. . . . He was flat against the floor, sliding along on his belly. . . . It was dark, yet he could see objects around him shimmering in strange, vibrant colors. . . . He was turning his head. . . . At first glance, the corridor was empty . . . but no . . . a man was sitting on the floor ahead, his chin drooping onto his chest, his outline gleaming in the dark. . . .

Harry put out his tongue. . . . He tasted the man's scent on the air. . . . He was alive but drowsing . . . sitting in front of a door at the end of the corridor . . .

Harry longed to bite the man . . . but he must master the impulse.
. . . He had more important work to do. . . .

But the man was stirring . . . a silvery cloak fell from his legs as
he jumped to his feet; and Harry saw his vibrant, blurred outline
towering above him, saw a wand withdrawn from a belt. . . . He had
no choice. . . . He reared high from the floor and struck once, twice,
three times, plunging his fangs deeply into the man's flesh, feeling his
ribs splinter beneath his jaws, feeling the warm gush of blood. . . .

The man was yelling in pain . . . then he fell silent. . . . He slumped
backward against the wall. . . . Blood was splattering onto the floor. . . .

His forehead hurt terribly. . . . It was aching fit to burst. . . .

"Harry! HARRY!"

He opened his eyes. Every inch of his body was covered in icy
sweat; his bedcovers were twisted all around him like a straitjacket; he
felt as though a white-hot poker was being applied to his forehead.

"Harry!"

Ron was standing over him looking extremely frightened. There
were more figures at the foot of Harry's bed. He clutched his head in
his hands; the pain was blinding him. . . . He rolled right over and
vomited over the edge of the mattress.

"He's really ill," said a scared voice. "Should we call someone?"

"Harry! *Harry!*"

He had to tell Ron, it was very important that he tell him. . . . Taking great gulps of air, Harry pushed himself up in bed, willing himself
not to throw up again, the pain half-blinding him.

"Your dad," he panted, his chest heaving. "Your dad's . . . been
attacked. . . ."

"What?" said Ron uncomprehendingly.

"Your dad! He's been bitten, it's serious, there was blood everywhere. . . ."

"I'm going for help," said the same scared voice, and Harry heard
footsteps running out of the dormitory.

"Harry, mate," said Ron uncertainly, "you . . . you were just dreaming. . . ."

"No!" said Harry furiously; it was crucial that Ron understand. "It wasn't a dream . . . not an ordinary dream. . . . I was there, I saw it. . . . I *did* it. . . ."

He could hear Seamus and Dean muttering but did not care. The pain in his forehead was subsiding slightly, though he was still sweating and shivering feverishly. He retched again and Ron leapt backward out of the way.

"Harry, you're not well," he said shakily. "Neville's gone for help. . . ."

"I'm fine!" Harry choked, wiping his mouth on his pajamas and shaking uncontrollably. "There's nothing wrong with me, it's your dad you've got to worry about — we need to find out where he is — he's bleeding like mad — I was — it was a huge snake. . . ."

He tried to get out of bed but Ron pushed him back into it; Dean and Seamus were still whispering somewhere nearby. Whether one minute passed or ten, Harry did not know; he simply sat there shaking, feeling the pain recede very slowly from his scar. . . . Then there were hurried footsteps coming up the stairs, and he heard Neville's voice again.

"Over here, Professor . . ."

Professor McGonagall came hurrying into the dormitory in her tartan dressing gown, her glasses perched lopsidedly on the bridge of her bony nose.

"What is it, Potter? Where does it hurt?"

He had never been so pleased to see her; it was a member of the Order of the Phoenix he needed now, not someone fussing over him and prescribing useless potions.

"It's Ron's dad," he said, sitting up again. "He's been attacked by a snake and it's serious, I saw it happen."

"What do you mean, you saw it happen?" said Professor McGonagall, her dark eyebrows contracting.

"I don't know. . . . I was asleep and then I was there. . . ."

"You mean you dreamed this?"

"No!" said Harry angrily. Would none of them understand? "I was having a dream at first about something completely different, something stupid . . . and then this interrupted it. It was real, I didn't imagine it, Mr. Weasley was asleep on the floor and he was attacked by a gigantic snake, there was a load of blood, he collapsed, someone's got to find out where he is. . . ."

Professor McGonagall was gazing at him through her lopsided spectacles as though horrified at what she was seeing.

"I'm not lying, and I'm not mad!" Harry told her, his voice rising to a shout. "I tell you, I saw it happen!"

"I believe you, Potter," said Professor McGonagall curtly. "Put on your dressing-gown — we're going to see the headmaster."

ST. MUNGO'S HOSPITAL FOR MAGICAL MALADIES AND INJURIES

H arry was so relieved that she was taking him seriously that he did not hesitate, but jumped out of bed at once, pulled on his dressing gown, and pushed his glasses back onto his nose.

"Weasley, you ought to come too," said Professor McGonagall.

They followed Professor McGonagall past the silent figures of Neville, Dean, and Seamus, out of the dormitory, down the spiral stairs into the common room, through the portrait hole, and off along the Fat Lady's moonlit corridor. Harry felt as though the panic inside him might spill over at any moment; he wanted to run, to yell for Dumbledore. Mr. Weasley was bleeding as they walked along so sedately, and what if those fangs (Harry tried hard not to think "my fangs") had been poisonous? They passed Mrs. Norris, who turned her lamplike eyes upon them and hissed faintly, but Professor McGonagall said, "Shoo!" Mrs. Norris slunk away into the shadows, and in a few minutes they had reached the stone gargoyle guarding the entrance to Dumbledore's office.

"Fizzing Whizbee," said Professor McGonagall.

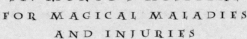

The gargoyle sprang to life and leapt aside; the wall behind it split in two to reveal a stone staircase that was moving continuously upward like a spiral escalator. The three of them stepped onto the moving stairs; the wall closed behind them with a thud, and they were moving upward in tight circles until they reached the highly polished oak door with the brass knocker shaped like a griffin.

Though it was now well past midnight, there were voices coming from inside the room, a positive babble of them. It sounded as though Dumbledore was entertaining at least a dozen people.

Professor McGonagall rapped three times with the griffin knocker, and the voices ceased abruptly as though someone had switched them all off. The door opened of its own accord and Professor McGonagall led Harry and Ron inside.

The room was in half darkness; the strange silver instruments standing on tables were silent and still rather than whirring and emitting puffs of smoke as they usually did. The portraits of old headmasters and headmistresses covering the walls were all snoozing in their frames. Behind the door, a magnificent red-and-gold bird the size of a swan dozed on its perch with its head under its wing.

"Oh, it's you, Professor McGonagall . . . and . . . *ah.*"

Dumbledore was sitting in a high-backed chair behind his desk; he leaned forward into the pool of candlelight illuminating the papers laid out before him. He was wearing a magnificently embroidered purple-and-gold dressing gown over a snowy-white nightshirt, but seemed wide awake, his penetrating light-blue eyes fixed intently upon Professor McGonagall.

"Professor Dumbledore, Potter has had a . . . well, a nightmare," said Professor McGonagall. "He says . . ."

"It wasn't a nightmare," said Harry quickly.

Professor McGonagall looked around at Harry, frowning slightly.

"Very well, then, Potter, you tell the headmaster about it."

"I . . . well, I *was* asleep. . . ." said Harry and even in his terror and his desperation to make Dumbledore understand he felt slightly irritated that the headmaster was not looking at him, but examining his own interlocked fingers. "But it wasn't an ordinary dream . . . it was real. . . . I saw it happen. . . ." He took a deep breath, "Ron's dad — Mr. Weasley — has been attacked by a giant snake."

The words seemed to reverberate in the air after he had said them, slightly ridiculous, even comic. There was a pause in which Dumbledore leaned back and stared meditatively at the ceiling. Ron looked from Harry to Dumbledore, white-faced and shocked.

"How did you see this?" Dumbledore asked quietly, still not looking at Harry.

"Well . . . I don't know," said Harry, rather angrily — what did it matter? "Inside my head, I suppose —"

"You misunderstand me," said Dumbledore, still in the same calm tone. "I mean . . . can you remember — er — where you were positioned as you watched this attack happen? Were you perhaps standing beside the victim, or else looking down on the scene from above?"

This was such a curious question that Harry gaped at Dumbledore; it was almost as though he knew . . .

"I was the snake," he said. "I saw it all from the snake's point of view. . . ."

Nobody else spoke for a moment, then Dumbledore, now looking at Ron, who was still whey-faced, said in a new and sharper voice, "Is Arthur seriously injured?"

"*Yes,*" said Harry emphatically — why were they all so slow on the uptake, did they not realize how much a person bled when fangs that long pierced their side? And why could Dumbledore not do him the courtesy of looking at him?

But Dumbledore stood up so quickly that Harry jumped, and addressed one of the old portraits hanging very near the ceiling.

"Everard?" he said sharply. "And you too, Dilys!"

A sallow-faced wizard with short, black bangs and an elderly witch with long silver ringlets in the frame beside him, both of whom seemed to have been in the deepest of sleeps, opened their eyes immediately.

"You were listening?" said Dumbledore.

The wizard nodded, the witch said, "Naturally."

"The man has red hair and glasses," said Dumbledore. "Everard, you will need to raise the alarm, make sure he is found by the right people —"

Both nodded and moved sideways out of their frames, but instead of emerging in neighboring pictures (as usually happened at Hogwarts), neither reappeared; one frame now contained nothing but a backdrop of dark curtain, the other a handsome leather armchair. Harry noticed that many of the other headmasters and mistresses on the walls, though snoring and drooling most convincingly, kept sneaking peeks at him under their eyelids, and he suddenly understood who had been talking when they had knocked.

"Everard and Dilys were two of Hogwarts's most celebrated Heads," Dumbledore said, now sweeping around Harry, Ron, and Professor McGonagall and approaching the magnificent sleeping bird on his perch beside the door. "Their renown is such that both have portraits hanging in other important Wizarding institutions. As they are free to move between their own portraits they can tell us what may be happening elsewhere. . . ."

"But Mr. Weasley could be anywhere!" said Harry.

"Please sit down, all three of you," said Dumbledore, as though Harry had not spoken. "Everard and Dilys may not be back for several minutes. . . . Professor McGonagall, if you could draw up extra chairs . . ."

Professor McGonagall pulled her wand from the pocket of her dressing gown and waved it; three chairs appeared out of thin air, straight-backed and wooden, quite unlike the comfortable chintz armchairs that Dumbledore had conjured back at Harry's hearing.

Harry sat down, watching Dumbledore over his shoulder. Dumbledore was now stroking Fawkes's plumed golden head with one finger. The phoenix awoke immediately. He stretched his beautiful head high and observed Dumbledore through bright, dark eyes.

"We will need," said Dumbledore very quietly to the bird, "a warning."

There was a flash of fire and the phoenix had gone.

Dumbledore now swooped down upon one of the fragile silver instruments whose function Harry had never known, carried it over to his desk, sat down facing them again, and tapped it gently with the tip of his wand.

The instrument tinkled into life at once with rhythmic clinking noises. Tiny puffs of pale green smoke issued from the minuscule silver tube at the top. Dumbledore watched the smoke closely, his brow furrowed, and after a few seconds, the tiny puffs became a steady stream of smoke that thickened and coiled in the air. . . . A serpent's head grew out of the end of it, opening its mouth wide. Harry wondered whether the instrument was confirming his story: He looked eagerly at Dumbledore for a sign that he was right, but Dumbledore did not look up.

"Naturally, naturally," murmured Dumbledore apparently to himself, still observing the stream of smoke without the slightest sign of surprise. "But in essence divided?"

Harry could make neither head nor tail of this question. The smoke serpent, however, split itself instantly into two snakes, both coiling and undulating in the dark air. With a look of grim satisfaction Dumbledore gave the instrument another gentle tap with his wand: The clinking noise slowed and died, and the smoke serpents grew faint, became a formless haze, and vanished.

Dumbledore replaced the instrument upon its spindly little table; Harry saw many of the old headmasters in the portraits follow him with their eyes, then, realizing that Harry was watching them, hastily pretend to be sleeping again. Harry wanted to ask what the strange silver instrument was for, but before he could do so, there was a shout from the top of the wall to their right; the wizard called Everard had reappeared in his portrait, panting slightly.

"Dumbledore!"

"What news?" said Dumbledore at once.

"I yelled until someone came running," said the wizard, who was mopping his brow on the curtain behind him, "said I'd heard something moving downstairs — they weren't sure whether to believe me but went down to check — you know there are no portraits down there to watch from. Anyway, they carried him up a few minutes later. He doesn't look good, he's covered in blood, I ran along to Elfrida Cragg's portrait to get a good view as they left —"

"Good," said Dumbledore as Ron made a convulsive movement, "I take it Dilys will have seen him arrive, then —"

And moments later, the silver-ringletted witch had reappeared in her picture too; she sank, coughing, into her armchair and said, "Yes, they've taken him to St. Mungo's, Dumbledore. . . . They carried him past under my portrait. . . . He looks bad. . . ."

"Thank you," said Dumbledore. He looked around at Professor McGonagall.

"Minerva, I need you to go and wake the other Weasley children."

"Of course. . . ."

Professor McGonagall got up and moved swiftly to the door; Harry cast a sideways glance at Ron, who was now looking terrified.

"And Dumbledore — what about Molly?" said Professor McGonagall, pausing at the door.

"That will be a job for Fawkes when he has finished keeping a lookout for anybody approaching," said Dumbledore. "But she may already know . . . that excellent clock of hers . . ."

Harry knew Dumbledore was referring to the clock that told, not the time, but the whereabouts and conditions of the various Weasley family members, and with a pang he thought that Mr. Weasley's hand must, even now, be pointing at "mortal peril." But it was very late. . . . Mrs. Weasley was probably asleep, not watching the clock. . . . And he felt cold as he remembered Mrs. Weasley's boggart turning into Mr. Weasley's lifeless body, his glasses askew, blood running down his face. . . . But Mr. Weasley wasn't going to die. . . . He couldn't. . . .

Dumbledore was now rummaging in a cupboard behind Harry and Ron. He emerged from it carrying a blackened old kettle, which he placed carefully upon his desk. He raised his wand and murmured *"Portus"*; for a moment the kettle trembled, glowing with an odd blue light, then it quivered to a rest, as solidly black as ever.

Dumbledore marched over to another portrait, this time of a clever-looking wizard with a pointed beard, who had been painted wearing the Slytherin colors of green and silver and was apparently sleeping so deeply that he could not hear Dumbledore's voice when he attempted to rouse him.

"Phineas. *Phineas.*"

And now the subjects of the portraits lining the room were no longer pretending to be asleep; they were shifting around in their frames, the better to watch what was happening. When the clever-looking wizard continued to feign sleep, some of them shouted his name too.

"Phineas! *Phineas!* PHINEAS!"

He could not pretend any longer; he gave a theatrical jerk and opened his eyes wide.

"Did someone call?"

"I need you to visit your other portrait again, Phineas," said Dumbledore. "I've got another message."

"Visit my other portrait?" said Phineas in a reedy voice, giving a long, fake yawn (his eyes traveling around the room and focusing upon Harry). "Oh no, Dumbledore, I am too tired tonight. . . ."

Something about Phineas's voice was familiar to Harry. Where had

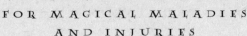
he heard it before? But before he could think, the portraits on the surrounding walls broke into a storm of protest.

"Insubordination, sir!" roared a corpulent, red-nosed wizard, brandishing his fists. "Dereliction of duty!"

"We are honor-bound to give service to the present headmaster of Hogwarts!" cried a frail-looking old wizard whom Harry recognized as Dumbledore's predecessor, Armando Dippet. "Shame on you, Phineas!"

"Shall I persuade him, Dumbledore?" called a gimlet-eyed witch, raising an unusually thick wand that looked not unlike a birch rod.

"Oh, very *well*," said the wizard called Phineas, eyeing this wand slightly apprehensively, "though he may well have destroyed my picture by now, he's done most of the family —"

"Sirius knows not to destroy your portrait," said Dumbledore, and Harry realized immediately where he had heard Phineas's voice before: issuing from the apparently empty frame in his bedroom in Grimmauld Place. "You are to give him the message that Arthur Weasley has been gravely injured and that his wife, children, and Harry Potter will be arriving at his house shortly. Do you understand?"

"Arthur Weasley, injured, wife and children and Harry Potter coming to stay," recited Phineas in a bored voice. "Yes, yes . . . very well. . . ."

He sloped away into the frame of the portrait and disappeared from view at the very moment that the study door opened again. Fred, George, and Ginny were ushered inside by Professor McGonagall, all three of them looking disheveled and shocked, still in their night things.

"Harry — what's going on?" asked Ginny, who looked frightened. "Professor McGonagall says you saw Dad hurt —"

"Your father has been injured in the course of his work for the Order of the Phoenix," said Dumbledore before Harry could speak. "He has been taken to St. Mungo's Hospital for Magical Maladies and Injuries. I am sending you back to Sirius's house, which is much more convenient for the hospital than the Burrow. You will meet your mother there."

"How're we going?" asked Fred, looking shaken. "Floo powder?"

"No," said Dumbledore, "Floo powder is not safe at the moment, the Network is being watched. You will be taking a Portkey." He indicated the old kettle lying innocently on his desk. "We are just waiting for Phineas Nigellus to report back. . . . I wish to be sure that the coast is clear before sending you —"

There was a flash of flame in the very middle of the office, leaving behind a single golden feather that floated gently to the floor.

"It is Fawkes's warning," said Dumbledore, catching the feather as it fell. "She must know you're out of your beds. . . . Minerva, go and head her off — tell her any story —"

Professor McGonagall was gone in a swish of tartan.

"He says he'll be delighted," said a bored voice behind Dumbledore; the wizard called Phineas had reappeared in front of his Slytherin banner. "My great-great-grandson has always had odd taste in houseguests. . . ."

"Come here, then," Dumbledore said to Harry and the Weasleys. "And quickly, before anyone else joins us . . ."

Harry and the others gathered around Dumbledore's desk.

"You have all used a Portkey before?" asked Dumbledore, and they nodded, each reaching out to touch some part of the blackened kettle. "Good. On the count of three then . . . one . . . two . . ."

It happened in a fraction of a second: In the infinitesimal pause before Dumbledore said "three," Harry looked up at him — they were very close together — and Dumbledore's clear blue gaze moved from the Portkey to Harry's face.

At once, Harry's scar burned white-hot, as though the old wound had burst open again — and unbidden, unwanted, but terrifyingly strong, there rose within Harry a hatred so powerful he felt, for that

instant, that he would like nothing better than to strike — to bite —
to sink his fangs into the man before him —

"... *three*."

He felt a powerful jerk behind his navel, the ground vanished from
beneath his feet, his hand was glued to the kettle; he was banging into
the others as all sped forward in a swirl of colors and a rush of wind,
the kettle pulling them onward and then —

His feet hit the ground so hard that his knees buckled, the kettle
clattered to the ground and somewhere close at hand a voice said, "Back
again, the blood traitor brats, is it true their father's dying . . . ?"

"OUT!" roared a second voice.

Harry scrambled to his feet and looked around; they had arrived
in the gloomy basement kitchen of number twelve, Grimmauld
Place. The only sources of light were the fire and one guttering candle, which illuminated the remains of a solitary supper. Kreacher
was disappearing through the door to the hall, looking back at them
malevolently as he hitched up his loincloth; Sirius was hurrying toward them all, looking anxious. He was unshaven and still in his day
clothes; there was also a slightly Mundungus-like whiff of stale drink
about him.

"What's going on?" he said, stretching out a hand to help Ginny
up. "Phineas Nigellus said Arthur's been badly injured —"

"Ask Harry," said Fred.

"Yeah, I want to hear this for myself," said George.

The twins and Ginny were staring at him. Kreacher's footsteps had
stopped on the stairs outside.

"It was —" Harry began; this was even worse than telling McGonagall and Dumbledore. "I had a — a kind of — vision. . . ."

And he told them all that he had seen, though he altered the story
so that it sounded as though he had watched from the sidelines as the
snake attacked, rather than from behind the snake's own eyes. . . .

Ron, who was still very white, gave him a fleeting look, but did not speak. When Harry had finished, Fred, George, and Ginny continued to stare at him for a moment. Harry did not know whether he was imagining it or not, but he fancied there was something accusatory in their looks. Well, if they were going to blame him for just seeing the attack, he was glad he had not told them that he had been inside the snake at the time. . . .

"Is Mum here?" said Fred, turning to Sirius.

"She probably doesn't even know what's happened yet," said Sirius. "The important thing was to get you away before Umbridge could interfere. I expect Dumbledore's letting Molly know now."

"We've got to go to St. Mungo's," said Ginny urgently. She looked around at her brothers; they were of course still in their pajamas. "Sirius, can you lend us cloaks or anything — ?"

"Hang on, you can't go tearing off to St. Mungo's!" said Sirius.

"'Course we can go to St. Mungo's if we want," said Fred, with a mulish expression, "he's our dad!"

"And how are you going to explain how you knew Arthur was attacked before the hospital even let his wife know?"

"What does that matter?" said George hotly.

"It matters because we don't want to draw attention to the fact that Harry is having visions of things that are happening hundreds of miles away!" said Sirius angrily. "Have you any idea what the Ministry would make of that information?"

Fred and George looked as though they could not care less what the Ministry made of anything. Ron was still white-faced and silent. Ginny said, "Somebody else could have told us. . . . We could have heard it somewhere other than Harry. . . ."

"Like who?" said Sirius impatiently. "Listen, your dad's been hurt while on duty for the Order and the circumstances are fishy enough without his children knowing about it seconds after it happened, you could seriously damage the Order's —"

"We don't care about the dumb Order!" shouted Fred.

"It's our dad dying we're talking about!" yelled George.

"Your father knew what he was getting into, and he won't thank you for messing things up for the Order!" said Sirius angrily in his turn. "This is how it is — this is why you're not in the Order — you don't understand — there are things worth dying for!"

"Easy for you to say, stuck here!" bellowed Fred. "I don't see you risking your neck!"

The little color remaining in Sirius's face drained from it. He looked for a moment as though he would quite like to hit Fred, but when he spoke, it was in a voice of determined calm. "I know it's hard, but we've all got to act as though we don't know anything yet. We've got to stay put, at least until we hear from your mother, all right?"

Fred and George still looked mutinous. Ginny, however, took a few steps over to the nearest chair and sank into it. Harry looked at Ron, who made a funny movement somewhere between a nod and shrug, and they sat down too. The twins glared at Sirius for another minute, then took seats on either side of Ginny.

"That's right," said Sirius encouragingly, "come on, let's all . . . let's all have a drink while we're waiting. *Accio Butterbeer!*"

He raised his wand as he spoke and half a dozen bottles came flying toward them out of the pantry, skidded along the table, scattering the debris of Sirius's meal, and stopped neatly in front of the six of them. They all drank, and for a while the only sounds were those of the crackling of the kitchen fire and the soft thud of their bottles on the table.

Harry was only drinking to have something to do with his hands. His stomach was full of horrible hot, bubbling guilt. They would not be here if it were not for him; they would all still be asleep in bed. And it was no good telling himself that by raising the alarm he had ensured that Mr. Weasley was found, because there was also the inescapable business of it being he who had attacked Mr. Weasley in the first place. . . .

Don't be stupid, you haven't got fangs, he told himself, trying to keep calm, though the hand on his butterbeer bottle was shaking. *You were lying in bed, you weren't attacking anyone. . . .*

But then, what just happened in Dumbledore's office? he asked himself. *I felt like I wanted to attack Dumbledore too. . . .*

He put the bottle down on the table a little harder than he meant to, so that it slopped over onto the table. No one took any notice. Then a burst of fire in midair illuminated the dirty plates in front of them and as they gave cries of shock, a scroll of parchment fell with a thud onto the table, accompanied by a single golden phoenix tail feather.

"Fawkes!" said Sirius at once, snatching up the parchment. "That's not Dumbledore's writing — it must be a message from your mother — here —"

He thrust the letter into George's hand, who ripped it open and read aloud, *"Dad is still alive. I am setting out for St. Mungo's now. Stay where you are. I will send news as soon as I can. Mum."*

George looked around the table.

"Still alive . . ." he said slowly. "But that makes it sound . . ."

He did not need to finish the sentence. It sounded to Harry too as though Mr. Weasley was hovering somewhere between life and death. Still exceptionally pale, Ron stared at the back of his mother's letter as though it might speak words of comfort to him. Fred pulled the parchment out of George's hands and read it for himself, then looked up at Harry, who felt his hand shaking on his butterbeer bottle again and clenched it more tightly to stop the trembling.

If Harry had ever sat through a longer night than this one he could not remember it. Sirius suggested once that they all go to bed, but without any real conviction, and the Weasleys' looks of disgust were answer enough. They mostly sat in silence around the table, watching the candle wick sinking lower and lower into liquid wax, now and then raising bottles to their lips, speaking only to check the time, to

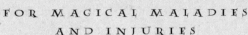

wonder aloud what was happening, and to reassure one another that if there was bad news, they would know straightaway, for Mrs. Weasley must long since have arrived at St. Mungo's.

Fred fell into a doze, his head sagging sideways onto his shoulder. Ginny was curled like a cat on her chair, but her eyes were open; Harry could see them reflecting the firelight. Ron was sitting with his head in his hands, whether awake or asleep it was impossible to tell. And he and Sirius looked at each other every so often, intruders upon the family grief, waiting . . . waiting . . .

And then, at ten past five in the morning by Ron's watch, the door swung open and Mrs. Weasley entered the kitchen. She was extremely pale, but when they all turned to look at her, Fred, Ron, and Harry half-rising from their chairs, she gave a wan smile.

"He's going to be all right," she said, her voice weak with tiredness. "He's sleeping. We can all go and see him later. Bill's sitting with him now, he's going to take the morning off work."

Fred fell back into his chair with his hands over his face. George and Ginny got up, walked swiftly over to their mother, and hugged her. Ron gave a very shaky laugh and downed the rest of his butterbeer in one.

"Breakfast!" said Sirius loudly and joyfully, jumping to his feet. "Where's that accursed house-elf? Kreacher! KREACHER!"

But Kreacher did not answer the summons.

"Oh, forget it, then," muttered Sirius, counting the people in front of him. "So it's breakfast for — let's see — seven . . . Bacon and eggs, I think, and some tea, and toast —"

Harry hurried over to the stove to help. He did not want to intrude upon the Weasleys' happiness, and he dreaded the moment when Mrs. Weasley would ask him to recount his vision. However, he had barely taken plates from the dresser when Mrs. Weasley lifted them out of his hands and pulled him into a hug.

"I don't know what would have happened if it hadn't been for you,

Harry," she said in a muffled voice. "They might not have found Arthur for hours, and then it would have been too late, but thanks to you he's alive and Dumbledore's been able to think up a good cover story for Arthur being where he was, you've no idea what trouble he would have been in otherwise, look at poor Sturgis. . . ."

Harry could hardly stand her gratitude, but fortunately she soon released him to turn to Sirius and thank him for looking after her children through the night. Sirius said that he was very pleased to have been able to help, and hoped they would all stay with him as long as Mr. Weasley was in hospital.

"Oh, Sirius, I'm so grateful. . . . They think he'll be there a little while and it would be wonderful to be nearer . . . Of course, that might mean we're here for Christmas. . . ."

"The more the merrier!" said Sirius with such obvious sincerity that Mrs. Weasley beamed at him, threw on an apron, and began to help with breakfast.

"Sirius," Harry muttered, unable to stand it a moment longer. "Can I have a quick word? Er — *now?*"

He walked into the dark pantry and Sirius followed. Without preamble Harry told his godfather every detail of the vision he had had, including the fact that he himself had been the snake who had attacked Mr. Weasley.

When he paused for breath, Sirius said, "Did you tell Dumbledore this?"

"Yes," said Harry impatiently, "but he didn't tell me what it meant. Well, he doesn't tell me anything anymore. . . ."

"I'm sure he would have told you if it was anything to worry about," said Sirius steadily.

"But that's not all," said Harry in a voice only a little above a whisper. "Sirius, I . . . I think I'm going mad. . . . Back in Dumbledore's office, just before we took the Portkey . . . for a couple of seconds there I thought I was a snake, I *felt* like one — my scar really hurt when I was looking at Dumbledore — Sirius, I wanted to attack him —"

He could only see a sliver of Sirius's face; the rest was in darkness.

"It must have been the aftermath of the vision, that's all," said Sirius. "You were still thinking of the dream or whatever it was and —"

"It wasn't that," said Harry, shaking his head. "It was like something rose up inside me, like there's a *snake* inside me —"

"You need to sleep," said Sirius firmly. "You're going to have breakfast and then go upstairs to bed, and then you can go and see Arthur after lunch with the others. You're in shock, Harry; you're blaming yourself for something you only witnessed, and it's lucky you *did* witness it or Arthur might have died. Just stop worrying. . . ."

He clapped Harry on the shoulder and left the pantry, leaving Harry standing alone in the dark.

Everyone but Harry spent the rest of the morning sleeping. He went up to the bedroom he had shared with Ron over the summer, but while Ron crawled into bed and was asleep within minutes, Harry sat fully clothed, hunched against the cold metal bars of the bedstead, keeping himself deliberately uncomfortable, determined not to fall into a doze, terrified that he might become the serpent again in his sleep and awake to find that he had attacked Ron, or else slithered through the house after one of the others. . . .

When Ron woke up, Harry pretended to have enjoyed a refreshing nap too. Their trunks arrived from Hogwarts while they were eating lunch, so that they could dress as Muggles for the trip to St. Mungo's. Everybody except Harry was riotously happy and talkative as they changed out of their robes into jeans and sweatshirts, and they greeted Tonks and Mad-Eye, who had turned up to escort them across London, gleefully laughing at the bowler hat Mad-Eye was wearing at an angle to conceal his magical eye and assuring him, truthfully, that Tonks, whose hair was short and bright pink again, would attract far less attention on the underground.

Tonks was very interested in Harry's vision of the attack on Mr. Weasley, something he was not remotely interested in discussing.

"There isn't any *Seer* blood in your family, is there?" she inquired curiously, as they sat side by side on a train rattling toward the heart of the city.

"No," said Harry, thinking of Professor Trelawney and feeling insulted.

"No," said Tonks musingly, "no, I suppose it's not really prophecy you're doing, is it? I mean, you're not seeing the future, you're seeing the present. . . . It's odd, isn't it? Useful, though . . ."

Harry did not answer; fortunately they got out at the next stop, a station in the very heart of London, and in the bustle of leaving the train he was able to allow Fred and George to get between himself and Tonks, who was leading the way. They all followed her up the escalator, Moody clunking along at the back of the group, his bowler tilted low and one gnarled hand stuck in between the buttons of his coat, clutching his wand. Harry thought he sensed the concealed eye staring hard at him; trying to deflect more questions about his dream he asked Mad-Eye where St. Mungo's was hidden.

"Not far from here," grunted Moody as they stepped out into the wintry air on a broad store-lined street packed with Christmas shoppers. He pushed Harry a little ahead of him and stumped along just behind; Harry knew the eye was rolling in all directions under the tilted hat. "Wasn't easy to find a good location for a hospital. Nowhere in Diagon Alley was big enough and we couldn't have it underground like the Ministry — unhealthy. In the end they managed to get hold of a building up here. Theory was sick wizards could come and go and just blend in with the crowd. . . ."

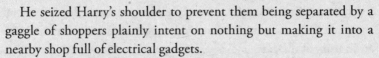
He seized Harry's shoulder to prevent them being separated by a gaggle of shoppers plainly intent on nothing but making it into a nearby shop full of electrical gadgets.

"Here we go," said Moody a moment later.

They had arrived outside a large, old-fashioned, red brick department store called Purge and Dowse Ltd. The place had a shabby, miserable air; the window displays consisted of a few chipped dummies with their wigs askew, standing at random and modeling fashions at least ten years out of date. Large signs on all the dusty doors read CLOSED FOR REFURBISHMENT. Harry distinctly heard a large woman laden with plastic shopping bags say to her friend as they passed, "It's *never* open, that place. . . ."

"Right," said Tonks, beckoning them forward to a window displaying nothing but a particularly ugly female dummy whose false eyelashes were hanging off and who was modeling a green nylon pinafore dress. "Everybody ready?"

They nodded, clustering around her; Moody gave Harry another shove between the shoulder blades to urge him forward and Tonks leaned close to the glass, looking up at the very ugly dummy and said, her breath steaming up the glass, "Wotcher . . . We're here to see Arthur Weasley."

For a split second, Harry thought how absurd it was for Tonks to expect the dummy to hear her talking that quietly through a sheet of glass, when there were buses rumbling along behind her and all the racket of a street full of shoppers. Then he reminded himself that dummies could not hear anyway. Next second his mouth opened in shock as the dummy gave a tiny nod, beckoned its jointed finger, and Tonks had seized Ginny and Mrs. Weasley by the elbows, stepped right through the glass and vanished.

Fred, George, and Ron stepped after them; Harry glanced around at the jostling crowd; not one of them seemed to have a glance to spare for window displays as ugly as Purge and Dowse Ltd.'s, nor did any of them seem to have noticed that six people had just melted into thin air in front of them.

"C'mon," growled Moody, giving Harry yet another poke in the back and together they stepped forward through what felt like a sheet of cool water, emerging quite warm and dry on the other side.

There was no sign of the ugly dummy or the space where she had stood. They had arrived in what seemed to be a crowded reception area where rows of witches and wizards sat upon rickety wooden chairs, some looking perfectly normal and perusing out-of-date copies of *Witch Weekly,* others sporting gruesome disfigurements such as elephant trunks or extra hands sticking out of their chests. The room was scarcely less quiet than the street outside, for many of the patients were making very peculiar noises. A sweaty-faced witch in the center of the front row, who was fanning herself vigorously with a copy of the *Daily Prophet,* kept letting off a high-pitched whistle as steam came pouring out of her mouth, and a grubby-looking warlock in the corner clanged like a bell every time he moved, and with each clang his head vibrated horribly, so that he had to seize himself by the ears and hold it steady.

Witches and wizards in lime-green robes were walking up and down the rows, asking questions and making notes on clipboards like Umbridge's. Harry noticed the emblem embroidered on their chests: a wand and bone, crossed.

"Are they doctors?" he asked Ron quietly.

"Doctors?" said Ron, looking startled. "Those Muggle nutters that cut people up? Nah, they're Healers."

"Over here!" called Mrs. Weasley over the renewed clanging of the warlock in the corner, and they followed her to the queue in front of a plump blonde witch seated at a desk marked INQUIRIES. The wall behind her was covered in notices and posters saying things like A CLEAN CAULDRON KEEPS POTIONS FROM BECOMING POISONS and ANTIDOTES ARE ANTI-DON'TS UNLESS APPROVED BY A QUALIFIED HEALER.

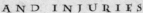
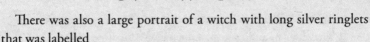
There was also a large portrait of a witch with long silver ringlets that was labelled

DILYS DERWENT

ST. MUNGO'S HEALER 1722–1741
HEADMISTRESS OF HOGWARTS SCHOOL OF
WITCHCRAFT AND WIZARDRY, 1741–1768

Dilys was eyeing the Weasley party as though counting them; when Harry caught her eye she gave a tiny wink, walked sideways out of her portrait, and vanished.

Meanwhile, at the front of the queue, a young wizard was performing an odd on-the-spot jig and trying, in between yelps of pain, to explain his predicament to the witch behind the desk.

"It's these — ouch — shoes my brother gave me — ow — they're eating my — OUCH — feet — look at them, there must be some kind of — AARGH — jinx on them and I can't — AAAAARGH — get them off —"

He hopped from one foot to the other as though dancing on hot coals.

"The shoes don't prevent you reading, do they?" said the blonde witch irritably, pointing at a large sign to the left of her desk. "You want Spell Damage, fourth floor. Just like it says on the floor guide. Next!"

The wizard hobbled and pranced sideways out of the way, the Weasley party moved forward a few steps and Harry read the floor guide:

ARTIFACT ACCIDENTS .... *Ground Floor*
(*Cauldron explosion, wand backfiring, broom crashes, etc.*)

CREATURE-INDUCED INJURIES .... *First Floor*
(*Bites, stings, burns, embedded spines, etc.*)

MAGICAL BUGS .... Second Floor
(Contagious maladies, e.g., dragon pox, vanishing sickness,
scrofungulus)

POTION AND PLANT POISONING............ Third Floor
(Rashes, regurgitation, uncontrollable giggling, etc.)

SPELL DAMAGE .... Fourth Floor
(Unliftable jinxes, hexes, and incorrectly applied charms, etc.)

VISITORS' TEAROOM AND HOSPITAL SHOP... Fifth Floor

If you are unsure where to go, incapable of normal speech, or
unable to remember why you are here, our Welcome Witch
will be pleased to help.

A very old, stooped wizard with a hearing trumpet had shuffled to
the front of the queue now.

"I'm here to see Broderick Bode!" he wheezed.

"Ward forty-nine, but I'm afraid you're wasting your time," said
the witch dismissively. "He's completely addled, you know, still thinks
he's a teapot. . . . Next!"

A harassed-looking wizard was holding his small daughter tightly
by the ankle while she flapped around his head using the immensely
large, feathery wings that had sprouted right out the back of her
romper suit.

"Fourth floor," said the witch in a bored voice, without asking, and
the man disappeared through the double doors beside the desk, holding his daughter like an oddly shaped balloon. "Next!"

Mrs. Weasley moved forward to the desk.

"Hello," she said. "My husband, Arthur Weasley, was supposed to
be moved to a different ward this morning, could you tell us — ?"

"Arthur Weasley?" said the witch, running her finger down a long list in front of her. "Yes, first floor, second door on the right, Dai Llewellyn ward."

"Thank you," said Mrs. Weasley. "Come on, you lot."

They followed through the double doors and along the narrow corridor beyond, which was lined with more portraits of famous Healers and lit by crystal bubbles full of candles that floated up on the ceiling, looking like giant soapsuds. More witches and wizards in lime-green robes walked in and out of the doors they passed; a foul-smelling yellow gas wafted into the passageway as they passed one door, and every now and then they heard distant wailing. They climbed a flight of stairs and entered the "Creature-Induced Injuries" corridor, where the second door on the right bore the words "DANGEROUS" DAI LLEWELLYN WARD: SERIOUS BITES. Underneath this was a card in a brass holder on which had been handwritten *Healer-in-Charge: Hippocrates Smethwyck, Trainee Healer: Augustus Pye.*

"We'll wait outside, Molly," Tonks said. "Arthur won't want too many visitors at once. . . . It ought to be just the family first."

Mad-Eye growled his approval of this idea and set himself with his back against the corridor wall, his magical eye spinning in all directions. Harry drew back too, but Mrs. Weasley reached out a hand and pushed him through the door, saying, "Don't be silly, Harry, Arthur wants to thank you. . . ."

The ward was small and rather dingy as the only window was narrow and set high in the wall facing the door. Most of the light came from more shining crystal bubbles clustered in the middle of the ceiling. The walls were of panelled oak and there was a portrait of a rather vicious-looking wizard on the wall, captioned URQUHART RACKHARROW, 1612–1697, INVENTOR OF THE ENTRAIL-EXPELLING CURSE.

There were only three patients. Mr. Weasley was occupying the bed at the far end of the ward beside the tiny window. Harry was pleased and relieved to see that he was propped up on several pillows and reading the

Daily Prophet by the solitary ray of sunlight falling onto his bed. He looked around as they walked toward him and, seeing whom it was, beamed.

"Hello!" he called, throwing the *Prophet* aside. "Bill just left, Molly, had to get back to work, but he says he'll drop in on you later. . . ."

"How are you, Arthur?" asked Mrs. Weasley, bending down to kiss his cheek and looking anxiously into his face. "You're still looking a bit peaky. . . ."

"I feel absolutely fine," said Mr. Weasley brightly, holding out his good arm to give Ginny a hug. "If they could only take the bandages off, I'd be fit to go home."

"Why can't they take them off, Dad?" asked Fred.

"Well, I start bleeding like mad every time they try," said Mr. Weasley cheerfully, reaching across for his wand, which lay on his bedside cabinet, and waving it so that six extra chairs appeared at his bedside to seat them all. "It seems there was some rather unusual kind of poison in that snake's fangs that keeps wounds open. . . . They're sure they'll find an antidote, though, they say they've had much worse cases than mine, and in the meantime I just have to keep taking a Blood-Replenishing Potion every hour. But that fellow over there," he said, dropping his voice and nodding toward the bed opposite in which a man lay looking green and sickly and staring at the ceiling. "Bitten by a *werewolf*, poor chap. No cure at all."

"A werewolf?" whispered Mrs. Weasley, looking alarmed. "Is he safe in a public ward? Shouldn't he be in a private room?"

"It's two weeks till full moon," Mr. Weasley reminded her quietly. "They've been talking to him this morning, the Healers, you know, trying to persuade him he'll be able to lead an almost normal life. I said to him — didn't mention names, of course — but I said I knew a werewolf personally, very nice man, who finds the condition quite easy to manage. . . ."

"What did he say?" asked George.

"Said he'd give me another bite if I didn't shut up," said Mr. Weasley sadly. "And that woman over *there*," he indicated the only other occupied bed, which was right beside the door, "won't tell the Healers what bit her, which makes us all think it must have been something she was handling illegally. Whatever it was took a real chunk out of her leg, *very* nasty smell when they take off the dressings."

"So, you going to tell us what happened, Dad?" asked Fred, pulling his chair closer to the bed.

"Well, you already know, don't you?" said Mr. Weasley, with a significant smile at Harry. "It's very simple — I'd had a very long day, dozed off, got sneaked up on, and bitten."

"Is it in the *Prophet,* you being attacked?" asked Fred, indicating the newspaper Mr. Weasley had cast aside.

"No, of course not," said Mr. Weasley, with a slightly bitter smile, "the Ministry wouldn't want everyone to know a dirty great serpent got —"

"Arthur!" said Mrs. Weasley warningly.

"— got — er — me," Mr. Weasley said hastily, though Harry was quite sure that was not what he had meant to say.

"So where were you when it happened, Dad?" asked George.

"That's my business," said Mr. Weasley, though with a small smile. He snatched up the *Daily Prophet,* shook it open again and said, "I was just reading about Willy Widdershins's arrest when you arrived. You know Willy turned out to be behind those regurgitating toilets last summer? One of his jinxes backfired, the toilet exploded, and they found him lying unconscious in the wreckage covered from head to foot in —"

"When you say you were 'on duty,'" Fred interrupted in a low voice, "what were you doing?"

"You heard your father," whispered Mrs. Weasley, "we are not discussing this here! Go on about Willy Widdershins, Arthur —"

"Well, don't ask me how, but he actually got off on the toilet charge," said Mr. Weasley grimly. "I can only suppose gold changed hands —"

"You were guarding it, weren't you?" said George quietly. "The weapon? The thing You-Know-Who's after?"

"George, be quiet!" snapped Mrs. Weasley.

"Anyway," said Mr. Weasley in a raised voice, "this time Willy's been caught selling biting doorknobs to Muggles, and I don't think he'll be able to worm his way out of it because according to this article, two Muggles have lost fingers and are now in St. Mungo's for emergency bone regrowth and memory modification. Just think of it, Muggles in St. Mungo's! I wonder which ward they're in?"

And he looked eagerly around as though hoping to see a signpost.

"Didn't you say You-Know-Who's got a snake, Harry?" asked Fred, looking at his father for a reaction. "A massive one? You saw it the night he returned, didn't you?"

"That's enough," said Mrs. Weasley crossly. "Mad-Eye and Tonks are outside, Arthur, they want to come and see you. And you lot can wait outside," she added to her children and Harry. "You can come and say good-bye afterward. Go on. . . ."

They trooped back into the corridor. Mad-Eye and Tonks went in and closed the door of the ward behind them. Fred raised his eyebrows.

"Fine," he said coolly, rummaging in his pockets, "be like that. Don't tell us anything."

"Looking for these?" said George, holding out what looked like a tangle of flesh-colored string.

"You read my mind," said Fred, grinning. "Let's see if St. Mungo's puts Imperturbable Charms on its ward doors, shall we?"

He and George disentangled the string and separated five Extendable Ears from each other. Fred and George handed them around. Harry hesitated to take one.

"Go on, Harry, take it! You saved Dad's life, if anyone's got the right to eavesdrop on him it's you. . . ."

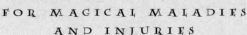
Grinning in spite of himself, Harry took the end of the string and inserted it into his ear as the twins had done.

"Okay, go!" Fred whispered.

The flesh-colored strings wriggled like long skinny worms, then snaked under the door. For a few seconds Harry could hear nothing, then he heard Tonks whispering as clearly as though she were standing right beside him.

". . . they searched the whole area but they couldn't find the snake anywhere, it just seems to have vanished after it attacked you, Arthur. . . . But You-Know-Who can't have expected a snake to get in, can he?"

"I reckon he sent it as a lookout," growled Moody, "'cause he's not had any luck so far, has he? No, I reckon he's trying to get a clearer picture of what he's facing and if Arthur hadn't been there the beast would've had much more time to look around. So Potter says he saw it all happen?"

"Yes," said Mrs. Weasley. She sounded rather uneasy. "You know, Dumbledore seems almost to have been waiting for Harry to see something like this. . . ."

"Yeah, well," said Moody, "there's something funny about the Potter kid, we all know that."

"Dumbledore seemed worried about Harry when I spoke to him this morning," whispered Mrs. Weasley.

"'Course he's worried," growled Moody. "The boy's seeing things from inside You-Know-Who's snake. . . . Obviously, Potter doesn't realize what that means, but if You-Know-Who's possessing him —"

Harry pulled the Extendable Ear out of his own, his heart hammering very fast and heat rushing up his face. He looked around at the others. They were all staring at him, the strings still trailing from their ears, looking suddenly fearful.

CHRISTMAS ON THE CLOSED WARD

Was this why Dumbledore would no longer meet Harry's eyes? Did he expect to see Voldemort staring out of them, afraid, perhaps, that their vivid green might turn suddenly to scarlet, with catlike slits for pupils? Harry remembered how the snakelike face of Voldemort had once forced itself out of the back of Professor Quirrell's head, and he ran his hand over the back of his own, wondering what it would feel like if Voldemort burst out of his skull. . . .

He felt dirty, contaminated, as though he were carrying some deadly germ, unworthy to sit on the underground train back from the hospital with innocent, clean people whose minds and bodies were free of the taint of Voldemort. . . . He had not merely seen the snake, he had *been* the snake, he knew it now. . . .

And then a truly terrible thought occurred to him, a memory bobbing to the surface of his mind, one that made his insides writhe and squirm like serpents. . . .

"What's he after apart from followers?"

"Stuff he can only get by stealth . . . like a weapon. Something he didn't have last time."

I'm the weapon, Harry thought, and it was as though poison were pumping through his veins, chilling him, bringing him out in a sweat as he swayed with the train through the dark tunnel. *I'm the one Voldemort's trying to use, that's why they've got guards around me everywhere I go, it's not for my protection, it's for other people's, only it's not working, they can't have someone on me all the time at Hogwarts. . . . I did attack Mr. Weasley last night, it was me, Voldemort made me do it and he could be inside me, listening to my thoughts right now. . . .*

"Are you all right, Harry, dear?" whispered Mrs. Weasley, leaning across Ginny to speak to him as the train rattled along through its dark tunnel. "You don't look very well. Are you feeling sick?"

They were all watching him. He shook his head violently and stared up at an advertisement for home insurance.

"Harry, dear, are you *sure* you're all right?" said Mrs. Weasley in a worried voice, as they walked around the unkempt patch of grass in the middle of Grimmauld Place. "You look ever so pale. . . . Are you sure you slept this morning? You go upstairs to bed right now, and you can have a couple of hours' sleep before dinner, all right?"

He nodded; here was a ready-made excuse not to talk to any of the others, which was precisely what he wanted, so when she opened the front door he proceeded straight past the troll's leg umbrella stand and up the stairs and hurried into his and Ron's bedroom.

Here he began to pace up and down, past the two beds and Phineas Nigellus's empty portrait, his brain teeming and seething with questions and ever more dreadful ideas. . . .

How had he become a snake? Perhaps he was an Animagus. . . . No, he couldn't be, he would know. . . . perhaps *Voldemort* was an Animagus. . . . *Yes,* thought Harry, *that would fit, he* would *turn into a snake of course . . . and when he's possessing me, then we both transform. . . . That still doesn't explain how come I got to London and back to my bed in the space of about five minutes, though. . . . But then Voldemort's about the most powerful wizard in the world, apart from*

Dumbledore, it's probably no problem at all to him to transport people like that. . . .

And then, with a terrible stab of panic he thought, *but this is insane — if Voldemort's possessing me, I'm giving him a clear view into the headquarters of the Order of the Phoenix right now! He'll know who's in the Order and where Sirius is . . . and I've heard loads of stuff I shouldn't have, everything Sirius told me the first night I was here. . . .*

There was only one thing for it: He would have to leave Grimmauld Place straightaway. He would spend Christmas at Hogwarts without the others, which would keep them safe over the holidays at least. . . . But no, that wouldn't do, there were still plenty of people at Hogwarts to maim and injure, what if it was Seamus, Dean, or Neville next time? He stopped his pacing and stood staring at Phineas Nigellus's empty frame. A leaden sensation was settling in the pit of his stomach. He had no alternative: He was going to have to return to Privet Drive, cut himself off from other wizards entirely. . . .

Well, if he had to do it, he thought, there was no point hanging around. Trying with all his might not to think how the Dursleys were going to react when they found him on their doorstep six months earlier than they had expected, he strode over to his trunk, slammed the lid shut and locked it, then glanced around automatically for Hedwig before remembering that she was still at Hogwarts — well, her cage would be one less thing to carry — he seized one end of his trunk and had dragged it halfway toward the door when a sneaky voice said, "Running away, are we?"

He looked around. Phineas Nigellus had appeared upon the canvas of his portrait and was leaning against the frame, watching Harry with an amused expression on his face.

"Not running away, no," said Harry shortly, dragging his trunk a few more feet across the room.

"I thought," said Phineas Nigellus, stroking his pointed beard, "that to belong in Gryffindor House you were supposed to be *brave*?

It looks to me as though you would have been better off in my own House. We Slytherins are brave, yes, but not stupid. For instance, given the choice, we will always choose to save our own necks."

"It's not my own neck I'm saving," said Harry tersely, tugging the trunk over a patch of particularly uneven, moth-eaten carpet right in front of the door.

"Oh I *see*," said Phineas Nigellus, still stroking his beard. "This is no cowardly flight — you are being *noble*."

Harry ignored him. His hand was on the doorknob when Phineas Nigellus said lazily, "I have a message for you from Albus Dumbledore."

Harry spun around.

"What is it?"

"Stay where you are."

"I haven't moved!" said Harry, his hand still upon the doorknob. "So what's the message?"

"I have just given it to you, dolt," said Phineas Nigellus smoothly. "Dumbledore says, *'Stay where you are.'*"

"Why?" said Harry eagerly, dropping the end of his trunk. "Why does he want me to stay? What else did he say?"

"Nothing whatsoever," said Phineas Nigellus, raising a thin black eyebrow as though he found Harry impertinent.

Harry's temper rose to the surface like a snake rearing from long grass. He was exhausted, he was confused beyond measure, he had experienced terror, relief, and then terror again in the last twelve hours, and still Dumbledore did not want to talk to him!

"So that's it, is it?" he said loudly. "*Stay there?* That's all anyone could tell me after I got attacked by those dementors too! Just stay put while the grown-ups sort it out, Harry! We won't bother telling you anything, though, because your tiny little brain might not be able to cope with it!"

"You know," said Phineas Nigellus, even more loudly than Harry, "this is precisely why I *loathed* being a teacher! Young people are so infernally convinced that they are absolutely right about everything. Has it not occurred to you, my poor puffed-up popinjay, that there might be an excellent reason why the headmaster of Hogwarts is not confiding every tiny detail of his plans to you? Have you never paused, while feeling hard-done-by, to note that following Dumbledore's orders has never yet led you into harm? No. No, like all young people, you are quite sure that you alone feel and think, you alone recognize danger, you alone are the only one clever enough to realize what the Dark Lord may be planning. . . ."

"He *is* planning something to do with me, then?" said Harry swiftly.

"Did I say that?" said Phineas Nigellus, idly examining his silk gloves. "Now, if you will excuse me, I have better things to do than to listen to adolescent agonizing. . . . Good day to you. . . ."

And he strolled into his frame and out of sight.

"Fine, go then!" Harry bellowed at the empty frame. "And tell Dumbledore thanks for nothing!"

The empty canvas remained silent. Fuming, Harry dragged his trunk back to the foot of his bed, then threw himself facedown upon the moth-eaten covers, his eyes shut, his body heavy and aching. . . .

He felt he had journeyed miles and miles. . . . It seemed impossible that less than twenty-four hours ago Cho Chang had been approaching him under the mistletoe. . . . He was so tired. . . . He was scared to sleep . . . yet he did not know how long he could fight it. . . . Dumbledore had told him to stay. . . . That must mean he was allowed to sleep. . . . But he was scared. . . . What if it happened again . . . ?

He was sinking into shadows. . . .

It was as though a film in his head had been waiting to start. He was walking down a deserted corridor toward a plain black door, past rough stone walls, torches, and an open doorway onto a flight of stone steps leading downstairs on the left. . . .

He reached the black door but could not open it. . . . He stood gazing at it, desperate for entry. . . . Something he wanted with all his heart lay beyond. . . . A prize beyond his dreams. . . . If only his scar would stop prickling . . . then he would be able to think more clearly. . . .

"Harry," said Ron's voice, from far, far away, "Mum says dinner's ready, but she'll save you something if you want to stay in bed. . . ."

Harry opened his eyes, but Ron had already left the room.

He doesn't want to be on his own with me, Harry thought. *Not after what he heard Moody say . . .*

He supposed none of them would want him there anymore now that they knew what was inside him. . . .

He would not go down to dinner; he would not inflict his company upon them. He turned over onto his other side and after a while dropped back off to sleep, waking much later in the early hours of the morning, with his insides aching with hunger, and Ron snoring in the next bed. Squinting around the room he saw the dark outline of Phineas Nigellus standing again in his portrait and it occurred to Harry that Dumbledore had probably set Phineas Nigellus to watch over him, in case he attacked somebody else.

The feeling of being unclean intensified. He half wished he had not obeyed Dumbledore and stayed. . . . If this was how life was going to be in Grimmauld Place from now on, maybe he would be better off in Privet Drive after all.

Everybody else spent the following morning putting up Christmas decorations. Harry could not remember Sirius ever being in such a good mood; he was actually singing carols, apparently delighted that he was to have company over Christmas. Harry could hear his voice echoing up through the floor in the cold and empty drawing room where he was sitting alone, watching the sky outside the windows growing whiter, threatening snow, all the time feeling a savage pleasure that he was giving the others the opportunity to keep talking about him, as they were bound to be doing. When he heard Mrs.

Weasley calling his name softly up the stairs around lunchtime he retreated farther upstairs and ignored her.

It was around six o'clock in the evening that the doorbell rang and Mrs. Black started screaming again. Assuming that Mundungus or some other Order member had come to call, Harry merely settled himself more comfortably against the wall of Buckbeak the hippogriff's room where he was hiding, trying to ignore how hungry he felt as he fed Buckbeak dead rats. It came as a slight shock when somebody hammered hard on the door a few minutes later.

"I know you're in there," said Hermione's voice. "Will you please come out? I want to talk to you."

"What are *you* doing here?" Harry asked her, pulling open the door, as Buckbeak resumed his scratching at the straw-strewn floor for any fragments of rat he might have dropped. "I thought you were skiing with your mum and dad."

"Well, to tell the truth, skiing's not *really* my thing," said Hermione. "So I've come for Christmas." There was snow in her hair and her face was pink with cold. "But don't tell Ron that, I told him it's really good because he kept laughing so much. Anyway, Mum and Dad are a bit disappointed, but I've told them that everyone who's serious about the exams is staying at Hogwarts to study. They want me to do well, they'll understand. Anyway," she said briskly, "let's go to your bedroom, Ron's mum's lit a fire in there and she's sent up sandwiches."

Harry followed her back to the second floor. When he entered the bedroom he was rather surprised to see both Ron and Ginny waiting for them, sitting on Ron's bed.

"I came on the Knight Bus," said Hermione airily, pulling off her jacket before Harry had time to speak. "Dumbledore told me what had happened first thing yesterday morning, but I had to wait for term to end officially before setting off. Umbridge is already livid that you lot disappeared right under her nose, even though Dumbledore told her Mr. Weasley was in St. Mungo's, and he'd given you all permission to visit. So . . ."

She sat down next to Ginny, and the two girls and Ron looked up at Harry.

"How're you feeling?" asked Hermione.

"Fine," said Harry stiffly.

"Oh, don't lie, Harry," she said impatiently. "Ron and Ginny say you've been hiding from everyone since you got back from St. Mungo's."

"They do, do they?" said Harry, glaring at Ron and Ginny. Ron looked down at his feet but Ginny seemed quite unabashed.

"Well, you have!" she said. "And you won't look at any of us!"

"It's you lot who won't look at me!" said Harry angrily.

"Maybe you're taking it in turns to look and keep missing each other," suggested Hermione, the corners of her mouth twitching.

"Very funny," snapped Harry, turning away.

"Oh, stop feeling all misunderstood," said Hermione sharply. "Look, the others have told me what you overheard last night on the Extendable Ears —"

"Yeah?" growled Harry, his hands deep in his pockets as he watched the snow now falling thickly outside. "All been talking about me, have you? Well, I'm getting used to it. . . ."

"We wanted to talk *to you*, Harry," said Ginny, "but as you've been hiding ever since we got back —"

"I didn't want anyone to talk to me," said Harry, who was feeling more and more nettled.

"Well, that was a bit stupid of you," said Ginny angrily, "seeing as you don't know anyone but me who's been possessed by You-Know-Who, and I can tell you how it feels."

Harry remained quite still as the impact of these words hit him. Then he turned on the spot to face her.

"I forgot," he said.

"Lucky you," said Ginny coolly.

"I'm sorry," Harry said, and he meant it. "So . . . so do you think I'm being possessed, then?"

"Well, can you remember everything you've been doing?" Ginny asked. "Are there big blank periods where you don't know what you've been up to?"

Harry racked his brains.

"No," he said.

"Then You-Know-Who hasn't ever possessed you," said Ginny simply. "When he did it to me, I couldn't remember what I'd been doing for hours at a time. I'd find myself somewhere and not know how I got there."

Harry hardly dared believe her, yet his heart was lightening almost in spite of himself.

"That dream I had about your dad and the snake, though —"

"Harry, you've had these dreams before," Hermione said. "You had flashes of what Voldemort was up to last year."

"This was different," said Harry, shaking his head. "I was inside that snake. It was like I *was* the snake. . . . What if Voldemort somehow transported me to London — ?"

"One day," said Hermione, sounding thoroughly exasperated, "you'll read *Hogwarts: A History,* and perhaps that will remind you that you can't Apparate or Disapparate inside Hogwarts. Even Voldemort couldn't just make you fly out of your dormitory, Harry."

"You didn't leave your bed, mate," said Ron. "I saw you thrashing around in your sleep about a minute before we could wake you up. . . ."

Harry started pacing up and down the room again, thinking. What they were all saying was not only comforting, it made sense. . . . Without really thinking he took a sandwich from the plate on the bed and crammed it hungrily into his mouth. . . .

I'm not the weapon after all, thought Harry. His heart swelled with happiness and relief, and he felt like joining in as they heard Sirius tramping past their door toward Buckbeak's room, singing "God Rest Ye Merry, Hippogriffs" at the top of his voice.

How could he have dreamed of returning to Privet Drive for Christmas? Sirius's delight at having the house full again, and especially at having Harry back, was infectious. He was no longer their sullen host of the summer; now he seemed determined that everyone should enjoy themselves as much, if not more, than they would have done at Hogwarts, and he worked tirelessly in the run-up to Christmas Day, cleaning and decorating with their help, so that by the time they all went to bed on Christmas Eve the house was barely recognizable. The tarnished chandeliers were no longer hung with cobwebs but with garlands of holly and gold and silver streamers; magical snow glittered in heaps over the threadbare carpets; a great Christmas tree, obtained by Mundungus and decorated with live fairies, blocked Sirius's family tree from view; and even the stuffed elf heads on the hall wall wore Father Christmas hats and beards.

Harry awoke on Christmas morning to find a stack of presents at the foot of his bed and Ron already halfway through opening his own, rather larger, pile.

"Good haul this year," he informed Harry through a cloud of paper. "Thanks for the Broom Compass, it's excellent, beats Hermione's — she's got me a *homework planner* —"

Harry sorted through his presents and found one with Hermione's handwriting on it. She had given him too a book that resembled a diary, except that it said things like *"Do it today or later you'll pay!"* every time he opened a page.

Sirius and Lupin had given Harry a set of excellent books entitled *Practical Defensive Magic and Its Use Against the Dark Arts,* which had superb, moving color illustrations of all the counterjinxes and hexes it described. Harry flicked through the first volume eagerly; he could see it was going to be highly useful in his plans for the D.A. Hagrid had sent a furry brown wallet that had fangs, which were presumably supposed to be an antitheft device, but unfortunately prevented Harry putting any money in without getting his fingers ripped off. Tonks's present was a small, working model of a Firebolt, which Harry watched fly around the room, wishing he still had his full-size version; Ron had given him an enormous box of Every-Flavor Beans; Mr. and Mrs. Weasley the usual hand-knitted jumper and some mince pies; and Dobby, a truly dreadful painting that Harry suspected had been done by the elf himself. He had just turned it upside down to see whether it looked better that way when, with a loud *crack*, Fred and George Apparated at the foot of his bed.

"Merry Christmas," said George. "Don't go downstairs for a bit."

"Why not?" said Ron.

"Mum's crying again," said Fred heavily. "Percy sent back his Christmas jumper."

"Without a note," added George. "Hasn't asked how Dad is or visited him or anything. . . ."

"We tried to comfort her," said Fred, moving around the bed to look at Harry's portrait. "Told her Percy's nothing more than a humongous pile of rat droppings —"

"— didn't work," said George, helping himself to a Chocolate Frog. "So Lupin took over. Best let him cheer her up before we go down for breakfast, I reckon."

"What's that supposed to be anyway?" asked Fred, squinting at Dobby's painting. "Looks like a gibbon with two black eyes."

"It's Harry!" said George, pointing at the back of the picture. "Says so on the back!"

"Good likeness," said Fred, grinning. Harry threw his new homework diary at him; it hit the wall opposite and fell to the floor where it said happily, *"If you've dotted the i's and crossed the t's then you may do whatever you please!"*

They got up and dressed; they could hear various inhabitants of the house calling "Merry Christmas" to each other. On their way downstairs they met Hermione. "Thanks for the book, Harry!" she said happily. "I've been wanting that *New Theory of Numerology* for ages! And that perfume is really unusual, Ron."

"No problem," said Ron. "Who's that for anyway?" he added, nodding at the neatly wrapped present she was carrying.

"Kreacher," said Hermione brightly.

"It had better not be clothes!" said Ron warningly. "You know what Sirius said, Kreacher knows too much, we can't set him free!"

"It isn't clothes," said Hermione, "although if I had my way I'd certainly give him something to wear other than that filthy old rag. No, it's a patchwork quilt, I thought it would brighten up his bedroom."

"What bedroom?" said Harry, dropping his voice to a whisper as they were passing the portrait of Sirius's mother.

"Well, Sirius says it's not so much a bedroom, more a kind of — *den*," said Hermione. "Apparently he sleeps under the boiler in that cupboard off the kitchen."

Mrs. Weasley was the only person in the basement when they arrived there. She was standing at the stove and sounded as though she had a bad head cold when she wished them Merry Christmas, and they all averted their eyes.

"So, this is Kreacher's bedroom?" said Ron, strolling over to a dingy door in the corner opposite the pantry which Harry had never seen open.

"Yes," said Hermione, now sounding a little nervous. "Er . . . I think we'd better knock . . ."

Ron rapped the door with his knuckles but there was no reply.

"He must be sneaking around upstairs," he said, and without further ado pulled open the door. *"Urgh."*

Harry peered inside. Most of the cupboard was taken up with a very large and old-fashioned boiler, but in the foot's space underneath the pipes Kreacher had made himself something that looked like a nest. A jumble of assorted rags and smelly old blankets were piled on the floor and the small dent in the middle of it showed where Kreacher curled up to sleep every night. Here and there among the material were stale bread crusts and moldy old bits of cheese. In a far corner glinted small objects and coins that Harry guessed Kreacher had saved, magpielike, from Sirius's purge of the house, and he had also managed to retrieve the silver-framed family photographs that Sirius had thrown away over the summer. Their glass might be shattered, but still the little black-and-white people inside them peered haughtily up at him, including — he felt a little jolt in his stomach — the dark, heavy-lidded woman whose trial he had witnessed in Dumbledore's Pensieve: Bellatrix Lestrange. By the looks of it, hers was Kreacher's favorite photograph; he had placed it to the fore of all the others and had mended the glass clumsily with Spellotape.

"I think I'll just leave his present here," said Hermione, laying the package neatly in the middle of the depression in the rags and blankets and closing the door quietly. "He'll find it later, that'll be fine. . . ."

"Come to think of it," said Sirius, emerging from the pantry carrying a large turkey as they closed the cupboard door, "has anyone actually seen Kreacher lately?"

"I haven't seen him since the night we came back here," said Harry. "You were ordering him out of the kitchen."

"Yeah . . ." said Sirius, frowning. "You know, I think that's the last time I saw him, too. . . . He must be hiding upstairs somewhere. . . ."

"He couldn't have left, could he?" said Harry. "I mean, when you said 'out,' maybe he thought you meant, get out of the house?"

"No, no, house-elves can't leave unless they're given clothes, they're tied to their family's house," said Sirius.

"They can leave the house if they really want to," Harry contradicted him. "Dobby did, he left the Malfoys' to give me warnings three years ago. He had to punish himself afterward, but he still managed it."

Sirius looked slightly disconcerted for a moment, then said, "I'll look for him later, I expect I'll find him upstairs crying his eyes out over my mother's old bloomers or something. . . . Of course, he might have crawled into the airing cupboard and died. . . . But I mustn't get my hopes up. . . ."

Fred, George, and Ron laughed; Hermione, however, looked reproachful.

Once they had had their Christmas lunch, the Weasleys and Harry and Hermione were planning to pay Mr. Weasley another visit, escorted by Mad-Eye and Lupin. Mundungus turned up in time for Christmas pudding and trifle, having managed to "borrow" a car for the occasion, as the Underground did not run on Christmas Day. The car, which Harry doubted very much had been taken with the knowledge or consent of its owner, had had a similar Enlarging Spell put upon it as the Weasleys' old Ford Anglia; although normally proportioned outside, ten people with Mundungus driving were able to fit into it quite comfortably. Mrs. Weasley hesitated at the point of getting inside; Harry knew that her disapproval of Mundungus was battling with her dislike of traveling without magic; finally the cold outside and her children's pleading triumphed, and she settled herself into the backseat between Fred and Bill with good grace.

The journey to St. Mungo's was quite quick, as there was very little traffic on the roads. A small trickle of witches and wizards were creeping furtively up the otherwise deserted street to visit the hospital. Harry and the others got out of the car, and Mundungus drove off around the corner to wait for them; they strolled casually toward the window where the dummy in green nylon stood, then, one by one, stepped through the glass.

The reception area looked pleasantly festive: The crystal orbs that illuminated St. Mungo's had been turned to red and gold so that they became gigantic, glowing Christmas baubles; holly hung around every doorway, and shining white Christmas trees covered in magical snow and icicles glittered in every corner, each topped with a gleaming gold star. It was less crowded than the last time they had been there, although halfway across the room Harry found himself shunted aside by a witch with a walnut jammed up her left nostril.

"Family argument, eh?" smirked the blonde witch behind the desk. "You're the third I've seen today . . . Spell Damage, fourth floor . . ."

They found Mr. Weasley propped up in bed with the remains of his turkey dinner on a tray in his lap and a rather sheepish expression on his face.

"Everything all right, Arthur?" asked Mrs. Weasley, after they had all greeted Mr. Weasley and handed over their presents.

"Fine, fine," said Mr. Weasley, a little too heartily. "You — er — haven't seen Healer Smethwyck, have you?"

"No," said Mrs. Weasley suspiciously, "why?"

"Nothing, nothing," said Mr. Weasley airily, starting to unwrap his pile of gifts. "Well, everyone had a good day? What did you all get for Christmas? Oh, *Harry* — this is absolutely *wonderful* —"

For he had just opened Harry's gift of fuse-wire and screwdrivers. Mrs. Weasley did not seem entirely satisfied with Mr. Weasley's answer. As her husband leaned over to shake Harry's hand, she peered at the bandaging under his nightshirt.

"Arthur," she said, with a snap in her voice like a mousetrap, "you've had your bandages changed. Why have you had your bandages changed a day early, Arthur? They told me they wouldn't need doing until tomorrow."

"What?" said Mr. Weasley, looking rather frightened and pulling the bed covers higher up his chest. "No, no — it's nothing — it's — I —"

He seemed to deflate under Mrs. Weasley's piercing gaze.

"Well — now don't get upset, Molly, but Augustus Pye had an idea. . . . He's the Trainee Healer, you know, lovely young chap and very interested in . . . um . . . complementary medicine. . . . I mean, some of these old Muggle remedies . . . well, they're called *stitches,* Molly, and they work very well on — on Muggle wounds —"

Mrs. Weasley let out an ominous noise somewhere between a shriek and a snarl. Lupin strolled away from the bed and over to the werewolf, who had no visitors and was looking rather wistfully at the crowd around Mr. Weasley; Bill muttered something about getting himself a cup of tea and Fred and George leapt up to accompany him, grinning.

"Do you mean to tell me," said Mrs. Weasley, her voice growing louder with every word and apparently unaware that her fellow visitors were scurrying for cover, "that you have been messing about with Muggle remedies?"

"Not messing about, Molly, dear," said Mr. Weasley imploringly. "It was just — just something Pye and I thought we'd try — only, most unfortunately — well, with these particular kinds of wounds — it doesn't seem to work as well as we'd hoped —"

"Meaning?"

"Well . . . well, I don't know whether you know what — what stitches are?"

"It sounds as though you've been trying to sew your skin back together," said Mrs. Weasley with a snort of mirthless laughter, "but even you, Arthur, wouldn't be *that* stupid —"

"I fancy a cup of tea too," said Harry, jumping to his feet.

Hermione, Ron, and Ginny almost sprinted to the door with him. As it swung closed behind them, they heard Mrs. Weasley shriek, "WHAT DO YOU MEAN, THAT'S THE GENERAL IDEA?"

"Typical Dad," said Ginny, shaking her head as they set off up the corridor. "Stitches . . . I ask you . . ."

"Well, you know, they do work well on non-magical wounds," said Hermione fairly. "I suppose something in that snake's venom dissolves them or something. . . . I wonder where the tearoom is?"

"Fifth floor," said Harry, remembering the sign over the Welcome Witch's desk.

They walked along the corridor through a set of double doors and found a rickety staircase lined with more portraits of brutal-looking Healers. As they climbed it, the various Healers called out to them, diagnosing odd complaints and suggesting horrible remedies. Ron was seriously affronted when a medieval wizard called out that he clearly had a bad case of spattergroit.

"And what's that supposed to be?" he asked angrily, as the Healer pursued him through six more portraits, shoving the occupants out of the way.

"'Tis a most grievous affliction of the skin, young master, that will leave you pockmarked and more gruesome even than you are now —"

"Watch who you're calling gruesome!" said Ron, his ears turning red.

"The only remedy is to take the liver of a toad, bind it tight about your throat, stand naked by the full moon in a barrel of eels' eyes —"

"I have not got spattergroit!"

"But the unsightly blemishes upon your visage, young master —"

"They're freckles!" said Ron furiously. "Now get back in your own picture and leave me alone!"

He rounded on the others, who were all keeping determinedly straight faces.

"What floor's this?"

"I think it's the fifth," said Hermione.

"Nah, it's the fourth," said Harry, "one more —"

But as he stepped onto the landing he came to an abrupt halt, staring at the small window set into the double doors that marked the start of a corridor signposted SPELL DAMAGE. A man was peering out at them all with his nose pressed against the glass. He had wavy blond hair, bright blue eyes, and a broad vacant smile that revealed dazzlingly white teeth.

"Blimey!" said Ron, also staring at the man.

"Oh my goodness," said Hermione suddenly, sounding breathless. "Professor Lockhart!"

Their ex-Defense Against the Dark Arts teacher pushed open the doors and moved toward them, wearing a long lilac dressing gown.

"Well, hello there!" he said. "I expect you'd like my autograph, would you?"

"Hasn't changed much, has he?" Harry muttered to Ginny, who grinned.

"Er — how are you, Professor?" said Ron, sounding slightly guilty. It had been Ron's malfunctioning wand that had damaged Professor Lockhart's memory so badly that he had landed here in the first place, though, as Lockhart had been attempting to permanently wipe Harry and Ron's memories at the time, Harry's sympathy was limited.

"I'm very well indeed, thank you!" said Lockhart exuberantly, pulling a rather battered peacock-feather quill from his pocket. "Now, how many autographs would you like? I can do joined-up writing now, you know!"

"Er — we don't want any at the moment, thanks," said Ron, raising his eyebrows at Harry, who asked, "Professor, should you be wandering around the corridors? Shouldn't you be in a ward?"

The smile faded slowly from Lockhart's face. For a few moments he gazed intently at Harry, then he said, "Haven't we met?"

"Er . . . yeah, we have," said Harry. "You used to teach us at Hogwarts, remember?"

"Teach?" repeated Lockhart, looking faintly unsettled. "Me? Did I?"

And then the smile reappeared upon his face so suddenly it was rather alarming. "Taught you everything you know, I expect, did I? Well, how about those autographs, then? Shall we say a round dozen, you can give them to all your little friends then and nobody will be left out!"

But just then a head poked out of a door at the far end of the corridor and a voice said, "Gilderoy, you naughty boy, where have you wandered off to?"

A motherly looking Healer wearing a tinsel wreath in her hair came bustling up the corridor, smiling warmly at Harry and the others.

"Oh Gilderoy, you've got visitors! How *lovely*, and on Christmas Day too! Do you know, he *never* gets visitors, poor lamb, and I can't think why, he's such a sweetie, aren't you?"

"We're doing autographs!" Gilderoy told the Healer with another glittering smile. "They want loads of them, won't take no for an answer! I just hope we've got enough photographs!"

"Listen to him," said the Healer, taking Lockhart's arm and beaming fondly at him as though he were a precocious two-year-old. "He was rather well known a few years ago; we very much hope that this liking for giving autographs is a sign that his memory might be coming back a little bit. Will you step this way? He's in a closed ward, you know, he must have slipped out while I was bringing in the Christmas presents, the door's usually kept locked . . . not that he's dangerous! But," she lowered her voice to a whisper, "bit of a danger to himself, bless him. . . . Doesn't know who he is, you see, wanders off and can't remember how to get back. . . . It *is* nice of you to have come to see him —"

"Er," said Ron, gesturing uselessly at the floor above, "actually, we were just — er —"

But the Healer was smiling expectantly at them, and Ron's feeble mutter of "going to have a cup of tea" trailed away into nothingness. They looked at one another rather hopelessly and then followed Lockhart and his Healer along the corridor.

"Let's not stay long," Ron said quietly.

The Healer pointed her wand at the door of the Janus Thickey ward and muttered *"Alohomora."* The door swung open and she led the way inside, keeping a firm grasp on Gilderoy's arm until she had settled him into an armchair beside his bed.

"This is our long-term resident ward," she informed Harry, Ron, Hermione, and Ginny in a low voice. "For permanent spell damage, you know. Of course, with intensive remedial potions and charms and a bit of luck, we can produce some improvement. . . . Gilderoy does seem to be getting back some sense of himself, and we've seen a real improvement in Mr. Bode, he seems to be regaining the power of speech very well, though he isn't speaking any language we recognize yet. . . . Well, I must finish giving out the Christmas presents, I'll leave you all to chat. . . ."

Harry looked around; this ward bore unmistakable signs of being a permanent home to its residents. They had many more personal effects around their beds than in Mr. Weasley's ward; the wall around Gilderoy's headboard, for instance, was papered with pictures of himself, all beaming toothily and waving at the new arrivals. He had autographed many of them to himself in disjointed, childish writing. The moment he had been deposited in his chair by the Healer, Gilderoy pulled a fresh stack of photographs toward him, seized a quill, and started signing them all feverishly.

"You can put them in envelopes," he said to Ginny, throwing the signed pictures into her lap one by one as he finished them. "I am not forgotten, you know, no, I still receive a very great deal of fan mail. . . . Gladys Gudgeon writes *weekly*. . . . I just wish I knew *why*. . . ." He paused, looking faintly puzzled, then beamed again and returned to his signing with renewed vigor. "I suspect it is simply my good looks. . . ."

A sallow-skinned, mournful-looking wizard lay in the bed opposite, staring at the ceiling; he was mumbling to himself and seemed quite unaware of anything around him. Two beds along was a woman whose entire head was covered in fur; Harry remembered something similar happening to Hermione during their second year, although fortunately the damage, in her case, had not been permanent. At the far end of the ward flowery curtains had been drawn around two beds to give the occupants and their visitors some privacy.

"Here you are, Agnes," said the Healer brightly to the furry-faced woman, handing her a small pile of Christmas presents. "See, not forgotten, are you? And your son's sent an owl to say he's visiting tonight, so that's nice, isn't it?"

Agnes gave several loud barks.

"And look, Broderick, you've been sent a potted plant and a lovely calendar with a different fancy hippogriff for each month, they'll brighten things up, won't they?" said the Healer, bustling along to the mumbling man, setting a rather ugly plant with long, swaying tentacles on the bedside cabinet and fixing the calendar to the wall with her wand. "And — oh, Mrs. Longbottom, are you leaving already?"

Harry's head spun round. The curtains had been drawn back from the two beds at the end of the ward and two visitors were walking back down the aisle between the beds: a formidable-looking old witch wearing a long green dress, a moth-eaten fox fur, and a pointed hat decorated with what was unmistakably a stuffed vulture and, trailing behind her looking thoroughly depressed — *Neville*.

With a sudden rush of understanding, Harry realized who the people in the end beds must be. He cast around wildly for some means of distracting the others so that Neville could leave the ward unnoticed and unquestioned, but Ron had looked up at the sound of the name "Longbottom" too, and before Harry could stop him had called, *"Neville!"*

Neville jumped and cowered as though a bullet had narrowly missed him.

"It's us, Neville!" said Ron brightly, getting to his feet. "Have you seen? Lockhart's here! Who've you been visiting?"

"Friends of yours, Neville, dear?" said Neville's grandmother graciously, bearing down upon them all.

Neville looked as though he would rather be anywhere in the world but here. A dull purple flush was creeping up his plump face and he was not making eye contact with any of them.

"Ah, yes," said his grandmother, peering at Harry and sticking out a shriveled, clawlike hand for him to shake. "Yes, yes, I know who you are, of course. Neville speaks most highly of you."

"Er — thanks," said Harry, shaking hands. Neville did not look at him, but stared at his own feet, the color deepening in his face all the while.

"And you two are clearly Weasleys," Mrs. Longbottom continued, proffering her hand regally to Ron and Ginny in turn. "Yes, I know your parents — not well, of course — but fine people, fine people . . . and you must be Hermione Granger?"

Hermione looked rather startled that Mrs. Longbottom knew her name, but shook hands all the same.

"Yes, Neville's told me all about you. Helped him out of a few sticky spots, haven't you? He's a good boy," she said, casting a sternly appraising look down her rather bony nose at Neville, "but he hasn't got his father's talent, I'm afraid to say. . . ." And she jerked her head in the direction of the two beds at the end of the ward, so that the stuffed vulture on her hat trembled alarmingly.

"What?" said Ron, looking amazed (Harry wanted to stamp on Ron's foot, but that sort of thing was much harder to bring off unnoticed when you were wearing jeans rather than robes). "Is that your *dad* down the end, Neville?"

"What's this?" said Mrs. Longbottom sharply. "Haven't you told your friends about your parents, Neville?"

Neville took a deep breath, looked up at the ceiling, and shook his head. Harry could not remember ever feeling sorrier for anyone, but he could not think of any way of helping Neville out of the situation.

"Well, it's nothing to be ashamed of!" said Mrs. Longbottom angrily. "You should be *proud*, Neville, *proud*! They didn't give their health and their sanity so their only son would be ashamed of them, you know!"

"I'm not ashamed," said Neville very faintly, still looking anywhere but at Harry and the others. Ron was now standing on tiptoe to look over at the inhabitants of the two beds.

"Well, you've got a funny way of showing it!" said Mrs. Longbottom. "My son and his wife," she said, turning haughtily to Harry, Ron, Hermione, and Ginny, "were tortured into insanity by You-Know-Who's followers."

Hermione and Ginny both clapped their hands over their mouths. Ron stopped craning his neck to catch a glimpse of Neville's parents and looked mortified.

"They were Aurors, you know, and very well respected within the Wizarding community," Mrs. Longbottom went on. "Highly gifted, the pair of them. I — yes, Alice dear, what is it?"

Neville's mother had come edging down the ward in her nightdress. She no longer had the plump, happy-looking face Harry had seen in Moody's old photograph of the original Order of the Phoenix. Her face was thin and worn now, her eyes seemed overlarge, and her hair, which had turned white, was wispy and dead-looking. She did not seem to want to speak, or perhaps she was not able to, but she made timid motions toward Neville, holding something in her outstretched hand.

"Again?" said Mrs. Longbottom, sounding slightly weary. "Very well, Alice dear, very well — Neville, take it, whatever it is. . . ."

But Neville had already stretched out his hand, into which his mother dropped an empty Drooble's Blowing Gum wrapper.

"Very nice, dear," said Neville's grandmother in a falsely cheery voice, patting his mother on the shoulder. But Neville said quietly, "Thanks Mum."

His mother tottered away, back up the ward, humming to herself. Neville looked around at the others, his expression defiant, as though daring them to laugh, but Harry did not think he'd ever found anything less funny in his life.

"Well, we'd better get back," sighed Mrs. Longbottom, drawing on long green gloves. "Very nice to have met you all. Neville, put that wrapper in the bin, she must have given you enough of them to paper your bedroom by now. . . ."

But as they left, Harry was sure he saw Neville slip the wrapper into his pocket.

The door closed behind them.

"I never knew," said Hermione, who looked tearful.

"Nor did I," said Ron rather hoarsely.

"Nor me," whispered Ginny.

They all looked at Harry.

"I did," he said glumly. "Dumbledore told me but I promised I wouldn't mention it . . . that's what Bellatrix Lestrange got sent to Azkaban for, using the Cruciatus Curse on Neville's parents until they lost their minds."

"Bellatrix Lestrange did that?" whispered Hermione, horrified. "That woman Kreacher's got a photo of in his den?"

There was a long silence, broken by Lockhart's angry voice. "Look, I didn't learn joined-up writing for nothing, you know!"

OCCLUMENCY

Kreacher, it transpired, had been lurking in the attic. Sirius said he had found him up there, covered in dust, no doubt looking for more relics of the Black family to hide in his cupboard. Though Sirius seemed satisfied with this story, it made Harry uneasy. Kreacher seemed to be in a better mood on his reappearance, his bitter muttering had subsided somewhat, and he submitted to orders more docilely than usual, though once or twice Harry caught the house-elf staring avidly at him, always looking quickly away when he saw that Harry had noticed.

Harry did not mention his vague suspicions to Sirius, whose cheerfulness was evaporating fast now that Christmas was over. As the date of their departure back to Hogwarts drew nearer, he became more and more prone to what Mrs. Weasley called "fits of the sullens," in which he would become taciturn and grumpy, often withdrawing to Buckbeak's room for hours at a time. His gloom seeped through the house, oozing under doorways like some noxious gas, so that all of them became infected by it.

Harry did not want to leave Sirius all alone again with only Kreacher for company. In fact, for the first time in his life, he was not looking forward to returning to Hogwarts. Going back to school would mean placing himself once again under the tyranny of Dolores Umbridge, who had no doubt managed to force through another dozen decrees in their absence. Then there was no Quidditch to look forward to now that he had been banned; there was every likelihood that their burden of homework would increase as the exams drew even nearer; Dumbledore remained as remote as ever; in fact, if it had not been for the D.A., Harry felt he might have gone to Sirius and begged him to let him leave Hogwarts and remain in Grimmauld Place.

Then, on the very last day of the holidays, something happened that made Harry positively dread his return to school.

"Harry dear," said Mrs. Weasley, poking her head into his and Ron's bedroom, where the pair of them were playing wizard chess watched by Hermione, Ginny, and Crookshanks, "could you come down to the kitchen? Professor Snape would like a word with you."

Harry did not immediately register what she had said; one of his castles was engaged in a violent tussle with a pawn of Ron's, and he was egging it on enthusiastically.

"Squash him — *squash him,* he's only a pawn, you idiot — sorry, Mrs. Weasley, what did you say?"

"Professor Snape, dear. In the kitchen. He'd like a word."

Harry's mouth fell open in horror. He looked around at Ron, Hermione, and Ginny, all of whom were gaping back at him. Crookshanks, whom Hermione had been restraining with difficulty for the past quarter of an hour, leapt gleefully upon the board and set the pieces running for cover, squealing at the top of their voices.

"Snape?" said Harry blankly.

"*Professor* Snape, dear," said Mrs. Weasley reprovingly. "Now come on, quickly, he says he can't stay long."

"What's he want with you?" said Ron, looking unnerved as Mrs. Weasley withdrew from the room.

"You haven't done anything, have you?"

"No!" said Harry indignantly, racking his brains to think what he could have done that would make Snape pursue him to Grimmauld Place. Had his last piece of homework perhaps earned a T?

He pushed open the kitchen door a minute or two later to find Sirius and Snape both seated at the long kitchen table, glaring in opposite directions. The silence between them was heavy with mutual dislike. A letter lay open on the table in front of Sirius.

"Er," said Harry to announce his presence.

Snape looked around at him, his face framed between curtains of greasy black hair.

"Sit down, Potter."

"You know," said Sirius loudly, leaning back on his rear chair legs and speaking to the ceiling, "I think I'd prefer it if you didn't give orders here, Snape. It's my house, you see."

An ugly flush suffused Snape's pallid face. Harry sat down in a chair beside Sirius, facing Snape across the table.

"I was supposed to see you alone, Potter," said Snape, the familiar sneer curling his mouth, "but Black —"

"I'm his godfather," said Sirius, louder than ever.

"I am here on Dumbledore's orders," said Snape, whose voice, by contrast, was becoming more and more quietly waspish, "but by all means stay, Black, I know you like to feel . . . involved."

"What's that supposed to mean?" said Sirius, letting his chair fall back onto all four legs with a loud bang.

"Merely that I am sure you must feel — ah — frustrated by the fact that you can do nothing *useful*," Snape laid a delicate stress on the word, "for the Order."

It was Sirius's turn to flush. Snape's lip curled in triumph as he turned to Harry.

"The headmaster has sent me to tell you, Potter, that it is his wish for you to study Occlumency this term."

"Study what?" said Harry blankly.

Snape's sneer became more pronounced.

"Occlumency, Potter. The magical defense of the mind against external penetration. An obscure branch of magic, but a highly useful one."

Harry's heart began to pump very fast indeed. Defense against external penetration? But he was not being possessed, they had all agreed on that. . . .

"Why do I have to study Occlu — thing?" he blurted out.

"Because the headmaster thinks it a good idea," said Snape smoothly. "You will receive private lessons once a week, but you will not tell anybody what you are doing, least of all Dolores Umbridge. You understand?"

"Yes," said Harry. "Who's going to be teaching me?"

Snape raised an eyebrow.

"I am," he said.

Harry had the horrible sensation that his insides were melting. Extra lessons with Snape — what on earth had he done to deserve this? He looked quickly around at Sirius for support.

"Why can't Dumbledore teach Harry?" asked Sirius aggressively. "Why you?"

"I suppose because it is a headmaster's privilege to delegate less enjoyable tasks," said Snape silkily. "I assure you I did not beg for the job." He got to his feet. "I will expect you at six o'clock on Monday evening, Potter. My office. If anybody asks, you are taking Remedial Potions. Nobody who has seen you in my classes could deny you need them."

He turned to leave, his black traveling cloak billowing behind him.

"Wait a moment," said Sirius, sitting up straighter in his chair.

Snape turned back to face them, sneering.

"I am in rather a hurry, Black . . . unlike you, I do not have unlimited leisure time. . . ."

"I'll get to the point, then," said Sirius, standing up. He was rather taller than Snape who, Harry noticed, had balled his fist in the pocket of his cloak over what Harry was sure was the handle of his wand. "If I hear you're using these Occlumency lessons to give Harry a hard time, you'll have me to answer to."

"How touching," Snape sneered. "But surely you have noticed that Potter is very like his father?"

"Yes, I have," said Sirius proudly.

"Well then, you'll know he's so arrogant that criticism simply bounces off him," Snape said sleekly.

Sirius pushed his chair roughly aside and strode around the table toward Snape, pulling out his wand as he went; Snape whipped out his own. They were squaring up to each other, Sirius looking livid, Snape calculating, his eyes darting from Sirius's wand-tip to his face.

"Sirius!" said Harry loudly, but Sirius appeared not to hear him.

"I've warned you, *Snivellus*," said Sirius, his face barely a foot from Snape's, "I don't care if Dumbledore thinks you've reformed, I know better —"

"Oh, but why don't you tell him so?" whispered Snape. "Or are you afraid he might not take the advice of a man who has been hiding inside his mother's house for six months very seriously?"

"Tell me, how is Lucius Malfoy these days? I expect he's delighted his lapdog's working at Hogwarts, isn't he?"

"Speaking of dogs," said Snape softly, "did you know that Lucius Malfoy recognized you last time you risked a little jaunt outside? Clever idea, Black, getting yourself seen on a safe station platform . . . gave you a cast-iron excuse not to leave your hidey-hole in future, didn't it?"

Sirius raised his wand.

"NO!" Harry yelled, vaulting over the table and trying to get in between them, "Sirius, don't —"

"Are you calling me a coward?" roared Sirius, trying to push Harry out of the way, but Harry would not budge.

"Why, yes, I suppose I am," said Snape.

"Harry — get — out — of — it!" snarled Sirius, pushing him out of the way with his free hand.

The kitchen door opened and the entire Weasley family, plus Hermione, came inside, all looking very happy, with Mr. Weasley walking proudly in their midst dressed in a pair of striped pajamas covered by a mackintosh.

"Cured!" he announced brightly to the kitchen at large. "Completely cured!"

He and all the other Weasleys froze on the threshold, gazing at the scene in front of them, which was also suspended in mid-action, both Sirius and Snape looking toward the door with their wands pointing into each other's faces and Harry immobile between them, a hand stretched out to each of them, trying to force them apart.

"Merlin's beard," said Mr. Weasley, the smile sliding off his face, "what's going on here?"

Both Sirius and Snape lowered their wands. Harry looked from one to the other. Each wore an expression of utmost contempt, yet the unexpected entrance of so many witnesses seemed to have brought them to their senses. Snape pocketed his wand and swept back across the kitchen, passing the Weasleys without comment. At the door he looked back.

"Six o'clock Monday evening, Potter."

He was gone. Sirius glared after him, his wand at his side.

"But what's been going on?" asked Mr. Weasley again.

"Nothing, Arthur," said Sirius, who was breathing heavily as though he had just run a long distance. "Just a friendly little chat between two old school friends. . . ." With what looked like an enormous effort, he smiled. "So . . . you're cured? That's great news, really great. . . ."

"Yes, isn't it?" said Mrs. Weasley, leading her husband forward into a chair. "Healer Smethwyck worked his magic in the end, found an antidote to whatever that snake's got in its fangs, and Arthur's learned his lesson about dabbling in Muggle medicine, *haven't you, dear?*" she added, rather menacingly.

"Yes, Molly dear," said Mr. Weasley meekly.

That night's meal should have been a cheerful one with Mr. Weasley back amongst them; Harry could tell Sirius was trying to make it so, yet when his godfather was not forcing himself to laugh loudly at Fred and George's jokes or offering everyone more food, his face fell back into a moody, brooding expression. Harry was separated from him by Mundungus and Mad-Eye, who had dropped in to offer Mr. Weasley their congratulations; he wanted to talk to Sirius, to tell him that he should not listen to a word Snape said, that Snape was goading him deliberately and that the rest of them did not think Sirius was a coward for doing as Dumbledore told him and remaining in Grimmauld Place, but he had no opportunity to do so, and wondered occasionally, eyeing the ugly look on Sirius's face, whether he would have dared to even if he had the chance. Instead he told Ron and Hermione under his voice about having to take Occlumency lessons with Snape.

"Dumbledore wants to stop you having those dreams about Voldemort," said Hermione at once. "Well, you won't be sorry not to have them anymore, will you?"

"Extra lessons with Snape?" said Ron, sounding aghast. "I'd rather have the nightmares!"

They were to return to Hogwarts on the Knight Bus the following day, escorted once again by Tonks and Lupin, both of whom were eating breakfast in the kitchen when Harry, Ron, and Hermione arrived there next morning. The adults seemed to have been midway through a whispered conversation when the door opened; all of them looked around hastily and fell silent.

After a hurried breakfast they pulled on jackets and scarves against the chilly gray January morning. Harry had an unpleasant constricted sensation in his chest; he did not want to say good-bye to Sirius. He had a bad feeling about this parting; he did not know when they would next see each other and felt that it was incumbent upon him to say something to Sirius to stop him doing anything stupid — Harry was worried that Snape's accusation of cowardice had stung Sirius so badly he might even now be planning some foolhardy trip beyond Grimmauld Place. Before he could think of what to say, however, Sirius had beckoned him to his side.

"I want you to take this," he said quietly, thrusting a badly wrapped package roughly the size of a paperback book into Harry's hands.

"What is it?" Harry asked.

"A way of letting me know if Snape's giving you a hard time. No, don't open it in here!" said Sirius, with a wary look at Mrs. Weasley, who was trying to persuade the twins to wear hand-knitted mittens. "I doubt Molly would approve — but I want you to use it if you need me, all right?"

"Okay," said Harry, stowing the package away in the inside pocket of his jacket, but he knew he would never use whatever it was. It would not be he, Harry, who lured Sirius from his place of safety, no matter how foully Snape treated him in their forthcoming Occlumency classes.

"Let's go, then," said Sirius, clapping Harry on the shoulder and smiling grimly, and before Harry could say anything else, they were heading upstairs, stopping before the heavily chained and bolted front door, surrounded by Weasleys.

"Good-bye, Harry, take care," said Mrs. Weasley, hugging him.

"See you Harry, and keep an eye out for snakes for me!" said Mr. Weasley genially, shaking his hand.

"Right — yeah," said Harry distractedly. It was his last chance to tell Sirius to be careful; he turned, looked into his godfather's face and opened his mouth to speak, but before he could do so Sirius was giving him a brief, one-armed hug. He said gruffly, "Look after yourself, Harry," and next moment Harry found himself being shunted out into the icy winter air, with Tonks (today heavily disguised as a tall, tweedy woman with iron-gray hair) chivvying him down the steps.

The door of number twelve slammed shut behind them. They followed Lupin down the front steps. As he reached the pavement, Harry looked around. Number twelve was shrinking rapidly as those on either side of it stretched sideways, squeezing it out of sight; one blink later, it had gone.

"Come on, the quicker we get on the bus the better," said Tonks, and Harry thought there was nervousness in the glance she threw around the square. Lupin flung out his right arm.

BANG.

A violently purple, triple-decker bus had appeared out of thin air in front of them, narrowly avoiding the nearest lamppost, which jumped backward out of its way.

A thin, pimply, jug-eared youth in a purple uniform leapt down onto the pavement and said, "Welcome to the —"

"Yes, yes, we know, thank you," said Tonks swiftly. "On, on, get on —"

And she shoved Harry forward toward the steps, past the conductor, who goggled at Harry as he passed.

"'Ere — it's 'Arry — !"

"If you shout his name I will curse you into oblivion," muttered Tonks menacingly, now shunting Ginny and Hermione forward.

"I've always wanted to go on this thing," said Ron happily, joining Harry on board and looking around.

It had been evening the last time Harry had traveled by Knight Bus and its three decks had been full of brass bedsteads. Now, in the early morning, it was crammed with an assortment of mismatched chairs grouped haphazardly around windows. Some of these appeared to have fallen over when the bus stopped abruptly in Grimmauld Place; a few witches and wizards were still getting to their feet, grumbling, and somebody's shopping bag had slid the length of the bus; an unpleasant mixture of frog spawn, cockroaches, and custard creams was scattered all over the floor.

"Looks like we'll have to split up," said Tonks briskly, looking around for empty chairs. "Fred, George, and Ginny, if you just take those seats at the back . . . Remus can stay with you. . . ."

She, Harry, Ron, and Hermione proceeded up to the very top deck, where there were two chairs at the very front of the bus and two at the back. Stan Shunpike, the conductor, followed Harry and Ron eagerly to the back. Heads turned as Harry passed and when he sat down, he saw all the faces flick back to the front again.

As Harry and Ron handed Stan eleven Sickles each, the bus set off again, swaying ominously. It rumbled around Grimmauld Square, weaving on and off the pavement, then, with another tremendous BANG, they were all flung backward; Ron's chair toppled right over and Pigwidgeon, who had been on his lap, burst out of his cage and flew twittering wildly up to the front of the bus where he fluttered down upon Hermione's shoulder instead. Harry, who had narrowly avoided falling by seizing a candle bracket, looked out of the window: they were now speeding down what appeared to be a motorway.

"Just outside Birmingham," said Stan happily, answering Harry's unasked question as Ron struggled up from the floor. "You keepin' well, then, 'Arry? I seen your name in the paper loads over the summer, but it weren't never nuffink very nice. . . . I said to Ern, I said, ''e didn't seem like a nutter when we met 'im, just goes to show, dunnit?'"

He handed over their tickets and continued to gaze, enthralled, at Harry; apparently Stan did not care how nutty somebody was if they were famous enough to be in the paper. The Knight Bus swayed alarmingly, overtaking a line of cars on the inside. Looking toward the front of the bus Harry saw Hermione cover her eyes with her hands, Pigwidgeon still swaying happily on her shoulder.

BANG.

Chairs slid backward again as the Knight Bus jumped from the Birmingham motorway to a quiet country lane full of hairpin bends. Hedgerows on either side of the road were leaping out of their way as they mounted the verges. From here they moved to a main street in the middle of a busy town, then to a viaduct surrounded by tall hills, then to a windswept road between high-rise flats, each time with a loud BANG.

"I've changed my mind," muttered Ron, picking himself up from the floor for the sixth time, "I never want to ride on here again."

"Listen, it's 'Ogwarts stop after this," said Stan brightly, swaying toward them. "That bossy woman up front 'oo got on with you, she's given us a little tip to move you up the queue. We're just gonna let Madam Marsh off first, though —" There was more retching from downstairs, followed by a horrible spattering sound. "She's not feeling 'er best."

A few minutes later the Knight Bus screeched to a halt outside a small pub, which squeezed itself out of the way to avoid a collision. They could hear Stan ushering the unfortunate Madam Marsh out of the bus and the relieved murmurings of her fellow passengers on the second deck. The bus moved on again, gathering speed, until —

BANG.

They were rolling through a snowy Hogsmeade. Harry caught a glimpse of the Hog's Head down its side street, the severed boar's head sign creaking in the wintry wind. Flecks of snow hit the large window at the front of the bus. At last they rolled to a halt outside the gates to Hogwarts.

Lupin and Tonks helped them off the bus with their luggage and then got off to say good-bye. Harry glanced up at the three decks of the Knight Bus and saw all the passengers staring down at them, noses flat against the windows.

"You'll be safe once you're in the grounds," said Tonks, casting a careful eye around at the deserted road. "Have a good term, okay?"

"Look after yourselves," said Lupin, shaking hands all round and reaching Harry last. "And listen . . ." He lowered his voice while the rest of them exchanged last-minute good-byes with Tonks, "Harry, I know you don't like Snape, but he is a superb Occlumens and we all — Sirius included — want you to learn to protect yourself, so work hard, all right?"

"Yeah, all right," said Harry heavily, looking up into Lupin's prematurely lined face. "See you, then . . ."

The six of them struggled up the slippery drive toward the castle dragging their trunks. Hermione was already talking about knitting a few elf hats before bedtime. Harry glanced back when they reached the oak front doors; the Knight Bus had already gone, and he half-wished, given what was coming the following day, that he was still on board.

Harry spent most of the next day dreading the evening. His morning Potions lesson did nothing to dispel his trepidation, as Snape was as unpleasant as ever, and Harry's mood was further lowered by the fact that members of the D.A. were continually approaching him in the corridors between classes, asking hopefully whether there would be a meeting that night.

"I'll let you know when the next one is," Harry said over and over again, "but I can't do it tonight, I've got to go to — er — Remedial Potions. . . ."

"You take *Remedial Potions*?" asked Zacharias Smith superciliously, having cornered Harry in the entrance hall after lunch. "Good Lord, you must be terrible, Snape doesn't usually give extra lessons, does he?"

As Smith strode away in an annoyingly buoyant fashion, Ron glared after him.

"Shall I jinx him? I can still get him from here," he said, raising his wand and taking aim between Smith's shoulder blades.

"Forget it," said Harry dismally. "It's what everyone's going to think, isn't it? That I'm really stup —"

"Hi, Harry," said a voice behind him. He turned around and found Cho standing there.

"Oh," said Harry as his stomach leapt uncomfortably. "Hi."

"We'll be in the library, Harry," said Hermione firmly, and she seized Ron above the elbow and dragged him off toward the marble staircase.

"Had a good Christmas?" asked Cho.

"Yeah, not bad," said Harry.

"Mine was pretty quiet," said Cho. For some reason, she was looking rather embarrassed. "Erm . . . there's another Hogsmeade trip next month, did you see the notice?"

"What? Oh no, I haven't checked the notice board since I got back. . . ."

"Yes, it's on Valentine's Day. . . ."

"Right," said Harry, wondering why she was telling him this. "Well, I suppose you want to — ?"

"Only if you do," she said eagerly.

Harry stared. He had been about to say "I suppose you want to know when the next D.A. meeting is?" but her response did not seem to fit.

"I — er —" he said.

"Oh, it's okay if you don't," she said, looking mortified. "Don't worry. I-I'll see you around."

She walked away. Harry stood staring after her, his brain working frantically. Then something clunked into place.

"Cho! Hey — CHO!"

He ran after her, catching her halfway up the marble staircase.

"Er — d'you want to come into Hogsmeade with me on Valentine's Day?"

"Oooh, yes!" she said, blushing crimson and beaming at him.

"Right . . . well . . . that's settled then," said Harry, and feeling that the day was not going to be a complete loss after all, he headed off to the library to pick up Ron and Hermione before their afternoon lessons, walking in a rather bouncy way himself.

By six o'clock that evening, however, even the glow of having successfully asked out Cho Chang was insufficient to lighten the ominous feelings that intensified with every step Harry took toward Snape's office.

He paused outside the door when he reached it, wishing he were almost anywhere else, then, taking a deep breath, knocked, and entered.

It was a shadowy room lined with shelves bearing hundreds of glass jars in which floated slimy bits of animals and plants, suspended in variously colored potions. In a corner stood the cupboard full of ingredients that Snape had once accused Harry — not without reason — of robbing. Harry's attention was drawn toward the desk, however, where a shallow stone basin engraved with runes and symbols lay in a pool of candlelight. Harry recognized it at once — Dumbledore's Pensieve. Wondering what on earth it was doing here, he jumped when Snape's cold voice came out of the corner.

"Shut the door behind you, Potter."

Harry did as he was told with the horrible feeling that he was imprisoning himself as he did so. When he turned back to face the room Snape had moved into the light and was pointing silently at the chair opposite his desk. Harry sat down and so did Snape, his cold black eyes fixed unblinkingly upon Harry, dislike etched in every line of his face.

"Well, Potter, you know why you are here," he said. "The headmaster has asked me to teach you Occlumency. I can only hope that you prove more adept at it than Potions."

"Right," said Harry tersely.

"This may not be an ordinary class, Potter," said Snape, his eyes narrowed malevolently, "but I am still your teacher and you will therefore call me 'sir' or 'Professor' at all times."

"Yes . . . *sir*," said Harry.

"Now, Occlumency. As I told you back in your dear godfather's kitchen, this branch of magic seals the mind against magical intrusion and influence."

"And why does Professor Dumbledore think I need it, sir?" said Harry, looking directly into Snape's dark, cold eyes and wondering whether he would answer.

Snape looked back at him for a moment and then said contemptuously, "Surely even you could have worked that out by now, Potter? The Dark Lord is highly skilled at Legilimency —"

"What's that? *Sir?*"

"It is the ability to extract feelings and memories from another person's mind —"

"He can read minds?" said Harry quickly, his worst fears confirmed.

"You have no subtlety, Potter," said Snape, his dark eyes glittering. "You do not understand fine distinctions. It is one of the shortcomings that makes you such a lamentable potion-maker."

Snape paused for a moment, apparently to savor the pleasure of insulting Harry, before continuing, "Only Muggles talk of 'mind reading.' The mind is not a book, to be opened at will and examined at leisure. Thoughts are not etched on the inside of skulls, to be perused by any invader. The mind is a complex and many-layered thing, Potter . . . or at least, most minds are. . . ." He smirked. "It is true, however, that those who have mastered Legilimency are able, under certain conditions, to delve into the minds of their victims and to interpret their findings correctly. The Dark Lord, for instance, almost always knows when somebody is lying to him. Only those skilled at Occlumency are able to shut down those feelings and memories that contradict the lie, and so utter falsehoods in his presence without detection."

Whatever Snape said, Legilimency sounded like mind reading to Harry and he did not like the sound of it at all.

"So he could know what we're thinking right now? Sir?"

"The Dark Lord is at a considerable distance and the walls and grounds of Hogwarts are guarded by many ancient spells and charms to ensure the bodily and mental safety of those who dwell within them," said Snape. "Time and space matter in magic, Potter. Eye contact is often essential to Legilimency."

"Well then, why do I have to learn Occlumency?"

Snape eyed Harry, tracing his mouth with one long, thin finger as he did so.

"The usual rules do not seem to apply with you, Potter. The curse that failed to kill you seems to have forged some kind of connection between you and the Dark Lord. The evidence suggests that at times, when your mind is most relaxed and vulnerable — when you are asleep, for instance — you are sharing the Dark Lord's thoughts and emotions. The headmaster thinks it inadvisable for this to continue. He wishes me to teach you how to close your mind to the Dark Lord."

Harry's heart was pumping fast again. None of this added up.

"But why does Professor Dumbledore want to stop it?" he asked abruptly. "I don't like it much, but it's been useful, hasn't it? I mean . . . I saw that snake attack Mr. Weasley and if I hadn't, Professor Dumbledore wouldn't have been able to save him, would he? Sir?"

Snape stared at Harry for a few moments, still tracing his mouth with his finger. When he spoke again, it was slowly and deliberately, as though he weighed every word.

"It appears that the Dark Lord has been unaware of the connection between you and himself until very recently. Up till now it seems that you have been experiencing his emotions and sharing his thoughts without his being any the wiser. However, the vision you had shortly before Christmas —"

"The one with the snake and Mr. Weasley?"

"Do not interrupt me, Potter," said Snape in a dangerous voice. "As I was saying . . . the vision you had shortly before Christmas represented such a powerful incursion upon the Dark Lord's thoughts —"

"I saw inside the snake's head, not his!"

"I thought I just told you not to interrupt me, Potter?"

But Harry did not care if Snape was angry; at last he seemed to be getting to the bottom of this business. He had moved forward in his chair so that, without realizing it, he was perched on the very edge, tense as though poised for flight.

"How come I saw through the snake's eyes if it's Voldemort's thoughts I'm sharing?"

"Do not say the Dark Lord's name!" spat Snape.

There was a nasty silence. They glared at each other across the Pensieve.

"Professor Dumbledore says his name," said Harry quietly.

"Dumbledore is an extremely powerful wizard," Snape muttered. "While *he* may feel secure enough to use the name . . . the rest of us . . ." He rubbed his left forearm, apparently unconsciously, on the spot where Harry knew the Dark Mark was burned into his skin.

"I just wanted to know," Harry began again, forcing his voice back to politeness, "why —"

"You seem to have visited the snake's mind because that was where the Dark Lord was at that particular moment," snarled Snape. "He was possessing the snake at the time and so you dreamed you were inside it too. . . ."

"And Vol — he — realized I was there?"

"It seems so," said Snape coolly.

"How do you know?" said Harry urgently. "Is this just Professor Dumbledore guessing, or — ?"

"I told you," said Snape, rigid in his chair, his eyes slits, "to call me 'sir.'"

"Yes, sir," said Harry impatiently, "but how do you know — ?"

"It is enough that we know," said Snape repressively. "The important point is that the Dark Lord is now aware that you are gaining access to his thoughts and feelings. He has also deduced that the process is likely to work in reverse; that is to say, he has realized that he might be able to access your thoughts and feelings in return —"

"And he might try and make me do things?" asked Harry. *"Sir?"* he added hurriedly.

"He might," said Snape, sounding cold and unconcerned. "Which brings us back to Occlumency."

Snape pulled out his wand from an inside pocket of his robes and Harry tensed in his chair, but Snape merely raised the wand to his temple and placed its tip into the greasy roots of his hair. When he withdrew it, some silvery substance came away, stretching from temple to wand like a thick gossamer strand, which broke as he pulled the wand away from it and fell gracefully into the Pensieve, where it swirled silvery white, neither gas nor liquid. Twice more Snape raised the wand to his temple and deposited the silvery substance into the stone basin, then, without offering any explanation of his behavior, he picked up the Pensieve carefully, removed it to a shelf out of their way and returned to face Harry with his wand held at the ready.

"Stand up and take out your wand, Potter."

Harry got to his feet feeling nervous. They faced each other with the desk between them.

"You may use your wand to attempt to disarm me, or defend yourself in any other way you can think of," said Snape.

"And what are you going to do?" Harry asked, eyeing Snape's wand apprehensively.

"I am about to attempt to break into your mind," said Snape softly. "We are going to see how well you resist. I have been told that you have already shown aptitude at resisting the Imperius Curse. . . . You will find that similar powers are needed for this. . . . Brace yourself, now. . . . *Legilimens!*"

Snape had struck before Harry was ready, before Harry had even begun to summon any force of resistance: the office swam in front of his eyes and vanished, image after image was racing through his mind like a flickering film so vivid it blinded him to his surroundings. . . .

He was five, watching Dudley riding a new red bicycle, and his heart was bursting with jealousy. . . . He was nine, and Ripper the bulldog was chasing him up a tree and the Dursleys were laughing below on the lawn. . . . He was sitting under the Sorting Hat, and it was telling him he would do well in Slytherin. . . . Hermione was lying in the hospital wing, her face covered with thick black hair. . . . A hundred dementors were closing in on him beside the dark lake. . . . Cho Chang was drawing nearer to him under the mistletoe. . . .

No, said a voice in Harry's head, as the memory of Cho drew nearer, *you're not watching that, you're not watching it, it's private —*

He felt a sharp pain in his knee. Snape's office had come back into view and he realized that he had fallen to the floor; one of his knees had collided painfully with the leg of Snape's desk. He looked up at Snape, who had lowered his wand and was rubbing his wrist. There was an angry weal there, like a scorch mark.

"Did you mean to produce a Stinging Hex?" asked Snape coolly.

"No," said Harry bitterly, getting up from the floor.

"I thought not," said Snape contemptuously. "You let me get in too far. You lost control."

"Did you see everything I saw?" Harry asked, unsure whether he wanted to hear the answer.

"Flashes of it," said Snape, his lip curling. "To whom did the dog belong?"

"My Aunt Marge," Harry muttered, hating Snape.

"Well, for a first attempt that was not as poor as it might have been," said Snape, raising his wand once more. "You managed to stop me eventually, though you wasted time and energy shouting. You must remain focused. Repel me with your brain and you will not need to resort to your wand."

"I'm trying," said Harry angrily, "but you're not telling me how!"

"Manners, Potter," said Snape dangerously. "Now, I want you to close your eyes."

Harry threw him a filthy look before doing as he was told. He did not like the idea of standing there with his eyes shut while Snape faced him, carrying a wand.

"Clear your mind, Potter," said Snape's cold voice. "Let go of all emotion. . . ."

But Harry's anger at Snape continued to pound through his veins like venom. Let go of his anger? He could as easily detach his legs. . . .

"You're not doing it, Potter. . . . You will need more discipline than this. . . . Focus, now. . . ."

Harry tried to empty his mind, tried not to think, or remember, or feel. . . .

"Let's go again . . . on the count of three . . . one — two — three — *Legilimens!*"

A great black dragon was rearing in front of him. . . . His father and mother were waving at him out of an enchanted mirror. . . . Cedric Diggory was lying on the ground with blank eyes staring at him. . . .

"NOOOOOOO!"

He was on his knees again, his face buried in his hands, his brain aching as though someone had been trying to pull it from his skull.

"Get up!" said Snape sharply. "Get up! You are not trying, you are making no effort, you are allowing me access to memories you fear, handing me weapons!"

Harry stood up again, his heart thumping wildly as though he had really just seen Cedric dead in the graveyard. Snape looked paler than usual, and angrier, though not nearly as angry as Harry was.

"I — am — making — an — effort," he said through clenched teeth.

"I told you to empty yourself of emotion!"

"Yeah? Well, I'm finding that hard at the moment," Harry snarled.

"Then you will find yourself easy prey for the Dark Lord!" said Snape savagely. "Fools who wear their hearts proudly on their sleeves, who cannot control their emotions, who wallow in sad memories and allow themselves to be provoked this easily — weak people, in other words — they stand no chance against his powers! He will penetrate your mind with absurd ease, Potter!"

"I am not weak," said Harry in a low voice, fury now pumping through him so that he thought he might attack Snape in a moment.

"Then prove it! Master yourself!" spat Snape. "Control your anger, discipline your mind! We shall try again! Get ready, now! *Legilimens!*"

He was watching Uncle Vernon hammering the letter box shut. . . . A hundred dementors were drifting across the lake in the grounds toward him. . . . He was running along a windowless passage with Mr. Weasley. . . . They were drawing nearer to the plain black door at the end of the corridor. . . . Harry expected to go through it . . . but Mr. Weasley led him off to the left, down a flight of stone steps. . . .

"I KNOW! I KNOW!"

He was on all fours again on Snape's office floor, his scar was prickling unpleasantly, but the voice that had just issued from his mouth was triumphant. He pushed himself up again to find Snape staring at him, his wand raised. It looked as though, this time, Snape had lifted the spell before Harry had even tried to fight back.

"What happened then, Potter?" he asked, eyeing Harry intently.

"I saw — I remembered," Harry panted. "I've just realized . . ."

"Realized what?" asked Snape sharply.

Harry did not answer at once; he was still savoring the moment of blinding realization as he rubbed his forehead. . . .

He had been dreaming about a windowless corridor ending in a locked door for months, without once realizing that it was a real place. Now, seeing the memory again, he knew that all along he had been dreaming about the corridor down which he had run with Mr. Weasley on the twelfth of August as they hurried to the courtrooms in the Ministry. It was the corridor leading to the Department of Mysteries, and Mr. Weasley had been there the night that he had been attacked by Voldemort's snake. . . .

He looked up at Snape.

"What's in the Department of Mysteries?"

"What did you say?" Snape asked quietly and Harry saw, with deep satisfaction, that Snape was unnerved.

"I said, what's in the Department of Mysteries, *sir*?" Harry said.

"And why," said Snape slowly, "would you ask such a thing?"

"Because," said Harry, watching Snape closely for a reaction, "that corridor I've just seen — I've been dreaming about it for months — I've just recognized it — it leads to the Department of Mysteries . . . and I think Voldemort wants something from —"

"*I have told you not to say the Dark Lord's name!*"

They glared at each other. Harry's scar seared again, but he did not care. Snape looked agitated. When he spoke again he sounded as though he was trying to appear cool and unconcerned.

"There are many things in the Department of Mysteries, Potter, few of which you would understand and none of which concern you, do I make myself plain?"

"Yes," Harry said, still rubbing his prickling scar, which was becoming more painful.

"I want you back here same time on Wednesday, and we will continue work then."

"Fine," said Harry. He was desperate to get out of Snape's office and find Ron and Hermione.

"You are to rid your mind of all emotion every night before sleep — empty it, make it blank and calm, you understand?"

"Yes," said Harry, who was barely listening.

"And be warned, Potter . . . I shall know if you have not practiced . . ."

"Right," Harry mumbled. He picked up his schoolbag, swung it over his shoulder, and hurried toward the office door. As he opened it he glanced back at Snape, who had his back to Harry and was scooping his own thoughts out of the Pensieve with the tip of his wand and replacing them carefully inside his own head. Harry left without another word, closing the door carefully behind him, his scar still throbbing painfully.

Harry found Ron and Hermione in the library, where they were working on Umbridge's most recent ream of homework. Other students, nearly all of them fifth years, sat at lamp-lit tables nearby, noses close to books, quills scratching feverishly, while the sky outside the mullioned windows grew steadily blacker. The only other sound was the slight squeaking of one of Madam Pince's shoes as the librarian prowled the aisles menacingly, breathing down the necks of those touching her precious books.

Harry felt shivery; his scar was still aching, he felt almost feverish. When he sat down opposite Ron and Hermione he caught sight of himself in the window opposite. He was very white, and his scar seemed to be showing up more clearly than usual.

"How did it go?" Hermione whispered, and then, looking concerned, "Are you all right, Harry?"

"Yeah . . . fine . . . I dunno," said Harry impatiently, wincing as pain shot through his scar again. "Listen . . . I've just realized something. . . ."

And he told them what he had just seen and deduced.

"So . . . so, are you saying . . ." whispered Ron, as Madam Pince swept past, squeaking slightly, "that the weapon — the thing You-Know-Who's after — is in the Ministry of Magic?"

"In the Department of Mysteries, it's got to be," Harry whispered. "I saw that door when your dad took me down to the courtrooms for my hearing and it's definitely the same one he was guarding when the snake bit him."

Hermione let out a long, slow sigh. "Of course," she breathed.

"Of course what?" said Ron rather impatiently.

"Ron, think about it. . . . Sturgis Podmore was trying to get through a door at the Ministry of Magic. . . . It must have been that one, it's too much of a coincidence!"

"How come Sturgis was trying to break in when he's on our side?" said Ron.

"Well, I don't know," Hermione admitted. "That *is* a bit odd. . . ."

"So what's in the Department of Mysteries?" Harry asked Ron. "Has your dad ever mentioned anything about it?"

"I know they call the people who work in there 'Unspeakables,'" said Ron, frowning. "Because no one really seems to know what they do in there. . . . Weird place to have a weapon . . ."

"It's not weird at all, it makes perfect sense," said Hermione. "It will be something top secret that the Ministry has been developing, I expect. . . . Harry, are you sure you're all right?"

For Harry had just run both his hands hard over his forehead as though trying to iron it.

"Yeah . . . fine . . ." he said, lowering his hands, which were trembling. "I just feel a bit . . . I don't like Occlumency much. . . ."

"I expect anyone would feel shaky if they'd had their mind attacked over and over again," said Hermione sympathetically. "Look, let's get back to the common room, we'll be a bit more comfortable there. . . ."

But the common room was packed and full of shrieks of laughter and excitement; Fred and George were demonstrating their latest bit of joke shop merchandise.

"Headless Hats!" shouted George, as Fred waved a pointed hat decorated with a fluffy pink feather at the watching students. "Two Galleons each — watch Fred, now!"

Fred swept the hat onto his head, beaming. For a second he merely looked rather stupid, then both hat and head vanished.

Several girls screamed, but everyone else was roaring with laughter.

"And off again!" shouted George, and Fred's hand groped for a moment in what seemed to be thin air over his shoulder; then his head reappeared as he swept the pink-feathered hat from it again.

"How do those hats work, then?" said Hermione, distracted from her homework and watching Fred and George. "I mean, obviously it's some kind of Invisibility Spell, but it's rather clever to have extended the field of invisibility beyond the boundaries of the charmed object. . . . I'd imagine the charm wouldn't have a very long life though. . . ."

Harry did not answer; he was still feeling ill.

"I'm going to have to do this tomorrow," he muttered, pushing the books he had just taken out of his bag back inside it.

"Well, write it in your homework planner then!" said Hermione encouragingly. "So you don't forget!"

Harry and Ron exchanged looks as he reached into his bag, withdrew the planner and opened it tentatively.

"Don't leave it till later, you big second-rater!" chided the book as Harry scribbled down Umbridge's homework. Hermione beamed at it.

"I think I'll go to bed," said Harry, stuffing the homework planner back into his bag and making a mental note to drop it in the fire the first opportunity he got.

He walked across the common room, dodging George, who tried to put a Headless Hat on him, and reached the peace and cool of the stone staircase to the boys' dormitories. He was feeling sick again, just as he had the night he had had the vision of the snake, but thought that if he could just lie down for a while he would be all right.

He opened the door of his dormitory and was one step inside it when he experienced pain so severe he thought that someone must have sliced into the top of his head. He did not know where he was, whether he was standing or lying down, he did not even know his own name. . . .

Maniacal laughter was ringing in his ears. . . . He was happier than he had been in a very long time. . . . Jubilant, ecstatic, triumphant . . . A wonderful, wonderful thing had happened. . . .

"Harry? HARRY!"

Someone had hit him around the face. The insane laughter was punctuated with a cry of pain. The happiness was draining out of him, but the laughter continued. . . .

He opened his eyes and as he did so, he became aware that the wild laughter was coming out of his own mouth. The moment he realized this, it died away; Harry lay panting on the floor, staring up at the ceiling, the scar on his forehead throbbing horribly. Ron was bending over him, looking very worried.

"What happened?" he said.

"I . . . dunno . . ." Harry gasped, sitting up again. "He's really happy . . . really happy . . ."

"You-Know-Who is?"

"Something good's happened," mumbled Harry. He was shaking as badly as he had done after seeing the snake attack Mr. Weasley and felt very sick. "Something he's been hoping for."

The words came, just as they had back in the Gryffindor changing room, as though a stranger was speaking them through Harry's mouth, yet he knew they were true. He took deep breaths, willing himself not to vomit all over Ron. He was very glad that Dean and Seamus were not here to watch this time.

"Hermione told me to come and check on you," said Ron in a low voice, helping Harry to his feet. "She says your defenses will be low at the moment, after Snape's been fiddling around with your mind. . . . Still, I suppose it'll help in the long run, won't it?"

He looked doubtfully at Harry as he helped him toward bed. Harry nodded without any conviction and slumped back on his pillows, aching all over from having fallen to the floor so often that evening, his scar still prickling painfully. He could not help feeling that his first foray into Occlumency had weakened his mind's resistance rather than strengthening it, and he wondered, with a feeling of great trepidation, what had happened to make Lord Voldemort the happiest he had been in fourteen years.

THE BEETLE AT BAY

Harry's question was answered the very next morning. When Hermione's *Daily Prophet* arrived she smoothed it out, gazed for a moment at the front page, and then gave a yelp that caused everyone in the vicinity to stare at her.

"What?" said Harry and Ron together.

For an answer she spread the newspaper on the table in front of them and pointed at ten black-and-white photographs that filled the whole of the front page, nine showing wizards' faces and the tenth, a witch's. Some of the people in the photographs were silently jeering; others were tapping their fingers on the frame of their pictures, looking insolent. Each picture was captioned with a name and the crime for which the person had been sent to Azkaban.

Antonin Dolohov, read the legend beneath a wizard with a long, pale, twisted face who was sneering up at Harry, *convicted of the brutal murders of Gideon and Fabian Prewett.*

Augustus Rookwood, said the caption beneath a pockmarked man with greasy hair who was leaning against the edge of his picture, looking bored, *convicted of leaking Ministry of Magic Secrets to He-Who-Must-Not-Be-Named*.

But Harry's eyes were drawn to the picture of the witch. Her face had leapt out at him the moment he had seen the page. She had long, dark hair that looked unkempt and straggly in the picture, though he had seen it sleek, thick, and shining. She glared up at him through heavily lidded eyes, an arrogant, disdainful smile playing around her thin mouth. Like Sirius, she retained vestiges of great good looks, but something — perhaps Azkaban — had taken most of her beauty.

Bellatrix Lestrange, convicted of the torture and permanent incapacitation of Frank and Alice Longbottom.

Hermione nudged Harry and pointed at the headline over the pictures, which Harry, concentrating on Bellatrix, had not yet read.

MASS BREAKOUT FROM AZKABAN
MINISTRY FEARS BLACK IS "RALLYING POINT"
FOR OLD DEATH EATERS

"Black?" said Harry loudly. "Not — ?"

"*Shhh!*" whispered Hermione desperately. "Not so loud — just read it!"

> The Ministry of Magic announced late last night that there has been a mass breakout from Azkaban.
>
> Speaking to reporters in his private office, Cornelius Fudge, Minister of Magic, confirmed that ten high-security prisoners escaped in the early hours of yesterday evening, and that he has already informed the Muggle Prime Minister of the dangerous nature of these individuals.
>
> "We find ourselves, most unfortunately, in the same position we were two and a half years ago when

the murderer Sirius Black escaped," said Fudge last
night. "Nor do we think the two breakouts are unrelated. An escape of this magnitude suggests outside
help, and we must remember that Black, as the first
person ever to break out of Azkaban, would be ideally
placed to help others follow in his footsteps. We think
it likely that these individuals, who include Black's
cousin, Bellatrix Lestrange, have rallied around Black
as their leader. We are, however, doing all we can to
round up the criminals and beg the magical community to remain alert and cautious. On no account
should any of these individuals be approached."

"There you are, Harry," said Ron, looking awestruck. "That's why
he was happy last night. . . ."

"I don't believe this," snarled Harry, "Fudge is blaming the breakout on *Sirius*?"

"What other options does he have?" said Hermione bitterly. "He
can hardly say, 'Sorry everyone, Dumbledore warned me this might
happen, the Azkaban guards have joined Lord Voldemort' — stop
whimpering, Ron — 'and now Voldemort's worst supporters have broken out too.' I mean, he's spent a good six months telling everyone
you and Dumbledore are liars, hasn't he?"

Hermione ripped open the newspaper and began to read the report
inside while Harry looked around the Great Hall. He could not understand why his fellow students were not looking scared or at least
discussing the terrible piece of news on the front page, but very few of
them took the newspaper every day like Hermione. There they all
were, talking about homework and Quidditch and who knew what
other rubbish, and outside these walls ten more Death Eaters had
swollen Voldemort's ranks. . . .

He glanced up at the staff table. It was a different story here:

Dumbledore and Professor McGonagall were deep in conversation, both looking extremely grave. Professor Sprout had the *Prophet* propped against a bottle of ketchup and was reading the front page with such concentration that she was not noticing the gentle drip of egg yolk falling into her lap from her stationary spoon. Meanwhile, at the far end of the table, Professor Umbridge was tucking into a bowl of porridge. For once her pouchy toad's eyes were not sweeping the Great Hall looking for misbehaving students. She scowled as she gulped down her food and every now and then she shot a malevolent glance up the table to where Dumbledore and McGonagall were talking so intently.

"Oh my —" said Hermione wonderingly, still staring at the newspaper.

"What now?" said Harry quickly; he was feeling jumpy.

"It's . . . *horrible*," said Hermione, looking shaken. She folded back page ten of the newspaper and handed it back to Harry and Ron.

TRAGIC DEMISE OF
MINISTRY OF MAGIC WORKER

St. Mungo's Hospital promised a full inquiry last night after Ministry of Magic worker Broderick Bode, 49, was discovered dead in his bed, strangled by a potted-plant. Healers called to the scene were unable to revive Mr. Bode, who had been injured in a workplace accident some weeks prior to his death.

Healer Miriam Strout, who was in charge of Mr. Bode's ward at the time of the incident, has been suspended on full pay and was unavailable for comment yesterday, but a spokeswizard for the hospital said in a statement, "St. Mungo's deeply regrets the death of Mr. Bode, whose health was improving steadily prior to this tragic accident.

"We have strict guidelines on the decorations permitted on our wards but it appears that Healer Strout, busy over the Christmas period, overlooked the dangers of the plant on Mr. Bode's bedside table. As his speech and mobility improved, Healer Strout encouraged Mr. Bode to look after the plant himself, unaware that it was not an innocent Flitterbloom, but a cutting of Devil's Snare, which, when touched by the convalescent Mr. Bode, throttled him instantly.

"St. Mungo's is as yet unable to account for the presence of the plant on the ward and asks any witch or wizard with information to come forward."

"Bode . . ." said Ron. "*Bode.* It rings a bell. . . ."

"We saw him," Hermione whispered. "In St. Mungo's, remember? He was in the bed opposite Lockhart's, just lying there, staring at the ceiling. And we saw the Devil's Snare arrive. She — the Healer — said it was a Christmas present. . . ."

Harry looked back at the story. A feeling of horror was rising like bile in his throat.

"How come we didn't recognize Devil's Snare . . . ? We've seen it before . . . we could've stopped this from happening . . ."

"Who expects Devil's Snare to turn up in a hospital disguised as a potted plant?" said Ron sharply. "It's not our fault, whoever sent it to the bloke is to blame! They must be a real prat, why didn't they check what they were buying?"

"Oh come on, Ron!" said Hermione shakily, "I don't think anyone could put Devil's Snare in a pot and not realize it tries to kill whoever touches it? This — this was murder. . . . A clever murder, as well. . . . If the plant was sent anonymously, how's anyone ever going to find out who did it?"

Harry was not thinking about Devil's Snare. He was remembering taking the lift down to the ninth level of the Ministry on the day of his hearing, and the sallow-faced man who had got in on the Atrium level.

"I met Bode," he said slowly. "I saw him at the Ministry with your dad . . ."

Ron's mouth fell open.

"I've heard Dad talk about him at home! He was an Unspeakable — he worked in the Department of Mysteries!"

They looked at one another for a moment, then Hermione pulled the newspaper back toward her, closed it, glared for a moment at the pictures of the ten escaped Death Eaters on the front, then leapt to her feet.

"Where are you going?" said Ron, startled.

"To send a letter," said Hermione, swinging her bag onto her shoulder. "It . . . well, I don't know whether . . . but it's worth trying . . . and I'm the only one who can . . ."

"I *hate* it when she does that," grumbled Ron as he and Harry got up from the table and made their own, slower way out of the Great Hall. "Would it kill her to tell us what she's up to for once? It'd take her about ten more seconds — hey, Hagrid!"

Hagrid was standing beside the doors into the entrance hall, waiting for a crowd of Ravenclaws to pass. He was still as heavily bruised as he had been on the day he had come back from his mission to the giants and there was a new cut right across the bridge of his nose.

"All righ', you two?" he said, trying to muster a smile but managing only a kind of pained grimace.

"Are you okay, Hagrid?" asked Harry, following him as he lumbered after the Ravenclaws.

"Fine, fine," said Hagrid with a feeble assumption of airiness; he waved a hand and narrowly missed concussing a frightened-looking Professor Vector, who was passing. "Jus' busy, yeh know, usual stuff —

lessons ter prepare — couple o' salamanders got scale rot — an' I'm on probation," he mumbled.

"*You're on probation?*" said Ron very loudly, so that many students passing looked around curiously. "Sorry — I mean — you're on probation?" he whispered.

"Yeah," said Hagrid. "'S'no more'n I expected, ter tell yeh the truth. Yeh migh' not've picked up on it, bu' that inspection didn' go too well, yeh know . . . anyway," he sighed deeply. "Bes' go an rub a bit more chili powder on them salamanders or their tails'll be hangin' off 'em next. See yeh, Harry . . . Ron . . ."

He trudged away, out the front doors and down the stone steps into the damp grounds. Harry watched him go, wondering how much more bad news he could stand.

The fact that Hagrid was now on probation became common knowledge within the school over the next few days, but to Harry's indignation, hardly anybody appeared to be upset about it; indeed, some people, Draco Malfoy prominent among them, seemed positively gleeful. As for the freakish death of an obscure Department of Mysteries employee in St. Mungo's, Harry, Ron, and Hermione seemed to be the only people who knew or cared. There was only one topic of conversation in the corridors now: the ten escaped Death Eaters, whose story had finally filtered through the school from those few people who read the newspapers. Rumors were flying that some of the convicts had been spotted in Hogsmeade, that they were supposed to be hiding out in the Shrieking Shack and that they were going to break into Hogwarts, just as Sirius Black had done.

Those who came from Wizarding families had grown up hearing the names of these Death Eaters spoken with almost as much fear as Voldemort's; the crimes they had committed during the days of Voldemort's reign of terror were legendary. There were relatives of their victims among the Hogwarts students, who now found themselves the unwilling objects of a gruesome sort of reflected fame as they walked the corridors: Susan Bones, who had an uncle, aunt, and cousins who had all died at the hands of one of the ten, said miserably during Herbology that she now had a good idea what it felt like to be Harry.

"And I don't know how you stand it, it's horrible," she said bluntly, dumping far too much dragon manure on her tray of Screechsnap seedlings, causing them to wriggle and squeak in discomfort.

It was true that Harry was the subject of much renewed muttering and pointing in the corridors these days, yet he thought he detected a slight difference in the tone of the whisperers' voices. They sounded curious rather than hostile now, and once or twice he was sure he overheard snatches of conversation that suggested that the speakers were not satisfied with the *Prophet*'s version of how and why ten Death Eaters had managed to break out of Azkaban fortress. In their confusion and fear, these doubters now seemed to be turning to the only other explanation available to them, the one that Harry and Dumbledore had been expounding since the previous year.

It was not only the students' mood that had changed. It was now quite common to come across two or three teachers conversing in low, urgent whispers in the corridors, breaking off their conversations the moment they saw students approaching.

"They obviously can't talk freely in the staffroom anymore," said Hermione in a low voice, as she, Harry, and Ron passed Professors McGonagall, Flitwick, and Sprout huddled together outside the Charms classroom one day. "Not with Umbridge there."

"Reckon they know anything new?" said Ron, gazing back over his shoulder at the three teachers.

"If they do, we're not going to hear about it, are we?" said Harry angrily. "Not after Decree . . . What number are we on now?"

For new signs had appeared on the house notice boards the morning after news of the Azkaban breakout:

——— BY ORDER OF ———

The High Inquisitor of Hogwarts

Teachers are hereby banned from giving students any information that is not strictly related to the subjects they are paid to teach.

The above is in accordance with
Educational Decree Number Twenty-six.

Signed:

Dolores Jane Umbridge

HIGH INQUISITOR

This latest decree had been the subject of a great number of jokes among the students. Lee Jordan had pointed out to Umbridge that by the terms of the new rule she was not allowed to tell Fred and George off for playing Exploding Snap in the back of the class.

"Exploding Snap's got nothing to do with Defense Against the Dark Arts, Professor! That's not information relating to your subject!"

When Harry next saw Lee, the back of his hand was bleeding rather badly. Harry recommended essence of murtlap.

Harry had thought that the breakout from Azkaban might have humbled Umbridge a little, that she might have been abashed at the catastrophe that had occurred right under her beloved Fudge's nose. It seemed, however, to have only intensified her furious desire to bring every aspect of life at Hogwarts under her personal control. She seemed determined at the very least to achieve a sacking before long, and the only question was whether it would be Professor Trelawney or Hagrid who went first.

Every single Divination and Care of Magical Creatures lesson was now conducted in the presence of Umbridge and her clipboard. She lurked by the fire in the heavily perfumed tower room, interrupting Professor Trelawney's increasingly hysterical talks with difficult questions about Ornithomancy and Heptomology, insisting that she predict students' answers before they gave them and demanding that she demonstrate her skill at the crystal ball, the tea leaves, and the rune stones in turn. Harry thought that Professor Trelawney might soon crack under the strain; several times he passed her in the corridors (in itself a very unusual occurrence as she generally remained in her tower room), muttering wildly to herself, wringing her hands, and shooting terrified glances over her shoulder, all the time giving off a powerful smell of cooking sherry. If he had not been so worried about Hagrid, he would have felt sorry for her — but if one of them was to be ousted out of a job, there could be only one choice for Harry as to who should remain.

Unfortunately, Harry could not see that Hagrid was putting up a better show than Trelawney. Though he seemed to be following Hermione's advice and had shown them nothing more frightening than a crup, a creature indistinguishable from a Jack Russell terrier except for its forked tail, since before Christmas, he also seemed to have lost his nerve. He was oddly distracted and jumpy in lessons, losing the thread of what he was saying while talking to the class, answering questions wrongly and glancing anxiously at Umbridge all the time. He was also more distant with Harry, Ron, and Hermione than he had ever been before, expressly forbidding them to visit him after dark.

"If she catches yeh, it'll be all of our necks on the line," he told them flatly, and with no desire to do anything that jeopardized his job further, they abstained from walking down to his hut in the evenings.

It seemed to Harry that Umbridge was steadily depriving him of everything that made his life at Hogwarts worth living: visits to Hagrid's house, letters from Sirius, his Firebolt, and Quidditch. He took his revenge the only way he had: redoubling his efforts for the D.A.

Harry was pleased to see that all of them, even Zacharias Smith, had been spurred to work harder than ever by the news that ten more Death Eaters were now on the loose, but in nobody was this improvement more pronounced than in Neville. The news of his parents' attacker's escape had wrought a strange and even slightly alarming change in him. He had not once mentioned his meeting with Harry, Ron, and Hermione on the closed ward in St. Mungo's, and taking their lead from him, they had kept quiet about it too. Nor had he said anything on the subject of Bellatrix and her fellow torturers' escape; in fact, he barely spoke during D.A. meetings anymore, but worked relentlessly on every new jinx and countercurse Harry taught them, his plump face screwed up in concentration, apparently indifferent to injuries or accidents, working harder than anyone else in the room. He was improving so fast it was quite unnerving and when Harry taught them the Shield Charm, a means of deflecting minor jinxes so that they rebounded upon the attacker, only Hermione mastered the charm faster than Neville.

In fact Harry would have given a great deal to be making as much progress at Occlumency as Neville was making during D.A. meetings. Harry's sessions with Snape, which had started badly enough, were not improving; on the contrary, Harry felt he was getting worse with every lesson.

Before he had started studying Occlumency, his scar had prickled occasionally, usually during the night, or else following one of those strange flashes of Voldemort's thoughts or moods that he experienced every now and then. Nowadays, however, his scar hardly ever stopped prickling, and he often felt lurches of annoyance or cheerfulness that were unrelated to what was happening to him at the time, which were always accompanied by a particularly painful twinge from his scar. He had the horrible impression that he was slowly turning into a kind of aerial that was tuned in to tiny fluctuations in Voldemort's mood, and he was sure he could date this increased sensitivity firmly from his first Occlumency lesson with Snape. What was more, he was now dreaming about walking down the corridor toward the entrance to the Department of Mysteries almost every night, dreams that always culminated in him standing longingly in front of the plain black door.

"Maybe it's a bit like an illness," said Hermione, looking concerned when Harry confided in her and Ron. "A fever or something. It has to get worse before it gets better."

"It's lessons with Snape that are making it worse," said Harry flatly. "I'm getting sick of my scar hurting, and I'm getting bored walking down that corridor every night." He rubbed his forehead angrily. "I just wish the door would open, I'm sick of standing staring at it —"

"That's not funny," said Hermione sharply. "Dumbledore doesn't want you to have dreams about that corridor at all, or he wouldn't have asked Snape to teach you Occlumency. You're just going to have to work a bit harder in your lessons."

"I am working!" said Harry, nettled. "You try it sometime, Snape trying to get inside your head, it's not a bundle of laughs, you know!"

"Maybe . . ." said Ron slowly.

"Maybe what?" said Hermione rather snappishly.

"Maybe it's not Harry's fault he can't close his mind," said Ron darkly.

"What do you mean?" said Hermione.

"Well, maybe Snape isn't really trying to help Harry. . . ."

Harry and Hermione stared at him. Ron looked darkly and meaningfully from one to the other.

"Maybe," he said again in a lower voice, "he's actually trying to open Harry's mind a bit wider . . . make it easier for You-Know —"

"Shut up, Ron," said Hermione angrily. "How many times have

you suspected Snape, and when have you *ever* been right? Dumbledore trusts him, he works for the Order, that ought to be enough."

"He used to be a Death Eater," said Ron stubbornly. "And we've never seen proof that he *really* swapped sides. . . ."

"Dumbledore trusts him," Hermione repeated. "And if we can't trust Dumbledore, we can't trust anyone."

With so much to worry about and so much to do — startling amounts of homework that frequently kept the fifth years working until past midnight, secret D.A. meetings, and regular classes with Snape — January seemed to be passing alarmingly fast. Before Harry knew it, February had arrived, bringing with it wetter and warmer weather and the prospect of the second Hogsmeade visit of the year. Harry had had very little time to spare on conversations with Cho since they had agreed to visit the village together, but suddenly found himself facing a Valentine's Day spent entirely in her company.

On the morning of the fourteenth he dressed particularly carefully. He and Ron arrived at breakfast just in time for the arrival of the post owls. Hedwig was not there — not that he had expected her — but Hermione was tugging a letter from the beak of an unfamiliar brown owl as they sat down.

"And about time! If it hadn't come today . . ." she said eagerly, tearing open the envelope and pulling out a small piece of parchment. Her eyes sped from left to right as she read through the message and a grimly pleased expression spread across her face.

"Listen, Harry," she said, looking up at him. "This is really important. . . . Do you think you could meet me in the Three Broomsticks around midday?"

"Well . . . I dunno," said Harry dubiously. "Cho might be expecting me to spend the whole day with her. We never said what we were going to do."

"Well, bring her along if you must," said Hermione urgently. "But will you come?"

"Well . . . all right, but why?"

"I haven't got time to tell you now, I've got to answer this quickly —"

And she hurried out of the Great Hall, the letter clutched in one hand and a piece of uneaten toast in the other.

"Are you coming?" Harry asked Ron, but he shook his head, looking glum.

"I can't come into Hogsmeade at all, Angelina wants a full day's training. Like it's going to help — we're the worst team I've ever seen. You should see Sloper and Kirke, they're pathetic, even worse than I am." He heaved a great sigh. "I dunno why Angelina won't just let me resign. . . ."

"It's because you're good when you're on form, that's why," said Harry irritably.

He found it very hard to be sympathetic to Ron's plight when he himself would have given almost anything to be playing in the forthcoming match against Hufflepuff. Ron seemed to notice Harry's tone, because he did not mention Quidditch again during breakfast, and there was a slight frostiness in the way they said good-bye to each other shortly afterward. Ron departed for the Quidditch pitch and Harry, after attempting to flatten his hair while staring at his reflection in the back of a teaspoon, proceeded alone to the entrance hall to meet Cho, feeling very apprehensive and wondering what on earth they were going to talk about.

She was waiting for him a little to the side of the oak front doors, looking very pretty with her hair tied back in a long ponytail. Harry's feet seemed to be too big for his body as he walked toward her, and he was suddenly horribly aware of his arms and how stupid they looked swinging at his sides.

"Hi," said Cho slightly breathlessly.

"Hi," said Harry.

They stared at each other for a moment, then Harry said, "Well — er — shall we go, then?"

"Oh — yes . . ."

They joined the queue of people being signed out by Filch, occasionally catching each other's eye and grinning shiftily, but not talking to each other. Harry was relieved when they reached the fresh air, finding it easier to walk along in silence than just stand there looking awkward. It was a fresh, breezy sort of day and as they passed the Quidditch stadium, Harry glimpsed Ron and Ginny skimming over the stands and felt a horrible pang that he was not up there with them. . . .

"You really miss it, don't you?" said Cho.

He looked around and saw her watching him.

"Yeah," sighed Harry. "I do."

"Remember the first time we played against each other?" she asked him.

"Yeah," said Harry, grinning. "You kept blocking me."

"And Wood told you not to be a gentleman and knock me off my broom if you had to," said Cho, smiling reminiscently. "I heard he got taken on by Pride of Portree, is that right?"

"Nah, it was Puddlemere United, I saw him at the World Cup last year."

"Oh, I saw you there too, remember? We were on the same campsite. It was really good, wasn't it?"

The subject of the Quidditch World Cup carried them all the way down the drive and out through the gates. Harry could hardly believe how easy it was to talk to her, no more difficult, in fact, than talking to Ron and Hermione, and he was just starting to feel confident and cheerful when a large gang of Slytherin girls passed them, including Pansy Parkinson.

"Potter and Chang!" screeched Pansy to a chorus of snide giggles. "Urgh, Chang, I don't think much of your taste. . . . At least Diggory was good-looking!"

They sped up, talking and shrieking in a pointed fashion with many exaggerated glances back at Harry and Cho, leaving an embarrassed silence in their wake. Harry could think of nothing else to say about Quidditch, and Cho, slightly flushed, was watching her feet.

"So . . . where d'you want to go?" Harry asked as they entered Hogsmeade. The High Street was full of students ambling up and down, peering into the shop windows and messing about together on the pavements.

"Oh . . . I don't mind," said Cho, shrugging. "Um . . . shall we just have a look in the shops or something?"

They wandered toward Dervish and Banges. A large poster had been stuck up in the window and a few Hogsmeaders were looking at it. They moved aside when Harry and Cho approached and Harry found himself staring once more at the ten pictures of the escaped Death Eaters. The poster ("By Order of the Ministry of Magic") offered a thousand-Galleon reward to any witch or wizard with information relating to the recapture of any of the convicts pictured.

"It's funny, isn't it," said Cho in a low voice, also gazing up at the pictures of the Death Eaters. "Remember when that Sirius Black escaped, and there were dementors all over Hogsmeade looking for him? And now ten Death Eaters are on the loose and there aren't dementors anywhere. . . ."

"Yeah," said Harry, tearing his eyes away from Bellatrix Lestrange's face to glance up and down the High Street. "Yeah, it is weird. . . ."

He was not sorry that there were no dementors nearby, but now he came to think of it, their absence was highly significant. They had not only let the Death Eaters escape, they were not bothering to look for them. . . . It looked as though they really were outside Ministry control now.

The ten escaped Death Eaters were staring out of every shop window he and Cho passed. It started to rain as they passed Scrivenshaft's; cold, heavy drops of water kept hitting Harry's face and the back of his neck.

"Um . . . d'you want to get a coffee?" said Cho tentatively, as the rain began to fall more heavily.

"Yeah, all right," said Harry, looking around. "Where — ?"

"Oh, there's a really nice place just up here, haven't you ever been to Madam Puddifoot's?" she said brightly, and she led him up a side road and into a small tea shop that Harry had never noticed before. It was a cramped, steamy little place where everything seemed to have been decorated with frills or bows. Harry was reminded unpleasantly of Umbridge's office.

"Cute, isn't it?" said Cho happily.

"Er . . . yeah," said Harry untruthfully.

"Look, she's decorated it for Valentine's Day!" said Cho, indicating a number of golden cherubs that were hovering over each of the small, circular tables, occasionally throwing pink confetti over the occupants.

"Aaah . . ."

They sat down at the last remaining table, which was situated in the steamy window. Roger Davies, the Ravenclaw Quidditch Captain, was sitting about a foot and a half away with a pretty blonde girl. They were holding hands. The sight made Harry feel uncomfortable, particularly when, looking around the tea shop, he saw that it was full of nothing but couples, all of them holding hands. Perhaps Cho would expect him to hold *her* hand.

"What can I get you, m'dears?" said Madam Puddifoot, a very stout woman with a shiny black bun, squeezing between their table and Roger Davies's with great difficulty.

"Two coffees, please," said Cho.

In the time it took for their coffees to arrive, Roger Davies and his girlfriend started kissing over their sugar bowl. Harry wished they wouldn't; he felt that Davies was setting a standard with which Cho would soon expect him to compete. He felt his face growing hot and tried staring out of the window, but it was so steamed up he could not see the street outside. To postpone the moment when he had to look at Cho he stared up at the ceiling as though examining the paintwork and received a handful of confetti in the face from their hovering cherub.

After a few more painful minutes Cho mentioned Umbridge; Harry seized on the subject with relief and they passed a few happy moments abusing her, but the subject had already been so thoroughly canvassed during D.A. meetings it did not last very long. Silence fell again. Harry was very conscious of the slurping noises coming from the table next door and cast wildly around for something else to say.

"Er . . . listen, d'you want to come with me to the Three Broomsticks at lunchtime? I'm meeting Hermione Granger there."

Cho raised her eyebrows.

"You're meeting Hermione Granger? Today?"

"Yeah. Well, she asked me to, so I thought I would. D'you want to come with me? She said it wouldn't matter if you did."

"Oh . . . well . . . that was nice of her."

But Cho did not sound as though she thought it was nice at all; on the contrary, her tone was cold and all of a sudden she looked rather forbidding.

A few more minutes passed in total silence, Harry drinking his coffee so fast that he would soon need a fresh cup. Next door, Roger Davies and his girlfriend seemed glued together by the lips.

Cho's hand was lying on the table beside her coffee, and Harry was feeling a mounting pressure to take hold of it. *Just do it,* he told himself, as a fount of mingled panic and excitement surged up inside his chest. *Just reach out and grab it.* . . . Amazing how much more difficult it was to extend his arm twelve inches and touch her hand than to snatch a speeding Snitch from midair . . .

But just as he moved his hand forward, Cho took hers off the table.

She was now watching Roger Davies kissing his girlfriend with a mildly interested expression.

"He asked me out, you know," she said in a quiet voice. "A couple of weeks ago. Roger. I turned him down, though."

Harry, who had grabbed the sugar bowl to excuse his sudden lunging movement across the table, could not think why she was telling him this. If she wished she were sitting at the table next door being heartily kissed by Roger Davies, why had she agreed to come out with him?

He said nothing. Their cherub threw another handful of confetti over them; some of it landed in the last cold dregs of coffee Harry had been about to drink.

"I came in here with Cedric last year," said Cho.

In the second or so it took for him to take in what she had said, Harry's insides had become glacial. He could not believe she wanted to talk about Cedric now, while kissing couples surrounded them and a cherub floated over their heads.

Cho's voice was rather higher when she spoke again.

"I've been meaning to ask you for ages. . . . Did Cedric — did he m-m-mention me at all before he died?"

This was the very last subject on earth Harry wanted to discuss, and least of all with Cho.

"Well — no —" he said quietly. "There — there wasn't time for him to say anything. Erm . . . so . . . d'you . . . d'you get to see a lot of Quidditch in the holidays? You support the Tornados, right?"

His voice sounded falsely bright and cheery. To his horror, he saw that her eyes were swimming with tears again, just as they had been after the last D.A. meeting before Christmas.

"Look," he said desperately, leaning in so that nobody else could overhear, "let's not talk about Cedric right now. . . . Let's talk about something else. . . ."

But this, apparently, was quite the wrong thing to say.

"I thought," she said, tears spattering down onto the table. "I thought *you'd* u-u-understand! I *need* to talk about it! Surely you n-need to talk about it t-too! I mean, you saw it happen, d-didn't you?"

Everything was going nightmarishly wrong; Roger Davies' girlfriend had even unglued herself to look around at Cho crying.

"Well — I have talked about it," Harry said in a whisper, "to Ron and Hermione, but —"

"Oh, you'll talk to Hermione Granger!" she said shrilly, her face now shining with tears, and several more kissing couples broke apart to stare. "But you won't talk to me! P-perhaps it would be best if we just . . . just p-paid and you went and met up with Hermione G-Granger, like you obviously want to!"

Harry stared at her, utterly bewildered, as she seized a frilly napkin and dabbed at her shining face with it.

"Cho?" he said weakly, wishing Roger would seize his girlfriend and start kissing her again to stop her goggling at him and Cho.

"Go on, leave!" she said, now crying into the napkin. "I don't know why you asked me out in the first place if you're going to make arrangements to meet other girls right after me. . . . How many are you meeting after Hermione?"

"It's not like that!" said Harry, and he was so relieved at finally understanding what she was annoyed about that he laughed, which he realized a split second too late was a mistake.

Cho sprang to her feet. The whole tearoom was quiet, and everybody was watching them now.

"I'll see you around, Harry," she said dramatically, and hiccuping slightly she dashed to the door, wrenched it open, and hurried off into the pouring rain.

"Cho!" Harry called after her, but the door had already swung shut behind her with a tuneful tinkle.

There was total silence within the tea shop. Every eye was upon

Harry. He threw a Galleon down onto the table, shook pink confetti out of his eyes, and followed Cho out of the door.

It was raining hard now, and she was nowhere to be seen. He simply did not understand what had happened; half an hour ago they had been getting along fine.

"Women!" he muttered angrily, sloshing down the rain-washed street with his hands in his pockets. "What did she want to talk about Cedric for anyway? Why does she always want to drag up a subject that makes her act like a human hosepipe?"

He turned right and broke into a splashy run, and within minutes he was turning into the doorway of the Three Broomsticks. He knew he was too early to meet Hermione, but he thought it likely there would be someone in here with whom he could spend the intervening time. He shook his wet hair out of his eyes and looked around. Hagrid was sitting alone in a corner, looking morose.

"Hi, Hagrid!" he said, when he had squeezed through the crammed tables and pulled up a chair beside him.

Hagrid jumped and looked down at Harry as though he barely recognized him. Harry saw that he had two fresh cuts on his face and several new bruises.

"Oh, it's you, Harry," said Hagrid. "You all righ'?"

"Yeah, I'm fine," lied Harry; in fact, next to this battered and mournful-looking Hagrid, he felt he did not have much to complain about. "Er — are you okay?"

"Me?" said Hagrid. "Oh yeah, I'm grand, Harry, grand. . . ."

He gazed into the depths of his pewter tankard, which was the size of a large bucket, and sighed. Harry did not know what to say to him. They sat side by side in silence for a moment. Then Hagrid said abruptly, "In the same boat, you an' me, aren' we, Harry?"

"Er —" said Harry.

"Yeah . . . I've said it before. . . . Both outsiders, like," said Hagrid, nodding wisely. "An' both orphans. Yeah . . . both orphans."

He took a great swig from his tankard.

"Makes a diff'rence, havin' a decent family," he said. "Me dad was decent. An' your mum an' dad were decent. If they'd lived, life woulda bin diff'rent, eh?"

"Yeah . . . I s'pose," said Harry cautiously. Hagrid seemed to be in a very strange mood.

"Family," said Hagrid gloomily. "Whatever yeh say, blood's important. . . ."

And he wiped a trickle of it out of his eye.

"Hagrid," said Harry, unable to stop himself, "where are you getting all these injuries?"

"Eh?" said Hagrid, looking startled. "Wha' injuries?"

"All those!" said Harry, pointing at Hagrid's face.

"Oh . . . tha's jus' normal bumps an' bruises, Harry," said Hagrid dismissively. "I got a rough job."

He drained his tankard, set it back upon the table, and got to his feet.

"I'll be seein' yeh, Harry. . . . Take care now. . . ."

And he lumbered out of the pub looking wretched and then disappeared into the torrential rain. Harry watched him go, feeling miserable. Hagrid was unhappy and he was hiding something, but he seemed determined not to accept help. What was going on? But before Harry could think about the matter any further, he heard a voice calling his name.

"Harry! Harry, over here!"

Hermione was waving at him from the other side of the room. He got up and made his way toward her through the crowded pub. He was still a few tables away when he realized that Hermione was not alone; she was sitting at a table with the unlikeliest pair of drinking mates he could ever have imagined: Luna Lovegood and none other than Rita Skeeter, ex-journalist on the *Daily Prophet* and one of Hermione's least favorite people in the world.

"You're early!" said Hermione, moving along to give him room to sit down. "I thought you were with Cho, I wasn't expecting you for another hour at least!"

"Cho?" said Rita at once, twisting around in her seat to stare avidly at Harry. "A *girl*?"

She snatched up her crocodile-skin handbag and groped within it.

"It's none of *your* business if Harry's been with a hundred girls," Hermione told Rita coolly. "So you can put that away right now."

Rita had been on the point of withdrawing an acid-green quill from her bag. Looking as though she had been forced to swallow Stinksap, she snapped her bag shut again.

"What are you up to?" Harry asked, sitting down and staring from Rita to Luna to Hermione.

"Little Miss Perfect was just about to tell me when you arrived," said Rita, taking a large slurp of her drink. "I suppose I'm allowed to *talk* to him, am I?" she shot at Hermione.

"Yes, I suppose you are," said Hermione coldly.

Unemployment did not suit Rita. The hair that had once been set in elaborate curls now hung lank and unkempt around her face. The scarlet paint on her two-inch talons was chipped and there were a couple of false jewels missing from her winged glasses. She took another great gulp of her drink and said out of the corner of her mouth, "Pretty girl, is she, Harry?"

"One more word about Harry's love life and the deal's off and that's a promise," said Hermione irritably.

"What deal?" said Rita, wiping her mouth on the back of her hand. "You haven't mentioned a deal yet, Miss Prissy, you just told me to turn up. Oh, one of these days . . ." She took a deep shuddering breath.

"Yes, yes, one of these days you'll write more horrible stories about Harry and me," said Hermione indifferently. "Find someone who cares, why don't you?"

"They've run plenty of horrible stories about Harry this year without my help," said Rita, shooting a sideways look at him over the top of her glass and adding in a rough whisper, "How has that made you feel, Harry? Betrayed? Distraught? Misunderstood?"

"He feels angry, of course," said Hermione in a hard, clear voice. "Because he's told the Minister of Magic the truth and the Minister's too much of an idiot to believe him."

"So you actually stick to it, do you, that He-Who-Must-Not-Be-Named is back?" said Rita, lowering her glass and subjecting Harry to a piercing stare while her finger strayed longingly to the clasp of the crocodile bag. "You stand by all this garbage Dumbledore's been telling everybody about You-Know-Who returning and you being the sole witness — ?"

"I wasn't the sole witness," snarled Harry. "There were a dozen-odd Death Eaters there as well. Want their names?"

"I'd love them," breathed Rita, now fumbling in her bag once more and gazing at him as though he was the most beautiful thing she had ever seen. "A great bold headline: '*Potter Accuses . . .*' A subheading: '*Harry Potter Names Death Eaters Still Among Us.*' And then, beneath a nice big photograph of you: '*Disturbed teenage survivor of You-Know-Who's attack, Harry Potter, 15, caused outrage yesterday by accusing respectable and prominent members of the Wizarding community of being Death Eaters. . . .*'"

The Quick-Quotes Quill was actually in her hand and halfway to her mouth when the rapturous expression died out of her face.

"But of course," she said, lowering the quill and looking daggers at Hermione, "Little Miss Perfect wouldn't want that story out there, would she?"

"As a matter of fact," said Hermione sweetly, "that's exactly what Little Miss Perfect *does* want."

Rita stared at her. So did Harry. Luna, on the other hand, sang, "Weasley Is Our King" dreamily under her breath and stirred her drink with a cocktail onion on a stick.

"You *want* me to report what he says about He-Who-Must-Not-Be-Named?" Rita asked Hermione in a hushed voice.

"Yes, I do," said Hermione. "The true story. All the facts. Exactly as Harry reports them. He'll give you all the details, he'll tell you the names of the undiscovered Death Eaters he saw there, he'll tell you what Voldemort looks like now — oh, get a grip on yourself," she added contemptuously, throwing a napkin across the table, for at the sound of Voldemort's name, Rita had jumped so badly that she had slopped half her glass of firewhisky down herself.

Rita blotted the front of her grubby raincoat, still staring at Hermione. Then she said baldly, "The *Prophet* wouldn't print it. In case you haven't noticed, nobody believes his cock-and-bull story. Everyone thinks he's delusional. Now, if you let me write the story from that angle —"

"We don't need another story about how Harry's lost his marbles!" said Hermione angrily. "We've had plenty of those already, thank you! I want him given the opportunity to tell the truth!"

"There's no market for a story like that," said Rita coldly.

"You mean the *Prophet* won't print it because Fudge won't let them," said Hermione irritably.

Rita gave Hermione a long, hard look. Then, leaning forward across the table toward her, she said in a businesslike tone, "All right, Fudge is leaning on the *Prophet,* but it comes to the same thing. They won't print a story that shows Harry in a good light. Nobody wants to read it. It's against the public mood. This last Azkaban breakout has got people quite worried enough. People just don't want to believe You-Know-Who's back."

"So the *Daily Prophet* exists to tell people what they want to hear, does it?" said Hermione scathingly.

Rita sat up straight again, her eyebrows raised, and drained her glass of firewhisky.

"The *Prophet* exists to sell itself, you silly girl," she said coldly.

"My dad thinks it's an awful paper," said Luna, chipping into the conversation unexpectedly. Sucking on her cocktail onion, she gazed at Rita with her enormous, protuberant, slightly mad eyes. "He publishes important stories that he thinks the public needs to know. He doesn't care about making money."

Rita looked disparagingly at Luna.

"I'm guessing your father runs some stupid little village newsletter?" she said. "'Twenty-five Ways to Mingle with Muggles' and the dates of the next Bring-and-Fly Sale?"

"No," said Luna, dipping her onion back into her gillywater, "he's the editor of *The Quibbler.*"

Rita snorted so loudly that people at a nearby table looked around in alarm.

"'Important stories he thinks the public needs to know'?" she said witheringly. "I could manure my garden with the contents of that rag."

"Well, this is your chance to raise the tone of it a bit, isn't it?" said Hermione pleasantly. "Luna says her father's quite happy to take Harry's interview. That's who'll be publishing it."

Rita stared at them both for a moment and then let out a great whoop of laughter.

"*The Quibbler!*" she said, cackling. "You think people will take him seriously if he's published in *The Quibbler?*"

"Some people won't," said Hermione in a level voice. "But the *Daily Prophet*'s version of the Azkaban breakout had some gaping holes in it. I think a lot of people will be wondering whether there isn't a better explanation of what happened, and if there's an alternative story available, even if it is published in a" — she glanced sideways at Luna — "in a — well, an *unusual* magazine — I think they might be rather keen to read it."

Rita did not say anything for a while, but eyed Hermione shrewdly, her head a little to one side.

"All right, let's say for a moment I'll do it," she said abruptly. "What kind of fee am I going to get?"

"I don't think Daddy exactly pays people to write for the magazine," said Luna dreamily. "They do it because it's an honor, and, of course, to see their names in print."

Rita Skeeter looked as though the taste of Stinksap was strong in her mouth again as she rounded on Hermione. "I'm supposed to do this *for free*?"

"Well, yes," said Hermione calmly, taking a sip of her drink. "Otherwise, as you very well know, I will inform the authorities that you are an unregistered Animagus. Of course, the *Prophet* might give you rather a lot for an insider's account of life in Azkaban. . . ."

Rita looked as though she would have liked nothing better than to seize the paper umbrella sticking out of Hermione's drink and thrust it up her nose.

"I don't suppose I've got any choice, have I?" said Rita, her voice shaking slightly. She opened her crocodile bag once more, withdrew a piece of parchment, and raised her Quick-Quotes Quill.

"Daddy will be pleased," said Luna brightly. A muscle twitched in Rita's jaw.

"Okay, Harry?" said Hermione, turning to him. "Ready to tell the public the truth?"

"I suppose," said Harry, watching Rita balancing the Quick-Quotes Quill at the ready on the parchment between them.

"Fire away, then, Rita," said Hermione serenely, fishing a cherry out of the bottom of her glass.

SEEN AND UNFORESEEN

Luna said vaguely that she did not know how soon Rita's interview with Harry would appear in *The Quibbler*, that her father was expecting a lovely long article on recent sightings of Crumple-Horned Snorkacks. "And, of course, that'll be a very important story, so Harry's might have to wait for the following issue," said Luna.

Harry had not found it an easy experience to talk about the night when Voldemort had returned. Rita had pressed him for every little detail, and he had given her everything he could remember, knowing that this was his one big opportunity to tell the world the truth. He wondered how people would react to the story. He guessed that it would confirm a lot of people in the view that he was completely insane, not least because his story would be appearing alongside utter rubbish about Crumple-Horned Snorkacks. But the breakout of Bellatrix Lestrange and her fellow Death Eaters had given Harry a burning desire to do something, whether it worked or not. . . .

"Can't wait to see what Umbridge thinks of you going public," said Dean, sounding awestruck at dinner on Monday night. Seamus was shoveling down large amounts of chicken-and-ham pie on Dean's other side, but Harry knew he was listening.

"It's the right thing to do, Harry," said Neville, who was sitting opposite him. He was rather pale, but went on in a low voice, "It must have been . . . tough . . . talking about it. . . . Was it?"

"Yeah," mumbled Harry, "but people have got to know what Voldemort's capable of, haven't they?"

"That's right," said Neville, nodding, "and his Death Eaters too . . . People should know. . . ."

Neville left his sentence hanging and returned to his baked potato. Seamus looked up, but when he caught Harry's eye he looked quickly back at his plate again. After a while Dean, Seamus, and Neville departed for the common room, leaving Harry and Hermione at the table waiting for Ron, who had not yet had dinner because of Quidditch practice.

Cho Chang walked into the hall with her friend Marietta. Harry's stomach gave an unpleasant lurch, but she did not look over at the Gryffindor table and sat down with her back to him.

"Oh, I forgot to ask you," said Hermione brightly, glancing over at the Ravenclaw table, "what happened on your date with Cho? How come you were back so early?"

"Er . . . well, it was . . ." said Harry, pulling a dish of rhubarb crumble toward him and helping himself to seconds, "a complete fiasco, now you mention it."

And he told her what had happened in Madam Puddifoot's Tea Shop.

". . . so then," he finished several minutes later, as the final bit of crumble disappeared, "she jumps up, right, and says 'I'll see you around, Harry,' and runs out of the place!" He put down his spoon and looked at Hermione. "I mean, what was all that about? What was going on?"

Hermione glanced over at the back of Cho's head and sighed. "Oh, Harry," she said sadly. "Well, I'm sorry, but you were a bit tactless."

"*Me,* tactless?" said Harry, outraged. "One minute we were getting on fine, next minute she was telling me that Roger Davies asked her out, and how she used to go and snog Cedric in that stupid tea shop — how was I supposed to feel about that?"

"Well, you see," said Hermione, with the patient air of one explaining that one plus one equals two to an overemotional toddler, "you shouldn't have told her that you wanted to meet me halfway through your date."

"But, but," spluttered Harry, "but — you told me to meet you at twelve and to bring her along, how was I supposed to do that without telling her — ?"

"You should have told her differently," said Hermione, still with that maddeningly patient air. "You should have said it was really annoying, but I'd *made* you promise to come along to the Three Broomsticks, and you really didn't want to go, you'd much rather spend the whole day with her, but unfortunately you thought you really ought to meet me and would she please, please come along with you, and hopefully you'd be able to get away more quickly? And it might have been a good idea to mention how ugly you think I am too," Hermione added as an afterthought.

"But I don't think you're ugly," said Harry, bemused.

Hermione laughed.

"Harry, you're worse than Ron. . . . Well, no, you're not," she sighed, as Ron himself came stumping into the Hall splattered with mud and looking grumpy. "Look — you upset Cho when you said you were going to meet me, so she tried to make you jealous. It was her way of trying to find out how much you liked her."

"Is that what she was doing?" said Harry as Ron dropped onto the bench opposite them and pulled every dish within reach toward himself. "Well, wouldn't it have been easier if she'd just asked me whether I liked her better than you?"

"Girls don't often ask questions like that," said Hermione.

"Well, they should!" said Harry forcefully. "Then I could've just told her I fancy her, and she wouldn't have had to get herself all worked up again about Cedric dying!"

"I'm not saying what she did was sensible," said Hermione, as Ginny joined them, just as muddy as Ron and looking equally disgruntled. "I'm just trying to make you see how she was feeling at the time."

"You should write a book," Ron told Hermione as he cut up his potatoes, "translating mad things girls do so boys can understand them."

"Yeah," said Harry fervently, looking over at the Ravenclaw table. Cho had just got up; still not looking at him, she left the Great Hall. Feeling rather depressed, he looked back at Ron and Ginny. "So, how was Quidditch practice?"

"It was a nightmare," said Ron in a surly voice.

"Oh come on," said Hermione, looking at Ginny, "I'm sure it wasn't that —"

"Yes, it was," said Ginny. "It was appalling. Angelina was nearly in tears by the end of it."

Ron and Ginny went off for baths after dinner; Harry and Hermione returned to the busy Gryffindor common room and their usual pile of homework. Harry had been struggling with a new star chart for Astronomy for half an hour when Fred and George turned up.

"Ron and Ginny not here?" asked Fred, looking around as he pulled up a chair and, when Harry shook his head, he said, "Good. We were watching their practice. They're going to be slaughtered. They're complete rubbish without us."

"Come on, Ginny's not bad," said George fairly, sitting down next to Fred. "Actually, I dunno how she got so good, seeing how we never let her play with us. . . ."

"She's been breaking into your broom shed in the garden since the age of six and taking each of your brooms out in turn when you weren't looking," said Hermione from behind her tottering pile of Ancient Rune books.

"Oh," said George, looking mildly impressed. "Well — that'd explain it."

"Has Ron saved a goal yet?" asked Hermione, peering over the top of *Magical Hieroglyphs and Logograms.*

"Well, he can do it if he doesn't think anyone's watching him," said Fred, rolling his eyes. "So all we have to do is ask the crowd to turn their backs and talk among themselves every time the Quaffle goes up his end on Saturday."

He got up again and moved restlessly to the window, staring out across the dark grounds.

"You know, Quidditch was about the only thing in this place worth staying for."

Hermione cast him a stern look.

"You've got exams coming!"

"Told you already, we're not fussed about N.E.W.T.s," said Fred. "The Snackboxes are ready to roll, we found out how to get rid of those boils, just a couple of drops of murtlap essence sorts them, Lee put us onto it. . . ."

George yawned widely and looked out disconsolately at the cloudy night sky.

"I dunno if I even want to watch this match. If Zacharias Smith beats us I might have to kill myself."

"Kill him, more like," said Fred firmly.

"That's the trouble with Quidditch," said Hermione absentmindedly, once again bent over her Rune translation, "it creates all this bad feeling and tension between the Houses."

She looked up to find her copy of *Spellman's Syllabary* and caught Fred, George, and Harry looking at her with expressions of mingled disgust and incredulity on their faces.

"Well, it does!" she said impatiently. "It's only a game, isn't it?"

"Hermione," said Harry, shaking his head, "you're good on feelings and stuff, but you just don't understand about Quidditch."

"Maybe not," she said darkly, returning to her translation again, "but at least my happiness doesn't depend on Ron's goalkeeping ability."

And though Harry would rather have jumped off the Astronomy Tower than admit it to her, by the time he had watched the game the following Saturday he would have given any number of Galleons not to care about Quidditch either.

The very best thing you could say about the match was that it was short; the Gryffindor spectators had to endure only twenty-two minutes of agony. It was hard to say what the worst thing was: Harry thought it was a close-run contest between Ron's fourteenth failed save, Sloper missing the Bludger but hitting Angelina in the mouth with his bat, and Kirke shrieking and falling backward off his broom as Zacharias Smith zoomed at him carrying the Quaffle. The miracle was that Gryffindor only lost by ten points: Ginny managed to snatch the Snitch from right under Hufflepuff Seeker Summerby's nose, so that the final score was two hundred and forty versus two hundred and thirty.

"Good catch," Harry told Ginny back in the common room, where the atmosphere closely resembled that of a particularly dismal funeral.

"I was lucky," she shrugged. "It wasn't a very fast Snitch and Summerby's got a cold, he sneezed and closed his eyes at exactly the wrong moment. Anyway, once you're back on the team —"

"Ginny, I've got a lifelong ban."

"You're banned as long as Umbridge is in the school," Ginny corrected him. "There's a difference. Anyway, once you're back, I think I'll try out for Chaser. Angelina and Alicia are both leaving next year and I prefer goal-scoring to Seeking anyway."

Harry looked over at Ron, who was hunched in a corner, staring at his knees, a bottle of butterbeer clutched in his hand.

"Angelina still won't let him resign," Ginny said, as though reading Harry's mind. "She says she knows he's got it in him."

Harry liked Angelina for the faith she was showing in Ron, but at the same time thought it would really be kinder to let him leave the team. Ron had left the pitch to another booming chorus of "Weasley Is Our King" sung with great gusto by the Slytherins, who were now favorites to win the Quidditch Cup.

Fred and George wandered over.

"I haven't got the heart to take the mickey out of him, even," said Fred, looking over at Ron's crumpled figure. "Mind you . . . when he missed the fourteenth . . ."

He made wild motions with his arms as though doing an upright doggy-paddle.

"Well, I'll save it for parties, eh?"

Ron dragged himself up to bed shortly after this. Out of respect for his feelings, Harry waited a while before going up to the dormitory himself, so that Ron could pretend to be asleep if he wanted to. Sure enough, when Harry finally entered the room Ron was snoring a little too loudly to be entirely plausible.

Harry got into bed, thinking about the match. It had been immensely frustrating watching from the sidelines. He was quite impressed by Ginny's performance but he felt that if he had been playing he could have caught the Snitch sooner. . . . There had been a moment when it had been fluttering near Kirke's ankle; if she hadn't hesitated, she might have been able to scrape a win for Gryffindor. . . .

Umbridge had been sitting a few rows below Harry and Hermione. Once or twice she had turned squatly in her seat to look at him, her wide toad's mouth stretched in what he thought had been a gloating smile. The memory of it made him feel hot with anger as he lay there in the dark. After a few minutes, however, he remembered that he was supposed to be emptying his mind of all emotion before he slept, as Snape kept instructing him at the end of every Occlumency lesson.

He tried for a moment or two, but the thought of Snape on top of memories of Umbridge merely increased his sense of grumbling resentment, and he found himself focusing instead on how much he loathed the pair of them. Slowly, Ron's snores died away, replaced by the sound of deep, slow breathing. It took Harry much longer to get to sleep; his body was tired, but it took his brain a long time to close down.

He dreamed that Neville and Professor Sprout were waltzing around the Room of Requirement while Professor McGonagall played the bagpipes. He watched them happily for a while, then decided to go and find the other members of the D.A. . . .

But when he left the room he found himself facing, not the tapestry of Barnabas the Barmy, but a torch burning in its bracket on a stone wall. He turned his head slowly to the left. There, at the far end of the windowless passage, was a plain, black door.

He walked toward it with a sense of mounting excitement. He had the strangest feeling that this time he was going to get lucky at last, and find the way to open it. . . . He was feet from it and saw with a leap of excitement that there was a glowing strip of faint blue light down the right-hand side. . . . The door was ajar. . . . He stretched out his hand to push it wide and —

Ron gave a loud, rasping, genuine snore, and Harry awoke abruptly with his right hand stretched in front of him in the darkness, to open a door that was hundreds of miles away. He let it fall with a feeling of mingled disappointment and guilt. He knew he should not have seen the door, but at the same time, felt so consumed with curiosity about what was behind it that he could not help feeling annoyed with Ron. . . . If he could have saved his snore for just another minute . . .

* * *

They entered the Great Hall for breakfast at exactly the same moment as the post owls on Monday morning. Hermione was not the only person eagerly awaiting her *Daily Prophet*: Nearly everyone was eager for more news about the escaped Death Eaters, who, despite many reported sightings, had still not been caught. She gave the delivery owl a Knut and unfolded the newspaper eagerly while Harry helped himself to orange juice; as he had only received one note during the entire year he was sure, when the first owl landed with a thud in front of him, that it had made a mistake.

"Who're you after?" he asked it, languidly removing his orange juice from underneath its beak and leaning forward to see the recipient's name and address:

> Harry Potter
> Great Hall
> Hogwarts School

Frowning, he made to take the letter from the owl, but before he could do so, three, four, five more owls had fluttered down beside it and were jockeying for position, treading in the butter, knocking over the salt, and each attempting to give him their letters first.

"What's going on?" Ron asked in amazement, as the whole of Gryffindor table leaned forward to watch as another seven owls landed amongst the first ones, screeching, hooting, and flapping their wings.

"Harry!" said Hermione breathlessly, plunging her hands into the feathery mass and pulling out a screech owl bearing a long, cylindrical package. "I think I know what this means — open this one first!"

Harry ripped off the brown packaging. Out rolled a tightly furled copy of March's edition of *The Quibbler*. He unrolled it to see his own face grinning sheepishly at him from the front cover. In large red letters across his picture were the words:

HARRY POTTER SPEAKS OUT AT LAST: THE TRUTH ABOUT HE-WHO-MUST-NOT-BE-NAMED AND THE NIGHT I SAW HIM RETURN

"It's good, isn't it?" said Luna, who had drifted over to the Gryffindor table and now squeezed herself onto the bench between Fred and Ron. "It came out yesterday, I asked Dad to send you a free copy. I expect all these," she waved a hand at the assembled owls still scrabbling around on the table in front of Harry, "are letters from readers."

"That's what I thought," said Hermione eagerly, "Harry, d'you mind if we — ?"

"Help yourself," said Harry, feeling slightly bemused.

Ron and Hermione both started ripping open envelopes.

"This one's from a bloke who thinks you're off your rocker," said Ron, glancing down his letter. "Ah well . . ."

"This woman recommends you try a good course of Shock Spells at St. Mungo's," said Hermione, looking disappointed and crumpling up a second.

"This one looks okay, though," said Harry slowly, scanning a long letter from a witch in Paisley. "Hey, she says she believes me!"

"This one's in two minds," said Fred, who had joined in the letter-opening with enthusiasm. "Says you don't come across as a mad person, but he really doesn't want to believe You-Know-Who's back so he doesn't know what to think now. . . . Blimey, what a waste of parchment . . ."

"Here's another one you've convinced, Harry!" said Hermione excitedly. "'Having read your side of the story I am forced to the conclusion that the *Daily Prophet* has treated you very unfairly. . . . Little though I want to think that He-Who-Must-Not-Be-Named has re-turned, I am forced to accept that you are telling the truth. . . .' Oh this is wonderful!"

"Another one who thinks you're barking," said Ron, throwing a crumpled letter over his shoulder, "but this one says you've got her converted, and she now thinks you're a real hero — she's put in a photograph too — wow —"

"What is going on here?" said a falsely sweet, girlish voice.

Harry looked up with his hands full of envelopes. Professor Umbridge was standing behind Fred and Luna, her bulging toad's eyes scanning the mess of owls and letters on the table in front of Harry. Behind her he saw many of the students watching them avidly.

"Why have you got all these letters, Mr. Potter?" she asked slowly.

"Is that a crime now?" said Fred loudly. "Getting mail?"

"Be careful, Mr. Weasley, or I shall have to put you in detention," said Umbridge. "Well, Mr. Potter?"

Harry hesitated, but he did not see how he could keep what he had done quiet; it was surely only a matter of time before a copy of *The Quibbler* came to Umbridge's attention.

"People have written to me because I gave an interview," said Harry. "About what happened to me last June."

For some reason he glanced up at the staff table as he said this. He had the strangest feeling that Dumbledore had been watching him a second before, but when he looked, Dumbledore seemed to be absorbed in conversation with Professor Flitwick.

"An interview?" repeated Umbridge, her voice thinner and higher than ever. "What do you mean?"

"I mean a reporter asked me questions and I answered them," said Harry. "Here —"

And he threw the copy of *The Quibbler* at her. She caught it and stared down at the cover. Her pale, doughy face turned an ugly, patchy violet.

"When did you do this?" she asked, her voice trembling slightly.

"Last Hogsmeade weekend," said Harry.

She looked up at him, incandescent with rage, the magazine shaking in her stubby fingers.

"There will be no more Hogsmeade trips for you, Mr. Potter," she whispered. "How you dare . . . how you could . . ." She took a deep breath. "I have tried again and again to teach you not to tell lies. The message, apparently, has still not sunk in. Fifty points from Gryffindor and another week's worth of detentions."

She stalked away, clutching *The Quibbler* to her chest, the eyes of many students following her.

By mid-morning enormous signs had been put up all over the school, not just on House notice boards, but in the corridors and classrooms too.

───── BY ORDER OF ─────

𝔗𝔥𝔢 𝔥𝔦𝔤𝔥 𝔦𝔫𝔮𝔲𝔦𝔰𝔦𝔱𝔬𝔯 𝔬𝔣 𝔥𝔬𝔤𝔴𝔞𝔯𝔱𝔰

Any student found in possession of the magazine *The Quibbler* will be expelled.

The above is in accordance with
Educational Decree Number Twenty-seven.

Signed:

Dolores Jane Umbridge

HIGH INQUISITOR

For some reason, every time Hermione caught sight of one of these signs she beamed with pleasure.

"What exactly are you so happy about?" Harry asked her.

"Oh Harry, don't you see?" Hermione breathed. "If she could have done one thing to make absolutely sure that every single person in this school will read your interview, it was banning it!"

And it seemed that Hermione was quite right. By the end of that day, though Harry had not seen so much as a corner of *The Quibbler* anywhere in the school, the whole place seemed to be quoting the interview at each other; Harry heard them whispering about it as they queued up outside classes, discussing it over lunch and in the back of lessons, while Hermione even reported that every occupant of the cubicles in the girls' toilets had been talking about it when she nipped in there before Ancient Runes.

"And then they spotted me, and obviously they know I know you, so they were bombarding me with questions," Hermione told Harry, her eyes shining, "and Harry, I think they believe you, I really do, I think you've finally got them convinced!"

Meanwhile Professor Umbridge was stalking the school, stopping students at random and demanding that they turn out their books and pockets. Harry knew she was looking for copies of *The Quibbler*, but the students were several steps ahead of her. The pages carrying Harry's interview had been bewitched to resemble extracts from textbooks if anyone but themselves read it, or else wiped magically blank until they wanted to peruse it again. Soon it seemed that every single person in the school had read it.

The teachers were, of course, forbidden from mentioning the interview by Educational Decree Number Twenty-six, but they found ways to express their feelings about it all the same. Professor Sprout awarded Gryffindor twenty points when Harry passed her a watering can; a beaming Professor Flitwick pressed a box of squeaking sugar mice on him at the end of Charms, said *"Shh!"* and hurried away; and Professor Trelawney broke into hysterical sobs during Divination and announced to the startled class, and a very disapproving Umbridge, that Harry was *not* going to suffer an early death after all, but would live to a ripe old age, become Minister of Magic, and have twelve children.

But what made Harry happiest was Cho catching up with him as he was hurrying along to Transfiguration the next day. Before he knew what had happened her hand was in his and she was breathing in his ear, "I'm really, really sorry. That interview was so brave . . . it made me cry."

He was sorry to hear she had shed even more tears over it, but very glad they were on speaking terms again, and even more pleased when she gave him a swift kiss on the cheek and hurried off again. And unbelievably, no sooner had he arrived outside Transfiguration than something just as good happened: Seamus stepped out of the queue to face him.

"I just wanted to say," he mumbled, squinting at Harry's left knee, "I believe you. And I've sent a copy of that magazine to me mam."

If anything more was needed to complete Harry's happiness, it was Malfoy, Crabbe, and Goyle's reactions. He saw them with their heads together later that afternoon in the library, together with a weedy-looking boy Hermione whispered was called Theodore Nott. They looked around at Harry as he browsed the shelves for the book he needed on Partial Vanishment, and Goyle cracked his knuckles threateningly and Malfoy whispered something undoubtedly malevolent to Crabbe. Harry knew perfectly well why they were acting like this: He had named all of their fathers as Death Eaters.

"And the best bit is," whispered Hermione gleefully as they left the library, "they can't contradict you, because they can't admit they've read the article!"

To cap it all, Luna told him over dinner that no copy of *The Quibbler* had ever sold out faster.

"Dad's reprinting!" she told Harry, her eyes popping excitedly. "He can't believe it, he says people seem even more interested in this than the Crumple-Horned Snorkacks!"

Harry was a hero in the Gryffindor common room that night; daringly, Fred and George had put an Enlargement Charm on the front cover of *The Quibbler* and hung it on the wall, so that Harry's giant head gazed down upon the proceedings, occasionally saying things like "The Ministry are morons" and "Eat dung, Umbridge" in a booming voice. Hermione did not find this very amusing; she said it interfered with her concentration, and ended up going to bed early out of irritation. Harry had to admit that the poster was not quite as funny after an hour or two, especially when the talking spell had started to wear off, so that it merely shouted disconnected words like "Dung" and "Umbridge" at more and more frequent intervals in a progressively higher voice. In fact it started to make his head ache and his scar began prickling uncomfortably again. To disappointed moans from the many people who were sitting around him, asking him to relive his interview for the umpteenth time, he announced that he too needed an early night.

The dormitory was empty when he reached it. He rested his forehead for a moment against the cool glass of the window beside his bed; it felt soothing against his scar. Then he undressed and got into bed, wishing his headache would go away. He also felt slightly sick. He rolled over onto his side, closed his eyes, and fell asleep almost at once. . . .

He was standing in a dark, curtained room lit by a single branch of candles. His hands were clenched on the back of a chair in front of him. They were long-fingered and white as though they had not seen sunlight for years and looked like large, pale spiders against the dark velvet of the chair.

Beyond the chair, in a pool of light cast upon the floor by the candles, knelt a man in black robes.

"I have been badly advised, it seems," said Harry, in a high, cold voice that pulsed with anger.

"Master, I crave your pardon. . . ." croaked the man kneeling on the floor. The back of his head glimmered in the candlelight. He seemed to be trembling.

"I do not blame you, Rookwood," said Harry in that cold, cruel voice.

He relinquished his grip upon the chair and walked around it, closer to the man cowering upon the floor, until he stood directly over him in the darkness, looking down from a far greater height than usual.

"You are sure of your facts, Rookwood?" asked Harry.

"Yes, my Lord, yes . . . I used to work in the department after — after all. . . ."

"Avery told me Bode would be able to remove it."

"Bode could never have taken it, Master. . . . Bode would have known he could not. . . . Undoubtedly that is why he fought so hard against Malfoy's Imperius Curse. . . ."

"Stand up, Rookwood," whispered Harry.

The kneeling man almost fell over in his haste to obey. His face was pockmarked; the scars were thrown into relief by the candlelight. He remained a little stooped when standing, as though halfway through a bow, and he darted terrified looks up at Harry's face.

"You have done well to tell me this," said Harry. "Very well . . . I have wasted months on fruitless schemes, it seems. . . . But no matter . . . We begin again, from now. You have Lord Voldemort's gratitude, Rookwood. . . ."

"My Lord . . . yes, my Lord," gasped Rookwood, his voice hoarse with relief.

"I shall need your help. I shall need all the information you can give me."

"Of course, my Lord, of course . . . anything . . ."

"Very well . . . you may go. Send Avery to me."

Rookwood scurried backward, bowing, and disappeared through a door.

Left alone in the dark room, Harry turned toward the wall. A cracked, age-spotted mirror hung on the wall in the shadows. Harry moved toward it. His reflection grew larger and clearer in the darkness. . . . A face whiter than a skull . . . red eyes with slits for pupils . . .

"NOOOOOOOOO!"

"What?" yelled a voice nearby.

Harry flailed around madly, became entangled in the hangings, and fell out of his bed. For a few seconds he did not know where he was; he was convinced that he was about to see the white, skull-like face looming at him out of the dark again, then Ron's voice spoke very near to him.

"Will you stop acting like a maniac, and I can get you out of here!"

Ron wrenched the hangings apart, and Harry stared up at him in the moonlight, as he lay flat on his back, his scar searing with pain. Ron looked as though he had just been getting ready for bed; one arm was out of his robes.

"Has someone been attacked again?" asked Ron, pulling Harry roughly to his feet. "Is it Dad? Is it that snake?"

"No — everyone's fine —" gasped Harry, whose forehead felt as though it was on fire again. "Well . . . Avery isn't. . . . He's in trouble. . . . He gave him the wrong information. . . . He's really angry. . . ."

Harry groaned and sank, shaking, onto his bed, rubbing his scar.

"But Rookwood's going to help him now. . . . He's on the right track again. . . ."

"What are you talking about?" said Ron, sounding scared. "D'you mean . . . did you just see You-Know-Who?"

"I *was* You-Know-Who," said Harry, and he stretched out his hands in the darkness and held them up to his face to check that they were no longer deathly white and long-fingered. "He was with Rookwood, he's one of the Death Eaters who escaped from Azkaban, remember? Rookwood's just told him Bode couldn't have done it. . . ."

"Done what?"

"Remove something. . . . He said Bode would have known he couldn't have done it. . . . Bode was under the Imperius Curse. . . . I think he said Malfoy's dad put it on him. . . ."

"Bode was bewitched to remove something?" Ron said. "But — Harry, that's got to be —"

"The weapon," Harry finished the sentence for him. "I know."

The dormitory door opened; Dean and Seamus came in. Harry swung his legs back into bed. He did not want to look as though anything odd had just happened, seeing as Seamus had only just stopped thinking Harry was a nutter.

"Did you say," murmured Ron, putting his head close to Harry's on the pretense of helping himself to water from the jug on his bedside table, "that you *were* You-Know-Who?"

"Yeah," said Harry quietly.

Ron took an unnecessarily large gulp of water. Harry saw it spill over his chin onto his chest.

"Harry," he said, as Dean and Seamus clattered around noisily, pulling off their robes, and talking, "you've got to tell —"

"I haven't got to tell anyone," said Harry shortly. "I wouldn't have seen it at all if I could do Occlumency. I'm supposed to have learned to shut this stuff out. That's what they want."

By "they" he meant Dumbledore. He got back into bed and rolled over onto his side with his back to Ron and after a while he heard Ron's mattress creak as he lay back down too. His scar began to burn; he bit hard on his pillow to stop himself making a noise. Somewhere, he knew, Avery was being punished. . . .

Harry and Ron waited until break next morning to tell Hermione exactly what had happened. They wanted to be absolutely sure they could not be overheard. Standing in their usual corner of the cool and breezy courtyard, Harry told her every detail of the dream he could remember. When he had finished, she said nothing at all for a few moments, but stared with a kind of painful intensity at Fred and George, who were both headless and selling their magical hats from under their cloaks on the other side of the yard.

"So that's why they killed him," she said quietly, withdrawing her gaze from Fred and George at last. "When Bode tried to steal this weapon, something funny happened to him. I think there must be defensive spells on it, or around it, to stop people from touching it. That's why he was in St. Mungo's, his brain had gone all funny and he couldn't talk. But remember what the Healer told us? He was recovering. And they couldn't risk him getting better, could they? I mean, the shock of whatever happened when he touched that weapon probably made the Imperius Curse lift. Once he'd got his voice back, he'd explain what he'd been doing, wouldn't he? They would have known he'd been sent to steal the weapon. Of course, it would have been easy for Lucius Malfoy to put the curse on him. Never out of the Ministry, is he?"

"He was even hanging around that day I had my hearing," said Harry. "In the — hang on . . ." he said slowly. "He was in the Department of Mysteries corridor that day! Your dad said he was probably trying to sneak down and find out what happened in my hearing, but what if —"

"Sturgis," gasped Hermione, looking thunderstruck.

"Sorry?" said Ron, looking bewildered.

"Sturgis Podmore," said Hermione, breathlessly. "Arrested for trying to get through a door. Lucius Malfoy got him too. I bet he did it the day you saw him there, Harry. Sturgis had Moody's Invisibility Cloak, right? So what if he was standing guard by the door, invisible, and Malfoy heard him move, or guessed he was there, or just did the Imperius Curse on the off chance that a guard was there? So when Sturgis next had an opportunity — probably when it was his turn on guard duty again — he tried to get into the department to steal the weapon for Voldemort — Ron, be quiet — but he got caught and sent to Azkaban. . . ."

She gazed at Harry.

"And now Rookwood's told Voldemort how to get the weapon?"

"I didn't hear all the conversation, but that's what it sounded like," said Harry. "Rookwood used to work there. . . . Maybe Voldemort'll send Rookwood to do it?"

Hermione nodded, apparently still lost in thought. Then, quite abruptly, she said, "But you shouldn't have seen this at all, Harry."

"What?" he said, taken aback.

"You're supposed to be learning how to close your mind to this sort of thing," said Hermione, suddenly stern.

"I know I am," said Harry. "But —"

"Well, I think we should just try and forget what you saw," said Hermione firmly. "And you ought to put in a bit more effort on your Occlumency from now on."

The week did not improve as it progressed: Harry received two more D's in Potions, was still on tenterhooks that Hagrid might get the sack, and could not stop himself from dwelling on the dream in which he had seen Voldemort, though he did not bring it up with Ron and Hermione again because he did not want another telling-off from Hermione. He wished very much that he could have talked to Sirius about it, but that was out of the question, so he tried to push the matter to the back of his mind.

Unfortunately, the back of his mind was no longer the secure place it had once been.

"Get up, Potter."

A couple of weeks after his dream of Rookwood, Harry was to be found, yet again, kneeling on the floor of Snape's office, trying to clear his head. He had just been forced, yet again, to relive a stream of very early memories he had not even realized he still had, most of them concerning humiliations Dudley and his gang had inflicted upon him in primary school.

"That last memory," said Snape. "What was it?"

"I don't know," said Harry, getting wearily to his feet. He was finding it increasingly difficult to disentangle separate memories from the rush of images and sound that Snape kept calling forth. "You mean the one where my cousin tried to make me stand in the toilet?"

"No," said Snape softly. "I mean the one concerning a man kneeling in the middle of a darkened room. . . ."

"It's . . . nothing," said Harry.

Snape's dark eyes bored into Harry's. Remembering what Snape had said about eye contact being crucial to Legilimency, Harry blinked and looked away.

"How do that man and that room come to be inside your head, Potter?" said Snape.

"It —" said Harry, looking everywhere but at Snape, "it was — just a dream I had."

"A dream," repeated Snape.

There was a pause during which Harry stared fixedly at a large dead frog suspended in a purple liquid in its jar.

"You do know why we are here, don't you, Potter?" said Snape in a low, dangerous voice. "You do know why I am giving up my evenings to this tedious job?"

"Yes," said Harry stiffly.

"Remind me why we are here, Potter."

"So I can learn Occlumency," said Harry, now glaring at a dead eel.

"Correct, Potter. And dim though you may be" — Harry looked back at Snape, hating him — "I would have thought that after two months' worth of lessons you might have made some progress. How many other dreams about the Dark Lord have you had?"

"Just that one," lied Harry.

"Perhaps," said Snape, his dark, cold eyes narrowing slightly, "perhaps you actually enjoy having these visions and dreams, Potter. Maybe they make you feel special — important?"

"No, they don't," said Harry, his jaw set and his fingers clenched tightly around the handle of his wand.

"That is just as well, Potter," said Snape coldly, "because you are neither special nor important, and it is not up to you to find out what the Dark Lord is saying to his Death Eaters."

"No — that's your job, isn't it?" Harry shot at him.

He had not meant to say it; it had burst out of him in temper. For a long moment they stared at each other, Harry convinced he had gone too far. But there was a curious, almost satisfied expression on Snape's face when he answered.

"Yes, Potter," he said, his eyes glinting. "That is my job. Now, if you are ready, we will start again. . . ."

He raised his wand. "One — two — three — *Legilimens!*"

A hundred dementors were swooping toward Harry across the lake in the grounds. . . . He screwed up his face in concentration. . . . They were coming closer. . . . He could see the dark holes beneath their hoods . . . yet he could also see Snape standing in front of him, his eyes fixed upon Harry's face, muttering under his breath. . . . And somehow, Snape was growing clearer, and the dementors were growing fainter . . .

Harry raised his own wand.

"Protego!"

Snape staggered; his wand flew upward, away from Harry — and suddenly Harry's mind was teeming with memories that were not his — a hook-nosed man was shouting at a cowering woman, while a small dark-haired boy cried in a corner. . . . A greasy-haired teenager sat alone in a dark bedroom, pointing his wand at the ceiling, shooting down flies. . . . A girl was laughing as a scrawny boy tried to mount a bucking broomstick —

"ENOUGH!"

Harry felt as though he had been pushed hard in the chest; he took several staggering steps backward, hit some of the shelves covering Snape's walls and heard something crack. Snape was shaking slightly, very white in the face.

The back of Harry's robes were damp. One of the jars behind him had broken when he fell against it; the pickled slimy thing within was swirling in its draining potion.

"*Reparo!*" hissed Snape, and the jar sealed itself once more. "Well, Potter . . . that was certainly an improvement. . . ." Panting slightly, Snape straightened the Pensieve in which he had again stored some of his thoughts before starting the lesson, almost as though checking that they were still there. "I don't remember telling you to use a Shield Charm . . . but there is no doubt that it was effective. . . ."

Harry did not speak; he felt that to say anything might be dangerous. He was sure he had just broken into Snape's memories, that he had just seen scenes from Snape's childhood, and it was unnerving to think that the crying little boy who had watched his parents shouting was actually standing in front of him with such loathing in his eyes. . . .

"Let's try again, shall we?" said Snape.

Harry felt a thrill of dread: He was about to pay for what had just happened, he was sure of it. They moved back into position with the desk between them, Harry feeling he was going to find it much harder to empty his mind this time. . . .

"On the count of three, then," said Snape, raising his wand once more. "One — two —"

Harry did not have time to gather himself together and attempt to clear his mind, for Snape had already cried "*Legilimens!*"

He was hurtling along the corridor toward the Department of

Mysteries, past the blank stone walls, past the torches — the plain black door was growing ever larger; he was moving so fast he was going to collide with it, he was feet from it and he could see that chink of faint blue light again —

The door had flown open! He was through it at last, inside a black-walled, black-floored circular room lit with blue-flamed candles, and there were more doors all around him — he needed to go on — but which door ought he to take — ?

"POTTER!"

Harry opened his eyes. He was flat on his back again with no memory of having gotten there; he was also panting as though he really had run the length of the Department of Mysteries corridor, really had sprinted through the black door and found the circular room. . . .

"Explain yourself!" said Snape, who was standing over him, looking furious.

"I . . . dunno what happened," said Harry truthfully, standing up. There was a lump on the back of his head from where he had hit the ground and he felt feverish. "I've never seen that before. I mean, I told you, I've dreamed about the door . . . but it's never opened before. . . ."

"You are not working hard enough!"

For some reason, Snape seemed even angrier than he had done two minutes before, when Harry had seen into his own memories.

"You are lazy and sloppy, Potter, it is small wonder that the Dark Lord —"

"Can you tell me something, *sir*?" said Harry, firing up again. "Why do you call Voldemort the Dark Lord, I've only ever heard Death Eaters call him that —"

Snape opened his mouth in a snarl — and a woman screamed from somewhere outside the room.

Snape's head jerked upward; he was gazing at the ceiling.

"What the — ?" he muttered.

Harry could hear a muffled commotion coming from what he thought might be the entrance hall. Snape looked around at him, frowning.

"Did you see anything unusual on your way down here, Potter?"

Harry shook his head. Somewhere above them, the woman screamed again. Snape strode to his office door, his wand still held at the ready, and swept out of sight. Harry hesitated for a moment, then followed.

The screams were indeed coming from the entrance hall; they grew louder as Harry ran toward the stone steps leading up from the dungeons. When he reached the top he found the entrance hall packed. Students had come flooding out of the Great Hall, where dinner was still in progress, to see what was going on. Others had crammed themselves onto the marble staircase. Harry pushed forward through a knot of tall Slytherins and saw that the onlookers had formed a great ring, some of them looking shocked, others even frightened. Professor McGonagall was directly opposite Harry on the other side of the hall; she looked as though what she was watching made her feel faintly sick.

Professor Trelawney was standing in the middle of the entrance hall with her wand in one hand and an empty sherry bottle in the other, looking utterly mad. Her hair was sticking up on end, her glasses were lopsided so that one eye was magnified more than the other; her innumerable shawls and scarves were trailing haphazardly from her shoulders, giving the impression that she was falling apart at the seams. Two large trunks lay on the floor beside her, one of them upside down; it looked very much as though it had been thrown down the stairs after her. Professor Trelawney was staring, apparently terrified, at something Harry could not see but that seemed to be standing at the foot of the stairs.

"No!" she shrieked. "NO! This cannot be happening. . . . It cannot . . . I refuse to accept it!"

"You didn't realize this was coming?" said a high girlish voice, sounding callously amused, and Harry, moving slightly to his right, saw that Trelawney's terrifying vision was nothing other than Professor Umbridge. "Incapable though you are of predicting even tomorrow's weather, you must surely have realized that your pitiful performance during my inspections, and lack of any improvement, would make it inevitable you would be sacked?"

"You c-can't!" howled Professor Trelawney, tears streaming down her face from behind her enormous lenses, "you c-can't sack me! I've b-been here sixteen years! H-Hogwarts is m-my h-home!"

"It *was* your home," said Professor Umbridge, and Harry was revolted to see the enjoyment stretching her toadlike face as she watched Professor Trelawney sink, sobbing uncontrollably, onto one of her trunks, "until an hour ago, when the Minister of Magic countersigned the order for your dismissal. Now kindly remove yourself from this hall. You are embarrassing us."

But she stood and watched, with an expression of gloating enjoyment, as Professor Trelawney shuddered and moaned, rocking backward and forward on her trunk in paroxysms of grief. Harry heard a sob to his left and looked around. Lavender and Parvati were both crying silently, their arms around each other. Then he heard footsteps. Professor McGonagall had broken away from the spectators, marched straight up to Professor Trelawney and was patting her firmly on the back while withdrawing a large handkerchief from within her robes.

"There, there, Sybill . . . Calm down. . . . Blow your nose on this. . . . It's not as bad as you think, now. . . . You are not going to have to leave Hogwarts. . . ."

"Oh really, Professor McGonagall?" said Umbridge in a deadly voice, taking a few steps forward. "And your authority for that statement is . . . ?"

"That would be mine," said a deep voice.

The oak front doors had swung open. Students beside them scuttled out of the way as Dumbledore appeared in the entrance. What he had been doing out in the grounds Harry could not imagine, but there was something impressive about the sight of him framed in the doorway against an oddly misty night. Leaving the doors wide behind him, he strode forward through the circle of onlookers toward the place where Professor Trelawney sat, tearstained and trembling, upon her trunk, Professor McGonagall alongside her.

"Yours, Professor Dumbledore?" said Umbridge with a singularly unpleasant little laugh. "I'm afraid you do not understand the position. I have here" — she pulled a parchment scroll from within her robes — "an Order of Dismissal signed by myself and the Minister of Magic. Under the terms of Educational Decree Number Twenty-three, the High Inquisitor of Hogwarts has the power to inspect, place upon probation, and sack any teacher she — that is to say, I — feel is not performing up to the standard required by the Ministry of Magic. I have decided that Professor Trelawney is not up to scratch. I have dismissed her."

To Harry's very great surprise, Dumbledore continued to smile. He looked down at Professor Trelawney, who was still sobbing and choking on her trunk, and said, "You are quite right, of course, Professor Umbridge. As High Inquisitor you have every right to dismiss my teachers. You do not, however, have the authority to send them away from the castle. I am afraid," he went on, with a courteous little bow, "that the power to do that still resides with the headmaster, and it is my wish that Professor Trelawney continue to live at Hogwarts."

At this, Professor Trelawney gave a wild little laugh in which a hiccup was barely hidden.

"No — no, I'll g-go, Dumbledore! I sh-shall l-leave Hogwarts and s-seek my fortune elsewhere —"

"No," said Dumbledore sharply. "It is my wish that you remain, Sybill."

He turned to Professor McGonagall.

"Might I ask you to escort Sybill back upstairs, Professor McGonagall?"

"Of course," said McGonagall. "Up you get, Sybill. . . ."

Professor Sprout came hurrying forward out of the crowd and grabbed Professor Trelawney's other arm. Together they guided her past Umbridge and up the marble stairs. Professor Flitwick went scurrying after them, his wand held out before him; he squeaked, *"Locomotor trunks!"* and Professor Trelawney's luggage rose into the air and proceeded up the staircase after her, Professor Flitwick bringing up the rear.

Professor Umbridge was standing stock-still, staring at Dumbledore, who continued to smile benignly.

"And what," she said in a whisper that nevertheless carried all around the entrance hall, "are you going to do with her once I appoint a new Divination teacher who needs her lodgings?"

"Oh, that won't be a problem," said Dumbledore pleasantly. "You see, I have already found us a new Divination teacher, and he will prefer lodgings on the ground floor."

"You've found — ?" said Umbridge shrilly. *"You've* found? Might I remind you, Dumbledore, that under Educational Decree Twenty-two —"

"— the Ministry has the right to appoint a suitable candidate if — and only if — the headmaster is unable to find one," said Dumbledore. "And I am happy to say that on this occasion I have succeeded. May I introduce you?"

He turned to face the open front doors, through which night mist was now drifting. Harry heard hooves. There was a shocked murmur around the hall and those nearest the doors hastily moved even farther backward, some of them tripping over in their haste to clear a path for the newcomer.

Through the mist came a face Harry had seen once before on a dark, dangerous night in the Forbidden Forest: white-blond hair and astonishingly blue eyes, the head and torso of a man joined to the palomino body of a horse.

"This is Firenze," said Dumbledore happily to a thunderstruck Umbridge. "I think you'll find him suitable."

THE CENTAUR AND THE SNEAK

I'll bet you wish you hadn't given up Divination now, don't you, Hermione?" asked Parvati, smirking.

It was breakfast time a few days after the sacking of Professor Trelawney, and Parvati was curling her eyelashes around her wand and examining the effect in the back of her spoon. They were to have their first lesson with Firenze that morning.

"Not really," said Hermione indifferently, who was reading the *Daily Prophet*. "I've never really liked horses."

She turned a page of the newspaper, scanning its columns.

"He's not a horse, he's a centaur!" said Lavender, sounding shocked.

"A *gorgeous* centaur . . ." sighed Parvati.

"Either way, he's still got four legs," said Hermione coolly. "Anyway, I thought you two were all upset that Trelawney had gone?"

"We are!" Lavender assured her. "We went up to her office to see her, we took her some daffodils — not the honking ones that Sprout's got, nice ones. . . ."

"How is she?" asked Harry.

"Not very good, poor thing," said Lavender sympathetically. "She was crying and saying she'd rather leave the castle forever than stay here if Umbridge is still here, and I don't blame her. Umbridge was horrible to her, wasn't she?"

"I've got a feeling Umbridge has only just started being horrible," said Hermione darkly.

"Impossible," said Ron, who was tucking into a large plate of eggs and bacon. "She can't get any worse than she's been already."

"You mark my words, she's going to want revenge on Dumbledore for appointing a new teacher without consulting her," said Hermione, closing the newspaper. "Especially another part-human. You saw the look on her face when she saw Firenze. . . ."

After breakfast Hermione departed for her Arithmancy class and Harry and Ron followed Parvati and Lavender into the entrance hall, heading for Divination.

"Aren't we going up to North Tower?" asked Ron, looking puzzled, as Parvati bypassed the marble staircase.

Parvati looked scornfully over her shoulder at him.

"How d'you expect Firenze to climb that ladder? We're in classroom eleven now, it was on the notice board yesterday."

Classroom eleven was situated in the ground-floor corridor leading off the entrance hall on the opposite side to the Great Hall. Harry knew it to be one of those classrooms that were never used regularly, and that it therefore had the slightly neglected feeling of a cupboard or storeroom. When he entered it right behind Ron, and found himself right in the middle of a forest clearing, he was therefore momentarily stunned.

"What the — ?"

The classroom floor had become springily mossy and trees were growing out of it; their leafy branches fanned across the ceiling and windows, so that the room was full of slanting shafts of soft, dappled, green light. The students who had already arrived were sitting on the earthy floor with their backs resting against tree trunks or boulders, arms wrapped around their knees or folded tightly across their chests, looking rather nervous. In the middle of the room, where there were no trees, stood Firenze.

"Harry Potter," he said, holding out a hand when Harry entered.

"Er — hi," said Harry, shaking hands with the centaur, who surveyed him unblinkingly through those astonishingly blue eyes but did not smile. "Er — good to see you . . ."

"And you," said the centaur, inclining his white-blond head. "It was foretold that we would meet again."

Harry noticed that there was the shadow of a hoof-shaped bruise on Firenze's chest. As he turned to join the rest of the class upon the floor, he saw that they were all looking at him with awe, apparently deeply impressed that he was on speaking terms with Firenze, whom they seemed to find intimidating.

When the door was closed and the last student had sat down upon a tree stump beside the wastepaper basket, Firenze gestured around the room.

"Professor Dumbledore has kindly arranged this classroom for us," said Firenze, when everyone had settled down, "in imitation of my natural habitat. I would have preferred to teach you in the Forbidden Forest, which was — until Monday — my home . . . but this is not possible."

"Please — er — sir —" said Parvati breathlessly, raising her hand, "why not? We've been in there with Hagrid, we're not frightened!"

"It is not a question of your bravery," said Firenze, "but of my position. I can no longer return to the forest. My herd has banished me."

"Herd?" said Lavender in a confused voice, and Harry knew she was thinking of cows. "What — oh!" Comprehension dawned on her face. "There are *more of you?*" she said, stunned.

"Did Hagrid breed you, like the thestrals?" asked Dean eagerly.

Firenze turned his head very slowly to face Dean, who seemed to realize at once that he had said something very offensive.

"I didn't — I meant — sorry," he finished in a hushed voice.

"Centaurs are not the servants or playthings of humans," said Firenze quietly. There was a pause, then Parvati raised her hand again.

"Please, sir . . . why have the other centaurs banished you?"

"Because I have agreed to work for Professor Dumbledore," said Firenze. "They see this as a betrayal of our kind."

Harry remembered how, nearly four years ago, the centaur Bane had shouted at Firenze for allowing Harry to ride to safety upon his back, calling him a "common mule." He wondered whether it had been Bane who had kicked Firenze in the chest.

"Let us begin," said Firenze. He swished his long palomino tail, raised his hand toward the leafy canopy overhead then lowered it slowly, and as he did so, the light in the room dimmed, so that they now seemed to be sitting in a forest clearing by twilight, and stars emerged upon the ceiling. There were *oohs* and gasps, and Ron said audibly, "Blimey!"

"Lie back upon the floor," said Firenze in his calm voice, "and observe the heavens. Here is written, for those who can see, the fortune of our races."

Harry stretched out on his back and gazed upward at the ceiling. A twinkling red star winked at him from overhead.

"I know that you have learned the names of the planets and their moons in Astronomy," said Firenze's calm voice, "and that you have mapped the stars' progress through the heavens. Centaurs have unraveled the mysteries of these movements over centuries. Our findings teach us that the future may be glimpsed in the sky above us. . . ."

"Professor Trelawney did Astrology with us!" said Parvati excitedly, raising her hand in front of her so that it stuck up in the air as she lay on her back. "Mars causes accidents and burns and things like that, and when it makes an angle to Saturn, like now" — she drew a right angle in the air above her — "that means that people need to be extra careful when handling hot things —"

"That," said Firenze calmly, "is human nonsense."

Parvati's hand fell limply to her side.

"Trivial hurts, tiny human accidents," said Firenze, as his hooves thudded over the mossy floor. "These are of no more significance than the scurryings of ants to the wide universe, and are unaffected by planetary movements."

"Professor Trelawney —" began Parvati, in a hurt and indignant voice.

"— is a human," said Firenze simply. "And is therefore blinkered and fettered by the limitations of your kind."

Harry turned his head very slightly to look at Parvati. She looked very offended, as did several of the people surrounding her.

"Sybill Trelawney may have Seen, I do not know," continued Firenze, and Harry heard the swishing of his tail again as he walked up and down before them, "but she wastes her time, in the main, on the self-flattering nonsense humans call fortune-telling. I, however, am here to explain the wisdom of centaurs, which is impersonal and impartial. We watch the skies for the great tides of evil or change that are sometimes marked there. It may take ten years to be sure of what we are seeing."

Firenze pointed to the red star directly above Harry.

"In the past decade, the indications have been that Wizard-kind is living through nothing more than a brief calm between two wars. Mars, bringer of battle, shines brightly above us, suggesting that the fight must break out again soon. How soon, centaurs may attempt to divine by the burning of certain herbs and leaves, by the observation of fume and flame. . . ."

It was the most unusual lesson Harry had ever attended. They did indeed burn sage and mallowsweet there on the classroom floor, and Firenze told them to look for certain shapes and symbols in the pungent fumes, but he seemed perfectly unconcerned that not one of them could see any of the signs he described, telling them that humans were hardly ever good at this, that it took centaurs years and years to become competent, and finished by telling them that it was foolish to put too much faith in such things anyway, because even centaurs sometimes read them wrongly. He was nothing like any human teacher Harry had ever had. His priority did not seem to be to teach them what he knew, but rather to impress upon them that nothing, not even centaurs' knowledge, was foolproof.

"He's not very definite on anything, is he?" said Ron in a low voice, as they put out their mallowsweet fire. "I mean, I could do with a few more details about this war we're about to have, couldn't you?"

The bell rang right outside the classroom door and everyone jumped; Harry had completely forgotten that they were still inside the castle, quite convinced that he was really in the forest. The class filed out, looking slightly perplexed; Harry and Ron were on the point of following them when Firenze called, "Harry Potter, a word, please."

Harry turned. The centaur advanced a little toward him. Ron hesitated.

"You may stay," Firenze told him. "But close the door, please."

Ron hastened to obey.

"Harry Potter, you are a friend of Hagrid's, are you not?" said the centaur.

"Yes," said Harry.

"Then give him a warning from me. His attempt is not working. He would do better to abandon it."

"His attempt is not working?" Harry repeated blankly.

"And he would do better to abandon it," said Firenze, nodding. "I would warn Hagrid myself, but I am banished — it would be unwise for me to go too near the forest now — Hagrid has troubles enough, without a centaurs' battle."

"But — what's Hagrid attempting to do?" said Harry nervously.

Firenze looked at Harry impassively.

"Hagrid has recently rendered me a great service," said Firenze, "and he has long since earned my respect for the care he shows all living creatures. I shall not betray his secret. But he must be brought to his senses. The attempt is not working. Tell him, Harry Potter. Good day to you."

The happiness Harry had felt in the aftermath of *The Quibbler* interview had long since evaporated. As a dull March blurred into a squally April, his life seemed to have become one long series of worries and problems again.

Umbridge had continued attending all Care of Magical Creatures lessons, so it had been very difficult to deliver Firenze's warning to Hagrid. At last Harry had managed it by pretending he had lost his copy of *Fantastic Beasts and Where to Find Them* and doubling back after class one day. When he passed on Firenze's message, Hagrid gazed at him for a moment through his puffy, blackened eyes, apparently taken aback. Then he seemed to pull himself together.

"Nice bloke, Firenze," he said gruffly, "but he don' know what he's talkin' abou' on this. The attemp's comin' on fine."

"Hagrid, what're you up to?" asked Harry seriously. "Because you've got to be careful, Umbridge has already sacked Trelawney and if you ask me, she's on a roll. If you're doing anything you shouldn't be —"

"There's things more importan' than keepin' a job," said Hagrid, though his hands shook slightly as he said this and a basin full of knarl droppings crashed to the floor. "Don' worry abou' me, Harry, jus' get along now, there's a good lad. . . ."

Harry had no choice but to leave Hagrid mopping up the dung all over his floor, but he felt thoroughly dispirited as he trudged back up to the castle.

Meanwhile, as the teachers and Hermione persisted in reminding them, the O.W.L.s were drawing ever nearer. All the fifth years were suffering from stress to some degree, but Hannah Abbott became the first to receive a Calming Draught from Madam Pomfrey after she burst into tears during Herbology and sobbed that she was too stupid to take exams and wanted to leave school now.

If it had not been for the D.A. lessons, Harry thought he would have been extremely unhappy. He sometimes felt that he was living for the hours he spent in the Room of Requirement, working hard but thoroughly enjoying himself at the same time, swelling with pride as he looked around at his fellow D.A. members and saw how far they had come. Indeed, Harry sometimes wondered how Umbridge was going to react when all the members of the D.A. received "Outstanding" in their Defense Against the Dark Arts O.W.L.s.

They had finally started work on Patronuses, which everybody had been very keen to practice, though as Harry kept reminding them, producing a Patronus in the middle of a brightly lit classroom when they were not under threat was very different to producing it when confronted by something like a dementor.

"Oh, don't be such a killjoy," said Cho brightly, watching her silvery swan-shaped Patronus soar around the Room of Requirement during their last lesson before Easter. "They're so pretty!"

"They're not supposed to be pretty, they're supposed to protect you," said Harry patiently. "What we really need is a boggart or something; that's how I learned, I had to conjure a Patronus while the boggart was pretending to be a dementor —"

"But that would be really scary!" said Lavender, who was shooting puffs of silver vapor out of the end of her wand. "And I still — can't — do it!" she added angrily.

Neville was having trouble too. His face was screwed up in concentration, but only feeble wisps of silver smoke issued from his wand-tip.

"You've got to think of something happy," Harry reminded him.

"I'm trying," said Neville miserably, who was trying so hard his round face was actually shining with sweat.

"Harry, I think I'm doing it!" yelled Seamus, who had been

brought along to his first ever D.A. meeting by Dean. "Look — ah — it's gone. . . . But it was definitely something hairy, Harry!"

Hermione's Patronus, a shining silver otter, was gamboling around her.

"They *are* sort of nice, aren't they?" she said, looking at it fondly.

The door of the Room of Requirement opened and then closed again; Harry looked around to see who had entered, but there did not seem to be anybody there. It was a few moments before he realized that the people close to the door had fallen silent. Next thing he knew, something was tugging at his robes somewhere near the knee. He looked down and saw, to his very great astonishment, Dobby the house-elf peering up at him from beneath his usual eight hats.

"Hi, Dobby!" he said. "What are you — what's wrong?"

For the elf's eyes were wide with terror and he was shaking. The members of the D.A. closest to Harry had fallen silent now: Everybody in the room was watching Dobby. The few Patronuses people had managed to conjure faded away into silver mist, leaving the room looking much darker than before.

"Harry Potter, sir . . ." squeaked the elf, trembling from head to foot, "Harry Potter, sir . . . Dobby has come to warn you . . . but the house-elves have been warned not to tell . . ."

He ran headfirst at the wall: Harry, who had some experience of Dobby's habits of self-punishment, made to seize him, but Dobby merely bounced off the stone, cushioned by his eight hats. Hermione and a few of the other girls let out squeaks of fear and sympathy.

"What's happened, Dobby?" Harry asked, grabbing the elf's tiny arm and holding him away from anything with which he might seek to hurt himself.

"Harry Potter . . . she . . . she . . ."

Dobby hit himself hard on the nose with his free fist: Harry seized that too.

"Who's 'she,' Dobby?"

But he thought he knew — surely only one "she" could induce such fear in Dobby? The elf looked up at him, slightly cross-eyed, and mouthed wordlessly.

"Umbridge?" asked Harry, horrified.

Dobby nodded, then tried to bang his head off Harry's knees; Harry held him at bay.

"What about her? Dobby — she hasn't found out about this — about us — about the D.A.?"

He read the answer in the elf's stricken face. His hands held fast by Harry, the elf tried to kick himself and sank to his knees.

"Is she coming?" Harry asked quietly.

Dobby let out a howl. "Yes, Harry Potter, yes!"

Harry straightened up and looked around at the motionless, terrified people gazing at the thrashing elf.

"WHAT ARE YOU WAITING FOR?" Harry bellowed. "RUN!"

They all pelted toward the exit at once, forming a scrum at the door, then people burst through; Harry could hear them sprinting along the corridors and hoped they had the sense not to try and make it all the way to their dormitories. It was only ten to nine, if they just took refuge in the library or the Owlery, which were both nearer —

"Harry, come on!" shrieked Hermione from the center of the knot of people now fighting to get out.

He scooped up Dobby, who was still attempting to do himself serious injury, and ran with the elf in his arms to join the back of the queue.

"Dobby — this is an order — get back down to the kitchen with the other elves, and if she asks you whether you warned me, lie and say no!" said Harry. "And I forbid you to hurt yourself!" he added, dropping the elf as he made it over the threshold at last and slamming the door behind him.

"Thank you, Harry Potter!" squeaked Dobby, and he streaked off.

Harry glanced left and right, the others were all moving so fast that he caught only glimpses of flying heels at either end of the corridor before they vanished. He started to run right; there was a boys' bathroom up ahead, he could pretend he'd been in there all the time if he could just reach it —

"AAARGH!"

Something caught him around the ankles and he fell spectacularly, skidding along on his front for six feet before coming to a halt. Someone behind him was laughing. He rolled over onto his back and saw Malfoy concealed in a niche beneath an ugly dragon-shaped vase.

"Trip Jinx, Potter!" he said. "Hey, Professor — PROFESSOR! I've got one!"

Umbridge came bustling around the far corner, breathless but wearing a delighted smile.

"It's him!" she said jubilantly at the sight of Harry on the floor. "Excellent, Draco, excellent, oh, very good — fifty points to Slytherin! I'll take him from here. . . . Stand up, Potter!"

Harry got to his feet, glaring at the pair of them. He had never seen Umbridge looking so happy. She seized his arm in a vicelike grip and turned, beaming broadly, to Malfoy. "You hop along and see if you can round up anymore of them, Draco," she said. "Tell the others to look in the library — anybody out of breath — check the bathrooms, Miss Parkinson can do the girls' ones — off you go — and you," she added in her softest, most dangerous voice, as Malfoy walked away. "You can come with me to the headmaster's office, Potter."

They were at the stone gargoyle within minutes. Harry wondered how many of the others had been caught. He thought of Ron — Mrs. Weasley would kill him — and of how Hermione would feel if she was expelled before she could take her O.W.L.s. And it had been Seamus's very first meeting . . . and Neville had been getting so good. . . .

"Fizzing Whizbee," sang Umbridge, and the stone gargoyle jumped aside, the wall behind split open, and they ascended the moving stone staircase. They reached the polished door with the griffin knocker, but Umbridge did not bother to knock, she strode straight inside, still holding tight to Harry.

The office was full of people. Dumbledore was sitting behind his desk, his expression serene, the tips of his long fingers together. Professor McGonagall stood rigidly beside him, her face extremely tense. Cornelius Fudge, Minister of Magic, was rocking backward and forward on his toes beside the fire, apparently immensely pleased with the situation. Kingsley Shacklebolt and a tough-looking wizard Harry did not recognize with very short, wiry hair were positioned on either side of the door like guards, and the freckled, bespectacled form of Percy Weasley hovered excitedly beside the wall, a quill and a heavy scroll of parchment in his hands, apparently poised to take notes.

The portraits of old headmasters and mistresses were not shamming sleep tonight. All of them were watching what was happening below, alert and serious. As Harry entered, a few flitted into neighboring frames and whispered urgently into their neighbors' ears.

Harry pulled himself free of Umbridge's grasp as the door swung shut behind them. Cornelius Fudge was glaring at him with a kind of vicious satisfaction upon his face.

"Well," he said. "Well, well, well . . ."

Harry replied with the dirtiest look he could muster. His heart drummed madly inside him, but his brain was oddly cool and clear.

"He was heading back to Gryffindor Tower," said Umbridge. There was an indecent excitement in her voice, the same callous pleasure Harry had heard as she watched Professor Trelawney dissolving with misery in the entrance hall. "The Malfoy boy cornered him."

"Did he, did he?" said Fudge appreciatively. "I must remember to tell Lucius. Well, Potter . . . I expect you know why you are here?"

Harry fully intended to respond with a defiant "yes": His mouth had opened and the word was half formed when he caught sight of

Dumbledore's face. Dumbledore was not looking directly at Harry; his eyes were fixed upon a point just over his shoulder, but as Harry stared at him, he shook his head a fraction of an inch to each side.

Harry changed direction mid-word.

"Yeh — no."

"I beg your pardon?" said Fudge.

"No," said Harry, firmly.

"You *don't* know why you are here?"

"No, I don't," said Harry.

Fudge looked incredulously from Harry to Professor Umbridge; Harry took advantage of his momentary inattention to steal another quick look at Dumbledore, who gave the carpet the tiniest of nods and the shadow of a wink.

"So you have no idea," said Fudge in a voice positively sagging with sarcasm, "why Professor Umbridge has brought you to this office? You are not aware that you have broken any school rules?"

"School rules?" said Harry. "No."

"Or Ministry decrees?" amended Fudge angrily.

"Not that I'm aware of," said Harry blandly.

His heart was still hammering very fast. It was almost worth telling these lies to watch Fudge's blood pressure rising, but he could not see how on earth he would get away with them. If somebody had tipped off Umbridge about the D.A. then he, the leader, might as well be packing his trunk right now.

"So it's news to you, is it," said Fudge, his voice now thick with anger, "that an illegal student organization has been discovered within this school?"

"Yes, it is," said Harry, hoisting an unconvincing look of innocent surprise onto his face.

"I think, Minister," said Umbridge silkily from beside him, "we might make better progress if I fetch our informant."

"Yes, yes, do," said Fudge, nodding, and he glanced maliciously at Dumbledore as Umbridge left the room. "There's nothing like a good witness, is there, Dumbledore?"

"Nothing at all, Cornelius," said Dumbledore gravely, inclining his head.

There was a wait of several minutes, in which nobody looked at each other, then Harry heard the door open behind him. Umbridge moved past him into the room, gripping by the shoulder Cho's curly-haired friend Marietta, who was hiding her face in her hands.

"Don't be scared, dear, don't be frightened," said Professor Umbridge softly, patting her on the back, "it's quite all right, now. You have done the right thing. The Minister is very pleased with you. He'll be telling your mother what a good girl you've been. Marietta's mother, Minister," she added, looking up at Fudge, "is Madam Edgecombe from the Department of Magical Transportation. Floo Network office — she's been helping us police the Hogwarts fires, you know."

"Jolly good, jolly good!" said Fudge heartily. "Like mother, like daughter, eh? Well, come on, now, dear, look up, don't be shy, let's hear what you've got to — galloping gargoyles!"

As Marietta raised her head, Fudge leapt backward in shock, nearly landing himself in the fire. He cursed and stamped on the hem of his cloak, which had started to smoke, and Marietta gave a wail and pulled the neck of her robes right up to her eyes, but not before the whole room had seen that her face was horribly disfigured by a series of close-set purple pustules that had spread across her nose and cheeks to form the word "SNEAK."

"Never mind the spots now, dear," said Umbridge impatiently, "just take your robes away from your mouth and tell the Minister —"

But Marietta gave another muffled wail and shook her head frantically.

"Oh, very well, you silly girl, *I'll* tell him," snapped Umbridge. She hitched her sickly smile back onto her face and said, "Well, Minister,

Miss Edgecombe here came to my office shortly after dinner this evening and told me she had something she wanted to tell me. She said that if I proceeded to a secret room on the seventh floor, sometimes known as the Room of Requirement, I would find out something to my advantage. I questioned her a little further and she admitted that there was to be some kind of meeting there. Unfortunately at that point this hex," she waved impatiently at Marietta's concealed face, "came into operation and upon catching sight of her face in my mirror the girl became too distressed to tell me any more."

"Well, now," said Fudge, fixing Marietta with what he evidently imagined was a kind and fatherly look. "It is very brave of you, my dear, coming to tell Professor Umbridge, you did exactly the right thing. Now, will you tell me what happened at this meeting? What was its purpose? Who was there?"

But Marietta would not speak. She merely shook her head again, her eyes wide and fearful.

"Haven't we got a counterjinx for this?" Fudge asked Umbridge impatiently, gesturing at Marietta's face. "So she can speak freely?"

"I have not yet managed to find one," Umbridge admitted grudgingly, and Harry felt a surge of pride in Hermione's jinxing ability. "But it doesn't matter if she won't speak, I can take up the story from here.

"You will remember, Minister, that I sent you a report back in October that Potter had met a number of fellow students in the Hog's Head in Hogsmeade —"

"And what is your evidence for that?" cut in Professor McGonagall.

"I have testimony from Willy Widdershins, Minerva, who happened to be in the bar at the time. He was heavily bandaged, it is true, but his hearing was quite unimpaired," said Umbridge smugly. "He heard every word Potter said and hastened straight to the school to report to me —"

"Oh, so *that's* why he wasn't prosecuted for setting up all those regurgitating toilets!" said Professor McGonagall, raising her eyebrows. "What an interesting insight into our justice system!"

"Blatant corruption!" roared the portrait of the corpulent, red-nosed wizard on the wall behind Dumbledore's desk. "The Ministry did not cut deals with petty criminals in my day, no sir, they did not!"

"Thank you, Fortescue, that will do," said Dumbledore softly.

"The purpose of Potter's meeting with these students," continued Professor Umbridge, "was to persuade them to join an illegal society, whose aim was to learn spells and curses the Ministry has decided are inappropriate for school-age —"

"I think you'll find you're wrong there, Dolores," said Dumbledore quietly, peering at her over the half-moon spectacles perched halfway down his crooked nose.

Harry stared at him. He could not see how Dumbledore was going to talk him out of this one; if Willy Widdershins had indeed heard every word he said in the Hog's Head there was simply no escaping it.

"Oho!" said Fudge, bouncing up and down on the balls of his feet again. "Yes, do let's hear the latest cock-and-bull story designed to pull Potter out of trouble! Go on, then, Dumbledore, go on — Willy Widdershins was lying, was he? Or was it Potter's identical twin in the Hog's Head that day? Or is there the usual simple explanation involving a reversal of time, a dead man coming back to life, and a couple of invisible dementors?"

Percy Weasley let out a hearty laugh.

"Oh, very good, Minister, very good!"

Harry could have kicked him. Then he saw, to his astonishment, that Dumbledore was smiling gently too.

"Cornelius, I do not deny — and nor, I am sure, does Harry — that he was in the Hog's Head that day, nor that he was trying to recruit students to a Defense Against the Dark Arts group. I am merely pointing out that Dolores is quite wrong to suggest that such a group was, at that time, illegal. If you remember, the Ministry decree banning all student societies was not put into effect until two days after Harry's Hogsmeade meeting, so he was not breaking any rules in the Hog's Head at all."

Percy looked as though he had been struck in the face by something very heavy. Fudge remained motionless in mid-bounce, his mouth hanging open.

Umbridge recovered first.

"That's all very fine, Headmaster," she said, smiling sweetly. "But we are now nearly six months on from the introduction of Educational Decree Number Twenty-four. If the first meeting was not illegal, all those that have happened since most certainly are."

"Well," said Dumbledore, surveying her with polite interest over the top of his interlocked fingers, "they certainly *would* be, if they *had* continued after the decree came into effect. Do you have any evidence that these meetings continued?"

As Dumbledore spoke, Harry heard a rustle behind him and rather thought Kingsley whispered something. He could have sworn too that he felt something brush against his side, a gentle something like a draft or bird wings, but looking down he saw nothing there.

"Evidence?" repeated Umbridge with that horrible wide toadlike smile. "Have you not been listening, Dumbledore? Why do you think Miss Edgecombe is here?"

"Oh, can she tell us about six months' worth of meetings?" said Dumbledore, raising his eyebrows. "I was under the impression that she was merely reporting a meeting tonight."

"Miss Edgecombe," said Umbridge at once, "tell us how long these meetings have been going on, dear. You can simply nod or shake your head, I'm sure that won't make the spots worse. Have they been happening regularly over the last six months?"

Harry felt a horrible plummeting in his stomach. This was it, they had hit a dead end of solid evidence that not even Dumbledore would be able to shift aside. . . .

"Just nod or shake your head, dear," Umbridge said coaxingly to Marietta. "Come on, now, that won't activate the jinx further. . . ."

Everyone in the room was gazing at the top of Marietta's face. Only her eyes were visible between the pulled up robes and her curly fringe. Perhaps it was a trick of the firelight, but her eyes looked oddly blank. And then — to Harry's utter amazement — Marietta shook her head.

Umbridge looked quickly at Fudge and then back at Marietta.

"I don't think you understood the question, did you, dear? I'm asking whether you've been going to these meetings for the past six months? You have, haven't you?"

Again, Marietta shook her head.

"What do you mean by shaking your head, dear?" said Umbridge in a testy voice.

"I would have thought her meaning was quite clear," said Professor McGonagall harshly. "There have been no secret meetings for the past six months. Is that correct, Miss Edgecombe?"

Marietta nodded.

"But there was a meeting tonight!" said Umbridge furiously. "There was a meeting, Miss Edgecombe, you told me about it, in the Room of Requirement! And Potter was the leader, was he not, Potter organized it, Potter — *why are you shaking your head, girl?*"

"Well, usually when a person shakes their head," said McGonagall coldly, "they mean 'no.' So unless Miss Edgecombe is using a form of sign language as yet unknown to humans —"

Professor Umbridge seized Marietta, pulled her around to face her, and began shaking her very hard. A split second later Dumbledore was on his feet, his wand raised. Kingsley started forward and Umbridge leapt back from Marietta, waving her hands in the air as though they had been burned.

"I cannot allow you to manhandle my students, Dolores," said Dumbledore, and for the first time, he looked angry.

"You want to calm yourself, Madam Umbridge," said Kingsley in his deep, slow voice. "You don't want to get yourself into trouble now."

"No," said Umbridge breathlessly, glancing up at the towering figure of Kingsley. "I mean, yes — you're right, Shacklebolt — I — I forgot myself."

Marietta was standing exactly where Umbridge had released her. She seemed neither perturbed by Umbridge's sudden attack, nor relieved by her release. She was still clutching her robe up to her oddly blank eyes, staring straight ahead of her. A sudden suspicion connected to Kingsley's whisper and the thing he had felt shoot past him sprang into Harry's mind.

"Dolores," said Fudge, with the air of trying to settle something once and for all, "the meeting tonight — the one we know definitely happened —"

"Yes," said Umbridge, pulling herself together, "yes . . . well, Miss Edgecombe tipped me off and I proceeded at once to the seventh floor, accompanied by certain *trustworthy* students, so as to catch those in the meeting red-handed. It appears that they were forewarned of my arrival, however, because when we reached the seventh floor they were running in every direction. It does not matter, however. I have all their names here, Miss Parkinson ran into the Room of Requirement for me to see if they had left anything behind. . . . We needed evidence and the room provided . . ."

And to Harry's horror, she withdrew from her pocket the list of names that had been pinned upon the Room of Requirement's wall and handed it to Fudge.

"The moment I saw Potter's name on the list, I knew what we were dealing with," she said softly.

"Excellent," said Fudge, a smile spreading across his face. "Excellent, Dolores. And . . . by thunder . . ."

He looked up at Dumbledore, who was still standing beside Marietta, his wand held loosely in his hand.

"See what they've named themselves?" said Fudge quietly. *"Dumbledore's Army."*

Dumbledore reached out and took the piece of parchment from Fudge. He gazed at the heading scribbled by Hermione months before and for a moment seemed unable to speak. Then he looked up, smiling.

"Well, the game is up," he said simply. "Would you like a written confession from me, Cornelius — or will a statement before these witnesses suffice?"

Harry saw McGonagall and Kingsley look at each other. There was fear in both faces. He did not understand what was going on, and neither, apparently, did Fudge.

"Statement?" said Fudge slowly. "What — I don't — ?"

"Dumbledore's Army, Cornelius," said Dumbledore, still smiling as he waved the list of names before Fudge's face. "Not Potter's Army. *Dumbledore's Army.*"

"But — but —"

Understanding blazed suddenly in Fudge's face. He took a horrified step backward, yelped, and jumped out of the fire again.

"You?" he whispered, stamping again on his smoldering cloak.

"That's right," said Dumbledore pleasantly.

"You organized this?"

"I did," said Dumbledore.

"You recruited these students for — for your army?"

"Tonight was supposed to be the first meeting," said Dumbledore, nodding. "Merely to see whether they would be interested in joining me. I see now that it was a mistake to invite Miss Edgecombe, of course."

Marietta nodded. Fudge looked from her to Dumbledore, his chest swelling.

"Then you *have* been plotting against me!" he yelled.

"That's right," said Dumbledore cheerfully.

"NO!" shouted Harry.

Kingsley flashed a look of warning at him, McGonagall widened her eyes threateningly, but it had suddenly dawned upon Harry what Dumbledore was about to do, and he could not let it happen.

"No — Professor Dumbledore!"

"Be quiet, Harry, or I am afraid you will have to leave my office," said Dumbledore calmly.

"Yes, shut up, Potter!" barked Fudge, who was still ogling Dumbledore with a kind of horrified delight. "Well, well, well — I came here tonight expecting to expel Potter and instead —"

"Instead you get to arrest me," said Dumbledore, smiling. "It's like losing a Knut and finding a Galleon, isn't it?"

"Weasley!" cried Fudge, now positively quivering with delight, "Weasley, have you written it all down, everything he's said, his confession, have you got it?"

"Yes, sir, I think so, sir!" said Percy eagerly, whose nose was splattered with ink from the speed of his note-taking.

"The bit about how he's been trying to build up an army against the Ministry, how he's been working to destabilize me?"

"Yes, sir, I've got it, yes!" said Percy, scanning his notes joyfully.

"Very well, then," said Fudge, now radiant with glee. "Duplicate your notes, Weasley, and send a copy to the *Daily Prophet* at once. If we send a fast owl we should make the morning edition!" Percy dashed from the room, slamming the door behind him, and Fudge turned back to Dumbledore. "You will now be escorted back to the Ministry, where you will be formally charged and then sent to Azkaban to await trial!"

"Ah," said Dumbledore gently, "yes. Yes, I thought we might hit that little snag."

"Snag?" said Fudge, his voice still vibrating with joy. "I see no snag, Dumbledore!"

"Well," said Dumbledore apologetically, "I'm afraid I do."

"Oh really?"

"Well — it's just that you seem to be laboring under the delusion that I am going to — what is the phrase? 'Come quietly.' I am afraid I am not going to come quietly at all, Cornelius. I have absolutely no intention of being sent to Azkaban. I could break out, of course — but what a waste of time, and frankly, I can think of a whole host of things I would rather be doing."

Umbridge's face was growing steadily redder, she looked as though she was being filled with boiling water. Fudge stared at Dumbledore with a very silly expression on his face, as though he had just been stunned by a sudden blow and could not quite believe it had happened. He made a small choking noise and then looked around at Kingsley and the man with short gray hair, who alone of everyone in the room had remained entirely silent so far. The latter gave Fudge a reassuring nod and moved forward a little, away from the wall. Harry saw his hand drift, almost casually, toward his pocket.

"Don't be silly, Dawlish," said Dumbledore kindly. "I'm sure you are an excellent Auror, I seem to remember that you achieved 'Outstanding' in all your N.E.W.T.s, but if you attempt to — er — 'bring me in' by force, I will have to hurt you."

The man called Dawlish blinked, looking rather foolish. He looked toward Fudge again, but this time seemed to be hoping for a clue as to what to do next.

"So," sneered Fudge, recovering himself, "you intend to take on Dawlish, Shacklebolt, Dolores, and myself single-handed, do you, Dumbledore?"

"Merlin's beard, no," said Dumbledore, smiling. "Not unless you are foolish enough to force me to."

"He will not be single-handed!" said Professor McGonagall loudly, plunging her hand inside her robes.

"Oh yes he will, Minerva!" said Dumbledore sharply. "Hogwarts needs you!"

"Enough of this rubbish!" said Fudge, pulling out his own wand. "Dawlish! Shacklebolt! *Take him!*"

A streak of silver light flashed around the room. There was a bang like a gunshot, and the floor trembled. A hand grabbed the scruff of Harry's neck and forced him down on the floor as a second silver flash went off — several of the portraits yelled, Fawkes screeched, and a cloud of dust filled the air. Coughing in the dust, Harry saw a dark figure fall to the ground with a crash in front of him. There was a shriek and a thud and somebody cried, "No!" Then the sound of breaking glass, frantically scuffling footsteps, a groan — and silence.

Harry struggled around to see who was half-strangling him and saw Professor McGonagall crouched beside him. She had forced both him and Marietta out of harm's way. Dust was still floating gently down through the air onto them. Panting slightly, Harry saw a very tall figure moving toward them.

"Are you all right?" said Dumbledore.

"Yes!" said Professor McGonagall, getting up and dragging Harry and Marietta with her.

The dust was clearing. The wreckage of the office loomed into view: Dumbledore's desk had been overturned, all of the spindly tables had been knocked to the floor, their silver instruments in pieces. Fudge, Umbridge, Kingsley, and Dawlish lay motionless on the floor. Fawkes the phoenix soared in wide circles above them, singing softly.

"Unfortunately, I had to hex Kingsley too, or it would have looked very suspicious," said Dumbledore in a low voice. "He was remarkably quick on the uptake, modifying Miss Edgecombe's memory like that while everyone was looking the other way — thank him for me, won't you, Minerva?

"Now, they will all awake very soon and it will be best if they do not know that we had time to communicate — you must act as though no time has passed, as though they were merely knocked to the ground, they will not remember —"

"Where will you go, Dumbledore?" whispered Professor McGonagall. "Grimmauld Place?"

"Oh no," said Dumbledore with a grim smile. "I am not leaving to go into hiding. Fudge will soon wish he'd never dislodged me from Hogwarts, I promise you. . . ."

"Professor Dumbledore . . ." Harry began.

He did not know what to say first: how sorry he was that he had started the D.A. in the first place and caused all this trouble, or how terrible he felt that Dumbledore was leaving to save him from expulsion? But Dumbledore cut him off before he could say another word.

"Listen to me, Harry," he said urgently, "you must study Occlumency as hard as you can, do you understand me? Do everything Professor Snape tells you and practice it particularly every night before sleeping so that you can close your mind to bad dreams — you will understand why soon enough, but you must promise me —"

The man called Dawlish was stirring. Dumbledore seized Harry's wrist.

"Remember — close your mind —"

But as Dumbledore's fingers closed over Harry's skin, a pain shot through the scar on his forehead, and he felt again that terrible, snakelike longing to strike Dumbledore, to bite him, to hurt him —

"— you will understand," whispered Dumbledore.

Fawkes circled the office and swooped low over him. Dumbledore released Harry, raised his hand, and grasped the phoenix's long golden tail. There was a flash of fire and the pair of them had gone.

"Where is he?" yelled Fudge, pushing himself up from the ground. *"Where is he?"*

"I don't know!" shouted Kingsley, also leaping to his feet.

"Well, he can't have Disapparated!" cried Umbridge. "You can't inside this school —"

"The stairs!" cried Dawlish, and he flung himself upon the door, wrenched it open, and disappeared, followed closely by Kingsley and

Umbridge. Fudge hesitated, then got to his feet slowly, brushing dust from his front. There was a long and painful silence.

"Well, Minerva," said Fudge nastily, straightening his torn shirt-sleeve, "I'm afraid this is the end of your friend Dumbledore."

"You think so, do you?" said Professor McGonagall scornfully.

Fudge seemed not to hear her. He was looking around at the wrecked office. A few of the portraits hissed at him; one or two even made rude hand gestures.

"You'd better get those two off to bed," said Fudge, looking back at Professor McGonagall with a dismissive nod toward Harry and Marietta.

She said nothing, but marched Harry and Marietta to the door. As it swung closed behind them, Harry heard Phineas Nigellus's voice.

"You know, Minister, I disagree with Dumbledore on many counts . . . but you cannot deny he's got style. . . ."

SNAPE'S WORST MEMORY

— BY ORDER OF —

The Ministry of Magic

Dolores Jane Umbridge (High Inquisitor) has replaced Albus Dumbledore as Head of Hogwarts School of Witchcraft and Wizardry.

The above is in accordance with
Educational Decree Number Twenty-eight.

Signed:

Cornelius Oswald Fudge

MINISTER OF MAGIC

The notices had gone up all over the school overnight, but they did not explain how every single person within the castle seemed to know that Dumbledore had overcome two Aurors, the High Inquisitor, the Minister of Magic, and his Junior Assistant to escape. No matter where Harry went within the castle next day, the sole topic of conversation was Dumbledore's flight, and though some of the details might have gone awry in the retelling (Harry overheard one second-year girl assuring another that Fudge was now lying in St. Mungo's with a pumpkin for a head), it was surprising how accurate the rest of their information was. Everybody seemed aware, for instance, that Harry and Marietta were the only students to have witnessed the scene in Dumbledore's office, and as Marietta was now in the hospital wing, Harry found himself besieged with requests to give a firsthand account wherever he went.

"Dumbledore will be back before long," said Ernie Macmillan confidently on the way back from Herbology after listening intently to Harry's story. "They couldn't keep him away in our second year and they won't be able to this time. The Fat Friar told me . . ." He dropped his voice conspiratorially, so that Harry, Ron, and Hermione had to lean closer to him to hear, ". . . that Umbridge tried to get back into his office last night after they'd searched the castle and grounds for him. Couldn't get past the gargoyle. The Head's office has sealed itself against her." Ernie smirked. "Apparently she had a right little tantrum. . . ."

"Oh, I expect she really fancied herself sitting up there in the Head's office," said Hermione viciously, as they walked up the stone steps into the entrance hall. "Lording it over all the other teachers, the stupid puffed-up, power-crazy old —"

"Now, do you *really* want to finish that sentence, Granger?"

Draco Malfoy had slid out from behind the door, followed by Crabbe and Goyle. His pale, pointed face was alight with malice.

"Afraid I'm going to have to dock a few points from Gryffindor and Hufflepuff," he drawled.

"You can't take points from fellow prefects, Malfoy," said Ernie at once.

"I know *prefects* can't dock points from each other," sneered Malfoy; Crabbe and Goyle sniggered. "But members of the Inquisitorial Squad —"

"The *what?*" said Hermione sharply.

"The Inquisitorial Squad, Granger," said Malfoy, pointing toward a tiny silver *I* upon his robes just beneath his prefect's badge. "A select group of students who are supportive of the Ministry of Magic, hand-picked by Professor Umbridge. Anyway, members of the Inquisitorial Squad *do* have the power to dock points. . . . So, Granger, I'll have five from you for being rude about our new headmistress. . . . Macmillan, five for contradicting me. . . . Five because I don't like you, Potter . . . Weasley, your shirt's untucked, so I'll have another five for that. . . . Oh yeah, I forgot, you're a Mudblood, Granger, so ten for that. . . ."

Ron pulled out his wand, but Hermione pushed it away, whispering, "Don't!"

"Wise move, Granger," breathed Malfoy. "New Head, new times . . . Be good now, Potty . . . Weasel King . . ."

He strode away, laughing heartily with Crabbe and Goyle.

"He was bluffing," said Ernie, looking appalled. "He can't be allowed to dock points . . . that would be ridiculous. . . . It would completely undermine the prefect system. . . ."

But Harry, Ron, and Hermione had turned automatically toward the giant hourglasses set in niches along the wall behind them, which recorded the House points. Gryffindor and Ravenclaw had been neck and neck in the lead that morning. Even as they watched, stones flew upward, reducing the amounts in the lower bulbs. In fact, the only glass that seemed unchanged was the emerald-filled one of Slytherin.

"Noticed, have you?" said Fred's voice.

He and George had just come down the marble staircase and joined Harry, Ron, Hermione, and Ernie in front of the hourglasses.

"Malfoy just docked us all about fifty points," said Harry furiously, as they watched several more stones fly upward from the Gryffindor hourglass.

"Yeah, Montague tried to do us during break," said George.

"What do you mean, 'tried'?" said Ron quickly.

"He never managed to get all the words out," said Fred, "due to the fact that we forced him headfirst into that Vanishing Cabinet on the first floor."

Hermione looked very shocked.

"But you'll get into terrible trouble!"

"Not until Montague reappears, and that could take weeks, I dunno where we sent him," said Fred coolly. "Anyway . . . we've decided we don't care about getting into trouble anymore."

"Have you ever?" asked Hermione.

"'Course we have," said George. "Never been expelled, have we?"

"We've always known where to draw the line," said Fred.

"We might have put a toe across it occasionally," said George.

"But we've always stopped short of causing real mayhem," said Fred.

"But now?" said Ron tentatively.

"Well, now —" said George.

"— what with Dumbledore gone —" said Fred.

"— we reckon a bit of mayhem —" said George.

"— is exactly what our dear new Head deserves," said Fred.

"You mustn't!" whispered Hermione. "You really mustn't! She'd love a reason to expel you!"

"You don't get it, Hermione, do you?" said Fred, smiling at her. "We don't care about staying anymore. We'd walk out right now if we weren't determined to do our bit for Dumbledore first. So anyway," he checked his watch, "phase one is about to begin. I'd get in the Great Hall for lunch if I were you, that way the teachers will see you can't have had anything to do with it."

"Anything to do with what?" said Hermione anxiously.

"You'll see," said George. "Run along, now."

Fred and George turned away and disappeared in the swelling crowd descending the stairs toward lunch. Looking highly disconcerted, Ernie muttered something about unfinished Transfiguration homework and scurried away.

"I think we *should* get out of here, you know," said Hermione nervously. "Just in case . . ."

"Yeah, all right," said Ron, and the three of them moved toward the doors to the Great Hall, but Harry had barely glimpsed today's ceiling of scudding white clouds when somebody tapped him on the shoulder and, turning, he found himself almost nose to nose with Filch, the caretaker. He took several hasty steps backward; Filch was best viewed at a distance.

"The headmistress would like to see you, Potter," he leered.

"I didn't do it," said Harry stupidly, thinking of whatever Fred and George were planning. Filch's jowls wobbled with silent laughter.

"Guilty conscience, eh?" he wheezed. "Follow me. . . ."

Harry glanced back at Ron and Hermione, who were both looking worried. He shrugged and followed Filch back into the entrance hall, against the tide of hungry students.

Filch seemed to be in an extremely good mood; he hummed creakily under his breath as they climbed the marble staircase. As they reached the first landing he said, "Things are changing around here, Potter."

"I've noticed," said Harry coldly.

"Yerse . . . I've been telling Dumbledore for years and years he's too soft with you all," said Filch, chuckling nastily. "You filthy little beasts would never have dropped Stinkpellets if you'd known I had it in my power to whip you raw, would you, now? Nobody would have thought of throwing Fanged Frisbees down the corridors if I could've strung you up by the ankles in my office, would they? But when Educational Decree Twenty-nine comes in, Potter, I'll be allowed to do them things. . . . *And* she's asked the Minister to sign an order for the expulsion of Peeves. . . . Oh, things are going to be very different around here with *her* in charge. . . ."

Umbridge had obviously gone to some lengths to get Filch on her side, Harry thought, and the worst of it was that he would probably prove an important weapon; his knowledge of the school's secret passageways and hiding places was probably second only to the Weasley twins.

"Here we are," he said, leering down at Harry as he rapped three times upon Professor Umbridge's door and pushed it open. "The Potter boy to see you, ma'am."

Umbridge's office, so very familiar to Harry from his many detentions, was the same as usual except for the large wooden block lying across the front of her desk on which golden letters spelled the word HEADMISTRESS; also his Firebolt, and Fred's and George's Cleansweeps, which he saw with a pang were now chained and padlocked to a stout iron peg in the wall behind the desk. Umbridge was sitting behind the desk, busily scribbling upon some of her pink parchment, but looked up and smiled widely at their entrance.

"Thank you, Argus," she said sweetly.

"Not at all, ma'am, not at all," said Filch, bowing as low as his rheumatism would permit, and exiting backward.

"Sit," said Umbridge curtly, pointing toward a chair, and Harry sat. She continued to scribble for a few moments. He watched some of the foul kittens gamboling around the plates over her head, wondering what fresh horror she had in store for him.

"Well now," she said finally, setting down her quill and looking like a toad about to swallow a particularly juicy fly. "What would you like to drink?"

"What?" said Harry, quite sure he had misheard her.

"To drink, Mr. Potter," she said, smiling still more widely. "Tea? Coffee? Pumpkin juice?"

As she named each drink, she gave her short wand a wave, and a cup or glass of it appeared upon her desk.

"Nothing, thank you," said Harry.

"I wish you to have a drink with me," she said, her voice becoming more dangerously sweet. "Choose one."

"Fine . . . tea then," said Harry, shrugging.

She got up and made quite a performance of adding milk with her back to him. She then bustled around the desk with it, smiling in sinisterly sweet fashion.

"There," she said, handing it to him. "Drink it before it gets cold, won't you? Well, now, Mr. Potter . . . I thought we ought to have a little chat, after the distressing events of last night."

He said nothing. She settled herself back into her seat and waited. When several long moments had passed in silence, she said gaily, "You're not drinking up!"

He raised the cup to his lips and then, just as suddenly, lowered it. One of the horrible painted kittens behind Umbridge had great round blue eyes just like Mad-Eye Moody's magical one, and it had just occurred to Harry what Mad-Eye would say if he ever heard that Harry had drunk anything offered by a known enemy.

"What's the matter?" said Umbridge, who was still watching him. "Do you want sugar?"

"No," said Harry.

He raised the cup to his lips again and pretended to take a sip, though keeping his mouth tightly closed. Umbridge's smile widened.

"Good," she whispered. "Very good. Now then . . ." She leaned forward a little. *"Where is Albus Dumbledore?"*

"No idea," said Harry promptly.

"Drink up, drink up," she said, still smiling. "Now, Mr. Potter, let us not play childish games. I know that you know where he has gone. You and Dumbledore have been in this together from the beginning. Consider your position, Mr. Potter. . . ."

"I don't know where he is."

Harry pretended to drink again.

"Very well," said Umbridge, looking displeased. "In that case, you will kindly tell me the whereabouts of Sirius Black."

Harry's stomach turned over and his hand holding the teacup shook so that the cup rattled in its saucer. He tilted the cup to his mouth with his lips pressed together, so that some of the hot liquid trickled down onto his robes.

"I don't know," he said a little too quickly.

"Mr. Potter," said Umbridge, "let me remind you that it was I who almost caught the criminal Black in the Gryffindor fire in October. I know perfectly well it was you he was meeting and if I had had any proof neither of you would be at large today, I promise you. I repeat, Mr. Potter . . . Where is Sirius Black?"

"No idea," said Harry loudly. "Haven't got a clue."

They stared at each other so long that Harry felt his eyes watering. Then she stood up.

"Very well, Potter, I will take your word for it this time, but be warned: The might of the Ministry stands behind me. All channels of communication in and out of this school are being monitored. A Floo Network Regulator is keeping watch over every fire in Hogwarts — except my own, of course. My Inquisitorial Squad is opening and reading all owl post entering and leaving the castle. And Mr. Filch is observing all secret passages in and out of the castle. If I find a shred of evidence . . ."

BOOM!

The very floor of the office shook; Umbridge slipped sideways, clutching her desk for support, looking shocked.

"What was — ?"

She was gazing toward the door; Harry took the opportunity to empty his almost full cup of tea into the nearest vase of dried flowers. He could hear people running and screaming several floors below.

"Back to lunch with you, Potter!" cried Umbridge, raising her wand and dashing out of the office. Harry gave her a few seconds' start then hurried after her to see what the source of all the uproar was.

It was not difficult to find. One floor down, pandemonium reigned. Somebody (and Harry had a very shrewd idea who) had set off what seemed to be an enormous crate of enchanted fireworks.

Dragons comprised entirely of green-and-gold sparks were soaring up and down the corridors, emitting loud fiery blasts and bangs as they went. Shocking-pink Catherine wheels five feet in diameter were whizzing lethally through the air like so many flying saucers. Rockets with long tails of brilliant silver stars were ricocheting off the walls. Sparklers were writing swearwords in midair of their own accord. Firecrackers were exploding like mines everywhere Harry looked, and instead of burning themselves out, fading from sight, or fizzling to a halt, these pyrotechnical miracles seemed to be gaining in energy and momentum the longer he watched.

Filch and Umbridge were standing, apparently transfixed with horror, halfway down the stairs. As Harry watched, one of the larger Catherine wheels seemed to decide that what it needed was more room to maneuver; it whirled toward Umbridge and Filch with a sinister *wheeeeeeeeee*. Both adults yelled with fright and ducked and it soared straight out of the window behind them and off across the grounds. Meanwhile, several of the dragons and a large purple bat that was smoking ominously took advantage of the open door at the end of the corridor to escape toward the second floor.

"Hurry, Filch, hurry!" shrieked Umbridge. "They'll be all over the school unless we do something — *Stupefy!*"

A jet of red light shot out of the end of her wand and hit one of the rockets. Instead of freezing in midair, it exploded with such force that it blasted a hole in a painting of a soppy-looking witch in the middle of a meadow — she ran for it just in time, reappearing seconds later squashed into the painting next door, where a couple of wizards playing cards stood up hastily to make room for her.

"Don't Stun them, Filch!" shouted Umbridge angrily, for all the world as though it had been his suggestion.

"Right you are, Headmistress!" wheezed Filch, who was a Squib and could no more have Stunned the fireworks than swallowed them. He dashed to a nearby cupboard, pulled out a broom, and began swatting at the fireworks in midair; within seconds the head of the broom was ablaze.

Harry had seen enough. Laughing, he ducked down low, ran to a door he knew was concealed behind a tapestry a little way along the corridor and slipped through it to find Fred and George hiding just behind it, listening to Umbridge's and Filch's yells and quaking with suppressed mirth.

"Impressive," Harry said quietly, grinning. "Very impressive . . . You'll put Dr. Filibuster out of business, no problem. . . ."

"Cheers," whispered George, wiping tears of laughter from his face. "Oh, I hope she tries Vanishing them next. . . . They multiply by ten every time you try. . . ."

The fireworks continued to burn and to spread all over the school that afternoon. Though they caused plenty of disruption, particularly the firecrackers, the other teachers did not seem to mind them very much.

"Dear, dear," said Professor McGonagall sardonically, as one of the dragons soared around her classroom, emitting loud bangs and exhaling flame. "Miss Brown, would you mind running along to the headmistress and informing her that we have an escaped firework in our classroom?"

The upshot of it all was that Professor Umbridge spent her first afternoon as headmistress running all over the school answering the summonses of the other teachers, none of whom seemed able to rid their rooms of the fireworks without her. When the final bell rang and the students were heading back to Gryffindor Tower with their bags, Harry saw, with immense satisfaction, a disheveled and soot-blackened Umbridge tottering sweaty-faced from Professor Flitwick's classroom.

"Thank you so much, Professor!" said Professor Flitwick in his squeaky little voice. "I could have got rid of the sparklers myself, of course, but I wasn't sure whether I had the *authority*. . . ."

Beaming, he closed his classroom door in her snarling face.

Fred and George were heroes that night in the Gryffindor common room. Even Hermione fought her way through the excited crowd around them to congratulate them.

"They were wonderful fireworks," she said admiringly.

"Thanks," said George, looking both surprised and pleased. "Weasleys' Wildfire Whiz-Bangs. Only thing is, we used our whole stock, we're going to have to start again from scratch now. . . ."

"It was worth it, though," said Fred, who was taking orders from clamoring Gryffindors. "If you want to add your name to the waiting list, Hermione, it's five Galleons for your Basic Blaze box and twenty for the Deflagration Deluxe. . . ."

Hermione returned to the table where Harry and Ron were sitting staring at their schoolbags as though hoping their homework might spring out of it and start doing itself.

"Oh, why don't we have a night off?" said Hermione brightly, as a silver-tailed Weasley rocket zoomed past the window. "After all, the Easter holidays start on Friday, we'll have plenty of time then. . . ."

"Are you feeling all right?" Ron asked, staring at her in disbelief.

"Now you mention it," said Hermione happily, "d'you know . . . I think I'm feeling a bit . . . *rebellious*."

Harry could still hear the distant *bangs* of escaped firecrackers when he and Ron went up to bed an hour later, and as he got undressed a sparkler floated past the tower, still resolutely spelling out the word "POO."

He got into bed, yawning. With his glasses off, the occasional firework still passing the window became blurred, looking like sparkling clouds, beautiful and mysterious against the black sky. He turned onto his side, wondering how Umbridge was feeling about her first day in Dumbledore's job, and how Fudge would react when he heard that the school had spent most of the day in a state of advanced disruption. . . . Smiling to himself, he closed his eyes. . . .

The whizzes and bangs of escaped fireworks in the grounds seemed to be growing more distant . . . or perhaps he, Harry, was simply speeding away from them. . . .

He had fallen right into the corridor leading to the Department of Mysteries. He was speeding toward the plain black door. . . . *Let it open. . . . Let it open. . . .*

It did. He was inside the circular room lined with doors. . . . He crossed it, placed his hand upon an identical door, and it swung inward. . . .

Now he was in a long, rectangular room full of an odd, mechanical clicking. There were dancing flecks of light on the walls but he did not pause to investigate. . . . He had to go on. . . .

There was a door at the far end. . . . It too opened at his touch. . . .

And now he was in a dimly lit room as high and wide as a church, full of nothing but rows and rows of towering shelves, each laden with small, dusty, spun-glass spheres. . . . Now Harry's heart was beating fast with excitement. . . . He knew where to go. . . . He ran forward, but his footsteps made no noise in the enormous, deserted room. . . .

There was something in this room he wanted very, very much. . . .

Something he wanted. . . . or somebody else wanted. . . .

His scar was hurting. . . .

BANG! Harry awoke instantly, confused and angry. The dark dormitory was full of the sound of laughter.

"Cool!" said Seamus, who was silhouetted against the window.

"I think one of those Catherine wheels hit a rocket and it's like they mated, come and see!"

Harry heard Ron and Dean scramble out of bed for a better look. He lay quite still and silent while the pain in his scar subsided and disappointment washed over him. He felt as though a wonderful treat had been snatched from him at the very last moment. . . . He had got so close that time. . . .

Glittering, pink-and-silver winged piglets were now soaring past the windows of Gryffindor Tower. Harry lay and listened to the appreciative whoops of Gryffindors in the dormitories below them. His stomach gave a sickening jolt as he remembered that he had Occlumency the following evening. . . .

Harry spent the whole of the next day dreading what Snape was going to say if he found out how much farther into the Department of Mysteries he had penetrated during his last dream. With a surge of guilt he realized that he had not practiced Occlumency once since their last lesson: There had been too much going on since Dumbledore had left. He was sure he would not have been able to empty his mind even if he had tried. He doubted, however, whether Snape would accept that excuse. . . .

He attempted a little last-minute practice during classes that day, but it was no good, Hermione kept asking him what was wrong whenever he fell silent trying to rid himself of all thought and emotion and, after all, the best moment to empty his brain was not while teachers were firing review questions at the class.

Resigned to the worst, he set off for Snape's office after dinner. Halfway across the entrance hall, however, Cho came hurrying up to him.

"Over here," said Harry, glad of a reason to postpone his meeting with Snape and beckoning her across to the corner of the entrance hall where the giant hourglasses stood. Gryffindor's was now almost empty. "Are you okay? Umbridge hasn't been asking you about the D.A., has she?"

"Oh no," said Cho hurriedly. "No, it was only . . . Well, I just wanted to say . . . Harry, I never dreamed Marietta would tell. . . ."

"Yeah, well," said Harry moodily. He did feel Cho might have chosen her friends a bit more carefully. It was small consolation that the last he had heard, Marietta was still up in the hospital wing and Madam Pomfrey had not been able to make the slightest improvement to her pimples.

"She's a lovely person really," said Cho. "She just made a mistake —"

Harry looked at her incredulously.

"*A lovely person who made a mistake?* She sold us all out, including you!"

"Well . . . we all got away, didn't we?" said Cho pleadingly. "You know, her mum works for the Ministry, it's really difficult for her —"

"Ron's dad works for the Ministry too!" Harry said furiously. "And in case you hadn't noticed, he hasn't got 'sneak' written across *his* face —"

"That was a really horrible trick of Hermione Granger's," said Cho fiercely. "She should have told us she'd jinxed that list —"

"I think it was a brilliant idea," said Harry coldly. Cho flushed and her eyes grew brighter.

"Oh yes, I forgot — of course, if it was darling *Hermione's* idea —"

"Don't start crying again," said Harry warningly.

"I wasn't going to!" she shouted.

"Yeah . . . well . . . good," he said. "I've got enough to cope with at the moment."

"Go and cope with it then!" she said furiously, turning on her heel and stalking off.

Fuming, Harry descended the stairs to Snape's dungeon, and though he knew from experience how much easier it would be for

Snape to penetrate his mind if he arrived angry and resentful, he succeeded in nothing but thinking of a few more good things he should have said to Cho about Marietta before reaching the dungeon door.

"You're late, Potter," said Snape coldly, as Harry closed the door behind him.

Snape was standing with his back to Harry, removing, as usual, certain of his thoughts and placing them carefully in Dumbledore's Pensieve. He dropped the last silvery strand into the stone basin and turned to face Harry.

"So," he said. "Have you been practicing?"

"Yes," Harry lied, looking carefully at one of the legs of Snape's desk.

"Well, we'll soon find out, won't we?" said Snape smoothly. "Wand out, Potter."

Harry moved into his usual position, facing Snape with the desk between them. His heart was pumping fast with anger at Cho and anxiety about how much Snape was about to extract from his mind.

"On the count of three then," said Snape lazily. "One — two —"

Snape's office door banged open and Draco Malfoy sped in.

"Professor Snape, sir — oh — sorry —"

Malfoy was looking at Snape and Harry in some surprise.

"It's all right, Draco," said Snape, lowering his wand. "Potter is here for a little Remedial Potions."

Harry had not seen Malfoy look so gleeful since Umbridge had turned up to inspect Hagrid.

"I didn't know," he said, leering at Harry, who knew his face was burning. He would have given a great deal to be able to shout the truth at Malfoy — or, even better, to hit him with a good curse.

"Well, Draco, what is it?" asked Snape.

"It's Professor Umbridge, sir — she needs your help," said Malfoy. "They've found Montague, sir. He's turned up jammed inside a toilet on the fourth floor."

"How did he get in there?" demanded Snape.

"I don't know, sir, he's a bit confused. . . ."

"Very well, very well — Potter," said Snape, "we shall resume this lesson tomorrow evening instead."

He turned and swept from his office. Malfoy mouthed *"Remedial Potions?"* at Harry behind Snape's back before following him.

Seething, Harry replaced his wand inside his robes and made to leave the room. At least he had twenty-four more hours in which to practice; he knew he ought to feel grateful for the narrow escape, though it was hard that it came at the expense of Malfoy telling the whole school that he needed Remedial Potions. . . .

He was at the office door when he saw it: a patch of shivering light dancing on the door frame. He stopped, looking at it, reminded of something. . . . Then he remembered: It was a little like the lights he had seen in his dream last night, the lights in the second room he had walked through on his journey through the Department of Mysteries.

He turned around. The light was coming from the Pensieve sitting on Snape's desk. The silver-white contents were ebbing and swirling within. Snape's thoughts . . . things he did not want Harry to see if he broke through Snape's defenses accidentally. . . .

Harry gazed at the Pensieve, curiosity welling inside him. . . . What was it that Snape was so keen to hide from Harry?

The silvery lights shivered on the wall. . . . Harry took two steps toward the desk, thinking hard. Could it possibly be information about the Department of Mysteries that Snape was determined to keep from him?

Harry looked over his shoulder, his heart now pumping harder and faster than ever. How long would it take Snape to release Montague from the toilet? Would he come straight back to his office afterward, or accompany Montague to the hospital wing? Surely the latter . . . Montague was Captain of the Slytherin Quidditch team, Snape would want to make sure he was all right. . . .

Harry walked the remaining few feet to the Pensieve and stood over it, gazing into its depths. He hesitated, listening, then pulled out his wand again. The office and the corridor beyond were completely silent. He gave the contents of the Pensieve a small prod with the end of his wand.

The silvery stuff within began to swirl very fast. Harry leaned forward over it and saw that it had become transparent. He was, once again, looking down into a room as though through a circular window in the ceiling. . . . In fact, unless he was much mistaken, he was looking down upon the Great Hall. . . .

His breath was actually fogging the surface of Snape's thoughts. . . . His brain seemed to be in limbo. . . . It would be insane to do the thing that he was so strongly tempted to do. . . . He was trembling. . . . Snape could be back at any moment . . . but Harry thought of Cho's anger, of Malfoy's jeering face, and a reckless daring seized him.

He took a great gulp of breath and plunged his face into the surface of Snape's thoughts. At once, the floor of the office lurched, tipping Harry headfirst into the Pensieve. . . .

He was falling through cold blackness, spinning furiously as he went, and then —

He was standing in the middle of the Great Hall, but the four House tables were gone. Instead there were more than a hundred smaller tables, all facing the same way, at each of which sat a student, head bent low, scribbling on a roll of parchment. The only sound was the scratching of quills and the occasional rustle as somebody adjusted their parchment. It was clearly exam time.

Sunshine was streaming through the high windows onto the bent heads, which shone chestnut and copper and gold in the bright light. Harry looked around carefully. Snape had to be here somewhere. . . . This was *his* memory. . . .

And there he was, at a table right behind Harry. Harry stared. Snape-the-teenager had a stringy, pallid look about him, like a plant kept in the dark. His hair was lank and greasy and was flopping onto the table, his hooked nose barely half an inch from the surface of the parchment as he scribbled. Harry moved around behind Snape and read the heading of the examination paper:

DEFENSE AGAINST THE DARK ARTS —
ORDINARY WIZARDING LEVEL

So Snape had to be fifteen or sixteen, around Harry's own age. His hand was flying across the parchment; he had written at least a foot more than his closest neighbors, and yet his writing was minuscule and cramped.

"Five more minutes!"

The voice made Harry jump; turning, he saw the top of Professor Flitwick's head moving between the desks a short distance away. Professor Flitwick was walking past a boy with untidy black hair . . . very untidy black hair. . . .

Harry moved so quickly that, had he been solid, he would have knocked desks flying. Instead he seemed to slide, dreamlike, across two aisles and up a third. The back of the black-haired boy's head drew nearer and nearer. . . . He was straightening up now, putting down his quill, pulling his roll of parchment toward him so as to re-read what he had written. . . .

Harry stopped in front of the desk and gazed down at his fifteen-year-old father.

Excitement exploded in the pit of his stomach: It was as though he was looking at himself but with deliberate mistakes. James's eyes were hazel, his nose was slightly longer than Harry's, and there was no scar on his forehead, but they had the same thin face, same mouth, same eyebrows. James's hair stuck up at the back exactly as Harry's did, his hands could have been Harry's, and Harry could tell that when James stood up, they would be within an inch of each other's heights.

James yawned hugely and rumpled up his hair, making it even

messier than it had been. Then, with a glance toward Professor Flitwick, he turned in his seat and grinned at a boy sitting four seats behind him.

With another shock of excitement, Harry saw Sirius give James the thumbs-up. Sirius was lounging in his chair at his ease, tilting it back on two legs. He was very good-looking; his dark hair fell into his eyes with a sort of casual elegance neither James's nor Harry's could ever have achieved, and a girl sitting behind him was eyeing him hopefully, though he didn't seem to have noticed. And two seats along from this girl — Harry's stomach gave another pleasurable squirm — was Remus Lupin. He looked rather pale and peaky (was the full moon approaching?) and was absorbed in the exam: As he reread his answers he scratched his chin with the end of his quill, frowning slightly.

So that meant Wormtail had to be around here somewhere too . . . and sure enough, Harry spotted him within seconds: a small, mousy-haired boy with a pointed nose. Wormtail looked anxious; he was chewing his fingernails, staring down at his paper, scuffing the ground with his toes. Every now and then he glanced hopefully at his neighbor's paper. Harry stared at Wormtail for a moment, then back at James, who was now doodling on a bit of scrap parchment. He had drawn a Snitch and was now tracing the letters L. E. What did they stand for?

"Quills down, please!" squeaked Professor Flitwick. "That means you too, Stebbins! Please remain seated while I collect your parchment! *Accio!*"

More than a hundred rolls of parchment zoomed into the air and into Professor Flitwick's outstretched arms, knocking him backward off his feet. Several people laughed. A couple of students at the front desks got up, took hold of Professor Flitwick beneath the elbows, and lifted him onto his feet again.

"Thank you . . . thank you," panted Professor Flitwick. "Very well, everybody, you're free to go!"

Harry looked down at his father, who had hastily crossed out the L. E. he had been embellishing, jumped to his feet, stuffed his quill and the exam question paper into his bag, which he slung over his back, and stood waiting for Sirius to join him.

Harry looked around and glimpsed Snape a short way away, moving between the tables toward the doors into the entrance hall, still absorbed in his own examination paper. Round-shouldered yet angular, he walked in a twitchy manner that recalled a spider, his oily hair swinging about his face.

A gang of chattering girls separated Snape from James and Sirius, and by planting himself in the midst of this group, Harry managed to keep Snape in sight while straining his ears to catch the voices of James and his friends.

"Did you like question ten, Moony?" asked Sirius as they emerged into the entrance hall.

"Loved it," said Lupin briskly. "'Give five signs that identify the werewolf.' Excellent question."

"D'you think you managed to get all the signs?" said James in tones of mock concern.

"Think I did," said Lupin seriously, as they joined the crowd thronging around the front doors eager to get out into the sunlit grounds. "One: He's sitting on my chair. Two: He's wearing my clothes. Three: His name's Remus Lupin . . .'"

Wormtail was the only one who didn't laugh.

"I got the snout shape, the pupils of the eyes, and the tufted tail," he said anxiously, "but I couldn't think what else —"

"How thick are you, Wormtail?" said James impatiently. "You run round with a werewolf once a month —"

"Keep your voice down," implored Lupin.

Harry looked anxiously behind him again. Snape remained close by, still buried in his examination questions; but this was Snape's memory, and Harry was sure that if Snape chose to wander off in a different direction once outside in the grounds, he, Harry, would not be able to follow James any farther. To his intense relief, however, when James and his three friends strode off down the lawn toward the lake, Snape followed, still poring over the paper and apparently with no fixed idea of where he was going. By jogging a little ahead of him, Harry managed to maintain a close watch on James and the others.

"Well, I thought that paper was a piece of cake," he heard Sirius say. "I'll be surprised if I don't get Outstanding on it at least."

"Me too," said James. He put his hand in his pocket and took out a struggling Golden Snitch.

"Where'd you get that?"

"Nicked it," said James casually. He started playing with the Snitch, allowing it to fly as much as a foot away and seizing it again; his reflexes were excellent. Wormtail watched him in awe.

They stopped in the shade of the very same beech tree on the edge of the lake where Harry, Ron, and Hermione had spent a Sunday finishing their homework, and threw themselves down on the grass.

Harry looked over his shoulder yet again and saw, to his delight, that Snape had settled himself on the grass in the dense shadows of a clump of bushes. He was as deeply immersed in the O.W.L. paper as ever, which left Harry free to sit down on the grass between the beech and the bushes and watch the foursome under the tree.

The sunlight was dazzling on the smooth surface of the lake, on the bank of which the group of laughing girls who had just left the Great Hall were sitting with shoes and socks off, cooling their feet in the water.

Lupin had pulled out a book and was reading. Sirius stared around at the students milling over the grass, looking rather haughty and bored, but very handsomely so. James was still playing with the Snitch, letting it zoom farther and farther away, almost escaping but always grabbed at the last second. Wormtail was watching him with his mouth open. Every time James made a particularly difficult catch,

Wormtail gasped and applauded. After five minutes of this, Harry wondered why James didn't tell Wormtail to get a grip on himself, but James seemed to be enjoying the attention. Harry noticed his father had a habit of rumpling up his hair as though to make sure it did not get too tidy, and also that he kept looking over at the girls by the water's edge.

"Put that away, will you?" said Sirius finally, as James made a fine catch and Wormtail let out a cheer. "Before Wormtail wets himself from excitement."

Wormtail turned slightly pink but James grinned.

"If it bothers you," he said, stuffing the Snitch back in his pocket. Harry had the distinct impression that Sirius was the only one for whom James would have stopped showing off.

"I'm bored," said Sirius. "Wish it was full moon."

"You might," said Lupin darkly from behind his book. "We've still got Transfiguration, if you're bored you could test me. . . . Here." He held out his book.

Sirius snorted. "I don't need to look at that rubbish, I know it all."

"This'll liven you up, Padfoot," said James quietly. "Look who it is. . . ."

Sirius's head turned. He had become very still, like a dog that has scented a rabbit.

"Excellent," he said softly. *"Snivellus."*

Harry turned to see what Sirius was looking at.

Snape was on his feet again, and was stowing the O.W.L. paper in his bag. As he emerged from the shadows of the bushes and set off across the grass, Sirius and James stood up. Lupin and Wormtail remained sitting: Lupin was still staring down at his book, though his eyes were not moving and a faint frown line had appeared between his eyebrows. Wormtail was looking from Sirius and James to Snape with a look of avid anticipation on his face.

"All right, Snivellus?" said James loudly.

Snape reacted so fast it was as though he had been expecting an attack: Dropping his bag, he plunged his hand inside his robes, and his wand was halfway into the air when James shouted, *"Expelliarmus!"*

Snape's wand flew twelve feet into the air and fell with a little thud in the grass behind him. Sirius let out a bark of laughter.

"Impedimenta!" he said, pointing his wand at Snape, who was knocked off his feet, halfway through a dive toward his own fallen wand.

Students all around had turned to watch. Some of them had gotten to their feet and were edging nearer to watch. Some looked apprehensive, others entertained.

Snape lay panting on the ground. James and Sirius advanced on him, wands up, James glancing over his shoulder at the girls at the water's edge as he went. Wormtail was on his feet now, watching hungrily, edging around Lupin to get a clearer view.

"How'd the exam go, Snivelly?" said James.

"I was watching him, his nose was touching the parchment," said Sirius viciously. "There'll be great grease marks all over it, they won't be able to read a word."

Several people watching laughed; Snape was clearly unpopular. Wormtail sniggered shrilly. Snape was trying to get up, but the jinx was still operating on him; he was struggling, as though bound by invisible ropes.

"You — wait," he panted, staring up at James with an expression of purest loathing. "You — wait. . . ."

"Wait for what?" said Sirius coolly. "What're you going to do, Snivelly, wipe your nose on us?"

Snape let out a stream of mixed swearwords and hexes, but his wand being ten feet away nothing happened.

"Wash out your mouth," said James coldly. *"Scourgify!"*

Pink soap bubbles streamed from Snape's mouth at once; the froth was covering his lips, making him gag, choking him —

"Leave him ALONE!"

James and Sirius looked around. James's free hand jumped to his hair again.

It was one of the girls from the lake edge. She had thick, dark red hair that fell to her shoulders and startlingly green almond-shaped eyes — Harry's eyes.

Harry's mother . . .

"All right, Evans?" said James, and the tone of his voice was suddenly pleasant, deeper, more mature.

"Leave him alone," Lily repeated. She was looking at James with every sign of great dislike. "What's he done to you?"

"Well," said James, appearing to deliberate the point, "it's more the fact that he *exists,* if you know what I mean. . . ."

Many of the surrounding watchers laughed, Sirius and Wormtail included, but Lupin, still apparently intent on his book, didn't, and neither did Lily.

"You think you're funny," she said coldly. "But you're just an arrogant, bullying toerag, Potter. Leave him *alone.*"

"I will if you go out with me, Evans," said James quickly. "Go on . . . Go out with me, and I'll never lay a wand on old Snivelly again."

Behind him, the Impediment Jinx was wearing off. Snape was beginning to inch toward his fallen wand, spitting out soapsuds as he crawled.

"I wouldn't go out with you if it was a choice between you and the giant squid," said Lily.

"Bad luck, Prongs," said Sirius briskly, turning back to Snape. "OY!"

But too late; Snape had directed his wand straight at James; there was a flash of light and a gash appeared on the side of James's face, spattering his robes with blood. James whirled about; a second flash of light later, Snape was hanging upside down in the air, his robes falling over his head to reveal skinny, pallid legs and a pair of graying underpants.

Many people in the small crowd watching cheered. Sirius, James, and Wormtail roared with laughter.

Lily, whose furious expression had twitched for an instant as though she was going to smile, said, "Let him down!"

"Certainly," said James and he jerked his wand upward. Snape fell into a crumpled heap on the ground. Disentangling himself from his robes, he got quickly to his feet, wand up, but Sirius said, *"Petrificus Totalus!"* and Snape keeled over again at once, rigid as a board.

"LEAVE HIM ALONE!" Lily shouted. She had her own wand out now. James and Sirius eyed it warily.

"Ah, Evans, don't make me hex you," said James earnestly.

"Take the curse off him, then!"

James sighed deeply, then turned to Snape and muttered the countercurse.

"There you go," he said, as Snape struggled to his feet again, "you're lucky Evans was here, Snivellus —"

"I don't need help from filthy little Mudbloods like her!"

Lily blinked. "Fine," she said coolly. "I won't bother in future. And I'd wash your pants if I were you, *Snivellus*."

"Apologize to Evans!" James roared at Snape, his wand pointed threateningly at him.

"I don't want *you* to make him apologize," Lily shouted, rounding on James. "You're as bad as he is. . . ."

"What?" yelped James. "I'd NEVER call you a — you-know-what!"

"Messing up your hair because you think it looks cool to look like you've just got off your broomstick, showing off with that stupid Snitch, walking down corridors and hexing anyone who annoys you just because you can — I'm surprised your broomstick can get off the ground with that fat head on it. You make me SICK."

She turned on her heel and hurried away.

"Evans!" James shouted after her, "Hey, EVANS!"

But she didn't look back.

"What is it with her?" said James, trying and failing to look as though this was a throwaway question of no real importance to him.

"Reading between the lines, I'd say she thinks you're a bit conceited, mate," said Sirius.

"Right," said James, who looked furious now, "right —"

There was another flash of light, and Snape was once again hanging upside down in the air.

"Who wants to see me take off Snivelly's pants?"

But whether James really did take off Snape's pants, Harry never found out. A hand had closed tight over his upper arm, closed with a pincerlike grip. Wincing, Harry looked around to see who had hold of him, and saw, with a thrill of horror, a fully grown, adult-sized Snape standing right beside him, white with rage.

"Having fun?"

Harry felt himself rising into the air. The summer's day evaporated around him, he was floating upward through icy blackness, Snape's hand still tight upon his upper arm. Then, with a swooping feeling as though he had turned head over heels in midair, his feet hit the stone floor of Snape's dungeon, and he was standing again beside the Pensieve on Snape's desk in the shadowy, present-day Potions master's study.

"So," said Snape, gripping Harry's arm so tightly Harry's hand was starting to feel numb. "So . . . been enjoying yourself, Potter?"

"N-no . . ." said Harry, trying to free his arm.

It was scary: Snape's lips were shaking, his face was white, his teeth were bared.

"Amusing man, your father, wasn't he?" said Snape, shaking Harry so hard that his glasses slipped down his nose.

"I — didn't —"

Snape threw Harry from him with all his might. Harry fell hard onto the dungeon floor.

"You will not tell anybody what you saw!" Snape bellowed.

"No," said Harry, getting to his feet as far from Snape as he could. "No, of course I w —"

"Get out, get out, I don't want to see you in this office ever again!"

And as Harry hurtled toward the door, a jar of dead cockroaches exploded over his head. He wrenched the door open and flew away up the corridor, stopping only when he had put three floors between himself and Snape. There he leaned against the wall, panting, and rubbing his bruised arm.

He had no desire at all to return to Gryffindor Tower so early, nor to tell Ron and Hermione what he had just seen. What was making Harry feel so horrified and unhappy was not being shouted at or having jars thrown at him — it was that he knew how it felt to be humiliated in the middle of a circle of onlookers, knew exactly how Snape had felt as his father had taunted him, and that judging from what he had just seen, his father had been every bit as arrogant as Snape had always told him.

CAREER ADVICE

"B ut why haven't you got Occlumency lessons anymore?" said Hermione, frowning.

"I've *told* you," Harry muttered. "Snape reckons I can carry on by myself now I've got the basics. . . ."

"So you've stopped having funny dreams?" said Hermione skeptically.

"Pretty much," said Harry, not looking at her.

"Well, I don't think Snape should stop until you're absolutely sure you can control them!" said Hermione indignantly. "Harry, I think you should go back to him and ask —"

"No," said Harry forcefully. "Just drop it, Hermione, okay?"

It was the first day of the Easter holidays and Hermione, as was her custom, had spent a large part of the day drawing up study schedules for the three of them. Harry and Ron had let her do it — it was easier than arguing with her and, in any case, they might come in useful.

Ron had been startled to discover that there were only six weeks left until their exams.

"How can that come as a shock?" Hermione demanded, as she tapped each little square on Ron's schedule with her wand so that it flashed a different color according to its subject.

"I dunno . . ." said Ron, "there's been a lot going on. . . ."

"Well, there you are," she said, handing him his schedule, "if you follow that you should do fine."

Ron looked down it gloomily, but then brightened.

"You've given me an evening off every week!"

"That's for Quidditch practice," said Hermione.

The smile faded from Ron's face.

"What's the point?" he said. "We've got about as much chance of winning the Quidditch Cup this year as Dad's got of becoming Minister of Magic. . . ."

Hermione said nothing. She was looking at Harry, who was staring blankly at the opposite wall of the common room while Crookshanks pawed at his hand, trying to get his ears scratched.

"What's wrong, Harry?"

"What?" he said quickly. "Nothing . . ."

He seized his copy of *Defensive Magical Theory* and pretended to be looking something up in the index. Crookshanks gave him up as a bad job and slunk away under Hermione's chair.

"I saw Cho earlier," said Hermione tentatively, "and she looked really miserable too. . . . Have you two had a row again?"

"Wha — oh yeah, we have," said Harry, seizing gratefully on the excuse.

"What about?"

"That sneak friend of hers, Marietta," said Harry.

"Yeah, well, I don't blame you!" said Ron angrily, setting down his study schedule. "If it hadn't been for her . . ."

Ron went into a rant about Marietta Edgecombe, which Harry found helpful. All he had to do was look angry, nod, and say "yeah" and "that's right" whenever Ron drew breath, leaving his mind free to dwell, ever more miserably, on what he had seen in the Pensieve.

He felt as though the memory of it was eating him from inside. He had been so sure that his parents had been wonderful people that he never had the slightest difficulty in disbelieving Snape's aspersions on his father's character. Hadn't people like Hagrid and Sirius *told* Harry how wonderful his father had been? (*Yeah, well, look what Sirius was like himself,* said a nagging voice inside Harry's head. . . . *He was as bad, wasn't he?*) Yes, he had once overheard Professor McGonagall saying that his father and Sirius had been troublemakers at school, but she had described them as forerunners of the Weasley twins, and Harry could not imagine Fred and George dangling someone upside down for the fun of it . . . not unless they really loathed them . . . Perhaps Malfoy, or somebody who really deserved it . . .

Harry tried to make a case for Snape having deserved what he had suffered at James's hands — but hadn't Lily asked, "What's he done to you?" And hadn't James replied, "It's more the fact that he *exists,* if you know what I mean?" Hadn't James started it all simply because Sirius said he was bored? Harry remembered Lupin saying back in Grimmauld Place that Dumbledore had made him prefect in the hope that he would be able to exercise some control over James and Sirius. . . . But in the Pensieve, he had sat there and let it all happen. . . .

Harry reminded himself that Lily had intervened; his mother had been decent, yet the memory of the look on her face as she had shouted at James disturbed him quite as much as anything else. She had clearly loathed James and Harry simply could not understand how they could have ended up married. Once or twice he even wondered whether James had forced her into it. . . .

For nearly five years the thought of his father had been a source of comfort, of inspiration. Whenever someone had told him he was like

James he had glowed with pride inside. And now . . . now he felt cold and miserable at the thought of him.

The weather grew breezier, brighter, and warmer as the holidays passed, but Harry was stuck with the rest of the fifth and seventh years, who were all trapped inside, traipsing back and forth to the library. Harry pretended that his bad mood had no other cause but the approaching exams, and as his fellow Gryffindors were sick of studying themselves, his excuse went unchallenged.

"Harry, I'm talking to you, can you hear me?"

"Huh?"

He looked around. Ginny Weasley, looking very windswept, had joined him at the library table where he had been sitting alone. It was late on Sunday evening; Hermione had gone back to Gryffindor Tower to review Ancient Runes; Ron had Quidditch practice.

"Oh hi," said Harry, pulling his books back toward him. "How come you're not at practice?"

"It's over," said Ginny. "Ron had to take Jack Sloper up to the hospital wing."

"Why?"

"Well, we're not sure, but we *think* he knocked himself out with his own bat." She sighed heavily. "Anyway . . . a package just arrived, it's only just got through Umbridge's new screening process. . . ."

She hoisted a box wrapped in brown paper onto the table; it had clearly been unwrapped and carelessly rewrapped, and there was a scribbled note across it in red ink, reading INSPECTED AND PASSED BY THE HOGWARTS HIGH INQUISITOR.

"It's Easter eggs from Mum," said Ginny. "There's one for you. . . . There you go. . . ."

She handed him a handsome chocolate egg decorated with small, iced Snitches and, according to the packaging, containing a bag of Fizzing Whizbees. Harry looked at it for a moment, then, to his horror, felt a hard lump rise in his throat.

"Are you okay, Harry?" asked Ginny quietly.

"Yeah, I'm fine," said Harry gruffly. The lump in his throat was painful. He did not understand why an Easter egg should have made him feel like this.

"You seem really down lately," Ginny persisted. "You know, I'm sure if you just *talked* to Cho . . ."

"It's not Cho I want to talk to," said Harry brusquely.

"Who is it, then?" asked Ginny.

"I . . ."

He glanced around to make quite sure that nobody was listening; Madam Pince was several shelves away, stamping out a pile of books for a frantic-looking Hannah Abbott.

"I wish I could talk to Sirius," he muttered. "But I know I can't."

More to give himself something to do than because he really wanted any, Harry unwrapped his Easter egg, broke off a large bit, and put it into his mouth.

"Well," said Ginny slowly, helping herself to a bit of egg too, "if you really want to talk to Sirius, I expect we could think of a way to do it. . . ."

"Come on," said Harry hopelessly. "With Umbridge policing the fires and reading all our mail?"

"The thing about growing up with Fred and George," said Ginny thoughtfully, "is that you sort of start thinking anything's possible if you've got enough nerve."

Harry looked at her. Perhaps it was the effect of the chocolate — Lupin had always advised eating some after encounters with dementors — or simply because he had finally spoken aloud the wish that had been burning inside him for a week, but he felt a bit more hopeful. . . .

"WHAT DO YOU THINK YOU ARE DOING?"

"Oh damn," whispered Ginny, jumping to her feet. "I forgot —"

Madam Pince was swooping down upon them, her shriveled face contorted with rage.

"Chocolate in the library!" she screamed. "Out — *out* — OUT!"

And whipping out her wand, she caused Harry's books, bag, and ink bottle to chase him and Ginny from the library, whacking them repeatedly over the head as they ran.

As though to underline the importance of their upcoming examinations, a batch of pamphlets, leaflets, and notices concerning various Wizarding careers appeared on the tables in Gryffindor Tower shortly before the end of the holidays, along with yet another notice on the board, which read:

CAREER ADVICE

All fifth years will be required to attend a short meeting with their Head of House during the first week of the Summer term, in which they will be given the opportunity to discuss their future careers. Times of individual appointments are listed below.

Harry looked down the list and found that he was expected in Professor McGonagall's office at half-past two on Monday, which would mean missing most of Divination. He and the other fifth years spent a considerable part of the final weekend of the Easter break reading all the career information that had been left there for their perusal.

"Well, I don't fancy Healing," said Ron on the last evening of the holidays. He was immersed in a leaflet that carried the crossed bone-and-wand emblem of St. Mungo's on its front. "It says here you need at least an E at N.E.W.T. level in Potions, Herbology, Transfiguration, Charms, and Defense Against the Dark Arts. I mean . . . blimey. . . . Don't want much, do they?"

"Well, it's a very responsible job, isn't it?" said Hermione absently. She was poring over a bright pink-and-orange leaflet that was headed SO YOU THINK YOU'D LIKE TO WORK IN MUGGLE RELATIONS? "You don't seem to need many qualifications to liaise with Muggles. . . . All they want is an O.W.L. in Muggle Studies. . . . *'Much more important is your enthusiasm, patience, and a good sense of fun!'"*

"You'd need more than a good sense of fun to liaise with my uncle," said Harry darkly. "Good sense of when to duck, more like . . ." He was halfway through a pamphlet on Wizard banking. "Listen to this:

"'Are you seeking a challenging career involving travel, adventure, and substantial, danger-related treasure bonuses? Then consider a position with Gringotts Wizarding Bank, who are currently recruiting Curse-Breakers for thrilling opportunities abroad. . . .' They want Arithmancy, though. . . . You could do it, Hermione!"

"I don't much fancy banking," said Hermione vaguely, now immersed in HAVE YOU GOT WHAT IT TAKES TO TRAIN SECURITY TROLLS?

"Hey," said a voice in Harry's ear. He looked around; Fred and George had come to join them. "Ginny's had a word with us about you," said Fred, stretching out his legs on the table in front of them and causing several booklets on careers with the Ministry of Magic to slide off onto the floor. "She says you need to talk to Sirius?"

"What?" said Hermione sharply, freezing with her hand halfway toward picking up MAKE A BANG AT THE DEPARTMENT OF MAGICAL ACCIDENTS AND CATASTROPHES.

"Yeah . . ." said Harry, trying to sound casual, "yeah, I thought I'd like —"

"Don't be so ridiculous," said Hermione, straightening up and looking at him as though she could not believe her eyes. "With Umbridge groping around in the fires and frisking all the owls?"

"Well, we think we can find a way around that," said George, stretching and smiling. "It's a simple matter of causing a diversion. Now, you might have noticed that we have been rather quiet on the mayhem front during the Easter holidays?"

"What was the point, we asked ourselves, of disrupting leisure time?" continued Fred. "No point at all, we answered ourselves. And of course, we'd have messed up people's studying too, which would be the very last thing we'd want to do."

He gave Hermione a sanctimonious little nod. She looked rather taken aback by this thoughtfulness.

"But it's business as usual from tomorrow," Fred continued briskly. "And if we're going to be causing a bit of uproar, why not do it so that Harry can have his chat with Sirius?"

"Yes, but *still,*" said Hermione with an air of explaining something very simple to somebody very obtuse, "even if you *do* cause a diversion, how is Harry supposed to talk to him?"

"Umbridge's office," said Harry quietly.

He had been thinking about it for a fortnight and could think of no alternative; Umbridge herself had told him that the only fire that was not being watched was her own.

"Are — you — insane?" said Hermione in a hushed voice.

Ron had lowered his leaflet on jobs in the cultivated fungus trade and was watching the conversation warily.

"I don't think so," said Harry, shrugging.

"And how are you going to get in there in the first place?"

Harry was ready for this question.

"Sirius's knife," he said.

"Excuse me?"

"Christmas before last Sirius gave me a knife that'll open any lock," said Harry. "So even if she's bewitched the door so *Alohomora* won't work, which I bet she has —"

"What do you think about this?" Hermione demanded of Ron, and Harry was reminded irresistibly of Mrs. Weasley appealing to her husband during Harry's first dinner in Grimmauld Place.

"I dunno," said Ron, looking alarmed at being asked to give an opinion. "If Harry wants to do it, it's up to him, isn't it?"

"Spoken like a true friend and Weasley," said Fred, clapping Ron hard on the back. "Right, then. We're thinking of doing it tomorrow, just after lessons, because it should cause maximum impact if everybody's in the corridors — Harry, we'll set it off in the east wing somewhere, draw her right away from her own office — I reckon we should be able to guarantee you, what, twenty minutes?" he said, looking at George.

"Easy," said George.

"What sort of diversion is it?" asked Ron.

"You'll see, little bro," said Fred, as he and George got up again. "At least, you will if you trot along to Gregory the Smarmy's corridor round about five o'clock tomorrow."

Harry awoke very early the next day, feeling almost as anxious as he had done on the morning of his hearing at the Ministry of Magic. It was not only the prospect of breaking into Umbridge's office and using her fire to speak to Sirius that was making him feel nervous, though that was certainly bad enough — today also happened to be the first time he would be in close proximity with Snape since Snape had thrown him out of his office, as they had Potions that day.

After lying in bed for a while thinking about the day ahead, Harry got up very quietly and moved across to the window beside Neville's bed, staring out on a truly glorious morning. The sky was a clear, misty, opalescent blue. Directly ahead of him, Harry could see the towering beech tree below which his father had once tormented Snape. He was not sure what Sirius could possibly say to him that would make up for what he had seen in the Pensieve, but he was desperate to hear Sirius's own account of what had happened, to know of any mitigating factors there might have been, any excuse at all for his father's behavior. . . .

Something caught Harry's attention: movement on the edge of the Forbidden Forest. Harry squinted into the sun and saw Hagrid emerging from between the trees. He seemed to be limping. As Harry watched, Hagrid staggered to the door of his cabin and disappeared inside it. Harry watched the cabin for several minutes. Hagrid did not emerge again, but smoke furled from the chimney, so Hagrid could not be so badly injured that he was unequal to stoking the fire. . . .

Harry turned away from the window, headed back to his trunk, and started to dress.

With the prospect of forcing entry into Umbridge's office ahead, Harry had never expected the day to be a restful one, but he had not reckoned on Hermione's almost continual attempts to dissuade him from what he was planning to do at five o'clock. For the first time ever, she was at least as inattentive to Professor Binns in History of Magic as Harry and Ron were, keeping up a stream of whispered admonitions that Harry tried very hard to ignore.

". . . and if she does catch you there, apart from being expelled, she'll be able to guess you've been talking to Snuffles and this time I expect she'll *force* you to drink Veritaserum and answer her questions. . . ."

"Hermione," said Ron in a low and indignant voice, "are you going to stop telling Harry off and listen to Binns, or am I going to have to take notes instead?"

"You take notes for a change, it won't kill you!"

By the time they reached the dungeons, neither Harry nor Ron was speaking to Hermione any longer. Undeterred, she took advantage of their silence to maintain an uninterrupted flow of dire warnings, all uttered under her breath in a vehement hiss that caused Seamus to waste five whole minutes checking his cauldron for leaks.

Snape, meanwhile, seemed to have decided to act as though Harry were invisible. Harry was, of course, well used to this tactic, as it was one of Uncle Vernon's favorites, and on the whole was grateful he had to suffer nothing worse. In fact, compared to what he usually had to endure from Snape in the way of taunts and snide remarks, he found the new approach something of an improvement and was pleased to find that when left well alone, he was able to concoct an Invigoration Draught quite easily. At the end of the lesson he scooped some of the potion into a flask, corked it, and took it up to Snape's desk for mark-ing, feeling that he might at last have scraped an E.

He had just turned away when he heard a smashing noise; Malfoy gave a gleeful yell of laughter. Harry whipped around again. His po-tion sample lay in pieces on the floor, and Snape was watching him with a look of gloating pleasure.

"Whoops," he said softly. "Another zero, then, Potter . . ."

Harry was too incensed to speak. He strode back to his cauldron, intending to fill another flask and force Snape to mark it, but saw to his horror that the rest of the contents had vanished.

"I'm sorry!" said Hermione with her hands over her mouth. "I'm really sorry, Harry, I thought you'd finished, so I cleared up!"

Harry could not bring himself to answer. When the bell rang he hurried out of the dungeon without a backward glance and made sure that he found himself a seat between Neville and Seamus for lunch so that Hermione could not start nagging him about using Umbridge's office again.

He was in such a bad mood by the time that he got to Divina-tion that he had quite forgotten his career appointment with Professor McGonagall, remembering only when Ron asked him why he wasn't in her office. He hurtled back upstairs and arrived out of breath, only a few minutes late.

"Sorry, Professor," he panted, as he closed the door. "I forgot. . . ."

"No matter, Potter," she said briskly, but as she spoke, somebody else sniffed from the corner. Harry looked around.

Professor Umbridge was sitting there, a clipboard on her knee, a fussy little pie-frill around her neck, and a small, horribly smug smile on her face.

"Sit down, Potter," said Professor McGonagall tersely. Her hands shook slightly as she shuffled the many pamphlets littering her desk.

Harry sat down with his back to Umbridge and did his best to pre-tend he could not hear the scratching of her quill on her clipboard.

"Well, Potter, this meeting is to talk over any career ideas you might have, and to help you decide which subjects you should continue into sixth and seventh years," said Professor McGonagall. "Have you had any thoughts about what you would like to do after you leave Hogwarts?"

"Er," said Harry.

He was finding the scratching noise from behind him very distracting.

"Yes?" Professor McGonagall prompted Harry.

"Well, I thought of, maybe, being an Auror," Harry mumbled.

"You'd need top grades for that," said Professor McGonagall, extracting a small, dark leaflet from under the mass on her desk and opening it. "They ask for a minimum of five N.E.W.T.s, and nothing under 'Exceeds Expectations' grade, I see. Then you would be required to undergo a stringent series of character and aptitude tests at the Auror office. It's a difficult career path, Potter; they only take the best. In fact, I don't think anybody has been taken on in the last three years."

At this moment Professor Umbridge gave a very tiny cough, as though she was trying to see how quietly she could do it. Professor McGonagall ignored her.

"You'll want to know which subjects you ought to take, I suppose?" she went on, talking a little more loudly than before.

"Yes," said Harry. "Defense Against the Dark Arts, I suppose?"

"Naturally," said Professor McGonagall crisply. "I would also advise —"

Professor Umbridge gave another cough, a little more audible this time. Professor McGonagall closed her eyes for a moment, opened them again, and continued as though nothing had happened.

"I would also advise Transfiguration, because Aurors frequently need to Transfigure or Untransfigure in their work. And I ought to tell you now, Potter, that I do not accept students into my N.E.W.T.

classes unless they have achieved 'Exceeds Expectations' or higher at Ordinary Wizarding Level. I'd say you're averaging 'Acceptable' at the moment, so you'll need to put in some good hard work before the exams to stand a chance of continuing. Then you ought to do Charms, always useful, and Potions. Yes, Potter, Potions," she added, with the merest flicker of a smile. "Poisons and antidotes are essential study for Aurors. And I must tell you that Professor Snape absolutely refuses to take students who get anything other than 'Outstanding' in their O.W.L.s, so —"

Professor Umbridge gave her most pronounced cough yet.

"May I offer you a cough drop, Dolores?" Professor McGonagall asked curtly, without looking at Professor Umbridge.

"Oh no, thank you very much," said Umbridge, with that simpering laugh Harry hated so much. "I just wondered whether I could make the teensiest interruption, Minerva?"

"I daresay you'll find you can," said Professor McGonagall through tightly gritted teeth.

"I was just wondering whether Mr. Potter has *quite* the temperament for an Auror?" said Professor Umbridge sweetly.

"Were you?" said Professor McGonagall haughtily. "Well, Potter," she continued, as though there had been no interruption, "if you are serious in this ambition, I would advise you to concentrate hard on bringing your Transfiguration and Potions up to scratch. I see Professor Flitwick has graded you between 'Acceptable' and 'Exceeds Expectations' for the last two years, so your Charm work seems satisfactory; as for Defense Against the Dark Arts, your marks have been generally high, Professor Lupin in particular thought you — *are you quite sure you wouldn't like a cough drop, Dolores?*"

"Oh, no need, thank you, Minerva," simpered Professor Umbridge, who had just coughed her loudest yet. "I was just concerned that you might not have Harry's most recent Defense Against the Dark Arts marks in front of you. I'm quite sure I slipped in a note . . ."

"What, this thing?" said Professor McGonagall in a tone of revulsion, as she pulled a sheet of pink parchment from between the leaves of Harry's folder. She glanced down it, her eyebrows slightly raised, then placed it back into the folder without comment.

"Yes, as I was saying, Potter, Professor Lupin thought you showed a pronounced aptitude for the subject, and obviously for an Auror —"

"Did you not understand my note, Minerva?" asked Professor Umbridge in honeyed tones, quite forgetting to cough.

"Of course I understood it," said Professor McGonagall, her teeth clenched so tightly that the words came out a little muffled.

"Well, then, I am confused. . . . I'm afraid I don't quite understand how you can give Mr. Potter false hope that —"

"False hope?" repeated Professor McGonagall, still refusing to look round at Professor Umbridge. "He has achieved high marks in all his Defense Against the Dark Arts tests —"

"I'm terribly sorry to have to contradict you, Minerva, but as you will see from my note, Harry has been achieving very poor results in his classes with me —"

"I should have made my meaning plainer," said Professor McGonagall, turning at last to look Umbridge directly in the eyes. "He has achieved high marks in all Defense Against the Dark Arts tests set by a competent teacher."

Professor Umbridge's smile vanished as suddenly as a lightbulb blowing. She sat back in her chair, turned a sheet on her clipboard, and began scribbling very fast indeed, her bulging eyes rolling from side to side. Professor McGonagall turned back to Harry, her thin nostrils flared, her eyes burning.

"Any questions, Potter?"

"Yes," said Harry. "What sort of character and aptitude tests do the Ministry do on you, if you get enough N.E.W.T.s?"

"Well, you'll need to demonstrate the ability to react well to pressure and so forth," said Professor McGonagall, "perseverance and dedication, because Auror training takes a further three years, not to mention very high skills in practical defense. It will mean a lot more study even after you've left school, so unless you're prepared to —"

"I think you'll also find," said Umbridge, her voice very cold now, "that the Ministry looks into the records of those applying to be Aurors. Their criminal records."

"— unless you're prepared to take even more exams after Hogwarts, you should really look at another —"

"— which means that this boy has as much chance of becoming an Auror as Dumbledore has of ever returning to this school."

"A very good chance, then," said Professor McGonagall.

"Potter has a criminal record," said Umbridge loudly.

"Potter has been cleared of all charges," said Professor McGonagall, even more loudly.

Professor Umbridge stood up. She was so short that this did not make a great deal of difference, but her fussy, simpering demeanor had given place to a hard fury that made her broad, flabby face look oddly sinister.

"Potter has no chance whatsoever of becoming an Auror!"

Professor McGonagall got to her feet too, and in her case this was a much more impressive move. She towered over Professor Umbridge.

"Potter," she said in ringing tones, "I will assist you to become an Auror if it is the last thing I do! If I have to coach you nightly I will make sure you achieve the required results!"

"The Minister of Magic will never employ Harry Potter!" said Umbridge, her voice rising furiously.

"There may well be a new Minister of Magic by the time Potter is ready to join!" shouted Professor McGonagall.

"Aha!" shrieked Professor Umbridge, pointing a stubby finger at McGonagall. "Yes! Yes, yes, yes! Of course! That's what you want, isn't it, Minerva McGonagall? You want Cornelius Fudge replaced by Albus Dumbledore! You think you'll be where I am, don't you, Senior Undersecretary to the Minister and headmistress to boot!"

"You are raving," said Professor McGonagall, superbly disdainful. "Potter, that concludes our career consultation."

Harry swung his bag over his shoulder and hurried out of the room, not daring to look at Umbridge. He could hear her and Professor McGonagall continuing to shout at each other all the way back along the corridor.

Professor Umbridge was still breathing as though she had just run a race when she strode into their Defense Against the Dark Arts lesson that afternoon.

"I hope you've thought better of what you were planning to do, Harry," Hermione whispered, the moment they had opened their books to chapter thirty-four ("Non-Retaliation and Negotiation"). "Umbridge looks like she's in a really bad mood already. . . ."

Every now and then Umbridge shot glowering looks at Harry, who kept his head down, staring at *Defensive Magical Theory,* his eyes unfocused, thinking. . . .

He could just imagine Professor McGonagall's reaction if he were caught trespassing in Professor Umbridge's office mere hours after she had vouched for him. . . . There was nothing to stop him simply going back to Gryffindor Tower and hoping that sometime during the next summer holiday he would have a chance to ask Sirius about the scene he had witnessed in the Pensieve. . . . Nothing, except that the thought of taking this sensible course of action made him feel as though a lead weight had dropped into his stomach. . . . And then there was the matter of Fred and George, whose diversion was already planned, not to mention the knife Sirius had given him, which was currently residing in his schoolbag along with his father's old Invisibility Cloak. . . .

But the fact remained that if he were caught . . .

"Dumbledore sacrificed himself to keep you in school, Harry!" whispered Hermione, raising her book to hide her face from Umbridge. "And if you get thrown out today it will all have been for nothing!"

He could abandon the plan and simply learn to live with the memory of what his father had done on a summer's day more than twenty years ago. . . .

And then he remembered Sirius in the fire upstairs in the Gryffindor common room. . . . "You're less like your father than I thought. . . . The risk would've been what made it fun for James. . . ."

But did he want to be like his father anymore?

"Harry, don't do it, please don't do it!" Hermione said in anguished tones as the bell rang at the end of the class.

He did not answer; he did not know what to do. Ron seemed determined to give neither his opinion nor his advice. He would not look at Harry, though when Hermione opened her mouth to try dissuading Harry some more, he said in a low voice, "Give it a rest, okay? He can make up his own mind."

Harry's heart beat very fast as he left the classroom. He was halfway along the corridor outside when he heard the unmistakable sounds of a diversion going off in the distance. There were screams and yells reverberating from somewhere above them. People exiting the classrooms all around Harry were stopping in their tracks and looking up at the ceiling fearfully —

Then Umbridge came pelting out of her classroom as fast as her short legs would carry her. Pulling out her wand, she hurried off in the opposite direction: It was now or never.

"Harry — please!" said Hermione weakly.

But he had made up his mind — hitching his bag more securely onto his shoulder he set off at a run, weaving in and out of students now hurrying in the opposite direction, off to see what all the fuss was about in the east wing. . . .

Harry reached the corridor where Umbridge's office was situated and found it deserted. Dashing behind a large suit of armor whose helmet creaked around to watch him, he pulled open his bag, seized Sirius's knife, and donned the Invisibility Cloak. He then crept slowly and carefully back out from behind the suit of armor and along the corridor until he reached Umbridge's door.

He inserted the blade of the magical knife into the crack around it and moved it gently up and down, then withdrew it. There was a tiny *click,* and the door swung open. He ducked inside the office, closed the door quickly behind him, and looked around.

It was empty; nothing was moving except the horrible kittens on the plates continuing to frolic on the wall above the confiscated broomsticks.

Harry pulled off his Cloak and, striding over to the fireplace, found what he was looking for within seconds: a small box containing glittering Floo powder.

He crouched down in front of the empty grate, his hands shaking. He had never done this before, though he thought he knew how it must work. Sticking his head into the fireplace, he took a large pinch of powder and dropped it onto the logs stacked neatly beneath him. They exploded at once into emerald-green flames.

"Number twelve, Grimmauld Place!" Harry said loudly and clearly.

It was one of the most curious sensations he had ever experienced; he had traveled by Floo powder before, of course, but then it had been his entire body that had spun around and around in the flames through the network of Wizarding fireplaces that stretched over the country: This time, his knees remained firm upon the cold floor of Umbridge's office, and only his head hurtled through the emerald fire. . . .

And then, abruptly as it had begun, the spinning stopped. Feeling rather sick and as though he was wearing an exceptionally hot muffler around his head, Harry opened his eyes to find that he was looking up out of the kitchen fireplace at the long, wooden table, where a man sat poring over a piece of parchment.

"Sirius?"

The man jumped and looked around. It was not Sirius, but Lupin.

"Harry!" he said, looking thoroughly shocked. "What are you — what's happened, is everything all right?"

"Yeah," said Harry. "I just wondered — I mean, I just fancied a — a chat with Sirius."

"I'll call him," said Lupin, getting to his feet, still looking perplexed. "He went upstairs to look for Kreacher, he seems to be hiding in the attic again. . . ."

And Harry saw Lupin hurry out of the kitchen. Now he was left with nothing to look at but the chair and table legs. He wondered why Sirius had never mentioned how very uncomfortable it was to speak out of the fire — his knees were already objecting painfully to their prolonged contact with Umbridge's hard stone floor.

Lupin returned with Sirius at his heels moments later.

"What is it?" said Sirius urgently, sweeping his long dark hair out of his eyes and dropping to the ground in front of the fire, so that he and Harry were on a level; Lupin knelt down too, looking very concerned. "Are you all right? Do you need help?"

"No," said Harry, "it's nothing like that. . . . I just wanted to talk . . . about my dad. . . ."

They exchanged a look of great surprise, but Harry did not have time to feel awkward or embarrassed; his knees were becoming sorer by the second, and he guessed that five minutes had already passed from the start of the diversion — George had only guaranteed him twenty. He therefore plunged immediately into the story of what he had seen in the Pensieve.

When he had finished, neither Sirius nor Lupin spoke for a moment. Then Lupin said quietly, "I wouldn't like you to judge your father on what you saw there, Harry. He was only fifteen —"

"I'm fifteen!" said Harry heatedly.

"Look, Harry," said Sirius placatingly, "James and Snape hated each other from the moment they set eyes on each other, it was just one of those things, you can understand that, can't you? I think James was everything Snape wanted to be — he was popular, he was good at Quidditch, good at pretty much everything. And Snape was just this little oddball who was up to his eyes in the Dark Arts and James — whatever else he may have appeared to you, Harry — always hated the Dark Arts."

"Yeah," said Harry, "but he just attacked Snape for no good reason, just because — well, just because you said you were bored," he finished with a slightly apologetic note in his voice.

"I'm not proud of it," said Sirius quickly.

Lupin looked sideways at Sirius and then said, "Look, Harry, what you've got to understand is that your father and Sirius were the best in the school at whatever they did — everyone thought they were the height of cool — if they sometimes got a bit carried away —"

"If we were sometimes arrogant little berks, you mean," said Sirius.

Lupin smiled.

"He kept messing up his hair," said Harry in a pained voice.

Sirius and Lupin laughed.

"I'd forgotten he used to do that," said Sirius affectionately.

"Was he playing with the Snitch?" said Lupin eagerly.

"Yeah," said Harry, watching uncomprehendingly as Sirius and Lupin beamed reminiscently. "Well . . . I thought he was a bit of an idiot."

"Of course he was a bit of an idiot!" said Sirius bracingly. "We were all idiots! Well — not Moony so much," he said fairly, looking at Lupin, but Lupin shook his head.

"Did I ever tell you to lay off Snape?" he said. "Did I ever have the guts to tell you I thought you were out of order?"

"Yeah, well," said Sirius, "you made us feel ashamed of ourselves sometimes. . . . That was something. . . ."

"And," said Harry doggedly, determined to say everything that was on his mind now he was here, "he kept looking over at the girls by the lake, hoping they were watching him!"

"Oh, well, he always made a fool of himself whenever Lily was around," said Sirius, shrugging. "He couldn't stop himself showing off whenever he got near her."

"How come she married him?" Harry asked miserably. "She hated him!"

"Nah, she didn't," said Sirius.

"She started going out with him in seventh year," said Lupin.

"Once James had deflated his head a bit," said Sirius.

"And stopped hexing people just for the fun of it," said Lupin.

"Even Snape?" said Harry.

"Well," said Lupin slowly, "Snape was a special case. I mean, he never lost an opportunity to curse James, so you couldn't really expect James to take that lying down, could you?"

"And my mum was okay with that?"

"She didn't know too much about it, to tell you the truth," said Sirius. "I mean, James didn't take Snape on dates with her and jinx him in front of her, did he?"

Sirius frowned at Harry, who was still looking unconvinced.

"Look," he said, "your father was the best friend I ever had, and he was a good person. A lot of people are idiots at the age of fifteen. He grew out of it."

"Yeah, okay," said Harry heavily. "I just never thought I'd feel sorry for Snape."

"Now you mention it," said Lupin, a faint crease between his eyebrows, "how did Snape react when he found you'd seen all this?"

"He told me he'd never teach me Occlumency again," said Harry indifferently, "like that's a big disappoint —"

"He WHAT?" shouted Sirius, causing Harry to jump and inhale a mouthful of ashes.

"Are you serious, Harry?" said Lupin quickly. "He's stopped giving you lessons?"

"Yeah," said Harry, surprised at what he considered a great overreaction. "But it's okay, I don't care, it's a bit of a relief to tell you the —"

"I'm coming up there to have a word with Snape!" said Sirius forcefully and he actually made to stand up, but Lupin wrenched him back down again.

"If anyone's going to tell Snape it will be me!" he said firmly. "But Harry, first of all, you're to go back to Snape and tell him that on no account is he to stop giving you lessons — when Dumbledore hears —"

"I can't tell him that, he'd kill me!" said Harry, outraged. "You didn't see him when we got out of the Pensieve —"

"Harry, there is nothing so important as you learning Occlumency!" said Lupin sternly. "Do you understand me? Nothing!"

"Okay, okay," said Harry, thoroughly discomposed, not to mention annoyed. "I'll . . . I'll try and say something to him. . . . But it won't be . . ."

He fell silent. He could hear distant footsteps.

"Is that Kreacher coming downstairs?"

"No," said Sirius, glancing behind him. "It must be somebody your end . . ."

Harry's heart skipped several beats.

"I'd better go!" he said hastily and he pulled his head backward out of Grimmauld Place's fire. For a moment his head seemed to be revolving on his shoulders, and then he found himself kneeling in front of Umbridge's fire with his head firmly back on, watching the emerald flames flicker and die.

"Quickly, quickly!" he heard a wheezy voice mutter right outside the office door. "Ah, she's left it open. . . ."

Harry dived for the Invisibility Cloak and had just managed to pull it back over himself when Filch burst into the office. He looked absolutely delighted about something and was talking to himself feverishly as he crossed the room, pulled open a drawer in Umbridge's desk, and began rifling through the papers inside it.

"Approval for Whipping . . . Approval for Whipping . . . I can do it at last. . . . They've had it coming to them for years. . . ."

He pulled out a piece of parchment, kissed it, then shuffled rapidly back out of the door, clutching it to his chest.

Harry leapt to his feet and, making sure that he had his bag and the Invisibility Cloak was completely covering him, he wrenched open the door and hurried out of the office after Filch, who was hobbling along faster than Harry had ever seen him go.

One landing down from Umbridge's office and Harry thought it was safe to become visible again; he pulled off the Cloak, shoved it in his bag and hurried onward. There was a great deal of shouting and movement coming from the entrance hall. He ran down the marble staircase and found what looked like most of the school assembled there.

It was just like the night when Trelawney had been sacked. Students were standing all around the walls in a great ring (some of them, Harry noticed, covered in a substance that looked very like Stinksap); teachers and ghosts were also in the crowd. Prominent among the onlookers were members of the Inquisitorial Squad, who were all looking exceptionally pleased with themselves, and Peeves, who was bobbing overhead, gazed down upon Fred and George, who stood in the middle of the floor with the unmistakable look of two people who had just been cornered.

"So!" said Umbridge triumphantly, whom Harry realized was

standing just a few stairs in front of him, once more looking down upon her prey. "So . . . you think it amusing to turn a school corridor into a swamp, do you?"

"Pretty amusing, yeah," said Fred, looking back up at her without the slightest sign of fear.

Filch elbowed his way closer to Umbridge, almost crying with happiness.

"I've got the form, Headmistress," he said hoarsely, waving the piece of parchment Harry had just seen him take from her desk. "I've got the form and I've got the whips waiting. . . . Oh, let me do it now. . . ."

"Very good, Argus," she said. "You two," she went on, gazing down at Fred and George, "are about to learn what happens to wrongdoers in my school."

"You know what?" said Fred. "I don't think we are."

He turned to his twin.

"George," said Fred, "I think we've outgrown full-time education."

"Yeah, I've been feeling that way myself," said George lightly.

"Time to test our talents in the real world, d'you reckon?" asked Fred.

"Definitely," said George.

And before Umbridge could say a word, they raised their wands and said together, *"Accio Brooms!"*

Harry heard a loud crash somewhere in the distance. Looking to his left he ducked just in time — Fred and George's broomsticks, one still trailing the heavy chain and iron peg with which Umbridge had fastened them to the wall, were hurtling along the corridor toward their owners. They turned left, streaked down the stairs, and stopped sharply in front of the twins, the chain clattering loudly on the flagged stone floor.

"We won't be seeing you," Fred told Professor Umbridge, swinging his leg over his broomstick.

"Yeah, don't bother to keep in touch," said George, mounting his own.

Fred looked around at the assembled students, and at the silent, watchful crowd.

"If anyone fancies buying a Portable Swamp, as demonstrated upstairs, come to number ninety-three, Diagon Alley — Weasleys' Wizard Wheezes," he said in a loud voice. "Our new premises!"

"Special discounts to Hogwarts students who swear they're going to use our products to get rid of this old bat," added George, pointing at Professor Umbridge.

"STOP THEM!" shrieked Umbridge, but it was too late. As the Inquisitorial Squad closed in, Fred and George kicked off from the floor, shooting fifteen feet into the air, the iron peg swinging dangerously below. Fred looked across the hall at the poltergeist bobbing on his level above the crowd.

"Give her hell from us, Peeves."

And Peeves, whom Harry had never seen take an order from a student before, swept his belled hat from his head and sprang to a salute as Fred and George wheeled about to tumultuous applause from the students below and sped out of the open front doors into the glorious sunset.

GRAWP

The story of Fred and George's flight to freedom was retold so often over the next few days that Harry could tell it would soon become the stuff of Hogwarts legend. Within a week, even those who had been eyewitnesses were half-convinced that they had seen the twins dive-bomb Umbridge on their brooms, pelting her with Dungbombs before zooming out of the doors. In the immediate aftermath of their departure there was a great wave of talk about copying them, so that Harry frequently heard students saying things like, "Honestly, some days I just feel like jumping on my broom and leaving this place," or else, "One more lesson like that and I might just do a Weasley. . . ."

Fred and George had made sure that nobody was likely to forget them very soon. For one thing, they had not left instructions on how to remove the swamp that now filled the corridor on the fifth floor of the east wing. Umbridge and Filch had been observed trying different means of removing it but without success. Eventually the area was roped off and Filch, gnashing his teeth furiously, was given the task of punting students across it to their classrooms. Harry was certain that teachers like McGonagall or Flitwick could have removed the swamp in an instant, but just as in the case of Fred and George's Wildfire Whiz-Bangs, they seemed to prefer to watch Umbridge struggle.

Then there were the two large broom-shaped holes in Umbridge's office door, through which Fred and George's Cleansweeps had smashed to rejoin their masters. Filch fitted a new door and removed Harry's Firebolt to the dungeons where, it was rumored, Umbridge had set an armed security troll to guard it. However, her troubles were far from over.

Inspired by Fred and George's example, a great number of students were now vying for the newly vacant positions of Troublemakers-in-Chief. In spite of the new door, somebody managed to slip a hairy-snouted niffler into Umbridge's office, which promptly tore the place apart in its search for shiny objects, leapt on Umbridge on her reentrance, and tried to gnaw the rings off her stubby fingers. Dungbombs and Stinkpellets were dropped so frequently in the corridors that it became the new fashion for students to perform Bubble-Head Charms on themselves before leaving lessons, which ensured them a supply of fresh clean air, even though it gave them all the peculiar appearance of wearing upside-down goldfish bowls on their heads.

Filch prowled the corridors with a horsewhip ready in his hands, desperate to catch miscreants, but the problem was that there were now so many of them that he did not know which way to turn. The Inquisitorial Squad were attempting to help him, but odd things kept happening to its members. Warrington of the Slytherin Quidditch team reported to the hospital wing with a horrible skin complaint that made him look as though he had been coated in cornflakes. Pansy Parkinson, to Hermione's delight, missed all her lessons the following day, as she had sprouted antlers.

Meanwhile it became clear just how many Skiving Snackboxes Fred and George had managed to sell before leaving Hogwarts. Umbridge only had to enter her classroom for the students assembled there to faint, vomit, develop dangerous fevers, or else spout blood from both nostrils. Shrieking with rage and frustration she attempted to trace the mysterious symptoms to their source, but the students told her stubbornly they were suffering "Umbridge-itis." After putting four successive classes in detention and failing to discover their secret she was forced to give up and allow the bleeding, swooning, sweating, and vomiting students to leave her classes in droves.

But not even the users of the Snackboxes could compete with that master of chaos, Peeves, who seemed to have taken Fred's parting words deeply to heart. Cackling madly, he soared through the school, upending tables, bursting out of blackboards, and toppling statues and vases. Twice he shut Mrs. Norris inside suits of armor, from which she was rescued, yowling loudly, by the furious caretaker. He smashed lanterns and snuffed out candles, juggled burning torches over the heads of screaming students, caused neatly stacked piles of parchment to topple into fires or out of windows, flooded the second floor when he pulled off all the taps in the bathrooms, dropped a bag of tarantulas in the middle of the Great Hall during breakfast and, whenever he fancied a break, spent hours at a time floating along after Umbridge and blowing loud raspberries every time she spoke.

None of the staff but Filch seemed to be stirring themselves to help her. Indeed, a week after Fred and George's departure Harry witnessed Professor McGonagall walking right past Peeves, who was determinedly loosening a crystal chandelier, and could have sworn he heard her tell the poltergeist out of the corner of her mouth, "It unscrews the other way."

To cap matters, Montague had still not recovered from his sojourn in the toilet. He remained confused and disorientated and his parents were to be observed one Tuesday morning striding up the front drive, looking extremely angry.

"Should we say something?" said Hermione in a worried voice, pressing her cheek against the Charms window so that she could see

Mr. and Mrs. Montague marching inside. "About what happened to him? In case it helps Madam Pomfrey cure him?"

" 'Course not, he'll recover," said Ron indifferently.

"Anyway, more trouble for Umbridge, isn't it?" said Harry in a satisfied voice.

He and Ron both tapped the teacups they were supposed to be charming with their wands. Harry's spouted four very short legs that would not reach the desk and wriggled pointlessly in midair. Ron's grew four very thin spindly legs that hoisted the cup off the desk with great difficulty, trembled for a few seconds, then folded, causing the cup to crack into two.

"*Reparo!*" said Hermione quickly, mending Ron's cup with a wave of her wand. "That's all very well, but what if Montague's permanently injured?"

"Who cares?" said Ron irritably, while his teacup stood drunkenly again, trembling violently at the knees. "Montague shouldn't have tried to take all those points from Gryffindor, should he? If you want to worry about anyone, Hermione, worry about me!"

"You?" she said, catching her teacup as it scampered happily away across the desk on four sturdy little willow-patterned legs and replacing it in front of her. "Why should I be worried about you?"

"When Mum's next letter finally gets through Umbridge's screening process," said Ron bitterly, now holding his cup up while its frail legs tried feebly to support its weight, "I'm going to be in deep trouble. I wouldn't be surprised if she's sent a Howler again."

"But —"

"It'll be my fault Fred and George left, you wait," said Ron darkly. "She'll say I should've stopped them leaving, I should've grabbed the ends of their brooms and hung on or something. . . . Yeah, it'll be all my fault. . . ."

"Well, if she *does* say that it'll be very unfair, you couldn't have done anything! But I'm sure she won't, I mean, if it's really true they've got premises in Diagon Alley now, they must have been planning this for ages. . . ."

"Yeah, but that's another thing, how did they get premises?" said Ron, hitting his teacup so hard with his wand that its legs collapsed again and it lay twitching before him. "It's a bit dodgy, isn't it? They'll need loads of Galleons to afford the rent on a place in Diagon Alley, she'll want to know what they've been up to, to get their hands on that sort of gold. . . ."

"Well, yes, that occurred to me too," said Hermione, allowing her teacup to jog in neat little circles around Harry's, whose stubby little legs were still unable to touch the desktop. "I've been wondering whether Mundungus has persuaded them to sell stolen goods or something awful. . . ."

"He hasn't," said Harry curtly.

"How do you know?" said Ron and Hermione together.

"Because —" Harry hesitated, but the moment to confess finally seemed to have come. There was no good to be gained in keeping silent if it meant anyone suspected that Fred and George were criminals. "Because they got the gold from me. I gave them my Triwizard winnings last June."

There was a shocked silence, then Hermione's teacup jogged right over the edge of the desk and smashed on the floor.

"Oh, Harry, you *didn't*!" she said.

"Yes, I did," said Harry mutinously. "And I don't regret it either — I didn't need the gold, and they'll be great at a joke shop. . . ."

"But this is excellent!" said Ron, looking thrilled. "It's all your fault, Harry — Mum can't blame me at all! Can I tell her?"

"Yeah, I suppose you'd better," said Harry dully. "'Specially if she thinks they're receiving stolen cauldrons or something. . . ."

Hermione said nothing at all for the rest of the lesson, but Harry had a shrewd suspicion that her self-restraint was bound to crack before long. Sure enough, once they had left the castle for break and were standing around in the weak May sunshine, she fixed Harry with a beady eye and opened her mouth with a determined air.

Harry interrupted her before she had even started.

"It's no good nagging me, it's done," he said firmly. "Fred and George have got the gold — spent a good bit of it too, by the sounds of it — and I can't get it back from them and I don't want to. So save your breath, Hermione."

"I wasn't going to say anything about Fred and George!" she said in an injured voice.

Ron snorted disbelievingly and Hermione threw him a very dirty look.

"No, I wasn't!" she said angrily. "As a matter of fact, I was going to ask Harry when he's going to go back to Snape and ask for Occlumency lessons again!"

Harry's heart sank. Once they had exhausted the subject of Fred and George's dramatic departure, which admittedly had taken many hours, Ron and Hermione had wanted to hear news of Sirius. As Harry had not confided in them the reason he had wanted to talk to Sirius in the first place, it had been hard to think of things to tell them. He had ended up saying to them truthfully that Sirius wanted Harry to resume Occlumency lessons. He had been regretting this ever since; Hermione would not let the subject drop and kept reverting to it when Harry least expected it.

"You can't tell me you've stopped having funny dreams," Hermione said now, "because Ron told me last night you were muttering in your sleep again. . . ."

Harry threw Ron a furious look. Ron had the grace to look ashamed of himself.

"You were only muttering a bit," he mumbled apologetically. "Something about 'just a bit farther.'"

"I dreamed I was watching you lot play Quidditch," Harry lied brutally. "I was trying to get you to stretch out a bit farther to grab the Quaffle."

Ron's ears went red. Harry felt a kind of vindictive pleasure: He had not, of course, dreamed anything of the sort.

Last night he had once again made the journey along the Department of Mysteries corridor. He had passed through the circular room, then the room full of clicking and dancing light, until he found himself again inside that cavernous room full of shelves on which were ranged dusty glass spheres. . . .

He had hurried straight toward row number ninety-seven, turned left, and ran along it. . . . It had probably been then that he had spoken aloud. . . . *Just a bit farther* . . . for he could feel his conscious self struggling to wake . . . and before he had reached the end of the row, he had found himself lying in bed again, gazing up at the canopy of his four-poster.

"You are *trying* to block your mind, aren't you?" said Hermione, looking beadily at Harry. "You are keeping going with your Occlumency?"

"Of course I am," said Harry, trying to sound as though this question was insulting, but not quite meeting her eye. The truth was that he was so intensely curious about what was hidden in that room full of dusty orbs that he was quite keen for the dreams to continue.

The problem was that with just under a month to go until the exams and every free moment devoted to studying, his mind seemed saturated with information when he went to bed so that he found it very difficult to get to sleep at all. When he did, his overwrought brain presented him most nights with stupid dreams about the exams. He also suspected that part of his mind — the part that often spoke in Hermione's voice — now felt guilty on the occasions it strayed down that corridor ending in the black door, and sought to wake him before he could reach journey's end.

"You know," said Ron, whose ears were still flaming red, "if Mon-

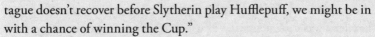
tague doesn't recover before Slytherin play Hufflepuff, we might be in with a chance of winning the Cup."

"Yeah, I s'pose so," said Harry, glad of a change of subject.

"I mean, we've won one, lost one — if Slytherin lose to Hufflepuff next Saturday —"

"Yeah, that's right," said Harry, losing track of what he was agreeing to: Cho Chang had just walked across the courtyard, determinedly not looking at him.

The final match of the Quidditch season, Gryffindor versus Ravenclaw, was to take place on the last weekend of May. Although Slytherin had been narrowly defeated by Hufflepuff in their last match, Gryffindor was not daring to hope for victory, due mainly (though of course nobody said it to him) to Ron's abysmal goalkeeping record. He, however, seemed to have found a new optimism.

"I mean, I can't get any worse, can I?" he told Harry and Hermione grimly over breakfast on the morning of the match. "Nothing to lose now, is there?"

"You know," said Hermione, as she and Harry walked down to the pitch a little later in the midst of a very excitable crowd, "I think Ron might do better without Fred and George around. They never exactly gave him a lot of confidence. . . ."

Luna Lovegood overtook them with what appeared to be a live eagle perched on top of her head.

"Oh gosh, I forgot!" said Hermione, watching the eagle flapping its wings as Luna walked serenely past a group of cackling and pointing Slytherins. "Cho will be playing, won't she?"

Harry, who had not forgotten this, merely grunted.

They found seats in the second to topmost row of the stands. It was a fine, clear day. Ron could not wish for better, and Harry found himself hoping against hope that Ron would not give the Slytherins cause for more rousing choruses of "Weasley Is Our King."

Lee Jordan, who had been very dispirited since Fred and George had left, was commentating as usual. As the teams zoomed out onto the pitches he named the players with something less than his usual gusto.

". . . Bradley . . . Davies . . . Chang," he said, and Harry felt his stomach perform, less of a back flip, more a feeble lurch as Cho walked out onto the pitch, her shiny black hair rippling in the slight breeze. He was not sure what he wanted to happen anymore, except that he could not stand any more rows. Even the sight of her chatting animatedly to Roger Davies as they prepared to mount their brooms caused him only a slight twinge of jealousy.

"And they're off!" said Lee. "And Davies takes the Quaffle immediately, Ravenclaw Captain Davies with the Quaffle, he dodges Johnson, he dodges Bell, he dodges Spinnet as well. . . . He's going straight for goal! He's going to shoot — and — and —" Lee swore very loudly. "And he's scored."

Harry and Hermione groaned with the rest of the Gryffindors. Predictably, horribly, the Slytherins on the other side of the stands began to sing:

> *Weasley cannot save a thing,*
> *He cannot block a single ring . . .*

"Harry," said a hoarse voice in Harry's ear. "Hermione . . ."

Harry looked around and saw Hagrid's enormous bearded face sticking between the seats; apparently he had squeezed his way all along the row behind, for the first and second years he had just passed had a ruffled, flattened look about them. For some reason, Hagrid was bent double as though anxious not to be seen, though he was still at least four feet taller than everybody else.

"Listen," he whispered, "can yeh come with me? Now? While ev'ryone's watchin' the match?"

"Er . . . can't it wait, Hagrid?" asked Harry. "Till the match is over?"

"No," said Hagrid. "No, Harry, it's gotta be now . . . while ev'ryone's lookin' the other way. . . . Please?"

Hagrid's nose was gently dripping blood. His eyes were both blackened. Harry had not seen him this close up since his return to the school; he looked utterly woebegone.

"'Course," said Harry at once, "'course we'll come. . . ."

He and Hermione edged back along their row of seats, causing much grumbling among the students who had to stand up for them. The people in Hagrid's row were not complaining, merely attempting to make themselves as small as possible.

"I 'ppreciate this, you two, I really do," said Hagrid as they reached the stairs. He kept looking around nervously as they descended toward the lawn below. "I jus' hope she doesn' notice us goin'. . . ."

"You mean Umbridge?" said Harry. "She won't, she's got her whole Inquisitorial Squad sitting with her, didn't you see? She must be expecting trouble at the match."

"Yeah, well, a bit o' trouble wouldn' hurt," said Hagrid, pausing to peer around the edge of the stands to make sure the stretch of lawn between there and his cabin was deserted. "Give us more time . . ."

"What is it, Hagrid?" said Hermione, looking up at him with a concerned expression on her face as they hurried across the lawn toward the edge of the forest.

"Yeh — yeh'll see in a mo'," said Hagrid, looking over his shoulder as a great roar rose from the stands behind them. "Hey — did someone jus' score?"

"It'll be Ravenclaw," said Harry heavily.

"Good . . . good . . ." said Hagrid distractedly. "Tha's good. . . ."

They had to jog to keep up with him as he strode across the lawn, looking around with every other step. When they reached his cabin, Hermione turned automatically left toward the front door; Hagrid, however, walked straight past it into the shade of the trees on the outermost edge of the forest, where he picked up a crossbow that was leaning against a tree. When he realized they were no longer with him, he turned.

"We're goin' in here," he said, jerking his shaggy head behind him.

"Into the forest?" said Hermione, perplexed.

"Yeah," said Hagrid. "C'mon now, quick, before we're spotted!"

Harry and Hermione looked at each other, then ducked into the cover of the trees behind Hagrid, who was already striding away from them into the green gloom, his crossbow over his arm. Harry and Hermione ran to catch up with him.

"Hagrid, why are you armed?" said Harry.

"Jus' a precaution," said Hagrid, shrugging his massive shoulders.

"You didn't bring your crossbow the day you showed us the thestrals," said Hermione timidly.

"Nah, well, we weren' goin' in so far then," said Hagrid. "An' anyway, tha' was before Firenze left the forest, wasn' it?"

"Why does Firenze leaving make a difference?" asked Hermione curiously.

"'Cause the other centaurs are good an' riled at me, tha's why," said Hagrid quietly, glancing around. "They used ter be — well, yeh couldn' call 'em friendly — but we got on all righ'. Kept 'emselves to 'emselves, bu' always turned up if I wanted a word. Not anymore . . ."

He sighed deeply.

"Firenze said that they're angry because he went to work for Dumbledore?" Harry asked, tripping on a protruding foot because he was busy watching Hagrid's profile.

"Yeah," said Hagrid heavily. "Well, angry doesn' cover it. Ruddy livid. If I hadn' stepped in, I reckon they'd've kicked Firenze ter death —"

"They attacked him?" said Hermione, sounding shocked.

"Yep," said Hagrid gruffly, forcing his way through several low-hanging branches. "He had half the herd onto him —"

"And you stopped it?" said Harry, amazed and impressed. "By yourself?"

"'Course I did, couldn't stand by an' watch 'em kill him, could I?" said Hagrid. "Lucky I was passin', really . . . an' I'd've thought Firenze mighta remembered tha' before he started sendin' me stupid warnin's!" he added hotly and unexpectedly.

Harry and Hermione looked at each other, startled, but Hagrid, scowling, did not elaborate.

"Anyway," he said, breathing a little more heavily than usual, "since then the other centaurs've bin livid with me an' the trouble is, they've got a lot of influence in the forest. . . . Cleverest creatures in here . . ."

"Is that why we're here, Hagrid?" asked Hermione. "The centaurs?"

"Ah no," said Hagrid, shaking his head dismissively, "no, it's not them. . . . Well, o' course, they could complicate the problem, yeah. . . . But yeh'll see what I mean in a bit. . . ."

On this incomprehensible note he fell silent and forged a little ahead, taking one stride for every three of theirs, so that they had great trouble keeping up with him.

The path was becoming increasingly overgrown and the trees grew so closely together as they walked farther and farther into the forest that it was as dark as dusk. They were soon a long way past the clearing where Hagrid had shown them the thestrals, but Harry felt no sense of unease until Hagrid stepped unexpectedly off the path and began wending his way in and out of trees toward the dark heart of the forest.

"Hagrid?" said Harry, fighting his way through thickly knotted brambles over which Hagrid had stepped easily and remembering very vividly what had happened to him on the other occasions he had stepped off the forest path. "Where are we going?"

"Bit further," said Hagrid over his shoulder. "C'mon, Harry. . . . We need ter keep together now. . . ."

It was a great struggle to keep up with Hagrid, what with branches and thickets of thorn through which Hagrid marched as easily as though they were cobwebs, but which snagged Harry and Hermione's robes, frequently entangling them so severely that they had to stop for minutes at a time to free themselves. Harry's arms and legs were soon covered in small cuts and scratches. They were so deep in the forest now that sometimes all Harry could see of Hagrid in the gloom was a massive dark shape ahead of him. Any sound seemed threatening in the muffled silence. The breaking of a twig echoed loudly and the tiniest rustle of movement, though it might have been made by an innocent sparrow, caused Harry to peer through the gloom for a culprit. It occurred to him that he had never managed to get this far into the forest without meeting some kind of creature — their absence struck him as rather ominous.

"Hagrid, would it be all right if we lit our wands?" said Hermione quietly.

"Er . . . all righ'," Hagrid whispered back. "In fact . . ."

He stopped suddenly and turned around; Hermione walked right into him and was knocked over backward. Harry caught her just before she hit the forest floor.

"Maybe we bes' jus' stop fer a momen', so I can . . . fill yeh in," said Hagrid. "Before we ge' there, like."

"Good!" said Hermione, as Harry set her back on her feet. They both murmured *"Lumos!"* and their wand-tips ignited. Hagrid's face swam through the gloom by the light of the two wavering beams and Harry saw that he looked nervous and sad again.

"Righ'," said Hagrid. "Well . . . see . . . the thing is . . ."

He took a great breath.

"Well, there's a good chance I'm goin' ter be gettin' the sack any day now," he said.

Harry and Hermione looked at each other, then back at him.

"But you've lasted this long —" Hermione said tentatively. "What makes you think —"

"Umbridge reckons it was me that put tha' niffler in her office."

"And was it?" said Harry, before he could stop himself.

"No, it ruddy well wasn'!" said Hagrid indignantly. "On'y anythin' ter do with magical creatures an' she thinks it's got somethin' ter do with me. Yeh know she's bin lookin' fer a chance ter get rid of me ever since I got back. I don' wan' ter go, o' course, but if it wasn' fer . . . well . . . the special circumstances I'm abou' ter explain to yeh, I'd leave righ' now, before she's go' the chance ter do it in front o' the whole school, like she did with Trelawney."

Harry and Hermione both made noises of protest, but Hagrid overrode them with a wave of one of his enormous hands.

"It's not the end o' the world, I'll be able ter help Dumbledore once I'm outta here, I can be useful ter the Order. An' you lot'll have Grubbly-Plank, yeh'll — yeh'll get through yer exams fine. . . ." His voice trembled and broke.

"Don' worry abou' me," he said hastily, as Hermione made to pat his arm. He pulled his enormous spotted handkerchief from the pocket of his waistcoat and mopped his eyes with it. "Look, I wouldn' be tellin' yer this at all if I didn' have ter. See, if I go . . . well, I can' leave withou' . . . withou' tellin' someone . . . because I'll — I'll need you two ter help me. An' Ron, if he's willin'."

"Of course we'll help you," said Harry at once. "What do you want us to do?"

Hagrid gave a great sniff and patted Harry wordlessly on the shoulder with such force that Harry was knocked sideways into a tree.

"I knew yeh'd say yes," said Hagrid into his handkerchief, "but I won' . . . never . . . forget . . . Well . . . c'mon . . . jus' a little bit further through here . . . Watch yerselves, now, there's nettles. . . ."

They walked on in silence for another fifteen minutes. Harry had opened his mouth to ask how much farther they had to go when Hagrid threw out his right arm to signal that they should stop.

"Really easy," he said softly. "Very quiet, now . . ."

They crept forward and Harry saw that they were facing a large, smooth mound of earth nearly as tall as Hagrid that he thought, with a jolt of dread, was sure to be the lair of some enormous animal. Trees had been ripped up at the roots all around the mound, so that it stood on a bare patch of ground surrounded by heaps of trunks and boughs that formed a kind of fence or barricade, behind which Harry, Hermione, and Hagrid now stood.

"Sleepin'," breathed Hagrid.

Sure enough, Harry could hear a distant, rhythmic rumbling that sounded like a pair of enormous lungs at work. He glanced sideways at Hermione, who was gazing at the mound with her mouth slightly open. She looked utterly terrified.

"Hagrid," she said in a whisper barely audible over the sound of the sleeping creature, "who is he?"

Harry found this an odd question. . . . "What is it?" was the one he had been planning on asking.

"Hagrid, you told us," said Hermione, her wand now shaking in her hand, "you told us none of them wanted to come!"

Harry looked from her to Hagrid and then, as realization hit him, he looked back at the mound with a small gasp of horror.

The great mound of earth, on which he, Hermione, and Hagrid could easily have stood, was moving slowly up and down in time with the deep, grunting breathing. It was not a mound at all. It was the curved back of what was clearly . . .

"Well — no — he didn' want ter come," said Hagrid, sounding desperate. "But I had ter bring him, Hermione, I had ter!"

"But why?" asked Hermione, who sounded as though she wanted to cry. "Why — what — oh, *Hagrid*!"

"I knew if I jus' got him back," said Hagrid, sounding close to tears himself, "an' — an' taught him a few manners — I'd be able ter take him outside an' show ev'ryone he's harmless!"

"Harmless!" said Hermione shrilly, and Hagrid made frantic hushing noises with his hands as the enormous creature before them grunted loudly and shifted in its sleep. "He's been hurting you all this time, hasn't he? That's why you've had all these injuries!"

"He don' know his own strength!" said Hagrid earnestly. "An' he's gettin' better, he's not fightin' so much anymore —"

"So this is why it took you two months to get home!" said Hermione distractedly. "Oh Hagrid, why did you bring him back if he didn't want to come, wouldn't he have been happier with his own people?"

"They were all bullyin' him, Hermione, 'cause he's so small!" said Hagrid.

"Small?" said Hermione. *"Small?"*

"Hermione, I couldn' leave him," said Hagrid, tears now trickling down his bruised face into his beard. "See — he's my brother!"

Hermione simply stared at him, her mouth open.

"Hagrid, when you say 'brother,'" said Harry slowly, "do you mean — ?"

"Well — half-brother," amended Hagrid. "Turns out me mother took up with another giant when she left me dad, an' she went an' had Grawp here —"

"Grawp?" said Harry.

"Yeah . . . well, tha's what it sounds like when he says his name," said Hagrid anxiously. "He don' speak a lot of English. . . . I've bin tryin' ter teach him. . . . Anyway, she don' seem ter have liked him much more'n she liked me. . . . See, with giantesses, what counts is producin' good big kids, and he's always been a bit on the runty side fer a giant — on'y sixteen foot —"

"Oh yes, tiny!" said Hermione, with a kind of hysterical sarcasm. "Absolutely minuscule!"

"He was bein' kicked around by all o' them — I jus' couldn' leave him —"

"Did Madame Maxime want to bring him back?" asked Harry.

"She — well, she could see it was right importan' ter me," said Hagrid, twisting his enormous hands. "Bu' — bu' she got a bit tired of him after a while, I must admit . . . so we split up on the journey home. . . . She promised not ter tell anyone though. . . ."

"How on earth did you get him back without anyone noticing?" said Harry.

"Well, tha's why it took so long, see," said Hagrid. "Could on'y travel by nigh' an' through wild country an' stuff. 'Course, he covers the ground pretty well when he wants ter, but he kep' wantin' ter go back. . . ."

"Oh Hagrid, why on earth didn't you let him!" said Hermione, flopping down onto a ripped-up tree and burying her face in her hands. "What do you think you're going to do with a violent giant who doesn't even want to be here!"

"Well, now — 'violent' — tha's a bit harsh," said Hagrid, still twisting his hands agitatedly. "I'll admit he mighta taken a couple o' swings at me when he's bin in a bad mood, but he's gettin' better, loads better, settlin' down well. . . ."

"What are those ropes for, then?" Harry asked.

He had just noticed ropes thick as saplings stretching from around the trunks of the largest nearby trees toward the place where Grawp lay curled on the ground with his back to them.

"You have to keep him tied up?" said Hermione faintly.

"Well . . . yeah . . ." said Hagrid, looking anxious. "See — it's like I say — he doesn' really know his strength —"

Harry understood now why there had been such a suspicious lack of any other living creature in this part of the forest.

"So what is it you want Harry and Ron and me to do?" Hermione asked apprehensively.

"Look after him," said Hagrid croakily. "After I'm gone."

Harry and Hermione exchanged miserable looks, Harry uncomfortably aware that he had already promised Hagrid that he would do whatever he asked.

"What — what does that involve, exactly?" Hermione inquired.

"Not food or anythin'!" said Hagrid eagerly. "He can get his own food, no problem. Birds an' deer an' stuff . . . No, it's company he needs. If I jus' knew someone was carryin' on tryin' ter help him a bit . . . teachin' him, yeh know . . ."

Harry said nothing, but turned to look back at the gigantic form lying asleep on the ground in front of them. Grawp had his back to them. Unlike Hagrid, who simply looked like a very oversize human, Grawp looked strangely misshapen. What Harry had taken to be a vast mossy boulder to the left of the great earthen mound he now recognized as Grawp's head. It was much larger in proportion to the body than a human head, almost perfectly round and covered with tightly curling, close-growing hair the color of bracken. The rim of a single large, fleshy ear was visible on top of the head, which seemed to sit, rather like Uncle Vernon's, directly upon the shoulders with little or no neck in between. The back, under what looked like a dirty brownish smock comprised of animal skins sewn roughly together, was very broad, and as Grawp slept, it seemed to strain a little at the rough seams of the skins. The legs were curled up under the body; Harry could see the soles of enormous, filthy, bare feet, large as sledges, resting one on top of the other on the earthy forest floor.

"You want us to teach him," Harry said in a hollow voice. He now understood what Firenze's warning had meant. *His attempt is not working. He would do better to abandon it.* Of course, the other creatures who lived in the forest would have heard Hagrid's fruitless attempts to teach Grawp English. . . .

"Yeah — even if yeh jus' talk ter him a bit," said Hagrid hopefully.

"'Cause I reckon, if he can talk ter people, he'll understand more that we all like him really, an' want him to stay. . . ."

Harry looked at Hermione, who peered back at him from between the fingers over her face.

"Kind of makes you wish we had Norbert back, doesn't it?" he said and she gave a very shaky laugh.

"Yeh'll do it, then?" said Hagrid, who did not seem to have caught what Harry had just said.

"We'll . . ." said Harry, already bound by his promise. "We'll try, Hagrid. . . ."

"I knew I could count on yeh, Harry," Hagrid said, beaming in a very watery way and dabbing at his face with his handkerchief again. "An' I don' wan' yeh ter put yerself out too much, like. . . . I know yeh've got exams. . . . If yeh could jus' nip down here in yer Invisibility Cloak maybe once a week an' have a little chat with him . . . I'll wake him up, then — introduce you —"

"Wha — no!" said Hermione, jumping up, "Hagrid, no, don't wake him, really, we don't need —"

But Hagrid had already stepped over the great trunk in front of them and was proceeding toward Grawp. When he was around ten feet away, he lifted a long, broken bough from the ground, smiled reassuringly over his shoulder at Harry and Hermione, and then poked Grawp hard in the middle of the back with the end of the bough.

The giant gave a roar that echoed around the silent forest. Birds in the treetops overhead rose twittering from their perches and soared away. In front of Harry and Hermione, meanwhile, the gigantic Grawp was rising from the ground, which shuddered as he placed an enormous hand upon it to push himself onto his knees and turned his head to see who and what had disturbed him.

"All righ', Grawpy?" said Hagrid in a would-be cheery voice, backing away with the long bough raised, ready to poke Grawp again. "Had a nice sleep, eh?"

Harry and Hermione retreated as far as they could while still keeping the giant within their sights. Grawp knelt between two trees he had not yet uprooted. They looked up into his startlingly huge face, which resembled a gray full moon swimming in the gloom of the clearing. It was as though the features had been hewn onto a great stone ball. The nose was stubby and shapeless, the mouth lopsided and full of misshapen yellow teeth the size of half-bricks. The small eyes were a muddy greenish-brown and just now were half gummed together with sleep. Grawp raised dirty knuckles as big as cricket balls to his eyes, rubbed vigorously, then, without warning, pushed himself to his feet with surprising speed and agility.

"Oh my . . ." Harry heard Hermione squeal, terrified, beside him.

The trees to which the other ends of the ropes around Grawp's wrists and ankles were attached creaked ominously. He was, as Hagrid had said, at least sixteen feet tall. Gazing blearily around, he reached out a hand the size of a beach umbrella, seized a bird's nest from the upper branches of a towering pine and turned it upside down with a roar of apparent displeasure that there was no bird in it — eggs fell like grenades toward the ground and Hagrid threw his arms over his head to protect himself.

"Anyway, Grawpy," shouted Hagrid, looking up apprehensively in case of further falling eggs, "I've brought some friends ter meet yeh. Remember, I told yeh I might? Remember, when I said I might have ter go on a little trip an' leave them ter look after yeh fer a bit? Remember that, Grawpy?"

But Grawp merely gave another low roar; it was hard to say whether he was listening to Hagrid or whether he even recognized the sounds Hagrid was making as speech. He had now seized the top of the pine tree and was pulling it toward him, evidently for the simple pleasure of seeing how far it would spring back when he let go.

"Now, Grawpy, don' do that!" shouted Hagrid. "Tha's how you ended up pullin' up the others —"

And sure enough, Harry could see the earth around the tree's roots beginning to crack.

"I got company fer yeh!" Hagrid shouted. "Company, see! Look down, yeh big buffoon, I brought yeh some friends!"

"Oh Hagrid, don't," moaned Hermione, but Hagrid had already raised the bough again and gave Grawp's knee a sharp poke.

The giant let go of the top of the pine tree, which swayed menacingly and deluged Hagrid with a rain of needles, and looked down.

"*This,*" said Hagrid, hastening over to where Harry and Hermione stood, "is Harry, Grawp! Harry Potter! He migh' be comin' ter visit yeh if I have ter go away, understand?"

The giant had only just realized that Harry and Hermione were there. They watched, in great trepidation, as he lowered his huge boulder of a head so that he could peer blearily at them.

"An' this is Hermione, see? Her —" Hagrid hesitated. Turning to Hermione he said, "Would yeh mind if he called yeh Hermy, Hermione? On'y it's a difficult name fer him ter remember. . . ."

"No, not at all," squeaked Hermione.

"This is Hermy, Grawp! An' she's gonna be comin' an' all! Is'n tha' nice? Eh? Two friends fer yeh ter — GRAWPY, NO!"

Grawp's hand had shot out of nowhere toward Hermione — Harry seized her and pulled her backward behind the tree, so that Grawp's fist scraped the trunk but closed on thin air.

"BAD BOY, GRAWPY!" Harry heard Hagrid yelling, as Hermione clung to Harry behind the tree, shaking and whimpering. "VERY BAD BOY! YEH DON' GRAB — OUCH!"

Harry poked his head out from around the trunk and saw Hagrid lying on his back, his hand over his nose. Grawp, apparently losing interest, had straightened up again and was again engaged in pulling back the pine as far as it would go.

"Righ'," said Hagrid thickly, getting up with one hand pinching his bleeding nose and the other grasping his crossbow. "Well . . . there yeh are. . . . Yeh've met him an' — an' now he'll know yeh when yeh come back. Yeah . . . well . . ."

He looked up at Grawp, who was now pulling back the pine with an expression of detached pleasure on his boulderish face; the roots were creaking as he ripped them away from the ground. . . .

"Well, I reckon tha's enough fer one day," said Hagrid. "We'll — er — we'll go back now, shall we?"

Harry and Hermione nodded. Hagrid shouldered his crossbow again and, still pinching his nose, led the way back into the trees.

Nobody spoke for a while, not even when they heard the distant crash that meant Grawp had pulled over the pine tree at last. Hermione's face was pale and set. Harry could not think of a single thing to say. What on earth was going to happen when somebody found out that Hagrid had hidden Grawp in the forest? And he had promised that he, Ron, and Hermione would continue Hagrid's totally pointless attempts to civilize the giant. . . . How could Hagrid, even with his immense capacity to delude himself that fanged monsters were lovably harmless, fool himself that Grawp would ever be fit to mix with humans?

"Hold it," said Hagrid abruptly, just as Harry and Hermione were struggling through a patch of thick knotgrass behind him. He pulled an arrow out of the quiver over his shoulder and fitted it into the crossbow. Harry and Hermione raised their wands; now that they had stopped walking, they too could hear movement close by.

"Oh blimey," said Hagrid quietly.

"I thought that we told you, Hagrid," said a deep male voice, "that you are no longer welcome here?"

A man's naked torso seemed for an instant to be floating toward them through the dappled green half-light. Then they saw that his waist joined smoothly with a horse's chestnut body. This centaur had a proud, high-cheekboned face and long black hair. Like Hagrid, he was armed: A quiverful of arrows and a long bow were slung over his shoulders.

"How are yeh, Magorian?" said Hagrid warily.

The trees behind the centaur rustled and four or five more emerged behind him. Harry recognized the black-bodied and bearded Bane, whom he had met nearly four years ago on the same night he had met Firenze. Bane gave no sign that he had ever seen Harry before.

"So," he said, with a nasty inflection in his voice, before turning immediately to Magorian. "We agreed, I think, what we would do if this human showed his face in the forest again?"

"'This human' now, am I?" said Hagrid testily. "Jus' fer stoppin' all of yeh committin' murder?"

"You ought not to have meddled, Hagrid," said Magorian. "Our ways are not yours, nor are our laws. Firenze has betrayed and dishonored us."

"I dunno how yeh work that out," said Hagrid impatiently. "He's done nothin' except help Albus Dumbledore —"

"Firenze has entered into servitude to humans," said a gray centaur with a hard, deeply lined face.

"*Servitude!*" said Hagrid scathingly. "He's doin' Dumbledore a favor is all —"

"He is peddling our knowledge and secrets among humans," said Magorian quietly. "There can be no return from such disgrace."

"If yeh say so," said Hagrid, shrugging, "but personally I think yeh're makin' a big mistake —"

"As are you, human," said Bane, "coming back into our forest when we warned you —"

"Now, you listen ter me," said Hagrid angrily. "I'll have less of the 'our' forest, if it's all the same ter you. It's not up ter you who comes an' goes in here —"

"No more is it up to you, Hagrid," said Magorian smoothly. "I shall let you pass today because you are accompanied by your young —"

"They're not his!" interrupted Bane contemptuously. "Students, Magorian, from up at the school! They have probably already profited from the traitor Firenze's teachings. . . ."

"Nevertheless," said Magorian calmly, "the slaughter of foals is a terrible crime. . . . We do not touch the innocent. Today, Hagrid, you pass. Henceforth, stay away from this place. You forfeited the friendship of the centaurs when you helped the traitor Firenze escape us."

"I won' be kept outta the fores' by a bunch of mules like you!" said Hagrid loudly.

"Hagrid," said Hermione in a high-pitched and terrified voice, as both Bane and the gray centaur pawed at the ground, "let's go, please let's go!"

Hagrid moved forward, but his crossbow was still raised and his eyes were still fixed threateningly upon Magorian.

"We know what you are keeping in the forest, Hagrid!" Magorian called after them, as the centaurs slipped out of sight. "And our tolerance is waning!"

Hagrid turned and gave every appearance of wanting to walk straight back to Magorian again.

"You'll tolerate him as long as he's here, it's as much his forest as yours!" he yelled, while Harry and Hermione both pushed with all their might against Hagrid's moleskin waistcoat in an effort to keep him moving forward. Still scowling, he looked down; his expression changed to mild surprise at the sight of them both pushing him. He seemed not to have felt it.

"Calm down, you two," he said, turning to walk on while they panted along behind him. "Ruddy old nags though, eh?"

"Hagrid," said Hermione breathlessly, skirting the patch of nettles they had passed on their way there, "if the centaurs don't want humans in the forest, it doesn't really look as though Harry and I will be able —"

"Ah, you heard what they said," said Hagrid dismissively. "They wouldn't hurt foals — I mean, kids. Anyway, we can' let ourselves be pushed around by that lot. . . ."

"Nice try," Harry murmured to Hermione, who looked crestfallen.

At last they rejoined the path and after another ten minutes, the trees began to thin. They were able to see patches of clear blue sky again and hear, in the distance, the definite sounds of cheering and shouting.

"Was that another goal?" asked Hagrid, pausing in the shelter of the trees as the Quidditch stadium came into view. "Or d'you reckon the match is over?"

"I don't know," said Hermione miserably. Harry saw that she looked much the worse for wear; her hair was full of bits of twig and leaves, her robes were ripped in several places and there were numerous scratches on her face and arms. He knew he could look little better.

"I reckon it's over, yeh know!" said Hagrid, still squinting toward the stadium. "Look — there's people comin' out already — if you two hurry yeh'll be able ter blend in with the crowd an' no one'll know you weren't there!"

"Good idea," said Harry. "Well . . . see you later, then, Hagrid. . . ."

"I don't believe him," said Hermione in a very unsteady voice, the moment they were out of earshot of Hagrid. "I don't believe him. I *really* don't believe him. . . ."

"Calm down," said Harry.

"Calm down!" she said feverishly. "A giant! A giant in the forest! And we're supposed to give him English lessons! Always assuming, of course, we can get past the herd of murderous centaurs on the way in and out! I — don't — *believe* — him!"

"We haven't got to do anything yet!" Harry tried to reassure her in a quiet voice, as they joined a stream of jabbering Hufflepuffs heading back toward the castle. "He's not asking us to do anything unless he gets chucked out and that might not even happen —"

"Oh come off it, Harry!" said Hermione angrily, stopping dead in her tracks so that the people behind her had to swerve to avoid her. "Of course he's going to be chucked out and to be perfectly honest, after what we've just seen, who can blame Umbridge?"

There was a pause in which Harry glared at her, and her eyes filled slowly with tears.

"You didn't mean that," said Harry quietly.

"No . . . well . . . all right . . . I didn't," she said, wiping her eyes angrily. "But why does he have to make life so difficult for himself — for *us*?"

"I dunno —"

> *Weasley is our King,*
> *Weasley is our King,*
> *He didn't let the Quaffle in,*
> *Weasley is our King . . .*

"And I wish they'd stop singing that stupid song," said Hermione miserably, "haven't they gloated enough?"

A great tide of students was moving up the sloping lawns from the pitch.

"Oh, let's get in before we have to meet the Slytherins," said Hermione.

> *Weasley can save anything,*
> *He never leaves a single ring,*
> *That's why Gryffindors all sing:*
> *Weasley is our King.*

"Hermione . . ." said Harry slowly.

The song was growing louder, but it was issuing not from a crowd of green-and-silver-clad Slytherins, but from a mass of red and gold moving slowly toward the castle, which was bearing a solitary figure upon its many shoulders. . . .

> *Weasley is our King,*
> *Weasley is our King,*
> *He didn't let the Quaffle in,*
> *Weasley is our King . . .*

"No!" said Hermione in a hushed voice.

"YES!" said Harry loudly.

"HARRY! HERMIONE!" yelled Ron, waving the silver Quidditch Cup in the air and looking quite beside himself. "WE DID IT! WE WON!"

They beamed up at him as he passed; there was a scrum at the door of the castle and Ron's head got rather badly bumped on the lintel, but nobody seemed to want to put him down. Still singing, the crowd squeezed itself into the entrance hall and out of sight. Harry and Hermione watched them go, beaming, until the last echoing strains of "Weasley Is Our King" died away. Then they turned to each other, their smiles fading.

"We'll save our news till tomorrow, shall we?" said Harry.

"Yes, all right," said Hermione wearily. "I'm not in any hurry. . . ."

They climbed the steps together. At the front doors both instinctively looked back at the Forbidden Forest. Harry was not sure whether it was his imagination or not, but he rather thought he saw a small cloud of birds erupting into the air over the treetops in the distance, almost as though the tree in which they had been nesting had just been pulled up by the roots.

O.W.L.S

Ron's euphoria at helping Gryffindor scrape the Quidditch Cup was such that he could not settle to anything next day. All he wanted to do was talk over the match and Harry and Hermione found it very difficult to find an opening in which to mention Grawp — not that either of them tried very hard; neither was keen to be the one to bring Ron back to reality in quite such a brutal fashion. As it was another fine, warm day, they persuaded him to join them in studying under the beech tree on the edge of the lake, where they stood less chance of being overheard than in the common room. Ron was not particularly keen on this idea at first; he was thoroughly enjoying being patted on the back by Gryffindors walking past his chair, not to mention the occasional outbursts of "Weasley Is Our King," but agreed after a while that some fresh air might do him good.

They spread their books out in the shade of the beech tree and sat down while Ron talked them through his first save of the match for what felt like the dozenth time.

"Well, I mean, I'd already let in that one of Davies's, so I wasn't feeling that confident, but I dunno, when Bradley came toward me, just out of nowhere, I thought — *you can do this!* And I had about a second to decide which way to fly, you know, because he looked like he was aiming for the right goal hoop — my right, obviously, his left — but I had a funny feeling that he was feinting, and so I took the chance and flew left — his right, I mean — and — well — you saw what happened," he concluded modestly, sweeping his hair back quite unnecessarily so that it looked interestingly windswept and glancing around to see whether the people nearest to them — a bunch of gossiping third-year Hufflepuffs — had heard him. "And then, when Chambers came at me about five minutes later — what?" Ron said, stopping mid-sentence at the look on Harry's face. "Why are you grinning?"

"I'm not," said Harry quickly, looking down at his Transfiguration notes and attempting to straighten his face. The truth was that Ron had just reminded Harry forcibly of another Gryffindor Quidditch player who had once sat rumpling his hair under this very tree. "I'm just glad we won, that's all."

"Yeah," said Ron slowly, savoring the words, "*we won.* Did you see the look on Chang's face when Ginny got the Snitch right out from under her nose?"

"I suppose she cried, did she?" said Harry bitterly.

"Well, yeah — more out of temper than anything, though . . ." Ron frowned slightly. "But you saw her chuck her broom away when she got back to the ground, didn't you?"

"Er —" said Harry.

"Well, actually . . . no, Ron," said Hermione with a heavy sigh, putting down her book and looking at him apologetically. "As a matter of fact, the only bit of the match Harry and I saw was Davies's first goal."

Ron's carefully ruffled hair seemed to wilt with disappointment.

"You didn't watch?" he said faintly, looking from one to the other. "You didn't see me make any of those saves?"

"Well — no," said Hermione, stretching out a placatory hand toward him. "But Ron, we didn't want to leave — we had to!"

"Yeah?" said Ron, whose face was growing rather red. "How come?"

"It was Hagrid," said Harry. "He decided to tell us why he's been covered in injuries ever since he got back from the giants. He wanted us to go into the forest with him, we had no choice, you know how he gets. . . . Anyway . . ."

The story was told in five minutes, by the end of which Ron's indignation had been replaced by a look of total incredulity.

"He brought one back and hid it in the forest?"

"Yep," said Harry grimly.

"No," said Ron, as though by saying this he could make it untrue. "No, he can't have. . . ."

"Well, he has," said Hermione firmly. "Grawp's about sixteen feet tall, enjoys ripping up twenty-foot pine trees, and knows me," she snorted, "as *Hermy*."

Ron gave a nervous laugh.

"And Hagrid wants us to . . . ?"

"Teach him English, yeah," said Harry.

"He's lost his mind," said Ron in an almost awed voice.

"Yes," said Hermione irritably, turning a page of *Intermediate Transfiguration* and glaring at a series of diagrams showing an owl turning into a pair of opera glasses. "Yes, I'm starting to think he has. But unfortunately, he made Harry and me promise."

"Well, you're just going to have to break your promise, that's all," said Ron firmly. "I mean, come on . . . We've got exams and we're about that far," he held up his hand to show thumb and forefinger a millimeter apart, "from being chucked out as it is. And anyway . . . remember Norbert? Remember Aragog? Have we ever come off better for mixing with any of Hagrid's monster mates?"

"I know, it's just that — we promised," said Hermione in a small voice.

Ron smoothed his hair flat again, looking preoccupied.

"Well," he sighed, "Hagrid hasn't been sacked yet, has he? He's hung on this long, maybe he'll hang on till the end of term and we won't have to go near Grawp at all."

The castle grounds were gleaming in the sunlight as though freshly painted; the cloudless sky smiled at itself in the smoothly sparkling lake, the satin-green lawns rippled occasionally in a gentle breeze: June had arrived, but to the fifth years this meant only one thing: Their O.W.L.s were upon them at last.

Their teachers were no longer setting them homework; lessons were devoted to reviewing those topics their teachers thought most likely to come up in the exams. The purposeful, feverish atmosphere drove nearly everything but the O.W.L.s from Harry's mind, though he did wonder occasionally during Potions lessons whether Lupin had ever told Snape that he must continue giving Harry Occlumency tuition: If he had, then Snape had ignored Lupin as thoroughly as he was now ignoring Harry. This suited Harry very well; he was quite busy and tense enough without extra classes with Snape, and to his relief Hermione was much too preoccupied these days to badger him about Occlumency. She was spending a lot of time muttering to herself and had not laid out any elf clothes for days.

She was not the only person acting oddly as the O.W.L.s drew steadily nearer. Ernie Macmillan had developed an irritating habit of interrogating people about their study habits.

"How many hours d'you think you're doing a day?" he demanded of Harry and Ron as they queued outside Herbology, a manic gleam in his eyes.

"I dunno," said Ron. "A few . . ."

"More or less than eight?"

"Less, I s'pose," said Ron, looking slightly alarmed.

"I'm doing eight," said Ernie, puffing out his chest. "Eight or nine.

I'm getting an hour in before breakfast every day. Eight's my average. I can do ten on a good weekend day. I did nine and a half on Monday. Not so good on Tuesday — only seven and a quarter. Then on Wednesday —"

Harry was deeply thankful that Professor Sprout ushered them into greenhouse three at that point, forcing Ernie to abandon his recital.

Meanwhile Draco Malfoy had found a different way to induce panic.

"Of course, it's not what you know," he was heard to tell Crabbe and Goyle loudly outside Potions a few days before the exams were to start, "it's who you know. Now, Father's been friendly with the head of the Wizarding Examinations Authority for years — old Griselda Marchbanks — we've had her round for dinner and everything. . . ."

"Do you think that's true?" Hermione whispered to Harry and Ron, looking frightened.

"Nothing we can do about it if it is," said Ron gloomily.

"I don't think it's true," said Neville quietly from behind them. "Because Griselda Marchbanks is a friend of my gran's, and she's never mentioned the Malfoys."

"What's she like, Neville?" asked Hermione at once. "Is she strict?"

"Bit like Gran, really," said Neville in a subdued voice.

"Knowing her won't hurt your chances though, will it?" Ron told him encouragingly.

"Oh, I don't think it will make any difference," said Neville, still more miserably. "Gran's always telling Professor Marchbanks I'm not as good as my dad. . . . Well . . . you saw what she's like at St. Mungo's. . . ."

Neville looked fixedly at the floor. Harry, Ron, and Hermione glanced at one another, but didn't know what to say. It was the first time that Neville had acknowledged that they had met at the Wizarding hospital.

Meanwhile a flourishing black-market trade in aids to concentration, mental agility, and wakefulness had sprung up among the fifth and seventh years. Harry and Ron were much tempted by the bottle of Baruffio's Brain Elixir offered to them by Ravenclaw sixth year Eddie Carmichael, who swore it was solely responsible for the nine "Outstanding" O.W.L.s he had gained the previous summer and was offering the whole pint for a mere twelve Galleons. Ron assured Harry he would reimburse him for his half the moment he left Hogwarts and got a job, but before they could close the deal, Hermione had confiscated the bottle from Carmichael and poured the contents down a toilet.

"Hermione, we wanted to buy that!" shouted Ron.

"Don't be stupid," she snarled. "You might as well take Harold Dingle's powdered dragon claw and have done with it."

"Dingle's got powdered dragon claw?" said Ron eagerly.

"Not anymore," said Hermione. "I confiscated that too. None of these things actually works you know —"

"Dragon claw does work!" said Ron. "It's supposed to be incredible, really gives your brain a boost, you come over all cunning for a few hours — Hermione, let me have a pinch, go on, it can't hurt —"

"This stuff can," said Hermione grimly. "I've had a look at it, and it's actually dried doxy droppings."

This information took the edge off Harry and Ron's desire for brain stimulants.

They received their examination schedules and details of the procedure for O.W.L.s during their next Transfiguration lesson.

"As you can see," Professor McGonagall told the class while they copied down the dates and times of their exams from the blackboard, "your O.W.L.s are spread over two successive weeks. You will sit the theory exams in the mornings and the practice in the afternoons. Your practical Astronomy examination will, of course, take place at night.

"Now, I must warn you that the most stringent Anti-Cheating Charms have been applied to your examination papers. Auto-Answer

Quills are banned from the examination hall, as are Remembralls, Detachable Cribbing Cuffs, and Self-Correcting Ink. Every year, I am afraid to say, seems to harbor at least one student who thinks that he or she can get around the Wizarding Examinations Authority's rules. I can only hope that it is nobody in Gryffindor. Our new — headmistress" — Professor McGonagall pronounced the word with the same look on her face that Aunt Petunia had whenever she was contemplating a particularly stubborn bit of dirt — "has asked the Heads of House to tell their students that cheating will be punished most severely — because, of course, your examination results will reflect upon the headmistress's new regime at the school. . . ."

Professor McGonagall gave a tiny sigh. Harry saw the nostrils of her sharp nose flare.

"However, that is no reason not to do your very best. You have your own futures to think about."

"Please, Professor," said Hermione, her hand in the air, "when will we find out our results?"

"An owl will be sent to you some time in July," said Professor McGonagall.

"Excellent," said Dean Thomas in an audible whisper, "so we don't have to worry about it till the holidays. . . ."

Harry imagined sitting in his bedroom in Privet Drive in six weeks' time, waiting for his O.W.L. results. Well, he thought, at least he would be sure of one bit of post next summer. . . .

Their first exam, Theory of Charms, was scheduled for Monday morning. Harry agreed to test Hermione after lunch on Sunday but regretted it almost at once. She was very agitated and kept snatching the book back from him to check that she had gotten the answer completely right, finally hitting him hard on the nose with the sharp edge of *Achievements in Charming*.

"Why don't you just do it yourself?" he said firmly, handing the book back to her, his eyes watering.

Meanwhile Ron was reading two years of Charms notes with his fingers in his ears, his lips moving soundlessly; Seamus was lying flat on his back on the floor, reciting the definition of a Substantive Charm, while Dean checked it against *The Standard Book of Spells, Grade 5;* and Parvati and Lavender, who were practicing basic locomotion charms, were making their pencil cases race each other around the edge of the table.

Dinner was a subdued affair that night. Harry and Ron did not talk much, but ate with gusto, having studied hard all day. Hermione on the other hand kept putting down her knife and fork and diving under the table for her bag, from which she would seize a book to check some fact or figure. Ron was just telling her that she ought to eat a decent meal or she would not sleep that night, when her fork slid from her limp fingers and landed with a loud tinkle on her plate.

"Oh, my goodness," she said faintly, staring into the entrance hall. "Is that them? Is that the examiners?"

Harry and Ron whipped around on their bench. Through the doors to the Great Hall they could see Umbridge standing with a small group of ancient-looking witches and wizards. Umbridge, Harry was pleased to see, looked rather nervous.

"Shall we go and have a closer look?" said Ron.

Harry and Hermione nodded and they hastened toward the double doors into the entrance hall, slowing down as they stepped over the threshold to walk sedately past the examiners. Harry thought Professor Marchbanks must be the tiny, stooped witch with a face so lined it looked as though it had been draped in cobwebs; Umbridge was speaking to her very deferentially. Professor Marchbanks seemed to be a little deaf; she was answering Umbridge very loudly considering that they were only a foot apart.

"Journey was fine, journey was fine, we've made it plenty of times before!" she said impatiently. "Now, I haven't heard from Dumbledore lately!" she added, peering around the hall as though hopeful he might suddenly emerge from a broom cupboard. "No idea where he is, I suppose?"

"None at all," said Umbridge, shooting a malevolent look at Harry, Ron, and Hermione, who were now dawdling around the foot of the stairs as Ron pretended to do up his shoelace. "But I daresay the Ministry of Magic will track him down soon enough. . . ."

"I doubt it," shouted tiny Professor Marchbanks, "not if Dumbledore doesn't want to be found! I should know. . . . Examined him personally in Transfiguration and Charms when he did N.E.W.T.s . . . Did things with a wand I'd never seen before . . ."

"Yes . . . well . . ." said Professor Umbridge as Harry, Ron, and Hermione dragged their feet up the marble staircase as slowly as they dared, "let me show you to the staffroom . . . I daresay you'd like a cup of tea after your journey. . . ."

It was an uncomfortable sort of an evening. Everyone was trying to do some last-minute studying but nobody seemed to be getting very far. Harry went to bed early but then lay awake for what felt like hours. He remembered his careers consultation and McGonagall's furious declaration that she would help him become an Auror if it was the last thing she did. . . . He wished he had expressed a more achievable ambition now that exam time was here. . . . He knew that he was not the only one lying awake, but none of the others in the dormitory spoke and finally, one by one, they fell asleep.

None of the fifth years talked very much at breakfast next day either. Parvati was practicing incantations under her breath while the salt cellar in front of her twitched, Hermione was rereading *Achievement in Charming* so fast that her eyes appeared blurred, and Neville kept dropping his knife and fork and knocking over the marmalade.

Once breakfast was over, the fifth and seventh years milled around in the entrance hall while the other students went off to lessons. Then, at half-past nine, they were called forward class by class to reenter the Great Hall, which was now arranged exactly as Harry had seen it in the Pensieve when his father, Sirius, and Snape had been taking their O.W.L.s. The four House tables had been removed and replaced instead with many tables for one, all facing the staff-table end of the Hall where Professor McGonagall stood facing them. When they were all seated and quiet she said, "You may begin," and turned over an enormous hourglass on the desk beside her, on which were also spare quills, ink bottles, and rolls of parchment.

Harry turned over his paper, his heart thumping hard. . . . Three rows to his right and four seats ahead, Hermione was already scribbling. . . . He lowered his eyes to the first question: *a) Give the incantation, and b) describe the wand movement required to make objects fly. . . .*

Harry had a fleeting memory of a club soaring high into the air and landing loudly on the thick skull of a troll. . . . Smiling slightly, he bent over the paper and began to write. . . .

"Well, it wasn't too bad, was it?" asked Hermione anxiously in the entrance hall two hours later, still clutching the exam paper. "I'm not sure I did myself justice on Cheering Charms, I just ran out of time — did you put in the countercharm for hiccups? I wasn't sure whether I ought to, it felt like too much — and on question twenty-three —"

"Hermione," said Ron sternly, "we've been through this before. . . . We're not going through every exam afterward, it's bad enough doing them once."

The fifth years ate lunch with the rest of the school (the four House tables reappeared over the lunch hour) and then trooped off into the small chamber beside the Great Hall, where they were to wait until called for their practical examination. As small groups of students were called forward in alphabetical order, those left behind muttered incantations and practiced wand movements, occasionally poking one another in the back or eye by mistake.

Hermione's name was called. Trembling, she left the chamber with

Anthony Goldstein, Gregory Goyle, and Daphne Greengrass. Students who had already been tested did not return afterward, so Harry and Ron had no idea how Hermione had done.

"She'll be fine — remember she got a hundred and twelve percent on one of our Charms tests?" said Ron.

Ten minutes later, Professor Flitwick called, "Parkinson, Pansy — Patil, Padma — Patil, Parvati — Potter, Harry."

"Good luck," said Ron quietly. Harry walked into the Great Hall, clutching his wand so tightly his hand shook.

"Professor Tofty is free, Potter," squeaked Professor Flitwick, who was standing just inside the door. He pointed Harry toward what looked like the very oldest and baldest examiner, who was sitting behind a small table in a far corner, a short distance from Professor Marchbanks, who was halfway through testing Draco Malfoy.

"Potter, is it?" said Professor Tofty, consulting his notes and peering over his pince-nez at Harry as he approached. "The famous Potter?"

Out of the corner of his eye, Harry distinctly saw Malfoy throw a scathing look over at him; the wine glass Malfoy had been levitating fell to the floor and smashed. Harry could not suppress a grin. Professor Tofty smiled back at him encouragingly.

"That's it," he said in his quavery old voice, "no need to be nervous. . . . Now, if I could ask you to take this eggcup and make it do some cartwheels for me. . . ."

On the whole Harry thought it went rather well; his Levitation Charm was certainly much better than Malfoy's had been, though he wished he had not mixed up the incantations for Color-Change and Growth Charms, so that the rat he was supposed to be turning orange swelled shockingly and was the size of a badger before Harry could rectify his mistake. He was glad Hermione had not been in the Hall at the time and neglected to mention it to her afterward. He could tell Ron, though; Ron had caused a dinner plate to mutate into a large mushroom and had no idea how it had happened.

There was no time to relax that night — they went straight to the common room after dinner and submerged themselves in studying for Transfiguration next day. Harry went to bed, his head buzzing with complex spell models and theories.

He forgot the definition of a Switching Spell during his written exam next morning, but thought his practical could have been a lot worse. At least he managed to vanish the whole of his iguana, whereas poor Hannah Abbott lost her head completely at the next table and somehow managed to multiply her ferret into a flock of flamingos, causing the examination to be halted for ten minutes while the birds were captured and carried out of the Hall.

They had their Herbology exam on Wednesday (other than a small bite from a Fanged Geranium, Harry felt he had done reasonably well) and then, on Thursday, Defense Against the Dark Arts. Here, for the first time, Harry felt sure he had passed. He had no problem with any of the written questions and took particular pleasure, during the practical examination, in performing all the counterjinxes and defensive spells right in front of Umbridge, who was watching coolly from near the doors into the entrance hall.

"Oh bravo!" cried Professor Tofty, who was examining Harry again, when Harry demonstrated a perfect boggart banishing spell. "Very good indeed! Well, I think that's all, Potter . . . unless . . ."

He leaned forward a little.

"I heard, from my dear friend Tiberius Ogden, that you can produce a Patronus? For a bonus point . . . ?"

Harry raised his wand, looked directly at Umbridge, and imagined her being sacked.

"*Expecto Patronum!*"

The silver stag erupted from the end of his wand and cantered the length of the hall. All of the examiners looked around to watch its progress and when it dissolved into silver mist, Professor Tofty clapped his veined and knotted hands enthusiastically.

"Excellent!" he said. "Very well, Potter, you may go!"

As Harry passed Umbridge beside the door their eyes met. There was a nasty smile playing around her wide, slack mouth, but he did not care. Unless he was very much mistaken (and he was not planning on saying it to anybody, in case he was), he had just achieved an "Outstanding" O.W.L.

On Friday, Harry and Ron had a day off while Hermione sat her Ancient Runes exam, and as they had the whole weekend in front of them, they permitted themselves a break from studying. They stretched and yawned beside the open window, through which warm summer air wafted over them as they played a desultory game of wizard chess. Harry could see Hagrid in the distance, teaching a class on the edge of the forest. He was trying to guess what creatures they were examining — he thought it must be unicorns, because the boys seemed to be standing back a little — when the portrait hole opened and Hermione clambered in, looking thoroughly bad tempered.

"How were the runes?" said Ron, yawning and stretching.

"I mistranslated 'ehwaz,'" said Hermione furiously. "It means 'partnership,' not 'defense,' I mixed it up with 'eihwaz.'"

"Ah well," said Ron lazily, "that's only one mistake, isn't it, you'll still get —"

"Oh shut up," said Hermione angrily, "it could be the one mistake that makes the difference between a pass and a fail. And what's more, someone's put another niffler in Umbridge's office, I don't know how they got it through that new door, but I just walked past there and Umbridge is shrieking her head off — by the sound of it, it tried to take a chunk out of her leg —"

"Good," said Harry and Ron together.

"It is *not* good!" said Hermione hotly. "She thinks it's Hagrid doing it, remember? And we do *not* want Hagrid chucked out!"

"He's teaching at the moment, she can't blame him," said Harry, gesturing out of the window.

"Oh, you're so *naive* sometimes, Harry, you really think Umbridge will wait for proof?" said Hermione, who seemed determined to be in a towering temper, and she swept off toward the girls' dormitories, banging the door behind her.

"Such a lovely, sweet-tempered girl," said Ron, very quietly, prodding his queen forward so that she could begin beating up one of Harry's knights.

Hermione's bad mood persisted for most of the weekend, though Harry and Ron found it quite easy to ignore as they spent most of Saturday and Sunday studying for Potions on Monday, the exam to which Harry was looking forward least and which he was sure would be the one that would be the downfall of his ambitions to become an Auror. Sure enough, he found the written exam difficult, though he thought he might have got full marks on the question about Polyjuice Potion: He could describe its effects extremely accurately, having taken it illegally in his second year.

The afternoon practical was not as dreadful as he had expected it to be. With Snape absent from the proceedings he found that he was much more relaxed than he usually was while making potions. Neville, who was sitting very near Harry, also looked happier than Harry had ever seen him during a Potions class. When Professor Marchbanks said, "Step away from your cauldrons, please, the examination is over," Harry corked his sample flask feeling that he might not have achieved a good grade but that he had, with luck, avoided a fail.

"Only four exams left," said Parvati Patil wearily as they headed back to Gryffindor common room.

"Only!" said Hermione snappishly. "*I've* got Arithmancy and it's probably the toughest subject there is!"

Nobody was foolish enough to snap back, so she was unable to vent her spleen on any of them and was reduced to telling off some first years for giggling too loudly in the common room.

Harry was determined to perform well in Tuesday's Care of Magical Creatures exam so as not to let Hagrid down. The practical examination took place in the afternoon on the lawn on the edge of the Forbidden Forest, where students were required to correctly identify the knarl hidden among a dozen hedgehogs (the trick was to offer them all milk in turn: knarls, highly suspicious creatures whose quills had many magical properties, generally went berserk at what they saw as an attempt to poison them); then demonstrate correct handling of a bowtruckle, feed and clean a fire-crab without sustaining serious burns, and choose, from a wide selection of food, the diet they would give a sick unicorn.

Harry could see Hagrid watching anxiously out of his cabin window. When Harry's examiner, a plump little witch this time, smiled at him and told him he could leave, Harry gave Hagrid a fleeting thumbs-up before heading back up to the castle.

The Astronomy theory exam on Wednesday morning went well enough; Harry was not convinced he had got the names of all of Jupiter's moons right, but was at least confident that none of them was inhabited by mice. They had to wait until evening for their practical Astronomy; the afternoon was devoted instead to Divination.

Even by Harry's low standards in Divination, the exam went very badly. He might as well have tried to see moving pictures in the desktop as in the stubbornly blank crystal ball; he lost his head completely during tea-leaf reading, saying it looked to him as though Professor Marchbanks would shortly be meeting a round, dark, soggy stranger, and rounded off the whole fiasco by mixing up the life and head lines on her palm and informing her that she ought to have died the previous Tuesday.

"Well, we were always going to fail that one," said Ron gloomily as they ascended the marble staircase. He had just made Harry feel rather better by telling him how he told the examiner in detail about the ugly man with a wart on his nose in his crystal ball, only to look up and realize he had been describing his examiner's reflection.

"We shouldn't have taken the stupid subject in the first place," said Harry.

"Still, at least we can give it up now."

"Yeah," said Harry. "No more pretending we care what happens when Jupiter and Uranus get too friendly . . ."

"And from now on, I don't care if my tea leaves spell *die, Ron, die* — I'm just chucking them in the bin where they belong."

Harry laughed just as Hermione came running up behind them. He stopped laughing at once, in case it annoyed her.

"Well, I think I've done all right in Arithmancy," she said, and Harry and Ron both sighed with relief. "Just time for a quick look over our star charts before dinner, then . . ."

When they reached the top of the Astronomy Tower at eleven o'clock they found a perfect night for stargazing, cloudless and still. The grounds were bathed in silvery moonlight, and there was a slight chill in the air. Each of them set up his or her telescope and, when Professor Marchbanks gave the word, proceeded to fill in the blank star chart he or she had been given.

Professors Marchbanks and Tofty strolled among them, watching as they entered the precise positions of the stars and planets they were observing. All was quiet except for the rustle of parchment, the occasional creak of a telescope as it was adjusted on its stand, and the scribbling of many quills. Half an hour passed, then an hour; the little squares of reflected gold light flickering on the ground below started to vanish as lights in the castle windows were extinguished.

As Harry completed the constellation Orion on his chart, however, the front doors of the castle opened directly below the parapet where he was standing, so that light spilled down the stone steps a little way across the lawn. Harry glanced down as he made a slight adjustment to the position of his telescope and saw five or six elongated shadows moving over the brightly lit grass before the doors swung shut and the lawn became a sea of darkness once more.

Harry put his eye back to his telescope and refocused it, now examining Venus. He looked down at his chart to enter the planet there, but something distracted him. Pausing with his quill suspended over the parchment, he squinted down into the shadowy grounds and saw half a dozen figures walking over the lawn. If they had not been moving, and the moonlight had not been gilding the tops of their heads, they would have been indistinguishable from the dark ground on which they stood. Even at this distance, Harry had a funny feeling that he recognized the walk of the squattest among them, who seemed to be leading the group.

He could not think why Umbridge would be taking a stroll outside past midnight, much less accompanied by five others. Then somebody coughed behind him, and he remembered that he was halfway through an exam. He had quite forgotten Venus's position — jamming his eye to his telescope, he found it again and was again on the point of entering it on his chart when, alert for any odd sound, he heard a distant knock that echoed through the deserted grounds, followed immediately by the muffled barking of a large dog.

He looked up, his heart hammering. There were lights on in Hagrid's windows and the people he had observed crossing the lawn were now silhouetted against them. The door opened and he distinctly saw six tiny but sharply defined figures walk over the threshold. The door closed again and there was silence.

Harry felt very uneasy. He glanced around to see whether Ron or Hermione had noticed what he had, but Professor Marchbanks came walking behind him at that moment, and not wanting to appear as though he was sneaking looks at anyone else's work, he hastily bent over his star chart and pretended to be adding notes to it while really peering over the top of the parapet toward Hagrid's cabin. Figures were now moving across the cabin windows, temporarily blocking the light.

He could feel Professor Marchbanks's eyes on the back of his neck and pressed his eye again to his telescope, staring up at the moon though he had marked its position an hour ago, but as Professor Marchbanks moved on he heard a roar from the distant cabin that echoed through the darkness right to the top of the Astronomy Tower. Several of the people around Harry ducked out from behind their telescopes and peered instead in the direction of Hagrid's cabin.

Professor Tofty gave another dry little cough.

"Try and concentrate, now, boys and girls," he said softly.

Most people returned to their telescopes. Harry looked to his left. Hermione was gazing transfixed at Hagrid's.

"Ahem — twenty minutes to go," said Professor Tofty.

Hermione jumped and returned at once to her star chart; Harry looked down at his own and noticed that he had mislabelled Venus as Mars. He bent to correct it.

There was a loud *BANG* from the grounds. Several people said "Ouch!" as they poked themselves in the face with the ends of their telescopes, hastening to see what was going on below.

Hagrid's door had burst open and by the light flooding out of the cabin they saw him quite clearly, a massive figure roaring and brandishing his fists, surrounded by six people, all of whom, judging by the tiny threads of red light they were casting in his direction, seemed to be attempting to Stun him.

"No!" cried Hermione.

"My dear!" said Professor Tofty in a scandalized voice. "This is an examination!"

But nobody was paying the slightest attention to their star charts anymore: Jets of red light were still flying beside Hagrid's cabin, yet somehow they seemed to be bouncing off him. He was still upright and still, as far as Harry could see, fighting. Cries and yells echoed across the grounds; a man yelled, "Be reasonable, Hagrid!" and Hagrid roared, "Reasonable be damned, yeh won' take me like this, Dawlish!"

Harry could see the tiny outline of Fang, attempting to defend Hagrid, leaping at the wizards surrounding him until a Stunning Spell caught him and he fell to the ground. Hagrid gave a howl of fury, lifted the culprit bodily from the ground, and threw him: The man flew what looked like ten feet and did not get up again. Hermione gasped, both hands over her mouth; Harry looked around at Ron and saw that he too was looking scared. None of them had ever seen Hagrid in a real temper before. . . .

"Look!" squealed Parvati, who was leaning over the parapet and pointing to the foot of the castle where the front doors seemed to have opened again; more light had spilled out onto the dark lawn and a single long black shadow was now rippling across the lawn.

"Now, really!" said Professor Tofty anxiously. "Only sixteen minutes left, you know!"

But nobody paid him the slightest attention: They were watching the person now sprinting toward the battle beside Hagrid's cabin.

"How dare you!" the figure shouted as she ran. "How *dare* you!"

"It's McGonagall!" whispered Hermione.

"Leave him alone! *Alone*, I say!" said Professor McGonagall's voice through the darkness. "On what grounds are you attacking him? He has done nothing, nothing to warrant such —"

Hermione, Parvati, and Lavender all screamed. No fewer than four Stunners had shot from the figures around the cabin toward Professor McGonagall. Halfway between cabin and castle the red beams collided with her. For a moment she looked luminous, illuminated by an eerie red glow, then was lifted right off her feet, landed hard on her back, and moved no more.

"Galloping gargoyles!" shouted Professor Tofty, who seemed to have forgotten the exam completely. "Not so much as a warning! Outrageous behavior!"

"COWARDS!" bellowed Hagrid, his voice carrying clearly to the top of the tower, and several lights flickered back on inside the castle. "RUDDY COWARDS! HAVE SOME O' THAT — AN' THAT —"

"Oh my —" gasped Hermione.

Hagrid took two massive swipes at his closest attackers; judging by their immediate collapse, they had been knocked cold. Harry saw him double over and thought for a moment that he had finally been overcome by a spell, but on the contrary, next moment Hagrid was standing again with what appeared to be a sack on his back — then Harry realized that Fang's limp body was draped around his shoulders.

"Get him, get him!" screamed Umbridge, but her remaining helper seemed highly reluctant to go within reach of Hagrid's fists. Indeed, he was backing away so fast he tripped over one of his unconscious colleagues and fell over. Hagrid had turned and begun to run with Fang still hung around his neck; Umbridge sent one last Stunning Spell after him but it missed, and Hagrid, running full-pelt toward the distant gates, disappeared into the darkness.

There was a long minute's quivering silence, everybody gazing openmouthed into the grounds. Then Professor Tofty's voice said feebly, "Um . . . five minutes to go, everybody . . ."

Though he had only filled in two-thirds of his chart, Harry was desperate for the end of the exam. When it came at last he, Ron, and Hermione forced their telescopes haphazardly back into their holders and dashed back down the spiral staircase. None of the students were going to bed — they were all talking loudly and excitedly at the foot of the stairs about what they had witnessed.

"That evil woman!" gasped Hermione, who seemed to be having difficulty talking due to rage. "Trying to sneak up on Hagrid in the dead of night!"

"She clearly wanted to avoid another scene like Trelawney's," said Ernie Macmillan sagely, squeezing over to join them.

"Hagrid did well, didn't he?" said Ron, who looked more alarmed than impressed. "How come all the spells bounced off him?"

"It'll be his giant blood," said Hermione shakily. "It's very hard to Stun a giant, they're like trolls, really tough. . . . But poor Professor McGonagall. . . . Four Stunners straight in the chest, and she's not exactly young, is she?"

"Dreadful, dreadful," said Ernie, shaking his head pompously. "Well, I'm off to bed. . . . 'Night, all . . ."

People around them were drifting away, still talking excitedly about what they had just seen.

"At least they didn't get to take Hagrid off to Azkaban," said Ron. "I 'spect he's gone to join Dumbledore, hasn't he?"

"I suppose so," said Hermione, who looked tearful. "Oh, this is awful, I really thought Dumbledore would be back before long, but now we've lost Hagrid too. . . ."

They traipsed back to the Gryffindor common room to find it full. The commotion out in the grounds had woken several people, who had hastened to rouse their friends. Seamus and Dean, who had arrived ahead of Harry, Ron, and Hermione, were now telling everyone what they had heard from the top of the Astronomy Tower.

"But why sack Hagrid now?" asked Angelina Johnson, shaking her head. "It's not like Trelawney, he's been teaching much better than usual this year!"

"Umbridge hates part-humans," said Hermione bitterly, flopping down into an armchair. "She was always going to try and get Hagrid out."

"And she thought Hagrid was putting nifflers in her office," piped up Katie Bell.

"Oh blimey," said Lee Jordan, covering his mouth. "It's me's been putting the nifflers in her office, Fred and George left me a couple, I've been levitating them in through her window. . . ."

"She'd have sacked him anyway," said Dean. "He was too close to Dumbledore."

"That's true," said Harry, sinking into an armchair beside Hermione's.

"I just hope Professor McGonagall's all right," said Lavender tearfully.

"They carried her back up to the castle, we watched through the dormitory window," said Colin Creevey. "She didn't look very well. . . ."

"Madam Pomfrey will sort her out," said Alicia Spinnet firmly. "She's never failed yet."

It was nearly four in the morning before the common room cleared. Harry felt wide awake — the image of Hagrid sprinting away into the dark was haunting him. He was so angry with Umbridge he could not think of a punishment bad enough for her, though Ron's suggestion of having her fed to a box of starving Blast-Ended Skrewts had its merits. He fell asleep contemplating hideous revenges and arose from bed three hours later feeling distinctly unrested.

Their final exam, History of Magic, was not to take place until that afternoon. Harry would very much have liked to go back to bed after breakfast, but he had been counting on the morning for a spot of last-minute studying, so instead he sat with his head in his hands by the common room window, trying hard not to doze off as he read through some of the notes stacked three-and-a-half feet high that Hermione had lent him.

The fifth years entered the Great Hall at two o'clock and took their places in front of their overturned examination papers. Harry felt exhausted. He just wanted this to be over so that he could go and sleep. Then tomorrow, he and Ron were going to go down to the Quidditch pitch — he was going to have a fly on Ron's broom and savor their freedom from studying. . . .

"Turn over your papers," said Professor Marchbanks from the front of the Hall, flicking over the giant hourglass. "You may begin. . . ."

Harry stared fixedly at the first question. It was several seconds before it occurred to him that he had not taken in a word of it; there was a wasp buzzing distractingly against one of the high windows. Slowly, tortuously, he began to write an answer.

He was finding it very difficult to remember names and kept confusing dates. He simply skipped question four: *In your opinion, did wand legislation contribute to, or lead to better control of, goblin riots of the eighteenth century?* thinking that he would go back to it if he had time at the end. He had a stab at question five: *How was the Statute of Secrecy breached in 1749 and what measures were introduced to prevent a recurrence?* but had a nagging suspicion that he had missed several important points. He had a feeling vampires had come into the story somewhere. . . .

He looked ahead for a question he could definitely answer and his eyes alighted upon number ten.

Describe the circumstances that led to the Formation of the International Confederation of Wizards and explain why the warlocks of Liechtenstein refused to join.

I know this, Harry thought, though his brain felt torpid and slack. He could visualize a heading, in Hermione's handwriting: *The Formation of the International Confederation of Wizards . . .* He had read these notes only this morning. . . .

He began to write, looking up now and again to check the large hourglass on the desk beside Professor Marchbanks. He was sitting right behind Parvati Patil, whose long dark hair fell below the back of her chair. Once or twice he found himself staring at the tiny golden lights that glistened in it when she moved her head very slightly and had to give his own head a little shake to clear it.

. . . the first Supreme Mugwump of the International Confederation

of Wizards was Pierre Bonaccord, but his appointment was contested by the Wizarding community of Liechtenstein, because —

All around Harry quills were scratching on parchment like scurrying, burrowing rats. The sun was very hot on the back of his head. What was it that Bonaccord had done to offend the wizards of Liechtenstein? Harry had a feeling it had something to do with trolls. . . . He gazed blankly at the back of Parvati's head again. If he could only perform Legilimency and open a window in the back of her head and see what it was about trolls that had caused the breach between Pierre Bonaccord and Liechtenstein. . . .

Harry closed his eyes and buried his face in his hands, so that the glowing red of his eyelids grew dark and cool. Bonaccord had wanted to stop troll-hunting and give the trolls rights . . . but Liechtenstein was having problems with a tribe of particularly vicious mountain trolls. . . . That was it. . . .

He opened his eyes; they stung and watered at the sight of the blazing-white parchment. Slowly he wrote two lines about the trolls then read through what he had done so far. It did not seem very informative or detailed, yet he was sure Hermione's notes on the confederation had gone on for pages and pages. . . .

He closed his eyes again, trying to see them, trying to remember. . . . The confederation had met for the first time in France, yes, he had written that already. . . .

Goblins had tried to attend and been ousted. . . . He had written that too. . . .

And nobody from Liechtenstein had wanted to come . . .

Think, he told himself, his face in his hands, while all around him quills scratched out never-ending answers and the sand trickled through the hourglass at the front. . . .

He was walking along the cool, dark corridor to the Department of Mysteries again, walking with a firm and purposeful tread, breaking occasionally into a run, determined to reach his destination at last. . . . The black door swung open for him as usual, and here he was in the circular room with its many doors. . . .

Straight across the stone floor and through the second door . . . patches of dancing light on the walls and floor and that odd mechanical clicking, but no time to explore, he must hurry. . . .

He jogged the last few feet to the third door, which swung open just like the others. . . .

Once again he was in the cathedral-sized room full of shelves and glass spheres. . . . His heart was beating very fast now. . . . He was going to get there this time. . . . When he reached number ninety-seven he turned left and hurried along the aisle between two rows. . . .

But there was a shape on the floor at the very end, a black shape moving upon the floor like a wounded animal. . . . Harry's stomach contracted with fear . . . with excitement. . . .

A voice issued from his own mouth, a high, cold voice empty of any human kindness, "Take it for me. . . . Lift it down, now. . . . I cannot touch it . . . but you can. . . ."

The black shape upon the floor shifted a little. Harry saw a long-fingered white hand clutching a wand rise on the end of his own arm . . . heard the high, cold voice say, *"Crucio!"*

The man on the floor let out a scream of pain, attempted to stand but fell back, writhing. Harry was laughing. He raised his wand, the curse lifted, and the figure groaned and became motionless.

"Lord Voldemort is waiting. . . ."

Very slowly, his arms trembling, the man on the ground raised his shoulders a few inches and lifted his head. His face was bloodstained and gaunt, twisted in pain yet rigid with defiance. . . .

"You'll have to kill me," whispered Sirius.

"Undoubtedly I shall in the end," said the cold voice. "But you will fetch it for me first, Black. . . . You think you have felt pain thus far?

Think again. . . . We have hours ahead of us and nobody to hear you scream. . . ."

But somebody screamed as Voldemort lowered his wand again; somebody yelled and fell sideways off a hot desk onto the cold stone floor. Harry hit the ground and awoke, still yelling, his scar on fire, as the Great Hall erupted all around him.

OUT OF THE FIRE

I'm not going. . . . I don't need the hospital wing. . . . I don't want . . ."

He was gibbering, trying to pull away from Professor Tofty, who was looking at him with much concern, and who had just helped Harry out into the entrance hall while the students all around them stared.

"I'm — I'm fine, sir," Harry stammered, wiping the sweat from his face. "Really . . . I just fell asleep. . . . Had a nightmare . . ."

"Pressure of examinations!" said the old wizard sympathetically, patting Harry shakily on the shoulder. "It happens, young man, it happens! Now, a cooling drink of water, and perhaps you will be ready to return to the Great Hall? The examination is nearly over, but you may be able to round off your last answer nicely?"

"Yes," said Harry wildly. "I mean . . . no . . . I've done — done as much as I can, I think. . . ."

"Very well, very well," said the old wizard gently. "I shall go and collect your examination paper, and I suggest that you go and have a nice lie down. . . ."

"I'll do that," said Harry, nodding vigorously. "Thanks very much."

He waited for the second when the old man's heels disappeared over the threshold into the Great Hall, then ran up the marble staircase and then more staircases toward the hospital wing, hurtling along the corridors so fast that the portraits he passed muttered reproaches, and burst through the double doors like a hurricane, causing Madam Pomfrey, who had been spooning some bright blue liquid into Montague's open mouth, to shriek in alarm.

"Potter, what do you think you're doing?"

"I need to see Professor McGonagall," gasped Harry, the breath tearing his lungs. "Now . . . It's urgent. . . ."

"She's not here, Potter," said Madam Pomfrey sadly. "She was transferred to St. Mungo's this morning. Four Stunning Spells straight to the chest at her age? It's a wonder they didn't kill her."

"She's . . . gone?" said Harry, stunned.

The bell rang just outside the dormitory, and he heard the usual distant rumbling of students starting to flood out into the corridors above and below him. He remained quite still, looking at Madam Pomfrey. Terror was rising inside him.

There was nobody left to tell. Dumbledore had gone, Hagrid had gone, but he had always expected Professor McGonagall to be there, irascible and inflexible, perhaps, but always dependably, solidly present. . . .

"I don't wonder you're shocked, Potter," said Madam Pomfrey with a kind of fierce approval in her face. "As if one of them could have Stunned Minerva McGonagall face on by daylight! Cowardice, that's what it was. . . . Despicable cowardice . . . If I wasn't worried what would happen to you students without me, I'd resign in protest. . . ."

"Yes," said Harry blankly.

He strode blindly from the hospital wing into the teeming corridor where he stood, buffeted by the crowd, the panic expanding inside him like poison gas so that his head swam and he could not think what to do. . . .

Ron and Hermione, said a voice in his head.

He was running again, pushing students out of the way, oblivious to their angry protests and shouts. He sprinted back down two floors and was at the top of the marble staircase when he saw them hurrying toward him.

"Harry!" said Hermione at once, looking very frightened. "What happened? Are you all right? Are you ill?"

"Where have you been?" demanded Ron.

"Come with me," Harry said quickly. "Come on, I've got to tell you something. . . ."

He led them along the first-floor corridor, peering through doorways, and at last found an empty classroom into which he dived, closing the door behind Ron and Hermione the moment they were inside and leaning against it, facing them.

"Voldemort's got Sirius."

"What?"

"How d'you — ?"

"Saw it. Just now. When I fell asleep in the exam."

"But — but where? How?" said Hermione, whose face was white.

"I dunno how," said Harry. "But I know exactly where. There's a room in the Department of Mysteries full of shelves covered in these little glass balls, and they're at the end of row ninety-seven . . . He's trying to use Sirius to get whatever it is he wants from in there. . . . He's torturing him. . . . Says he'll end by killing him . . ."

Harry found his voice was shaking, as were his knees. He moved over to a desk and sat down on it, trying to master himself.

"How're we going to get there?" he asked them.

There was a moment's silence. Then Ron said, "G-get there?"

"Get to the Department of Mysteries, so we can rescue Sirius!" Harry said loudly.

"But — Harry . . ." said Ron weakly.

"What? *What?*" said Harry.

He could not understand why they were both gaping at him as though he was asking them something unreasonable.

"Harry," said Hermione in a rather frightened voice, "er . . . how . . . how did Voldemort get into the Ministry of Magic without anybody realizing he was there?"

"How do I know?" bellowed Harry. "The question is how *we're* going to get in there!"

"But . . . Harry, think about this," said Hermione, taking a step toward him, "it's five o'clock in the afternoon. . . . The Ministry of Magic must be full of workers. . . . How would Voldemort and Sirius have got in without being seen? Harry . . . they're probably the two most wanted wizards in the world. . . . You think they could get into a building full of Aurors undetected?"

"I dunno, Voldemort used an Invisibility Cloak or something!" Harry shouted. "Anyway, the Department of Mysteries has always been completely empty whenever I've been —"

"You've never been there, Harry," said Hermione quietly. "You've dreamed about the place, that's all."

"They're not normal dreams!" Harry shouted in her face, standing up and taking a step closer to her in turn. He wanted to shake her. "How d'you explain Ron's dad then, what was all that about, how come I knew what had happened to him?"

"He's got a point," said Ron quietly, looking at Hermione.

"But this is just — just so *unlikely!*" said Hermione desperately. "Harry, how on earth could Voldemort have got hold of Sirius when he's been in Grimmauld Place all the time?"

"Sirius might've cracked and just wanted some fresh air," said Ron, sounding worried. "He's been desperate to get out of that house for ages —"

"But why," Hermione persisted, "why on earth would Voldemort want to use *Sirius* to get the weapon, or whatever the thing is?"

"I dunno, there could be loads of reasons!" Harry yelled at her. "Maybe Sirius is just someone Voldemort doesn't care about seeing hurt —"

"You know what, I've just thought of something," said Ron in a hushed voice. "Sirius's brother was a Death Eater, wasn't he? Maybe he told Sirius the secret of how to get the weapon!"

"Yeah — and that's why Dumbledore's been so keen to keep Sirius locked up all the time!" said Harry.

"Look, I'm sorry," cried Hermione, "but neither of you are making sense, and we've got no proof for any of this, no proof Voldemort and Sirius are even there —"

"Hermione, Harry's seen them!" said Ron, rounding on her.

"Okay," she said, looking frightened yet determined, "I've just got to say this. . . ."

"What?"

"You . . . This isn't a criticism, Harry! But you do . . . sort of . . . I mean — don't you think you've got a bit of a — a — *saving-people-thing*?" she said.

He glared at her. "And what's that supposed to mean, a 'saving-people-thing'?"

"Well . . . you . . ." She looked more apprehensive than ever. "I mean . . . last year, for instance . . . in the lake . . . during the Tournament . . . you shouldn't have . . . I mean, you didn't need to save that little Delacour girl. . . . You got a bit . . . carried away . . ."

A wave of hot, prickly anger swept Harry's body — how could she remind him of that blunder now?

". . . I mean, it was really great of you and everything," said Hermione quickly, looking positively petrified at the look on Harry's face. "Everyone thought it was a wonderful thing to do —"

"That's funny," said Harry in a trembling voice, "because I definitely remember Ron saying I'd wasted time *acting the hero*. . . . Is that what you think this is? You reckon I want to act the hero again?"

"No, no, no!" said Hermione, looking aghast. "That's not what I mean at all!"

"Well, spit out what you've got to say, because we're wasting time here!" Harry shouted.

"I'm trying to say — Voldemort knows you, Harry! He took Ginny down into the Chamber of Secrets to lure you there, it's the kind of thing he does, he knows you're the — the sort of person who'd go to Sirius's aid! What if he's just trying to get you into the Department of Myst — ?"

"Hermione, it doesn't matter if he's done it to get me there or not — they've taken McGonagall to St. Mungo's, there isn't anyone left from the Order at Hogwarts who we can tell, and if we don't go, Sirius is dead!"

"But Harry — what if your dream was — was just that, a dream?"

Harry let out a roar of frustration. Hermione actually stepped back from him, looking alarmed.

"You don't get it!" Harry shouted at her. "I'm not having nightmares, I'm not just dreaming! What d'you think all the Occlumency was for, why d'you think Dumbledore wanted me prevented from seeing these things? Because they're REAL, Hermione — Sirius is trapped — I've seen him — Voldemort's got him, and no one else knows, and that means we're the only ones who can save him, and if you don't want to do it, fine, but I'm going, understand? And if I remember rightly, you didn't have a problem with my *saving-people-thing* when it was you I was saving from the dementors, or" — he rounded on Ron — "when it was your sister I was saving from the basilisk —"

"I never said I had a problem!" said Ron heatedly.

"But Harry, you've just said it," said Hermione fiercely. "Dumbledore wanted you to learn to shut these things out of your mind, if you'd done Occlumency properly you'd never have seen this —"

"IF YOU THINK I'M JUST GOING TO ACT LIKE I HAVEN'T SEEN —"

"Sirius told you there was nothing more important than you learning to close your mind!"

"WELL, I EXPECT HE'D SAY SOMETHING DIFFERENT IF HE KNEW WHAT I'D JUST —"

The classroom door opened. Harry, Ron, and Hermione whipped around. Ginny walked in, looking curious, followed by Luna, who as usual looked as though she had drifted in accidentally.

"Hi," said Ginny uncertainly. "We recognized Harry's voice — what are you yelling about?"

"Never you mind," said Harry roughly.

Ginny raised her eyebrows.

"There's no need to take that tone with me," she said coolly. "I was only wondering whether I could help."

"Well, you can't," said Harry shortly.

"You're being rather rude, you know," said Luna serenely.

Harry swore and turned away. The very last thing he wanted now was a conversation with Luna Lovegood.

"Wait," said Hermione suddenly. "Wait . . . Harry, they *can* help."

Harry and Ron looked at her.

"Listen," she said urgently, "Harry, we need to establish whether Sirius really has left headquarters —"

"I've told you, I saw —"

"Harry, I'm begging you, please!" said Hermione desperately. "Please let's just check that Sirius isn't at home before we go charging off to London — if we find out he's not there then I swear I won't try and stop you, I'll come, I'll d-do whatever it takes to try and save him —"

"Sirius is being tortured NOW!" shouted Harry. "We haven't got time to waste —"

"But if this is a trick of V-Voldemort's — Harry, we've got to check, we've got to —"

"How?" Harry demanded. "How're we going to check?"

"We'll have to use Umbridge's fire and see if we can contact him," said Hermione, who looked positively terrified at the thought. "We'll draw Umbridge away again, but we'll need lookouts, and that's where we can use Ginny and Luna."

Though clearly struggling to understand what was going on, Ginny said immediately, "Yeah, we'll do it," and Luna said, "When you say 'Sirius,' are you talking about Stubby Boardman?"

Nobody answered her.

"Okay," Harry said aggressively to Hermione, "Okay, if you can think of a way of doing this quickly, I'm with you, otherwise I'm going to the Department of Mysteries right now —"

"The Department of Mysteries?" said Luna, looking mildly surprised. "But how are you going to get there?"

Again, Harry ignored her.

"Right," said Hermione, twisting her hands together and pacing up and down between the desks. "Right . . . well . . . One of us has to go and find Umbridge and — and send her off in the wrong direction, keep her away from her office. They could tell her — I don't know — that Peeves is up to something awful as usual. . . ."

"I'll do it," said Ron at once. "I'll tell her Peeves is smashing up the Transfiguration department or something, it's miles away from her office. Come to think of it, I could probably persuade Peeves to do it if I met him on the way. . . ."

It was a mark of the seriousness of the situation that Hermione made no objection to the smashing up of the Transfiguration department.

"Okay," she said, her brow furrowed as she continued to pace.

"Now, we need to keep students away from her office while we force entry, or some Slytherin's bound to go and tip her off. . . ."

"Luna and I can stand at either end of the corridor," said Ginny promptly, "and warn people not to go down there because someone's let off a load of Garroting Gas." Hermione looked surprised at the readiness with which Ginny had come up with this lie. Ginny shrugged and said, "Fred and George were planning to do it before they left."

"Okay," said Hermione, "well then, Harry, you and I will be under the Invisibility Cloak, and we'll sneak into the office and you can talk to Sirius —"

"He's not there, Hermione!"

"I mean, you can — can check whether Sirius is at home or not while I keep watch, I don't think you should be in there alone, Lee's already proved the window's a weak spot, sending those nifflers through it."

Even through his anger and impatience Harry recognized Hermione's offer to accompany him into Umbridge's office as a sign of solidarity and loyalty.

"I . . . okay, thanks," he muttered.

"Right, well, even if we do all of that, I don't think we're going to be able to bank on more than five minutes," said Hermione, looking relieved that Harry seemed to have accepted the plan, "not with Filch and the wretched Inquisitorial Squad floating around."

"Five minutes'll be enough," said Harry. "C'mon, let's go —"

"*Now?*" said Hermione, looking shocked.

"Of course now!" said Harry angrily. "What did you think, we're going to wait until after dinner or something? Hermione, Sirius is being tortured *right now*!"

"I — oh all right," she said desperately. "You go and get the Invisibility Cloak and we'll meet you at the end of Umbridge's corridor, okay?"

Harry did not answer, but flung himself out of the room and began to fight his way through the milling crowds outside. Two floors up he met Seamus and Dean, who hailed him jovially and told him they were planning a dusk-till-dawn end-of-exams celebration in the common room. Harry barely heard them. He scrambled through the portrait hole while they were still arguing about how many black-market butterbeers they would need and was climbing back out of it, the Invisibility Cloak and Sirius's knife secure in his bag, before they noticed he had left them.

"Harry, d'you want to chip in a couple of Galleons? Harold Dingle reckons he could sell us some firewhisky. . . ."

But Harry was already tearing away back along the corridor, and a couple of minutes later was jumping the last few stairs to join Ron, Hermione, Ginny, and Luna, who were huddled together at the end of Umbridge's corridor.

"Got it," he panted. "Ready to go, then?"

"All right," whispered Hermione as a gang of loud sixth years passed them. "So Ron — you go and head Umbridge off. . . . Ginny, Luna, if you can start moving people out of the corridor. . . . Harry and I will get the Cloak on and wait until the coast is clear. . . ."

Ron strode away, his bright red hair visible right to the end of the passage. Meanwhile, Ginny's equally vivid head bobbed between the jostling students surrounding them in the other direction, trailed by Luna's blonde one.

"Get over here," muttered Hermione, tugging at Harry's wrist and pulling him back into a recess where the ugly stone head of a medieval wizard stood muttering to itself on a column. "Are — are you sure you're okay, Harry? You're still very pale. . . ."

"I'm fine," he said shortly, tugging the Invisibility Cloak from out of his bag. In truth, his scar was aching, but not so badly that he thought Voldemort had yet dealt Sirius a fatal blow. It had hurt much worse than this when Voldemort had been punishing Avery. . . .

"Here," he said. He threw the Invisibility Cloak over both of them and they stood listening carefully over the Latin mumblings of the bust in front of them.

"You can't come down here!" Ginny was calling to the crowd. "No, sorry, you're going to have to go round by the swiveling staircase, someone's let off Garroting Gas just along here —"

They could hear people complaining; one surly voice said, "I can't see no gas . . ."

"That's because it's colorless," said Ginny in a convincingly exasperated voice, "but if you want to walk through it, carry on, then we'll have your body as proof for the next idiot who didn't believe us. . . ."

Slowly the crowd thinned. The news about the Garroting Gas seemed to have spread — people were not coming this way anymore. When at last the surrounding area was quite clear, Hermione said quietly, "I think that's as good as we're going to get, Harry — come on, let's do it."

Together they moved forward, covered by the Cloak. Luna was standing with her back to them at the far end of the corridor. As they passed Ginny, Hermione whispered, "Good one . . . don't forget the signal . . ."

"What's the signal?" muttered Harry, as they approached Umbridge's door.

"A loud chorus of 'Weasley Is Our King' if they see Umbridge coming," replied Hermione, as Harry inserted the blade of Sirius's knife in the crack between door and wall. The lock clicked open, and they entered the office.

The garish kittens were basking in the late afternoon sunshine warming their plates, but otherwise the office was as still and empty as last time. Hermione breathed a sigh of relief.

"I thought she might have added extra security after the second niffler. . . ."

They pulled off the Cloak. Hermione hurried over to the window and stood out of sight, peering down into the grounds with her wand out. Harry dashed over to the fireplace, seized the pot of Floo powder, and threw a pinch into the grate, causing emerald flames to burst into life there. He knelt down quickly, thrust his head into the dancing fire, and cried, "Number twelve, Grimmauld Place!"

His head began to spin as though he had just got off a fairground ride though his knees remained firmly planted upon the cold office floor. He kept his eyes screwed up against the whirling ash, and when the spinning stopped, he opened them to find himself looking out upon the long, cold kitchen of Grimmauld Place.

There was nobody there. He had expected this, yet was not prepared for the molten wave of dread and panic that seemed to burst through his stomach floor at the sight of the deserted room.

"Sirius?" he shouted. "Sirius, are you there?"

His voice echoed around the room, but there was no answer except a tiny scuffing sound to the right of the fire.

"Who's there?" he called, wondering whether it was just a mouse.

Kreacher the house-elf came creeping into view. He looked highly delighted about something, though he seemed to have recently sustained a nasty injury to both hands, which were heavily bandaged.

"It's the Potter boy's head in the fire," Kreacher informed the empty kitchen, stealing furtive, oddly triumphant glances at Harry. "What has he come for, Kreacher wonders?"

"Where's Sirius, Kreacher?" Harry demanded.

The house-elf gave a wheezy chuckle. "Master has gone out, Harry Potter."

"Where's he gone? *Where's he gone, Kreacher?*"

Kreacher merely cackled.

"I'm warning you!" said Harry, fully aware that his scope for inflicting punishment upon Kreacher was almost nonexistent in this position. "What about Lupin? Mad-Eye? Any of them, are any of them here?"

"Nobody here but Kreacher!" said the elf gleefully, and turning away from Harry he began to walk slowly toward the door at the end of the kitchen. "Kreacher thinks he will have a little chat with his Mistress now, yes, he hasn't had a chance in a long time, Kreacher's Master has been keeping him away from her —"

"Where has Sirius gone?" Harry yelled after the elf. *"Kreacher, has he gone to the Department of Mysteries?"*

Kreacher stopped in his tracks. Harry could just make out the back of his bald head through the forest of chair legs before him.

"Master does not tell poor Kreacher where he is going," said the elf quietly.

"But you know!" shouted Harry. "Don't you? You know where he is!"

There was a moment's silence, then the elf let out his loudest cackle yet. "Master will not come back from the Department of Mysteries!" he said gleefully. "Kreacher and his Mistress are alone again!"

And he scurried forward and disappeared through the door to the hall.

"You — !"

But before he could utter a single curse or insult, Harry felt a great pain at the top of his head. He inhaled a lot of ash and, choking, found himself being dragged backward through the flames until, with a horrible abruptness, he was staring up into the wide, pallid face of Professor Umbridge, who had dragged him backward out of the fire by the hair and was now bending his neck back as far as it would go as though she was going to slit his throat.

"You think," she whispered, bending Harry's neck back even farther, so that he was looking up at the ceiling above him, "that after two nifflers I was going to let one more foul, scavenging little creature enter my office without my knowledge? I had Stealth Sensoring Spells placed all around my doorway after the last one got in, you foolish boy. Take his wand," she barked at someone he could not see, and he felt a hand grope inside the chest pocket of his robes and remove the wand. "Hers too . . ."

Harry heard a scuffle over by the door and knew that Hermione had just had her wand wrested from her as well.

"I want to know why you are in my office," said Umbridge, shaking the fist clutching his hair so that he staggered.

"I was — trying to get my Firebolt!" Harry croaked.

"Liar." She shook his head again. "Your Firebolt is under strict guard in the dungeons, as you very well know, Potter. You had your head in my fire. With whom have you been communicating?"

"No one —" said Harry, trying to pull away from her. He felt several hairs part company with his scalp.

"*Liar!*" shouted Umbridge. She threw him from her, and he slammed into the desk. Now he could see Hermione pinioned against the wall by Millicent Bulstrode. Malfoy was leaning on the windowsill, smirking as he threw Harry's wand into the air one-handed and then caught it again.

There was a commotion outside and several large Slytherins entered, each gripping Ron, Ginny, Luna, and — to Harry's bewilderment — Neville, who was trapped in a stranglehold by Crabbe and looked in imminent danger of suffocation. All four of them had been gagged.

"Got 'em all," said Warrington, shoving Ron roughly forward into the room. "*That* one," he poked a thick finger at Neville, "tried to stop me taking *her*," he pointed at Ginny, who was trying to kick the shins of the large Slytherin girl holding her, "so I brought him along too."

"Good, good," said Umbridge, watching Ginny's struggles. "Well, it looks as though Hogwarts will shortly be a Weasley-free zone, doesn't it?"

Malfoy laughed loudly and sycophantically. Umbridge gave her wide, complacent smile and settled herself into a chintz-covered armchair, blinking up at her captives like a toad in a flowerbed.

"So, Potter," she said. "You stationed lookouts around my office and you sent this buffoon," she nodded at Ron, and Malfoy laughed even louder, "to tell me the poltergeist was wreaking havoc in the Transfiguration department when I knew perfectly well that he was busy smearing ink on the eyepieces of all the school telescopes, Mr. Filch having just informed me so.

"Clearly, it was very important for you to talk to somebody. Was it Albus Dumbledore? Or the half-breed, Hagrid? I doubt it was Minerva McGonagall, I hear she is still too ill to talk to anyone. . . ."

Malfoy and a few of the other members of the Inquisitorial Squad laughed some more at that. Harry found he was so full of rage and hatred he was shaking.

"It's none of your business who I talk to," he snarled.

Umbridge's slack face seemed to tighten.

"Very well," she said in her most dangerous and falsely sweet voice. "Very well, Mr. Potter . . . I offered you the chance to tell me freely. You refused. I have no alternative but to force you. Draco — fetch Professor Snape."

Malfoy stowed Harry's wand inside his robes and left the room smirking, but Harry hardly noticed. He had just realized something; he could not believe he had been so stupid as to forget it. He had thought that all the members of the Order, all those who could help him save Sirius, were gone — but he had been wrong. There was still a member of the Order of the Phoenix at Hogwarts — Snape.

There was silence in the office except for the fidgetings and scufflings resultant from the Slytherins' efforts to keep Ron and the others under control. Ron's lip was bleeding onto Umbridge's carpet as he struggled against Warrington's half nelson. Ginny was still trying to stamp on the feet of the sixth-year girl who had both her upper arms in a tight grip. Neville was turning steadily more purple in the face while tugging at Crabbe's arms, and Hermione was attempting vainly to throw Millicent Bulstrode off her. Luna, however, stood limply by the side of her captor, gazing vaguely out of the window as though rather bored by the proceedings.

Harry looked back at Umbridge, who was watching him closely. He kept his face deliberately smooth and blank as footsteps were heard in the corridor outside and Draco Malfoy came back into the room, holding open the door for Snape.

"You wanted to see me, Headmistress?" said Snape, looking around at all the pairs of struggling students with an expression of complete indifference.

"Ah, Professor Snape," said Umbridge, smiling widely and standing up again. "Yes, I would like another bottle of Veritaserum, as quick as you can, please."

"You took my last bottle to interrogate Potter," he said, observing her coolly through his greasy curtains of black hair. "Surely you did not use it all? I told you that three drops would be sufficient."

Umbridge flushed.

"You can make some more, can't you?" she said, her voice becoming more sweetly girlish as it always did when she was furious.

"Certainly," said Snape, his lip curling. "It takes a full moon cycle to mature, so I should have it ready for you in around a month."

"A month?" squawked Umbridge, swelling toadishly. "A *month*? But I need it this evening, Snape! I have just found Potter using my fire to communicate with a person or persons unknown!"

"Really?" said Snape, showing his first, faint sign of interest as he looked around at Harry. "Well, it doesn't surprise me. Potter has never shown much inclination to follow school rules."

His cold, dark eyes were boring into Harry's, who met his gaze unflinchingly, concentrating hard on what he had seen in his dream, willing Snape to read it in his mind, to understand . . .

"I wish to interrogate him!" shouted Umbridge angrily, and Snape looked away from Harry back into her furiously quivering face. "I wish you to provide me with a potion that will force him to tell me the truth!"

"I have already told you," said Snape smoothly, "that I have no further stocks of Veritaserum. Unless you wish to poison Potter — and I assure you I would have the greatest sympathy with you if you did — I cannot help you. The only trouble is that most venoms act too fast to give the victim much time for truth-telling. . . ."

Snape looked back at Harry, who stared at him, frantic to communicate without words.

Voldemort's got Sirius in the Department of Mysteries, he thought desperately. *Voldemort's got Sirius —*

"You are on probation!" shrieked Professor Umbridge, and Snape looked back at her, his eyebrows slightly raised. "You are being deliberately unhelpful! I expected better, Lucius Malfoy always speaks most highly of you! Now get out of my office!"

Snape gave her an ironic bow and turned to leave. Harry knew his last chance of letting the Order know what was going on was walking out of the door.

"He's got Padfoot!" he shouted. "He's got Padfoot at the place where it's hidden!"

Snape had stopped with his hand on Umbridge's door handle.

"Padfoot?" cried Professor Umbridge, looking eagerly from Harry to Snape. "What is Padfoot? Where what is hidden? What does he mean, Snape?"

Snape looked around at Harry. His face was inscrutable. Harry could not tell whether he had understood or not, but he did not dare speak more plainly in front of Umbridge.

"I have no idea," said Snape coldly. "Potter, when I want nonsense shouted at me I shall give you a Babbling Beverage. And Crabbe, loosen your hold a little, if Longbottom suffocates it will mean a lot of tedious paperwork, and I am afraid I shall have to mention it on your reference if ever you apply for a job."

He closed the door behind him with a snap, leaving Harry in a state of worse turmoil than before: Snape had been his very last hope. He looked at Umbridge, who seemed to be feeling the same way; her chest was heaving with rage and frustration.

"Very well," she said, and she pulled out her wand. "Very well . . . I am left with no alternative. . . . This is more than a matter of school discipline. . . . This is an issue of Ministry security. . . . Yes . . . yes . . ."

She seemed to be talking herself into something. She was shifting her weight nervously from foot to foot, staring at Harry, beating her wand against her empty palm and breathing heavily. Harry felt horribly powerless without his own wand as he watched her.

"You are forcing me, Potter. . . . I do not want to," said Umbridge, still moving restlessly on the spot, "but sometimes circumstances justify the use . . . I am sure the Minister will understand that I had no choice. . . ."

Malfoy was watching her with a hungry expression on his face.

"The Cruciatus Curse ought to loosen your tongue," said Umbridge quietly.

"No!" shrieked Hermione. "Professor Umbridge — it's illegal" — but Umbridge took no notice. There was a nasty, eager, excited look on her face that Harry had never seen before. She raised her wand.

"The Minister wouldn't want you to break the law, Professor Umbridge!" cried Hermione.

"What Cornelius doesn't know won't hurt him," said Umbridge, who was now panting slightly as she pointed her wand at different parts of Harry's body in turn, apparently trying to decide what would hurt the most. "He never knew I ordered dementors after Potter last summer, but he was delighted to be given the chance to expel him, all the same. . . ."

"It was *you*?" gasped Harry. "*You* sent the dementors after me?"

"*Somebody* had to act," breathed Umbridge, as her wand came to rest pointing directly at Harry's forehead. "They were all bleating about silencing you somehow — discrediting you — but I was the one who actually *did* something about it. . . . Only you wriggled out of that one, didn't you, Potter? Not today, though, not now . . ."

And taking a deep breath, she cried, "*Cruc —*"

"NO!" shouted Hermione in a cracked voice from behind Millicent Bulstrode. "No — Harry — Harry, we'll have to tell her!"

"No way!" yelled Harry, staring at the little of Hermione he could see.

"We'll have to, Harry, she'll force it out of you anyway, what's . . . what's the point . . . ?"

And Hermione began to cry weakly into the back of Millicent Bulstrode's robes. Millicent stopped trying to squash her against the wall immediately and dodged out of her way looking disgusted.

"Well, well, well!" said Umbridge, looking triumphant. "Little Miss Question-All is going to give us some answers! Come on then, girl, come on!"

"Er — my — nee — no!" shouted Ron through his gag.

Ginny was staring at Hermione as though she had never seen her before; Neville, still choking for breath, was gazing at her too. But Harry had just noticed something. Though Hermione was sobbing desperately into her hands, there was no trace of a tear. . . .

"I'm — I'm sorry everyone," said Hermione. "But — I can't stand it —"

"That's right, that's right, girl!" said Umbridge, seizing Hermione by the shoulders, thrusting her into the abandoned chintz chair and leaning over her. "Now then . . . with whom was Potter communicating just now?"

"Well," gulped Hermione into her hands, "well, he was *trying* to speak to Professor Dumbledore. . . ."

Ron froze, his eyes wide; Ginny stopped trying to stamp on her Slytherin captor's toes; even Luna looked mildly surprised. Fortunately, the attention of Umbridge and her minions was focused too exclusively upon Hermione to notice these suspicious signs.

"Dumbledore?" said Umbridge eagerly. "You know where Dumbledore is, then?"

"Well . . . no!" sobbed Hermione. "We've tried the Leaky Cauldron in Diagon Alley and the Three Broomsticks and even the Hog's Head —"

"Idiot girl, Dumbledore won't be sitting in a pub when the whole Ministry's looking for him!" shouted Umbridge, disappointment etched in every sagging line of her face.

"But — but we needed to tell him something important!" wailed Hermione, holding her hands more tightly over her face, not, Harry knew, out of anguish, but to disguise the continued absence of tears.

"Yes?" said Umbridge with a sudden resurgence of excitement. "What was it you wanted to tell him?"

"We . . . we wanted to tell him it's r-ready!" choked Hermione.

"What's ready?" demanded Umbridge, and now she grabbed Hermione's shoulders again and shook her slightly. "What's ready, girl?"

"The . . . the weapon," said Hermione.

"Weapon? Weapon?" said Umbridge, and her eyes seemed to pop with excitement. "You have been developing some method of resistance? A weapon you could use against the Ministry? On Professor Dumbledore's orders, of course?"

"Y-y-yes," gasped Hermione. "But he had to leave before it was finished and n-n-now we've finished it for him, and we c-c-can't find him t-t-to tell him!"

"What kind of weapon is it?" said Umbridge harshly, her stubby hands still tight on Hermione's shoulders.

"We don't r-r-really understand it," said Hermione, sniffing loudly. "We j-j-just did what P-P-Professor Dumbledore told us t-t-to do . . ."

Umbridge straightened up, looking exultant.

"Lead me to the weapon," she said.

"I'm not showing . . . *them*," said Hermione shrilly, looking around at the Slytherins through her fingers.

"It is not for you to set conditions," said Professor Umbridge harshly.

"Fine," said Hermione, now sobbing into her hands again, "fine . . . let them see it, I hope they use it on you! In fact, I wish you'd invite loads and loads of people to come and see! Th-that would serve you right — oh, I'd love it if the wh-whole school knew where it was, and how to u-use it, and then if you annoy any of them they'll be able to s-sort you out!"

These words had a powerful impact on Umbridge. She glanced swiftly and suspiciously around at her Inquisitorial Squad, her bulging eyes resting for a moment on Malfoy, who was too slow to disguise the look of eagerness and greed that had appeared on his face.

Umbridge contemplated Hermione for another long moment and then spoke in what she clearly thought was a motherly voice. "All right, dear, let's make it just you and me . . . and we'll take Potter too, shall we? Get up, now —"

"Professor," said Malfoy eagerly, "Professor Umbridge, I think some of the squad should come with you to look after —"

"I am a fully qualified Ministry official, Malfoy, do you really think

I cannot manage two wandless teenagers alone?" asked Umbridge sharply. "In any case, it does not sound as though this weapon is something that schoolchildren should see. You will remain here until I return and make sure none of these" — she gestured around at Ron, Ginny, Neville, and Luna — "escape."

"All right," said Malfoy, looking sulky and disappointed.

"And you two can go ahead of me and show me the way," said Umbridge, pointing at Harry and Hermione with her wand. "Lead on. . . ."

FIGHT AND FLIGHT

arry had no idea what Hermione was planning, or even whether she had a plan. He walked half a pace behind her as they headed down the corridor outside Umbridge's office, knowing it would look very suspicious if he appeared not to know where they were going. He did not dare attempt to talk to her; Umbridge was walking so closely behind them that he could hear her ragged breathing.

Hermione led the way down the stairs into the entrance hall. The din of loud voices and the clatter of cutlery on plates echoed from out of the double doors to the Great Hall. It seemed incredible to Harry that twenty feet away were people who were enjoying dinner, celebrating the end of exams, not a care in the world. . . .

Hermione walked straight out of the oak front doors and down the stone steps into the balmy evening air. The sun was falling toward the tops of the trees in the Forbidden Forest now as Hermione marched purposefully across the grass, Umbridge jogging to keep up. Their long dark shadows rippled over the grass behind them like cloaks.

"It's hidden in Hagrid's hut, is it?" said Umbridge eagerly in Harry's ear.

"Of course not," said Hermione scathingly. "Hagrid might have set it off accidentally."

"Yes," said Umbridge, whose excitement seemed to be mounting. "Yes, he would have done, of course, the great half-breed oaf. . . ."

She laughed. Harry felt a strong urge to swing around and seize her by the throat, but resisted. His scar was throbbing in the soft evening air but it had not yet burned white-hot, as he knew it would if Voldemort had moved in for the kill. . . .

"Then . . . where is it?" asked Umbridge, with a hint of uncertainty in her voice as Hermione continued to stride toward the forest.

"In there, of course," said Hermione, pointing into the dark trees. "It had to be somewhere that students weren't going to find it accidentally, didn't it?"

"Of course," said Umbridge, though she sounded a little apprehensive now. "Of course . . . very well, then . . . you two stay ahead of me."

"Can we have your wand, then, if we're going first?" Harry asked her.

"No, I don't think so, Mr. Potter," said Umbridge sweetly, poking him in the back with it. "The Ministry places a rather higher value on my life than yours, I'm afraid."

As they reached the cool shade of the first trees, Harry tried to catch Hermione's eye; walking into the forest without wands seemed to him to be more foolhardy than anything they had done so far this evening. She, however, merely gave Umbridge a contemptuous glance and plunged straight into the trees, moving at such a pace that Umbridge, with her shorter legs, had difficulty in keeping up.

"Is it very far in?" Umbridge asked, as her robe ripped on a bramble.

"Oh yes," said Hermione. "Yes, it's well hidden."

Harry's misgivings increased. Hermione was not taking the path they had followed to visit Grawp, but the one he had followed three years ago to the lair of the monster Aragog. Hermione had not been with him on that occasion; he doubted she had any idea what danger lay at the end of it.

"Er — are you sure this is the right way?" he asked her pointedly.

"Oh yes," she said in a steely voice, crashing through the undergrowth with what he thought was a wholly unnecessary amount of noise. Behind them, Umbridge tripped over a fallen sapling. Neither of them paused to help her up again; Hermione merely strode on, calling loudly over her shoulder, "It's a bit further in!"

"Hermione, keep your voice down," Harry muttered, hurrying to catch up with her. "Anything could be listening in here —"

"I want us heard," she answered quietly, as Umbridge jogged noisily after them. "You'll see. . . ."

They walked on for what seemed a long time, until they were once again so deep into the forest that the dense tree canopy blocked out all light. Harry had the feeling he had had before in the forest, one of being watched by unseen eyes. . . .

"How much further?" demanded Umbridge angrily from behind him.

"Not far now!" shouted Hermione, as they emerged into a dim, dank clearing. "Just a little bit —"

An arrow flew through the air and landed with a menacing thud in the tree just over her head. The air was suddenly full of the sound of hooves. Harry could feel the forest floor trembling; Umbridge gave a little scream and pushed him in front of her like a shield —

He wrenched himself free of her and turned. Around fifty centaurs were emerging on every side, their bows raised and loaded, pointing at Harry, Hermione, and Umbridge, who backed slowly into the center of the clearing, Umbridge uttering odd little whimpers of terror. Harry looked sideways at Hermione. She was wearing a triumphant smile.

"Who are you?" said a voice.

Harry looked left. The chestnut-bodied centaur called Magorian was walking toward them out of the circle; his bow, like the others', was raised. On Harry's right, Umbridge was still whimpering, her wand trembling violently as she pointed it at the advancing centaur.

"I asked you who are you, human," said Magorian roughly.

"I am Dolores Umbridge!" said Umbridge in a high-pitched, terrified voice. "Senior Undersecretary to the Minister of Magic and Headmistress and High Inquisitor of Hogwarts!"

"You are from the Ministry of Magic?" said Magorian, as many of the centaurs in the surrounding circle shifted restlessly.

"That's right!" said Umbridge in an even higher voice. "So be very careful! By the laws laid down by the Department for the Regulation and Control of Magical Creatures, any attack by half-breeds such as yourselves on a human —"

"*What* did you call us?" shouted a wild-looking black centaur, whom Harry recognized as Bane. There was a great deal of angry muttering and tightening of bowstrings around them.

"Don't call them that!" Hermione said furiously, but Umbridge did not appear to have heard her. Still pointing her shaking wand at Magorian, she continued, "Law Fifteen B states clearly that 'Any attack by a magical creature who is deemed to have near-human intelligence, and therefore considered responsible for its actions —'"

"'Near-human intelligence'?" repeated Magorian, as Bane and several others roared with rage and pawed the ground. "We consider that a great insult, human! Our intelligence, thankfully, far outstrips your own —"

"What are you doing in our forest?" bellowed the hard-faced gray centaur whom Harry and Hermione had seen on their last trip into the forest. "Why are you here?"

"*Your* forest?" said Umbridge, shaking now not only with fright but also, it seemed, with indignation. "I would remind you that you live here only because the Ministry of Magic permits you certain areas of land —"

An arrow flew so close to her head that it caught at her mousy hair in passing. She let out an earsplitting scream and threw her hands over her head while some of the centaurs bellowed their approval and others laughed raucously. The sound of their wild, neighing laughter echoing around the dimly lit clearing and the sight of their pawing hooves was extremely unnerving.

"Whose forest is it now, human?" bellowed Bane.

"Filthy half-breeds!" she screamed, her hands still tight over her head. "Beasts! Uncontrolled animals!"

"Be quiet!" shouted Hermione, but it was too late — Umbridge pointed her wand at Magorian and screamed, *"Incarcerous!"*

Ropes flew out of midair like thick snakes, wrapping themselves tightly around the centaur's torso and trapping his arms. He gave a cry of rage and reared onto his hind legs, attempting to free himself, while the other centaurs charged.

Harry grabbed Hermione and pulled her to the ground. Facedown on the forest floor he knew a moment of terror as hooves thundered around him, but the centaurs leapt over and around them, bellowing and screaming with rage.

"Nooooo!" he heard Umbridge shriek. "Noooooo . . . I am Senior Undersecretary . . . you cannot . . . unhand me, you animals . . . nooooo!"

He saw a flash of red light and knew that she had attempted to Stun one of them — then she screamed very loudly. Lifting his head a few inches, Harry saw that Umbridge had been seized from behind by Bane and lifted high into the air, wriggling and yelling with fright. Her wand fell from her hand to the ground and Harry's heart leapt, if he could just reach it —

But as he stretched out a hand toward it, a centaur's hoof descended upon the wand and it broke cleanly in half.

"Now!" roared a voice in Harry's ear and a thick hairy arm descended from thin air and dragged him upright; Hermione too had been pulled to her feet. Over the plunging, many-colored backs and heads of the centaurs Harry saw Umbridge being borne away through the trees by Bane, still screaming nonstop; her voice grew fainter and fainter until they could no longer hear it over the trampling of hooves surrounding them.

"And these?" said the hard-faced, gray centaur holding Hermione.

"They are young," said a slow, doleful voice from behind Harry. "We do not attack foals."

"They brought her here, Ronan," replied the centaur who had such a firm grip on Harry. "And they are not so young. . . . He is nearing manhood, this one. . . ."

He shook Harry by the neck of his robes.

"Please," said Hermione breathlessly, "please, don't attack us, we don't think like her, we aren't Ministry of Magic employees! We only came in here because we hoped you'd drive her off for us —"

Harry knew at once from the look on the face of the gray centaur holding Hermione that she had made a terrible mistake in saying this. The gray centaur threw back his head, his back legs stamping furiously, and bellowed, "You see, Ronan? They already have the arrogance of their kind! So we were to do your dirty work, were we, human girl? We were to act as your servants, drive away your enemies like obedient hounds?"

"No!" said Hermione in a horrorstruck squeak. "Please — I didn't mean that! I just hoped you'd be able to — to help us —"

But she seemed to be going from bad to worse.

"We do not help humans!" snarled the centaur holding Harry, tightening his grip and rearing a little at the same time, so that Harry's feet left the ground momentarily. "We are a race apart and proud to be so. . . . We will not permit you to walk from here, boasting that we did your bidding!"

"We're not going to say anything like that!" Harry shouted. "We know you didn't do anything because we wanted you to —"

But nobody seemed to be listening to him. A bearded centaur toward the back of the crowd shouted, "They came here unasked, they must pay the consequences!"

A roar of approval met these words and a dun-colored centaur shouted, "They can join the woman!"

"You said you didn't hurt the innocent!" shouted Hermione, real tears sliding down her face now. "We haven't done anything to hurt you, we haven't used wands or threats, we just want to go back to school, please let us go back —"

"We are not all like the traitor Firenze, human girl!" shouted the gray centaur, to more neighing roars of approval from his fellows. "Perhaps you thought us pretty talking horses? We are an ancient people who will not stand wizard invasions and insults! We do not recognize your laws, we do not acknowledge your superiority, we are —"

But they did not hear what else centaurs were, for at that moment there came a crashing noise on the edge of the clearing so loud that all of them — Harry, Hermione, and the fifty or so centaurs filling the clearing — looked around. Harry's centaur let him fall to the ground again as his hands flew to his bow and quiver of arrows; Hermione had been dropped too, and Harry hurried toward her as two thick tree trunks parted ominously and the monstrous form of Grawp the giant appeared in the gap.

The centaurs nearest him backed into those behind. The clearing was now a forest of bows and arrows waiting to be fired, all pointing upward at the enormous grayish face now looming over them from just beneath the thick canopy of branches. Grawp's lopsided mouth was gaping stupidly. They could see his bricklike yellow teeth glimmering in the half-light, his dull sludge-colored eyes narrowed as he squinted down at the creatures at his feet. Broken ropes trailed from both ankles.

He opened his mouth even wider.

"Hagger."

Harry did not know what "hagger" meant, or what language it was from, nor did he much care — he was watching Grawp's feet, which were almost as long as Harry's whole body. Hermione gripped his arm tightly; the centaurs were quite silent, staring up at the giant, whose huge, round head moved from side to side as he continued to peer amongst them as though looking for something he had dropped.

"*Hagger!*" he said again, more insistently.

"Get away from here, giant!" called Magorian. "You are not welcome among us!"

These words seemed to make no impression whatsoever on Grawp. He stooped a little (the centaurs' arms tensed on their bows) and then bellowed, "HAGGER!"

A few of the centaurs looked worried now. Hermione, however, gave a gasp.

"Harry!" she whispered. "I think he's trying to say 'Hagrid'!"

At this precise moment Grawp caught sight of them, the only two humans in a sea of centaurs. He lowered his head another foot or so, staring intently at them. Harry could feel Hermione shaking as Grawp opened his mouth wide again and said, in a deep, rumbling voice, "Hermy."

"Goodness," said Hermione, gripping Harry's arm so tightly it was growing numb and looking as though she was about to faint, "he — he remembered!"

"HERMY!" roared Grawp. "WHERE HAGGER?"

"I don't know!" squealed Hermione, terrified. "I'm sorry, Grawp, I don't know!"

"GRAWP WANT HAGGER!"

One of the giant's massive hands swooped down upon them — Hermione let out a real scream, ran a few steps backward and fell over. Wandless, Harry braced himself to punch, kick, bite, or whatever else it took as the hand flew toward him and knocked a snow-white centaur off his legs.

It was what the centaurs had been waiting for — Grawp's outstretched fingers were a foot from Harry when fifty arrows went soaring through the air at the giant, peppering his enormous face, causing him to howl with pain and rage and straighten up again, rubbing his face with his enormous hands, breaking off the arrow shafts but forcing the heads in still deeper.

He yelled and stamped his enormous feet and the centaurs scattered out of the way. Pebble-sized droplets of Grawp's blood showered Harry as he pulled Hermione to her feet and the pair of them ran as fast as they could for the shelter of the trees. Once there they looked back — Grawp was snatching blindly at the centaurs as blood ran all down his face; they were retreating in disorder, galloping away through the trees on the other side of the clearing. As Harry and Hermione watched, Grawp gave another roar of fury and plunged after them, smashing more trees aside as he went.

"Oh no," said Hermione, quaking so badly that her knees gave way. "Oh, that was horrible. And he might kill them all. . . ."

"I'm not that fussed, to be honest," said Harry bitterly.

The sounds of the galloping centaurs and the blundering giant were growing fainter and fainter. As Harry listened to them his scar gave another great throb and a wave of terror swept over him.

They had wasted so much time — they were even further from rescuing Sirius than they had been when he had had the vision. Not only had Harry managed to lose his wand but they were stuck in the middle of the Forbidden Forest with no means of transport whatsoever.

"Smart plan," he spat at Hermione, keen to release some of his fury. "Really smart plan. Where do we go from here?"

"We need to get back up to the castle," said Hermione faintly.

"By the time we've done that, Sirius'll probably be dead!" said Harry, kicking a nearby tree in temper; there was a high-pitched chattering overhead and he looked up to see an angry bowtruckle flexing its long twiglike fingers at him.

"Well, we can't do anything without wands," said Hermione hopelessly, dragging herself up again. "Anyway, Harry, how exactly were you planning to get all the way to London?"

"Yeah, we were just wondering that," said a familiar voice from behind her.

Harry and Hermione moved instinctively together, peering through the trees, as Ron came into sight, with Ginny, Neville, and Luna hurrying along behind him. All of them looked a little the worse for wear — there were several long scratches running the length of Ginny's cheek, a large purple lump was swelling above Neville's right eye, Ron's lip was bleeding worse than ever — but all were looking rather pleased with themselves.

"So," said Ron, pushing aside a low-hanging branch and holding out Harry's wand, "had any ideas?"

"How did you get away?" asked Harry in amazement, taking his wand from Ron.

"Couple of Stunners, a Disarming Charm, Neville brought off a really nice little Impediment Jinx," said Ron airily, now handing back Hermione's wand too. "But Ginny was best, she got Malfoy — Bat-Bogey Hex — it was superb, his whole face was covered in the great flapping things. Anyway, we saw you heading into the forest out of the window and followed. What've you done with Umbridge?"

"She got carried away," said Harry. "By a herd of centaurs."

"And they left you behind?" asked Ginny, looking astonished.

"No, they got chased off by Grawp," said Harry.

"Who's Grawp?" Luna asked interestedly.

"Hagrid's little brother," said Ron promptly. "Anyway, never mind that now. Harry, what did you find out in the fire? Has You-Know-Who got Sirius or — ?"

"Yes," said Harry, as his scar gave another painful prickle, "and I'm sure Sirius is still alive, but I can't see how we're going to get there to help him."

They all fell silent, looking rather scared. The problem facing them seemed insurmountable.

"Well, we'll have to fly, won't we?" said Luna in the closest thing to a matter-of-fact voice Harry had ever heard her use.

"Okay," said Harry irritably, rounding on her, "first of all, 'we' aren't doing anything if you're including yourself in that, and second of all, Ron's the only one with a broomstick that isn't being guarded by a security troll, so —"

"I've got a broom!" said Ginny.

"Yeah, but you're not coming," said Ron angrily.

"Excuse me, but I care what happens to Sirius as much as you do!" said Ginny, her jaw set so that her resemblance to Fred and George was suddenly striking.

"You're too —" Harry began.

"I'm three years older than you were when you fought You-Know-Who over the Sorcerer's Stone," she said fiercely, "and it's because of me Malfoy's stuck back in Umbridge's office with giant flying bogeys attacking him —"

"Yeah, but —"

"We were all in the D.A. together," said Neville quietly. "It was all supposed to be about fighting You-Know-Who, wasn't it? And this is the first chance we've had to do something real — or was that all just a game or something?"

"No — of course it wasn't —" said Harry impatiently.

"Then we should come too," said Neville simply. "We want to help."

"That's right," said Luna, smiling happily.

Harry's eyes met Ron's. He knew that Ron was thinking exactly what he was: If he could have chosen any members of the D.A. in addition to himself, Ron, and Hermione to join him in the attempt to rescue Sirius, he would not have picked Ginny, Neville, or Luna.

"Well, it doesn't matter anyway," said Harry frustratedly, "because we still don't know how to get there —"

"I thought we'd settled that?" said Luna maddeningly. "We're flying!"

"Look," said Ron, barely containing his anger, "you might be able to fly without a broomstick but the rest of us can't sprout wings whenever we —"

"There are other ways of flying than with broomsticks," said Luna serenely.

"I s'pose we're going to ride on the back of the Kacky Snorgle or whatever it is?" Ron demanded.

"The Crumple-Horned Snorkack can't fly," said Luna in a dignified voice, "but *they* can, and Hagrid says they're very good at finding places their riders are looking for."

Harry whirled around. Standing between two trees, their white eyes gleaming eerily, were two thestrals, watching the whispered conversation as though they understood every word.

"Yes!" he whispered, moving toward them. They tossed their reptilian heads, throwing back long black manes, and Harry stretched out his hand eagerly and patted the nearest one's shining neck. How could he ever have thought them ugly?

"Is it those mad horse things?" said Ron uncertainly, staring at a point slightly to the left of the thestral Harry was patting. "Those ones you can't see unless you've watched someone snuff it?"

"Yeah," said Harry.

"How many?"

"Just two."

"Well, we need three," said Hermione, who was still looking a little shaken, but determined just the same.

"Four, Hermione," said Ginny, scowling.

"I think there are six of us, actually," said Luna calmly, counting.

"Don't be stupid, we can't all go!" said Harry angrily. "Look, you three" — he pointed at Neville, Ginny, and Luna — "you're not involved in this, you're not —"

They burst into more protests. His scar gave another, more painful, twinge. Every moment they delayed was precious; he did not have time to argue.

"Okay, fine, it's your choice," he said curtly. "But unless we can find more thestrals you're not going to be able —"

"Oh, more of them will come," said Ginny confidently, who like Ron was squinting in quite the wrong direction, apparently under the impression that she was looking at the horses.

"What makes you think that?"

"Because in case you hadn't noticed, you and Hermione are both covered in blood," she said coolly, "and we know Hagrid lures thestrals with raw meat, so that's probably why these two turned up in the first place. . . ."

Harry felt a soft tug on his robes at that moment and looked down to see the closest thestral licking his sleeve, which was damp with Grawp's blood.

"Okay, then," he said, a bright idea occurring. "Ron and I will take these two and go ahead, and Hermione can stay here with you three and she'll attract more thestrals —"

"I'm not staying behind!" said Hermione furiously.

"There's no need," said Luna, smiling. "Look, here come more now. . . . You two must really smell. . . ."

Harry turned. No fewer than six or seven thestrals were picking their way through the trees now, their great leathery wings folded tight to their bodies, their eyes gleaming through the darkness. He had no excuse now. . . .

"All right," he said angrily, "pick one and get on, then."

THE DEPARTMENT
OF MYSTERIES

H arry wound his hand tightly into the mane of the nearest thestral, placed a foot on a stump nearby and scrambled clumsily onto the horse's silken back. It did not object, but twisted its head around, fangs bared, and attempted to continue its eager licking of his robes.

He found there was a way of lodging his knees behind the wing joints that made him feel more secure and looked around at the others. Neville had heaved himself over the back of the next thestral and was now attempting to swing one short leg over the creature's back. Luna was already in place, sitting sidesaddle and adjusting her robes as though she did this every day. Ron, Hermione, and Ginny, however, were still standing motionless on the spot, openmouthed and staring.

"What?" he said.

"How're we supposed to get on?" said Ron faintly. "When we can't see the things?"

"Oh it's easy," said Luna, sliding obligingly from her thestral and marching over to him, Hermione, and Ginny. "Come here. . . ."

She pulled them over to the other thestrals standing around and
one by one managed to help them onto the backs of their mounts.
All three looked extremely nervous as she wound their hands into the
horses' manes and told them to grip tightly before getting back onto
her own steed.

"This is mad," Ron said faintly, moving his free hand gingerly up
and down his horse's neck. "Mad . . . if I could just see it —"

"You'd better hope it stays invisible," said Harry darkly. "We all
ready, then?"

They all nodded and he saw five pairs of knees tighten beneath
their robes.

"Okay . . ."

He looked down at the back of his thestral's glossy black head and
swallowed. "Ministry of Magic, visitors' entrance, London, then," he
said uncertainly. "Er . . . if you know . . . where to go . . ."

For a moment his thestral did nothing at all. Then, with a sweeping movement that nearly unseated him, the wings on either side extended, the horse crouched slowly and then rocketed upward so fast
and so steeply that Harry had to clench his arms and legs tightly
around the horse to avoid sliding backward over its bony rump. He
closed his eyes and put his face down into the horse's silky mane as
they burst through the topmost branches of the trees and soared out
into a bloodred sunset.

Harry did not think he had ever moved so fast: The thestral
streaked over the castle, its wide wings hardly beating. The cooling air
was slapping Harry's face; eyes screwed up against the rushing wind,
he looked around and saw his five fellows soaring along behind him,
each of them bent as low as possible into the neck of their thestral to
protect themselves from its slipstream.

They were over the Hogwarts grounds, they had passed Hogsmeade. Harry could see mountains and gullies below them. In the

falling darkness Harry saw small collections of lights as they passed over more villages, then a winding road on which a single car was beetling its way home through the hills. . . .

"This is bizarre!" Harry heard Ron yell from somewhere behind him, and he imagined how it must feel to be speeding along at this height with no visible means of support. . . .

Twilight fell: The sky turned to a light, dusky purple littered with tiny silver stars, and soon it was only the lights of Muggle towns that gave them any clue of how far from the ground they were or how very fast they were traveling. Harry's arms were wrapped tightly around his horse's neck as he willed it to go even faster. How much time had elapsed since he had seen Sirius lying on the Department of Mysteries floor? How much longer would he be able to resist Voldemort? All Harry knew for sure was that Sirius had neither done as Voldemort wanted, nor died, for he was convinced that either outcome would cause him to feel Voldemort's jubilation or fury course through his own body, making his scar sear as painfully as it had on the night Mr. Weasley was attacked. . . .

On they flew through the gathering darkness; Harry's face felt stiff and cold, his legs numb from gripping the thestral's sides so tightly, but he did not dare shift positions lest he slip. . . . He was deaf from the thundering in his ears and his mouth was dry and frozen from the rush of cold night air. He had lost all sense of how far they had come; all his faith was in the beast below him, still streaking purposefully through the night, barely flapping its wings as it sped ever onward. . . .

If they were too late . . .

He's still alive, he's still fighting, I can feel it. . . .

If Voldemort decided Sirius was not going to crack . . .

I'd know. . . .

Harry's stomach gave a jolt. The thestral's head was suddenly pointing toward the ground and he had actually slid forward a few inches along its neck. They were descending at last. . . . He heard one of the girls shriek behind him and twisted around dangerously but could see no sign of a falling body. . . . Presumably they had received a shock from the change of position, just as he had. . . .

And now bright orange lights were growing larger and rounder on all sides. They could see the tops of buildings, streams of headlights like luminous insect eyes, squares of pale yellow that were windows. Quite suddenly, it seemed, they were hurtling toward the pavement. Harry gripped the thestral with every last ounce of his strength, braced for a sudden impact, but the horse touched the dark ground as lightly as a shadow and Harry slid from his back, looking around at the street where the overflowing dumpster still stood a short way from the vandalized telephone box, both drained of color in the flat orange glare of the streetlights.

Ron landed a short way away and toppled immediately off his thestral onto the pavement.

"Never again," he said, struggling to his feet. He made as though to stride away from his thestral, but, unable to see it, collided with its hindquarters and almost fell over again. "Never, ever again . . . that was the worst —"

Hermione and Ginny touched down on either side of him. Both slid off their mounts a little more gracefully than Ron, though with similar expressions of relief at being back on firm ground. Neville jumped down, shaking, but Luna dismounted smoothly.

"Where do we go from here, then?" she asked Harry in a politely interested voice, as though this was all a rather interesting day-trip.

"Over here," he said. He gave his thestral a quick, grateful pat, then led the way quickly to the battered telephone box and opened the door. "Come *on!*" he urged the others as they hesitated.

Ron and Ginny marched in obediently; Hermione, Neville, and Luna squashed themselves in after them; Harry took one glance back at the thestrals, now foraging for scraps of rotten food inside the dumpster, then forced himself into the box after Luna.

"Whoever's nearest the receiver, dial six two four four two!" he said.

Ron did it, his arm bent bizarrely to reach the dial. As it whirred back into place the cool female voice sounded inside the box, "Welcome to the Ministry of Magic. Please state your name and business."

"Harry Potter, Ron Weasley, Hermione Granger," Harry said very quickly, "Ginny Weasley, Neville Longbottom, Luna Lovegood . . . We're here to save someone, unless your Ministry can do it first!"

"Thank you," said the cool female voice. "Visitors, please take the badges and attach them to the front of your robes."

Half a dozen badges slid out of the metal chute where returned coins usually appeared. Hermione scooped them up and handed them mutely to Harry over Ginny's head; he glanced at the topmost one.

HARRY POTTER
RESCUE MISSION

"Visitor to the Ministry, you are required to submit to a search and present your wand for registration at the security desk, which is located at the far end of the Atrium."

"Fine!" Harry said loudly, as his scar gave another throb. "Now can we *move*?"

The floor of the telephone box shuddered and the pavement rose up past the glass windows of the telephone box. The scavenging thestrals were sliding out of sight, blackness closed over their heads, and with a dull grinding noise they sank down into the depths of the Ministry of Magic.

A chink of soft golden light hit their feet and, widening, rose up their bodies. Harry bent his knees and held his wand as ready as he could in such cramped conditions, peering through the glass to see whether anybody was waiting for them in the Atrium, but it seemed to be completely empty. The light was dimmer than it had been by day. There were no fires burning under the mantelpieces set into the walls, but he saw as the lift slid smoothly to a halt that golden symbols continued to twist sinuously in the dark blue ceiling.

"The Ministry of Magic wishes you a pleasant evening," said the woman's voice.

The door of the telephone box burst open; Harry toppled out of it, followed by Neville and Luna. The only sound in the Atrium was the steady rush of water from the golden fountain, where jets from the wands of the witch and wizard, the point of the centaur's arrow, the tip of the goblin's hat, and the house-elf's ears continued to gush into the surrounding pool.

"Come on," said Harry quietly and the six of them sprinted off down the hall, Harry in the lead, past the fountain, toward the desk where the security man who had weighed Harry's wand had sat and which was now deserted.

Harry felt sure that there ought to be a security person there, sure that their absence was an ominous sign, and his feeling of foreboding increased as they passed through the golden gates to the lifts. He pressed the nearest down button and a lift clattered into sight almost immediately, the golden grilles slid apart with a great, echoing clanking, and they dashed inside. Harry stabbed the number nine button, the grilles closed with a bang, and the lift began to descend, jangling and rattling. Harry had not realized how noisy the lifts were on the day that he had come with Mr. Weasley — he was sure that the din would raise every security person within the building, yet when the lift halted, the cool female voice said, "Department of Mysteries," and the grilles slid open again, they stepped out into the corridor where nothing was moving but the nearest torches, flickering in the rush of air from the lift.

Harry turned toward the plain black door. After months and months of dreaming about it, he was here at last. . . .

"Let's go," he whispered, and he led the way down the corridor, Luna right behind him, gazing around with her mouth slightly open.

"Okay, listen," said Harry, stopping again within six feet of the door. "Maybe . . . maybe a couple of people should stay here as a — as a lookout, and —"

"And how're we going to let you know something's coming?" asked Ginny, her eyebrows raised. "You could be miles away."

"We're coming with you, Harry," said Neville.

"Let's get on with it," said Ron firmly.

Harry still did not want to take them all with him, but it seemed he had no choice. He turned to face the door and walked forward. Just as it had in his dream, it swung open and he marched forward, leading the others over the threshold.

They were standing in a large, circular room. Everything in here was black including the floor and ceiling — identical, unmarked, handle-less black doors were set at intervals all around the black walls, interspersed with branches of candles whose flames burned blue, their cool, shimmering light reflected in the shining marble floor so that it looked as though there was dark water underfoot.

"Someone shut the door," Harry muttered.

He regretted giving this order the moment Neville had obeyed it. Without the long chink of light from the torch-lit corridor behind them, the place became so dark that for a moment the only things they could see were the bunches of shivering blue flames on the walls and their ghostly reflections in the floor below.

In his dream, Harry had always walked purposefully across this room to the door immediately opposite the entrance and walked on. But there were around a dozen doors here. Just as he was gazing ahead at the doors opposite him, trying to decide which was the right one, there was a great rumbling noise and the candles began to move side-ways. The circular wall was rotating.

Hermione grabbed Harry's arm as though frightened the floor might move too, but it did not. For a few seconds the blue flames around them were blurred to resemble neon lines as the wall sped around and then, quite as suddenly as it had started, the rumbling stopped and everything became stationary once again.

Harry's eyes had blue streaks burned into them; it was all he could see.

"What was that about?" whispered Ron fearfully.

"I think it was to stop us knowing which door we came in from," said Ginny in a hushed voice.

Harry realized at once that she was right: He could no sooner have picked the exit from the other doors than located an ant upon the jet-black floor. Meanwhile, the door through which they needed to proceed could be any of the dozen surrounding them.

"How're we going to get back out?" said Neville uncomfortably.

"Well, that doesn't matter now," said Harry forcefully, blinking to try and erase the blue lines from his vision, and clutching his wand tighter than ever. "We won't need to get out till we've found Sirius —"

"Don't go calling for him, though!" Hermione said urgently, but Harry had never needed her advice less; his instinct was to keep as quiet as possible for the time being.

"Where do we go, then, Harry?" Ron asked.

"I don't —" Harry began. He swallowed. "In the dreams I went through the door at the end of the corridor from the lifts into a dark room — that's this one — and then I went through another door into a room that kind of . . . glitters. We should try a few doors," he said hastily. "I'll know the right way when I see it. C'mon."

He marched straight at the door now facing him, the others following close behind him, set his left hand against its cool, shining surface, raised his wand, ready to strike the moment it opened, and pushed. It swung open easily.

After the darkness of the first room, the lamps hanging low on golden chains from this ceiling gave the impression that this long rectangular room was much brighter, though there were no glittering, shimmering lights such as Harry had seen in his dreams. The place was quite empty except for a few desks and, in the very middle of the room, an enormous glass tank of deep-green water, big enough for all of them to swim in, which contained a number of pearly white objects that were drifting around lazily in the liquid.

"What're those things?" whispered Ron.

"Dunno," said Harry.

"Are they fish?" breathed Ginny.

"Aquavirius maggots!" said Luna excitedly. "Dad said the Ministry were breeding —"

"No," said Hermione. She sounded odd. She moved forward to look through the side of the tank. "They're brains."

"Brains?"

"Yes . . . I wonder what they're doing with them?"

Harry joined her at the tank. Sure enough, there could be no mistake now that he saw them at close quarters. Glimmering eerily they drifted in and out of sight in the depths of the green water, looking something like slimy cauliflowers.

"Let's get out of here," said Harry. "This isn't right, we need to try another door —"

"There are doors here too," said Ron, pointing around the walls. Harry's heart sank; how big was this place?

"In my dream I went through that dark room into the second one," he said. "I think we should go back and try from there."

So they hurried back into the dark, circular room; the ghostly shapes of the brains were now swimming before Harry's eyes instead of the blue candle flames.

"Wait!" said Hermione sharply, as Luna made to close the door of the brain room behind them. *"Flagrate!"*

She drew with her wand in midair and a fiery X appeared on the door. No sooner had the door clicked shut behind them than there was a great rumbling, and once again the wall began to revolve very fast, but now there was a great red-gold blur in amongst the faint blue, and when all became still again, the fiery cross still burned, showing the door they had already tried.

"Good thinking," said Harry. "Okay, let's try this one —"

Again he strode directly at the door facing him and pushed it open, his wand still raised, the others at his heels.

This room was larger than the last, dimly lit and rectangular, and the center of it was sunken, forming a great stone pit some twenty feet below them. They were standing on the topmost tier of what seemed to be stone benches running all around the room and descending in steep steps like an amphitheater, or the courtroom in which Harry had been tried by the Wizengamot. Instead of a chained chair, however, there was a raised stone dais in the center of the lowered floor, and upon this dais stood a stone archway that looked so ancient, cracked, and crumbling that Harry was amazed the thing was still standing. Unsupported by any surrounding wall, the archway was hung with a tattered black curtain or veil which, despite the complete stillness of the cold surrounding air, was fluttering very slightly as though it had just been touched.

"Who's there?" said Harry, jumping down onto the bench below. There was no answering voice, but the veil continued to flutter and sway.

"Careful!" whispered Hermione.

Harry scrambled down the benches one by one until he reached the stone bottom of the sunken pit. His footsteps echoed loudly as he walked slowly toward the dais. The pointed archway looked much taller from where he stood now than when he had been looking down on it from above. Still the veil swayed gently, as though somebody had just passed through it.

"Sirius?" Harry spoke again, but much more quietly now that he was nearer.

He had the strangest feeling that there was someone standing right behind the veil on the other side of the archway. Gripping his wand very tightly, he edged around the dais, but there was nobody there. All that could be seen was the other side of the tattered black veil.

"Let's go," called Hermione from halfway up the stone steps. "This isn't right, Harry, come on, let's go. . . ."

She sounded scared, much more scared than she had in the room where the brains swam, yet Harry thought the archway had a kind of beauty about it, old though it was. The gently rippling veil intrigued him; he felt a very strong inclination to climb up on the dais and walk through it.

"Harry, let's go, okay?" said Hermione more forcefully.

"Okay," he said, but he did not move. He had just heard something. There were faint whispering, murmuring noises coming from the other side of the veil.

"What are you saying?" he said very loudly, so that the words echoed all around the surrounding stone benches.

"Nobody's talking, Harry!" said Hermione, now moving over to him.

"Someone's whispering behind there," he said, moving out of her reach and continuing to frown at the veil. "Is that you, Ron?"

"I'm here, mate," said Ron, appearing around the side of the archway.

"Can't anyone else hear it?" Harry demanded, for the whispering and murmuring was becoming louder; without really meaning to put it there, he found his foot was on the dais.

"I can hear them too," breathed Luna, joining them around the side of the archway and gazing at the swaying veil. "There are people *in there*!"

"What do you mean, '*in there*'?" demanded Hermione, jumping down from the bottom step and sounding much angrier than the occasion warranted. "There isn't any '*in there*,' it's just an archway, there's no room for anybody to be there — Harry, stop it, come away —"

She grabbed his arm and pulled, but he resisted.

"Harry, we are supposed to be here for Sirius!" she said in a high-pitched, strained voice.

"Sirius," Harry repeated, still gazing, mesmerized, at the continuously swaying veil. "Yeah . . ."

And then something slid back into place in his brain: Sirius, captured, bound, and tortured, and he was staring at this archway. . . .

He took several paces back from the dais and wrenched his eyes from the veil.

"Let's go," he said.

"That's what I've been trying to — well, come on, then!" said Hermione, and she led the way back around the dais. On the other side, Ginny and Neville were staring, apparently entranced, at the veil too. Without speaking, Hermione took hold of Ginny's arm, Ron Neville's, and they marched them firmly back to the lowest stone bench and clambered all the way back up to the door.

"What d'you reckon that arch was?" Harry asked Hermione as they regained the dark circular room.

"I don't know, but whatever it was, it was dangerous," she said firmly, again inscribing a fiery cross upon the door.

Once more the wall spun and became still again. Harry approached a door at random and pushed. It did not move.

"What's wrong?" said Hermione.

"It's . . . locked . . ." said Harry, throwing his weight at the door, but it did not budge.

"This is it, then, isn't it?" said Ron excitedly, joining Harry in the attempt to force the door open. "Bound to be!"

"Get out of the way!" said Hermione sharply. She pointed her wand at the place where a lock would have been on an ordinary door and said, *"Alohomora!"*

Nothing happened.

"Sirius's knife!" said Harry, and he pulled it out from inside his robes and slid it into the crack between the door and the wall. The others all watched eagerly as he ran it from top to bottom, withdrew it, and then flung his shoulder again at the door. It remained as firmly shut as ever. What was more, when Harry looked down at the knife, he saw that the blade had melted.

"Right, we're leaving that room," said Hermione decisively.

"But what if that's the one?" said Ron, staring at it with a mixture of apprehension and longing.

"It can't be, Harry could get through all the doors in his dream," said Hermione, marking the door with another fiery cross as Harry replaced the now-useless handle of Sirius's knife in his pocket.

"You know what could be in there?" said Luna eagerly, as the wall started to spin yet again.

"Something blibbering, no doubt," said Hermione under her breath, and Neville gave a nervous little laugh.

The wall slid back to a halt and Harry, with a feeling of increasing desperation, pushed the next door open.

"*This is it!*"

He knew it at once by the beautiful, dancing, diamond-sparkling light. As Harry's eyes became more accustomed to the brilliant glare he saw clocks gleaming from every surface, large and small, grandfather and carriage, hanging in spaces between the bookcases or standing on desks ranging the length of the room, so that a busy, relentless ticking filled the place like thousands of minuscule, marching footsteps. The source of the dancing, diamond-bright light was a towering crystal bell jar that stood at the far end of the room.

"This way!"

Harry's heart was pumping frantically now that he knew they were on the right track. He led the way forward down the narrow space between the lines of the desks, heading, as he had done in his dream, for the source of the light, the crystal bell jar quite as tall as he was that stood on a desk and appeared to be full of a billowing, glittering wind.

"Oh *look!*" said Ginny, as they drew nearer, pointing at the very heart of the bell jar.

Drifting along in the sparkling current inside was a tiny, jewel-bright egg. As it rose in the jar it cracked open and a hummingbird emerged, which was carried to the very top of the jar, but as it fell on the draft, its feathers became bedraggled and damp again, and by the time it had been borne back to the bottom of the jar it had been enclosed once more in its egg.

"Keep going!" said Harry sharply, because Ginny showed signs of wanting to stop and watch the egg's progress back into a bird.

"You dawdled enough by that old arch!" she said crossly, but followed him past the bell jar to the only door behind it.

"This is it," Harry said again, and his heart was now pumping so hard and fast he felt it must interfere with his speech. "It's through here —"

He glanced around at them all. They had their wands out and looked suddenly serious and anxious. He looked back at the door and pushed. It swung open.

They were there, they had found the place: high as a church and full of nothing but towering shelves covered in small, dusty, glass orbs. They glimmered dully in the light issuing from more candle brackets set at intervals along the shelves. Like those in the circular room behind them, their flames were burning blue. The room was very cold.

Harry edged forward and peered down one of the shadowy aisles between two rows of shelves. He could not hear anything nor see the slightest sign of movement.

"You said it was row ninety-seven," whispered Hermione.

"Yeah," breathed Harry, looking up at the end of the closest row. Beneath the branch of blue-glowing candles protruding from it glimmered the silver figure 53.

"We need to go right, I think," whispered Hermione, squinting to the next row. "Yes . . . that's fifty-four. . . ."

"Keep your wands out," Harry said softly.

They crept forward, staring behind them as they went on down the long alleys of shelves, the farther ends of which were in near total darkness. Tiny, yellowing labels had been stuck beneath each glass orb on the shelf. Some of them had a weird, liquid glow; others were as dull and dark within as blown lightbulbs.

They passed row eighty-four . . . eighty-five . . . Harry was listening hard for the slightest sound of movement, but Sirius might be gagged now, or else unconscious . . . *or,* said an unbidden voice inside his head, *he might already be dead. . . .*

I'd have felt it, he told himself, his heart now hammering against his Adam's apple. *I'd already know. . . .*

"Ninety-seven!" whispered Hermione.

They stood grouped around the end of the row, gazing down the alley beside it. There was nobody there.

"He's right down at the end," said Harry, whose mouth had become slightly dry. "You can't see properly from here. . . ."

And he led them forward, between the towering rows of glass balls, some of which glowed softly as they passed. . . .

"He should be near here," whispered Harry, convinced that every step was going to bring the ragged form of Sirius into view upon the darkened floor. "Anywhere here . . . really close . . ."

"Harry?" said Hermione tentatively, but he did not want to respond. His mouth was very dry now.

"Somewhere about . . . here . . ." he said.

They had reached the end of the row and emerged into more dim candlelight. There was nobody there at all. All was echoing, dusty silence.

"He might be . . ." Harry whispered hoarsely, peering down the alley next door. "Or maybe . . ." He hurried to look down the one beyond that.

"Harry?" said Hermione again.

"What?" he snarled.

"I . . . I don't think Sirius is here."

Nobody spoke. Harry did not want to look at any of them. He felt sick. He did not understand why Sirius was not here. He had to be here. This was where he, Harry, had seen him. . . .

He ran up the space at the end of the rows, staring down them. Empty aisle after empty aisle flickered past. He ran the other way, back past his staring companions. There was no sign of Sirius anywhere, nor any hint of a struggle.

"Harry?" Ron called.

"What?"

He did not want to hear what Ron had to say, did not want to hear Ron tell him he had been stupid, or suggest that they ought to go back to Hogwarts. But the heat was rising in his face and he felt as though he would like to skulk down here in the darkness for a long while before facing the brightness of the Atrium above and the others' accusing stares. . . .

"Have you seen this?" said Ron.

"What?" said Harry, but eagerly this time — it had to be a sign that Sirius had been there, a clue — he strode back to where they were all standing, a little way down row ninety-seven, but found nothing except Ron staring at one of the dusty glass spheres on the shelves.

"What?" Harry repeated glumly.

"It's — it's got your name on," said Ron.

Harry moved a little closer. Ron was pointing at one of the small glass spheres that glowed with a dull inner light, though it was very dusty and appeared not to have been touched for many years.

"My name?" said Harry blankly.

He stepped forward. Not as tall as Ron, he had to crane his neck to read the yellowish label affixed to the shelf right beneath the dusty glass ball. In spidery writing was written a date of some sixteen years previously, and below that:

S. P. T. to A. P. W. B. D.

Dark Lord

and (?) Harry Potter

Harry stared at it.

"What is it?" Ron asked, sounding unnerved. "What's your name doing down here?"

He glanced along at the other labels on that stretch of shelf.

"I'm not here," he said, sounding perplexed. "None of the rest of us are here. . . ."

"Harry, I don't think you should touch it," said Hermione sharply, as he stretched out his hand.

"Why not?" he said. "It's something to do with me, isn't it?"

"Don't, Harry," said Neville suddenly. Harry looked around at him. Neville's round face was shining slightly with sweat. He looked as though he could not take much more suspense.

"It's got my name on," said Harry.

And feeling slightly reckless, he closed his fingers around the dusty ball's surface. He had expected it to feel cold, but it did not. On the contrary, it felt as though it had been lying in the sun for hours, as though the glow of light within was warming it. Expecting, even hoping, that something dramatic was going to happen, something exciting that might make their long and dangerous journey worthwhile after all, he lifted the glass ball down from its shelf and stared at it.

Nothing whatsoever happened. The others moved in closer around Harry, gazing at the orb as he brushed it free of the clogging dust.

And then, from right behind them, a drawling voice said, "Very good, Potter. Now turn around, nice and slowly, and give that to me."

BEYOND THE VEIL

Black shapes were emerging out of thin air all around them, blocking their way left and right; eyes glinted through slits in hoods, a dozen lit wand-tips were pointing directly at their hearts. Ginny gave a gasp of horror.

"To me, Potter," repeated the drawling voice of Lucius Malfoy as he held out his hand, palm up.

Harry's insides plummeted sickeningly. They were trapped and outnumbered two to one.

"To me," said Malfoy yet again.

"Where's Sirius?" Harry said.

Several of the Death Eaters laughed. A harsh female voice from the midst of the shadowy figures to Harry's left said triumphantly, "The Dark Lord always knows!"

"Always," echoed Malfoy softly. "Now, give me the prophecy, Potter."

"I want to know where Sirius is!"

"I want to know where Sirius is!" mimicked the woman to his left. She and her fellow Death Eaters had closed in so that they were

mere feet away from Harry and the others, the light from their wands dazzling Harry's eyes.

"You've got him," said Harry, ignoring the rising panic in his chest, the dread he had been fighting since they had first entered the ninety-seventh row. "He's here. I know he is."

"The little baby woke up fwightened and fort what it dweamed was twoo," said the woman in a horrible, mock-baby voice. Harry felt Ron stir beside him.

"Don't do anything," he muttered. "Not yet —"

The woman who had mimicked him let out a raucous scream of laughter.

"You hear him? *You hear him?* Giving instructions to the other children as though he thinks of fighting us!"

"Oh, you don't know Potter as I do, Bellatrix," said Malfoy softly. "He has a great weakness for heroics; the Dark Lord understands this about him. *Now give me the prophecy, Potter.*"

"I know Sirius is here," said Harry, though panic was causing his chest to constrict and he felt as though he could not breathe properly. *"I know you've got him!"*

More of the Death Eaters laughed, though the woman still laughed loudest of all.

"It's time you learned the difference between life and dreams, Potter," said Malfoy. "Now give me the prophecy, or we start using wands."

"Go on, then," said Harry, raising his own wand to chest height. As he did so, the five wands of Ron, Hermione, Neville, Ginny, and Luna rose on either side of him. The knot in Harry's stomach tightened. If Sirius really was not here, he had led his friends to their deaths for no reason at all. . . .

But the Death Eaters did not strike.

"Hand over the prophecy and no one need get hurt," said Malfoy coolly.

It was Harry's turn to laugh.

"Yeah, right!" he said. "I give you this — prophecy, is it? And you'll just let us skip off home, will you?"

The words were hardly out of his mouth when the female Death Eater shrieked, *"Accio Proph —"*

Harry was just ready for her. He shouted *"Protego!"* before she had finished her spell, and though the glass sphere slipped to the tips of his fingers he managed to cling on to it.

"Oh, he knows how to play, little bitty baby Potter," she said, her mad eyes staring through the slits in her hood. "Very well, then —"

"I TOLD YOU, NO!" Lucius Malfoy roared at the woman. "If you smash it — !"

Harry's mind was racing. The Death Eaters wanted this dusty spun-glass sphere. He had no interest in it. He just wanted to get them all out of this alive, make sure that none of his friends paid a terrible price for his stupidity . . .

The woman stepped forward, away from her fellows, and pulled off her hood. Azkaban had hollowed Bellatrix Lestrange's face, making it gaunt and skull-like, but it was alive with a feverish, fanatical glow.

"You need more persuasion?" she said, her chest rising and falling rapidly. "Very well — take the smallest one," she ordered the Death Eaters beside her. "Let him watch while we torture the little girl. I'll do it."

Harry felt the others close in around Ginny. He stepped sideways so that he was right in front of her, the prophecy held up to his chest.

"You'll have to smash this if you want to attack any of us," he told Bellatrix. "I don't think your boss will be too pleased if you come back without it, will he?"

She did not move; she merely stared at him, the tip of her tongue moistening her thin mouth.

"So," said Harry, "what kind of prophecy are we talking about anyway?"

He could not think what to do but to keep talking. Neville's arm was pressed against his, and he could feel him shaking. He could feel one of the other's quickened breath on the back of his head. He was hoping they were all thinking hard about ways to get out of this, because his mind was blank.

"What kind of prophecy?" repeated Bellatrix, the grin fading from her face. "You jest, Harry Potter."

"Nope, not jesting," said Harry, his eyes flicking from Death Eater to Death Eater, looking for a weak link, a space through which they could escape. "How come Voldemort wants it?"

Several of the Death Eaters let out low hisses.

"You dare speak his name?" whispered Bellatrix.

"Yeah," said Harry, maintaining his tight grip on the glass ball, expecting another attempt to bewitch it from him. "Yeah, I've got no problem saying Vol —"

"Shut your mouth!" Bellatrix shrieked. "You dare speak his name with your unworthy lips, you dare besmirch it with your half-blood's tongue, you dare —"

"Did you know he's a half-blood too?" said Harry recklessly. Hermione gave a little moan in his ear. "Voldemort? Yeah, his mother was a witch but his dad was a Muggle — or has he been telling you lot he's pureblood?"

"*STUPEF —*"

"*NO!*"

A jet of red light had shot from the end of Bellatrix Lestrange's wand, but Malfoy had deflected it. His spell caused hers to hit the shelf a foot to the left of Harry and several of the glass orbs there shattered.

Two figures, pearly white as ghosts, fluid as smoke, unfurled themselves from the fragments of broken glass upon the floor and each began to speak. Their voices vied with each other, so that only fragments of what they were saying could be heard over Malfoy and Bellatrix's shouts.

"*. . . at the Solstice will come a new . . .*" said the figure of an old, bearded man.

"DO NOT ATTACK! WE NEED THE PROPHECY!"

"He dared — he dares —" shrieked Bellatrix incoherently. "— He stands there — filthy half-blood —"

"WAIT UNTIL WE'VE GOT THE PROPHECY!" bawled Malfoy.

"*. . . and none will come after . . .*" said the figure of a young woman.

The two figures that had burst from the shattered spheres had melted into thin air. Nothing remained of them or their erstwhile homes but fragments of glass upon the floor. They had, however, given Harry an idea. The problem was going to be conveying it to the others.

"You haven't told me what's so special about this prophecy I'm supposed to be handing over," he said, playing for time. He moved his foot slowly sideways, feeling around for someone else's.

"Do not play games with us, Potter," said Malfoy.

"I'm not playing games," said Harry, half his mind on the conversation, half on his wandering foot. And then he found someone's toes and pressed down upon them. A sharp intake of breath behind him told him they were Hermione's.

"What?" she whispered.

"Dumbledore never told you that the reason you bear that scar was hidden in the bowels of the Department of Mysteries?" said Malfoy sneeringly.

"I — what?" said Harry, and for a moment he quite forgot his plan. "What about my scar?"

"*What?*" whispered Hermione more urgently behind him.

"Can this be?" said Malfoy, sounding maliciously delighted; some of the Death Eaters were laughing again, and under cover of their laughter, Harry hissed to Hermione, moving his lips as little as possible, "Smash shelves —"

"Dumbledore never told you?" Malfoy repeated. "Well, this explains why you didn't come earlier, Potter, the Dark Lord wondered why —"

"— when I say go —"

"— you didn't come running when he showed you the place where it was hidden in your dreams. He thought natural curiosity would make you want to hear the exact wording. . . ."

"Did he?" said Harry. Behind him he felt rather than heard Hermione passing his message to the others and he sought to keep talking, to distract the Death Eaters. "So he wanted me to come and get it, did he? Why?"

"*Why?*" Malfoy sounded incredulously delighted. "Because the only people who are permitted to retrieve a prophecy from the Department of Mysteries, Potter, are those about whom it was made, as the Dark Lord discovered when he attempted to use others to steal it for him."

"And why did he want to steal a prophecy about me?"

"About both of you, Potter, about both of you . . . Haven't you ever wondered why the Dark Lord tried to kill you as a baby?"

Harry stared into the slitted eyeholes through which Malfoy's gray eyes were gleaming. Was this prophecy the reason Harry's parents had died, the reason he carried his lightning-bolt scar? Was the answer to all of this clutched in his hand?

"Someone made a prophecy about Voldemort and me?" he said quietly, gazing at Lucius Malfoy, his fingers tightening over the warm glass sphere in his hand. It was hardly larger than a Snitch and still gritty with dust. "And he's made me come and get it for him? Why couldn't he come and get it himself?"

"Get it himself?" shrieked Bellatrix on a cackle of mad laughter.

"The Dark Lord, walk into the Ministry of Magic, when they are so sweetly ignoring his return? The Dark Lord, reveal himself to the Aurors, when at the moment they are wasting their time on my dear cousin?"

"So he's got you doing his dirty work for him, has he?" said Harry. "Like he tried to get Sturgis to steal it — and Bode?"

"Very good, Potter, very good . . ." said Malfoy slowly. "But the Dark Lord knows you are not unintell —"

"NOW!" yelled Harry.

Five different voices behind him bellowed *"REDUCTO!"* Five curses flew in five different directions and the shelves opposite them exploded as they hit. The towering structure swayed as a hundred glass spheres burst apart, pearly-white figures unfurled into the air and floated there, their voices echoing from who knew what long-dead past amid the torrent of crashing glass and splintered wood now raining down upon the floor —

"RUN!" Harry yelled, and as the shelves swayed precariously and more glass spheres began to pour from above, he seized a handful of Hermione's robes and dragged her forward, one arm over his head as chunks of shelf and shards of glass thundered down upon them. A Death Eater lunged forward through the cloud of dust and Harry elbowed him hard in the masked face. They were all yelling, there were cries of pain, thunderous crashes as the shelves collapsed upon themselves, weirdly echoing fragments of the Seers unleashed from their spheres —

Harry found the way ahead clear and saw Ron, Ginny, and Luna sprint past him, their arms over their heads. Something heavy struck him on the side of the face but he merely ducked his head and sprinted onward; a hand caught him by the shoulder; he heard Hermione shout *"Stupefy!"* and the hand released him at once.

They were at the end of row ninety-seven; Harry turned right and began to sprint in earnest. He could hear footsteps right behind him and Hermione's voice urging Neville on. The door through which they had come was ajar straight ahead, Harry could see the glittering light of the bell jar, he pelted through it, the prophecy still clutched tight and safe in his hand, waited for the others to hurtle over the threshold before slamming the door behind them —

"*Colloportus!*" gasped Hermione and the door sealed itself with an odd squelching noise.

"Where — where are the others?" gasped Harry.

He had thought that Ron, Luna, and Ginny had been ahead of them, that they would be waiting in this room, but there was nobody there.

"They must have gone the wrong way!" whispered Hermione, terror in her face.

"Listen!" whispered Neville.

Footsteps and shouts echoed from behind the door they had just sealed. Harry put his ear close to the door to listen and heard Lucius Malfoy roar: "Leave Nott, *leave him, I say,* the Dark Lord will not care for Nott's injuries as much as losing that prophecy — Jugson, come back here, we need to organize! We'll split into pairs and search, and don't forget, be gentle with Potter until we've got the prophecy, you can kill the others if necessary — Bellatrix, Rodolphus, you take the left, Crabbe, Rabastan, go right — Jugson, Dolohov, the door straight ahead — Macnair and Avery, through here — Rookwood, over there — Mulciber, come with me!"

"What do we do?" Hermione asked Harry, trembling from head to foot.

"Well, we don't stand here waiting for them to find us, for a start," said Harry. "Let's get away from this door. . . ."

They ran, quietly as they could, past the shimmering bell jar where the tiny egg was hatching and unhatching, toward the exit into the circular hallway at the far end of the room. They were almost there when Harry heard something large and heavy collide with the door Hermione had charmed shut.

"Stand aside!" said a rough voice. *"Alohomora!"*

As the door flew open, Harry, Hermione, and Neville dived under desks. They could see the bottom of the two Death Eaters' robes drawing nearer, their feet moving rapidly.

"They might've run straight through to the hall," said the rough voice.

"Check under the desks," said another.

Harry saw the knees of the Death Eaters bend. Poking his wand out from under the desk he shouted, *"STUPEFY!"*

A jet of red light hit the nearest Death Eater; he fell backward into a grandfather clock and knocked it over. The second Death Eater, however, had leapt aside to avoid Harry's spell and now pointed his own wand at Hermione, who had crawled out from under the desk to get a better aim.

"Avada —"

Harry launched himself across the floor and grabbed the Death Eater around the knees, causing him to topple and his aim to go awry. Neville overturned his desk in his anxiety to help; pointing his wand wildly at the struggling pair he cried, *"EXPELLIARMUS!"*

Both Harry's and the Death Eater's wands flew out of their hands and soared back toward the entrance to the Hall of Prophecy; both scrambled to their feet and charged after them, the Death Eater in front and Harry hot on his heels, Neville bringing up the rear, plainly horrorstruck at what he had done.

"Get out of the way, Harry!" yelled Neville, clearly determined to repair the damage.

Harry flung himself sideways as Neville took aim again and shouted, *"STUPEFY!"*

The jet of red light flew right over the Death Eater's shoulder and hit a glass-fronted cabinet on the wall full of variously shaped hourglasses. The cabinet fell to the floor and burst apart, glass flying everywhere, then sprang back up onto the wall, fully mended, then fell down again, and shattered —

The Death Eater had snatched up his wand, which lay on the floor beside the glittering bell jar. Harry ducked down behind another desk as the man turned — his mask had slipped so that he could not see, he ripped it off with his free hand and shouted, *"STUP —"*

"STUPEFY!" screamed Hermione, who had just caught up with them. The jet of red light hit the Death Eater in the middle of his chest; he froze, his arm still raised, his wand fell to the floor with a clatter and he collapsed backward toward the bell jar. Harry expected to hear a *clunk,* for the man to hit solid glass and slide off the jar onto the floor, but instead, his head sank through the surface of the bell jar as though it was nothing but a soap bubble and he came to rest, sprawled on his back on the table, with his head lying inside the jar full of glittering wind.

"Accio Wand!" cried Hermione. Harry's wand flew from a dark corner into her hand and she threw it to him.

"Thanks," he said, "right, let's get out of —"

"Look out!" said Neville, horrified, staring at the Death Eater's head in the bell jar.

All three of them raised their wands again, but none of them struck. They were all gazing, openmouthed, appalled, at what was happening to the man's head.

It was shrinking very fast, growing balder and balder, the black hair and stubble retracting into his skull, his cheeks smooth, his skull round and covered with a peachlike fuzz. . . .

A baby's head now sat grotesquely on top of the thick, muscled neck of the Death Eater as he struggled to get up again. But even as they watched, their mouths open, the head began to swell to its previous proportions again, thick black hair was sprouting from the pate and chin. . . .

"It's time," said Hermione in an awestruck voice. *"Time . . ."*

The Death Eater shook his ugly head again, trying to clear it, but before he could pull himself together again, it began to shrink back to babyhood once more. . . .

There was a shout from a room nearby, then a crash and a scream.

"RON?" Harry yelled, turning quickly from the monstrous transformation taking place before them. "GINNY? LUNA?"

"Harry!" Hermione screamed.

The Death Eater had pulled his head out of the bell jar. His appearance was utterly bizarre, his tiny baby's head bawling loudly while his thick arms flailed dangerously in all directions, narrowly missing Harry, who ducked. Harry raised his wand but to his amazement Hermione seized his arm.

"You can't hurt a baby!"

There was no time to argue the point. Harry could hear more footsteps growing louder from the Hall of Prophecy they had just left and knew, too late, that he ought not to have shouted and given away their position.

"Come on!" he said again, and leaving the ugly baby-headed Death Eater staggering behind them, they took off for the door that stood ajar at the other end of the room, leading back into the black hallway.

They had run halfway toward it when Harry saw through the open door two more Death Eaters running across the black room toward them. Veering left he burst instead into a small, dark, cluttered office and slammed the door behind them.

"Collo —" began Hermione, but before she could complete the spell the door had burst open again and the two Death Eaters had come hurtling inside. With a cry of triumph, both yelled, *"IMPEDIMENTA!"*

Harry, Hermione, and Neville were all knocked backward off their feet. Neville was thrown over the desk and disappeared from view,

Hermione smashed into a bookcase and was promptly deluged in a cascade of heavy books; the back of Harry's head slammed into the stone wall behind him, tiny lights burst in front of his eyes, and for a moment he was too dizzy and bewildered to react.

"WE'VE GOT HIM!" yelled the Death Eater nearest Harry, "IN AN OFFICE OFF —"

"*Silencio!*" cried Hermione, and the man's voice was extinguished. He continued to mouth through the hole in his mask, but no sound came out; he was thrust aside by his fellow.

"*Petrificus Totalus!*" shouted Harry, as the second Death Eater raised his wand. His arms and legs snapped together and he fell forward, facedown onto the rug at Harry's feet, stiff as a board and unable to move at all.

"Well done, Ha —"

But the Death Eater Hermione had just struck dumb made a sudden slashing movement with his wand from which flew a streak of what looked like purple flame. It passed right across Hermione's chest; she gave a tiny "oh!" as though of surprise and then crumpled onto the floor where she lay motionless.

"HERMIONE!"

Harry fell to his knees beside her as Neville crawled rapidly toward her from under the desk, his wand held up in front of him. The Death Eater kicked out hard at Neville's head as he emerged — his foot broke Neville's wand in two and connected with his face — Neville gave a howl of pain and recoiled, clutching his mouth and nose. Harry twisted around, his own wand held high, and saw that the Death Eater had ripped off his mask and was pointing his wand directly at Harry, who recognized the long, pale, twisted face from the *Daily Prophet*: Antonin Dolohov, the wizard who had murdered the Prewetts.

Dolohov grinned. With his free hand, he pointed from the prophecy still clutched in Harry's hand, to himself, then at Hermione.

Though he could no longer speak his meaning could not have been clearer: *Give me the prophecy, or you get the same as her. . . .*

"Like you won't kill us all the moment I hand it over anyway!" said Harry.

A whine of panic inside his head was preventing him thinking properly. He had one hand on Hermione's shoulder, which was still warm, yet did not dare look at her properly. *Don't let her be dead, don't let her be dead, it's my fault if she's dead. . . .*

"Whaddever you do, Harry," said Neville fiercely from under the desk, lowering his hands to show a clearly broken nose and blood pouring down his mouth and chin, "don'd gib it to him!"

Then there was a crash outside the door, and Dolohov looked over his shoulder — the baby-headed Death Eater had appeared in the doorway, his head bawling, his great fists still flailing uncontrollably at everything around him.

Harry seized his chance: *"PETRIFICUS TOTALUS!"*

The spell hit Dolohov before he could block it, and he toppled forward across his comrade, both of them rigid as boards and unable to move an inch.

"Hermione," Harry said at once, shaking her as the baby-headed Death Eater blundered out of sight again. "Hermione, wake up. . . ."

"Whaddid he do to her?" said Neville, crawling out from under the desk again to kneel at her other side, blood streaming from his rapidly swelling nose.

"I dunno. . . ."

Neville groped for Hermione's wrist.

"Dat's a pulse, Harry, I'b sure id is. . . ."

Such a powerful wave of relief swept through Harry that for a moment he felt light-headed.

"She's alive?"

"Yeah, I dink so. . . ."

There was a pause in which Harry listened hard for the sounds of more footsteps, but all he could hear were the whimpers and blunderings of the baby Death Eater in the next room.

"Neville, we're not far from the exit," Harry whispered. "We're right next to that circular room. . . . If we can just get you across it and find the right door before any more Death Eaters come, I'll bet you can get Hermione up the corridor and into the lift. . . . Then you could find someone. . . . Raise the alarm . . ."

"And whad are you going do do?" said Neville, mopping his bleeding nose with his sleeve and frowning at Harry.

"I've got to find the others," said Harry.

"Well, I'b going do find dem wid you," said Neville firmly.

"But Hermione —"

"We'll dake her wid us," said Neville firmly. "I'll carry her — you're bedder at fighding dem dan I ab —"

He stood up and seized one of Hermione's arms, glared at Harry, who hesitated, then grabbed the other and helped hoist Hermione's limp form over Neville's shoulders.

"Wait," said Harry, snatching up Hermione's wand from the floor and shoving it into Neville's hand, "you'd better take this. . . ."

Neville kicked aside the broken fragments of his own wand as they walked slowly toward the door.

"My gran's going do kill be," said Neville thickly, blood spattering from his nose as he spoke, "dat was by dad's old wand. . . ."

Harry stuck his head out of the door and looked around cautiously. The baby-headed Death Eater was screaming and banging into things, toppling grandfather clocks and overturning desks, bawling and confused, while the glass cabinet that Harry now suspected had contained Time-Turners continued to fall, shatter, and repair itself on the wall behind them.

"He's never going to notice us," he whispered. "C'mon . . . keep close behind me. . . ."

They crept out of the office and back toward the door into the black hallway, which now seemed completely deserted. They walked a few steps forward, Neville tottering slightly due to Hermione's weight. The door of the Time Room swung shut behind them, and the walls began to rotate once more. The recent blow on the back of Harry's head seemed to have unsteadied him; he narrowed his eyes, swaying slightly, until the walls stopped moving again. With a sinking heart Harry saw that Hermione's fiery crosses had faded from the doors.

"So which way d'you reck — ?"

But before they could make a decision as to which way to try, a door to their right sprang open and three people fell out of it.

"Ron!" croaked Harry, dashing toward them. "Ginny — are you all — ?"

"Harry," said Ron, giggling weakly, lurching forward, seizing the front of Harry's robes and gazing at him with unfocused eyes. "There you are. . . . Ha ha ha . . . You look funny, Harry. . . . You're all messed up. . . ."

Ron's face was very white and something dark was trickling from the corner of his mouth. Next moment his knees had given way, but he still clutched the front of Harry's robes, so that Harry was pulled into a kind of bow.

"Ginny?" Harry said fearfully. "What happened?"

But Ginny shook her head and slid down the wall into a sitting position, panting and holding her ankle.

"I think her ankle's broken, I heard something crack," whispered Luna, who was bending over her and who alone seemed to be unhurt. "Four of them chased us into a dark room full of planets, it was a very odd place, some of the time we were just floating in the dark —"

"Harry, we saw Uranus up close!" said Ron, still giggling feebly. "Get it, Harry? We saw Uranus — ha ha ha —"

A bubble of blood grew at the corner of Ron's mouth and burst.

"Anyway, one of them grabbed Ginny's foot, I used the Reductor Curse and blew up Pluto in his face, but . . ."

Luna gestured hopelessly at Ginny, who was breathing in a very shallow way, her eyes still closed.

"And what about Ron?" said Harry fearfully, as Ron continued to giggle, still hanging off the front of Harry's robes.

"I don't know what they hit him with," said Luna sadly, "but he's gone a bit funny, I could hardly get him along at all. . . ."

"Harry," said Ron, pulling Harry's ear down to his mouth and still giggling weakly, "you know who this girl is, Harry? She's Loony . . . Loony Lovegood . . . ha ha ha . . ."

"We've got to get out of here," said Harry firmly. "Luna, can you help Ginny?"

"Yes," said Luna, sticking her wand behind her ear for safekeeping, putting an arm around Ginny's waist and pulling her up.

"It's only my ankle, I can do it myself!" said Ginny impatiently, but next moment she had collapsed sideways and grabbed Luna for support. Harry pulled Ron's arm over his shoulder just as, so many months ago, he had pulled Dudley's. He looked around: They had a one-in-twelve chance of getting the exit right the first time —

He heaved Ron toward a door; they were within a few feet of it when another door across the hall burst open and three Death Eaters sped into the hall, led by Bellatrix Lestrange.

"*There they are!*" she shrieked.

Stunning Spells shot across the room: Harry smashed his way through the door ahead, flung Ron unceremoniously from him, and ducked back to help Neville in with Hermione. They were all over the threshold just in time to slam the door against Bellatrix.

"*Colloportus!*" shouted Harry, and he heard three bodies slam into the door on the other side.

"It doesn't matter!" said a man's voice. "There are other ways in — WE'VE GOT THEM, THEY'RE HERE!"

Harry spun around. They were back in the Brain Room and, sure enough, there were doors all around the walls. He could hear footsteps in the hall behind them as more Death Eaters came running to join the first.

"Luna — Neville — help me!"

The three of them tore around the room, sealing the doors as they went: Harry crashed into a table and rolled over the top of it in his haste to reach the next door.

"Colloportus!"

There were footsteps running along behind the doors; every now and then another heavy body would launch itself against one, so it creaked and shuddered. Luna and Neville were bewitching the doors along the opposite wall — then, as Harry reached the very top of the room, he heard Luna cry, *"Collo — aaaaaaaaargh . . ."*

He turned in time to see her flying through the air. Five Death Eaters were surging into the room through the door she had not reached in time; Luna hit a desk, slid over its surface and onto the floor on the other side where she lay sprawled, as still as Hermione.

"Get Potter!" shrieked Bellatrix, and she ran at him. He dodged her and sprinted back up the room; he was safe as long as they thought they might hit the prophecy —

"Hey!" said Ron, who had staggered to his feet and was now tottering drunkenly toward Harry, giggling. "Hey, Harry, there are *brains* in here, ha ha ha, isn't that weird, Harry?"

"Ron, get out of the way, get down —"

But Ron had already pointed his wand at the tank.

"Honest, Harry, they're brains — look — *Accio Brain!*"

The scene seemed momentarily frozen. Harry, Ginny, and Neville and each of the Death Eaters turned in spite of themselves to watch the top of the tank as a brain burst from the green liquid like a leaping fish. For a moment it seemed suspended in midair, then it soared toward Ron, spinning as it came, and what looked like ribbons of moving images flew from it, unraveling like rolls of film —

"Ha ha ha, Harry, look at it —" said Ron, watching it disgorge its gaudy innards. "Harry, come and touch it, bet it's weird —"

"RON, NO!"

Harry did not know what would happen if Ron touched the tentacles of thought now flying behind the brain, but he was sure it would not be anything good. He darted forward but Ron had already caught the brain in his outstretched hands.

The moment they made contact with his skin, the tentacles began wrapping themselves around Ron's arms like ropes.

"Harry, look what's happen — no — no, I don't like it — no, stop — *stop* —"

But the thin ribbons were spinning around Ron's chest now. He tugged and tore at them as the brain was pulled tight against him like an octopus's body.

"*Diffindo!*" yelled Harry, trying to sever the feelers wrapping themselves tightly around Ron before his eyes, but they would not break. Ron fell over, still thrashing against his bonds.

"Harry, it'll suffocate him!" screamed Ginny, immobilized by her broken ankle on the floor — then a jet of red light flew from one of the Death Eater's wands and hit her squarely in the face. She keeled over sideways and lay there unconscious.

"*STUBEFY!*" shouted Neville, wheeling around and waving Hermione's wand at the oncoming Death Eaters. "*STUBEFY, STUBEFY!*"

But nothing happened — one of the Death Eaters shot their own Stunning Spell at Neville; it missed him by inches. Harry and Neville were now the only two left fighting the five Death Eaters, two of whom sent streams of silver light like arrows past them that left craters in the wall behind them. Harry ran for it as Bellatrix Lestrange sprinted right at him. Holding the prophecy high above his head he sprinted back up the room; all he could think of doing was to draw the Death Eaters away from the others.

It seemed to have worked. They streaked after him, knocking chairs and tables flying but not daring to bewitch him in case they hurt the prophecy, and he dashed through the only door still open, the one through which the Death Eaters themselves had come. Inwardly praying that Neville would stay with Ron — find some way of releasing him — he ran a few feet into the new room and felt the floor vanish —

He was falling down steep stone step after steep stone step, bouncing on every tier until at last, with a crash that knocked all the breath out of his body, he landed flat on his back in the sunken pit where the stone archway stood on its dais. The whole room was ringing with the Death Eaters' laughter. He looked up and saw the five who had been in the Brain Room descending toward him, while as many more emerged through other doorways and began leaping from bench to bench toward him. Harry got to his feet though his legs were trembling so badly they barely supported him. The prophecy was still miraculously unbroken in his left hand, his wand clutched tightly in his right. He backed away, looking around, trying to keep all the Death Eaters within his sights. The back of his legs hit something solid; he had reached the dais where the archway stood. He climbed backward onto it.

The Death Eaters all halted, gazing at him. Some were panting as hard as he was. One was bleeding badly; Dolohov, freed of the full Body-Bind, was leering, his wand pointing straight at Harry's face.

"Potter, your race is run," drawled Lucius Malfoy, pulling off his mask. "Now hand me the prophecy like a good boy. . . ."

"Let — let the others go, and I'll give it to you!" said Harry desperately.

A few of the Death Eaters laughed.

"You are not in a position to bargain, Potter," said Lucius Malfoy, his pale face flushed with pleasure. "You see, there are ten of us and only one of you . . . or hasn't Dumbledore ever taught you how to count?"

"He's dot alone!" shouted a voice from above them. "He's still god be!"

Harry's heart sank. Neville was scrambling down the stone benches toward them, Hermione's wand held fast in his trembling hand.

"Neville — no — go back to Ron —"

"STUBEFY!" Neville shouted again, pointing his wand at each Death Eater in turn, "STUBEFY! STUBE —"

One of the largest Death Eaters seized Neville from behind, pinioning his arms to his sides. He struggled and kicked; several of the Death Eaters laughed.

"It's Longbottom, isn't it?" sneered Lucius Malfoy. "Well, your grandmother is used to losing family members to our cause. . . . Your death will not come as a great shock. . . ."

"Longbottom?" repeated Bellatrix, and a truly evil smile lit her gaunt face. "Why, I have had the pleasure of meeting your parents, boy. . . ."

"I DOE YOU HAB!" roared Neville, and he fought so hard against his captor's encircling grip that the Death Eater shouted, "Someone Stun him!"

"No, no, no," said Bellatrix. She looked transported, alive with excitement as she glanced at Harry, then back at Neville. "No, let's see how long Longbottom lasts before he cracks like his parents. . . . Unless Potter wants to give us the prophecy —"

"DON'D GIB ID DO DEM!" roared Neville, who seemed beside himself, kicking and writhing as Bellatrix drew nearer to him and his captor, her wand raised. "DON'D GIB ID DO DEM, HARRY!"

Bellatrix raised her wand. "Crucio!"

Neville screamed, his legs drawn up to his chest so that the Death Eater holding him was momentarily holding him off the ground. The Death Eater dropped him and he fell to the floor, twitching and screaming in agony.

"That was just a taster!" said Bellatrix, raising her wand so that Neville's screams stopped and he lay sobbing at her feet. She turned and gazed up at Harry. "Now, Potter, either give us the prophecy, or watch your little friend die the hard way!"

Harry did not have to think; there was no choice. The prophecy was hot with the heat from his clutching hand as he held it out. Malfoy jumped forward to take it.

Then, high above them, two more doors burst open and five more people sprinted into the room: Sirius, Lupin, Moody, Tonks, and Kingsley.

Malfoy turned and raised his wand, but Tonks had already sent a Stunning Spell right at him. Harry did not wait to see whether it had made contact, but dived off the dais out of the way. The Death Eaters were completely distracted by the appearance of the members of the Order, who were now raining spells down upon them as they jumped from step to step toward the sunken floor: Through the darting bodies, the flashes of light, Harry could see Neville crawling along. He dodged another jet of red light and flung himself flat on the ground to reach Neville.

"Are you okay?" he yelled, as another spell soared inches over their heads.

"Yes," said Neville, trying to pull himself up.

"And Ron?"

"I dink he's all right — he was still fighding the brain when I left —"

The stone floor between them exploded as a spell hit it, leaving a crater right where Neville's hand had been seconds before. Both scrambled away from the spot, then a thick arm came out of nowhere, seized Harry around the neck and pulled him upright, so that his toes were barely touching the floor.

"Give it to me," growled a voice in his ear, "give me the prophecy —"

The man was pressing so tightly on Harry's windpipe that he could not breathe — through watering eyes he saw Sirius dueling with a Death Eater some ten feet away. Kingsley was fighting two at once; Tonks, still halfway up the tiered seats, was firing spells down at Bellatrix — nobody seemed to realize that Harry was dying. . . . He turned his wand backward toward the man's side, but had no breath to utter an incantation, and the man's free hand was groping toward the hand in which Harry was grasping the prophecy —

"AARGH!"

Neville had come lunging out of nowhere: Unable to articulate a spell, he had jabbed Hermione's wand hard into the eyehole of the Death Eater's mask. The man relinquished Harry at once with a howl of pain and Harry whirled around to face him and gasped, *"STUPEFY!"*

The Death Eater keeled over backward and his mask slipped off. It was Macnair, Buckbeak's would-be killer, one of his eyes now swollen and bloodshot.

"Thanks!" Harry said to Neville, pulling him aside as Sirius and his Death Eater lurched past, dueling so fiercely that their wands were blurs. Then Harry's foot made contact with something round and hard and he slipped — for a moment he thought he had dropped the prophecy, then saw Moody's magic eye spinning away across the floor.

Its owner was lying on his side, bleeding from the head, and his attacker was now bearing down upon Harry and Neville: Dolohov, his long pale face twisted with glee.

"Tarantallegra!" he shouted, his wand pointing at Neville, whose legs went immediately into a kind of frenzied tap dance, unbalancing him and causing him to fall to the floor again. "Now, Potter —"

He made the same slashing movement with his wand that he had used on Hermione just as Harry yelled, *"Protego!"*

Harry felt something streak across his face like a blunt knife but the force of it knocked him sideways, and he fell over Neville's jerking legs, but the Shield Charm had stopped the worst of the spell.

Dolohov raised his wand again. *"Accio Proph —"*

Sirius hurtled out of nowhere, rammed Dolohov with his shoulder, and sent him flying out of the way. The prophecy had again flown to the tips of Harry's fingers but he had managed to cling to it. Now Sirius and Dolohov were dueling, their wands flashing like swords, sparks flying from their wand tips —

Dolohov drew back his wand to make the same slashing movement he had used on Harry and Hermione. Springing up, Harry yelled, *"Petrificus Totalus!"* Once again, Dolohov's arms and legs snapped together and he keeled over backward, landing with a crash on his back.

"Nice one!" shouted Sirius, forcing Harry's head down as a pair of Stunning Spells flew toward them. "Now I want you to get out of —"

They both ducked again. A jet of green light had narrowly missed Sirius; across the room Harry saw Tonks fall from halfway up the stone steps, her limp form toppling from stone seat to stone seat, and Bellatrix, triumphant, running back toward the fray.

"Harry, take the prophecy, grab Neville, and run!" Sirius yelled, dashing to meet Bellatrix. Harry did not see what happened next: Kingsley swayed across his field of vision, battling with the pockmarked Rookwood, now mask-less; another jet of green light flew over Harry's head as he launched himself toward Neville —

"Can you stand?" he bellowed in Neville's ear, as Neville's legs jerked and twitched uncontrollably. "Put your arm round my neck —"

Neville did so — Harry heaved — Neville's legs were still flying in every direction, they would not support him and then, out of nowhere, a man lunged at them. Both fell backward, Neville's legs waving wildly like an overturned beetle's, Harry with his left arm held up in the air to try and save the small glass ball from being smashed.

"The prophecy, give me the prophecy, Potter!" snarled Lucius Malfoy's voice in his ear, and Harry felt the tip of Malfoy's wand pressing hard between his ribs.

"No — get — off — me . . . Neville — catch it!"

Harry flung the prophecy across the floor, Neville spun himself around on his back and scooped the ball to his chest. Malfoy pointed the wand instead at Neville, but Harry jabbed his own wand back over his shoulder and yelled, *"Impedimenta!"*

Malfoy was blasted off his back. As Harry scrambled up again he looked around and saw Malfoy smash into the dais on which Sirius and Bellatrix were now dueling. Malfoy aimed his wand at Harry and Neville again, but before he could draw breath to strike, Lupin had jumped between them.

"Harry, round up the others and GO!"

Harry seized Neville by the shoulder of his robes and lifted him bodily onto the first tier of stone steps. Neville's legs twitched and jerked and would not support his weight. Harry heaved again with all the strength he possessed and they climbed another step —

A spell hit the stone bench at Harry's heel. It crumbled away and he fell back to the step below: Neville sank onto the bench above, his legs still jerking and thrashing, and thrust the prophecy into his pocket.

"Come on!" said Harry desperately, hauling at Neville's robes. "Just try and push with your legs —"

He gave another stupendous heave and Neville's robes tore all along the left seam — the small spun-glass ball dropped from his pocket and before either of them could catch it, one of Neville's floundering feet kicked it. It flew some ten feet to their right and smashed on the step beneath them. As both of them stared at the place where it had broken, appalled at what had happened, a pearly-white figure with hugely magnified eyes rose into the air, unnoticed by any but them. Harry could see its mouth moving, but in all the crashes and screams and yells surrounding them, not one word of the prophecy could he hear. The figure stopped speaking and dissolved into nothingness.

"Harry, I'b sorry!" cried Neville, his face anguished as his legs continued to flounder, "I'b so sorry, Harry, I didn'd bean do —"

"It doesn't matter!" Harry shouted. "Just try and stand, let's get out of —"

"Dubbledore!" said Neville, his sweaty face suddenly transported, staring over Harry's shoulder.

"What?"

"DUBBLEDORE!"

Harry turned to look where Neville was staring. Directly above them, framed in the doorway from the Brain Room, stood Albus Dumbledore, his wand aloft, his face white and furious. Harry felt a kind of electric charge surge through every particle of his body — *they were saved.*

Dumbledore had already sped past Neville and Harry, who had no more thoughts of leaving, when the Death Eaters nearest realized Dumbledore was there, and yelled to the others. One of the Death Eaters ran for it, scrabbling like a monkey up the stone steps opposite. Dumbledore's spell pulled him back as easily and effortlessly as though he had hooked him with an invisible line —

Only one couple were still battling, apparently unaware of the new arrival. Harry saw Sirius duck Bellatrix's jet of red light: He was laughing at her. "Come on, you can do better than that!" he yelled, his voice echoing around the cavernous room.

The second jet of light hit him squarely on the chest.

The laughter had not quite died from his face, but his eyes widened in shock.

Harry released Neville, though he was unaware of doing so. Harry jumped to the ground, pulling out his wand, as Dumbledore turned to the dais too.

It seemed to take Sirius an age to fall. His body curved in a graceful arc as he sank backward through the ragged veil hanging from the arch. . . .

And Harry saw the look of mingled fear and surprise on his godfather's wasted, once-handsome face as he fell through the ancient doorway and disappeared behind the veil, which fluttered for a moment as though in a high wind and then fell back into place.

Harry heard Bellatrix Lestrange's triumphant scream, but knew it meant nothing — Sirius had only just fallen through the archway, he would reappear from the other side any second. . . .

But Sirius did not reappear.

"SIRIUS!" Harry yelled, "SIRIUS!"

Harry's breath was coming in searing gasps. Sirius must be just behind the curtain, he, Harry, would pull him back out again. . . .

But as he sprinted toward the dais, Lupin grabbed Harry around the chest, holding him back.

"There's nothing you can do, Harry —"

"Get him, save him, he's only just gone through!"

"It's too late, Harry —"

"We can still reach him —"

Harry struggled hard and viciously, but Lupin would not let go. . . .

"There's nothing you can do, Harry . . . nothing. . . . He's gone."

THE ONLY ONE
HE EVER FEARED

He hasn't gone!" Harry yelled.

He did not believe it, he would not believe it; still he fought Lupin with every bit of strength he had: Lupin did not understand, people hid behind that curtain, he had heard them whispering the first time he had entered the room — Sirius was hiding, simply lurking out of sight —

"SIRIUS!" he bellowed, "SIRIUS!"

"He can't come back, Harry," said Lupin, his voice breaking as he struggled to contain Harry. "He can't come back, because he's d —"

"HE — IS — NOT — DEAD!" roared Harry. "SIRIUS!"

There was movement going on around them, pointless bustling, the flashes of more spells. To Harry it was meaningless noise, the deflected curses flying past them did not matter, nothing mattered except that Lupin stop pretending that Sirius, who was standing feet from them behind that old curtain, was not going to emerge at any moment, shaking back his dark hair and eager to reenter the battle —

Lupin dragged Harry away from the dais, Harry still staring at the archway, angry at Sirius now for keeping him waiting —

But some part of him realized, even as he fought to break free from Lupin, that Sirius had never kept him waiting before. . . . Sirius had risked everything, always, to see Harry, to help him. . . . If Sirius was not reappearing out of that archway when Harry was yelling for him as though his life depended on it, the only possible explanation was that he could not come back. . . . That he really was . . .

Dumbledore had most of the remaining Death Eaters grouped in the middle of the room, seemingly immobilized by invisible ropes. Mad-Eye Moody had crawled across the room to where Tonks lay and was attempting to revive her. Behind the dais there were still flashes of light, grunts, and cries — Kingsley had run forward to continue Sirius's duel with Bellatrix.

"Harry?"

Neville had slid down the stone benches one by one to the place where Harry stood. Harry was no longer struggling against Lupin, who maintained a precautionary grip on his arm nevertheless.

"Harry . . . I'b really sorry. . . ." said Neville. His legs were still dancing uncontrollably. "Was dat man — was Sirius Black a — a friend of yours?"

Harry nodded.

"Here," said Lupin quietly, and pointing his wand at Neville's legs he said, *"Finite."* The spell was lifted. Neville's legs fell back onto the floor and remained still. Lupin's face was pale. "Let's — let's find the others. Where are they all, Neville?"

Lupin turned away from the archway as he spoke. It sounded as though every word was causing him pain.

"Dey're all back dere," said Neville. "A brain addacked Ron bud I dink he's all righd — and Herbione's unconscious, bud we could feel a bulse —"

There was a loud bang and a yell from behind the dais. Harry saw Kingsley, yelling in pain, hit the ground. Bellatrix Lestrange turned tail and ran as Dumbledore whipped around. He aimed a spell at her but she deflected it. She was halfway up the steps now —

"Harry — no!" cried Lupin, but Harry had already ripped his arm from Lupin's slackened grip.

"SHE KILLED SIRIUS!" bellowed Harry. "SHE KILLED HIM — I'LL KILL HER!"

And he was off, scrambling up the stone benches. People were shouting behind him but he did not care. The hem of Bellatrix's robes whipped out of sight ahead and they were back in the room where the brains were swimming. . . .

She aimed a curse over her shoulder. The tank rose into the air and tipped. Harry was deluged in the foul-smelling potion within. The brains slipped and slid over him and began spinning their long, colored tentacles, but he shouted, *"Wingardium Leviosa!"* and they flew into the air away from him. Slipping and sliding he ran on toward the door. He leapt over Luna, who was groaning on the floor, past Ginny, who said, "Harry — what — ?" past Ron, who giggled feebly, and Hermione, who was still unconscious. He wrenched open the door into the circular black hall and saw Bellatrix disappearing through a door on the other side of the room — beyond her was the corridor leading back to the lifts.

He ran, but she had slammed the door behind her and the walls had begun to rotate again. Once more he was surrounded by streaks of blue light from the whirling candelabra.

"Where's the exit?" he shouted desperately, as the wall rumbled to a halt again. "Where's the way out?"

The room seemed to have been waiting for him to ask. The door right behind him flew open, and the corridor toward the lifts stretched ahead of him, torch-lit and empty. He ran. . . .

He could hear a lift clattering ahead of him. He sprinted up the passageway, swung around the corner, and slammed his fist onto the button to call a second lift. It jangled and banged lower and lower; the grilles slid open and Harry dashed inside, now hammering the button marked Atrium. The doors slid shut and he was rising. . . .

He forced his way out of the lift before the grilles were fully open and looked around. Bellatrix was almost at the telephone lift at the other end of the hall, but she looked back as he sprinted toward her, and aimed another spell at him. He dodged behind the Fountain of Magical Brethren; the spell zoomed past him and hit the wrought gold gates at the other end of the Atrium so that they rang like bells. There were no more footsteps. She had stopped running. He crouched behind the statues, listening.

"*Come out, come out, little Harry!*" she called in her mock-baby voice, which echoed off the polished wooden floors. "What did you come after me for, then? I thought you were here to avenge my dear cousin!"

"I am!" shouted Harry, and a score of ghostly Harrys seemed to chorus *I am! I am! I am!* all around the room.

"Aaaaaah . . . did you *love* him, little baby Potter?"

Hatred rose in Harry such as he had never known before. He flung himself out from behind the fountain and bellowed "*Crucio!*"

Bellatrix screamed. The spell had knocked her off her feet, but she did not writhe and shriek with pain as Neville had — she was already on her feet again, breathless, no longer laughing. Harry dodged behind the golden fountain again — her counterspell hit the head of the handsome wizard, which was blown off and landed twenty feet away, gouging long scratches into the wooden floor.

"Never used an Unforgivable Curse before, have you, boy?" she yelled. She had abandoned her baby voice now. "You need to *mean* them, Potter! You need to really want to cause pain — to enjoy it — righteous anger won't hurt me for long — I'll show you how it is done, shall I? I'll give you a lesson —"

Harry had been edging around the fountain on the other side. She screamed, "*Crucio!*" and he was forced to duck down again as the centaur's arm, holding its bow, spun off and landed with a crash on the floor a short distance from the golden wizard's head.

"Potter, you cannot win against me!" she cried. He could hear her moving to the right, trying to get a clear shot of him. He backed around the statue away from her, crouching behind the centaur's legs, his head level with the house-elf's. "I was and am the Dark Lord's most loyal servant, I learned the Dark Arts from him, and I know spells of such power that you, pathetic little boy, can never hope to compete —"

"*Stupefy!*" yelled Harry. He had edged right around to where the goblin stood beaming up at the now headless wizard and taken aim at her back as she peered around the fountain for him. She reacted so fast he barely had time to duck.

"*Protego!*"

The jet of red light, his own Stunning Spell, bounced back at him. Harry scrambled back behind the fountain, and one of the goblin's ears went flying across the room.

"Potter, I am going to give you one chance!" shouted Bellatrix. "Give me the prophecy — roll it out toward me now — and I may spare your life!"

"Well, you're going to have to kill me, because it's gone!" Harry roared — and as he shouted it, pain seared across his forehead. His scar was on fire again, and he felt a surge of fury that was quite unconnected with his own rage. "And he knows!" said Harry with a mad laugh to match Bellatrix's own. "Your dear old mate Voldemort knows it's gone! He's not going to be happy with you, is he?"

"What? What do you mean?" she cried, and for the first time there was fear in her voice.

"The prophecy smashed when I was trying to get Neville up the steps! What do you think Voldemort'll say about that, then?"

His scar seared and burned. . . . The pain of it was making his eyes stream. . . .

"LIAR!" she shrieked, but he could hear the terror behind the anger now. "YOU'VE GOT IT, POTTER, AND YOU WILL GIVE IT TO ME — *Accio Prophecy! ACCIO PROPHECY!*"

Harry laughed again because he knew it would incense her, the pain building in his head so badly he thought his skull might burst. He waved his empty hand from behind the one-eared goblin and withdrew it quickly as she sent another jet of green light flying at him.

"Nothing there!" he shouted. "Nothing to summon! It smashed and nobody heard what it said, tell your boss that —"

"No!" she screamed. "It isn't true, you're lying — MASTER, I TRIED, I TRIED — DO NOT PUNISH ME —"

"Don't waste your breath!" yelled Harry, his eyes screwed up against the pain in his scar, now more terrible than ever. "He can't hear you from here!"

"Can't I, Potter?" said a high, cold voice.

Harry opened his eyes.

Tall, thin, and black-hooded, his terrible snakelike face white and gaunt, his scarlet, slit-pupiled eyes staring . . . Lord Voldemort had appeared in the middle of the hall, his wand pointing at Harry who stood frozen, quite unable to move.

"So you smashed my prophecy?" said Voldemort softly, staring at Harry with those pitiless red eyes. "No, Bella, he is not lying. . . . I see the truth looking at me from within his worthless mind. . . . Months of preparation, months of effort . . . and my Death Eaters have let Harry Potter thwart me again. . . ."

"Master, I am sorry, I knew not, I was fighting the Animagus Black!" sobbed Bellatrix, flinging herself down at Voldemort's feet as he paced slowly nearer. "Master, you should know —"

"Be quiet, Bella," said Voldemort dangerously. "I shall deal with you in a moment. Do you think I have entered the Ministry of Magic to hear your sniveling apologies?"

"But Master — he is here — he is below —"

Voldemort paid no attention.

"I have nothing more to say to you, Potter," he said quietly. "You have irked me too often, for too long. *AVADA KEDAVRA!*"

Harry had not even opened his mouth to resist. His mind was blank, his wand pointing uselessly at the floor.

But the headless golden statue of the wizard in the fountain had sprung alive, leaping from its plinth, and landed on the floor with a crash between Harry and Voldemort. The spell merely glanced off its chest as the statue flung out its arms, protecting Harry.

"What — ?" said Voldemort, staring around. And then he breathed, "Dumbledore!"

Harry looked behind him, his heart pounding. Dumbledore was standing in front of the golden gates.

Voldemort raised his wand and sent another jet of green light at Dumbledore, who turned and was gone in a whirling of his cloak; next second he had reappeared behind Voldemort and waved his wand toward the remnants of the fountain; the other statues sprang to life too. The statue of the witch ran at Bellatrix, who screamed and sent spells streaming uselessly off its chest, before it dived at her, pinning her to the floor. Meanwhile, the goblin and the house-elf scuttled toward the fireplaces set along the wall, and the one-armed centaur galloped at Voldemort, who vanished and reappeared beside the pool. The headless statue thrust Harry backward, away from the fight, as Dumbledore advanced on Voldemort and the golden centaur cantered around them both.

"It was foolish to come here tonight, Tom," said Dumbledore calmly. "The Aurors are on their way —"

"By which time I shall be gone, and you dead!" spat Voldemort. He sent another Killing Curse at Dumbledore but missed, instead hitting the security guard's desk, which burst into flame.

Dumbledore flicked his own wand. The force of the spell that emanated from it was such that Harry, though shielded by his stone guard, felt his hair stand on end as it passed, and this time Voldemort was forced to conjure a shining silver shield out of thin air to deflect it. The spell, whatever it was, caused no visible damage to the shield, though a deep, gonglike note reverberated from it, an oddly chilling sound. . . .

"You do not seek to kill me, Dumbledore?" called Voldemort, his scarlet eyes narrowed over the top of the shield. "Above such brutality, are you?"

"We both know that there are other ways of destroying a man, Tom," Dumbledore said calmly, continuing to walk toward Voldemort as though he had not a fear in the world, as though nothing had happened to interrupt his stroll up the hall. "Merely taking your life would not satisfy me, I admit —"

"There is nothing worse than death, Dumbledore!" snarled Voldemort.

"You are quite wrong," said Dumbledore, still closing in upon Voldemort and speaking as lightly as though they were discussing the matter over drinks. Harry felt scared to see him walking along, undefended, shieldless. He wanted to cry out a warning, but his headless guard kept shunting him backward toward the wall, blocking his every attempt to get out from behind it. "Indeed, your failure to understand that there are things much worse than death has always been your greatest weakness —"

Another jet of green light flew from behind the silver shield. This time it was the one-armed centaur, galloping in front of Dumbledore, that took the blast and shattered into a hundred pieces, but before the fragments had even hit the floor, Dumbledore had drawn back his wand and waved it as though brandishing a whip. A long thin flame flew from the tip; it wrapped itself around Voldemort, shield and all. For a moment, it seemed Dumbledore had won, but then the fiery rope became a serpent, which relinquished its hold upon Voldemort at once and turned, hissing furiously, to face Dumbledore.

Voldemort vanished. The snake reared from the floor, ready to strike —

There was a burst of flame in midair above Dumbledore just as Voldemort reappeared, standing on the plinth in the middle of the pool where so recently the five statues had stood.

"Look out!" Harry yelled.

But even as he shouted, one more jet of green light had flown at Dumbledore from Voldemort's wand and the snake had struck —

Fawkes swooped down in front of Dumbledore, opened his beak wide, and swallowed the jet of green light whole. He burst into flame and fell to the floor, small, wrinkled, and flightless. At the same moment, Dumbledore brandished his wand in one, long, fluid movement — the snake, which had been an instant from sinking its fangs into him, flew high into the air and vanished in a wisp of dark smoke; the water in the pool rose up and covered Voldemort like a cocoon of molten glass —

For a few seconds Voldemort was visible only as a dark, rippling, faceless figure, shimmering and indistinct upon the plinth, clearly struggling to throw off the suffocating mass —

Then he was gone, and the water fell with a crash back into its pool, slopping wildly over the sides, drenching the polished floor.

"MASTER!" screamed Bellatrix.

Sure it was over, sure Voldemort had decided to flee, Harry made to run out from behind his statue guard, but Dumbledore bellowed, "Stay where you are, Harry!"

For the first time, Dumbledore sounded frightened. Harry could not see why. The hall was quite empty but for themselves, the sobbing Bellatrix still trapped under her statue, and the tiny baby Fawkes croaking feebly on the floor —

And then Harry's scar burst open. He knew he was dead: it was pain beyond imagining, pain past endurance —

He was gone from the hall, he was locked in the coils of a creature with red eyes, so tightly bound that Harry did not know where his body ended and the creature's began. They were fused together, bound by pain, and there was no escape —

And when the creature spoke, it used Harry's mouth, so that in his agony he felt his jaw move. . . .

"*Kill me now, Dumbledore.* . . ."

Blinded and dying, every part of him screaming for release, Harry felt the creature use him again. . . .

"*If death is nothing, Dumbledore, kill the boy.* . . ."

Let the pain stop, thought Harry. *Let him kill us. . . . End it, Dumbledore. . . . Death is nothing compared to this. . . .*

And I'll see Sirius again. . . .

And as Harry's heart filled with emotion, the creature's coils loosened, the pain was gone, Harry was lying facedown on the floor, his glasses gone, shivering as though he lay upon ice, not wood. . . .

And there were voices echoing through the hall, more voices than there should have been: Harry opened his eyes, saw his glasses lying at the heel of the headless statue that had been guarding him, but which now lay flat on its back, cracked and immobile. He put them on and raised his head an inch to find Dumbledore's crooked nose inches from his own.

"Are you all right, Harry?"

"Yes," said Harry, shaking so violently he could not hold his head up properly. "Yeah, I'm — where's Voldemort, where — who are all these — what's —"

The Atrium was full of people. The floor was reflecting emerald-green flames that had burst into life in all the fireplaces along one wall, and a stream of witches and wizards was emerging from them. As Dumbledore pulled him back to his feet, Harry saw the tiny gold statues of the house-elf and the goblin leading a stunned-looking Cornelius Fudge forward.

"He was there!" shouted a scarlet-robed man with a ponytail, who was pointing at a pile of golden rubble on the other side of the hall, where Bellatrix had lain trapped moments before. "I saw him, Mr. Fudge, I swear, it was You-Know-Who, he grabbed a woman and Disapparated!"

"I know, Williamson, I know, I saw him too!" gibbered Fudge, who was wearing pajamas under his pinstriped cloak and was gasping as though he had just run miles. "Merlin's beard — here — *here!* — in the Ministry of Magic! — great heavens above — it doesn't seem possible — my word — how can this be?"

"If you proceed downstairs into the Department of Mysteries, Cornelius," said Dumbledore, apparently satisfied that Harry was all right, and walking forward so that the newcomers realized he was there for the first time (a few of them raised their wands, others simply looked amazed; the statues of the elf and goblin applauded and Fudge jumped so much that his slipper-clad feet left the floor), "you will find several escaped Death Eaters contained in the Death Chamber, bound by an Anti-Disapparation Jinx and awaiting your decision as to what to do with them."

"Dumbledore!" gasped Fudge, apparently beside himself with amazement. "You — here — I — I —"

He looked wildly around at the Aurors he had brought with him, and it could not have been clearer that he was in half a mind to cry, "Seize him!"

"Cornelius, I am ready to fight your men — and win again!" said Dumbledore in a thunderous voice. "But a few minutes ago you saw proof, with your own eyes, that I have been telling you the truth for a year. Lord Voldemort has returned, you have been chasing the wrong men for twelve months, and it is time you listened to sense!"

"I — don't — well —" blustered Fudge, looking around as though hoping somebody was going to tell him what to do. When nobody did, he said, "Very well — Dawlish! Williamson! Go down to the Department of Mysteries and see . . . Dumbledore, you — you will need to tell me exactly — the Fountain of Magical Brethren — what happened?" he added in a kind of whimper, staring around at the floor, where the remains of the statues of the witch, wizard, and centaur now lay scattered.

"We can discuss that after I have sent Harry back to Hogwarts," said Dumbledore.

"Harry — *Harry Potter?*"

Fudge spun around and stared at Harry, who was still standing against the wall beside the fallen statue that had been guarding him during Dumbledore and Voldemort's duel.

"He-here?" said Fudge. "Why — what's all this about?"

"I shall explain everything," repeated Dumbledore, "when Harry is back at school."

He walked away from the pool to the place where the golden wizard's head lay on the floor. He pointed his wand at it and muttered, *"Portus."* The head glowed blue and trembled noisily against the wooden floor for a few seconds, then became still once more.

"Now see here, Dumbledore!" said Fudge, as Dumbledore picked up the head and walked back to Harry carrying it. "You haven't got authorization for that Portkey! You can't do things like that right in front of the Minister of Magic, you — you —"

His voice faltered as Dumbledore surveyed him magisterially over his half-moon spectacles.

"You will give the order to remove Dolores Umbridge from Hogwarts," said Dumbledore. "You will tell your Aurors to stop searching for my Care of Magical Creatures teacher so that he can return to work. I will give you . . ." Dumbledore pulled a watch with twelve hands from his pocket and glanced at it, "half an hour of my time tonight, in which I think we shall be more than able to cover the important points of what has happened here. After that, I shall need to return to my school. If you need more help from me you are, of course, more than welcome to contact me at Hogwarts. Letters addressed to the headmaster will find me."

Fudge goggled worse than ever. His mouth was open and his round face grew pinker under his rumpled gray hair.

"I — you —"

Dumbledore turned his back on him.

"Take this Portkey, Harry."

He held out the golden head of the statue, and Harry placed his hand upon it, past caring what he did next or where he went.

"I shall see you in half an hour," said Dumbledore quietly. "One . . . two . . . three . . ."

Harry felt the familiar sensation of a hook being jerked behind his navel. The polished wooden floor was gone from beneath his feet; the Atrium, Fudge, and Dumbledore had all disappeared, and he was flying forward in a whirlwind of color and sound. . . .

THE LOST PROPHECY

Harry's feet hit solid ground again; his knees buckled a little and the golden wizard's head fell with a resounding *clunk* to the floor. He looked around and saw that he had arrived in Dumbledore's office.

Everything seemed to have repaired itself during the headmaster's absence. The delicate silver instruments stood again upon the spindle-legged tables, puffing and whirring serenely. The portraits of the headmasters and headmistresses were snoozing in their frames, heads lolling back in armchairs or against the edge of their pictures. Harry looked through the window. There was a cool line of pale green along the horizon: Dawn was approaching.

The silence and the stillness, broken only by the occasional grunt or snuffle of a sleeping portrait, was unbearable to him. If his surroundings could have reflected the feelings inside him, the pictures would have been screaming in pain. He walked around the quiet, beautiful office, breathing quickly, trying not to think. But he had to think. . . . There was no escape. . . .

It was his fault Sirius had died; it was all his fault. If he, Harry, had not been stupid enough to fall for Voldemort's trick, if he had not been so convinced that what he had seen in his dream was real, if he had only opened his mind to the possibility that Voldemort was, as Hermione had said, banking on Harry's *love of playing the hero* . . .

It was unbearable, he would not think about it, he could not stand it. . . . There was a terrible hollow inside him he did not want to feel or examine, a dark hole where Sirius had been, where Sirius had vanished. He did not want to have to be alone with that great, silent space, he could not stand it —

A picture behind him gave a particularly loud grunting snore, and a cool voice said, "Ah . . . Harry Potter . . ."

Phineas Nigellus gave a long yawn, stretching his arms as he watched Harry with shrewd, narrow eyes.

"And what brings you here in the early hours of the morning?" said Phineas. "This office is supposed to be barred to all but the rightful headmaster. Or has Dumbledore sent you here? Oh, don't tell me . . ." He gave another shuddering yawn. "Another message for my worthless great-great-grandson?"

Harry could not speak. Phineas Nigellus did not know that Sirius was dead, but Harry could not tell him. To say it aloud would be to make it final, absolute, irretrievable.

A few more of the portraits had stirred now. Terror of being interrogated made Harry stride across the room and seize the doorknob.

It would not turn. He was shut in.

"I hope this means," said the corpulent, red-nosed wizard who hung on the wall behind Dumbledore's desk, "that Dumbledore will soon be back with us?"

Harry turned. The wizard was eyeing him with great interest. Harry nodded. He tugged again on the doorknob behind his back, but it remained immovable.

"Oh good," said the wizard. "It has been very dull without him, very dull indeed."

He settled himself on the thronelike chair on which he had been painted and smiled benignly upon Harry.

"Dumbledore thinks very highly of you, as I am sure you know," he said comfortably. "Oh yes. Holds you in great esteem."

The guilt filling the whole of Harry's chest like some monstrous, weighty parasite now writhed and squirmed. Harry could not stand this, he could not stand being Harry anymore. . . . He had never felt more trapped inside his own head and body, never wished so intensely that he could be somebody — anybody — else. . . .

The empty fireplace burst into emerald-green flame, making Harry leap away from the door, staring at the man spinning inside the grate. As Dumbledore's tall form unfolded itself from the fire, the wizards and witches on the surrounding walls jerked awake. Many of them gave cries of welcome.

"Thank you," said Dumbledore softly.

He did not look at Harry at first, but walked over to the perch beside the door and withdrew, from an inside pocket of his robes, the tiny, ugly, featherless Fawkes, whom he placed gently on the tray of soft ashes beneath the golden post where the full-grown Fawkes usually stood.

"Well, Harry," said Dumbledore, finally turning away from the baby bird, "you will be pleased to hear that none of your fellow students are going to suffer lasting damage from the night's events."

Harry tried to say "Good," but no sound came out. It seemed to him that Dumbledore was reminding him of the amount of damage he had caused by his actions tonight, and although Dumbledore was for once looking at him directly, and though his expression was kindly rather than accusatory, Harry could not bear to meet his eyes.

"Madam Pomfrey is patching everybody up now," said Dumbledore. "Nymphadora Tonks may need to spend a little time in St. Mungo's, but it seems that she will make a full recovery."

Harry contented himself with nodding at the carpet, which was growing lighter as the sky outside grew paler. He was sure that all the portraits around the room were listening eagerly to every word Dumbledore spoke, wondering where Dumbledore and Harry had been and why there had been injuries.

"I know how you are feeling, Harry," said Dumbledore very quietly.

"No, you don't," said Harry, and his voice was suddenly loud and strong. White-hot anger leapt inside him. Dumbledore knew *nothing* about his feelings.

"You see, Dumbledore?" said Phineas Nigellus slyly. "Never try to understand the students. They hate it. They would much rather be tragically misunderstood, wallow in self-pity, stew in their own —"

"That's enough, Phineas," said Dumbledore.

Harry turned his back on Dumbledore and stared determinedly out of the opposite window. He could see the Quidditch stadium in the distance. Sirius had appeared there once, disguised as the shaggy black dog, so he could watch Harry play. . . . He had probably come to see whether Harry was as good as James had been. . . . Harry had never asked him. . . .

"There is no shame in what you are feeling, Harry," said Dumbledore's voice. "On the contrary . . . the fact that you can feel pain like this is your greatest strength."

Harry felt the white-hot anger lick his insides, blazing in the terrible emptiness, filling him with the desire to hurt Dumbledore for his calmness and his empty words.

"My greatest strength, is it?" said Harry, his voice shaking as he stared out at the Quidditch stadium, no longer seeing it. "You haven't got a clue. . . . You don't know . . ."

"What don't I know?" asked Dumbledore calmly.

It was too much. Harry turned around, shaking with rage.

"I don't want to talk about how I feel, all right?"

"Harry, suffering like this proves you are still a man! This pain is part of being human —"

"THEN — I — DON'T — WANT — TO — BE — HUMAN!" Harry roared, and he seized one of the delicate silver instruments from the spindle-legged table beside him and flung it across the room. It shattered into a hundred tiny pieces against the wall. Several of the pictures let out yells of anger and fright, and the portrait of Armando Dippet said, *"Really!"*

"I DON'T CARE!" Harry yelled at them, snatching up a lunascope and throwing it into the fireplace. "I'VE HAD ENOUGH, I'VE SEEN ENOUGH, I WANT OUT, I WANT IT TO END, I DON'T CARE ANYMORE —"

He seized the table on which the silver instrument had stood and threw that too. It broke apart on the floor and the legs rolled in different directions.

"You do care," said Dumbledore. He had not flinched or made a single move to stop Harry demolishing his office. His expression was calm, almost detached. "You care so much you feel as though you will bleed to death with the pain of it."

"I — DON'T!" Harry screamed, so loudly that he felt his throat might tear, and for a second he wanted to rush at Dumbledore and break him too; shatter that calm old face, shake him, hurt him, make him feel some tiny part of the horror inside Harry.

"Oh yes, you do," said Dumbledore, still more calmly. "You have now lost your mother, your father, and the closest thing to a parent you have ever known. Of course you care."

"YOU DON'T KNOW HOW I FEEL!" Harry roared. "YOU — STANDING THERE — YOU —"

But words were no longer enough, smashing things was no more help. He wanted to run, he wanted to keep running and never look back, he wanted to be somewhere he could not see the clear blue eyes staring at him, that hatefully calm old face. He ran to the door, seized the doorknob again, and wrenched at it.

But the door would not open.

Harry turned back to Dumbledore.

"Let me out," he said. He was shaking from head to foot.

"No," said Dumbledore simply.

For a few seconds they stared at each other.

"Let me out," Harry said again.

"No," Dumbledore repeated.

"If you don't — if you keep me in here — if you don't let me —"

"By all means continue destroying my possessions," said Dumbledore serenely. "I daresay I have too many."

He walked around his desk and sat down behind it, watching Harry.

"Let me out," Harry said yet again, in a voice that was cold and almost as calm as Dumbledore's.

"Not until I have had my say," said Dumbledore.

"Do you — do you think I want to — do you think I give a — I DON'T CARE WHAT YOU'VE GOT TO SAY!" Harry roared. "I don't want to hear *anything* you've got to say!"

"You will," said Dumbledore sadly. "Because you are not nearly as angry with me as you ought to be. If you are to attack me, as I know you are close to doing, I would like to have thoroughly earned it."

"What are you talking — ?"

"It is *my* fault that Sirius died," said Dumbledore clearly. "Or I should say almost entirely my fault — I will not be so arrogant as to claim responsibility for the whole. Sirius was a brave, clever, and energetic man, and such men are not usually content to sit at home in hiding while they believe others to be in danger. Nevertheless, you should never have believed for an instant that there was any necessity for you to go to the Department of Mysteries tonight. If I had been open with you, Harry, as I should have been, you would have known a long time ago that Voldemort might try and lure you to the Department of Mysteries, and you would never have been tricked into going there tonight. And Sirius would not have had to come after you. That blame lies with me, and with me alone."

Harry was still standing with his hand on the doorknob but he was unaware of it. He was gazing at Dumbledore, hardly breathing, listening yet barely understanding what he was hearing.

"Please sit down," said Dumbledore. It was not an order, it was a request.

Harry hesitated, then walked slowly across the room now littered with silver cogs and fragments of wood and took the seat facing Dumbledore's desk.

"Am I to understand," said Phineas Nigellus slowly from Harry's left, "that my great-great-grandson — the last of the Blacks — is dead?"

"Yes, Phineas," said Dumbledore.

"I don't believe it," said Phineas brusquely.

Harry turned his head in time to see Phineas marching out of his portrait and knew that he had gone to visit his other painting in Grimmauld Place. He would walk, perhaps, from portrait to portrait, calling for Sirius through the house. . . .

"Harry, I owe you an explanation," said Dumbledore. "An explanation of an old man's mistakes. For I see now that what I have done, and not done, with regard to you, bears all the hallmarks of the failings of age. Youth cannot know how age thinks and feels. But old men are guilty if they forget what it was to be young . . . and I seem to have forgotten lately. . . ."

The sun was rising properly now. There was a rim of dazzling orange visible over the mountains and the sky above it was colorless and bright. The light fell upon Dumbledore, upon the silver of his eyebrows and beard, upon the lines gouged deeply into his face.

"I guessed, fifteen years ago," said Dumbledore, "when I saw the scar upon your forehead, what it might mean. I guessed that it might be the sign of a connection forged between you and Voldemort."

"You've told me this before, Professor," said Harry bluntly. He did not care about being rude. He did not care about anything very much anymore.

"Yes," said Dumbledore apologetically. "Yes, but you see — it is necessary to start with your scar. For it became apparent, shortly after you rejoined the magical world, that I was correct, and that your scar was giving you warnings when Voldemort was close to you, or else feeling powerful emotion."

"I know," said Harry wearily.

"And this ability of yours — to detect Voldemort's presence, even when he is disguised, and to know what he is feeling when his emotions are roused — has become more and more pronounced since Voldemort returned to his own body and his full powers."

Harry did not bother to nod. He knew all of this already.

"More recently," said Dumbledore, "I became concerned that Voldemort might realize that this connection between you exists. Sure enough, there came a time when you entered so far into his mind and thoughts that he sensed your presence. I am speaking, of course, of the night when you witnessed the attack on Mr. Weasley."

"Yeah, Snape told me," Harry muttered.

"*Professor* Snape, Harry," Dumbledore corrected him quietly. "But did you not wonder why it was not I who explained this to you? Why I did not teach you Occlumency? Why I had not so much as looked at you for months?"

Harry looked up. He could see now that Dumbledore looked sad and tired.

"Yeah," Harry mumbled. "Yeah, I wondered."

"You see," continued Dumbledore heavily, "I believed it could not be long before Voldemort attempted to force his way into your mind, to manipulate and misdirect your thoughts, and I was not eager to give him more incentives to do so. I was sure that if he realized that our relationship was — or had ever been — closer than that of headmaster and pupil, he would seize his chance to use you as a means to spy on me. I feared the uses to which he would put you, the possibility that he might try and possess you. Harry, I believe I was right to think that Voldemort would have made use of you in such a way. On those rare occasions when we had close contact, I thought I saw a shadow of him stir behind your eyes. . . . I was trying, in distancing myself from you, to protect you. An old man's mistake . . ."

Harry remembered the feeling that a dormant snake had risen in him, ready to strike, on those occasions when he and Dumbledore made eye contact.

"Voldemort's aim in possessing you, as he demonstrated tonight, would not have been my destruction. It would have been yours. He hoped, when he possessed you briefly a short while ago, that I would sacrifice you in the hope of killing him."

He sighed deeply. Harry was letting the words wash over him. He would have been so interested to know all this a few months ago, and now it was meaningless compared to the gaping chasm inside him that was the loss of Sirius, none of it mattered . . .

"Sirius told me that you felt Voldemort awake inside you the very night that you had the vision of Arthur Weasley's attack. I knew at once that my worst fears were correct: Voldemort from that point had realized he could use you. In an attempt to arm you against Voldemort's assaults on your mind, I arranged Occlumency lessons with Professor Snape."

He paused. Harry watched the sunlight, which was sliding slowly across the polished surface of Dumbledore's desk, illuminate a silver ink pot and a handsome scarlet quill. Harry could tell that the portraits all around them were awake and listening raptly to Dumbledore's explanation. He could hear the occasional rustle of robes, the slight clearing of a throat. Phineas Nigellus had still not returned. . . .

"Professor Snape discovered,". Dumbledore resumed, "that you had been dreaming about the door to the Department of Mysteries for months. Voldemort, of course, had been obsessed with the possibility of hearing the prophecy ever since he regained his body, and as he dwelled on the door, so did you, though you did not know what it meant.

"And then you saw Rookwood, who worked in the Department of Mysteries before his arrest, telling Voldemort what we had known all along — that the prophecies held in the Ministry of Magic are heavily protected. Only the people to whom they refer can lift them from the shelves without suffering madness. In this case, either Voldemort himself would have to enter the Ministry of Magic and risk revealing himself at last — or else you would have to take it for him. It became a matter of even greater urgency that you should master Occlumency."

"But I didn't," muttered Harry. He said it aloud to try and ease the dead weight of guilt inside him; a confession must surely relieve some of the terrible pressure squeezing his heart. "I didn't practice, I didn't bother, I could've stopped myself having those dreams, Hermione kept telling me to do it, if I had he'd never have been able to show me where to go, and — Sirius wouldn't — Sirius wouldn't —"

Something was erupting inside Harry's head: a need to justify himself, to explain —

"I tried to check he'd really taken Sirius, I went to Umbridge's office, I spoke to Kreacher in the fire, and he said Sirius wasn't there, he said he'd gone!"

"Kreacher lied," said Dumbledore calmly. "You are not his master, he could lie to you without even needing to punish himself. Kreacher intended you to go to the Ministry of Magic."

"He — he sent me on purpose?"

"Oh yes. Kreacher, I am afraid, has been serving more than one master for months."

"How?" said Harry blankly. "He hasn't been out of Grimmauld Place for years."

"Kreacher seized his opportunity shortly before Christmas," said Dumbledore, "when Sirius, apparently, shouted at him to 'get out.' He took Sirius at his word and interpreted this as an order to leave the house. He went to the only Black family member for whom he had any respect left. . . . Black's cousin Narcissa, sister of Bellatrix and wife of Lucius Malfoy."

"How do you know all this?" Harry said. His heart was beating very fast. He felt sick. He remembered worrying about Kreacher's odd absence over Christmas, remembered him turning up again in the attic. . . .

"Kreacher told me last night," said Dumbledore. "You see, when you gave Professor Snape that cryptic warning, he realized that you had had a vision of Sirius trapped in the bowels of the Department of Mysteries. He, like you, attempted to contact Sirius at once. I should explain that members of the Order of the Phoenix have more reliable methods of communicating than the fire in Dolores Umbridge's office. Professor Snape found that Sirius was alive and safe in Grimmauld Place.

"When, however, you did not return from your trip into the forest with Dolores Umbridge, Professor Snape grew worried that you still believed Sirius to be a captive of Lord Voldemort's. He alerted certain Order members at once."

Dumbledore heaved a great sigh and then said, "Alastor Moody, Nymphadora Tonks, Kingsley Shacklebolt, and Remus Lupin were at headquarters when he made contact. All agreed to go to your aid at once. Professor Snape requested that Sirius remain behind, as he needed somebody to remain at headquarters to tell me what had happened, for I was due there at any moment. In the meantime he, Professor Snape, intended to search the forest for you.

"But Sirius did not wish to remain behind while the others went to search for you. He delegated to Kreacher the task of telling me what had happened. And so it was that when I arrived in Grimmauld Place shortly after they had all left for the Ministry, it was the elf who told me — laughing fit to burst — where Sirius had gone."

"He was laughing?" said Harry in a hollow voice.

"Oh yes," said Dumbledore. "You see, Kreacher was not able to betray us totally. He is not Secret-Keeper for the Order, he could not give the Malfoys our whereabouts or tell them any of the Order's confidential plans that he had been forbidden to reveal. He was bound by the enchantments of his kind, which is to say that he could not disobey a direct order from his master, Sirius. But he gave Narcissa information of the sort that is very valuable to Voldemort, yet must have seemed much too trivial for Sirius to think of banning him from repeating it."

"Like what?" said Harry.

"Like the fact that the person Sirius cared most about in the world was you," said Dumbledore quietly. "Like the fact that you were coming to regard Sirius as a mixture of father and brother. Voldemort knew already, of course, that Sirius was in the Order, that you knew where he was — but Kreacher's information made him realize that the one person whom you would go to any lengths to rescue was Sirius Black."

Harry's lips were cold and numb.

"So . . . when I asked Kreacher if Sirius was there last night . . ."

"The Malfoys — undoubtedly on Voldemort's instructions — had told him he must find a way of keeping Sirius out of the way once you had seen the vision of Sirius being tortured. Then, if you decided to check whether Sirius was at home or not, Kreacher would be able to pretend he was not. Kreacher injured Buckbeak the hippogriff yesterday, and at the moment when you made your appearance in the fire, Sirius was upstairs trying to tend to him."

There seemed to be very little air in Harry's lungs, his breathing was quick and shallow.

"And Kreacher told you all this . . . and laughed?" he croaked.

"He did not wish to tell me," said Dumbledore. "But I am a sufficiently accomplished Legilimens myself to know when I am being lied to and I — persuaded him — to tell me the full story, before I left for the Department of Mysteries."

"And," whispered Harry, his hands curled in cold fists on his knees, "and Hermione kept telling us to be nice to him —"

"She was quite right, Harry," said Dumbledore. "I warned Sirius when we adopted twelve Grimmauld Place as our headquarters that Kreacher must be treated with kindness and respect. I also told him that Kreacher could be dangerous to us. I do not think that Sirius took me very seriously, or that he ever saw Kreacher as a being with feelings as acute as a human's —"

"Don't you blame — don't you — talk — about Sirius like —" Harry's breath was constricted, he could not get the words out properly. But the rage that had subsided so briefly had flared in him again; he would not let Dumbledore criticize Sirius. "Kreacher's a lying — foul — he deserved —"

"Kreacher is what he has been made by wizards, Harry," said Dumbledore. "Yes, he is to be pitied. His existence has been as miserable as your friend Dobby's. He was forced to do Sirius's bidding, because Sirius was the last of the family to which he was enslaved, but he felt no true loyalty to him. And whatever Kreacher's faults, it must be admitted that Sirius did nothing to make Kreacher's lot easier —"

"DON'T TALK ABOUT SIRIUS LIKE THAT!" Harry yelled.

He was on his feet again, furious, ready to fly at Dumbledore, who had plainly not understood Sirius at all, how brave he was, how much he had suffered . . .

"What about Snape?" Harry spat. "You're not talking about him, are you? When I told him Voldemort had Sirius he just sneered at me as usual —"

"Harry, you know that Professor Snape had no choice but to pretend not to take you seriously in front of Dolores Umbridge," said

Dumbledore steadily, "but as I have explained, he informed the Order as soon as possible about what you had said. It was he who deduced where you had gone when you did not return from the forest. It was he too who gave Professor Umbridge fake Veritaserum when she was attempting to force you to tell of Sirius's whereabouts. . . ."

Harry disregarded this; he felt a savage pleasure in blaming Snape, it seemed to be easing his own sense of dreadful guilt, and he wanted to hear Dumbledore agree with him.

"Snape — Snape g-goaded Sirius about staying in the house — he made out Sirius was a coward —"

"Sirius was much too old and clever to have allowed such feeble taunts to hurt him," said Dumbledore.

"Snape stopped giving me Occlumency lessons!" Harry snarled. "He threw me out of his office!"

"I am aware of it," said Dumbledore heavily. "I have already said that it was a mistake for me not to teach you myself, though I was sure, at the time, that nothing could have been more danger-ous than to open your mind even further to Voldemort while in my presence —"

"Snape made it worse, my scar always hurt worse after lessons with him —" Harry remembered Ron's thoughts on the subject and plunged on. "How do you know he wasn't trying to soften me up for Voldemort, make it easier for him to get inside my —"

"I trust Severus Snape," said Dumbledore simply. "But I forgot — another old man's mistake — that some wounds run too deep for the healing. I thought Professor Snape could overcome his feelings about your father — I was wrong."

"But that's okay, is it?" yelled Harry, ignoring the scandalized faces and disapproving mutterings of the portraits covering the walls. "It's okay for Snape to hate my dad, but it's not okay for Sirius to hate Kreacher?"

"Sirius did not hate Kreacher," said Dumbledore. "He regarded him as a servant unworthy of much interest or notice. Indifference and neglect often do much more damage than outright dislike. . . . The fountain we destroyed tonight told a lie. We wizards have mistreated and abused our fellows for too long, and we are now reaping our reward."

"SO SIRIUS DESERVED WHAT HE GOT, DID HE?" Harry yelled.

"I did not say that, nor will you ever hear me say it," Dumbledore replied quietly. "Sirius was not a cruel man, he was kind to house-elves in general. He had no love for Kreacher, because Kreacher was a living reminder of the home Sirius had hated."

"Yeah, he did hate it!" said Harry, his voice cracking, turning his back on Dumbledore and walking away. The sun was bright inside the room now, and the eyes of all the portraits followed him as he walked, without realizing what he was doing, without seeing the office at all. "You made him stay shut up in that house and he hated it, that's why he wanted to get out last night —"

"I was trying to keep Sirius alive," said Dumbledore quietly.

"People don't like being locked up!" Harry said furiously, rounding on him. "You did it to me all last summer —"

Dumbledore closed his eyes and buried his face in his long-fingered hands. Harry watched him, but this uncharacteristic sign of exhaustion, or sadness, or whatever it was from Dumbledore, did not soften him. On the contrary, he felt even angrier that Dumbledore was showing signs of weakness. He had no business being weak when Harry wanted to rage and storm at him.

Dumbledore lowered his hands and surveyed Harry through his half-moon glasses.

"It is time," he said, "for me to tell you what I should have told you five years ago, Harry. Please sit down. I am going to tell you everything. I ask only a little patience. You will have your chance to rage at me — to do whatever you like — when I have finished. I will not stop you."

Harry glared at him for a moment, then flung himself back into the chair opposite Dumbledore and waited. Dumbledore stared for a moment at the sunlit grounds outside the window, then looked back at Harry and said, "Five years ago you arrived at Hogwarts, Harry, safe and whole, as I had planned and intended. Well — not quite whole. You had suffered. I knew you would when I left you on your aunt and uncle's doorstep. I knew I was condemning you to ten dark and difficult years."

He paused. Harry said nothing.

"You might ask — and with good reason — why it had to be so. Why could some Wizarding family not have taken you in? Many would have done so more than gladly, would have been honored and delighted to raise you as a son.

"My answer is that my priority was to keep you alive. You were in more danger than perhaps anyone but myself realized. Voldemort had been vanquished hours before, but his supporters — and many of them are almost as terrible as he — were still at large, angry, desperate, and violent. And I had to make my decision too with regard to the years ahead. Did I believe that Voldemort was gone forever? No. I knew not whether it would be ten, twenty, or fifty years before he returned, but I was sure he would do so, and I was sure too, knowing him as I have done, that he would not rest until he killed you.

"I knew that Voldemort's knowledge of magic is perhaps more extensive than any wizard alive. I knew that even my most complex and powerful protective spells and charms were unlikely to be invincible if he ever returned to full power.

"But I knew too where Voldemort was weak. And so I made my decision. You would be protected by an ancient magic of which he knows, which he despises, and which he has always, therefore, underestimated — to his cost. I am speaking, of course, of the fact that your mother died to save you. She gave you a lingering protection he never expected, a protection that flows in your veins to this day. I put my trust, therefore, in your mother's blood. I delivered you to her sister, her only remaining relative."

"She doesn't love me," said Harry at once. "She doesn't give a damn —"

"But she took you," Dumbledore cut across him. "She may have taken you grudgingly, furiously, unwillingly, bitterly, yet still she took you, and in doing so, she sealed the charm I placed upon you. Your mother's sacrifice made the bond of blood the strongest shield I could give you."

"I still don't —"

"While you can still call home the place where your mother's blood dwells, there you cannot be touched or harmed by Voldemort. He shed her blood, but it lives on in you and her sister. Her blood became your refuge. You need return there only once a year, but as long as you can still call it home, there he cannot hurt you. Your aunt knows this. I explained what I had done in the letter I left, with you, on her doorstep. She knows that allowing you houseroom may well have kept you alive for the past fifteen years."

"Wait," said Harry. "Wait a moment."

He sat up straighter in his chair, staring at Dumbledore.

"You sent that Howler. You told her to remember — it was your voice —"

"I thought," said Dumbledore, inclining his head slightly, "that she might need reminding of the pact she had sealed by taking you. I suspected the dementor attack might have awoken her to the dangers of having you as a surrogate son."

"It did," said Harry quietly. "Well — my uncle more than her. He wanted to chuck me out, but after the Howler came she — she said I had to stay." He stared at the floor for a moment, then said, "But what's this got to do with . . ."

He could not say Sirius's name.

"Five years ago, then," continued Dumbledore, as though he had not paused in his story, "you arrived at Hogwarts, neither as happy nor as well nourished as I would have liked, perhaps, yet alive and healthy. You were not a pampered little prince, but as normal a boy as I could have hoped under the circumstances. Thus far, my plan was working well.

"And then . . . well, you will remember the events of your first year at Hogwarts quite as clearly as I do. You rose magnificently to the challenge that faced you, and sooner — much sooner — than I had anticipated, you found yourself face-to-face with Voldemort. You survived again. You did more. You delayed his return to full power and strength. You fought a man's fight. I was . . . prouder of you than I can say.

"Yet there was a flaw in this wonderful plan of mine," said Dumbledore. "An obvious flaw that I knew, even then, might be the undoing of it all. And yet, knowing how important it was that my plan should succeed, I told myself that I would not permit this flaw to ruin it. I alone could prevent this, so I alone must be strong. And here was my first test, as you lay in the hospital wing, weak from your struggle with Voldemort."

"I don't understand what you're saying," said Harry.

"Don't you remember asking me, as you lay in the hospital wing, why Voldemort had tried to kill you when you were a baby?"

Harry nodded.

"Ought I to have told you then?"

Harry stared into the blue eyes and said nothing, but his heart was racing again.

"You do not see the flaw in the plan yet? No . . . perhaps not. Well, as you know, I decided not to answer you. Eleven, I told myself, was much too young to know. I had never intended to tell you when you were eleven. The knowledge would be too much at such a young age.

"I should have recognized the danger signs then. I should have asked myself why I did not feel more disturbed that you had already asked me the question to which I knew, one day, I must give a terrible answer. I should have recognized that I was too happy to think that I did not have to do it on that particular day. . . . You were too young, much too young.

"And so we entered your second year at Hogwarts. And once again you met challenges even grown wizards have never faced. Once again you acquitted yourself beyond my wildest dreams. You did not ask me again, however, why Voldemort had left that mark upon you. We discussed your scar, oh yes. . . . We came very, very close to the subject. Why did I not tell you everything?

"Well, it seemed to me that twelve was, after all, hardly better than eleven to receive such information. I allowed you to leave my presence, bloodstained, exhausted but exhilarated, and if I felt a twinge of unease that I ought, perhaps, to have told you then, it was swiftly silenced. You were still so young, you see, and I could not find it in me to spoil that night of triumph. . . .

"Do you see, Harry? Do you see the flaw in my brilliant plan now? I had fallen into the trap I had foreseen, that I had told myself I could avoid, that I must avoid."

"I don't —"

"I cared about you too much," said Dumbledore simply. "I cared more for your happiness than your knowing the truth, more for your peace of mind than my plan, more for your life than the lives that might be lost if the plan failed. In other words, I acted exactly as Voldemort expects we fools who love to act.

"Is there a defense? I defy anyone who has watched you as I have —

and I have watched you more closely than you can have imagined — not to want to save you more pain than you had already suffered. What did I care if numbers of nameless and faceless people and creatures were slaughtered in the vague future, if in the here and now you were alive, and well, and happy? I never dreamed that I would have such a person on my hands.

"We entered your third year. I watched from afar as you struggled to repel dementors, as you found Sirius, learned what he was and rescued him. Was I to tell you then, at the moment when you had triumphantly snatched your godfather from the jaws of the Ministry? But now, at the age of thirteen, my excuses were running out. Young you might be, but you had proved you were exceptional. My conscience was uneasy, Harry. I knew the time must come soon. . . .

"But you came out of the maze last year, having watched Cedric Diggory die, having escaped death so narrowly yourself . . . and I did not tell you, though I knew, now Voldemort had returned, I must do it soon. And now, tonight, I know you have long been ready for the knowledge I have kept from you for so long, because you have proved that I should have placed the burden upon you before this. My only defense is this: I have watched you struggling under more burdens than any student who has ever passed through this school, and I could not bring myself to add another — the greatest one of all."

Harry waited, but Dumbledore did not speak.

"I still don't understand."

"Voldemort tried to kill you when you were a child because of a prophecy made shortly before your birth. He knew the prophecy had been made, though he did not know its full contents. He set out to kill you when you were still a baby, believing he was fulfilling the terms of the prophecy. He discovered, to his cost, that he was mistaken, when the curse intended to kill you backfired. And so, since his return to his body, and particularly since your extraordinary escape from him last year, he has been determined to hear that prophecy in its entirety. This is the weapon he has been seeking so assiduously since his return: the knowledge of how to destroy you."

The sun had risen fully now. Dumbledore's office was bathed in it. The glass case in which the sword of Godric Gryffindor resided gleamed white and opaque, the fragments of the instruments Harry had thrown to the floor glistened like raindrops, and behind him, the baby Fawkes made soft chirruping noises in his nest of ashes.

"The prophecy's smashed," Harry said blankly. "I was pulling Neville up those benches in the — the room where the archway was, and I ripped his robes and it fell. . . ."

"The thing that smashed was merely the record of the prophecy kept by the Department of Mysteries. But the prophecy was made to somebody, and that person has the means of recalling it perfectly."

"Who heard it?" asked Harry, though he thought he knew the answer already.

"I did," said Dumbledore. "On a cold, wet night sixteen years ago, in a room above the bar at the Hog's Head Inn. I had gone there to see an applicant for the post of Divination teacher, though it was against my inclination to allow the subject of Divination to continue at all. The applicant, however, was the great-great-granddaughter of a very famous, very gifted Seer, and I thought it common politeness to meet her. I was disappointed. It seemed to me that she had not a trace of the gift herself. I told her, courteously I hope, that I did not think she would be suitable for the post. I turned to leave."

Dumbledore got to his feet and walked past Harry to the black cabinet that stood beside Fawkes's perch. He bent down, slid back a catch, and took from inside it the shallow stone basin, carved with runes around the edges, in which Harry had seen his father tormenting Snape. Dumbledore walked back to the desk, placed the Pensieve upon it, and raised his wand to his own temple. From it, he withdrew silvery, gossamer-fine strands of thought clinging to the wand, and deposited them in the basin. He sat back down behind his desk and watched his thoughts swirl and drift inside the Pensieve for a moment. Then, with a sigh, he raised his wand and prodded the silvery substance with its tip.

A figure rose out of it, draped in shawls, her eyes magnified to enormous size behind her glasses, and she revolved slowly, her feet in the basin. But when Sybill Trelawney spoke, it was not in her usual ethereal, mystic voice, but in the harsh, hoarse tones Harry had heard her use once before.

"*THE ONE WITH THE POWER TO VANQUISH THE DARK LORD APPROACHES. . . . BORN TO THOSE WHO HAVE THRICE DEFIED HIM, BORN AS THE SEVENTH MONTH DIES . . . AND THE DARK LORD WILL MARK HIM AS HIS EQUAL, BUT HE WILL HAVE POWER THE DARK LORD KNOWS NOT . . . AND EITHER MUST DIE AT THE HAND OF THE OTHER FOR NEITHER CAN LIVE WHILE THE OTHER SURVIVES. . . . THE ONE WITH THE POWER TO VANQUISH THE DARK LORD WILL BE BORN AS THE SEVENTH MONTH DIES. . . .*"

The slowly revolving Professor Trelawney sank back into the silver mass below and vanished.

The silence within the office was absolute. Neither Dumbledore nor Harry nor any of the portraits made a sound. Even Fawkes had fallen silent.

"Professor Dumbledore?" Harry said very quietly, for Dumbledore, still staring at the Pensieve, seemed completely lost in thought. "It . . . did that mean . . . What did that mean?"

"It meant," said Dumbledore, "that the person who has the only chance of conquering Lord Voldemort for good was born at the end of July, nearly sixteen years ago. This boy would be born to parents who had already defied Voldemort three times."

Harry felt as though something was closing in upon him. His breathing seemed difficult again.

"It means — me?"

Dumbledore took a deep breath.

"The odd thing is, Harry," he said softly, "that it may not have meant you at all. Sybill's prophecy could have applied to two wizard boys, both born at the end of July that year, both of whom had parents in the Order of the Phoenix, both sets of parents having narrowly escaped Voldemort three times. One, of course, was you. The other was Neville Longbottom."

"But then . . . but then, why was it my name on the prophecy and not Neville's?"

"The official record was relabeled after Voldemort's attack on you as a child," said Dumbledore. "It seemed plain to the keeper of the Hall of Prophecy that Voldemort could only have tried to kill you because he knew you to be the one to whom Sybill was referring."

"Then — it might not be me?" said Harry.

"I am afraid," said Dumbledore slowly, looking as though every word cost him a great effort, "that there is no doubt that it *is* you."

"But you said — Neville was born at the end of July too — and his mum and dad —"

"You are forgetting the next part of the prophecy, the final identifying feature of the boy who could vanquish Voldemort. . . . Voldemort himself would 'mark him as his equal.' And so he did, Harry. He chose you, not Neville. He gave you the scar that has proved both blessing and curse."

"But he might have chosen wrong!" said Harry. "He might have marked the wrong person!"

"He chose the boy he thought most likely to be a danger to him," said Dumbledore. "And notice this, Harry. He chose, not the pureblood (which, according to his creed, is the only kind of wizard worth being or knowing), but the half-blood, like himself. He saw himself in you before he had ever seen you, and in marking you with that scar, he did not kill you, as he intended, but gave you powers, and a future, which have fitted you to escape him not once, but four times so far — something that neither your parents, nor Neville's parents, ever achieved."

"Why did he do it, then?" said Harry, who felt numb and cold. "Why did he try and kill me as a baby? He should have waited to see whether Neville or I looked more dangerous when we were older and tried to kill whoever it was then —"

"That might, indeed, have been the more practical course," said Dumbledore, "except that Voldemort's information about the prophecy was incomplete. The Hog's Head Inn, which Sybill chose for its cheapness, has long attracted, shall we say, a more interesting clientele than the Three Broomsticks. As you and your friends found out to your cost, and I to mine that night, it is a place where it is never safe to assume you are not being overheard. Of course, I had not dreamed, when I set out to meet Sybill Trelawney, that I would hear anything worth overhearing. My — our — one stroke of good fortune was that the eavesdropper was detected only a short way into the prophecy and thrown from the building."

"So he only heard . . . ?"

"He heard only the first part, the part foretelling the birth of a boy in July to parents who had thrice defied Voldemort. Consequently, he could not warn his master that to attack you would be to risk transferring power to you — again marking you as his equal. So Voldemort never knew that there might be danger in attacking you, that it might be wise to wait or to learn more. He did not know that you would have 'power the Dark Lord knows not' —"

"But I don't!" said Harry in a strangled voice. "I haven't any powers he hasn't got, I couldn't fight the way he did tonight, I can't possess people or — or kill them —"

"There is a room in the Department of Mysteries," interrupted Dumbledore, "that is kept locked at all times. It contains a force that is at once more wonderful and more terrible than death, than human intelligence, than forces of nature. It is also, perhaps, the most mysterious of the many subjects for study that reside there. It is the power held within that room that you possess in such quantities and which

Voldemort has not at all. That power took you to save Sirius tonight. That power also saved you from possession by Voldemort, because he could not bear to reside in a body so full of the force he detests. In the end, it mattered not that you could not close your mind. It was your heart that saved you."

Harry closed his eyes. If he had not gone to save Sirius, Sirius would not have died. . . . More to stave off the moment when he would have to think of Sirius again, Harry asked, without caring much about the answer, "The end of the prophecy . . . it was something about . . . *'neither can live . . .'*"

"*'. . . while the other survives,'*" said Dumbledore.

"So," said Harry, dredging up the words from what felt like a deep well of despair inside him, "so does that mean that . . . that one of us has got to kill the other one . . . in the end?"

"Yes," said Dumbledore.

For a long time, neither of them spoke. Somewhere far beyond the office walls, Harry could hear the sound of voices, students heading down to the Great Hall for an early breakfast, perhaps. It seemed impossible that there could be people in the world who still desired food, who laughed, who neither knew nor cared that Sirius Black was gone forever. Sirius seemed a million miles away already, even if a part of Harry still believed that if he had only pulled back that veil, he would have found Sirius looking back at him, greeting him, perhaps, with his laugh like a bark. . . .

"I feel I owe you another explanation, Harry," said Dumbledore hesitantly. "You may, perhaps, have wondered why I never chose you as a prefect? I must confess . . . that I rather thought . . . you had enough responsibility to be going on with."

Harry looked up at him and saw a tear trickling down Dumbledore's face into his long silver beard.

THE SECOND
WAR BEGINS

HE-WHO-MUST-NOT-BE-NAMED RETURNS

In a brief statement Friday night, Minister of Magic Cornelius Fudge confirmed that He-Who-Must-Not-Be-Named has returned to this country and is active once more.

"It is with great regret that I must confirm that the wizard styling himself Lord — well, you know who I mean — is alive and among us again," said Fudge, looking tired and flustered as he addressed reporters. "It is with almost equal regret that we report the mass revolt of the dementors of Azkaban, who have shown themselves averse to continuing in the Ministry's employ. We believe that the dementors are currently taking direction from Lord — Thingy.

"We urge the magical population to remain vigilant. The Ministry is currently publishing guides to elementary home and personal defense that will be delivered free to all Wizarding homes within the coming month."

The Minister's statement was met with dismay and alarm from the Wizarding community, which as recently as last Wednesday was receiving Ministry assurances that there was "no truth whatsoever in these persistent rumors that You-Know-Who is operating amongst us once more."

Details of the events that led to the Ministry turnaround are still hazy, though it is believed that He-Who-Must-Not-Be-Named and a select band of followers (known as Death Eaters) gained entry to the Ministry of Magic itself on Thursday evening.

Albus Dumbledore, newly reinstated headmaster of Hogwarts School of Witchcraft and Wizardry, reinstated member of the International Confederation of Wizards, and reinstated Chief Warlock of the Wizengamot, was unavailable for comment last night. He has insisted for a year that You-Know-Who was not dead, as was widely hoped and believed, but recruiting followers once more for a fresh attempt to seize power. Meanwhile the Boy Who Lived —

"There you are, Harry, I knew they'd drag you into it somehow," said Hermione, looking over the top of the paper at him.

They were in the hospital wing. Harry was sitting on the end of Ron's bed and they were both listening to Hermione read the front page of the *Sunday Prophet*. Ginny, whose ankle had been mended in a trice by Madam Pomfrey, was curled up at the foot of Hermione's bed; Neville, whose nose had likewise been returned to its normal size and shape, was in a chair between the two beds; and Luna, who had dropped in to visit clutching the latest edition of *The Quibbler*, was reading the magazine upside down and apparently not taking in a word Hermione was saying.

"He's 'the Boy Who Lived' again now, though, isn't he?" said Ron darkly. "Not such a show-off maniac anymore, eh?"

He helped himself to a handful of Chocolate Frogs from the immense pile on his bedside cabinet, threw a few to Harry, Ginny, and Neville, and ripped off the wrapper of his own with his teeth. There were still deep welts on his forearms where the brain's tentacles had wrapped around him. According to Madam Pomfrey, thoughts could leave deeper scarring than almost anything else, though since she had started applying copious amounts of Dr. Ubbly's Oblivious Unction, there seemed to be some improvement.

"Yes, they're very complimentary about you now, Harry," said Hermione, now scanning down the article. "*A lone voice of truth . . . perceived as unbalanced, yet never wavered in his story . . . forced to bear ridicule and slander . . .*' Hmmm," said Hermione, frowning, "I notice they don't mention the fact that it was them doing all the ridiculing and slandering, though. . . ."

She winced slightly and put a hand to her ribs. The curse Dolohov had used on her, though less effective than it would have been had he been able to say the incantation aloud, had nevertheless caused, in Madam Pomfrey's words, "quite enough damage to be going on with." Hermione was having to take ten different types of potion every day and although she was improving greatly, was already bored with the hospital wing.

"*'You-Know-Who's Last Attempt to Take Over, pages two to four, What the Ministry Should Have Told Us, page five, Why Nobody Listened to Albus Dumbledore, pages six to eight, Exclusive Interview with Harry Potter, page nine . . .*'Well," said Hermione, folding up the newspaper and throwing it aside, "it's certainly given them lots to write about. And that interview with Harry isn't exclusive, it's the one that was in *The Quibbler* months ago. . . ."

"Daddy sold it to them," said Luna vaguely, turning a page of *The Quibbler*. "He got a very good price for it too, so we're going to go on an expedition to Sweden this summer and see if we can catch a Crumple-Horned Snorkack."

Hermione seemed to struggle with herself for a moment, then said, "That sounds lovely."

Ginny caught Harry's eye and looked away quickly, grinning.

"So anyway," said Hermione, sitting up a little straighter and wincing again, "what's going on in school?"

"Well, Flitwick's got rid of Fred and George's swamp," said Ginny. "He did it in about three seconds. But he left a tiny patch under the window and he's roped it off —"

"Why?" said Hermione, looking startled.

"Oh, he just says it was a really good bit of magic," said Ginny, shrugging.

"I think he left it as a monument to Fred and George," said Ron through a mouthful of chocolate. "They sent me all these, you know," he told Harry, pointing at the small mountain of Frogs beside him. "Must be doing all right out of that joke shop, eh?"

Hermione looked rather disapproving and asked, "So has all the trouble stopped now Dumbledore's back?"

"Yes," said Neville, "everything's settled right back down again."

"I s'pose Filch is happy, is he?" asked Ron, propping a Chocolate Frog card featuring Dumbledore against his water jug.

"Not at all," said Ginny. "He's really, really miserable, actually. . . ." She lowered her voice to a whisper. "He keeps saying Umbridge was the best thing that ever happened to Hogwarts. . . ."

All six of them looked around. Professor Umbridge was lying in a bed opposite them, gazing up at the ceiling. Dumbledore had strode alone into the forest to rescue her from the centaurs. How he had done it — how he had emerged from the trees supporting Professor Umbridge without so much as a scratch on him — nobody knew, and

Umbridge was certainly not telling. Since she had returned to the castle she had not, as far as any of them knew, uttered a single word. Nobody really knew what was wrong with her either. Her usually neat mousy hair was very untidy and there were bits of twig and leaf in it, but otherwise she seemed to be quite unscathed.

"Madam Pomfrey says she's just in shock," whispered Hermione.

"Sulking, more like," said Ginny.

"Yeah, she shows signs of life if you do this," said Ron, and with his tongue he made soft clip-clopping noises. Umbridge sat bolt upright, looking wildly around.

"Anything wrong, Professor?" called Madam Pomfrey, poking her head around her office door.

"No . . . no . . . ," said Umbridge, sinking back into her pillows, "no, I must have been dreaming. . . ."

Hermione and Ginny muffled their laughter in the bedclothes.

"Speaking of centaurs," said Hermione, when she had recovered a little, "who's Divination teacher now? Is Firenze staying?"

"He's got to," said Harry, "the other centaurs won't take him back, will they?"

"It looks like he and Trelawney are both going to teach," said Ginny.

"Bet Dumbledore wishes he could've got rid of Trelawney for good," said Ron, now munching on his fourteenth Frog. "Mind you, the whole subject's useless if you ask me, Firenze isn't a lot better. . . ."

"How can you say that?" Hermione demanded. "After we've just found out that there are real prophecies?"

Harry's heart began to race. He had not told Ron, Hermione, or anyone else what the prophecy had contained. Neville had told them it had smashed while Harry was pulling him up the steps in the Death Room, and Harry had not yet corrected this impression. He was not ready to see their expressions when he told them that he must be either murderer or victim, there was no other way. . . .

"It is a pity it broke," said Hermione quietly, shaking her head.

"Yeah, it is," said Ron. "Still, at least You-Know-Who never found out what was in it either — where are you going?" he added, looking both surprised and disappointed as Harry stood up.

"Er — Hagrid's," said Harry. "You know, he just got back and I promised I'd go down and see him and tell him how you two are. . . ."

"Oh all right then," said Ron grumpily, looking out of the dormitory window at the patch of bright blue sky beyond. "Wish we could come . . ."

"Say hello to him for us!" called Hermione, as Harry proceeded down the ward. "And ask him what's happening about . . . about his little friend!"

Harry gave a wave of his hand to show he had heard and understood as he left the dormitory.

The castle seemed very quiet even for a Sunday. Everybody was clearly out in the sunny grounds, enjoying the end of their exams and the prospect of a last few days of term unhampered by studying or homework. Harry walked slowly along the deserted corridor, peering out of windows as he went. He could see people messing around in the air over the Quidditch pitch and a couple of students swimming in the lake, accompanied by the giant squid.

He was finding it hard at the moment to decide whether he wanted to be with people or not. Whenever he was in company he wanted to get away, and whenever he was alone he wanted company. He thought he might really go and visit Hagrid, though; he had not talked to him properly since he had returned. . . .

Harry had just descended the last marble step into the entrance hall when Malfoy, Crabbe, and Goyle emerged from a door on the right that Harry knew led down to the Slytherin common room. Harry stopped dead; so did Malfoy and the others. For a few moments, the only sounds were the shouts, laughter, and splashes drifting into the hall from the grounds through the open front doors.

Malfoy glanced around. Harry knew he was checking for signs of teachers. Then he looked back at Harry and said in a low voice, "You're dead, Potter."

Harry raised his eyebrows. "Funny," he said, "you'd think I'd have stopped walking around. . . ."

Malfoy looked angrier than Harry had ever seen him. He felt a kind of detached satisfaction at the sight of his pale, pointed face contorted with rage.

"You're going to pay," said Malfoy in a voice barely louder than a whisper. "*I'm* going to make you pay for what you've done to my father. . . ."

"Well, I'm terrified now," said Harry sarcastically. "I s'pose Lord Voldemort's just a warm-up act compared to you three — what's the matter?" he said, for Malfoy, Crabbe, and Goyle had all looked stricken at the sound of the name. "He's your dad's mate, isn't he? Not scared of him, are you?"

"You think you're such a big man, Potter," said Malfoy, advancing now, Crabbe and Goyle flanking him. "You wait. I'll have you. You can't land my father in prison —"

"I thought I just had," said Harry.

"The dementors have left Azkaban," said Malfoy quietly. "Dad and the others'll be out in no time. . . ."

"Yeah, I expect they will," said Harry. "Still, at least everyone knows what scumbags they are now —"

Malfoy's hand flew toward his wand, but Harry was too quick for him. He had drawn his own wand before Malfoy's fingers had even entered the pocket of his robes.

"Potter!"

The voice rang across the entrance hall; Snape had emerged from the staircase leading down to his office, and at the sight of him Harry felt a great rush of hatred beyond anything he felt toward Malfoy. . . . Whatever Dumbledore said, he would never forgive Snape . . . never . . .

"What are you doing, Potter?" said Snape coldly as ever, as he strode over to the four of them.

"I'm trying to decide what curse to use on Malfoy, sir," said Harry fiercely.

Snape stared at him.

"Put that wand away at once," he said curtly. "Ten points from Gryff —"

Snape looked toward the giant hourglasses on the walls and gave a sneering smile.

"Ah. I see there are no longer any points left in the Gryffindor hourglass to take away. In that case, Potter, we will simply have to —"

"Add some more?"

Professor McGonagall had just stumped up the stone steps into the castle. She was carrying a tartan carpetbag in one hand and leaning heavily on a walking stick with her other, but otherwise looked quite well.

"Professor McGonagall!" said Snape, striding forward. "Out of St. Mungo's, I see!"

"Yes, Professor Snape," said Professor McGonagall, shrugging off her traveling cloak, "I'm quite as good as new. You two — Crabbe — Goyle —"

She beckoned them forward imperiously and they came, shuffling their large feet and looking awkward.

"Here," said Professor McGonagall, thrusting her carpetbag into Crabbe's chest and her cloak into Goyle's, "take these up to my office for me."

They turned and stumped away up the marble staircase.

"Right then," said Professor McGonagall, looking up at the hourglasses on the wall, "well, I think Potter and his friends ought to have fifty points apiece for alerting the world to the return of You-Know-Who! What say you, Professor Snape?"

"What?" snapped Snape, though Harry knew he had heard perfectly well. "Oh — well — I suppose . . ."

"So that's fifty each for Potter, the two Weasleys, Longbottom, and Miss Granger," said Professor McGonagall, and a shower of rubies fell down into the bottom bulb of Gryffindor's hourglass as she spoke. "Oh — and fifty for Miss Lovegood, I suppose," she added, and a number of sapphires fell into Ravenclaw's glass. "Now, you wanted to take ten from Mr. Potter, I think, Professor Snape — so there we are. . . ."

A few rubies retreated into the upper bulb, leaving a respectable amount below nevertheless.

"Well, Potter, Malfoy, I think you ought to be outside on a glorious day like this," Professor McGonagall continued briskly.

Harry did not need telling twice. He thrust his wand back inside his robes and headed straight for the front doors without another glance at Snape and Malfoy.

The hot sun hit him with a blast as he walked across the lawns toward Hagrid's cabin. Students lying around on the grass sunbathing, talking, reading the *Sunday Prophet,* and eating sweets looked up at him as he passed. Some called out to him, or else waved, clearly eager to show that they, like the *Prophet,* had decided he was something of a hero. Harry said nothing to any of them. He had no idea how much they knew of what had happened three days ago, but he had so far avoided being questioned and preferred it that way.

He thought at first when he knocked on Hagrid's cabin door that he was out, but then Fang came charging around the corner and almost bowled him over with the enthusiasm of his welcome. Hagrid, it transpired, was picking runner beans in his back garden.

"All righ', Harry!" he said, beaming, when Harry approached the fence. "Come in, come in, we'll have a cup o' dandelion juice. . . ."

"How's things?" Hagrid asked him, as they settled down at his wooden table with a glass apiece of iced juice. "You — er — feelin' all righ', are yeh?"

Harry knew from the look of concern on Hagrid's face that he was not referring to Harry's physical well-being.

"I'm fine," Harry said quickly, because he could not bear to discuss the thing that he knew was in Hagrid's mind. "So, where've you been?"

"Bin hidin' out in the mountains," said Hagrid. "Up in a cave, like Sirius did when he —"

Hagrid broke off, cleared his throat gruffly, looked at Harry, and took a long draught of juice.

"Anyway, back now," he said feebly.

"You — you look better," said Harry, who was determined to keep the conversation moving away from Sirius.

"Wha'?" said Hagrid, raising a massive hand and feeling his face. "Oh — oh yeah. Well, Grawpy's loads better behaved now, loads. Seemed right pleased ter see me when I got back, ter tell yeh the truth. He's a good lad, really. . . . I've bin thinkin' abou' tryin' ter find him a lady friend, actually. . . ."

Harry would normally have tried to persuade Hagrid out of this idea at once. The prospect of a second giant taking up residence in the forest, possibly even wilder and more brutal than Grawp, was positively alarming, but somehow Harry could not muster the energy necessary to argue the point. He was starting to wish he was alone again, and with the idea of hastening his departure he took several large gulps of his dandelion juice, half emptying his glass.

"Ev'ryone knows you've bin tellin' the truth now, Harry," said Hagrid softly and unexpectedly. "Tha's gotta be better, hasn' it?"

Harry shrugged.

"Look . . ." Hagrid leaned toward him across the table, "I knew

Sirius longer 'n you did. . . . He died in battle, an' tha's the way he'd've wanted ter go —"

"He didn't want to go at all!" said Harry angrily.

Hagrid bowed his great shaggy head.

"Nah, I don' reckon he did," he said quietly. "But still, Harry . . . he was never one ter sit around at home an' let other people do the fightin'. He couldn' have lived with himself if he hadn' gone ter help —"

Harry leapt up again.

"I've got to go and visit Ron and Hermione in the hospital wing," he said mechanically.

"Oh," said Hagrid, looking rather upset. "Oh . . . all righ' then, Harry . . . Take care of yerself then, an' drop back in if yeh've got a mo. . . ."

"Yeah . . . right . . ."

Harry crossed to the door as fast as he could and pulled it open. He was out in the sunshine again before Hagrid had finished saying good-bye and walked away across the lawn. Once again, people called out to him as he passed. He closed his eyes for a few moments, wishing they would all vanish, that he could open his eyes and find himself alone in the grounds. . . .

A few days ago, before his exams had finished and he had seen the vision Voldemort had planted in his mind, he would have given almost anything for the Wizarding world to know that he had been telling the truth, for them to believe that Voldemort was back and know that he was neither a liar nor mad. Now, however . . .

He walked a short way around the lake, sat down on its bank, sheltered from the gaze of passersby behind a tangle of shrubs, and stared out over the gleaming water, thinking. . . .

Perhaps the reason he wanted to be alone was because he had felt isolated from everybody since his talk with Dumbledore. An invisible barrier separated him from the rest of the world. He was — he had always been — a marked man. It was just that he had never really understood what that meant. . . .

And yet sitting here on the edge of the lake, with the terrible weight of grief dragging at him, with the loss of Sirius so raw and fresh inside, he could not muster any great sense of fear. It was sunny and the grounds around him were full of laughing people, and even though he felt as distant from them as though he belonged to a different race, it was still very hard to believe as he sat here that his life must include, or end in, murder. . . .

He sat there for a long time, gazing out at the water, trying not to think about his godfather or to remember that it was directly across from here, on the opposite bank, that Sirius had collapsed trying to fend off a hundred dementors. . . .

The sun had fallen before he realized that he was cold. He got up and returned to the castle, wiping his face on his sleeve as he went.

Ron and Hermione left the hospital wing completely cured three days before the end of term. Hermione showed signs of wanting to talk about Sirius, but Ron tended to make hushing noises every time she mentioned his name. Harry was not sure whether or not he wanted to talk about his godfather yet; his wishes varied with his mood. He knew one thing, though: Unhappy as he felt at the moment, he would greatly miss Hogwarts in a few days' time when he was back at number four, Privet Drive. Even though he now understood exactly why he had to return there every summer, he did not feel any better about it. Indeed, he had never dreaded his return more.

Professor Umbridge left Hogwarts the day before the end of term. It seemed that she had crept out of the hospital wing during dinnertime, evidently hoping to depart undetected, but unfortunately for her, she met Peeves on the way, who seized his last chance to do as Fred had instructed and chased her gleefully from the premises, whacking her alternately with a walking stick and a sock full of chalk. Many students ran out into the entrance hall to watch her running away down the path, and the Heads of Houses tried only halfheartedly to restrain their pupils. Indeed, Professor McGonagall sank back into her chair at the staff table after a few feeble remonstrances and was clearly heard to express a regret that she could not run cheering after Umbridge herself, because Peeves had borrowed her walking stick.

Their last evening at school arrived; most people had finished packing and were already heading down to the end-of-term feast, but Harry had not even started.

"Just do it tomorrow!" said Ron, who was waiting by the door of their dormitory. "Come on, I'm starving. . . ."

"I won't be long. . . . Look, you go ahead. . . ."

But when the dormitory door closed behind Ron, Harry made no effort to speed up his packing. The very last thing he wanted to do was to attend the end-of-term feast. He was worried that Dumbledore would make some reference to him in his speech. He was sure to mention Voldemort's return; he had talked to them about it last year, after all. . . .

Harry pulled some crumpled robes out of the very bottom of his trunk to make way for folded ones and, as he did so, noticed a badly wrapped package lying in a corner of it. He could not think what it was doing there. He bent down, pulled it out from underneath his trainers, and examined it.

He realized what it was within seconds. Sirius had given it to him just inside the front door of twelve Grimmauld Place. *Use it if you need me, all right?*

Harry sank down onto his bed and unwrapped the package. Out fell a small, square mirror. It looked old; it was certainly dirty. Harry held it up to his face and saw his own reflection looking back at him.

He turned the mirror over. There on the reverse side was a scribbled note from Sirius.

This is a two-way mirror. I've got the other.
If you need to speak to me, just say my name
into it; you'll appear in my mirror and I'll be
able to talk in yours. James and I used to use
them when we were in separate detentions.

And Harry's heart began to race. He remembered seeing his dead parents in the Mirror of Erised four years ago. He was going to be able to talk to Sirius again, right now, he knew it —

He looked around to make sure there was nobody else there; the dormitory was quite empty. He looked back at the mirror, raised it in front of his face with trembling hands, and said, loudly and clearly, "Sirius."

His breath misted the surface of the glass. He held the mirror even closer, excitement flooding through him, but the eyes blinking back at him through the fog were definitely his own.

He wiped the mirror clear again and said, so that every syllable rang clearly through the room, "Sirius Black!"

Nothing happened. The frustrated face looking back out of the mirror was still, definitely, his own. . . .

Sirius didn't have his mirror on him when he went through the archway, said a small voice in Harry's head. *That's why it's not working. . . .*

Harry remained quite still for a moment, then hurled the mirror back into the trunk where it shattered. He had been convinced, for a whole, shining minute, that he was going to see Sirius, talk to him again. . . .

Disappointment was burning in his throat. He got up and began throwing his things pell-mell into the trunk on top of the broken mirror —

But then an idea struck him. . . . A better idea than a mirror . . . A much bigger, more important idea . . . How had he never thought of it before — why had he never asked?

He was sprinting out of the dormitory and down the spiral staircase, hitting the walls as he ran and barely noticing. He hurtled across the empty common room, through the portrait hole and off along the corridor, ignoring the Fat Lady, who called after him, "The feast is about to start, you know, you're cutting it very fine!"

But Harry had no intention of going to the feast . . .

How could it be that the place was full of ghosts whenever you didn't need one, yet now . . .

He ran down staircases and along corridors and met nobody either alive or dead. They were all, clearly, in the Great Hall. Outside his Charms classroom he came to a halt, panting and thinking disconsolately that he would have to wait until later, until after the end of the feast . . .

But just as he had given up hope he saw it — a translucent somebody drifting across the end of the corridor.

"Hey — hey Nick! NICK!"

The ghost stuck its head back out of the wall, revealing the extravagantly plumed hat and dangerously wobbling head of Sir Nicholas de Mimsy-Porpington.

"Good evening," he said, withdrawing the rest of his body from the solid stone and smiling at Harry. "I am not the only one who is late, then? Though," he sighed, "in rather different senses, of course . . ."

"Nick, can I ask you something?"

A most peculiar expression stole over Nearly Headless Nick's face as he inserted a finger in the stiff ruff at his neck and tugged it a little straighter, apparently to give himself thinking time. He desisted only when his partially severed neck seemed about to give way completely.

"Er — now, Harry?" said Nick, looking discomforted. "Can't it wait until after the feast?"

"No — Nick — please," said Harry, "I really need to talk to you. Can we go in here?"

Harry opened the door of the nearest classroom and Nearly Headless Nick sighed.

"Oh very well," he said, looking resigned. "I can't pretend I haven't been expecting it."

Harry was holding the door open for him, but he drifted through the wall instead.

"Expecting what?" Harry asked, as he closed the door.

"You to come and find me," said Nick, now gliding over to the window and looking out at the darkening grounds. "It happens, sometimes . . . when somebody has suffered a . . . loss."

"Well," said Harry, refusing to be deflected. "You were right, I've — I've come to find you."

Nick said nothing.

"It's —" said Harry, who was finding this more awkward than he had anticipated, "it's just — you're dead. But you're still here, aren't you?"

Nick sighed and continued to gaze out at the grounds.

"That's right, isn't it?" Harry urged him. "You died, but I'm talking to you. . . . You can walk around Hogwarts and everything, can't you?"

"Yes," said Nearly Headless Nick quietly, "I walk and talk, yes."

"So, you came back, didn't you?" said Harry urgently. "People can come back, right? As ghosts. They don't have to disappear completely. *Well?*" he added impatiently, when Nick continued to say nothing.

Nearly Headless Nick hesitated, then said, "Not everyone can come back as a ghost."

"What d'you mean?" said Harry quickly.

"Only . . . only wizards."

"Oh," said Harry, and he almost laughed with relief. "Well, that's okay then, the person I'm asking about is a wizard. So he can come back, right?"

Nick turned away from the window and looked mournfully at Harry. "He won't come back."

"Who?"

"Sirius Black," said Nick.

"But you did!" said Harry angrily. "You came back — you're dead and you didn't disappear —"

"Wizards can leave an imprint of themselves upon the earth, to walk palely where their living selves once trod," said Nick miserably. "But very few wizards choose that path."

"Why not?" said Harry. "Anyway — it doesn't matter — Sirius won't care if it's unusual, he'll come back, I know he will!"

And so strong was his belief that Harry actually turned his head to check the door, sure, for a split second, that he was going to see Sirius, pearly white and transparent but beaming, walking through it toward him.

"He will not come back," repeated Nick quietly. "He will have . . . gone on."

"What d'you mean, 'gone on'?" said Harry quickly. "Gone on where? Listen — what happens when you die, anyway? Where do you go? Why doesn't everyone come back? Why isn't this place full of ghosts? Why — ?"

"I cannot answer," said Nick.

"You're dead, aren't you?" said Harry exasperatedly. "Who can answer better than you?"

"I was afraid of death," said Nick. "I chose to remain behind. I sometimes wonder whether I oughtn't to have . . . Well, that is neither here nor there. . . . In fact, *I* am neither here nor there. . . ." He gave a small sad chuckle. "I know nothing of the secrets of death, Harry, for I chose my feeble imitation of life instead. I believe learned wizards study the matter in the Department of Mysteries —"

"Don't talk to me about that place!" said Harry fiercely.

"I am sorry not to have been more help," said Nick gently. "Well . . . well, do excuse me . . . the feast, you know . . ."

And he left the room, leaving Harry there alone, gazing blankly at the wall through which Nick had disappeared.

Harry felt almost as though he had lost his godfather all over again in losing the hope that he might be able to see or speak to him once more. He walked slowly and miserably back up through the empty castle, wondering whether he would ever feel cheerful again.

He had turned the corner toward the Fat Lady's corridor when he saw somebody up ahead fastening a note to a board on the wall. A second glance showed him that it was Luna. There were no good hiding places nearby, she was bound to have heard his footsteps, and in any case, Harry could hardly muster the energy to avoid anyone at the moment.

"Hello," said Luna vaguely, glancing around at him as she stepped back from the notice.

"How come you're not at the feast?" Harry asked.

"Well, I've lost most of my possessions," said Luna serenely. "People take them and hide them, you know. But as it's the last night, I really do need them back, so I've been putting up signs."

She gestured toward the notice board, upon which, sure enough, she had pinned a list of all her missing books and clothes, with a plea for their return.

An odd feeling rose in Harry — an emotion quite different from the anger and grief that had filled him since Sirius's death. It was a few moments before he realized that he was feeling sorry for Luna.

"How come people hide your stuff?" he asked her, frowning.

"Oh . . . well . . ." She shrugged. "I think they think I'm a bit odd, you know. Some people call me 'Loony' Lovegood, actually."

Harry looked at her and the new feeling of pity intensified rather painfully.

"That's no reason for them to take your things," he said flatly. "D'you want help finding them?"

"Oh no," she said, smiling at him. "They'll come back, they always do in the end. It was just that I wanted to pack tonight. Anyway . . . why aren't *you* at the feast?"

Harry shrugged. "Just didn't feel like it."

"No," said Luna, observing him with those oddly misty, protuberant eyes. "I don't suppose you do. That man the Death Eaters killed was your godfather, wasn't he? Ginny told me."

Harry nodded curtly, but found that for some reason he did not mind Luna talking about Sirius. He had just remembered that she too could see thestrals.

"Have you . . ." he began. "I mean, who . . . has anyone you've known ever died?"

"Yes," said Luna simply, "my mother. She was a quite extraordinary witch, you know, but she did like to experiment and one of her spells went rather badly wrong one day. I was nine."

"I'm sorry," Harry mumbled.

"Yes, it was rather horrible," said Luna conversationally. "I still feel very sad about it sometimes. But I've still got Dad. And anyway, it's not as though I'll never see Mum again, is it?"

"Er — isn't it?" said Harry uncertainly.

She shook her head in disbelief. "Oh, come on. You heard them, just behind the veil, didn't you?"

"You mean . . ."

"In that room with the archway. They were just lurking out of sight, that's all. You heard them."

They looked at each other. Luna was smiling slightly. Harry did not know what to say, or to think. Luna believed so many extraordinary things . . . yet he had been sure he had heard voices behind the veil too. . . .

"Are you sure you don't want me to help you look for your stuff?" he said.

"Oh no," said Luna. "No, I think I'll just go down and have some pudding and wait for it all to turn up. . . . It always does in the end. . . . Well, have a nice holiday, Harry."

"Yeah . . . yeah, you too."

She walked away from him, and as he watched her go, he found that the terrible weight in his stomach seemed to have lessened slightly.

The journey home on the Hogwarts Express next day was eventful in several ways. Firstly, Malfoy, Crabbe, and Goyle, who had clearly been waiting all week for the opportunity to strike without teacher witnesses, attempted to ambush Harry halfway down the train as he made his way back from the toilet. The attack might have succeeded had it not been for the fact that they unwittingly chose to stage the attack right outside a compartment full of D.A. members, who saw what was happening through the glass and rose as one to rush to Harry's aid. By the time Ernie Macmillan, Hannah Abbott, Susan Bones, Justin Finch-Fletchley, Anthony Goldstein, and Terry Boot had finished using a wide variety of the hexes and jinxes Harry had taught them, Malfoy, Crabbe, and Goyle resembled nothing so much as three gigantic slugs squeezed into Hogwarts uniforms as Harry, Ernie, and Justin hoisted them into the luggage rack and left them there to ooze.

"I must say, I'm looking forward to seeing Malfoy's mother's face when he gets off the train," said Ernie with some satisfaction, as he watched Malfoy squirm above him. Ernie had never quite got over the indignity of Malfoy docking points from Hufflepuff during his brief spell as a member of the Inquisitorial Squad.

"Goyle's mum'll be really pleased, though," said Ron, who had come to investigate the source of the commotion. "He's loads better-looking now. . . . Anyway, Harry, the food trolley's just stopped if you want anything. . . ."

Harry thanked the others and accompanied Ron back to their compartment, where he bought a large pile of Cauldron Cakes and Pumpkin Pasties. Hermione was reading the *Daily Prophet* again, Ginny was doing a quiz in *The Quibbler,* and Neville was stroking his *Mimbulus mimbletonia,* which had grown a great deal over the year and now made odd crooning noises when touched.

Harry and Ron whiled away most of the journey playing wizard chess while Hermione read out snippets from the *Prophet.* It was now full of articles about how to repel dementors, attempts by the Ministry to track down Death Eaters, and hysterical letters claiming that the writer had seen Lord Voldemort walking past their house that very morning. . . .

"It hasn't really started yet," sighed Hermione gloomily, folding up the newspaper again. "But it won't be long now. . . ."

"Hey, Harry," said Ron, nodding toward the glass window onto the corridor.

Harry looked around. Cho was passing, accompanied by Marietta Edgecombe, who was wearing a balaclava. His and Cho's eyes met for a moment. Cho blushed and kept walking. Harry looked back down at the chessboard just in time to see one of his pawns chased off its square by Ron's knight.

"What's — er — going on with you and her anyway?" Ron asked quietly.

"Nothing," said Harry truthfully.

"I — er — heard she's going out with someone else now," said Hermione tentatively.

Harry was surprised to find that this information did not hurt at all. Wanting to impress Cho seemed to belong to a past that was no longer quite connected with him. So much of what he had wanted before Sirius's death felt that way these days. . . . The week that had elapsed since he had last seen Sirius seemed to have lasted much, much longer: It stretched across two universes, the one with Sirius in it, and the one without.

"You're well out of it, mate," said Ron forcefully. "I mean, she's quite good-looking and all that, but you want someone a bit more cheerful."

"She's probably cheerful enough with someone else," said Harry, shrugging.

"Who's she with now anyway?" Ron asked Hermione, but it was Ginny who answered.

"Michael Corner," she said.

"Michael — but —" said Ron, craning around in his seat to stare at her. "But you were going out with him!"

"Not anymore," said Ginny resolutely. "He didn't like Gryffindor beating Ravenclaw at Quidditch and got really sulky, so I ditched him and he ran off to comfort Cho instead." She scratched her nose absently with the end of her quill, turned *The Quibbler* upside down, and began marking her answers. Ron looked highly delighted.

"Well, I always thought he was a bit of an idiot," he said, prodding his queen forward toward Harry's quivering castle. "Good for you. Just choose someone — better — next time."

He cast Harry an oddly furtive look as he said it.

"Well, I've chosen Dean Thomas, would you say he's better?" asked Ginny vaguely.

"WHAT?" shouted Ron, upending the chessboard. Crookshanks went plunging after the pieces and Hedwig and Pigwidgeon twittered and hooted angrily from overhead.

As the train slowed down in the approach to King's Cross, Harry thought he had never wanted to leave it less. He even wondered fleetingly what would happen if he simply refused to get off, but remained stubbornly sitting there until the first of September, when it would take him back to Hogwarts. When it finally puffed to a standstill, however, he lifted down Hedwig's cage and prepared to drag his trunk from the train as usual.

When the ticket inspector signaled to him, Ron, and Hermione that it was safe to walk through the magical barrier between platforms nine and ten, however, he found a surprise awaiting him on the other side: a group of people standing there to greet him whom he had not expected at all.

There was Mad-Eye Moody, looking quite as sinister with his bowler hat pulled low over his magical eye as he would have done without it, his gnarled hands clutching a long staff, his body wrapped in a voluminous traveling cloak. Tonks stood just behind him, her bright bubble-gum-pink hair gleaming in the sunlight filtering through the dirty glass station ceiling, wearing heavily patched jeans and a bright purple T-shirt bearing the legend THE WEIRD SISTERS. Next to Tonks was Lupin, his face pale, his hair graying, a long and threadbare overcoat covering a shabby jumper and trousers. At the front of the group stood Mr. and Mrs. Weasley, dressed in their Muggle best, and Fred and George, who were both wearing brand-new jackets in some lurid green, scaly material.

"Ron, Ginny!" called Mrs. Weasley, hurrying forward and hugging her children tightly. "Oh, and Harry dear — how are you?"

"Fine," lied Harry, as she pulled him into a tight embrace. Over her shoulder he saw Ron goggling at the twins' new clothes.

"What are *they* supposed to be?" he asked, pointing at the jackets.

"Finest dragon skin, little bro," said Fred, giving his zip a little tweak. "Business is booming and we thought we'd treat ourselves."

"Hello, Harry," said Lupin, as Mrs. Weasley let go of Harry and turned to greet Hermione.

"Hi," said Harry. "I didn't expect . . . what are you all doing here?"

"Well," said Lupin with a slight smile, "we thought we might have a little chat with your aunt and uncle before letting them take you home."

"I dunno if that's a good idea," said Harry at once.

"Oh, I think it is," growled Moody, who had limped a little closer. "That'll be them, will it, Potter?"

He pointed with his thumb over his shoulder; his magical eye was evidently peering through the back of his head and his bowler hat. Harry leaned an inch or so to the left to see where Mad-Eye was pointing and there, sure enough, were the three Dursleys, who looked positively appalled to see Harry's reception committee.

"Ah, Harry!" said Mr. Weasley, turning from Hermione's parents, whom he had been greeting enthusiastically, and who were taking it in turns to hug Hermione. "Well — shall we do it, then?"

"Yeah, I reckon so, Arthur," said Moody.

He and Mr. Weasley took the lead across the station toward the place where the Dursleys stood, apparently rooted to the floor. Hermione disengaged herself gently from her mother to join the group.

"Good afternoon," said Mr. Weasley pleasantly to Uncle Vernon, coming to a halt right in front of him. "You might remember me, my name's Arthur Weasley."

As Mr. Weasley had singlehandedly demolished most of the Dursleys' living room two years previously, Harry would have been very surprised if Uncle Vernon had forgotten him. Sure enough, Uncle Vernon turned a deeper shade of puce and glared at Mr. Weasley, but chose not to say anything, partly, perhaps, because the Dursleys were outnumbered two to one. Aunt Petunia looked both frightened and embarrassed. She kept glancing around, as though terrified somebody she knew would see her in such company. Dudley, meanwhile, seemed to be trying to look small and insignificant, a feat at which he was failing extravagantly.

"We thought we'd just have a few words with you about Harry," said Mr. Weasley, still smiling.

"Yeah," growled Moody. "About how he's treated when he's at your place."

Uncle Vernon's mustache seemed to bristle with indignation. Possibly because the bowler hat gave him the entirely mistaken impression that he was dealing with a kindred spirit, he addressed himself to Moody.

"I am not aware that it is any of your business what goes on in my house —"

"I expect what you're not aware of would fill several books, Dursley," growled Moody.

"Anyway, that's not the point," interjected Tonks, whose pink hair seemed to offend Aunt Petunia more than all the rest put together, for she closed her eyes rather than look at her. "The point is, if we find out you've been horrible to Harry —"

"— and make no mistake, we'll hear about it," added Lupin pleasantly.

"Yes," said Mr. Weasley, "even if you won't let Harry use the fellytone —"

"Telephone," whispered Hermione.

"Yeah, if we get any hint that Potter's been mistreated in any way, you'll have us to answer to," said Moody.

Uncle Vernon swelled ominously. His sense of outrage seemed to outweigh even his fear of this bunch of oddballs.

"Are you threatening me, sir?" he said, so loudly that passersby actually turned to stare.

"Yes, I am," said Mad-Eye, who seemed rather pleased that Uncle Vernon had grasped this fact so quickly.

"And do I look like the kind of man who can be intimidated?" barked Uncle Vernon.

"Well . . ." said Moody, pushing back his bowler hat to reveal his sinisterly revolving magical eye. Uncle Vernon leapt backward in horror and collided painfully with a luggage trolley. "Yes, I'd have to say you do, Dursley."

He turned from Uncle Vernon to Harry. "So, Potter . . . give us a shout if you need us. If we don't hear from you for three days in a row, we'll send someone along. . . ."

Aunt Petunia whimpered piteously. It could not have been plainer that she was thinking of what the neighbors would say if they caught sight of these people marching up the garden path.

"'Bye, then, Potter," said Moody, grasping Harry's shoulder for a moment with a gnarled hand.

"Take care, Harry," said Lupin quietly. "Keep in touch."

"Harry, we'll have you away from there as soon as we can," Mrs. Weasley whispered, hugging him again.

"We'll see you soon, mate," said Ron anxiously, shaking Harry's hand.

"Really soon, Harry," said Hermione earnestly. "We promise."

Harry nodded. He somehow could not find words to tell them what it meant to him, to see them all ranged there, on his side. Instead he smiled, raised a hand in farewell, turned around, and led the way out of the station toward the sunlit street, with Uncle Vernon, Aunt Petunia, and Dudley hurrying along in his wake.

JP MASCLET

J. K. ROWLING began writing stories when she was six years old. She started working on the Harry Potter sequence in 1990, when, she says, "the idea . . . simply fell into my head." The first book, *Harry Potter and the Sorcerer's Stone*, was published in the United Kingdom in 1997 and the United States in 1998. Since then, books in the Harry Potter series have been honored with many prizes, including the Anthony Award, the Hugo Award, the Bram Stoker Award, the Whitbread Children's Book Award, the Nestlé Smarties Book Prize, and the British Book Awards Children's Book of the Year, as well as *New York Times* Notable Book, ALA Notable Children's Book, and ALA Best Book for Young Adults citations. Ms. Rowling has also been named an Officer of the Order of the British Empire.

She lives in Scotland with her family.

MARY GRANDPRÉ has illustrated more than twenty beautiful books, including *Henry and Pawl and the Round Yellow Ball,* cowritten with her husband Tom Casmer; *Plum,* a collection of poetry by Tony Mitton; *Lucia and the Light,* by Phyllis Root; and the American editions of all seven Harry Potter novels. Her work has also appeared in *The New Yorker, The Atlantic Monthly,* and *The Wall Street Journal,* and her paintings and pastels have been shown in galleries across the United States.

Ms. GrandPré lives in Sarasota, Florida, with her family.

Harry Potter

Read all of Harry's Magical Adventures!

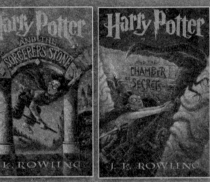

ARTHUR A. LEVINE BOOKS

SCHOLASTIC

www.scholastic.com/harrypotter